PENGUIN BOOKS

THE PORTABLE DANTE

Each volume in The Viking Portable Library either presents a representative selection from the works of a single outstanding writer or offers a comprehensive anthology on a special subject. Averaging 700 pages in length and designed for compactness and readability, these books fill a need not met by other compilations. All are edited by distinguished authorities, who have written introductory essays and included much other helpful material.

"The Viking Portables have done more for good reading and good writers than anything that has come along since I can remember."
—Arthur Mizener

Some Volumes in
THE VIKING PORTABLE LIBRARY

The Portable

DANTE

¶ THE DIVINE COMEDY, *complete,
translated by Laurence Binyon, with
notes from C. H. Grandgent*

¶ LA VITA NUOVA, *complete, trans-
lated by D. G. Rossetti*

¶ *Excerpts from the* RHYMES *and the*
LATIN PROSE WORKS

Edited, and with an Introduction, by
PAOLO MILANO

PENGUIN BOOKS

Penguin Books Ltd, Harmondsworth,
Middlesex, England
Penguin Books, 625 Madison Avenue,
New York, New York 10022, U.S.A.
Penguin Books Australia Ltd, Ringwood,
Victoria, Australia
Penguin Books Canada Limited, 2801 John Street,
Markham, Ontario, Canada L3R 1B4
Penguin Books (N.Z.) Ltd, 182–190 Wairau Road,
Auckland 10, New Zealand

First published in the United States of America by The Viking Press 1947
Paperbound edition published 1955
Revised edition published 1969
Reprinted 1970, 1971, 1973, 1974 (twice), 1975, 1976
Published in Penguin Books 1977
Reprinted 1978, 1979, 1981

LIBRARY OF CONGRESS CATALOGING IN PUBLICATION DATA
Dante Alighieri, 1265–1321.
The portable Dante.
Bibliography: p. 660.
CONTENTS: The Divine comedy, complete, translated
by L. Binyon, with notes from C. H. Grandgent—La vita
nuova, complete, translated by D. G. Rossetti.—
Excerpts from the Rhymes and the Latin prose works.
I. Milano, Paolo.   II. Binyon, Laurence, 1869–1943.
III. Rossetti, Dante Gabriel, 1828–1882.   IV. Title.
[PQ4315.A3B5 1977]   851'.1   77-7623
ISBN 0 14 015.032 3

Printed in the United States of America by
Kingsport Press, Inc., Kingsport, Tennessee
Set in Linotype Caledonia

Grateful acknowledgment is made to Mrs. Nicolete Gray and the
Society of Authors, London, for permission to use the text of Laurence
Binyon's translation of *The Divine Comedy* in this volume; to D. C.
Heath and Company, Boston, for the use of a number of the notes by
C. H. Grandgent in their edition of *La Divina Commedia*; to J. M.
Dent & Sons, Ltd., London and Toronto, for use of selections from
Dante's Latin Works translated by A. G. Ferrers Howell and Philip H.
Wicksteed; to The Clarendon Press, Oxford, for the lines from *Il Con-
tralto* translated by William Walrond Jackson; and to Harcourt, Brace
& Co., New York, for the excerpt from T. S. Eliot's *Selected Essays*.

Contents

Editor's Acknowledgments

I wish to add to the publisher's acknowledgment my own thanks to D. C. Heath & Co. for their generous permission to include in this volume a number of the excellent notes to the *Commedia* by the late C. H. Grandgent of Harvard. I am also grateful to J. M. Dent & Sons of London and Toronto for their permission to print selections from their edition of Dante's Latin Works.

My reliance on the work of the leading Dante scholars and critics has been too great to be simply called a debt, or to be acknowledged in detail. I should not, however, fail to mention with special gratitude the studies of Michele Barbi, Attilio Momigliano, C. H. Grandgent, and T. S. Eliot.

To my wife, Rachel Milano, who skillfully and patiently worked with me, I owe more than I can say or than she would admit.

Even more difficult to express is my last and deepest indebtedness. If an editor's job were something that could be dedicated, this volume would be inscribed to Alfred Kazin. He suggested this book, and assisted me at every step with the most sensitive advice and the friendliest encouragement. Whatever is valuable in my work is as much his as it is mine.

Queens College, New York, 1947   P. M.

Editor's Introduction

In his *Philosophical Dictionary* (1764), Voltaire wrote of Dante: "The Italians call him divine; but it is a hidden divinity—few people understand his oracles. He has commentators, which, perhaps, is another reason for his not being understood. His reputation will go on increasing, because scarce anybody reads him."

Contemptuous though it was of masterpieces more honored than read, Voltaire's prophecy of Dante's growing fame came true nevertheless. The lowest ebb of Dante's reputation had come in the eighteenth century, when Horace Walpole branded him as "extravagant, absurd, disgusting, in short a Methodist parson in Bedlam." Then a new glory sprang about the Florentine in the nineteenth century, followed in the twentieth by something that can only be called Dante's apotheosis. Commenting, in the early 1930's, upon the literary tastes of the first postwar generation, Edmund Wilson wrote: "As for the enthusiasm for Dante—to paraphrase the man in Hemingway's novel, there's been nothing like it since the Fratellinis." At the present time, if current comment is a reliable sign, Dante is the favorite "genius" of our intellectuals. Voltaire, however, would still have reason to wonder how many of Dante's worshipers have read not only what T. S. Eliot had to say about the *Divine Comedy*, but the poem itself. And had the Old Sage lived to witness our reversal of his verdict, he probably would still insist that the commentators enlighten instead of exalting, and that they devote themselves to Dante's art rather than to the cult of Dante.

II

Of Dante's life we know as little as we know of Shake-speare's. Yet the harmony between Dante's character and his work is such that the meager facts are almost enough for us. Only one generation later another Tuscan, Petrarch, was to initiate the split between the poet's life and his life in poetry, ushering in with mournful beauty the age of the "modern" writer. But those who usually dispose of Dante as a "medieval" poet must remember that his birth, in 1265, coincides with the establishment of the first articulate democracy of the Christian era—the free commune of Florence. Florence then became a burghers' republic, founded on an unsteady alliance between the merchant class (known as the Fat People) and the artisans (the Minute People), and governed by elected representatives of their trade unions, or guilds.

The old struggle between the Popes and the German monarchs of that kingdom which, centuries before Voltaire's gibe, was already "neither Holy, nor Roman, nor an Empire," had been joined in 1266 at the Battle of Benevento. Dante was a few months old when the Imperial power over Italy was broken, and the victory of the Church and its Guelf party over their opponents, the Ghibellines, seemed to be complete. The new democratic rulers of Florence were passionate Guelfs—that is, they sided with the Pope in opposing all Imperial interference in Italian affairs; but they were also jealous of their city's independence. Their major political problem, during Dante's life and for a while thereafter, was how to remain unflinchingly anti-Ghibelline and yet avoid subservience to the Pontiff. Any weakness toward the Emperor's party would have encouraged a return of

the feudal knights the Florentines had just dispossessed
and banished, while too close an alliance with the
power-seeking Papacy might have cost Florence her
leadership of the whole of Tuscany. When Dante was
"midway in the journey of this life," the conflicting
factions in Florence were two offshoots of the Guelf
party, called the Blacks and the Whites. To disregard
the family feuds complicating their rivalry, the middle-
class Blacks were ready to compromise with the Church
to gain power; the Whites, a strange grouping of petty
nobility and lower artisans, were for a steadfast, if un-
attainable, independence from both throne and altar.
History was not with the Whites; they were defeated,
and Dante with them.

Dante's family were impoverished city noblemen
who, unlike the feudal lords, were traditionally Guelf.
The Alighieris lived on the income from land and cattle,
but they resided within the walls of Florence. Dante
was hardly twelve when his father arranged for him a
future marriage with a young lady of more distinguished
nobility, Gemma Donati, who was to be accompanied
by some dowry. If Dante went, as is probable, to a
grammar school run by Franciscan friars, he must have
been influenced by their enlightened fervor and their
dislike for Church politics. What we do know of his
education is that he studied "rhetoric" under a philos-
opher and didactic poet, Brunetto Latini, whose name
would be remembered only by scholars, had Dante not
granted him immortality in a passage of the *Inferno*.
Ser Brunetto was the first, in the words of a chronicler,
to teach the Florentines "how to govern the republic
according to politics," or, as we would say, to lecture in
political science. In the *Commedia*, Dante meets him in
Hell, where Brunetto is being punished eternally with
those who committed sodomy. Dante himself makes no

reference to this most un-Christian sin. He is only over-whelmed by a flood of tenderness and gratitude, more like that of a son than of a pupil:

> Still in my heart stays, memory's dear inmate,
> The fatherly, kind image, paining now,
> Of you, when in the world, early and late,
>
> You taught me how man may eternal grow. . . .
> (*Inferno*, xv, 82-85)

(A passage of one of T. S. Eliot's *Four Quartets*, "Little Gidding," is patterned after this unequaled homage of a poet to his teacher, transcending all human weakness; but transposed, in the fashion of our time, from tender sorrow to grim despair.)

The crucial episodes of Dante's life, it is usually main-tained, are three: the sudden death of a young woman, a political purge in his native city, and the defeat and fall of an invading emperor. In weighing a poet's life, however, emphasis on mere events can be misleading. The death of Beatrice, Dante's banishment from Flor-ence, and the collapse of Henry VII's Italian campaign, are no more than symbols for a spiritual development that crosses such external landmarks only to rise beyond them altogether. It would be more enlightening to say that the three stages of Dante's intellectual growth were his early cult of Ideal Love, his mature endeavors as a philosopher and a scholar, and his final "mission" as a reformer and a prophet. To which it must be added that he was chiefly, and always, a poet.

Dante tells us, in *La Vita Nuova* ("The New Life"), that he had learned by himself, and early, "the art of discoursing with rhyme." We know that, as a young man, he corresponded with the troubadours, and that later his association with an elder friend and poet, Guido Cavalcanti, resulted in a new approach to poetry, "the sweet new style." For the Provençal poets, love was courtly and profane, and the burden of their poems was the complaint against the "hardness" of the Beloved— "to serve, to fear, to conceal." Then, with the troubadours, a religious note was added, and the Woman of their songs assumed angelic traits. Dante and Guido struck a new tone. What they discovered, or thought they had, was an intimate relation between the sentiment called love, and moral endeavor. With Dante, the "service of ladies," earthly or celestial, became devotion to the Only One—a thing of the mind as well as of the heart, and a passage to the higher life. The Beloved was both the guide to perfection and its incarnation. Such is the temper which gives the *Vita Nuova,* Dante's youthful book of collected lyrics, its poetic unity.

From a "service of Love" so austerely conceived, to the study of philosophy, the natural sciences and, of course, theology, the step was natural. In one of his minor works, *Il Convivio* ("The Banquet"), Dante tells movingly of his first enthusiasm for scholarship:

I who sought to console myself discovered not only a remedy for my tears, but also the words employed by authors and sciences and books; and as I pondered on them I judged surely that Philosophy, who was mistress of these authors, these sciences, and these books, must be a most exalted thing. And I imagined her as made in the likeness of a gentle Lady; and I could not think of her in actual shape as aught but compassionate, wherefore my sense did in truth gaze on her with such a will that I could hardly turn it away from her.

(*Il Convivio,* II, 13)

He would often spend the night on his books until, in his own words, "through greatly overtasking my sight by studious reading, I so weakened the visual spirits" that, in the hour before dawn, "the stars all appeared to me to be discolored by a kind of white haze."

The thirteenth century scholars, and Dante with them, were still under the spell of the recent and greatest feat of medieval philosophy—the final reconciliation of Aristotelian thought and Christian dogma worked out by Thomas Aquinas. To his immediate heirs, the "perennial philosophy" of Aquinas looked like a perfect cathedral that would require centuries to explore, and which no cultural earthquake could ever shake. Dante gloried in being among the first of its learned visitors. To maintain that truth might be changing or plural would have seemed to Dante more than a heresy, it would have been a philosophical absurdity. Once a truth had been revealed or established, to accept it and to comment upon it, with none of our modern concern for personal originality, was for Dante a plain intellectual duty.

Dante's marriage with Gemma Donati—the wife his father had chosen for him—probably occurred in 1291, when he was twenty-six. They had two sons, and one (or two) daughters. It has been much discussed, and still is obscure, whether Gemma, whom he never mentions in his works, joined Dante at any time during his two decades of uninterrupted exile. We know that in the last years of the poet's life a son and a daughter did.

In his late twenties and early thirties Dante became active and in a way prominent in Florentine politics. Florentine democrats, like the classic democrats of Athens, watched even their best rulers sharply and mistrustfully to keep them from becoming despots. Their chief magistrates, the Priors of the Guilds, held office for only two months; this led Dante to assure Florence, bitterly, that Athens and Sparta

> Showed but a small hint of the Commonweal
> Compared with thee, who dost so finely spin
> That in October thou providest thread

Which mid-November cannot hope to win. . . .
(*Purgatorio*, vi, 141-44)

In 1293, on a tide of democratic fervor, the Florentines excluded all citizens of noble birth from public office. Two years later, however, the stern measure was relaxed, and nominal membership in one of the guilds became sufficient. Dante, having joined the guild of physicians and apothecaries, could then hold various offices. Finally he was elected to the priorship for the summer of 1300.

At this point, Dante saw a solution to partisan strife in a strong measure—the banishment of the most sectarian chiefs of both factions. The Florentines followed his advice; one of the exiles was Dante's friend Guido Cavalcanti. But the Pope, Boniface VIII, eager for a showdown with the anti-Church party in Florence as well as in the rest of Tuscany, summoned to Italy a foreign army under Charles of Valois, a brother of Philip the Fair, the King of France. Dante was alarmed and outraged; he became one of the most outspoken critics of Boniface. When he was sent to the Pope as one of three envoys seeking to avert an armed decision, Boniface thought it clever to keep Dante in Rome month after month while the Blacks in Florence were being helped to power by the French armed "mediator" to whom they had opened the city gates.

Dante probably never saw Florence again. A year before, he had barely missed being excommunicated by the angry Pope. Now, at the beginning of 1302, he was condemned by the triumphant Blacks to pay a fine of five thousand florins and to be banished from Florence for two years. Two months later, when he refused to pay (and, by implication, plead guilty to the charge against him) the banishment was made perpetual, with provision that he be burnt alive should he be caught within the territory of the republic. The actual offense imputed to Dante was "barratry," that is, graft—a purely technical indictment not less vicious than the way it was leveled against him, "or someone of his party." Behind this legal language was a ruthless political purge. Dante never submitted, and he died a refugee.

In exile, Dante became, in his own words, a Florentine by birth, not in spirit (*"Florentinus natione, non moribus"*). He now regarded himself a citizen of Italy, or, rather, of the Christian world. He joined those "to whom the world is [their] native country, just as the sea is to the fish." His ordeal for twenty years, until his death at fifty-six, was bitter:

After it was the pleasure of the citizens of that fairest and most famous daughter of Rome, Florence, to cast me out of her dearest bosom . . . I have wandered through almost every region to which this tongue of ours extends, a stranger, almost a beggar, exposing to view against my will the stroke of fortune which is often wont unjustly to be charged to the account of the stricken. Truly I have been a ship without sail and without rudder, wafted to divers havens and inlets and shores, by the parching wind which woeful poverty exhales.

(*Il Convivio*, I, 3)

Thus Dante opened the long line of Europe's banished intellectuals—or, more exactly, he was the first to give political exile the dignity of an institution: "Exile given to me, I have taken as honor."

For a while, Dante shared the hopes of his fellow-Whites, who plotted a military comeback with the help of some city, or feudal lord, among Florence's rivals. But, disgusted by their intrigues, he soon broke with "the crew stupid and venomous," to make "a party of [himself] alone." Time and again he was offered chances to return. But the amnesty would have required a public atonement. He refused. "What then?" he wrote to a Florentine friend who sought his recall. "May I not gaze upon the mirror of the sun and stars wherever I may be? Can I not ponder on the sweetest truths wherever I may be beneath the heaven, but I must first make me inglorious?" The only hope that never deserted Dante was that his *Commedia* would open the gates of Florence to him:

> If ever it happen that the sacred song,
> Whereto both heaven and earth have set a hand,
> Whereby I am lean, these many years and long,
>
> O'ercome the cruelty which keeps me banned
> From the fair sheepfold where I slept, a lamb,
> Foe to the wolves that raven through the land,
>
> With different voice now, nor with fleece the same,
> Shall I return, poet, and at the fount
> Of my baptizing shall the chaplet claim.
> > (*Paradiso*, xxv, 1-10)

But his poetry was not a passport for him. For two decades Dante led the wandering life of a learned courtier. He lived, at least twice, in Verona, the guest in later years of Can Grande Della Scala, who was the leader of the Ghibelline League, and of whom Dante thought highly. He was in Bologna, in Padua, and finally in Ravenna. His powerful hosts would often avail themselves of his Latin to phrase an elaborate dispatch, or a flowery treaty with a neighboring town; they would occasionally send him on diplomatic missions. He certainly had leisure, since he wrote much and wonderfully. But he also was to learn "how bitter another's bread is"

> By tasting it, and how hard to the feet
> Another's stairs are, up and down to go.
> > (*Paradiso*, xvii, 59-60)

For three years, from 1310 to 1313, Dante's political hopes flared again. The disputed crown of the Holy Roman Empire had fallen upon the Count of Luxembourg, who became the Emperor Henry VII, to be hailed universally as a *rex pacificus*. When he descended into Italy at the head of an army, even the Pope, Clement V, who had backed his election, prodded the Italians to welcome him. No wonder that Dante saw in him the delivering, God-appointed Prince who would finally and justly separate the temporal power from the spiritual—in a word, the incarnation of Dante's own political dream. "O Italy!" Dante cried to all the princes of the country, "Henceforth rejoice! . . . Because thy bridegroom, . . . the most clement Henry, . . . is hastening to the bridal." Against the Florentines, who, reluctant to accept a foreign invader, were mobilizing against the Emperor most of Italy, Dante thundered: "Where ye think to defend the corridor of false liberty, there shall ye fall into the dungeons of true slavery." He then begged Henry, in a passionate letter, to show Florence no mercy, "to destroy the poisonous hydra." His crusade stopped only short of taking up arms himself against Florence, as many Whites did.

Henry's expedition failed miserably. The Pope, suddenly changing his mind, turned the King of Naples against the Emperor. Then, in 1313, when the outcome of the struggle was still uncertain, Henry died near Siena. The whole campaign collapsed, and with it Dante's hopes. The poet was left to his doctrinaire dream, and he probably wrote then his political treatise, *De Monarchia*—a prophetic vindication of the rights of Empire.

Dante's last years seem to have been serene. He spent them at Ravenna, in the house of Guido Novello da Polenta, a nephew of Francesca da Rimini. He had with him one of his sons, and his daughter, who had taken the veil and the name of Beatrice. He was the respected author of the *Inferno* and the *Purgatorio*, and of three scholarly works. The tradition is that he wrote the exalted last canto of his *Paradiso* shortly before his death, on September 14, 1321.

III

In that part of the book of my memory before the which is little that can be read, there is a rubric, saying, *Incipit Vita Nova* [Here beginneth the new life]. Under such rubric I find written many things; and among them the words which I purpose to copy into this little book; if not all of them, at least their substance.

Such is the intent of Dante's first work, plainly expressed in the opening lines. The *Vita Nuova* is the autobiography of a young man, as reflected in the sonnets and in the *canzoni* he has written so far. It is the first backward glance of a poet still in his twenties, who prunes and edits his work to reveal its place in his life and its meaning beyond literature. This is why the book, alternately in prose and verse, unfolds constantly on three levels: a poem, an account of the occasion that inspired it, and an analysis of its stylistic and spiritual quality. The depth of the experience is felt in the several meanings of *nuova*—"new," "renewed," "youthful."

"The New Life" revolves around Beatrice. She was not only Dante's Beatrice; she was also a real woman, the wife of a Florentine banker. We have no reason to question Dante's account of their first meeting, when she was eight and he nine, nor the psychological truth of his saying that "from that time forward, Love quite governed my soul." They met again nine years later, and Dante's exalted bondage was confirmed for life and beyond it. To conceal it, the young poet gave his attentions to another lady, who "was a screen for so much love on my part," whereupon Beatrice "denied me her most sweet salutation, in the which alone was my blessedness."

The other tenuous episodes of this record of a soul in love are the death of Beatrice's father, and Dante's dream of the impending death of his Beloved, which occurs a short time later. After the passing of Beatrice, Dante shared for a while his sorrow with a "compassionate lady," to whom he addressed a few sonnets, "and my eyes began to be gladdened overmuch with her company"; but soon he felt this to be a lapse, and renewed his dedication to Beatrice alone. The book ends on a "wonderful vision" of "such time as I discourse more worthily" of her, and on the hope "yet to write concerning her what has not been written of any woman." This is the announcement of the great work to come, and with it the *Commedia* is born.

Each turn in the course of his love is marked by a poem. Two or three of the sonnets, and as many *canzoni* perhaps, are among the purest and firmest of Western poetry; and yet the poetic vitality of "The New Life" lies rather in its prose. It is a kind of accompaniment, almost in the musical sense—a sweet-toned underlining of the meaning of love beyond love, and of poetry beyond its words. Dante captures here the sense of youth in the poet, and somehow releases the quality it has for all men. The boundaries between the heart and the mind, and between poetry and philosophy or poetry and religion, are still faint. Each event is continually the symbol of something higher that is to come, while every moment of daily life is fused into a rhythm of human longing. (In an ecstatic page, Dante marvels that a group of pilgrims passing through Florence should not perceive that the city is veiled in mourning for Beatrice.) Earthly love and aspiration beyond this world mingle creatively, and even melancholy is a kind of hope.

IV

Dante called his major work a "Comedy," because he had written it in Italian in a style removed from the "tragic" Latin, and also because it progressed from a dark beginning to redemption and hope. A later generation added the word *Divine*—that is, dealing with a sacred subject with superhuman excellence. The poem was first conceived as the final exaltation of Beatrice: her actual deification and enthronement in the Court of Heaven. This early purpose runs as a thread through the whole *Commedia*, and is triumphantly visible in the *Paradiso;* but it has been made part of a higher and complex design. For six centuries, this "design" of the *Commedia* has been the primary concern of the exponents, critics, and commentators who, from Boccaccio to C. H. Grandgent, have labored to uncover

> . . . the doctrines that for cloak
> Beneath the strangeness of the verses hide.
> (*Inferno,* ix, 62-63)

For them the *Commedia* is a palace that no one should enter without an absolute knowledge of its structure. Beginning usually with medieval cosmology (the motionless earth of the Ptolemaic system, the Hemisphere of Water, the Spheres of Air, of Fire, and of the Moon), the traditional commentator proceeds to examine the Three Kingdoms, as Dante built them. He describes the slopes of Hell with its circles and its rivers, the island-mountain of Purgatory, and the elaborate display of the Heavenly Spheres, and he traces painstakingly the steps of the poet's triple journey. Then follows Dante's conception of the sins and the virtues, and the origin of their classification, half-Aristotelian, half-Christian. And finally the reader is offered the key to the kingdom: the disclosure of the four meanings of the poem—the literal, the allegorical, the moral, and the anagogical. The *Commedia*, he is told, is an actual journey through the worlds beyond life, it is an allegory of the stages of a soul's redemption, it is a warning to mankind and a guide for the perplexed, and finally a prophecy of divine things to come.

Another, and more recent, kind of Dantean criticism leaves the system to the scholars, and analyzes the *Commedia* as metaphysical poetry. The most famous example of this in our time, and one that springs from the revival of English metaphysical poetry, is T. S. Eliot's. His views are a true rediscovery of the nature of Dante's achievement by a poet for whom the *Commedia* has been far more than a literary experience. But these views are articulated with so cautious a finesse that to summarize them in a few paragraphs would lead only to a distortion. This basic passage[1] from his main essay on Dante may prove more rewarding:

I do not recommend, in first reading the first canto of the *Inferno*, worrying about the identity of the Leopard, the Lion, or the She-Wolf. It is really better, at the start, not to know or care what they do mean. What we should consider is not so much the meaning of the images, but the reverse process, that which led a man having an idea to express it in images. We have to consider the type of mind which by nature and *practice* tended to express itself in allegory: and for a competent poet, allegory means *clear visual images*. And clear visual images are given much more intensity by having a meaning—we do not need to know

---

[1] From "Dante," in *Selected Essays* by *T. S. Eliot* (Harcourt Brace & Co., New York, 1932), p. 204.

what that meaning is, but in our awareness of the image we must be aware that the meaning is there too. Allegory is only one poetic method, but it is a method which has very great advantages.

Dante's is a *visual* imagination. It is a visual imagination in a different sense from that of a modern painter of still life: it is visual in the sense that he lived in an age in which men still saw visions. It was a psychological habit, the trick of which we have forgotten, but as good as any of our own. We have nothing but dreams, and we have forgotten that seeing visions—a practice now relegated to the aberrant and un-educated—was once a more significant, interesting, and disciplined kind of dreaming. We take it for granted that our dreams spring from below: possibly the quality of our dreams suffers in consequence.

All that I ask of the reader, at this point, is to clear his mind, if he can, of every prejudice against allegory, and to admit at least that it was not a device to enable the unin-spired to write verses, but really a mental habit, which when raised to the point of genius can make a great poet as well as a great mystic or saint.

This is a sensitive approach—an attempt to guide the reader whose esthetic horizon may be limited to roman-ticism and naturalism toward an understanding of a kind of poetry alien to the contemporary mind. At the opposite pole from Eliot's interpretation is the scholarly analysis of Dante's system, with its emphasis on cos-mology and philology. Traditional comment has a valu-able function—to provide the novice reader with nec-essary information. Yet both these approaches can be misleading, for each assumes that Dante's *intentions* coincide roughly with his poetic *achievement;* as a re-sult, the reader is so pressed, in both cases, to discover what Dante meant to say, that he may find it hard to see what is *in* the *Commedia,* what Dante did actually say.

Is there not a third way? A way of seeking in our own response concrete references against which to measure

Dante's beliefs and the ends he pursued? Let us begin with what a perceptive reader finds for himself, when he goes through the hundred cantos of the *Commedia* for the first time.

Our first, our dominating impression of the *Commedia* is that the poet's journey to the lives beyond is actually a representation of the ways of *this* world. The poem is so crowded with human events that we never feel we have really left the earth,

> The small round floor that makes us passionate . . .
> (*Paradiso,* xxii, 151)

The dramatic and the lyrical in the *Commedia* outweigh by far the didactic and the devotional. Moreover, the representation is so well rooted in human experience, so solid, that many critics falling under its spell have been quarreling for centuries about some of its physical details, as they would about a tangible reality. It is an irresistible illusion—it first conquered Dante himself. He pities, he admires, he quarrels, he weeps, he embraces—and so do his characters, though they are dead. Their sins or virtues recede into the background, which is pure idea; their life on earth is what counts, and this is what is constantly before us.

Take the most popular passage of the *Commedia*—Count Ugolino's episode (*Inferno,* xxxiii, 1-90), which Chaucer paraphrased. The treason for which the Count has been condemned to Hell is hardly mentioned; Dante sharply sets before us the slow horror of his death among his starving children. And in the case of Ulysses (*Inferno,* xxvi, 90-142), the glorification of his last defiant adventure is so passionate that Ulysses the hero cancels out Ulysses the sinner. Dante's Underworld and Overworld are poetic images of our earth. The poem is a triple gallery of timeless murals, an exalted account of a divinely conducted tour.

Dante is anything but a mystic; even his exaltation of St. Francis (in *Paradiso*, XI, 43-117) praises him as laboring for Christ in the vineyard of this world. The sins the poet confesses to are luxury and pride. He is not ashamed to be a partisan, and even in Heaven he bursts out freely in invectives. His Christ is never the Lamb, but Christ the Judge; and the whole *Commedia*, as Michelangelo so well perceived, is an anticipation of the Last Judgment. The subject of the poem is man's inveterate deviation from the path of God—that is, the human drama. The pagan world is as attractive to Dante as the Christian; and the martyrs of the Church, as Francesco De Sanctis and C. H. Grandgent have shown, excite him much less than the heroic suicides of ancient history. At the bottom of Hell, his three-mouthed Lucifer feasts insatiably not only on Judas, who sold Christ, but also on Brutus and Cassius, who betrayed Caesar.

It will thus seem natural to meet in the *Commedia*, not so much monsters and angels, as troubadours and bankers, popes and prostitutes, housewives and apostles —here a village pimp, there a pagan demigod. But even more, two whole cantos of the *Inferno* (the twenty-first and twenty-second) actually compose a farce—an exchange of billingsgate and knavish tricks among comic devils called "Curly-beard," or "Dog-scratcher," or "Badtail." We may marvel at the poet's keen interest in the trades and crafts—the tailor's, the shipbuilder's, the falconer's—or at his undeviating accuracy in every astronomical, chronological, mechanical, or physiological detail. The *Commedia* is not a vision by a mind in absolute contemplation, it is rooted in the immediate Christian world of the year 1300, as seen by a Tuscan exile.

Each of the three divisions of the triple poem (the *Inferno,* the *Purgatorio,* and the *Paradiso*) has a singular atmosphere of its own which provokes and defies definition. The reader who has just emerged, with Dante and Virgil, out of the pits of Hell onto the edge of the Island of Purgatory, feels, with the first lines, that he is breathing a different air; as he will again on entering the first heaven of Paradise.

It is traditional, and useful, to define these variations in Dante's poetic quality by saying that the *Inferno* is dramatic, the *Purgatorio* lyrical, and the *Paradiso* metaphysical. Similarly, the *Inferno* is often called the realm of fire, the *Purgatorio* the realm of music, and the *Paradiso* the realm of light. But all this is too easy. There is more to be gained in getting at Dante's attitude toward the characters he meets, as it varies from one kingdom to the other. In Hell, Dante is awestruck: his reverence for his guide, Virgil, is childlike, his contempt for the sinners is deeply felt, even vindictive; but he is still chiefly a spectator. He emerges fully as a person, as the protagonist in his own poem, only in the *Purgatorio.* This is his own kingdom; Purgatory is the true reflection of his condition on earth. In Paradise, Dante's personality fades again, but this time, so to speak, it fades forward: he longs to be one with the blessed, as they long to dissolve into God.

The sinners in Hell, to whom future hope is denied, are all still entangled in earthly vice; their spent life is their only concern. They uphold their actions—defiantly, ironically, cunningly. When shame overpowers them, it itself becomes an *evil* shame. All this makes the most famous figure in the *Inferno,* the poignant Francesca da Rimini, a kind of exception. Who can be blind to the beauty of her great episode?—*Inferno,* v, 73-142. Yet its popularity rests on a misunderstanding which began in the Romantic period. Sympathy for an ill-fated adultress is obviously a romantic theme, but we are wrong to think that this is the effect Dante desired. When Francesca ends the sorrowful account of her transgression, with Paolo weeping silently in the background, Dante faints "like a body falling dead," because the recognition of the force of passion *and* of the justice of divine punishment is more than his human frailty can bear.

The real, if evil, heroes of the *Inferno* are the Great Rebels—from the highest, Capaneus, who did violence to God himself, and who, not "ripened" even by a rain of fire:

> So that the rain tames him not, though so charred,
> *(Inferno,* XIV, 48)

> Bestial life pleased me, not of man,
> Mule that I was: for Vanni Fucci I am,
> Beast!
> *(Inferno,* XXIV, 124-26)

and screams,

> Raising his hands with both the figs on high:
> "Take thou them, God; at thee, at thee they aimed!"
> *(Inferno,* XXV, 2-3)

The dominant figure among these rebels is Farinata degli Uberti, the Ghibelline chief who stands upright in his tomb, confronting Dante,

> As if of Hell he had a great disdain.
> *(Inferno,* X, 35-36)

He is imprisoned in the circle of the heretics, condemned as a freethinker. Yet Dante cannot refuse homage to his magnanimity in Hell, nor to his relentless militancy on earth. Here is the poetry of contrast in Dante's own mind. Intellectually he prizes the Christian virtues—humility, temperance, obedience. Yet he cannot help admiring singleness of purpose and strength of will, whatever their end. Even a repentant Machiavellian has a strange appeal for him—Guido da Montefeltro (*Inferno*, xxvii), who reveals, in an unforgettable speech, the sophistry by which the Pope himself led Guido to forsake the Franciscan vows he had taken in his old age and then got him to trick a hostile city into submission. It is only natural that Dante's art in the *Inferno* should reach its peak in the Ulysses episode (*Inferno*, xxvi, 90-142), where the human craving for knowledge as a boundless experience, with its inherent tragedy, is exalted by the most austere poet of our culture.

"Repentance and Hope" might be the motto of the *Purgatorio*. They color it everywhere, and are so strongly felt as to be infused into the music of each line, speaking of humbleness of heart, renunciation; of the slow, sweet oblivion of that error called life (in Dante's Italian, *errore* stands not only for "error" in the English sense, but also for wandering). Is it not fitting that on the slopes of the Purgatory we should meet so many artists? As early as the second canto, we meet Casella— the poet's musician-friend, who is eager to hear again one of Dante's *canzoni*,

> . . . the enamoured song,
> Which used to soothe all wishes of my thought.
> (*Purgatorio*, ii, 107-108)

But the earthly visitor is not allowed to respond; he may not even embrace Casella's ethereal body. This theme of friendship and brotherhood runs throughout the *Purgatorio*. Its symbol is the embrace—which two fellow-

poets finally exchange when Virgil meets Sordello, a
Provençal troubadour. Virgil was born near Mantua,
and so was Sordello, twelve centuries later. They are
bound by poetry and their native city. Their mutual
readiness

>   . . . to acclaim
> His countryman and hail him there for friend
> Merely at the sweet sound of his city's name,
>   (*Purgatorio*, vi, 79-81)

inspires in Dante the most passionate lament over Italy's
misfortunes that has ever been written:

> Thou inn of sorrow, ah, trampled Italy!
> No Lady of domains, but brothel of shame!
> Ship without pilot on a storming sea! . . .
>   (*Purgatorio*, vi, 76-78)

Another Provençal poet is important in this section:
Arnaut Daniel (*Purgatorio*, xxvi, 136-148), who in
Purgatory must expiate sexual lust. Dante puts into his
mouth eight lines of Provençal which project the grief
and hope of one hung between atonement and re-
demption. (Every word of this speech has stirred a re-
sponse in T. S. Eliot's mind, and left some trace in his
poetry.)[1]

In the *Purgatorio*, all strife is felt from afar—its sound
is dimmed. For human conflict discolors the peace of
this other world, like the scar disfiguring that handsome
warrior, Manfred:

>   . . . blond
> He was, and beautiful, of noble mien;
> But one eye-brow was cleft by a great wound.
>   (*Purgatorio*, iii, 106-108)

---

[1] See *T. S. Eliot's Ash Wednesday*, iii. This section of the poem,
when first published separately, even bore the title "Som de l'Esca-
lina," an expression in Provençal used by Arnaut Daniel in Purga-
torio, xxvi.

An illegitimate son of Frederick II, and an enemy of the Papacy, Manfred had been defeated and slain in battle. But he has no hatred for the Church—he grieves only for his bones, which the Pope had ordered to be exhumed and cast like rubbish in the fields:

Now by the rains they are washed, by winds dispersed . . .
                                    (*Purgatorio*, III, 130)

Yet not even through the "malediction" of the Church, he adds,

                                    . . . is one lost
        So that eternal love cannot relent
        So long as hope has aught of green to boast.
                                    (*Purgatorio*, III, 133-35)

The noble prince's journey to Heaven may be long, but the goal is secure. This is not only Manfred's hope, it is the faith that gives the whole *Purgatorio* its poetic and spiritual light.

Until late in the nineteenth century, it was felt that Dante's confession of creative powerlessness before the Supreme Vision on which his poem closes:

    To the high imagination force now failed . . .
                                    (*Paradiso*, XXXIII, 142)

could well apply to most of the *Paradiso*. Dante the poet, it was thought, had surrendered to Dante the theologian, sacrificing art to doctrine. Our century has almost reversed this judgment. The rediscovery of English metaphysical poetry, the recognition of Gerard Manley Hopkins and Emily Dickinson, have led us to a quiet revolution in taste which has put the *Paradiso* on the highest altar of poetry. No sensitive critic would deny that in the *Paradiso* there are deserts without poetry. But one must also stress that when, as in most cantos, theology, political vision, and the metaphysical quest *are* made flesh, Dante's art reaches a sublimity not only unsurpassed, but forgotten, by the poets who came after him.

We can say of the sinners in the *Inferno* and the *Purgatorio* that they are "characters." We cannot often say this of the figures in the *Paradiso*. Those who appear before us to speak, question, or instruct, are emblems rather than persons. Blessedness, which is the union with God, is a state, and while it admits degrees and qualities, it cannot be shaped into individual traits. Yet Dante's dramatic power is so assertive that, recurrently, a real character will emerge before us. It is as if the poetic center had been moved to create him, in a kind of cosmic parabola that brings the reader back to earth for a while, only to lift him up again to the heavenly spheres.

Dante is a voyager in this realm, and a privileged one, for he sees that blessedness is a thing to be enjoyed, and he aspires to it after death. Yet, for the time being, he is intent only on *understanding* it. The surrender of reason to faith is only the culmination of the poem—its very exhaustion, when the word becomes silence. But before that point is reached, in virtually all the *Paradiso*, the human will to understand—in all the projections of intellectual and poetic power—is felt more deeply than ever. Dante gathers his forces around him toward a keener, and still keener perception:

> For the last labor, good Apollo, I pray,
> Make me so apt a vessel of thy power
> As is required for gift of thy loved bay.
>
> (*Paradiso,* i, 13-15)

His humility is very moving:

> But he who thinks how heavy a theme to grip
> Is here for mortal, shouldering such a weight,
> Will think no blame if sometimes the foot slip.
>
> (*Paradiso,* xxii, 64-66)

At moments he feels himself to be

> Working as the artist who has skill by dint
> Of his art's practice but a hand that shakes.
> > (*Paradiso*, XIII, 67-68)

In the *Paradiso*, the poet wishes to represent and to prophesy. On the one hand, he aims to capture the ineffable—how the blessed appear, and what they feel—not so much in its uniqueness as in its endless variety. His subject, frankly, is the anatomy of bliss. He conjures up all possible images from the realm of sounds, of colors, of odors; he finds hundreds of ways to tell us, wonderfully, that what he sees cannot be told. Beatrice's beauty in particular, and all it represents, are for him a symbol of what expression cannot attain:

> And if in speaking I had wealth not less
> Than in imagining, I would not dare
> To attempt the least part of her loveliness.
> > (*Paradiso*, XXXI, 37-39)

> If all of her that heretofore is said
> Could in a single perfect praise be quit,
> 'Twere still too narrow to suffice my need.
> > (*Paradiso*, XXX, 36-38)

Yet this reticence proves more powerful than any directness. For long stretches (Canto XXIII, for example) we are engulfed, with the blessed, in a stream of joy that overwhelms all our senses as much as theirs:

> Then as if dizzy with the spiced perfume
> They plunged into the enchanted eddy again . . .
> > (*Paradiso*, XXX, 67-69)

Thus the slow ascent toward the highest, as blessedness grows from sphere to sphere, is also a continuous heightening of Dante's imagination, up to that ultimate stillness which is its triumph.

On the other hand, Dante intends to establish intel-

lectually, and to disclose poetically, the nature of the
Church and of the Empire. Both are God-ordained
powers, and their history concerns the poet only to the
extent to which it displays their timeless essence. Their
present estrangement and conflict are a transgression
which Heaven mysteriously permits. But their future
reconciliation is already written in God's decrees—then
they will order themselves in a perfect hierarchy, the
Pope under the Emperor, and both under the divine
law.

> The inborn thirst, which never is allayed,
> For the God-moulded realm . . .
>
> *(Paradiso,* ii, 19-20)

is the deepest craving of man and nature, indeed their
very meaning, so that the whole universe lives in ex-
pectation. This is the ultimate thrust of Dante's insight,
in which representation and prophecy meet—and be-
come revelation. For revelation is the disclosure of
knowledge to man by supernatural agency. This is ex-
actly what Dante meant the *Commedia* to be. He
thought of himself as of a vehicle through whom God's
designs were to be made patent. To this task, he sum-
moned all his knowledge of nature (which is the child
of God), and all the power of art, which is

> Of the Godhead the grandchild, so to say,
>
> *(Inferno,* xi, 105)

since to him revelation was not the opposite of reason
and poetry, it was their consummation.

The last canto of the *Paradiso* is one of the summits
not only of Western art, but of man's spiritual endeavor.
It opens on a Prayer to the Blessed Virgin, which
Chaucer adapted in part—the most inspired a poet ever
wrote. It goes on to describe the vision of God—first his
concept, then his nature, and finally his presence—in

verses shot through by a light that is dazzling, yet seems to vanish before us at every moment, and in which the inexpressible and the undeniable mingle miraculously. Many masterpieces invite a catharsis; the *Commedia* includes us in an apotheosis.

v

What has been said so far may be convincing to those who know Dante in the original, who have savored the full Italian texture of his art. To read Dante in English is to feel his inner quality only indirectly, and not many translations have helped us to do that. Laurence Binyon's[1] version of the *Commedia* is an extraordinarily successful effort.

There are passages in the poem that have been rendered better by others; but I do not know of any other complete English version more continually, more faithfully, and more fruitfully sensitive. Binyon's rendering, in English triple rhyme, adheres to Dante's own meter —the arduous *terza rima,* without which the *Commedia* is unthinkable. Its language represents a backward reach into an older English, as Dante's is an older Italian. In the course of its more than thirteen thousand lines some unevenness may be traced; but Binyon never distorts the original style; he never takes us beyond the range of Dante's own voice. This is apparent when we see how a translator's romantic leanings (M. B. Ander-

---

[1] Laurence Binyon (1869-1943) was one of those rare men whose taste is as exquisite as their culture is wide. Keeper of prints and drawings in the British Museum, a famous Orientalist and a connoisseur of art and of literary history, a scholar in many fields (to say nothing of his knowledge of things Italian), he was a distinguished poet as well. He devoted to his version of the Divine Comedy the best of twenty years, and completed it shortly before his death.

son), his literalness (J. B. Fletcher), or his rhetoric (Longfellow) can disfigure a masterpiece. Those who have read Dante only in a prose translation can now rediscover him.

Laurence Binyon meant his version of the *Commedia* "to be read with pleasure as an English poem." To orient the reader, he prefaced the cantos with admirably concise "arguments," which are reprinted in this edition. But if the reader is actually to go through the poem without serious interruptions, he needs also a minimum of specific information such as only footnotes can supply. The best notes in English to the *Divine Comedy* are by the late C. H. Grandgent of Harvard, the greatest of American Dante scholars. A substantial number of the Grandgent notes are reprinted here, most of them condensed for this edition.

Those who do not know the poem in the original often ask: "How does Dante sound in Italian? What is his artistry like? Why is it great?" It is difficult to answer, but not impossible. For a person who knows some poetry deeply has in this knowledge a key to all poetry.

The main point about Dante is this: what he says is never more, is never less, than his *initial* and total response to the object before him. Art, for him, is the form that truth takes on when it is fully perceived (which is not true, though it may at first appear so, of all successful creation: think of Baroque art). Dante never indulges in fancy; he never adorns, or magnifies. As he thinks and sees (whether with his outer, or his inner, eye), so he writes. With him the poet is never an addition to the man, as is always the case with Romantics, and often even with Shakespeare. His sensory apprehension is so sure, and his intellectual grasp so direct, that he never doubts that he is at the very center of perception. This is probably the secret of Dante's celebrated conciseness. For him a figure, a feeling, a dramatic situation can only have one shape, one core, one meaning: how could he help being brief?

Take one of the supreme achievements of the *Inferno*, the story of Piero della Vigna, Frederick II's minister and devoted courtier, who, unjustly accused of treason by his Emperor-friend, killed himself to escape his agony. What a knot of conflicts for a modern psychologist to untangle! Yet Dante puts Piero's whole drama into one tercet, which gives us what we have been seeking—the very essence of a moral commitment:

> *L'animo mio per disdegnoso gusto,*
> *Credendo col morir fuggir disdegno,*
> *Ingiusto fece me contra me giusto.*

> My soul into disdainful temper thrust,
> Thinking by death to escape the world's disdain,
> Made me, the just, unto myself unjust.
>
> (*Inferno*, XIII, 70-72)

(Note that the Italian *"animo,"* which Binyon renders "soul," means precisely *both* the mind and the heart—the realm of the will and of the emotions. And that the Italian for "temper" is *"gusto,"* whose connotation, although by no means identical with our English "gusto," yet has some association with pleasure.) The same could be shown of many of the famed episodes—all dense, all pruned, if not all as unbelievably plain as the speech of Pia de' Tolomei (*Purgatorio*, V, 131-136)—a murder story *and* an elegy in six lines.

Dante's style—his brevity, and that trait which only a sculptural term, "relievo," can describe—depend intimately on the nature of the language he used, or rather, helped to create. Italian was in its infancy then; it was slowly emerging from a vernacular status and Dante molded it freely. His sense of words is not categorical, as ours often is (the scientific habit has made our modern languages invertebrate, with each term a ready-made dress for a mechanically corresponding concept). Compared with ours, Dante's vocabulary is poor—but happily so, since each word is loaded with meaning and rich in poetic resonance. His use of adjectives is the most sparing and, therefore, the most powerful in Italian literature. His main weapon is the verb—which passive minds neglect, and which he handles like a chisel. The most hackneyed image is still the most expressive: Dante doesn't draw, he carves.

The popular conception of Dante as a "medieval" poet is confusing. It rests either on a misapprehension (England and France were in fact still medieval in Dante's thirteenth century, but Italy no longer was), or on some hasty conclusions—after all, doesn't Dante believe in the Devil, and in scholastic logic, and in absolute monarchy? If we are attentive to Dante's true achievement—his art—we will find him much closer to the Renaissance than to the Middle Ages. Friedrich Engels was not too much off the mark, when, in an address to Italian Socialists, he called Dante the first universal mind of our modern era. Dante's contribution to poetry is parallel to his friend Giotto's in painting. They do not perfect a dying art; they cross the threshold onto a new one. And the cultural temper of their age is well defined in the term "pre-Renaissance."

Dante's peculiar asset as a poet is that of the true beginner who draws strength both from the absolutes of a deep-rooted tradition and from his soundings of the future. No view, therefore, is more dubious than the current one (so tainted with envy, especially when held by writers), that Dante was so good a poet because he could rely innocently on his unshakable Catholic faith.

This was by no means Dante's approach to art. It is doubtful that he could even have conceived a fallacy so peculiarly modern and romantic as that which holds that an artist can be favored by a stock of beliefs which for him remain beyond discussion. Dante would have rejected this as blasphemous for the religious man and dishonorable for the poet. He was happy to believe, for he was sure that the Catholic tenets were also *rationally* true. His was not Pascal's faith—a matter for the heart —nor, like him, was he "betting" on God. The structure of theology had to be tested in every part, and demonstrated in the light of reason; even the inscrutable dogmas had to be proved inscrutable. Furthermore, Dante appeals at every turn to human experience to confirm religious views. Is not the whole of the *Commedia* a cosmic demonstration of what, in Dante's belief, *happens* to those who err?

But the reader will ask: "Can Dante's poem be enjoyed in full by those who do not share his faith?" A captious answer could be that we do enjoy the Venus of Milo though the pagan gods have no reality for us. Yet the case *is* different, for Dante did not uphold, as in a way the Greeks did, the autonomy of art. "Art for art's sake" would have seemed to him even more senseless than damnable. His religious faith and his scholastic philosophy are an indissoluble part of his poetic universe. But though the content of his beliefs is one we may accept or refuse, they come to us as *an experience,* and one whose articulated form appeals to us as it did to him.

Take for example the classification of the sins and virtues upon which the *Commedia*—Dante's own Last Judgment—undoubtedly rests. It is not only a theological appraisal, it is an ethical and a psychological one. If on the first account we may not heed it, on the second or the third we must. When Dante's bitterest condemnation falls upon the slothful "who never were alive,"

> . . . the abject crew that were
> Odious to God and to his enemies,
>
> (*Inferno,* III, 62-63)

or when, apropos of nuns whom outsiders have forced to break their vows and leave the convent, he explains, by Church doctrine and his own art, that the victim of violence can rarely be excused, since by his passive acceptance he somehow collaborates with his oppressor:

> For the will cannot, if it will not, die,
> But does as in the fire's flame nature does
> Though violence wrest it thousand times awry.
>
> Should it, then, bend, little or much, it thus
> Abets the violence. . . .
>
> (*Paradiso,* IV, 76-80)

we feel that, possessed of his religious experience and going beyond it, Dante describes some permanent potential of human nature which the future can fill.

I say nothing of his political dream of universal peace, or of his luminous prophecy of a second Advent; they speak of the oldest, the strongest longing of humankind.

Not even a short introduction can avoid skirting the last, thorniest question. What is the role of allegory in the *Commedia?* An unexpected opponent of allegory in literature, Edgar Allan Poe, wrote once that allegory is acceptable only when "the suggested meaning runs through the obvious one in a *very* profound undercurrent, so as never to interfere with the upper one without our own volition, so as never to show itself unless *called* to the surface." Allegory, in other words, must be optional—a thought Dante himself expressed many times, and to which he was faithful. There is no doubt that he intended his *Commedia* to be accessible to, and variously valid for, different kinds of readers, some of whom would enjoy the "fable," while others would find their way to the higher meaning. This, however, does not explain *why* he gave the poem its composite structure, unfolding it simultaneously on several planes. The allegorical approach is by no means a device; it is the natural end of Dante's idea of art and a reflection of the peculiar integration of his mind. I hesitate to use our modern word "integration"—for all the associations it so mechanically provokes ("integration to," adjustment," etc.) are absolutely foreign to Dante. The man who may have commented on the choice of an envoy, as one story goes—"If I go, who will stay? And if I stay, who will go?"—certainly did not believe that the individual and society should be brought together at any price. He thought that both should submit to a superior truth, of which a patient search and a long love had made him the trustee.

At this point it will be easy to perceive that Dante's art is *also* allegorical, because he must allow it to function at the same time on all levels of human apprehension. The source of his greatness as a poet lies probably in his native feeling that the artist's creation is not only an esthetic act, but also a way of knowing, and a road to moral perfection. As a statement of the complexity of the artist's task this may sound obvious. But it is worth recalling, especially if one looks at the state of contemporary art. How much of it is at once beautiful, philosophically true, and morally edifying? A slow dissociation of these three qualities has been at work for centuries, and we are reduced to admire, as if in separate wings of a gallery, the flesh according to Matisse, the mind according to Picasso, and the heart according to Rouault. Twenty generations after Dante's time, we have traveled to the opposite end of history—we live in an age where the split between mind, matter, and soul (to use Dante's terms) has become so complete that we feel it is about to be reversed. This must account for the fascination Dante has for us. His peace of mind is our lost paradise.

It is a fact that our poets are ready, intellectually at least, to accept the lesson the achievement of the *Commedia* exemplifies so persuasively. They acknowledge, as Herbert Read once remarked, that "the poet is only capable of his intuitive experiences so long as he receives some sort of sanction from the procedure of thought. A positive poetry is possible when the esthetic intuitions of the poet co-operate with the thought of the philosopher (as in the case of Lucretius and Dante)."

How enviously we look up to a genius whose suffering was the effect of circumstances, or of the human condition, not of some contradiction within himself. We are eager to imitate this "poet of integrity," as Dante has been called. But we are also dangerously impatient. On one hand we know that the road is long (it may take centuries), on the other we are continually tempted to take any short-cut.

Some are ready to erase six centuries of Western history and take shelter under the wings of Catholic orthodoxy and behind the syllogisms of Aquinas, as if allegiance to Dante's Church, or to the frame of his beliefs, could grant them some semblance of his genius. It is a mirage. Those who believe it forget that Dante was a Catholic who enthroned his Beloved in the Empyrean at the side of God, who called the Church of his time the Harlot of Kings, and who prepared for a living Pope ("The Prince of the new Pharisees") a seat in Hell. They pass over Dante's genuine reverence for knowledge and science. Praising Dante's exaltation of the Catholic faith, they fail to see that active love of an ideal was to him the closest thing to faith.

Dante was one who held that every aspect of man's adventure on earth deserved to be reflected in poetry. In his poem of redemption he found place for the wisecrack of a harlot (*Inferno*, XVIII, 133-135), and for the most obscene expression of ironic disapproval (*Inferno*, XXI, 139). And, finally, he thought Cato of Utica

> . . . so much to be revered
> That no son owes a father more of awe
> (*Purgatorio*, I, 32-33)

that very Cato who killed himself as the last defender of the Roman republic, to seek

> . . . freedom, that so precious thing,
> How precious, he knows who for her will die.
> (*Purgatorio*, I, 71-72)

If the world is to see another poet whose moral fiber and universal mind are comparable to Dante's, it will only be in an age happily purged of the separateness which plagues our civilization and threatens its inner death.

Dante is peculiarly the poet of the whole; and we shall read him best when we have been made whole again, and in our own way. Meanwhile it may be enough to say, as Chaucer did six centuries ago:

> Of this tragedie it oghte ynough suffise;
> Whose wol here it in a lenger wise,
> Redeth the grete poete of Ytaille
> That highte Dant, for he kan al devyse
> From point to point, nat o word wol he faille.
> (*The Monk's Tale*, II, 461-465)

PAOLO MILANO

Some Dates in the Life of Dante

1265   Latter part of May: Birth in Florence of Dante (or Durante) Alighieri. Dante's mother died during his childhood, and his father, Alighiero di Bellincione d'Alighiero, had at least two children from a new marriage.

1274   First meeting of Dante and Beatrice.

1277   Dante's father arranges for his son a future marriage with a girl of noble birth, Gemma Donati. The dowry is fixed.

1283   Death of Dante's father.
May Day: Dante and Beatrice meet again and exchange greetings.

1289   June 11: Dante fights among the horsemen at the battle of Campaldino, where the forces of the Guelf League (Florence and Lucca) defeat the Ghibellines of Arezzo and Pisa.
December 31: Death of Beatrice's father, Folco Portinari.

1290   June 8: Death of Beatrice.

1291   Presumable date of Dante's marriage with Gemma Donati. They had two sons (Piero and Jacopo) and one or two daughters.

1292   Probable date of the composition of *La Vita Nuova*.

1294   February: Charles Martel, the Anjou prince, is given a solemn reception in Florence. Dante is among the knights who do him honor.

1295   July 6: Dante joins the guild of physicians and apothecaries to enter public life.

1295   November 1 (to April 30, 1296): Dante serves as a member of the "People's Council" of the Commune of Florence.

1300   May: Dante is sent as a special envoy to the city of San Gemignano.
June 15: Dante is elected a "Prior of the Guilds," one of the six chief magistrates of Florence.
September: An envoy of Boniface VIII, Cardinal d'Acquasparta, excommunicates all the Priors of Florence on the Pope's behalf. Dante is spared only because his term of office expired on August 15.

1301   October: Dante is sent to Rome, one of three envoys who are to negotiate an agreement with Boniface VIII.

1302   January 27: The Blacks, having seized power in Florence, condemn Dante to pay a fine of five thousand florins, to be banished from the city for two years, and to be forever excluded from public office. Dante learns of the sentence on his way back to Florence. His exile begins.

    March 10: Following Dante's refusal to appear in Florence and plead guilty, his banishment is made perpetual, and he is condemned to be burned alive, should he cross the territory of the Republic.

1303   Dante's sons are condemned to share their father's exile as soon as they reach their fourteenth year.

1304-   Dante works at *Il Convivio* ("The Banquet") and
1307   at *De Vulgari Eloquentia*.

1306   Dante is a guest, in Lunigiana, of Lord Moruello, Marquis of Malaspina. (See Epistle III.)

1310   Henry VII descends into Italy at the head of an army.

1311   September: An amnesty is granted to many White exiles. Dante is excluded.

1313   Sudden death of Henry VII near Siena, and collapse of his Italian campaign.

1314   Following the death of Pope Clement V, Dante addresses a passionate epistle to the Italian cardinals, urging them to bring the Papal see back from Avignon to Rome.

1312-   Probable date of the composition of *De Monar-*
1314   *chia*.

1315   Dante refuses to be recalled from exile. (See Epistle IX.)

    November 6: The Florentines confirm Dante's condemnation to death, this time including in the death sentence his two sons.

1315-   Dante lives in Verona as a guest of Can Grande
1321   Della Scala, a Ghibelline leader, and later in Ravenna. He works at the *Commedia*.

1320   Before an audience of learned clergymen in Verona, Dante discusses a topical problem of medieval physics—the respective height of water and earth on the surface of the planet ("*Quaestio de aqua et terra*").

1321   September 14 (or 13): Dante's death in Ravenna, in the house of Guido Novello da Polenta.

THE DIVINE COMEDY

Translated by Laurence Binyon

with notes from C H. Grandgent

This revised edition incorporates extensive corrections in *The Inferno* made by the translator before his death.

INFERNO

Canto I

It is the eve of Good Friday, 1300, and Dante is thirty-five years old. He comes to himself in the darkness of the wood of Error, not knowing how he had lost the true way. Gaining the foot of a hill, the Delectable Mountain, or hill of virtue, he is cheered by the morning sun, and begins the ascent, but is baffled by a Leopard (Lust), then dismayed by a Lion (Pride), and a She-Wolf (Avarice). Turning to run back to the valley, he is met by the spirit of Virgil, the poet of his adoration, who in the Vision typifies human wisdom. Virgil tells him that he cannot pass the She-Wolf, though a savior of Italy is one day to arise who will chase her into Hell; and Dante is to follow him and be shown the spirits who are in pain and have no hope, and the spirits who through pain are to come to bliss; and from these he will be led by another (Beatrice, Dante's early love, typifying Heavenly Wisdom) to see the spirits in Paradise. Dante follows in Virgil's steps.

Mɪᴅᴡᴀʏ life's journey I was made aware
    That I had strayed into a dark forest,
    And the right path appeared not anywhere.
Ah, tongue cannot describe how it oppressed,
    This wood, so harsh, dismal and wild, that fear
    At thought of it strikes now into my breast.
So bitter it is, death is scarce bitterer.

3

But, for the good it was my hap to find,
  I speak of the other things that I saw there.
I cannot well remember in my mind   10
  How I came thither, so was I immersed
  In sleep, when the true way I left behind.
But when my footsteps had attained the first
  Slope of a hill, at the end of that drear vale
  Which with such terror had my spirit pierced,
I looked up, and beheld its shoulders pale
  Already in clothing of that planet's light   17
  Which guideth men on all roads without fail.
Then had my bosom a little of respite
  From what had all the pool of my heart tost   20
  While I so piteously endured the night.
As one, whom pantings of his breath exhaust,
  Escaped from the deep water to the shore,
  Turns back and gazes on the danger crost,
So my mind, fleeing still and stricken sore,
  Turned back to gaze astonished on that pass
  Which none hath ever left alive before.
When my tired body had rested a brief space
  I trod anew the slope, desert and bare,
  With the firmer foot still in the lower place.   30
And at the ascent, as 't were on the first stair,
  Behold! a Leopard, very swift and light   32

---

17. "That planet": the sun, which is just rising. The sun, here and
elsewhere, typifies enlightenment, perhaps righteous choice, the
intelligent use of the free will.

30. This perplexing and much discussed line seems to describe the
act of cautiously feeling one's way up a slope.

32. When Dante tries to scale the hill, three beasts beset his path.
These animals evidently stand for Dante's vicious habits, which
prevent his reform. The ravening wolf is Incontinence of any
kind, the raging lion is Violence, the swift and stealthy leopard
is Fraud. We may understand, from the episode, that Dante could
perhaps have overcome the graver sins of Fraud and Violence,
but was unable, without heavenly aid, to rid himself of some of
the habits of Incontinence.

And covered with a hide of mottled hair.
And it would not depart, but opposite
  On my path faced me, so that many a time
  I turned me to go back, because of it.
The moment was the morning's earliest prime,
  And the sun mounted up, accompanied
  By those stars that with him began to climb   *39*
When divine Love first made through heaven to glide *40*
  Those things of beauty, so that hope I caught   *41*
  Of that wild creature with the gaudy hide.
The hour of time and the sweet season wrought
  Thus on me; yet not so much, but when appeared
  A Lion, terror to my heart he brought.
He seemed coming against me with head reared
  Ravening with hunger, and so terrible
  That the very air seemed of his breath afeared;
And a She-Wolf, that in her famished fell
  Looked all infuriate craving (she hath meant   *50*
  To many ere now that they in misery dwell)
On me with grimness of her aspect sent
  A burden that my spirit overpowered,
  So that I lost the hope of the ascent.
As one that is with lust of gain devoured,
  When comes the time that makes him lose, will rack
  His thoughts, lamenting all his hope deflowered,
To such state brought me, in dread of his attack,
  That restless beast, who by degrees perforce
  To where the Sun is silent drove me back.   *60*
While I was rushing on my downward course
  Suddenly on my sight there seemed to start
  One who appeared from a long silence hoarse.   *63*

39-41. *It was believed that when the universe was created, the heavenly bodies were placed in their vernal positions. The sun is in the sign of Aries from March 21 to April 20 inclusive.*
63. *At this crisis Reason, personified in Virgil, comes, at divine bid-*

When I beheld him in that great desert
   "Have pity on me!" I cried out to his face,
   "Whatsoever—shade or very man—thou art."
He answered me: "Not man; man once I was.
   My parents both were of the Lombard name,
   Of Mantua by their country and by their race.
Sub Julio was I born, though late I came: 70
   In Rome the good Augustus on me shone,
   In the time of the false Gods of lying fame.   72
Poet was I, and sang of that just son   73
   Of old Anchises, who came out from Troy
   After the burning of proud Ilion.
But thou, why turn'st thou back to such annoy?
   Why climbest not the Mount Delectable
   The cause and the beginning of all joy?"
"And art thou, then, that Virgil, and that well
   Which pours abroad so ample a stream of song?" 80
   I answered him abashed, with front that fell.
"O glory and light of all the poets' throng!
   May the ardent study and great love serve me now
   Which made me to peruse thy book so long!   84
Thou art my Master and my Author thou.
   Thou only art he from whom the noble style
   I took, wherein my merit men avow.
Regard yon beast from which I made recoil!
   Help me from her, renownèd sage, for she

---

ding, to the sinner's rescue. *The voice of Reason has not been heeded for so long that it comes faintly to the sinner's ear.*

70-71. "Sub Julio": *at the time of Julius Caesar; but so late that he was identified with the reign of Augustus, and not that of Caesar. Virgil was barely twenty-six when Caesar perished.*

72. *Repeatedly Virgil makes pathetic but always dignified and reticent allusion to his lack of Christianity and his consequent eternal exclusion from the presence of God.*

73. "That just son": *Aeneas.*

84. *We learn from Inf.* xx, 114 *that Dante knew the Aeneid by heart.*

Puts all my veins and pulses in turmoil."   90
"Needs must thou find another way to flee,"
    He answered, seeing my eyes with weeping fill,
    "If thou from this wild place wouldst get thee free;
Because this beast, at which thou criest still,
    Suffereth none to go upon her path,
    But hindereth and entangleth till she kill,
And hath a nature so perverse in wrath,
    Her craving maw never is satiated
    But after food the fiercer hunger hath.
Many are the creatures with whom she hath wed,   100
    And shall be yet more, till appear the Hound   *101*
    By whom in pain she shall be stricken dead.
He will not batten on pelf or fruitful ground,
    But wisdom, love, and virtue shall he crave.
    'Twixt Feltro and Feltro shall his folk abound.
He that abasèd Italy shall save,
    For which Euryalus, Turnus, Nisus died,
    For which her virgin blood Camilla gave.   *108*
And her through every city far and wide
    Back into Hell's deep dungeon shall he chase,   110
    Whence envy first let loose her ravening stride.
Wherefore I judge this fittest for thy case
    That I should lead thee, and thou follow in faith,

101-105. This Hound is obviously a redeemer who shall set the world aright. If we compare this passage with another prophecy in Purg. XXXIII, 40-45, it is tolerably clear that he is to be a temporal rather than a spiritual savior—a great Emperor, whose mission it shall be to establish the balance of power, restore justice, and guide erring humanity. Such an Emperor, destined to come at the end of the world, was not unknown to legend. As the prediction was still unfulfilled at the time of the writing, Dante naturally made it vague. We know that the poet entertained great hopes of the youthful leader, Can Grande della Scala, in Dante's last years the chief representative of the Imperial power in Italy. "Feltro and Feltro" may point to the towns of Feltre and Monte Feltro.

108. Camilla, a warrior virgin who fought against the Trojans.

To journey hence through an eternal place,
Where thou shalt hear cries of despairing breath,
    Shalt look on the ancient spirits in their pain,
    Such that each calls out for a second death.
And thou shalt see those who in fire refrain   *118*
    From sorrow, since their hope is in the end,
    Whensoever it be, to the blessèd to attain.   *120*
To whom if thou desirest to ascend
    There shall be a spirit worthier than I,   *122*
    When I depart, who shall thy steps befriend.
For that Lord Emperor who reigns on high,
    Because I was not to his law submiss,
    Wills not that I to his city come too nigh.
In every part he ruleth, and all is his,
    There is his city, there is his high seat:
    O happy, whom he chooseth for that bliss!"
And I to him: "O Poet, I entreat   *130*
    In the name of that God whom thou didst not know,
    So that I 'scape this ill and worse ill yet,
Lead me where thou hast spoken of but now,
    So that my eyes St. Peter's gate may find   *134*
    And those whom thou portrayest in such woe!"
Then he moved onward: and I went behind.

118-119. The souls in Purgatory.
122. Beatrice.
134. The gate of Purgatory, opened only to the elect.

Canto II

As the evening of the first day falls, Dante begins to doubt his courage for the journey. He recalls the visit to the underworld of Aeneas (told by Virgil in the Sixth Aeneid) and of St. Paul (the theme of a medieval legend) and declares himself unworthy to follow such as these. Virgil then discloses that Beatrice came from Heaven, prompted by Divine Grace, to ask him to rescue Dante from the dangers into which he has fallen. Dante's courage at once revives, and he accepts his mission.

THE day was going, and the darkened air
　　Was taking from its toil each animal
　　That is on the earth; I only, alone there,
Essayed to arm my spirit against all
　　The terror of the journey and pity's plea,
　　Which memory, that errs not, shall recall.
O Muses, O high Genius, strengthen me!
　　O Memory, that what I saw hast writ,
　　Here shall be made known thine integrity.
I began: "Poet, who guidest now my feet,　　10
　　Look if the virtue in me avail to endure
　　The arduous pass, ere thou trust me to it.
Thou sayest the father of Silvius went secure　　13
　　In his corruptible body, and that world knew

13-21. *This first visitor of the lower world is Father Aeneas, founder of Rome.*

Which Death knows not, of all his senses sure.
But if the Adversary of Sin that due
  Of favour gave him, weighing the high effect
  And who, and what, should be his great issue,
This seems not unmeet to the intellect;
  For he was born to father and prepare   20
  Rome and her Empire, as high Heaven's elect;
Both of which, the true history to declare,
  Were the foundations of that sainted spot
  Which is the seat of greatest Peter's heir.
By this adventure, whence thy praise he got,
  He learned things that for him were argument
  Of victory, and the Papal Mantle wrought.
Afterwards too the Chosen Vessel went   28
  The confirmation of that faith to bring
  Which is for way of our salvation meant.   30
But I, why go? By whose commissioning?
  I am not Aeneas, no, nor Paul: too weak
  I, and others also, deem me for this thing.
If I resign me, then, that world to seek,
  I fear the quest for folly be aspersed.
  Thou art wise and canst divine more than I speak."
And like one who unwills what he willed first
  And new thoughts change the intention that he had,
  So that his resolution is reversed,
So on that dim slope did my purpose fade
  For I with thinking had dulled down the zest
  That at the outset sprang so prompt and glad.
"If rightly I read the trouble in thy breast,"
  The shade of the Magnanimous replied,
  "With cowardice thy spirit is oppressed,
Which oftentimes a man hath mortified,
  So that it turns him back from noble deed,
  As with false seeing a beast will start aside.

---

28. "The Chosen Vessel" is St. Paul: Acts 9:15.

Now, that thy heart may from this fear be freed,
    Hear why I came and what I heard, and where,   50
    When first I felt the pity of thy need.
I was with those who are in suspense: and there   52
    A Lady of so great beauty and blessedness,   53
    I craved for her command, called me to her.
Her eyes so shone, the Morning Star shines less.
    And she began to speak, gentle and low,
    In the angel voice that did her soul express:
'O courteous Mantuan spirit, whom men fame so   58
    That thy renown yet lasts, and till Time end
    The motion of his hours, shall greater grow,   60
He that is my friend, but not fortune's friend,
    Halts on the lonely moor, by fear deterred,
    So that the path he dareth not ascend.
Already I fear he may so sore have erred
    That I have risen to succour him too late,
    From what of him in Heaven I have heard.
Go now, and with thy poet's speech ornate
    And what means else may rescue courage weak
    Help him, and me deliver of this care's weight.
I am Beatrice who send thee, him to seek.   70
    I come from that place for which now I sigh.
    It was love moved me and made my lips to speak.
Often to thy praise will I testify
    When I am come into my Lord's presence.'
    She then was silent; and I made reply:
'O Lady, who art the only virtue whence
    Mankind may overpass what is contained   77

52. "Who are in suspense": between Heaven and Hell, in Limbus.
53. "A Lady": Beatrice.
58. Virgil was born near Mantua.
70. Beatrice stands for Revelation, for which Dante's distorted mind
    must be prepared by Reason.
77. Mankind surpasses everything contained within the sphere of
    the moon (everything perishable) only through divine revelation,
    embodied in Beatrice.

Within the heaven of least circumference,
So welcome is the bidding thou hast deigned,
    That were it now done, it were done too slow.   80
    It needs but that thy wish should be explained:
But tell me why into this core of woe
    Thou shun'st not to descend, turning thy face
    From the ample air, whither thou yearn'st to go?'
'Since thou,' she answered, 'so much of this case
    Desirest knowledge, briefly shalt thou hear
    Why I shrink not to come into this place.
Those things that have the power to wound and sear,
    To them alone should due of dread be paid;
    To the others not, they are not things to fear.   90
I am by God so, in his mercy, made,
    That misery of yours touches me not,   92
    Nor in the scorch of this fire am I frayed.
A Lady in heaven is to such pity wrought   94
    By the hard pass, whereto I bid thee haste,
    That the strict law's remission she hath sought.
She called to her Lucy, and made request,   97
    Saying, Now thy faithful one hath need of thee:
    I entrust him to thee; and do thou the rest.
Lucy, the enemy of all cruelty,   100
    Arose and came and stood within my gaze
    There, where the ancient Rachel sat by me.   102
She spoke and said: Beatrice, God's true praise,
    Why helpest thou not him, who loved thee so
    That for thy sake he left the vile crowd's ways?

---

92. *The happiness of the blest is not marred by compassion for the damned.*

94. *"A Lady in heaven": the Virgin, who is not expressly named anywhere in the Inferno, Hell being a place where mercy does not enter.*

97. *Lucy has been regarded by almost all interpreters as the emblem of Grace—probably, as her name suggests, Illuminating Grace.*

102. *Rachel symbolized the contemplative life.*

Hearest thou not the plaining of his woe?
  Seëst thou not what death would him undo
  By that wild flood the sea may not o'ercrow?   *108*
None in the world was ever swift to ensue
  His good, or fly his hurt, as these my feet   110
  At once, after those words were uttered few,
Hasted to come down from my blessèd seat,
  Confiding in thy speech, so nobly graced,
  It honours both thee and those hearing it.'
Having said this, her footsteps she retraced,
  Turning from me her eyes that wept and shone;
  At sight of which she made me more to haste.
Thus I came to thee, as she desired, and won
  Thee from that ravening beast which would withhold
  The short way to the Beauteous Mount begun.   120
What is it, then, keeps thee? Why, why haltest cold?
  Why in thy heart nourishest fear so base?
  Why art thou not delivered, eager, bold,
When three such blessed Ladies of their grace
  Care in the court of Heaven for thy plight,
  And my words promise thee such good to embrace?"
As little flowers, that by the chill of night
  Are closed, prick up their stems drooping and bent,
  And to the early ray re-open white,
So was it with my courage fallen and spent;   130
  And I began, as one from bondage freed,
  So good a warmth about my body went:
"O most compassionate She, who helps my need!
  O courteous thou, who to that uttered word
  Didst listen, and to its truth so swift give heed!
Thou makest me so eager in accord
  With what thou say'st, and quickenest so my heart,

---

108. "The wild flood" *is perhaps the Acheron, the river of death
which flows beneath Dante's feet, and which does not empty into
the sea, but runs down through Hell.*

That to my first resolve I am restored.
Now it is one will moves us both; thou art
    Guide, master, lord!" These words to him I said, 140
    And then, perceiving that he made to start,
Began the desolate, arduous path to tread.

Canto III

*The poets pass through the door of Hell. And first,
in what is Hell's ante-room, they meet a confused
lamenting rabble: these are those, displeasing alike
to God and to his enemies, who pursued neither
good nor evil. Among them Dante recognizes him
"who made the great refusal," generally identified
with the Pope Celestine V, who, elected in 1294,
resigned a few months later in favor of Boniface
VIII, Dante's great enemy. Then they come to the
shores of Acheron, the river which circles the rim
of Hell before descending deeper; across it Charon
ferries the lost souls, but demurs to taking Dante in
his boat. A sudden earthquake throws Dante into
a trance.*

Gate of Hell

THROUGH ME THE WAY IS TO THE CITY OF WOE:
    THROUGH ME THE WAY INTO THE ETERNAL PAIN;
    THROUGH ME THE WAY AMONG THE LOST BELOW.
RIGHTEOUSNESS DID MY MAKER ON HIGH CONSTRAIN.
    ME DID DIVINE AUTHORITY UPREAR;   5
    ME SUPREME WISDOM AND PRIMAL LOVE SUSTAIN.   6

5-6. *Hell was made by the triune God—Father, Son, and Holy
Ghost, or Power, Wisdom, and Love.*

BEFORE I WAS, NO THINGS CREATED WERE   7
   SAVE THE ETERNAL, AND I ETERNAL ABIDE.   8
   RELINQUISH ALL HOPE, YE WHO ENTER HERE.

These words, of a dim colour, I espied   10
   Written above the lintel of a door.
   Whereat: "Master, the sense is hard," I cried.

And he, as one experienced in that lore:
   "Here all misgiving must thy mind reject.
   Here cowardice must die and be no more.

We are come to the place I told thee to expect,
   Where thou shouldst see the people whom pain stings
   And who have lost the good of the intellect."   18

His hand on mine, to uphold my falterings,
   With looks of cheer that bade me comfort keep,   20
   He led me on into the secret things.

Here lamentation, groans, and wailings deep
   Reverberated through the starless air,
   So that it made me at the beginning weep.

Uncouth tongues, horrible chatterings of despair,
   Shrill and faint cries, words of grief, tones of rage,
   And, with it all, smiting of hands, were there,

Making a tumult, nothing could assuage,
   To swirl in the air that knows not day or night,
   Like sand within the whirlwind's eddying cage.   30

And I, whose mind failed to discern aright,
   Said: "Master, what is it that my ear affrays?
   Who are these that seem so crushed beneath their
     plight?"

And he to me: "These miserable ways

7-8. "In the beginning God created the heaven and the earth. And
the earth was without form, and void" (Gen. 1:1-2). At this
point, apparently, Hell was created for the rebellious angels, who
sinned almost as soon as they were made. On the Judgment Day,
when all the wicked shall have been consigned to Hell, it will be
sealed up, and will remain unchanged forever.

18. "The good of the intellect" is the vision of God.

The forlorn spirits endure of those who spent
Life without infamy and without praise.
They are mingled with that caitiff rabblement
Of the angels, who rebelled not, yet avowed
To God no loyalty, on themselves intent.
Heaven chased them forth, lest, being there, they cloud
Its beauty, and the deep Hell refuses them,
For, beside these, the wicked might be proud."   42
And I: "Master, what is the grief extreme
Which makes them so their fortune execrate?"
He answered: "Brief words best their case beseem.
They have no hope of death: and their estate
Is so abased in the blind life they own
That they are envious of all others' fate.
Report of them the world permitteth none.
Mercy and Justice have them in disdain.
Let us not talk of them. Look, and pass on."   50
I, who looked, beheld a banner all a-strain,
Which moved, and, as it moved, so quickly spun
That never a respite it appeared to deign.
And after it I saw so many run,
I had not believed, they seemed so numberless,
That Death so great a legion had undone.
When I had marked some few among the press,
I chanced the shade of him to recognize
Who made the great refusal, in cowardice.   60
Forthwith I was assured, and knew mine eyes
Looked of a truth on the abject crew that were
Odious to God and to his enemies.

---

42. The guilty might derive some satisfaction from comparing themselves with these.
60. Without much doubt this is Celestine v, a pious hermit, who, after a long vacancy of the papal office, was elected Pope in July, 1294, but abdicated five months later, feeling himself physically and mentally unfit. Through his renunciation Boniface viii, Dante's chief enemy, became Pope.

These paltry, who never were alive, were bare
　　As to the body, and all about were stung
　　By stings of the wasps and hornets that were there.
Because of these, blood, from their faces sprung,
　　Was mingled with their tears and flowed to feast
　　The loathly worms about their feet that clung.
Then as my peering eyes made further quest,   70
　　I saw folk on the shore of a great stream.
　　"Master," I said, "make to me manifest
Who these are and what law constraineth them
　　Willingly to pass over and be gone,
　　If rightly I can discern by the faint gleam."
And he to me: "The things shall all be known
　　To thy understanding when our steps are stayed
　　Upon the mournful shores of Acheron."
Casting abashed eyes downward, and afraid
　　Lest that my words should some offence have
　　　　wrought,   80
　　I ceased from speech until the stream we made.
And toward us lo! arriving in a boat
　　An Ancient, white with hair upon him old,   83
　　Crying, "Woe to you, ye spirits misbegot!
Hope not that heaven ye ever shall behold.
　　I come to carry you to yon shore, and lead
　　Into the eternal darkness, heat and cold.
And thou who art there, a living spirit, with speed
　　Get hence, nor with these who are dead delay"—
　　But when he noted that I took no heed,   90
He said: "By another ferry, another way
　　Of entrance must thou seek to pass, not here.
　　Needs must a lighter vessel thee convey."
My Guide to him: "Charon, thy frowns forbear.   94

---

83. *The ancient boatman is Charon.*
94. *Charon sees that Dante is destined to be carried, after death, to*
　　Purgatory in the angel's boat described in Purg. ii, 40-51.

Thus is this thing willed there, where what is willed
  Can be accomplished. Further question spare."
Then were the shaggy cheeks from trouble stilled   97
  Of that old steersman on the livid fen
  Around whose eyes flames in a circle wheeled.
But those forlorn and naked spirits of men   100
  Changed colour, chattering with their teeth, all numb,
  Soon as the harsh words sounded in their ken.
They blasphemed God, blasphemed their mother's
        womb,
  The human kind, the place, the time, the seed
  Of their engendering, and their birth and doom;
Then weeping all together in their sad need
  Betook themselves to the accursed shore
  Which awaits each who of God takes no heed.
Charon, the demon, beckoning before,
  With eyes of glowing coal, assembles all: 110
  Whoever lags, he beats him with his oar.
And as the late leaves of November fall
  To earth, one after another, ever fewer,
  Till the bough sees its spoil gone past recall,
So by that river Adam's seed impure
  Cast themselves from the wharf, one after one,
  At signals, as the bird goes to the lure.   117
Thus are they borne across the water dun;
  And ere they disembark on the far strand
  On this another gathering is begun.   120
"Son," said the courteous Master, "understand
  That all those who have died in the anger of God
  Congregate hither out of every land.
And they are prompt to pass over the flood,
  For Divine Justice pricketh in them so

97-99. Charon, like most of the classical guardians retained in
Dante's Hell, becomes a demonic figure.
117. "The lure": the call by which the hunter lures it.

That fear is changed to longing in their blood.   *126*
By this way no good spirit is seen to go.
  Therefore if Charon doth of thee complain,
  What his words mean thou easily may'st know."
When he had ended, the whole shadowy plain   *130*
  Shuddered so strongly, that the terror past
  Still at the memory bathes me in sweat again.
Out of the tear-drenched earth came forth a blast
  That made a crimson flash before me leap
  And numbness over all my senses cast.
And I fell, like to one seized with a sleep.

Canto IV

*When the poet awakes he is on the farther side of
Acheron and on the brink of the great Abyss. He
descends with Virgil to the First Circle or Limbo,
where are the souls of the unbaptized and of the
virtuous heathen. Virgil describes the descent of
Christ into Limbo. In a part which is more lumi-
nous they are greeted by Homer and other chief
poets of antiquity; it is here that Virgil's own place
is. Farther on is a noble castle, where are seen
heroes and heroines of old, Aristotle, "the master of
them that know," and the philosophers, and other
famous spirits.*

RUMBLE of thunder upon my brain deep-drowsed
  So shook the sleep that at the heavy sound
  I started, like a man by force aroused.

126. *Any reality seems to them less intolerable than the apprehen-
sion.*

And my now rested eyes casting around
   I rose upright, with peering gaze intent
   To know the place wherein myself I found.
True it is, I stood on the edge of the descent
   Where the hollow of the gulf out of despair
   Amasses thunder of infinite lament.
Sombre, profound, and brimmed with vaporous air   10
   It was, so that I, seeking to pierce through
   To the very bottom, could see nothing there.
"Let us go down to the blind world below,"
   Began the Poet, on a sudden pale.
   "I shall be first, and thou behind me go."
And I, who had marked his colour so to quail,
   Said: "How shall I come where thou losest cheer
   Who art wont over my falterings to prevail?"
And he to me: "The misery that is here,
   Down among this folk, maketh my face wan   20
   With pity, which thine eyes mistake for fear.
Descend we: the long way constrains us on."
   So he entered, and he made me enter too,
   On the first circle that the abyss doth zone.
Here was no sound that the ear could catch of rue,
   Save only of sighs, that still as they complain
   Make the eternal air tremble anew.
And this rose from the sorrow, unracked by pain,
   That was in the great multitude below
   Of children and of women and of men.
The good Master to me: "Wouldst thou not know   30
   What spirits are these thou seest and hearest grieve?
   I'd have thee learn before thou farther go,
These sinned not: but the merit that they achieve   34
   Helps not, since baptism was not theirs, the gate
   Of that faith, which was given thee to believe.

---

34. "These sinned not": *Virgil will not have Dante suppose for a moment that his companions in Limbus have been evildoers.*

And if ere Christ they came, untimely in date,
   They worshipped not with right experience;
   And I myself am numbered in their state.
For such defect and for no other offence   40
   We are lost, and only in so far amerced
   That without hope we languish in suspense."
I, when I heard this, to the heart was pierced,
   Because I knew men to much virtue bred
   Whose spirits in that Limbo were athirst.
"Tell me, my Master, tell me, Sir!" I said,   46
   Seized with a longing wholly to be assured
   Of that faith wherein error cannot tread,
"Did ever any of those herein immured
   By his own or other's merit to bliss get free?"   50
   And he, aware what meant my covert word,
Answered: "I was yet new in this degree   52
   When I saw one in power crowned appear   53
   On whom the signs of victory were to see.
He took from us the shade of our first sire;   55
   Of his son Abel, and Noah of that same seed;
   Moses, the obedient and the law-giver;
The patriarch, Abraham, and the King, David;
   Israel with his father and with his sons;   59
   Rachel also, to win whom so much he did;   60
And many another; and made them blessed ones;

46-48. *As soon as Dante learns that Virgil's soul dwells in Limbus, he is eager to receive from this witness corroboration of the doctrine of the descent of Christ into Hell.*

52. *"I was yet new . . .": Virgil died in the year 19 B.C.*

53. *"I saw one . . . appear": Christ, who is never named in the Inferno.—"Crowned": doubtless a cruciform nimbus. After the crucifixion Christ went down into Hell, and took from Limbus the souls of the worthy people of the Old Testament.*

55. *"Our first sire" is Adam.*

59. *"Israel": Jacob; "his father": Isaac; "his sons": his twelve children.*

60. *To win Rachel, Jacob served Laban twice seven years: Gen. 29:18-28.*

And I would have thee know that, before these,
　There has been no human soul that he atones."　　63
We ceased not to go on by slow degrees,
　Though he spoke still, and past the wood had come,
　The wood I mean of spirits thick like trees,
And, since my slumber, had not advanced therefrom
　Far, when a radiant glow beyond us shone
　Which overcame a hemisphere of gloom.
A little distance from us it lay on,　　　　　　　70
　Yet not so much but that I saw in part
　What honourable folk that place had won.
"O thou that honourest Science and Art,
　Who are these that have such honour and acclaim
　That it removes them from the rest apart?"
And he to me: "The glory of the name　　　　　76
　Which sounds of them above in the earthly sphere
　Gains favour of Heaven which thus promoteth them."
Meanwhile a voice was sounding in my ear:　　79
　"Honour ye all the great Poet: his shade　　　80
　That had departed, now again is here."
After the voice had paused and silent stayed,
　I saw four great shades come with one accord.
　They had an aspect neither gay nor sad.
The good Master began to speak his word:
　"On him who bears the sword thine eyes now cast,　86
　Who comes before the others, as their lord.
He is Homer, who all poets hath surpassed.

---

63. *Before the descent of Christ all human souls went, if bad, to
Hell; if good, to Limbus. Since that time Christian souls penitent
at the moment of death have gone to Purgatory.*
76-78. *God allows the intelligence, by the good use of which they
won such renown on earth, to remain with them in the other
world.*
79. *We are not told which of the spirits utters the greeting to
Virgil.*
86. "On him who bears . . .": *Homer, who is depicted with a
sword because he sang of arms.*

The next who comes is Horace, satirist,
   Ovid the third, and Lucan is the last.   90
Because each nature doth with mine consist
   Through that name which the one voice glorifies
   They do me honour, and themselves not least."
Thus came that noble school before mine eyes
   Assembling round the lord of loftiest style
   Who over the others like an eagle flies.
After they had talked together a little while,
   They turned to me and welcoming signs displayed:
   At which salute I saw my Master smile.
And yet more honour unto me they paid,   100
   For me into their band did they invite,
   So that I a sixth amid such wisdom made.
Thus we went moving onwards toward the light
   Speaking such things as here were better mute,
   Though there to speak them was both meet and right.
Now came we to a Noble Castle's foot,
   With lofty walls seven times engirdled round,   *107*
   And a fair rivulet moated it about.
This we passed over as it had been dry ground.
   Through seven gates entering with those sages, lo! *110*
   A meadow of fresh verdure there I found.
On it were people with grave eyes and slow,
   And great authority was in their mien.
   They spoke seldom, with mild voices and low.
Thus we retired on one side that demesne
   Into an open, luminous, high place,

---

107. The "Noble Castle," or the Palace of Wisdom, is surrounded
by seven walls representing the four moral virtues (prudence,
temperance, fortitude, and justice) and the three intellectual vir-
tues (understanding, knowledge, and wisdom).
110. The gates probably symbolize the seven liberal arts of the
trivium (grammar; logic, rhetoric) and the quadrivium (music,
arithmetic, geometry, astronomy), which afford access to knowl-
edge.

So that they stood where they could all be seen.
There on the green enamel, face to face,
　Were shown me the great spirits, so that I
　Exalt myself to have enjoyed such grace.　　　　120
I saw Electra in a great company　　　　　　　121
　Among whom Hector and Aeneas were,
　And armèd Caesar with the falcon eye.
I saw Camilla and Penthesilea there　　　　　　124
　Over against them, and the Latian King;
　Lavinia his daughter sitting near;　　　　　　126
That Brutus who drove out the proud Tarquin;
　Lucrece, Cornelia, Julia, Marcia, four
　Together, and by himself the Saladin.　　　　129
When I had raised my eyes a little more,　　　　130
　I saw the Master of those who know: he sate　131
　Amid the sons Philosophy to him bore.
All do him honour, all eyes on him wait.
　Here I beheld Plato and Socrates
　Who of all are nearest to his high estate.
Democritus, whose world blind Chance decrees;
　Diogenes, Thales, Anaxagoras;　　　　　　137
　Zeno, Heraclitus, and Empedocles:
Him who was skilled the virtue of plants to class,
　Dioscorides, I saw; and Orpheus' shade;　　　140

---

121. Electra, daughter of Atlas, and mother of Dardanus who was
　the founder of Troy.
124. Camilla: a warrior maiden (cf. Inf., i, 108); Penthesilea: queen
　of the Amazons.
126-28. "Lavinia": wife of Aeneas; "Brutus": Lucius Junius Brutus,
　implacable foe of the Tarquins; "Lucrece": Lucretia, wife of Col-
　latinus; "Julia": daughter of Caesar, wife of Pompey; "Marcia":
　wife of Cato of Utica; "Cornelia": mother of the Gracchi.
129. "Saladin," the model of chivalry, was sultan of Egypt and Syria
　in the twelfth century. He is different in race and religion from
　those mentioned hitherto.
131. "The Master of those who know": Aristotle.
137. "Thales" was one of the seven wise men of Greece.
140. Orpheus is considered as a philosopher.

Tully's and Linus'; moral Seneca's;   *141*

Euclid, and Ptolemy, who the stars surveyed;   *142*

  Hippocrates, Avicenna, and Galen,   *143*

  Averroes also, who the Comment made.   *144*

I may not portray all in the full scene,

  Being hurried on so by the long theme's care,

  That oft the word comes short of the thing seen.

The band of six to two hath dwindled, where   *148*

  By another road the sage Escort inclines

  Out of the quiet into the trembling air.   150

I come to a place where there is naught that shines.

---

141. "Tully," or Cicero, was one of the first philosophers that Dante studied. "Linus": an imaginary Greek poet (other texts have "Livy," the Roman historian, who also wrote philosophical works). "Seneca" the moralist was thought to be a different person from the dramatist.

142. "Ptolemy," the great geographer and astronomer of Alexandria, who lived in the second century B.C.

143. "Hippocrates, Avicenna, and Galen": three famous physicians of Greece, Turkestan, and Mysia.

144. "Averroes": a Spanish Moor of the twelfth century, was a celebrated scholar and philosopher. Having read the works of Aristotle in ancient Syriac translations, he composed three commentaries on them; one of these was followed by St. Thomas.

148. The company of six dwindles to two—Virgil and Dante.

Canto V

The descent to the Second Circle, with which Hell proper begins. Here are the souls of carnal sinners. Minos, who presides over the entrance of Hell as Judge and assigns their places to the damned as they come in, at first refuses admittance to Dante, but is overawed by Virgil. The carnal sinners are blown about forever on stormy winds, and among

them Virgil points out famous lovers. Dante wishes
to speak with one pair, who are Francesca da Ri-
mini and Paolo Malatesta, brother of the husband
to whom for state reasons Francesca had been mar-
ried. Hearing Francesca's story Dante is so over-
come with pity that he faints.

From the first circle I thus descended down
   Into the second, which less space admits,
   And so much more pain that it stings to groan.
There Minos, hideously grinning, sits,
   Inspects the offences at the entering in,
   Judges and, as he girds himself, commits.
I mean, that when the ill-born spirit comes in
   Before his presence, it confesses all;
   Thereon that scrutinizer of each sin
Sees what place Hell holds for its fittest stall;   10
   Round him as many times his tail doth throw
   As the degrees he wills that it should fall.
Always before him stand they, row on row;
   To sentence comes each of the wretched train:
   They tell, and hear; and straight are whirled below.
"O thou, who comest to the home of pain,"
   Said Minos to me, when my face he spied,
   Leaving his business of the great Arraign,
"Beware in whom thou, entering, dost confide.
   Let not the broad approach thy feet ensnare."   20
   "Why criest thou out?" answered to him my Guide.
"Hinder thou not his destined steps. Forbear!
   Thus is the thing willed there, where what is willed
   Can be accomplished. Further question spare."
Now begin notes of wailing never stilled
   To pierce into my ear; now am I come
   Where thronging lamentations hold me thrilled.

I came into a place of all light dumb
    That bellows like a storm in the sea-deep
    When the thwart winds that strike it roar and hum. 30
The abysmal tempest that can never sleep
    Snatches the spirits and headlong hurries them,
    Beats and besets them with its whirling sweep.
When they arrive before the ruin, stream   34
    The cries up; there the wail is and the moan,
    There the divine omnipotence they blaspheme.
I learnt that in such restless violence blown
    This punishment the carnal sinners share
    Whose reason by desire was overthrown.
And as their beating wings the starlings bear   40
    At the cold season, in broad flocking flight,
    So those corrupted spirits were rapt in air
To and fro, down, up, driven in helpless plight,
    Comforted by no hope ever to lie
    At rest, nor even to bear a pain more light.
And as the cranes in long line streak the sky
    And in procession chant their mournful call,
    So I saw come with sound of wailing by
The shadows fluttering in the tempest's brawl.
    Whereat, "O Master, who are these," I said,   50
    "On whom the black winds with their scourges fall?"
"The first of those concerning whom thou hast prayed 52
    To know," he answered, "had dominion
    Of many tongues, which she as empress swayed.
With vice of luxury was she so undone,
    That she made lust a law by her decree,

---

34. "The ruin": as the pit narrows progressively toward the bottom,
the terraces correspondingly decrease in circumference. At one
point in the round of this shelf is a break, where the rock has
fallen. In Canto XII, 31-45, we are told that when Christ de-
scended into Hell, his coming was preceded by an earthquake,
which shook down the walls of the abyss in three spots.
52. "The first of those . . ." is Semiramis, queen of Assyria.

To obliterate the shame that she had won.
This is Semiramis: we read that she
    Came after Ninus, and had been his bride.
    She ruled the land the Soldan holds in fee.   60
That other is she who by her own hand died   61
    For Love's sake, to Sichaeus' urn untrue;
    Voluptuous Cleopatra comes beside.
See Helen, for whose sake the long years drew
    Ill after ill; see great Achilles there,
    Who fought with love in the end, and whom love
        slew.
See Paris, Tristram!" More than a thousand pair   67
    He with his finger pointing at shades of fame
    Showed me, whom love had power from life to tear
After that I had heard my Teacher name   70
    Each lady of old, with her enamoured knight,
    My thoughts were mazed, such pity upon me came.
I began: "Poet, I fain would, if I might,
    Speak with those two that hand in hand appear
    And, as they move, seem to the wind so light."
And he to me: "When they approach more near,
    Thou shalt see. By the love which is their guide
    Do thou entreat them then, and they will hear.
Soon as the wind's whirl made them nearer glide,
    I raised my voice up: "O tired spirits, come   80
    And speak with us, if that be not denied."
Eagerly as a pair of pigeons, whom
    Desire calls, and their will bears, as they fly
    On wide unfaltering wings to their sweet home,
So swerved those spirits from out the company
    Where Dido is, flying toward us underneath

---

61. "She who by her own hand died" is Dido. The story of her
fatal love for Aeneas (and her infidelity to the memory of her
dead husband Sichaeus) is told in Aeneid, IV.
67. "Paris": son of Priam. "Tristram": the hero of the most famous
medieval love romance.

The fell mirk; such a power had my fond cry.
"O kind and gracious creature that hast breath
    And comest journeying through the black air
    To us who made the earth bloody with our death,   90
Were but the world's King friend to us, a prayer
    Should from us both implore Him for thy peace
    Because thou hast taken pity on our despair.
Whether to speak or listen better please,
    We will speak with you, and hear and understand,
    Now while the lull'd wind spares a little ease.
The place where I was born sits on the strand   97
    Where Po descends to his peace, and with him takes
    All the other streams that follow him down the
        land.   99
Love, that in gentle heart so quickly wakes,   100
    Took him with this fair body, which from me
    Was torn: the way of it still hurts and aches.   102
Love, that to no loved one remits his fee,
    Took me with joy of him, so deep in-wrought,
    Even now it hath not left me, as thou dost see.
Love led us both to one death. He that sought
    And spilt our life—Cain's hell awaits him now."   107
    These words to us upon the wind were brought.
When I had heard those wounded spirits, my brow
    Sank downward, and I held it where it was,   110
    Until the Poet spoke: "What musest thou?"
And when I answered, I began: "Alas!
    How many sweet thoughts and what longings fain
    Led them into the lamentable pass!"

---

97. "The place where I was born": Ravenna, then only one mile
    from the sea and connected with the Po river by canals.
99. The tributaries are conceived as chasing the Po down to the sea.
102. "The way . . . and aches": because, murdered as she was with-
    out a chance to repent, she incurred eternal punishment.
107. "Cain's hell": the abode of traitors to kindred, at the bottom
    of Hell, which awaits Francesca's husband, Gian Ciotto.

I turned, and I began to speak again:
   "Francesca, the tears come into mine eyes
   For sorrow, and for pity of thy pain.
But tell me: in the time of the sweet sighs
   How did Love vouchsafe proof of what he is,
   And of the obscure yearnings make you wise?"   120
And she to me: "No grief surpasses this
   (And that thy Teacher understands full well)— *122*
   In the midst of misery to remember bliss.
But if thou so desire to know how fell
   The seed whose first root in our bosoms fed,
   I'll tell, as one who can but weep and tell.
One day together, for pastime, we read
   Of Launcelot, and how Love held him in thrall. *128*
   We were alone, and without any dread.
Sometimes our eyes, at the word's secret call,   130
   Met, and our cheeks a changing colour wore.
   But it was one page only that did all.
When we read how that smile, so thirsted for,
   Was kissed by such a lover, he that may
   Never from me be separated more
All trembling kissed my mouth. The book I say
   Was a Galahalt to us, and he beside   *137*
   That wrote the book. We read no more that day."
While the one spirit spoke thus, the other cried
   So lamentably, that the whole life fled   140
   For pity out of me, as if I died;
And I fell, like a body falling dead.

---

122. "Thy Teacher": Virgil, who was happy and glorious on earth,
and is now condemned to eternal exile.
128. "We read of Launcelot": the French prose romance of Launce-
lot of the Lake, which tells of the love of the hero for Guinevere,
wife of King Arthur.
137. "The book . . . was a Galahalt to us": Galahalt was the inter-
mediary who brought Launcelot and Guinevere together; Paolo
and Francesca had no such go-between—the book was their Gala-
halt, their guide to love.

Canto VI

*Dante awakes in the Third Circle, where an icy
rain falls on souls of the gluttonous, watched over
by Cerberus. A Florentine spirit named Ciacco
accosts him and prophesies about Florence and the
varying fortunes of the Black and White factions
in it.*

WHEN my mind came back, that had closed at sight
  Of those two kinsfolk in their misery bound,
  Pity of whom in sorrow had mazed me quite,
New torments, new tormented ones around,
  Whatever step I take, wherever strain
  My eyes, I see, peopling the shadowy ground.
I am now in the Third Circle of the Rain,
  Eternal, cold, accurst, and charged with woe.
  Its law and quality ever the same remain.
Big hail, and clots of muddied water, and snow   10
  Pour downward through the darkness of the air:
  The ground they beat stinks with the overflow.
Cerberus, cruel and uncouth monster, there
  Stretches his three throats out and hound-like bays
  Over the people embogged about his lair.
His beard is slobbered black, his red eyes blaze,   *16*

16-19. Gluttony, the next of the sins of Incontinence, is essentially
foul and selfish. It is a sin that robs men of their humanity,
making them unrecognizable to their friends. Its perfect embodi-
ment is Cerberus, the tormenting genius of the place.

His belly is big, his hands clawed; and with growl
　　The spirits he clutches, rends piecemeal and flays.
The rain provoketh them like dogs to howl.

　　They with one side the other strive to screen:　　20
　　Often they turn themselves, those sinners foul.
When we by Cerberus, the great Worm, were seen,
　　He showed the tusks within each grinning jaw:
　　He had no limb but quivered with his spleen.
My Guide spread out his palms, when this he saw,
　　And took up clods of earth, and with full fist
　　Crammed them into each madly ravening maw.
And like the craving dog whose barks persist
　　But whom the first full bites of food appease,
　　For all his fever is but to champ that grist,　　30
So was it with those squalid visages
　　Of demon Cerberus, who roars so loud
　　The spirits would fain that deafness gave them ease.
Now passed we on over the shadows bowed
　　Beneath the crushing rain, and our feet set
　　On seeming bodies, empty as a cloud.
They all lay grovelling prone amid the wet
　　Save one who sat up quickly and raised his head,
　　Seeing us pass before him, and our eyes met.
"O thou who through this drizzling hell art led,"　　40
　　He cried out, "recognize me if thou may'st,
　　For thou wast made before I was unmade."
And I to him: "The anguish which thou hast
　　It may be so obscures thee to my mind
　　That 'tis as if for me thou never wast.
But tell me: who art thou in such place confined
　　And to such punishment condemned, that though
　　Worse may be, none is of so loathsome kind."
And he to me: "Thy city, which brims so　　49
　　With envy that the sack is ripe to spill,　　50

49. "Thy city": Florence.

Contained me in the sunny life ye know.
You citizens called me Ciacco: I did ill.   52
   For the fell sin of gluttony I atone
   Thou seest how in the rain I suffer still.
And I, unhappy spirit, am not alone.
   For all of these are in like penal state
   For the like trespass." More he would speak none.
I answered him: "Ciacco, thy piteous fate
   Weighs on me so, it moves me to lament.
   But, if thou canst, tell me what things await   60
The citizens of the city that strife has rent,
   If any in it be just: and tell me why
   Such discord doth within it so ferment."
And he to me: "They from contention high   64
   Shall come to blood; the Party of the Woods
   With contumely shall force the other to fly.
Ere the third sun his annual course concludes,   67
   This one must fall and the other prevail, upborne 68
   By him who still tacks in alternate moods.   69
Long shall it hold high the proud front of scorn, 70
   Making the other with sore burdens bleed,
   Though with the shame of bondage it be torn.

---

52. "Ciacco": a Florentine renowned both for his gluttony and for his cleverness, who figures also in one of Boccaccio's tales, Decameron, IX, 8.

64-66. After long strife between the adherents of the Donati, representing the old aristocracy, and the followers of the Cerchi, who had come to Florence from the country and enriched themselves by commerce, blood was shed in an encounter on May 1, 1300. In June, 1301, the leaders of the Black or Donati party conspired against their opponents, and in consequence were exiled.

67. "Third sun": the third solar year, beginning January 1; the Florentine year began on March 25.

68. "The other prevail": the Blacks having gained the upper hand through the cunning of Boniface VIII and his pretended peacemaker, Charles of Valois, banished, between January 1 and October 1, 1302, some 600 Whites. Dante was sentenced on January 27, and again on March 10.

69. "Upborne by him . . .": Boniface.

Two indeed are just: but none to them gives heed.   73
   Pride, Envy, and Avarice are the triple spark
   Which sows in all those bosoms fiery seed."
Here ended he his lamentation dark.
   And I to him: "Continue, for I would
   Hear yet more from thee and thine instruction mark.
Farinata and Tegghiaio, who worthiest stood,
   Arrigo, Rusticucci, and Mosca, and those   80
   Others who fixed their will on doing good,
Where are they? What place found they at the
     close?
   For fain would I be certain, if I may,
   Whether they taste Hell's poison or Heaven's repose."
And he: "Among the blackest spirits they.
   Them may'st thou see, if thou so far descend,
   Whom other sins down to the bottom weigh.
But when thou art come to the sweet world, befriend
   My memory, and recall to men my fate.
   No more I tell thee: here I make an end."   90
He twisted then his eyes asquint from straight,
   Looked at me a little, and then bowed down his head
   And mid his blind companions fell prostrate.
My Guide spoke to me: "No more from that bed
   He wakes until the angel trumpet sounds   95
   When the stern Power shall make his advent dread.
They shall revisit then their sad grave-mounds,
   And each his flesh and his own shape resume,
   And hear what through eternity resounds."
Thus passed we on through the commingled gloom   100

---

73. "Two indeed are just": *in Florence, there are only two just men;
who these two are, we are not told.*
95. "Until the angel trumpet sounds": *on the Day of Judgment, at
the sound of the last trumpet, all souls in Heaven and Hell will
return to earth, resume their bodies, gather in the Valley of
Jehoshaphat, and listen to their eternal sentence; after which they
will go back to their respective places.*

Of the shadows and the rain with paces slow,
Touching a little on the life to come.
Wherefore I said: "Master, these pangs of woe—
Shall they be increased after the great Assize
Or stay scorching as now, or lesser grow?"
And he: "Turn to thy science and be wise. *106*
The more a thing perfected is, the more
It feels bliss, and in pain the sharper sighs.
Although the state of these accurst at core
Never indeed in true perfection ends, *110*
They look then to be nearer than before."
We made along that circle as round it bends,
Speaking much more than I repeat, till we
Attained the point whereat the road descends.
Here found we Plutus, the Great Enemy. *115*

106-111. "Turn to thy science": *i.e., to the philosophy of Aquinas.
If the bodiless soul cannot attain the utmost happiness, we may
infer that it cannot attain the utmost misery. It follows that the
pains of Hell will be severer after the Judgment, because, although
the word "perfection" cannot be fitly applied to "these accurst at
core," they expect to be more complete after the Great Day than
before it.*
115. "Plutus": *the god of wealth, who was not always distinguished,
even by the ancients, from Pluto.*

Canto VII

---

*Plutus, the ancient God of Riches (who seems to
be identified or confused by Dante with Pluto),
presides over the Fourth Circle. Here are the
Misers and the Spendthrifts, abusers of worldly
goods in different ways. They roll dead weights in
opposite directions and when they meet scold each
other. Dante inquires of the function of Fortune,*

*which Virgil explains. They arrive at the descent
into the Fifth Circle, accompanying the fall of a
stream which has worn a passage to form the
marsh of Styx below. Here are the Wrathful,
quarrelling in the mud, and the Sullen, sunk be-
neath it. The poets arrive at last at the foot of a
tower.*

"PAPE SATAN, aleppe, pape Satan!"   1
  That gentle sage who knew what all speech meant,
  When Plutus thus with clucking noise began,
Said for my comfort: "Fear not, nor repent
  Thy journey; for our descending of this rock
  Whatever power he hath shall not prevent."
He turned him to that swollen visage and spoke;
  "Cease, thou accursed Wolf, thy rage to spit!
  Within thyself consume it till thou choke.
Not without cause our journey is to the pit.   10
  There is it willed on high, where Michaël
  For the rebel arrogance took vengeance fit."   12
As sails that sudden gusts of tempest swell,
  Fall when the mast breaks, tangled past amend,
  So to the ground that cruel goblin fell.
Thus down to the fourth hollow we descend,
  Taking the more in of that bank of woe
  Wherein all the evil of the world is penned.
Ah! Divine Justice! Who crowds throe on throe,
  Toil upon toil, such as mine eyes now met?   20
  And why doth guilt of ours consume us so?
Like to the wave above Charybdis' threat   22

---

1. The first line is evidently intended to produce the effect of an
unintelligible jargon.
12. "The rebel arrogance": the revolt of the angels.
22. "Charybdis": in the Strait of Messina.

That breaks against the wave it meeteth there,
   So are the people here at counter set.
Here saw I troops more numerous than elsewhere
   With yells prolonged on this side and that side
   Rolling dead weights with full chest pushing square.
Smiting against each other in force they vied,
   Then wheeled about just there and rolled them back.
   "Why holdest thou?" "Why flingest away?" they
      cried.   30
Thus they return along the dismal track
   On either hand to the point opposite,
   And their refrain of scolding never slack.
Then everyone when he had compassed it
   Through his half-circle turned to the other mark,
   And my heart felt as though itself were hit.
"Master mine," said I, "lighten my mind's dark.
   Who are these? And all those that the tonsure wear,
   Those on our left side, were they each a clerk?"   39
And he: "All these in mind so squint-eyed were   40
   In their first life, that they were quite without
   All measure, whether to expend or spare.
Most clearly may'st thou tell this from their shout
   When they the two points of the circle have won
   Where contraries of guilt divide the rout.
Priests were they that no hairy cover have on
   Their heads, and Popes, and Cardinals, in whom
   Avarice hath its utmost mischief done."
And I: "Master, among this crew are some
   Whose faces surely I should recognize,   50
   Who were polluted with this evil scum."
And he to me: "Confused is thy surmise.
   The squalor that in life their senses shut

---

39. "Were they each a clerk?" *Clerics* form a large part of the
miserly host; *Dante was by no means alone in regarding avarice as
the besetting fault of the clergy.*

Now makes them too dim to be known of eyes.
For ever at one another must they butt.
    These from the grave shall rise up with fists tight,
    Those others with their very hair close-cut.
Ill-giving, ill-hoarding, lost for them the light
    Of the bright world, and in this scuffling caught.
    I beautify no words to tell their plight.   60
Now, my son, see to what a mock are brought
    The goods of Fortune's keeping, and how soon!
    Though to possess them still is all man's thought.
For all the gold that is beneath the moon,
    Or ever was, never could buy repose
    For one of those souls, faint to have that boon."
"Master," said I, "tell me from what power rose
    This Fortune upon whom thy word did glance.
    What is she, whose grasp doth the world's good enclose?"
And he to me: "How heavy the ignorance,   70
    O foolish creatures, that on you is laid!
    Hear now my judgment of her governance.
The wisdom that transcendeth all, and made
    The heavens and gave them guides to rule them right,   74
    So that each splendour should the other aid
With equal distribution of the light,
    In like sort also a general minister   77
    Set over this world's glory and fond delight,
From time to time those vain goods to transfer
    From people to people, and from class to class,   80
    Beyond cunning of mortals to deter.

---

74. "And gave them guides": *the angels, who govern the revolutions of the spheres.*

77. "A general minister": *Fortune, a power similar to the celestial intelligences that move the heavens. It is her mission to shift prosperity to and fro, without apparent plan, seeing that it remain not too long with one person, family, or nation.*

Hence the empire from that race to this must pass,
   In wax and wane obeying her decree
   Which lurketh like a snake hid in the grass.
She is past your wit to understand; but she
   Provideth, judgeth, governeth her own,
   As the other Gods do theirs in their degree.
To her mutations is no respite known.
   Necessity in her forbiddeth pause:
   Thus comes he oft who is raised or overthrown.   90
This is she who is cursed without a cause,
   And even from those hath maledictions got,
   Unjustly, of whom she should have won applause.
But she is in her bliss, and hears them not.
   In chime with the other primal creatures glad,   95
   She turns her sphere and tastes her blissful lot.   96
Descend we now to miseries more sad.
   The stars that when I set forth climbed on high   98
   Sink, and to stay too long my charge forbad."
To the other bank we crossed the circle, nigh   100
   Above a spring that boiled and overflowed
   Down through the cleft it wore to issue by.
Darker than blackest purple the water showed.
   We followed down the sombre stream's decline
   And reached the floor below by a strange road.
These sullen waves into a fen combine
   Called Styx, whenas the water's last descent   107
   Reaches the foot of that grey scarp malign.
And I who stood with fixed looks intent

---

95. "Primal creatures": the angels.
96. "Her sphere": the wheel, the traditional symbolic attribute of Fortune.
98. The stars which were rising in the east when they started have now crossed the meridian and begun to descend towards the west: it is past midnight. Virgil usually states the hour in astronomical terms.
107. The Styx was the most famous of the rivers of the classic lower world.

Saw muddied people in that slough who stuck,   110
    All naked and with brows in anger bent.
Not with hands only each the other struck
    But with the head and breast and heels that spurn:
    At one another with their teeth they pluck.
"Son," said the gracious Master, "here discern
    The souls of those whom anger stupefied.
    And I would have thee for a surety learn
That sobbing underneath the water abide
    People who make the surface bubble and froth,
    As the eye may tell, turned to whatever side.   120
Fixed in slime, groan they: 'We were sullen and wroth
    In the sweet air made glad by the Sun's fire;
    We fumed and smouldered inly, lapt in sloth,
And now we gloom and blacken in the mire.'
    This sad refrain they gurgle in their throat
    Because they cannot speak the words entire."
We 'twixt the dry bank and the putrid moat
    Compassed a wide arc of those waters sour,
    And still those swallowers of the filth we note.
At last we reached the basis of a tower.   130

---

130. Here, as frequently, Dante breaks his narrative at an interesting
point, using suspense as a means of heightening effect.

Canto VIII

---

*A signal flaming from the top of the tower is an-
swered at a distance, and Phlegyas comes hurrying
in his boat to take the poets across the marsh
of Styx, supposing them to be damned souls. On
the passage Filippo Argenti, a Florentine, tries to*

clutch the boat and is set on by his fellow-sinners,
to Dante's great satisfaction. Soon appears the red
city of Dis or Lucifer, wherein are punished the
more heinous sins. Fallen angels refuse the poets
admission, and even Virgil is discomfited.

I SAY, continuing, that as on we went,
  Long ere the foot of that high tower we hit,
  Our eyes were drawn up to its battlement
Because of two flames that we saw there lit,
  And yet another answering them discerned
  So far, the eye scarcely could distinguish it.
To the Sea of all Intelligence I turned,
  And spoke: "What says this beacon, and what replies
  That other fire, and by whom are they burned?"
And he to me: "Over the foul wave flies   10
  What is awaited: save it be withheld
  By the marsh-mist, thou'lt see it with thine eyes."
Never did arrow from the string propelled
  With such a vehemence the air divide
  As the small pinnace that I now beheld
Over the water toward us lightly glide;
  And at the helm a single steersman was.
  "Art thou arrived, fell spirit?" aloud he cried.
And my Lord answered, "Phlegyas, Phlegyas,   19
  Thou criest this time in vain. Take us for freight,   20
  But for no more than ferry of the morass."
As one who hearkens to some great deceit
  Done to him, and his spirit is inly frayed,
  So Phlegyas swelled in anger at his defeat.

---

19. The guardian of the *Fifth Circle* is the swift Phlegyas, who seems
to impersonate both furor and rancor. On earth he was a king of
the Lapithae, who, in a frenzy of rage against Apollo for the viola-
tion of his daughter, set fire to the temple at Delphi, and was
slain by the god. In the Commedia he is a boatman on the Styx.

My Guide stept down into the boat, and made
    Me to enter after him; nor till I trod
    Within it, did that vessel seem down-weighed.
Soon as my Guide and I the thwart bestrode,
    The ancient prow began to cleave anew
    The water, deeper than with other load.   30
As the dead channel we were running through,
    Before me rose one full of mud, and cried,
    "Who art thou, come before thy time is due?"
And I to him: "I come, but not abide.
    But who art thou, so beastly that has grown?"
    "I am one who weeps, thou seëst," he replied.
And I to him: "With weeping and with moan
    Stay on, accursed spirit! For though thou roll
    In all thy filth, yet thou to me art known."
Then he stretched both hands out to clutch the thole. 40
    Whereat, watchful, the Master at him struck,
    Saying, "Off! Away, with the other dogs to growl!"
And put his arms about my neck, and took
    And kissed my face. "Indignant soul," he said,
    "Blessed be she that bore thee and gave thee suck!
Arrogant in your world he held his head:
    Now there is none to speak of him good things.
    So is his shade here upon rages fed.
How many above there deem themselves great kings
    Now, who shall lie wallowing in mire like swine,   50
    Leaving a name that with dishonour rings!"
And I, "Master, my wishes much incline
    To see him plunged into this broth, before
    We pass the ferry and this lagoon's confine."
And he to me: "Ere that thou see the shore
    Thou shalt be satisfied. Fit it is, my son,   56

56-57. "Fit it is . . . that thou enjoy this thing thou cravest for."
St. Thomas, in his Summa, distinguishes from sinful rage the
righteous indignation that is aroused by the sight of wickedness.

That thou enjoy this thing thou cravest for."
A little after I saw such mangling done
  Upon him by the foul folk muddy-cheeked,
  I still praise God that sight to have looked upon. 60
"Have at Filippo Argenti!" they all shrieked.
  The spirit of the infuriate Florentine
  Turned biting and on himself his fury wreaked.
We left him. He gets no more word of mine.
  But on mine ears now smote a sound of moan,
  And I peered forth, its meaning to divine.
Said my good Master: "We begin, my son,
  To approach the city that is named of Dis.   68
  Sad people it holds, and a great garrison."
"Already," I said, "mine eye distinguishes   70
  Clearly its minarets within the vale,
  All red, as if they had come from furnaces."
And he to me: "This their exterior shell
  The eternal fire within them maketh red,
  Even as thou seest, in this low hollow of Hell."
We now arrived at the deep fosses' bed
  That moat about that place disconsolate:
  Of iron seemed the walls above my head.
Not before making circuit long and late,
  We came to a stop, and loud the boatman there   80
  Cried out to us: "Land now! Here is the gate."
Above I saw full thousand spirits in air
  Rained down from heaven, who angry as if betrayed
  Cried: "Who is this who without death can dare
The kingdom of the dead folk to invade?"

This justifiable anger is illustrated here by the attitude of Dante
toward one of the violently wrathful. The furious soul that so
incenses Dante is Filippo Argenti of Florence.
68. "The City of Dis," or Lower Hell, is the abiding-place of those
whose sins were due not to Incontinence of desire or temper but
to permanent evil disposition, Bestiality, and Malice. Their crimes
are the fruit of envy and pride.

And my sage Master, making sign to them
    Of his desire, a secret parley essayed.
Their great scorn then did they a little stem,
    And said: "Alone come! let that other plod
    Back, who so bold into this kingdom came.   90
Let him return the way his folly trod.
    Try, if he can: for here shalt thou remain
    Who hast brought him hither by so dark a road."
Think, Reader, if my heart misgave me then
    To hear the accursed words, for from that shore
    I thought not ever to return again.
"O my loved Guide, who seven times and more
    Hast me from peril that stood before me freed,
    And didst to sweet security restore,
Leave me not so undone in my hard need,   100
    And if we may no farther go, retrace
    The path," I cried, "with all we can of speed."
And that Lord, who had led me to this place,
    Said to me: "Fear not, for our passage none
    Can take from us! 'twas given us by such Grace.
But thou, wait for me here. Thy spirit fordone
    Feed upon good hope, and be comforted.
    I will not leave thee in the low world alone."
Thus goes away and leaves me to my dread
    The gentle Father, and I with doubting dwell,   110
    For Yes and No contend within my head.
What then he proffered them I could not tell;
    But not long stood he among them in debate
    When all rushed suddenly in again pell-mell.
So did our adversaries close the gate
    Upon my Lord's breast, who, shut out in scorn
    To me with slow steps turned back desolate.
His eyes upon the ground, and eyebrows shorn
    Of all boldness, "Oh," he exclaimed with sighs,
    "Who is it excludes me from the abodes forlorn?"   120

And then to me: "Although my anger rise,
   Be not dismayed, for I shall bring thee through,
   Whatever hindrance they within devise.
This frowardness of theirs is nothing new.   *124*
   They used it once at a less secret door
   Which standeth still without bars to undo.
Thou sawest the dead writing that it bore.
   And now, this side of it, comes hitherward
   Without guide down the circles one before   *129*
Whose might the place shall be to us unbarred."   *130*

124-126. "This frowardness of theirs is nothing new": The demons are still possessed by the pride that caused their original fall. Their insolence was shown at the outer gate of Hell, when they tried to oppose the descent of Christ.

129-130. The one who is descending from the gate to open the city is an angel. In the hour of need divine help is not lacking. A special grace descends upon the distracted spirit, and opens a way where all seemed hopeless.

Canto IX

Without some divine aid the poets are unable to enter the City. Above the walls suddenly appear the three Furies and threaten Dante with the Medusa head which turns those who see it to stone. At last appears with a sound of storm the Angel for whose aid Virgil has been waiting; he passes over the marsh, puts the demons to flight and opens the gate of the City. They pass within and find a plain covered with sepulchres, the lids of which are open and which are full of flames. These sepulchers contain the Heretics.

THE colour cowardice had painted pale
  Upon my cheek, seeing my Guide turn back,
  Made him more promptly his own hue countervail.
He stopt, like one who some far sound would track,
  List'ning: for but short distance could eye strive
  Into the dim air filmed with vapour black.
"Yet needs must that the victory we contrive,"
  He began; "if not, . . . we were promised aid . . .
  O how long seems it till that one arrive!"
Well I perceived how his beginning stayed,   10
  And how with other words the first he sought
  To cover, and with a difference overlaid.
Nevertheless his language on me wrought;
  For it may be the words he faltered on
  I drew to a worse meaning than his thought.
"Into this bottom of the shell's drear cone
  Comes ever any from the first degree,   17
  Whose only punishment is hope forgone?"
So did I question; and he answered me:
  "Rarely it chances that any of us essay   20
  This journey upon which I go with thee.
True it is that once ere now I came this way,
  By that Erichtho fearfully conjured   23
  Who summoned back the shadows to their clay.
To the body's loss not long was I inured
  When she made me to enter within that wall
  To fetch a spirit in Judas' circle immured.
That is the lowest and most dark place of all,

17. "From the first degree": the Limbus.
23. "By that Erichtho fearfully conjured": The Thessalian sorceress
Erichtho, Virgil declares, sent him, shortly after his death, to
fetch a soul from the pit of treachery. That witches had such
power over the departed, was firmly believed not merely by the
ancients but in Christian times down almost to our day.

Farthest from the Heaven that moveth all. I know   29
    Full well the way: let naught then thee appal.   30
This marsh, whose exhalation stinketh so,
    Girdles the dolorous city of the dead,
    Where without anger now we cannot go."
My memory hath not kept what more he said,
    Because mine eyes drew me all up where I stood
    To the high tower's top, palpitating red,
Where, all in a moment risen up, with blood
    Spotted on them, three hellish Furies frowned.
    Women they were in body and attitude,
And they were girt with bright green hydras round;   40
    For hair they had small snakes and horn'd vipers
    About the ghastness of their temples wound.
He recognizing well the ministers
    Who serve the queen of wailing without cease,
    Said to me: "Mark now the Erynnes fierce!
The Fury upon the left Megaera is;
    Alecto is she that clamours on the right;
    'Twixt them Tisiphone." Then he held his peace.
Each at her breast was clawing, and then would smite
    Her body with the palms: so loud their moan,   50
    I pressed close to the poet in my affright.
"Let come Medusa, and change we him to stone!"
    All with one voice, and eyes bent downward, said.
    "Ill made we Theseus his assault atone."   54
"Turn backwards. Keep thine eyes closed in thy head!
    For if thou with the Gorgon should'st be faced,
    There would be no return up from the dead."
Thus spoke the Master, and he himself made haste
    To turn me, and would not in my hands confide

---

29. "The Heaven that moveth all" is the Primum Mobile, the outer-
most of the revolving heavens.
54. Theseus, who had attempted to rescue Persephone from the
lower world, was himself rescued by Hercules.

But his own also on my eyelids placed.   60
O ye who have sane intellects for guide
  Consider well the doctrines that for cloak
  Beneath the strangeness of the verses hide!
And now upon the turbid waters broke
  A crash, terrible with re-echoings
  That into trembling either shore awoke.
It was a sound as of a wind that springs
  Impetuous, meeting air that's hot and dry,
  Which unrelaxing all the forest wrings,
Wrenches the boughs off, breaks and beats awry.   70
  Rolling the dust, imperiously it towers,
  And makes the wild beasts and the shepherds fly.
Freeing my eyes, he said: "Sharpen thy powers
  Of vision over the foam of the ancient lake,
  Where most the smoke is and the swart air lours."
As frogs before their enemy the snake
  Leap through the water, scattered at his threat,
  Till each squats on the bottom, there to quake,
So saw I thousand ruined spirits set
  In flight before one, who at easy pace   80
  Came and passed over Styx with soles unwet.
He waved the gross fumes from before his face,
  Moving often his left hand as he went;
  And only of that annoyance showed he trace.
Well did I know that he from Heaven was sent,
  And turned to the Master; and he signed his will
  That I should stand all quiet with head down-bent.
Ah, with what scorn his countenance seemed to fill!
  He came to the gate, and with a wand he held
  Set it wide open, unresisted still.   90
"O race contemptible, from Heaven expelled!"
  Began he then, on the malign threshold,
  "Why is your contumacy yet unquelled?
Why at that Will still spurn ye, as of old,

Whose infinite fulfilment naught frustrates
  And which hath oft increased your pains fourfold?
What profits it to butt against the Fates?
  Your Cerberus rues his chin peeled and throat
      scored   *98*
  For this, if ye remember, at yon gates."
Then on the unclean journey, without word   100
  Spoken to us, returned he, and looked like one
  By other business constrained and spurred
Than that of those before him; and thereon
  We moved, and toward the city made our way,
  Secure of what the sacred words had done.
We entered into it without any affray.
  And I who had desire to scrutinize
  What things, and how, within such fortress lay,
Soon as I was within, sent round my eyes
  And saw a wilderness on either hand   110
  Full of evil torments and of miseries.
Like as at Arles, where Rhone stagnates in sand,
  Like as at Pola, by Quarnaro Sound,
  That barriers Italy and bathes her strand,
Sepulchres make uneven all the ground,   *115*
  So here on every side were tombs arrayed,
  Only that here was bitterer burial found;
For scatterings of flame among them played
  Whereby they were so heated through and through
  That no craft needeth iron hotter made.   120
Their covers were all raised up in our view,

98-99. *Cerberus, having tried to obstruct Hercules, was chained by him and dragged outside of Hell.*
115. *"Sepulchres make uneven all the ground": At Arles, near the delta of the Rhone, and at Pola, in the south of Istria, were ancient burying-grounds. The graves at Arles, of Roman origin, were thought to be filled with the bodies of Christian heroes who had fallen in battle with the Saracens. Just outside the city, on that side, the current of the Rhone turns to an eddy.*

And out of them such harsh lamenting rose
As from a wretched and a wounded crew.
And I spoke: "Tell me, Master, who are those
Who, within these chests buried, so beseech
With grievous sighs compassion on their throes?"
And he: "The Arch-Heretics are here, with each
His following of all sects: and heavier load
These tombs have in them than thy thought can
    reach.
Here like with like is buried in one abode,   130
And less or more hot are the monuments."
Then to the right hand turning, our feet trod
Between those pangs and the high battlements.

Canto X

*Passing between the flaming sepulchers and the
rampart circling the city, Dante is accosted from
one of the tombs by Farinata, chief of the Ghibel-
lines of Florence, who foretells to Dante the length
of his exile and explains the nature of the fore-
knowledge possessed by the dead. He is inter-
rupted by his companion in the tomb, the father
of Guido Cavalcanti (Dante's greatest friend, poet
and son-in-law of Farinata), who not seeing Guido
with Dante is anxious to know if he is alive or
dead: but Dante does not enlighten him. In reply
to a question, Farinata says that Frederick II, the
emperor, "stupor mundi," whose half-Oriental
court in Sicily was so brilliant in the thirteenth
century, and the Cardinal Ottaviano degli
Ubaldini, are among the heretics entombed.*

Now journeying along a secret track
   Between the ramparts and the sufferers
   My Master goes, and I behind his back.
"O sovran Virtue, who down the circling tiers
   Of the impious leadest me where thou dost bid,
   Satisfy," I said, "the wish that in me stirs.
The people who in these sepulchres are hid,
   May they be seen? None watches; none keeps guard.
   And see! already raised is every lid."
And he to me: "All shall be fast and barred   10
   When from Jehosophat they shall hither hie   *11*
   Each with the body he left under the sward.
This is the quarter wherein buried lie
   Epicurus and all those his doctrine swayed,   *14*
   Who with the body make the soul to die.
Therefore unto the question thou hast made
   Here within soon shalt thou an answer find
   And also to the wish thou hast not betrayed."
And I: "I keep not from thee, Escort kind,
   My thought, save that, as thou too didst require   20
   Ere now, I speak but in few words my mind."
"Tuscan, who goest through the city of fire
   Alive, with comely speech upon thy tongue,
   Halt here, if thou wilt tarry at my desire.
The speech thou usest manifests thee sprung

---

11. *On the day of Judgment all souls, having recovered their bodies,
will gather in the Valley of Jehoshaphat, whence, after hearing
their sentence, they will return to Heaven or Hell.*

14. *Although all heresies are punished in this circle, the only one
that concerns Dante is that called "Epicurean," a name bestowed,
in his day, upon materialistic free-thinking which denied the im-
mortality of the soul and regarded a comfortable life as the high-
est good. There is grim irony in the eternal burial of sinners who
affirmed that the spirit perishes with the body. Epicurus himself,
pagan though he was, is with them.*

From that famed country which, it may be, I tried
　　Which I perhaps with too much trouble wrung."
Suddenly in my ear this sound was cried
　　From out one of those coffers; and I drew,
　　In fear, a little closer to my Guide.　　　　　　　30
And he to me spoke: "Turn! What dost thou do?
　　See Farinata, raising himself amain!　　　　　　32
　　From the waist all of him shall rise in view."
My gaze from him I could not now have ta'en:
　　And he rose up to front me, face and breast,
　　As if of Hell he had a great disdain.
With prompt, inspiriting hands my Guide then prest
　　Me towards him, past the other sepulchres,
　　Counselling: "Use the words thou findest
　　　　best."
When I was where his tomb its front uprears,　　　40
　　He looked at me a little, and with a kind
　　Of scorn he questioned: "Who were thy forbears?"
I, who had it to obey him in my mind,
　　Concealed nothing from him, but told all out,
　　At which his brows upward a little inclined:
Then he said: "Fiercely did they use to flout
　　Me and my forefathers; and since they spurned

---

32. *This famous heretic is Manente degli Uberti, called Farinata, chief of the Florentine Ghibellines, a wise and valiant leader, who died in 1264, a year before Dante's birth. In 1260 he had taken part in the battle of Montaperti, where the Guelfs of Florence suffered a fearful defeat from the Sienese, the exiled Ghibellines, and King Manfred's Germans. After this rout the neighboring towns and barons held a council at Empoli, and all but Farinata were in favor of destroying Florence; he, however, opposed the project so stoutly that it was abandoned. In 1283 the inquisitor, Salmone da Lucca, condemned him (nearly twenty years dead), his wife, his sons, and his grandsons, as heretics; his bones were cast out, his property confiscated and sold. His brave and haughty spirit is not quelled even by his fiery punishment: he appears with head and chest erect.*

My party, twice I scattered them in rout." *48*

"If they were chased, on all sides they returned,
Both times," I answered, "from adversities; *50*
But yours that art have not so rightly learned."

Beside him then a shadow by degrees *52*
Emerged, and was discovered to the chin:
I think he had raised himself upon his knees.

He looked around as if he had thought to win
Sight of some other who might be with me;
And when that hope was wholly quenched
within,

Cried weeping: "If through this blind prison, free,
Thou goest by virtue of thy nature's height,
Where is my son? Why is he not here with thee?" *60*

And I to him: " 'Tis not by my own right *61*
I come; he that waits yonder leads me here,
Of whom perhaps thy Guido had despite."

His words, and manner of penance, made appear
His name, as if I had read it on his brow,
Therefore my answer had I made thus clear.

Suddenly erect, he cried: "What saidest thou?
He *had?* Lives he not, then, in the sweet air?
Does the sun's light not strike upon him now?"

When of a certain pause he was aware *70*
Ere I replied, where he had risen to stand

---

*48-51. Farinata scattered the Guelfs in 1248 and 1260; but they re-
turned to Florence in 1251, after the death of Frederick II, and
in 1266, after the battle of Benevento; they then expelled the
Ghibellines, who never "rightly learned" the art of returning.*

*52. The "Shadow" is Cavalcante de' Cavalcanti, a noble and wealthy
Florentine, the father of that Guido whom Dante calls his "first
friend." This Guido Cavalcanti, a little older than Dante, was a
famous poet and student, and an ardent partisan.*

*61-63. Dante hastens to explain Guido's absence by the assurance
that it is not his own wit, but Virgil's, which directs him, adding
that Guido may not have duly esteemed the ancient sage.*

Down he fell backward, and so vanished there.
But, haughty of spirit, that other, at whose demand
   I had halted, changed not aspect, nor his head
   Moved, nor his side bent, no, nor stirred a hand.
"And if," continuing his own words, he said,
   "To learn that art they have so little wit,
   It tortureth me more than doth this bed.
But fifty times shall not afresh be lit   79
   The countenance of the Lady who reigns here   80
   Ere thou shalt know the cost of learning it.
And, so thou would'st return back to the dear
   Earth, tell me why in each of its decrees
   That people against my people is so severe?"   84
Then I: "The havoc and the butcheries   85
   That made the Arbia dyed all red to run
   Hath filled our temple with such litanies."
He sighed, shaking his head; and then spoke on:
   "In that I was not single; nor, I swear,
   Would I in ill cause with the rest have gone.   90
But single I was in that place yonder, where   91
   All on the ruin of Florence had agreed.
   I only with open face defended her."
"Ah, so may peace come also to thy seed,
   Resolve me," I prayed him, "this hard knot that ties
   My judgment in it, and the riddle read.
It seemeth, if I hear aright, your eyes
   Perceive beforehand what Time brings with him,
   But with the present ye use otherwise."

79-81. "The Lady who reigns here" is Hecate, who in the sky ap-
pears as the moon. Before fifty months have passed, Dante is to
learn how hard is the art of returning from exile.

84. In 1280, when most of the Ghibellines were allowed to come
back, several of the Uberti were expressly excluded.

85-86. "The butcheries" refers to the battle of Montaperti, be-
side the Arbia river (cf. the note at line 32).

91. "In that place yonder": at the diet of Empoli; (cf. the note at
line 32).

"We see like those for whom the light is dim," *100*
    He answered me, "the things that are remote;
    So much still shines for us the Lord Supreme.
When they come near, or are, then avails not
    Our understanding, and we know no more,
    Save what is told us, of your human lot.
Easily may'st thou understand, therefore,
    That all we have of knowledge shall be dead
    From that time when the Future shuts its door."
Then pricked in conscience for my fault, I said,
    "Will you not now acquaint that fallen one *110*
    His child is not yet from the living fled?
And if before to his answer I made none
    Tell him it was my thought that was not free,
    Being in that knot which now you have undone."
And now my Master was recalling me.
    Therefore more earnestly the spirit I prest
    To tell me who were those with him. And he:
"With more than a thousand I lie here opprest.
    Yonder the Second Frederic is inurned, *119*
    The Cardinal also: I speak not of the rest." *120*
With that he hid himself. My steps I turned
    Back toward the ancient Poet, pondering

100-108. *The damned, while aware of the past and indistinctly cognizant of the future, have no knowledge of present events on earth. Just how much the "present" embraces we are not told. After the Judgment Day, when earthly life shall cease and the foresight of lost souls shall thus come to an end, their blindness will be unrelieved.*

119. *The great Emperor Frederick* II (1194-1250), *who was long engaged in strife against the Papacy, was generally regarded as an Epicurean.*

120. *"The Cardinal" Ottaviano degli Ubaldini, apostolic legate in Lombardy and Romagna against Frederick, in the Kingdom of Naples against Manfred, was accused of unbelief and of sympathy with the Imperial cause. Several of the early commentators report him as saying: "If there is a soul, I have lost it for the Ghibellines."*

That saying wherein some menace I discerned.
He moved, and as we went: "What is this thing,"
　　He said to me, "which teases so thy mind?"
　　I satisfied him in his questioning.
"Keep in thy memory what thine ears divined
　　To be against thee," warned the Sage. "Attend
　　Now," and with finger lifted he enjoined:
"When thou before the radiance shalt bend   130
　　Of that Lady, whose beauteous eyes see all,   131
　　Thou shalt learn thy life's journey unto its end."
Then to the left he turned his steps; the wall
　　We quitted, toward the middle advancing by
　　A path that strikes into a valley's fall,
Wherefrom the fume rose noisome even thus high.

---

131. "Of that Lady": Beatrice.

Canto XI

---

*The descent to the next, the Seventh Circle, is now
before the poets; but the fetid stench arising from
it repels them so that they take refuge behind a
sepulcher. The opportunity is taken by Virgil to
explain to Dante the conformation of the lower
Hell, and the various kinds of guilt punished in
the several circles: the system being based on
Aristotle's classification, to whose Ethics Virgil
refers, and on Cicero's. Three kinds of violence
are punished in three separate rings of the Seventh
Circle, which they are next to visit. The fraudulent
are in the Eighth, those guilty of the special fraud
of treachery in the Ninth and lowest circle. Dante
will now have no need to ask for what crimes the
sinners he is to meet are chastised: but he fails to*

*understand at first why all the damned are not in
the City of Dis. Virgil explains that the sins of in-
continence, the punishment of which they have
already witnessed before entering the city, are less
offensive to God and so less grievously visited.*

O<small>N THE</small> edge of a circle of great broken stones
  Rimming a cliff, we came above the place
  Wherein are packed worse sins and deeper groans.

And here, because of the horrible excess
  Of stench thrown upward from the unfathomed pit,
  We drew, for refuge from its noisomeness,

Behind a monument, whereon was writ:
  "Pope Anastasius is here immured;   8
  Photinus lured him the true path to quit."

"We must delay, till somewhat be inured   10
  Our sense to the vile reek, ere we descend:
  Then shall it be more easily endured."

So spoke the Master. "That our time we spend
  Not vainly," I said, "some compensation find."
  And he: "Thou seest that I so intend."

"Son," he continued, "within these stones wind
  Three circlets, going down in three degrees,
  Even like those which thou hast left behind.

They are all filled with spirits accurst: of these
  That sight hereafter alone suffice thee, know   20
  Wherefore and how the pangs upon them seize.

Of all malice that makes of Heaven a foe
  The end is injury, and all such end won
  By force or fraud worketh another's woe.

---

8. *This is Anastasius* II, *who for many centuries was generally but
unjustly thought to have been induced by Photinus, deacon of
Thessalonica, to deny the divinity of Christ; it is likely that he
had been confused with the Byzantine emperor, Anastasius* I.

But since fraud is a vice of man's alone,
   It more offends God: so are lowest set
   The fraudulent, and the heavier is their groan.
All the first circle is for the violent; yet,
   As violence in its object is threefold,
   It is in three rings built, each separate.   30
To God, oneself, one's neighbour, it is told,
   May violence be done, both to their things
   And to themselves, as I shall clearly unfold.
Force on one's neighbour death and torment brings,
   And on his goods fire, ravage and reverse
   Of fortune, and the hurt extortion wrings.
The first round, then, tortures all murderers,
   And, each kind separate, those who with intent
   Of malice strike; robbers and plunderers.
A man may to himself be violent   40
   And to his own; in the next round, therefore,
   Must each inhabitant in vain repent
Who robs himself of your world, wastes his store
   Of wealth, gambles and squanders till all's gone
   And, where he should rejoice, laments the more.
Violence against the Deity may be done   46
   In the heart denying and blaspheming blind;
   In Nature, too, spurning his benison.
The smallest ring hath therefore sealed and signed
   For its own both Sodom's and Cahors' offence,   50
   And all who speak with scorn of God in mind.
Fraud, which so gnaweth at all men's conscience,
   A man may use on one who trusts him best
   And on him also who risks no confidence.
This latter mode seems only to arrest

46-48. "Violence . . . in nature": the sodomites, or homosexuals,
do violence to nature, the minister of God.
50. Cahors: a town in southern France, a notorious nest of usurers.
Usurers—that is, moneylenders—do violence to human industry,
the offspring of Nature.

The love which Nature meaneth to endure;
  Hence in the second circle huddled nest   57
Hypocrisy, flattery; they who would conjure
  By spells; and simony; the thief, the cheat,
  Pandars and barrators, and the like ordure.   60
In the other mode mankind the love forget
  Which Nature makes, and that love's after-dower
  Which doth the special trust and faith beget.
Hence in the smallest circle, at the core   64
  Of the Universe, where Dis in darkness reigns,
  Each traitor is consumed for evermore."
And I: "Most clearly thy discourse explains,
  Master, distinguishing by class and class,
  This pit and all the people it contains.
But tell me: those clogged in the slab morass,   70
  Those whom the wind drives and the hard rain galls,
  And they whom mutual cursing tongues harass,
Why are they not in the red city's walls   73
  Chastised, if to God's anger they be prey?
  And if not, why the woe that them befalls?"
And he to me: "Now wherefore goes astray
  Thy wit beyond its wont? or is thy thought
  On other things and turned another way?
Recall the words thou surely hast not forgot
  In which thy Ethics makes the matter plain   80
  Of the three dispositions Heaven wills not,

---

57. "The second circle: the second of the "circlets" of line 17, is
actually the eighth circle.
64. "The smallest circle": the ninth and last of the circles of Hell,
at the center of the whole material universe, where Dis, or Luci-
fer, is confined.
70-72. The sinners mentioned here are: the wrathful (fifth circle),
the lustful and the gluttonous (second and third circles), and the
avaricious and the prodigal (fourth circle).
73. "The red city" is the city of Dis, or Lower Hell.
80. "Thy Ethics": the Ethics of thy master, Aristotle, who enumer-
ates three evils to be avoided: malice, incontinence, bestiality.

Incontinence, and malice, and insane
  Bestiality; and how incontinence less
  Displeaseth God and less blame doth obtain.
If rightly to regard this thou address
  Thy mind, recalling who are they who smart
  Above there, in that outer wilderness,
Thou wilt perceive why they are placed apart
  From these fell spirits, and why with gentler blow
  The Divine Justice hammereth their heart."   90
"O Sun, who heal'st all troubled vision, and so
  Contentest me where thou dost certify,
  That to doubt pleaseth not less than to know,
Turn thee now yet a little back," said I,
  "To where thou sayest that usury doth offend
  The divine goodness, and the knot untie."
"Philosophy, to him who will attend,"   97
  Said he, "in divers places hath discerned
  How Nature her example and her end
From Divine Intellect and its art hath learned.   100
  And to thy Physics if good heed thou pay,   101
  Thou wilt find, after but few pages turned,
That your art follows her, far as it may,   103
  As scholar his master, so that your art is
  Of the Godhead the grandchild, so to say.
By these two, if thy memory Genesis
  Recalls, and its beginning, man hath need
  To gain his bread and foster earthly bliss.
But the usurer, since he will not thus proceed,
  Flouts Nature's follower and herself also,   110

---

97. "Philosophy": the works of Aristotle.
100. "Its art": the operation of the divine intelligence.
101. "Thy Physics": Aristotle's treatise on Physics (II, ii).
103-105. Human industry follows nature as far as it can, so that it is, so to speak, the grandchild of God.

Setting his wealth another way to breed. *111*
But follow now, for I am willed to go.

The Fishes quiver on the horizon air, *113*
And over Caurus all the Wain lies low.
Far on it is where we descend the stair."

---

111. The moneylender sets his hope on gain derived neither from nature nor from toil.
113. Virgil, as usual, indicates the hour (in Jerusalem) by a description of the sky, which, of course, is not visible from Hell. The time is three hours or more after midnight.

Canto XII

Down a steep slope of shattered rock (caused by the earthquake at the Crucifixion), guarded by the Minotaur, the poets clamber to the Seventh Circle and find at the bottom of the cliff a River of Blood (Phlegethon) which flows round the circle. Boiling in its stream are those who have been violent against others; this being the first ring of the circle. Centaurs trot about the bank and shoot those who emerge more than their punishment allows. Chiron, their chief, appoints Nessus to guide Dante across the shallowest part of the stream. On the way, Nessus points out certain conquerors, assassins and highwaymen; among them is Guy de Montfort, who avenged his father Simon's death by murdering Henry, son of Richard, Earl of Cornwall, "on God's bosom," i.e. in a church, during Mass, at Viterbo. Henry's heart was said to have been kept in a casket on London Bridge.

CRAGGY the place was where for our advance
  We must descend, and by such presence marred,
  That any eye would look on it askance.
Like to the desolation hitherward   4
  Of Trent, on Adige, which, by want of prop
  Or earthquake, has the river's flank all scarred,
For down to the level from the mountain-top
  The rock there is so ruined by its fall
  That one above might scramble down the slope;
Such was the passage down that shattered wall;   10
  And on the ragged coping of the pit
  We found the infamy of Crete a-sprawl   12
That was conceived in the cow's counterfeit;
  Who, when he saw us, on himself, with look
  Of one whom inward spleen convulses, bit.
Toward him my sage: "Thou think'st maybe the Duke   16
  Of Athens comes to master thee anew
  Who in the world above thy life-blood took.
Off, Monster! This one comes not with a clue
  Provided by thy sister, on thy track,   20
  But passes on, your penances to view."
As a bull bursts his tether to attack
  Just when he feels the stroke that makes an end
  And cannot charge but plunges forth and back,

4-5. "The desolation . . . of Trent": *our poet compares this vast slide with one in northeastern Italy.*

12. "The infamy of Crete" *is the Minotaur; half man and half beast, he was the offspring of a bull and Pasiphae, wife of King Minos of Crete, who satisfied her abnormal passion (inflicted by Venus as a curse) by enclosing herself in a wooden cow.*

16-17. "The Duke of Athens," *so called by Boccaccio, Chaucer, and Shakespeare, is the Athenian hero Theseus, who slew the Minotaur in the Labyrinth, guided by Ariadne, the daughter of Pasiphae and Minos.*

So did the Minotaur his fury spend;
   And watchful called my Guide: "To the passage!
    Haste!
   The while he storms, 'tis best that thou descend."
Thus climbed we downward on that splintered waste
   Of stones, that often slid beneath my tread
   With the unfamiliar weight upon them placed.   30
I went in thought: and "Peradventure," he said,
   "Thou musest on this ruin, guarded by
   The brute rage I but now discomfited.
I'ld have thee know that the other time when I
   Descended hither to the deeps of hell,
   The rock was not yet tumbled from on high.
But short while certainly, if I gauge it well,
   Ere He came, who the plunder made of Dis
   From those who in the upmost circle dwell,
On every deep and foul abyss   40
   Trembled so, that the universe I deemed   41
   Felt love, whereby, as some think oft it is,
The world has been to chaos cracked and seamed;
   And in that moment, here and otherwhere,   44
   This ancient rock down into ruin streamed.
But turn thine eyes to the valley, for draws near
   The river of blood, wherein are boiling they
   Who live by violence and on other's fear."
O blind greed and mad anger, all astray   49
   That in the short life goad us onward so,   50
   And in the eternal with such plungings pay!
I saw a wide fosse bent into a bow

41-43. *According to Empedocles, the four elements, mixed to-
gether, produced chaos; hate, separating the seeds, brought forth
from chaos all the things of the universe; love, by drawing the
seeds together, can restore chaos. Dante probably got his idea of
Empedocles from Aristotle.*
44. *"Otherwhere": in the circle of the lustful (Inf. v, 34).*
49. *The motives of violence to our fellow man are greed and wrath.*

Embaying all the level ground in front,
Even as my Guide already had made me know.
Between it and the scarp's base were at hunt
  Centaurs, who, armed with arrows, thronged the
          strand,   56
  Running as in the world once they were wont.
Seeing us descending, each one came to a stand:
  And from their company broke three, with bow
  And javelin ready chosen in the hand.   60
And one from far cried: "To what torment go
Ye that have come down by the headlong track?
Tell me from there; if not, I draw the bow."
My Master said: "Our answer will we make
  To Chiron yonder. In thee, to thy rue,   65
  Rashness did ever judgment overtake."
He touched me, and said: "This is that Nessus, who 67
  Died for the fair Deianira, and took
  Of himself vengeance by the shirt that slew.
He in the middle who on his breast doth look   70
  Is the great Chiron, who Achilles nursed;
  The other Pholus, whom such rages shook.   72
Round the fosse go their thousands; and soon pierced
  With arrows is whatever spirit writhes out
  From the blood higher than by his guilt immersed."
We drew near to these creatures fleet of foot;
  And Chiron took an arrow, and with the notch

---

56. Along the narrow bank run Centaurs, whose business it is to
keep the other souls in their proper place. These half-human
guardians are not depicted as hateful or repulsive, nor do they
seem to be demons.

65. Chiron, son of Saturn, skilled in surgery, was the preceptor of
Achilles.

67. Nessus, while trying to carry off Dejanira through the water, was
struck by an arrow from Hercules, her husband. To avenge him-
self, he left his bloody shirt with Dejanira, which afterwards
caused the death of Hercules.

72. Pholus figured in the battle between the Centaurs and the
Lapithae.

His beard upon his jaw-bones backward put.
When he had uncovered his great mouth thus much,
   He said to his companions: "Note ye how   80
   The one behind moves that which he doth touch?
The feet of the dead are not wont so to do."
   And my good Guide, now at the breast of him,
   Where the two forms into one nature grew,
Said, "Ay, he lives, and through the valley dim
   Solitary must I his steps escort.
   Necessity brings him to it, and not whim.
From singing alleluias in Heaven's court
   Came she who for this task commissioned me.   *89*
   He is no thief, nor I of thievish sort.   90
But by the Virtue on high, through whose decree
   I am bound upon so wild a journey, spare
   One of thy band, to bear us company,
That he may show the ford to us, and may bear
   Him on his back over to the other side.
   For he is no spirit, to walk upon the air."
Chiron upon his right breast turned and: "Guide
   Be thou," said he to Nessus; "if waylaid
   By another troop, compel it to avoid."
So with our guide we moved on unafraid   100
   By the red bubbles of the scalding ooze
   Wherein the boiled their loud lamenting made.
I saw people in it up to the very brows.
   And: "These are tyrants," said the great Centaur,
   "Who made of blood and plunder their carouse.
Here all their ruthless ravage they deplore—
   Alexander, and Dionysius fierce of heart,   *107*
   Who made for Sicily the years so sore.

---

89. Beatrice.
107. It is not known whether Dante meant Alexander the Great or
Alexander of Pherae, who was coupled with Dionysius as a typical
tyrant by Cicero. Dionysius ruled Syracuse from 407 to 367 B.C.

That forehead with the hair on it so swart
   Is Ezzelin; and the other, who is fair,   *110*
   Opizzo of Este, who, the truth to impart,   *111*
Was quenched by his unnatural son, up there."   *112*
   I turned to the poet, and he made reply:
   "To him first now, not me, thou may'st refer."
A little on, the Centaur paused anigh
   Another throng of sinners which appeared
   To stand above the seething stream throat-high.
And there a spirit whom no other neared   *118*
   He showed us, saying: "He on God's bosom
   Transfixt the heart still upon Thames revered."   *120*
Then saw I from the river emerging some
   Who could the head and even the chest uprear;
   And many I knew by this doom overcome.
Thus more and more the blood grew shallower
   Until it scorched only the feet below.
   For us the passage of the fosse was here.
"As on this side thou seest the boiling flow
   Its own continual diminution keep,
   So," said the Centaur, "I would have thee know
That on the other it shelves from deep to deep   *130*
   Along the bottom, till it resumes its way
   To where the tyrants are compelled to weep.
Here Divine Justice stings that Attila   *133*
   Who upon earth was the world's flail; and here

---

110. "Ezzelin": Ezzelino da Romano, who held extensive dominions in northeastern Italy in the first half of the thirteenth century, a notoriously cruel tyrant; he was called a son of Satan.
111. "Opizzo of Este," Marquis of Ferrara in the second half of the thirteenth century, was a hard ruler.
112. Virgil, to whom Dante turns in doubt, tells him that in this matter the Centaur is the best authority.
118. The "spirit whom no other neared" is Guy de Montfort (cf. the Argument of this canto).
133. Attila, King of the Huns, was called the "Scourge of God."

Pyrrhus and Sextus; and it milketh aye   *135*
With scald of pain the disimprisoned tear
   From Rinier of Corneto, who so warred,   *137*
   With Rinier Pazzo, on the traveller."
Then he turned backward, and repassed the ford.

Canto XIII

*Crossing Phlegethon by the ford, the poets arrive
in the Wood of the Suicides, who have become
withered and poisonous trees among which the
Harpies cry. Pier dalle Vigne, who rose to great
power and to be Frederick II's most intimate ad-
viser, then suddenly fell into disgrace and com-
mitted suicide, speaks from one of the trees and
tells Dante his story. Their talk is interrupted
by a rushing noise made by two spirits pursued by
hounds. These are Giacomo da Sant' Andrea, and
Lano, a Sienese, two notorious spendthrifts. An-
other spirit, unnamed and unknown, tells Dante
that he is of Florence, the city which had Mars for
its patron and by changing him for the Baptist was
thought to have incurred that god's malignity.*

NESSUS had not regained the bank beyond
   When we betook us onward from the shore
   To a wood, wherein no path was to be found.

135. Pyrrhus, King of Epirus, was a fearful enemy of the Romans.
   Sextus, son of Pompey, became a pirate.
137-138. Rinieri da Corneto and Rinieri de' Pazzi were two high-
   waymen apparently famous in the thirteenth century.

No green leaves there, but all of dim colour:
    Smooth branches none, but wry with knot and gnarl;
    No apples, but gaunt twigs with poison sour.
Not scrub or thicket rougher hides the snarl   7
    'Twixt Cecina and Corneto of the beasts
    That roaming them abhor the well-tilled marl.
Here have the savage Harpies made their nests   10
    Who chased the Trojans from the Strophades
    With prophecy of baleful prophecy of coming pests.
Wide wings, and human necks and visages,
    Clawed feet, and a gross belly plumed below,
    They make lament above on the strange trees.
"Before thou further dost adventure, know
    That thou art in the second ring, from which,"
    The gracious Master said, "thou canst not go
Until the terrible great sand thou reach.   19
    Thou shalt see here—therefore look well around— 20
    Things which may take the credence from my
        speech."
Even then I heard on all sides wailing sound,
    But of those making it saw no one nigh;
    Wherefore I stood still, in amazement bound.
I think he thought that I thought that the cry
    Of those so many voices came from folk
    Who 'mid those trees hid, at our coming shy.
So now the Master said: "If thy hand broke

7-9. Cecina, a town near Volterra, and Corneto, a town close to Civitavecchia, denote the northern and southern limits of the woody, swampy district known as Maremma. In Dante's time it was covered with dense forest.

10-12. The Harpies are voracious, filthy birds with maidens' faces. On the Strophades islands, off Messenia, where they dwelt, their foul presence repeatedly interrupted the Trojans' repast; and finally one of them uttered so threatening a prophecy that the warriors hastily departed.

19. "The terrible great sand": the third ring, consisting of a waste of sand, upon which falls a rain of fire.

A shoot from any branch, the thoughts that went
 With thy conjecture soon wouldst thou revoke."   30
Then I stretched forth my hand a little, and bent
 And plucked a puny branch from a great thorn.
 And the trunk cried out: "Why hast thou me rent?"
And when it grew embrowned with blood, so torn,
 It cried again: "Why hast thou wounded me?
 Wast thou without one breath of pity born?
Men were we, and are now turned each to a tree.
 If souls of serpents were within us penned,
 Still should compassion have been found in thee."
As a green brand, that burneth at one end,   40
 At the other drips and hisses from the wood
 Where the escaping wind and fire contend,
So from that broken splinter words and blood
 Together came: whereat, like one afraid,
 I let the tip fall and all silent stood.
"If he, O wounded spirit," my sage then said,
 "Had but been able to believe before
 What he has seen but in my verse portrayed,   48
He would not have stretched hand to hurt so sore;
 But the incredible thing moved me to prove   50
 To him what now I do myself deplore.
But tell him who thou wast; so that thereof
 To make amends, he may thy fame renew,
 Where grace permits him to return, above."
Then the trunk: "Thy sweet words so melt me through,
 My lips cannot keep silence; if to impart
 My tale I linger, may it not burden you.
I am he who held both keys of Frederick's heart,   58

---

48. "But in my verse . . .": i.e., in the story of Polydorus in Aeneid
III, 22-43.
58. "I am he . . .": Pier delle Vigne, who entered the court of
Frederick II as a notary, and so won the confidence and affection
of the sovereign that for over twenty years he was entrusted with
the most important affairs of the realm. In 1248, or 1249, he was

And to their wards so softly did apply,
  Locking and then unlocking with such art,   60
That few had privacy of him as I.
  So loyal was I to the proud office,
  That sleep and pulses both were lost thereby.
The whore that at the house where Caesar is   64
  Will ever her adulterous glances aim,
  Man's common bane, of courts the special vice,
The minds of all against me did inflame,
  And these, inflamed, inflamed my lord august
  Till my glad honours withered to sad shame.
My soul into disdainful temper thrust,   70
  Thinking by death to escape the world's disdain,
  Made me, the just, unto myself unjust.
But by the fresh roots that this tree sustain
  I swear that never troth unto my lord,
  So worthy of honour, did I vow in vain.
If either of you be to the world restored,
  Comfort my memory which still lies so low
  From the stroke dealt to it by Envy's sword."
The poet waited; then: "Since he is slow,
  Further to speak, and thou the hour hast got,   80
  Speak now and ask, if more thou wouldest know."
Then I to him: "Demand thou of him what
  Thou think'st will most my mind's desire appease.
  Such pity is in my heart, that I could not."
He resumed therefore: "So may this man ease,
  By doing of what thou dost entreat, thy pain,

---

accused and convicted of treason; his eyes were put out, and ac-
cording to one account he was condemned by the Emperor to be
led in derision, on an ass, from town to town. To escape dishonor,
he killed himself by dashing his head against a wall. Piero, as
Dante conceived him, is a magnanimous courtier, and most pa-
thetic in his unshaken devotion to the master who wronged him.
64. "The whore" is Envy, and the house of Caesar is the Imperial
court.

Now, O imprisoned spirit, may it please
To tell us how the soul becomes the grain
    Of this gnarled wood; tell us too, if thou may'st,
    Whether any from such limbs deliverance gain."   90
Then the trunk sighed out strongly until the blast
    Of breath became voice into language knit:
    "My answer into brief words shall be cast.
When the fierce spirit doth the body quit
    From which it hath with violence broken out,
    Minos consigns it to the seventh pit.
It falls into the wood, and there, without
    Place chosen for it but as fortune dole,
    Like any grain of spelt it comes to sprout,
Shoots up to a sapling and a forest bole;   100
    Then the Harpies feeding on its leaves, their nest,
    Make for it both pain and the pain's loop-hole   102
We shall go seek our spoils out, like the rest,
    But not to be again in them arrayed;
    He earns not that who himself hath dispossessed.
Hither shall we drag them through the grievous glade
    And on the boughs our bodies shall be strung,
    Each on the thorn-tree of its guilty shade."
We still upon the voice attentive hung,
    Supposing it desired to tell us more,   110
    When suddenly we heard a noise upsprung,
Like one who hears the coming of the boar
    And hunt behind it on his place intrude,
    And hears the branches crash and beasts' uproar.
And on the left hand lo! two spirits pursued,
    Naked and torn, who fled at speed so sick
    That all the ground with broken boughs they strewed.
The foremost: "O come now, Death, O come quick!"
    And the other, finding feet too slow to escape:
    "Thy heels made no such answer to the prick,   120

102. *By breaking the leaves, they provide an outlet.*

Lano, at Toppo jousts." And then, mayhap,   *121*
  Because the breath was failing in him, he
  Made of himself and of a bush one shape.
Behind, the wood was full, from tree to tree,
  Of great black mastiffs, running with such gust
  As greyhounds from their leashes slipping free.
Into him, as he crouched, their teeth they thrust
  And tore him all asunder, shred by shred,
  To carry his woeful limbs off as they lust.
My Guide now took me by the hand and led   *130*
  My steps up to the bush, that vainly sighed
  Lamenting through its fractures as they bled.
"O Giacomo da Sant' Andrea," it cried,   *133*
  "What blame have I of thy sins, or what good
  Get'st thou by coming in my screen to hide?"
The Master spoke, when by it now he stood:
  "Who wast thou who through all these wounds dost
    blow
  Thy sorrowful speech forth, mingled with thy blood?"
And he to us: "Ye spirits that witness how
  I have been with so great ignominy torn   *140*
  That these my leaves are severed from the bough,
Gather them close about the bush forlorn!
  My city is that which changed its first patron   *143*
  To choose the Baptist; for which act of scorn
He by his arts will ever make it groan;
  And were it not that Arno doth retain

---

121. *The spendthrift Lano of Siena perished in the battle of Pieve del Toppo. The speaker is Giacomo da Sant'Andrea.*

133. *The soul in the bush, whose identity is uncertain, addresses the second of the two runners, a mad prodigal.*

143. *"My city": Florence, whose first patron, according to tradition, was Mars. The new patron was John the Baptist, whose image adorned the florin. The Florentines gave up martial valor for money making.*

Upon her bridge some shadow of him in stone, *147*
Those citizens who the city built again
  On the ashes left by Attila's decree, *149*
  Would have expended all their toil in vain. 150
I made my gibbet of my own roof-tree." *151*

---

147. "Some shadow of him . . .": an old stone statue, supposed to represent the God of War, stood at the head of the Ponte Vecchio.
149. It was believed that Attila, King of the Huns, had destroyed Florence.
151. "Gibbet": place of execution. Two of the earliest commentators say that this sinner hanged himself with a girdle in his house.

Canto XIV

The third ring of the Seventh Circle is the ring of Burning Sand, which torments the violent against God, who lie supine; the violent against Nature and Art, who sit all huddled up; and the violent against Nature, who are forced to be continually moving: on all of them falls a fiery rain. Among the first group is Capaneus, one of the Seven Against Thebes, who retains his fierce rebellious spirit. Virgil guides Dante along the edge of the Wood of the Suicides, so as to avoid the burning sand which the wood encloses all round; and from the wood flows a red stream, apparently a branch of Phlegethon, which has petrified its banks, which are high, like dykes, and has the power of quenching the flames which fall on it. Virgil explains the origin and course of the rivers of Hell.

THE dearness of my native place perforce
  Constraining me, those scattered leaves I brought
  Back to him, who by now grew faint and hoarse.
Then came we where is the division wrought
  Between the first ring and the second: here
  Heaven's justice hath conceived a fearful thought.
To make the strangeness of the new things clear,
  I say we reached a waste, which from its bed
  Rejects all plants, and none permitteth near.
By the drear wood it is engarlanded   10
  Round, as the wood is by the dismal fosse.
  Here, at the very edge, our steps we stayed.
The ground was of a sand both dry and gross,
  Not different in its quality, I trow,
  From that the feet of Cato trod across.   15
O chastisement of God, how oughtest thou
  To be of each one feared who reads with awe
  What to my eyes was manifested now.
Many herds there of naked souls I saw,
  Who all bewept the misery on them come,   20
  And seemed to suffer under diverse law.
Supine lay some upon the ground; and some
  Were sitting in a huddle all compressed:
  Others were stirred continually to roam.
Those that moved much outnumbered all the rest,
  Those lying in torment fewer, but wailed their woe
  More loudly, seeing their pain was bitterest.
All over the wide sands descending slow
  Were rained dilated flakes of dropping fire;
  As without wind falls in the hills the snow.   30
Like to the flames which in the regions dire   31

15. *Cato led the remnants of Pompey's army across the Libyan des-
ert in 47* B.C.
31-36. *Dante apparently got this story from Albertus Magnus.*

Of India's heat on Alexander smote
    And on his host, falling to earth entire,
Whereat he made his men take careful thought
    To trample down the soil beneath their feet
    (Those single fires being readier to put out),
So was the falling of the eternal heat,
    By which, like tinder under steel, the sands
    Caught fire, and with a doubled torment beat.
Now here, now there, the miserable hands
    Were shaking off the scorchings without rest,
    As they were still renewed, in helpless dance.
I began: "Master, thou who conquerest
    All things, except only those demons hard
    That at the gate our entry did contest,
Who is that great spirit who seems not to regard
    The fire, and scowls disdainful on his bed,
    So that the rain tames him not, though so charred?"
And he himself, alert to what I said,
    And knowing that I asked of him, forthwith
    Cried: "What I was alive, that am I dead.
Though Jupiter should weary out his smith   52
    From whom, incensed, he took the bolt whereby
    On my last day he blasted through my pith,
And though he weary out all the rest who ply
    The black forge under Mongibello's vault,
    One after one, and 'Help, good Vulcan,' cry,
As at the fight at Phlegra, when his bolt
    At me with all his fury of hate he flung—

---

46. "That great spirit" is Capaneus, one of the seven kings who
    attacked Thebes; scaling the walls, whence his gigantic shadow
    frightened the city, he mocked at the gods and challenged Jupiter,
    who thereupon slew him with a thunderbolt.
52-60. Even though Jupiter should labor as he did in the battle
    against the giants, in the valley of Phlegra in Thessaly, he could
    not subdue the spirit of Capaneus.—"His smith": Vulcan.—"All
    the rest": the Cyclops, assistants of Vulcan.—"Mongibello": a
    Sicilian name for Aetna.

Yet in his vengeance shall he not exult!"   60
Then my Guide spoke with such a force of tongue
   As never had I heard him use before:
   "O Capaneus, in that thou still hast clung
To thine unquenched pride, thou art punished more.
   No torture but the thoughts that make thee rave
   Would be a pain proportioned to thy score."
Then turned to me, a gentler look he gave,
   Saying: "This spirit was one of those Seven Kings
   Who besieged Thebes, and had, and seems to have,
God in despite; and scorn upon Him flings.   70
   But, as I have told him, his revilings black
   For such a breast are fittest garnishings.
Now go behind me, and see that in my track
   Thy feet not on the burning sand be set,
   But by the wood's edge keep them always back."
Silent we came to where a rivulet
   From the wood's shadow gushing outward shows,
   Whereof the redness makes me shudder yet.
As from the Bulicame a streamlet goes   79
   Which 'mid themselves the sinful women share,   80
   So down across the sand this water flows.
The bottom, and the banks on each side, were,
   With the edges raised above it, become stone:
   Here then, I knew, should be our thoroughfare.
" 'Mid all the rest that I to thee have shown,
   Since by the gate we entered into hell,
   Of which the threshold is denied to none,
Thine eyes have seen nothing so notable
   As is the present stream, which has the might
   Within it all the flames above to quell."   90
These words my Guide spoke; wondering at the sight,

---

79. "Bulicame": a hot spring near Viterbo, frequented as a bath. The stream issuing from it was divided into separate baths for prostitutes, who were compelled to stay apart from the others.

I prayed him that he might vouchsafe me taste
Of that whereof he had vouchsafed appetite.
"In the mid sea a country lies, all waste,"
    He therefore now continued, "Crete by name,
    Under whose king the world of old was chaste.   *96*
There stands a mountain, Ida called, the same
    Which once with green leaf and glad water shone,
    Now desert, like a thing of mouldered fame.
This for the trusty cradle of her son   *100*
    Did Rhea choose of yore; and to protect
    His infant cries, had clamour made thereon.
Within the mount a great old man erect   *103*
    Looks out to Rome as if it were his glass;
    His shoulders Damietta's coast reject.   *105*
A head shapen of perfect gold he has;
    Of pure silver his arms are, and his breast:
    But to the fork he is of molten brass.
Thence down he is all of iron, proved the best,
    Except that the right foot is baked of clay,   *110*
    And on this, more than the other, doth he rest.
All portions of him save the gold betray
    Fissures that drop tears, oozing without end,
    Which through the cave, collecting, force their way.
Their streams cascading in this valley spend:
    Acheron they make, and Styx and Phlegethon;

---

96. *In the golden age, under Saturn.*

100-102. *Rhea, wife of Saturn, to save the infant Jupiter from his father, who devoured his sons, entrusted him to the Curetes, or Corybantes, in Crete; and when he cried, she had them drown the sound with noise.*

103. *"A great old man": in the island of Crete, is the figure of an aged man—a statue evidently representing humanity at its successive ages. Ever since the Golden Age mankind has been imperfect; therefore all the statue except the head is split by a crack. From this fissure flow the tears of the sinful generations of men; descending into Hell, they make the infernal streams.*

105. *"Damietta," an Egyptian city, represents the ancient, pagan world; "Rome" stands for the modern, Christian world.*

Then by this narrow conduit they descend
To where is no descending more; whereon
 They form Cocytus; and what manner of pool *119*
 It is, thou'lt see: words for it now I have none." 120
And I to him: "If from our own world full
It flows thus down, why doth it only appear
To us upon this selvage visible?"
And he: "Thou knowest the place is circular;
 And though, going ever leftward, so much space
 Thou hast travelled, and hast now descended far,
Much of the circle thou hast still to trace:
 Wherefore if sight of aught new we obtain,
 This ought not to bring wonder to thy face."
"O Master, where are found," I asked again, 130
 "Phlegethon and Lethe? of one thou speakest naught,
 And the other is formed, thou sayest, by this rain." *132*
"In all thy questions thou dost please my thought,"
 He answered; "but the red stream's boiling hiss *134*
 The answer of one might well to thee have taught.
Thou shalt see Lethe; but beyond the abyss,
 There where the spirits go, themselves to cleanse,
 When by their penitence guilt assoiled is."
Then he said: "It is time that we go hence,
 And quit the wood. See that thou follow me: 140
 The unscorched marge makes for our feet defence,
And over it no fire hath power to be."

---

119. The frozen Cocytus forms the bottom of Dante's Hell.
132. "This rain": the rain of tears that forms the stream.
134-135. The heat of this stream proves that it is Phlegethon.

Canto XV

Dante follows Virgil along one of the petrified high banks of the stream which crosses the sand; and as they go, they meet a troop of those who indulged unnatural lust (the "violent against nature"), and among them Dante recognizes Brunetto Latini, famous in Florence as a philosopher and man of learning and author of the Treasure. *They greet each other affectionately; Brunetto speaks warmly of Dante's merits, and severely of the ingratitude of Florence; Dante acknowledges in tender words all he owes to Brunetto and his writings. Among Brunetto's companions is a bishop transferred by Boniface VIII (servus servorum Dei was a style used by the Popes) from Florence to Vicenza: the first reference in the poem to the great pope whom Dante detested.*

Now one of the hard banks our footing bears,
  And the stream's smoke maketh a shadowy shield
  So that the fire both bank and water spares.
As 'twixt Wissant and Bruges the Flemings build,
  Dreading the tide that ever toward them pours,
  Their rampart that compels the waves to yield,
And as the Paduans do by Brenta's shores,   **7**
  Their villages and castles to make fast,
  Ere Chiarentana feel the sun's hot force,   **9**

7. The "Brenta" is a stream in northeastern Italy.
9. "Chiarentana": a mountainous region north of the Brenta. Its melting snows swell the river.

These dykes were fashioned of like mould and cast,　10
　Albeit the master, whoever it was that wrought,
　Had made them not so lofty nor so massed.
Already we were from the wood remote
　So far, that had my eyes turned back thereto
　They could not have had power the place to note,
When up to us now a band of spirits drew,
　Coming beside the bank; and scrutiny
　Each made of us, as men are wont to do
At dusk, when a new moon is in the sky;
　And at us, puckering their brows, they pried　20
　Like an old tailor at his needle's eye.
As thus by all that company we were eyed,
　One of them recognized me, and by the skirt
　Caught hold of me, and "O what marvell!" cried.
Soon as he touched me, I could no more avert
　Mine eyes, but on his visage scorched and sere
　Fixt them, until beneath the mask of hurt
Did the remembered lineaments appear.
　And to his face my hand inclining down,
　I answered, "Ser Brunetto, are you here?"　30
And he: "May it not displease thee, O my son,
　If Brunetto Latini turn with thee
　A little back, and let his troop go on."
I said: "That same thing most contenteth me.
　And if that I sit with you, you prefer,
　So will I do, if he I am with agree."
"O my son," said he, "of this herd, whoe'er
　One instant stops, an hundred years must lie
　Helpless against the fire a hand to stir;
Therefore go on, while at thy skirts go I　40
　And then rejoin my comrades in lament,
　Who as they go, their loss eternal sigh."
I dared not from the road make the descent
　To go level with him; but bowed my head

Like one who walketh inly reverent.
He began now: "What fate or fortune led
 Thee down into this place, ere thy last day?
 Who is it that thy steps hath piloted?"
"Above there in the clear world on my way,"
 I answered him, "lost in a vale of gloom,   50
 Before my age was full, I went astray.
But yester morn I turned my back therefrom.
 As I re-entered it, he came from far,   53
 And by this same path he shall guide me home."
And he to me: "If thou follow thy star,
 Thou'lt fail not glorious harbour at the end,
 If in the beautiful life I did not err.
And had Fate chosen my own years to extend,
 Seeing Heaven did on thee so benignly look,
 I had been with thee to hearten and befriend.   60
But that ungrateful, that malignant folk   61
 Who came of old down from Fiesole,   62
 And still smack of the mountain and the rock,
Will for thy good deeds turn thine enemy.
 And there is cause; among the acid sloes
 Ill fits that sweet figs fruit upon the tree.
Old fame on earth proclaims them envious,
 Arrogant, blind of eye and greedy of throat:
 Wipe thyself clean of all such ways as those.
Thy fortune keeps thee for such honoured note   70
 That either side will hunger in pursuit
 Of thee; but far shall grass be from the goat.
Let them their own selves tear in pieces, brute

---

53. "He came . . .": Dante avoids mentioning Virgil by name in
Hell.
61. "That malignant folk": the Florentines.
62. "Fiesole" is at the top of a steep hill near Florence. Catiline,
driven from Rome, took refuge there with his followers. When
the place was finally taken, tradition has it that the surviving in-
habitants, combining with a Roman colony, founded Florence.

Beasts of Fiesole, and not impede
If 'mid their rankness any scion shoot
In which reviveth still the sacred seed
    Of those true Romans who incorrupt remained   77
    When grew that nest of malice and of greed."
"Could all of my desire have been attained,"
    I answered him, "not yet from the estate   80
    Of our humanity had you been banned.
Still in my heart stays, memory's dear inmate,
    The fatherly kind image, paining now,
    Of you, when in the world, early and late,
You taught me how man may eternal grow.
    And whilst I breathe the air, it is most right
    My grateful tongue declare all that I owe.
What of my course you tell, that do I write
    And keep for a Lady with another text
    For her wise comment, if I of her win sight.   90
Of this much would I have you disperplext.
    I am prepared, so conscience not upbraid,
    For Fortune, whatsoe'er she purpose next.
Not new to these ears is such boding made.   94
    Therefore let Fortune turn her wheel to accord
    With her own pleasure, and the boor his spade."
Then over his right shoulder turned my Lord   97
    Backward and looked at me, and spoke anon:
    "He listens well who noteth well the word."
None the less I continue speaking on   100
    With Ser Brunetto, and I ask him who
    Of his companions highest note have won.
And he to me: "Of some 'tis well to know:
    But of the rest 'twere better naught be said;

77-78. *Dante believed that his own family belonged to the old Roman stock of Florence.*
94-95. *Let fate and men pursue their thoughtless course: this sounds like a proverbial phrase.*
97. "My Lord": *Virgil.*

So much talk, this short time, we must forgo.
Know then in brief, all these were scholars bred
    And clerks, and upon earth great fame they knew,
    And all by the same soilure forfeited.
Priscian goeth among that sorry crew,
    And Francesco d'Accorso; and didst thou crave
    Such scurf, thou mightest have seen and spoken to
Him who from Arno to Bacchiglion's wave
    By the servant of God's servants was transferred,
    And there his sinfully spent nerves outgave.
I would say more, but must not be deferred
    My going, and speech must end now; for I see
    Smoke of new dust there from the sand upstirred.
People are coming with whom I may not be.
    But let my Treasure (and I ask no more),   *119*
    Wherein I live still, be commended thee."   120
He turned, and seemed like, in the field before
    Verona, one of those who run the race
    For the green cloth; so seemed he running, nor   *123*
Seemed in the loser's but the winner's place.

109-110. "Priscian": the great Latin grammarian of the sixth century.
    "Francesco d'Accorso": a renowned jurist, lived in Bologna and in
    England, in the thirteenth century.
112. He "who from Arno" is, is Andrea di Mozzi, a bishop removed
    in 1295 by Boniface VIII (see the Argument).
119. My "Treasure": Brunetto Latini's main work.
123. In the annual games held in Verona in the thirteenth century
    the first prize in the foot-race was a green cloth.

Canto XVI

Three Florentines detach themselves from a troop
of spirits and hail Dante as their countryman. Of
the fate of two of them, Tegghiaio and Rusticucci,
whom he admired for their political uprightness,
he had already been told vaguely in Canto VI. They
ask if Florence is really so degenerate as they have
heard, and at Dante's answer depart sorrowfully.
The poets have now arrived at the place where the
stream falls roaring over into a great abyss: but
how are they to descend? Virgil takes the cord
which Dante wears as a girdle and throws it down
into the pit; and to Dante's astonishment a strange
monster floats up and poises itself on the brink of
the precipice.

ALREADY I had come to where the boom
   Of water falling into the other ring   2
   Was heard resounding like a bee-hive's hum,
When three shades parted, in their haste running
   Together, from a ʈroop that passed beside
   Beneath the rain that scorched them with its sting.
Toward us they ran and each with one voice cried:
   "Stop thou! Of our corrupted city's brood
   Thou seem'st, if by thy dress thou art not belied."
Ah me, what scars I saw, both old and crude,   10
   Upon their bodies burnt unto the bone!
   Even at the thought of it is my pain renewed.

---

2. "The other ring" is the eighth circle, separated from the seventh
by a mighty precipice.

My Teacher lent a grave ear to their moan,
    Turned his face to me, and then said, "Now give heed;
    For unto these should courtesy be shown.
Were it not for the arrowy fire indeed
    This place engenders, I would say for thee
    Rather than them 'twere fitting to make speed."
They, as we stood still, wailed their ancient dree
    Afresh, and when they had arrived quite close   **20**
    Made of themselves a wheel there, all the three.
As champions do, when stript and oiled they choose   **22**
    With the eye their hold and purchase, ere to get
    At grips they come with thrusting and with blows,
So, as they wheeled, each one his visage set
    Continually toward me, in such wise
    That the neck travelled counter to the feet.
And "If this crumbling region's miseries,"
    One began, "and our burnt and blackened fell
    Cause thee not our petitions to despise,   **30**
Let our renown incline thy heart to tell
    What man thou art whose living feet tread so
    Unterrified the thoroughfare of Hell.
He in whose steps thou seest me trample, although
    All naked now he goes, and parched and peeled,
    Was higher in degree than thou canst know.
Grandson of good Gualdrada, he upheld   **37**
    The name of Guido Guerra, and in his days
    Great service did with counsel and in the field.
The other who in the sand behind me stays   **40**
    Is Tegghiaio Aldobrandi, whose fame   **41**

---

22. "Champions": the wrestlers and boxers of ancient times.
37. "Gualdrada" was renowned for her beauty and modesty. Her grandson, Guido Guerra, was a distinguished Florentine Guelph.
41. Tegghiaio, of the Adimari family, was an illustrious citizen of Florence in the middle part of the thirteenth century. If his counsel had been heeded, his countrymen would have escaped the defeat of Montaperti in 1260.

Should in the world above have earned him praise.
And I who with them to the torment came
   Was Iacopo Rusticucci; and more than aught   *44*
   It is my fierce wife who hath brought me blame."
Could I a shelter from the fire have got
   I would have flung me down among them there,
   Nor had my Guide forbidden it, I thought;
But since I should have burnt from heel to hair,
   Terror prevailed that good will to constrain   *50*
   Which made me greedy their embrace to share.
Then I began: "Sorrow and not disdain
   Of your condition did my heart imbrue
   So deeply that not soon will fade the pain,
When this my lord spoke words wherefrom I drew
   Such thought as expectation in me nursed
   That there might be approaching such as you.
I am of your city; and always from the first
   Your names with honour did my heart recall
   And with affection heard your deeds rehearsed.   *60*
For the sweet apples, leaving soon the gall,
   I go, as promised me my trusted Guide,
   But to the centre needs that first I fall."
"So may thy spirit long time," he replied,
   "Sustain thy members and their motions fill,
   And so thy fame bright after thee abide,
Tell us if courtesy and valour still
   Dwell in our city, once their old resort,
   Or have they quite abandoned her to ill?
Guglielmo Borsiere, who time but short   *70*
   Has suffered with us, and is yonder gone
   With the others, grieves us sore by his report."

---

44. Of *Jacopo Rusticucci*, a contemporary of the other two, little is recorded. Nothing is known of his wife.
70. The newly arrived *Guglielmo Borsiere is known to us only through a story in Boccaccio's Decameron, 1, 8.*

"Because new men and sudden gains have sown
  In thee the seeds of luxury and pride,
  Florence, thou hast already cause to groan."
Thus, lifting up my countenance, I cried.
  The three, who knew they had their answer got,
  As men when truth is told, each other eyed.
"If other times thou canst so free of scot,"
  They all replied, "make answer in like case,   80
  Thus as thou list, thou art lucky in thy lot.
Therefore if thou escape this dismal pass
  And win to see the beauteous stars again,
  When it shall pleasure thee to say 'I was,'
See that thou speak of us to living men."
  Then broke they up their wheel, and as they fled
  Their nimble legs seemed wings upon the plain.
Truly an Amen could not have been said
  So quickly as those spirits disappeared:
  Wherefore it pleased my Master to be sped.   90
I followed him and after a little neared
  So close the falling water with its din
  That, speaking, we had scarce each other heard.
As that stream, which its own path doth begin   94
  From Monte Veso with an eastward aim
  Upon the left slope of the Apennine
And, Acquaqueta called, is still the same
  Till it descends into its nether bed
  And at Forlì is emptied of that name,
Resoundeth, falling in one full cascade   100
  Above St. Benedict of the Mountain, where

94-99. *The roaring cataract in Hell is compared to the noisy falls of
the Montone river. "Monte Veso" is Monviso. One of the three
upper branches of the Montone is the "Acquaqueta" which, at
Forlì, gives up that name, and merges into the Montone.*
100-103. *"St. Benedict" (San Benedetto dell' Alpi) is a little village.
The river roars because it falls over a single ledge, when it ought
to be caught by a thousand.*

A thousand their safe refuge might have made,
So, thundering from a bank and plunging sheer,
   That crimsoned water on our senses smote
   So that ere long it would have stunned the ear.
I had a cord that girdled me about,   *106*
   And one time had I thought within its noose
   To catch the leopard with the spotted coat.
When from my loins I had made it wholly loose,
   I gave it to my Guide, upcoiled and wound,   110
   Even as he commanded, for his use.
He bent him on the right side toward the ground,
   And some few paces from the precipice
   He flung it forth into that pit profound.
"Surely it must be something strange shall rise,"
   I inly said, "by this strange signal brought
   Which thus my Master follows with his eyes."
Ah, well should men be circumspection taught
   With those who see not only the deed done
   But with their mind look through into the
       thought.   120
He said to me: "There will come up anon
   What I expect, and what thou seest in dream
   Must soon be plain for sight to look upon."
Ever from truths which liker falsehood seem,
   Far as man may, one should his lips refrain,
   For, blameless, he yet hazards disesteem;
But speak I needs must here, and by the strain
   Of this my Comedy, reader, I aver—
   So may it some enduring favour gain—
That I saw through that gross and gloomy air   130
   Come swimming up a shape, miraculous
   To any mind, unshaken howsoe'er;

---

106. *The significance of the "cord" has been variously interpreted. It must stand for something upon which Dante at one time built false hopes, but now, at the command of Reason, discards.*

Like one who reappears from where he goes   *133*
   To undo the anchor which, far down, grapnels
   A rock or aught else hidden in the ooze;
Who stretches arms up, and draws in the heels.

Canto XVII

*The monster is Geryon, the emblem of Fraud, who
guards the Eighth Circle; and to this the poets are
now to descend on Geryon's back. But first Dante
goes alone to see a group of the third class of the
violent who are punished in the burning sand.
These are the Usurers, who are violent against
Nature and Art. Returning to Virgil he takes his
place on Geryon, who floats down the circular
abyss and brings them to the next circle.*

Behold the fell beast with the sharp tail curled
   That mountains, walls and armour pierces through!
   Behold him who corrupteth the whole world!"
Thus did my Master speak to me anew,
   And beckoned him that he should come ashore
   Where to the marbled causeway's end we drew.
And that obscene image of Fraud then bore
   Onward, and landed with his head and chest,
   But drew not up his tail upon the scaur.
His face was as a just man's, and expressed   10

133-136. *To the observer above, a diver, returning to the surface, is
foreshortened and magnified by the intervening water.*

The mildness that its outward aspect feigned;
  Like to a serpent's trunk was all the rest.
He had two paws, up to the armpits maned
  With hair; the neck and breast and either flank
  Were freaked with knots and little whorls ingrained.
Never did Turk or Tartar livelier prank
  With colour cloth, inlaid and overlaid;
  Such dyes Arachne's tissue never drank.   *18*
As sometimes on the shore a barge is stayed,
  That part in water lies and part on land;   *20*
  And as, where guzzling Germans dwell, to aid
His fishery, the beaver takes his stand,   *22*
  So that most evil of beasts leant on the stone
  Which with its rim encloses the great sand.
Out in the void flickered his tail alone,
  Twisting the venomed fork up in the air
  Which armed the point, as in the scorpion.
My Guide said, "Now must we a little bear
  Off from our path, far as that beast that, buoyed
  Upon the bank, couches in evil there."   *30*
Descending to the right hand we deployed,
  And made ten paces toward the margin, so
  That we might well the flame and sand avoid;
And soon as we came close upon him, lo!
  A little farther upon the sandy waste
  Were people sitting near the abyss a-row.   *36*
"Here," said to me my Master, "that thou may'st
  Bear with thee full experience of this ring,
  Go and observe the state of these; but haste!

---

18. "Arachne": *the famous weaver who challenged Minerva to a contest, and was turned into a spider.*
22. *It was believed that the beaver caught fish with its tail, by dangling it in the water. In the Middle Ages the beaver was associated with Germany.*
36. "Were people . . .": *the usurers, who did violence to human industry.*

Brief let thy talk be. I will with this thing   40
  Be parleying, till thou return again,
  That to his strong back he may let us cling."
Thus on the extreme border of the plain
  Of that seventh circle, all alone I went
  To where that folk were seated in their pain.
Through the eyes their grief in torrents was unpent.
  This side and that their hands twisted about,
  Some shield from flame or hot soil to invent.
Not otherwise the dogs in summer drought,
  When they are bitten by the fleas or flies,   50
  Defend themselves, either with paw or snout.
After I had scanned the faces with my eyes
  Of many on whom the dread fire falling smote,
  I found not one that I could recognize,
But saw on each a pouch, hung from the throat,
  With a certain colour and device impressed,
  And on it with their gaze they seemed to gloat.
As I came close to them, mine eyes at quest
  Saw azure on a yellow purse display
  A lion's face and figure for a crest.   60
Then as my look continued on its way
  Another, red as blood, I noted now
  Whereon was stampt a goose more white than whey.
And one, whose argent wallet with a sow,
  Azure and pregnant, was imprinted, cried:
  "What in this ditch of misery doest thou?
Get thee away, and as thou hast not yet died,
  Know, neighbour Vitaliano shall appear   68
  And come to seat himself at my left side.
Florentine these are, Paduan I, whose ear   70

---

60. The azure lion here, the goose on line 63, and the sow on line
64, are the arms of three well-known families of usurers.
68. Of "Vitaliano," the only one of the usurers mentioned by name,
we have no certain information.

Their cries belabour often as with blows,
 Shouting 'Let come the sovereign cavalier
Who brings the pouch with three goats where he
   goes.' "   73
 Then with his mouth he writhed and sudden sent
 His tongue out, like an ox that licks his nose.
And I, dreading my lord's admonishment,
 Lest longer stay should his displeasure meet,
 Turned and went back from those spirits spent.
I found my master, who had taken seat
 Already on that dread creature's haunches bare: 80
 "Be bold," he said, "and think not of retreat.
This way must serve us for the downward stair.
 Mount thou in front, I shall the middle take,
 Lest the tail, swindging, hurt thee unaware."
Like one whom shiverings of the quartan shake
 So that he has his nails already blue
 And starts at the mere sight of shade to quake,
So, when these words came to me, did I grue;
 But threat of shame, which makes a servant bold
 Before his good lord, heartened me anew.   90
On those great shoulders then I got me hold.
 I wished to say, only the voice came not
 As I had meant: "Thy arms about me fold."
But he who at other times my succour wrought
 In other peril, clasped me by the waist,
 Soon as I mounted, and my body caught.
Then he: "Move, Geryon, gently as thou may'st,
 Wide be thy wheelings, thy descending slow.
 Think on the unusual burden that thou hast."
As from shore glides the boat back, backward, so   100

---

73. "Three goats" were the arms of the Becchi family of Florence.
It is thought that the "sovereign cavalier" of usurers is Gianni
Buiamonte, the head of a money-lending company.

He launched himself from where he had come to
  lean;
And when he felt him wholly freed below,
His tail he turned there where his breast had been,
  And like an eel he moved it as to steer,
  And with his paws gathered the air between.
Verily I think there was not greater fear
  When Phaëthon his reins relaxing lost,   *107*
  Whereby heaven scorched, as ev'n now doth appear,
Or when faint Icarus felt his shoulders roast   *109*
  Disfeathered, as the warm'd wax was unbound. *110*
  And his sire cried to him, "An ill way thou go'st,"
Than was my terror when myself I found
  In the air all round about me and all alone,
  And save that beast all else from sight was drowned.
Slow, slowly he continueth swimming on,
  Wheels and descends, but naught of this appeared
  Save on my face a wind from under blown.
Already upon the right the stream I heard
  Roar horribly beneath us; and I lowered
  My head, and forth with eyes bent down I peered. 120
Then feared I the dismounting that was toward
  Yet more, for fires I saw, and crying keen
  I heard, so that my limbs all trembling cowered.
I saw, what heretofore I had not seen,
  The sinking and the wheeling, shown me by
  The nearing on all sides of bale and teen.
As falcon, after flying long and high,

107-108. *Phaeton, son of Phoebus, was carried away by the horses of
  the chariot of the sun, which he tried to drive. The sky, scorched
  by the runaway chariot, still shows traces of it in the Milky Way.*
109-111. *Daedalus, to escape from Crete, fashioned wings for his
  son Icarus and himself and fastened them on with wax. In spite of
  his father's warning, the boy flew so high that the sun melted the
  wax, and, losing his wings, he fell into the sea.*

That has no lure nor any bird in sight,
  And "Oh, thou stoopest" makes the falconer cry,
Weary descends where swift he started flight,   130
  Makes many a circle, and from his master far
  Goes sullen and disdainful to alight;
So Geryon at the bottom of the scar
  Set us beside the rock's foot, ribbed and rough,
  And when he was disburdened of our care
Like arrow from the string he bounded off.

Canto XVIII

---

*The Eighth Circle is divided into ten concentric
rings forming deep chasms called Malebolge or
Evil Pockets; in each of them a separate kind of
Fraud has its own punishment. From the circum-
ference of the circle to the central pit (leading to
the Ninth Circle) run "spokes" of rock which
bridge the chasms. In the first, or outermost, chasm
are two processions of sinners going opposite ways;
the first are panders, the second seducers. By
means of one of the bridges Dante passes to the
cliff above the next chasm or bolgia where are
flatterers immersed in filth.*

*The description of the ten chasms of the Eighth
Circle occupies this and the succeeding cantos as
far as the end of Canto XXX.*

HELL hath a region, Malebolge called.
  All stone and iron-coloured is the place,
  Like the round barrier wherewith it is walled.

Right in the middle of the baleful space
   There yawns a well exceeding deep and wide,
   Whose structure hereinafter I shall trace.
The margin therefore that remains beside,
   Between the well and the cliff's root, is round;
   And ten ravines the floor of it divide.
As is the form presented by the ground,   10
   Where for defence of tower and bastion
   Moat after moat is round a castle wound,
Here a like image to the eye was shown;
   And as the thresholds of the fortress send
   Their several bridges to the far bank thrown,
So from the bottom of the rock extend
   Bridges, upon the dykes and fosses based,
   Down to the well that knits them at their end.
In this place, shaken off from Geryon's waist,
   We found ourselves now, and the poet still   20
   Kept to the left and I behind him paced.
On the right hand I saw new sights of ill—
   New torments, new tormentors multiplied—
   Which, deep within it, the first pocket fill.
There were the naked sinners; on our side
   Of the middle of it they came, so that we met;   26
   On the other, went with us, at larger stride.
The Romans thus, by the great throngs beset   28
   In the year of Jubilee, found the people a mode
   To pass the bridge unjostled without let,   30

---

26. On the nearer side of the bottom of the ditch, the sinners, in
   their circling course, were coming towards us; on the further side,
   they were going with us, but faster than we walked.
28-34. In describing the double march of the lost souls, Dante re-
   calls a scene witnessed by many thousands in Rome in the Jubilee
   year of 1299-1300. A barrier was erected lengthwise along the
   bridge of Sant'Angelo, in order that the crowd going to and com-
   ing from St. Peter's might pass in opposite directions without
   interference.—"The castle": Castel Sant'Angelo.—"The Mount":
   Monte Giordano, a slight eminence on the left of the river.

So that on one side they are all bestowed
    Facing the Castle, and to St. Peter's fare;
    On the other toward the Mount they keep the road.
Along the dingy stone, now here, now there,
    I saw horned demons each with a great whip
    Who from behind smote on those sinners bare.
With what alacrity they made them skip
    At the first strokes! Ah, truly there was none
    Who waited for the third, nay second, stripe.
As I went on, my eyes encountered one;   40
    And "Before now" immediately I said
    "This face I have not lacked to look upon."
To scrutinize him, in my steps I stayed.
    And the most gentle Guide suffered me go
    Backward a space, and with me himself delayed.
And that scourged spirit thought to have hidden, so low
    He hung his head; but little did it avail.
    For "Thou," said I, "who the eyes dost downward
        throw,
Unless thou wear false features for a veil,
    Art Venedico Caccianemico, but   50
    What brings thee in the stinging brine to quail?"
And he to me: "My lips were liefer shut.
    But these thy words that bring me back so true
    The world that was, forbid me to be mute.
'Twas I who made Ghisolabella do   55
    The Marquis' will, however it may please
    Rumour the shameful story to construe.
Nor wail I here the only Bolognese.
    Nay, with us is the place so full, that not

---

50. "Venedico Caccianemico," was Podestà of Milan in 1275, of
Pistoia in 1283.
55-56. "Ghisolabella" was Venedico's sister. "The Marquis": Obizzo
da Este of Ferrara.

So many to say *sipa* (as our way is)   60
Twixt Sàvena and Reno now are taught.
  If thou wouldst have confirming proof of it
  Recall how greed of money on us hath wrought."
As he spoke thus, a demon at him beat
  With lifted lash: "Pandar away," he cried,
  "Here are no women thou canst use to cheat."
My Escort then I re-accompanied;
  And after some few steps we came anon
  To where a cliff projected from the side.
This without effort soon we climbed upon,   70
  And on the rough ridge, turning to the right,
  From those eternal circles we passed on.
When we were at that place where for the flight
  Of the scourged spirits it thereunder gapes,
  "Now," said the Master, "wait and let the sight   75
Strike on thee of the misbegotten shapes
  Whose faces heretofore have been withheld,
  For they have gone with us and in our steps."
From the ancient bridge the train we then beheld
  Of those who now facing to us-ward sped,   80
  Whom likewise the pursuing scourge compelled.
The kind Master, without my asking, said:
  "Look on that great one who advances now
  And seems in all his pain no tear to shed.
How regal still is the aspect of his brow!
  He is Jason, who by courage and by guile   86
  Bore off the Ram's fleece from the Colchian bough.

60-61. "Sipa" is an old Bolognese word for sia, often used for "yes."
Bologna lies between the two rivers, Savena and Reno. The num-
ber of Bolognese panders in this ditch exceeds the number of all
the living people who speak Bolognese.
75-78. Dante is now to look down, at the right, on the seducers,
whose faces he has not been able to see from the bank.
86. "Jason" despoiled the Colchians of the golden fleece.

Upon that quest he passed by Lemnos isle,
    After the women, pitilessly bold,   *89*
    Had given the males all unto slaughter vile.   *90*
There with fair pledges and with words of gold
    Did he cajole the young Hypsipyle,
    Who theretofore had all the rest cajoled.   *93*
Pregnant and lorn he left her by that sea.
    Such guilt so heavy a punishment endures;
    And also for Medea is paid the fee.   *96*
With him go all who practise the like lures.
    Be this sufficient for thee to have known
    Of the first valley and all whom it devours."
We had come to where the pathway, narrower
        grown,   100
    Crosses the second ridge, whereof the rock
    Is buttress to another arch of stone.
Here in the other chasm whining of folk
    We heard, who with a gobbling muzzle growled,
    While with their palms upon themselves they struck.
The banks were crusted over with a mould
    Clotted upon them from the mounting fume
    Which eyes and nose assaulted and befouled.
The bottom was so deep that through the gloom
    We saw nought, till by keeping on the road   110
    To the arch's summit we were on it come.
Thereon we stood, and in the hollow showed
    Down there a people slopt in excrement
    As if from human privies it had flowed.
And while I searched them with my eyes intent,
    A head, if clerk's or layman's none could tell,

---

89. *The women of Lemnos, forsaken by their husbands on account of a curse put upon them by Venus, agreed to murder all the males on the island.*
93. *"Hypsipyle" had saved her father, King Thoas, by pretending to have killed him.*
96. *"Medea" was beguiled by Jason.*

I saw, with ordure it was so besprent.
He cried to me: "Why does thy look so dwell
  On me more than the others in this sty?"
  And I: "Because, if I remember well,   120
I have seen thee before now with thy hair dry.
  Thou art Alessio Interminei   *122*
  Of Lucca; of all, then, thee I keenest eye."
And he, beating his pumpkin-pate, said: "See!
  Down to this dirt the flatteries without end,
  Which my tongue revelled in, have sunken me!"
Thereon my Guide: "Stretch forth thy face and bend
  A little forward, that thine eyes may meet
  The form, and features fully comprehend,
Of that dishevelled harlot soiled with sweat   130
  Who with her filthy nails scratches her side,
  Now crouching and now standing on her feet.
Thais is she, the whore who thus replied   *133*
  To her lover when 'Dost thank me much?' he said:
  'Ay, more than much, marvellously,' she cried.
And herewith let our sight be surfeited."

---

122. "Alessio Interminei" *belonged to a noble family of Lucca; we
know nothing in particular about him.*
133. "Thais," *the harlot, is a character in Terence's* Eunuchus, *to
whom her lover* Thraso, *has sent a present.*

Canto XIX

---

*The third chasm contains the Simonists, who are
each fixed head downwards in holes in the rock.
Dante speaks with Pope Nicholas III, who takes
him at first to be the still living Boniface VIII
(Pope from 1294 to 1303). Dante hated Boniface
and has here contrived an opportunity—not the*

only one in the poem, see also Canto XXVII—for speaking his mind. Nicholas tells how he promoted the interests of his family, the Orsini ("I was a son of the She-Bear"), and prophesies the advent in Hell of a Pope "from the West," i.e. France— Clement V, the Frenchman who transferred the Papal See to Avignon. Dante denounces Simonism to Nicholas in trenchant words. Virgil then carries him to the arch looking down on the next chasm.

O SIMON MAGUS, O lost wretches, led   *1*
  By thee, who prostitute the things that need,
  Being things of God, with goodness to be wed;
Who gape for gold and silver, mouths of greed!
  For you now must the trumpet blow the doom,
  For in the third chasm is your place decreed.
To the next hollow we had already come
  And, mounted on the bridge, were in that part
  Which hangs plumb over the middle of the tomb.
Wisdom supreme! how dost thou show thine art   10
  In heaven, in earth, and in the pit profound!
  How justly dost apportion sin's desert!
The livid stone upon the bottom I found
  Was full of holes, and also on each side,   *14*
  All of one breadth, and each of them was round.
They seemed to me not greater and not less wide
  Than those made in my beautiful St. John
  Wherein stand the baptizers to preside,

---

1. The sin punished in the third chasm is simony, the use of ecclesiastical office for private gain. It derives its name from the Simon Magus of Acts 8:9-24.

14. The burrows of the simonists are compared to the pits for baptizers in the Baptistry of Florence, which Dante lovingly calls "his beautiful St. John." Dante takes this occasion to declare that he once broke down one of these receptacles to save someone drowning inside.

One of which I, not many years agone,
    Broke, to save one who else had drowned therein.
    I stamp this true, to enlighten every one.
A sinner's feet from each mouth could be seen
    Protruding up, and legs that rose in sight
    Far as the calf: the rest remained within.
The soles of either foot were all alight,
    Wherefore the joints were quivering in such throes
    As had burst withy or grassy bonds outright.
As on things oiled the flame flickers and flows
    Moving only along their outer face,
    So was it there from the heels unto the toes.
"Who is this, Master, who most in all this place
    Writhes himself, quivering as he anguishes,
    And whom the licking flames more redly chase?"
And he to me: "If down the bank it please
    That I should bear thee, that which lies the lowest,
    Thou'lt learn of him and of his trespasses."
And I: "It pleaseth me where'er thou goest.
    Thou art my lord; thou knowest I will to do
    Only thy will; and the unsaid words thou knowest."
On the fourth causeway then we came, and so
    Turned and descended down by the left bank
    And reached the narrow, pitted floor below.
Nor did the master set me from his flank
    Until he had brought me to the hollow crack
    Where he was, who lamented with his shank.
"Whoe'er thou be who art planted like a stake
    With the head downward, O thou spirit undone,"
    I was now saying, "If thou art able, speak!"
I stood still like the friar confessing one
    Fixt in the earth for treacherous homicide   50
    Who calls him back, his death so to postpone;

---

50. "Fixt in the earth . . .": murderers were planted, head down-
wards, in a hole, and buried alive.

And "Dost thou stand already there," he cried,
   "Boniface, dost thou stand already there?   53
   By several years the Writ to me hath lied.
Art thou so quickly gorged with all the gear
   For which thou didst not shrink by guile to seize
   The beauteous Lady and then to havock her?"   57
I became like to those who, ill at ease,
   Not comprehending the answer to them made,
   Stand as if mocked, and words within them freeze. 60
"Make haste and say to him," then Virgil said,
   "I am not he thou thinkest, I am not he."
   And I replied to him as my master bade.
Whereat in every fibre from the knee
   The spirit shuddered, sighing in lament,
   And spoke: "What is it, then, thou wouldst ask of me?
If to learn who I am thou art so intent
   That for this cause thou hast crost the embankment,
      know
   That I in the Great Mantle apparelled went,
And of the She-Bear was true son, and so   70
   Persistent to advance the cubs, that I,
   Who pouched above, myself am pouched below.
Beneath my head are those who in simony
   Preceded me, thrust even deeper down
   In the stone's crannies they are pinioned by.
Thither I also, when arrives that one   76

---

53. *The speaker, Nicholas* III, *thinks that his successor in simony,
Boniface* VIII, *has arrived. But, as Boniface was not to die until
1303, the book of destiny seems to have lied.*

57. *"The beauteous Lady" is the Church, the Bride of Christ.*

70-71. *Giovanni Gaetano Orsini, Pope Nicholas* III *from 1277 to
1280, was notorious for his nepotism. Because of the fact that the
"She-Bear" was the cognizance in his family arms, Dante refers to
his relatives as "the cubs."*

76-87. *"That one" is Boniface. Nicholas has been there nearly
twenty years; Boniface's feet will burn only about eleven years,
from 1303 to 1314, when Clement* V *will die.—Clement* V, *the
"shepherd without law," was noted for his greed and licentious-*

For whom I took thee when I was moved to make
But now the sudden question, shall be thrown.
But longer already is the time I bake
    My soles and stay with legs above the chest   80
    Than, planted with red feet, he too shall quake.
For after him shall come out of the West
    A shepherd without law, of uglier deed,
    Above us both fit covering to be prest.
'Twill be another Jason, of whom we read
    In Maccabees; and as to him of old
    His king was soft, so France, by this one fee'd."
I know not if at this I was too bold,
    For in this strain his discourse I repaid.
    "Ah, tell me truth now, tell me how much gold   90
Our Lord of Peter requisition made
    Before he put the keys into his hand.
    'Follow me!' Surely nought but this he bade.
Nor Peter, no, nor the others did demand
    Gold from Mathias when he for that part   95
    Was chosen, from which the guilty soul was banned.
Stay thou then here; justly chastised thou art,
    And keep thou well the monies gotten ill
    Which gave thee against Charles so bold a heart. 99
And were it not that reverence rules me still   100
    For the supreme keys which when life was glad
    Thou heldest, and the office thou didst fill,
I'd have for thee words harder than I had;
    Such woe your avarice for the world doth spell,

---

ness, and became the unscrupulous tool of Philip the Fair of
France. In 1309 he transferred the Papal See to Avignon. Clement
is compared to the Jason of 2 Macc., who bought the high-
priesthood of King Antiochus. As Antiochus favored Jason, Philip
will have Clement made Pope.
95. "Mathias" was chosen apostle to fill the place of Judas.
99. From the beginning of his papacy, Nicholas was hostile to
Charles of Anjou.

Trampling the good and raising up the bad.
Such pastors did the Evangelist foretell
  When a-whoring with the kings before his sight
  She who sitteth upon the waters fell;   *108*
She who was born with seven heads of might,
  And ten horns for her sign of warrant bore,   110
  While still her spouse in virtue found delight.
A God of silver and gold ye have made to adore;
  And how do ye differ from the idolater
  Save that he worships one, and ye five-score?
Ah, Constantine, what evil fruit did bear   *115*
  Not thy conversion, but that dowry broad
  Thou on the first rich Father didst confer!"
And whether rage or conscience in him gnawed,
  The while to him in such a strain I sung,
  With both his feet fiercely he kicked abroad.   120
Of a truth I think it pleased my Guide, he hung
  Upon my lips with so content an eye,
  Hearing the sound of truth upon my tongue.
Therefore he took me in both his arms to lie,
  And when he had drawn me all upon his breast
  Mounted the path he had descended by.
Nor did he weary in holding me close-prest
  Until, where the steep arch the chasm bestrode
  From fourth to fifth ridge, he had climbed its crest.
Here softly he the burden of his load   130
  Soft on the rough and craggy cliff deposed
  Where to goats even it were a painful road.
Therefrom another valley was disclosed.

---

108. "She who sitteth . . ." See *Rev.* 17: "*I saw a woman sit upon
a scarlet coloured beast, full of names of blasphemy, having seven
heads and ten horns.*" Dante combines the woman with the beast,
and makes her the symbol of the corrupt Church.

115. *The Emperor Constantine was thought to have donated the
Western Empire to St. Sylvester, the first Pope to hold temporal
possessions.*

Canto XX

*Dante looks down on the fourth chasm of Male-
bolge, where the Sorcerers and Diviners go with
their faces twisted so as to look behind them.
Among these are Amphiaraus of Argos, one of the
Seven Against Thebes, Tiresias the Theban, Aruns
the Etruscan, and Manto, daughter of Tiresias,
who, according to the story now put in Virgil's
mouth, founded his native city of Mantua. Virgil
points out other diviners, among whom is Michael
Scot, a prominent figure at the court of Frederick
II in Sicily; then enjoins haste, as "Cain and his
Thorns," i.e. the "man in the moon," is setting
beyond Seville (Spain being conceived as the
Western boundary of the northern hemisphere, as
India or "Ganges" the Eastern).*

VERSE for fresh penances must I compose
　　To fill the first book's twentieth canto and tell
　　Of the submergéd spirits and their woes.
I was now stationed so that I could well
　　Look down into the new discovered deep
　　Bathed in the tears of anguish as they fell.
In the round valley I saw a people weep
　　As they came on, all silent, at the pace
　　Our Litanies in their processions keep.
When deeper down my eyes perused the place,　　10
　　Each appeared strangely to be wrenched awry
　　Between the upper chest and lower face.

For toward the reins the chin was screwed, whereby
  With gait reversed they were constrained to go,
  For to look forth this posture would deny.
Perhaps by palsy's overmastering throe
  Some may have been thus quite distorted, yet
  I ne'er saw such, nor think it could be so.
Reader, so God vouchsafe thee fruit to get
  Of what thou readest, think now in thy mind   20
  If I could keep my cheeks from being wet
When this our image in such twisted kind
  I saw, that tears out of their eyelids prest
  Ran down their buttocks by the cleft behind.
Truly I wept, leant up against the breast
  Of the hard granite, so that my Guide said:
  "Art thou then still so foolish, like the rest?
Here pity lives when it is rightly dead.
  What more impiety can he avow
  Whose heart rebelleth at God's judgment dread?   30
Lift up thy head, lift up, and see him now
  For whom in the eye of Thebes earth clove her floor:
  Whereat they all cried: 'Whither rushest thou,
Amphiaraus? Quittest thou the war?'   34
  And he stopt not upon his headlong track
  To Minos down, who clutcheth evermore.
Mark how the shoulders now his bosom make.
  Because he wished too far in front to see
  He looks behind and ever goeth back.
Behold Tiresias, who so changed that he   40
  Lost his male semblance and became woman,
  Causing the transformed members all to agree.

---

34. *The story of Amphiaraus, the augur, one of the seven kings who
besieged Thebes, is told by Statius in the Thebaid.*
40. *"Tiresias," a famous soothsayer of Thebes, having struck with
his stick two snakes that were together, became a woman; seven
years later, striking the same snakes again, he regained his male
form.*

And afterwards he needs must over again
  Strike with his rod the two convolvéd snakes
  Ere he could reassume the plumes of man.

With back to his belly, next his footing takes
  Aruns, who in hills of Luni, where his hoe   47
  The Carrarese plies and his dwelling makes

'Mid the white marbles, had the cave below
  For his abode, wherefrom the prospect wide   50
  Of stars and sea he had not to forgo.

And yonder she who both her breasts doth hide
  With her dishevelled tresses from thy view,
  And has all the hairy skin on the other side,

Was Manto, who searched many countries through,   55
  Then settled there where I was born; wherefore   56
  Listen awhile, as I would have thee do.

After her father had passed out by death's door
  And Bacchus' city in servitude was thralled,   59
  Over the world she roamed a long time more.   60

Above in beauteous Italy lieth, walled
  By the Alps behind it, Germany's confine
  Over Tiralli, a lake Benaco called.   63

Through a thousand springs is all between Pennine
  And Garda and Val Camonica besprent
  The land by streams that in that lake resign.

Midmost a place is where the pastor of Trent   67

47. Aruns was an Etruscan soothsayer of Caesar's time. The moun-
tain cave seems to be an invention of Dante, who was in Luni-
giana in 1306.
55. Manto was the daughter of Tiresias of Thebes.
56. "Where I was born": the city of Mantua. Here Virgil launches
forth into a lengthy account of the founding of his native place:
the town was named after Manto, who ended her long wander-
ings on the spot where it was afterwards built.
59. Bacchus was the son of the Thebean Semele. Thebes came un-
der the rule of the tyrant Creon.
63-65. "Benaco" is Lake Garda; Garda rises on the east of it, Val
Camonica is a long valley some distance west of it.
67. There is a point in or near the lake where the dioceses of Trent,

And he of Brescia and the Veronese
  Might give their blessing if that road they went.
Peschiera, beautiful and strong fortress,   70
  Sits where the shore around is lowest seen
  To front the Brescians and the Bergamese.
There down must slide what is not held within
  The bosom of Benaco, and below
  It swells to a river amid pastures green.
Soon as the water setteth head to flow,
  No more Benaco, Mincio it is named
  Far as Governol, where it meeteth Po.
Soon is his current on the level tamed
  And widens into shallows smooth as glass,   80
  Sometimes in summer for miasma blamed.
By that way did the unmellowed virgin pass,
  And saw land bare of any denizen
  Or tillage, in the midst of the morass.
There, to shun all communion with men,
  She stayed, her arts amid her thralls to ply;
  There lived she and left her body in that fen.
Afterwards those who dwelt dispersed anigh
  Drew to that spot which had for bastions
  The swampy pools that it was compassed by.   90
They reared the city over those dead bones,
  Calling it, after her who chose it first,
  Mantua, and sought no augury's response.
In it a denser populace was nursed
  Ere Casalodi's mad pride, overawed   95
  By Pinamonte's cunning was reversed.

Brescia, and Verona meet, so that any one of the three bishops
  might make the sign of the cross in that spot.
95. The Ghibelline Pinamonte Bonaccorsi treacherously advised the
  Guelf Count Alberto da Casalodi, lord of Mantua, to exile the
  nobles so as to win the favor of the people. Following this coun-
  sel and thus losing support, Casalodi was driven from the city,
  with much slaughter and banishment of the Guelfs.

Therefore I charge thee, if e'er thou hear abroad
  Given to my city other origin,
  Let false invention not the truth defraud."
And I: "Master, thy affirmations win   100
  Such certainty in me, that all else were
  As a dead coal that once had kindled been.
But tell me of those that pass, if any appear
  Of note, of whom thou knowest and canst speak;
  For only of this my wish is bent to hear."
Then he answered: "He whose beard juts from his cheek
  Over his dusky shoulders on each hand
  Was, when in Greece the males were so to seek   108
That hardly for the cradles they remained,
  An Augur: he with Calchas timed the blow   110
  Which was to sever the first cable's strand.
Eurypylus his name: and somewhere so   112
  Doth my high Tragedy tell the tale of him:
  Thou know'st it well who dost the whole well know.
The other, who looks about the flanks so slim,
  Was Michael Scot; and verily he knew   116
  The magic game and its false signs to limn.
See Guy Bonatti, see Asdente, who   118
  Would fain he had still attended to his cord
  And leather, but too late the choice must rue.   120
See the sad women, who the needle ignored,
  The shuttle and spindle, and with effigy
  And herb devised their sorceries abhorred.
But come, Cain and his thorns, reminding me,   124

---

108. *All the men of Greece had gone to the Trojan war.*
112-13. *Eurypylus assisted Calchas the soothsayer in determining "the right moment for cutting the first cable at Aulis," when the Greeks set sail from Troy.*—"My high Tragedy": Virgil's Aeneid.
116. *Michael Scot, the Scotch scholar, who lived many years at the court of Frederick II, had great repute as a sorcerer.*
118. *Guido Bonatti of Forlì was a famous astrologer. Asdente, a poor cobbler of Parma, was known far and wide as a prophet.*
124. *For "Cain and his thorns" see the Argument.*

Occupies of each hemisphere the bound
Already, and beyond Seville meets the sea.
Already yester-eve the moon was round:
Thou must remember, for she harmed thee not
That time when thou wast in the wood profound."
Thus as he spoke, we moved on from that spot.   130

Canto XXI

*The next chasm of Malebolge into which they look
is that of the Barrators and Peculators who made a
traffic of public offices. These are submerged in
a river of boiling pitch and are kept under by
a horde of demons armed with long hooks and
called Malebranche or Evil-Talons. These demons
threaten the poets, till Virgil appeases their chief,
who gives them directions (afterwards proved
false) and appoints ten of his band to escort them.*

From bridge to bridge we came, with other talk
Which to recite my Comedy hath no care,
Keeping the summit of the stony baulk.
Then stopt we, on Malebolge's following lair
To look, and other vain lamenting moil;
And marvellously dark I found it there.
As the Venetians in their arsenal boil   7

7-15. The mention of the pitch leads to a lifelike description of the
great arsenal, or shipyard, in Venice, famous during and after the
Middle Ages, where the sailors utilize the enforced idleness of
winter to repair their damaged craft.

The lumps of pitch in winter, stiff as glue,
  To caulk the ships whose timbers warp and spoil,
Since sail they cannot then; whereof in lieu,   10
  Some of a vessel worn with voyage plug
  The ribs, and others build their craft anew;
Some shape oars, others plait ropes, twist and tug,
  Some hammer at the poop, some at the prow,
  Or mend sails, one the jib and one the lug:
So, not by fire, but divine art knows how,
  Thick pitch down there boiled, and on every side
  The bank was slimed with the overbrimming slough.
The pitch I saw, but naught therein espied
  Except the bubbles which the boiling raised,   20
  And watched it all heave and comprest subside.
While downward fixedly thereon I gazed,
  My Guide, suddenly saying "Have a care!"
  Drew me to him from where I stood amazed.
I turned like one who cannot choose but dare
  Turn round to look on that which he must flee
  And who is undermined with sudden scare,
So that he puts not off his flight to see;
  And there I saw a black devil ascend
  The crag behind us, running easily.   30
Ah, what a grimness did his look portend!
  How sorely did his cruel gesture daunt,
  Light on his feet and with his wings opened!
His shoulder, that was sharp and arrogant,
  For burden a sinner by the haunches bore
  And by the ankle he gript the miscreant.
"Ye Evil-Claws," he cried down to the shore,
  Beneath. "An elder of Santa Zita! Ho!   *38*
  Thrust him well under while I go for more
To the city I filled with them to overflow.   40

---

38. The chief magistrates of Lucca were called Elders. Santa Zita
was the special patron saint of Lucca.

Barrators all, except Bonturo, and lief   *41*
  Would each for money make a Yes of No."
He flung him down, then wheeled along the cliff;
  And never from his leash did mastiff bound
  With more alacrity to chase a thief.
The sinner plunged, then rose and writhed him round.
  But covered by the bridge the Demons cried:
  "Here are no Holy Faces to be found;   *48*
Here's other diving than on Serchio side.
  Above the pitch then heave not up thy chin   50
  Unless thou care not from our hooks to hide."
With more than a hundred prongs for discipline
  They nicked him, crying, "There, thou dancer, lurk!
  There's privacy to try thy thieving in."
Just so the cooks bid underlings at work
  About the cauldron that they overlean
  Thrust down the flesh from floating with the fork.
The good Master: "That it may not be seen
  That thou art here, crouch in yon broken bay,
  So that the splinter serve thee for a screen.   60
And whatsoever violence they essay,
  Fear not; for I these matters well have conned,
  Having ere now been once in like affray."
The head now of the bridge he passed beyond;
  And when he set on the sixth bank his foot
  A stedfast front he needed to have owned.
With such a fury and such tempestuous bruit
  Wherewith the dogs rush out on the poor man
  When, halting, he for alms makes hurried suit,
From underneath the bridge those demons ran,   70
  And turned on him with crooks raised up on high.

---

41. "Except Bonturo" *is ironical: Bonturo Dati, boss of Lucca, was
the worst grafter of all.*
48-49. *The hunched-up shape of their victim suggests to the hu-
morous demons the attitude of prayer.—The Serchio is a stream
near Lucca.*

"Be none of you despiteful," he began;
"Before your grapnels upon me you try
   Let one of you come forth to hear me. Wait
   And then consider if those hooks you ply."
All cried: "Let Evil-Tail go!" And thereat
   One moved, and the others stayed firm where they
      stood,
   And came to him saying "What avails him that?"
"Thinkest thou, Evil-Tail, then, that I could,"
   My Master said, "have come secure thus far   80
   Against all opposition of your brood
Without divine will and propitious star?
   Let me pass on. 'Tis written in Heaven's book
   That I for another this wild path unbar."
Then was his pride so fallen that his hook
   He let drop at his feet and to the rest
   Exclaimed, "No more now! let him not be struck!"
My Guide to me: "O thou who cowerest
   Among the bridge's jags where thou hast crept
   Cowering, return, return now undistrest."   90
At which I moved and to him quickly stept.
   Whereon the devils thronged us all about,
   So that I feared the pact might not be kept.
Thus did I once the foot-men who marched out
   Under safe-conduct from Caprona see,   95
   Ringed by so many foemen, fear and doubt.
And to my Master with my whole body
   I drew close, turning not aside my head
   From the look of them, which seemed not good to
      me.
Their irons they lowered and to each other said,   100
   "Now shall I touch him on the rump?" and "Yes,"

---

95. "Caprona," a town on the Arno, surrendered in 1289 to the
troops of Lucca and Florence. It is evident from these lines that
Dante was serving with the Florentines.

Others would answer, "notch it for him red."
But he whom my Guide held in talk of peace
    Turned round immediately and looked askance,
    And "Touzlemane," he shouted, "cease there, cease!"
Then to us: "Further by this cliff advance   106
    Will not be possible, for the sixth arch there
    Lies shattered over all the ground's expanse.
And if it please you forward still to fare,
    Follow along this ridge; not far away   110
    Another cliff will give you passage clear.
Five hours later than this hour yesterday
    A thousand ten score sixty and six years
    Were ended, since the shattering of this way.
Thither, to watch if any take the airs
    Out of the pitch, I send some of my men.
    Follow them, nor have fear of any snares."
"Forth, Hellequin and Frostyharrow!" then
    That fiend continued, "and Dogsnarler, thou!
    And Beardabristle to command the ten.   120
Furnacewind follow, and Dragonspittle too,
    Fanged Swinewallow and Houndscratcher, and last
    Farfarel and raging Scarletfury, you.
See that keen eyes upon the pitch ye cast.
    Be these two safe, far as yon ridge of rock
    That all unbroken spans the antres vast."
"O Master, what is this?" In fear I spoke,
    "Alone, if thou the way know, let us start.
    Such escort's aid I care not to invoke.
If thou beest wary, as wontedly thou wert,   130
    Dost thou not see them, how they grind their teeth
    And with bent brows threaten us to our hurt?"

106-114. To entrap Dante and his too-confiding guide, the leader
of the Evil-Claws informs them that though the nearest bridge
over the following valley is broken, the next bridge will afford
them a safe passage. This arch was shattered, he says, when Christ
descended into Hell, 1266 years ago.

And he: "I'd have thee a brave spirit breathe.
  Let them grind on, and threaten what they durst.
  'Tis all for those rogues in the tar that seethe."
By the left bank they turned to go; but first,
  With tongue between his teeth protruded, each
  Made signal to his chief; and from him burst
A sound that made a trumpet of his breech.

Canto XXII

*The poets go along the stream with their escort,
one of whom catches a sinner who has emerged
from the pitch and holds him up by the hair. He is
a Navarrese called Ciampolo (the name however is
not given by Dante) and Virgil questions him. He
offers to bring sinners of Italian birth to speak with
them, and by a trick eludes the demons. Two of
the Malebranche then quarrel among themselves
and are left entangled in the pitch. This episode
seems introduced by way of humorous relief.*

I HAVE seen horsemen moving camp to arm
  For the assault, and mustering band by band,
  And other whiles retiring at the alarm;
I have seen prickers file across your land,
  O Aretines, and foray sweep pell-mell,   5
  The clash of tourneys, and the tilt-yard manned,

5. Dante was present at the battle of Campaldino, in 1289, when
the forces of Arezzo (the "Aretines") were defeated by those of
Florence and Lucca.

To trumpets now and now to beaten bell,
   To drums and turret-beacons from afar,
   Things native and outlandish things as well;
But never, I vow, to such a monstrous blare   10
   Did I see footmen march or horsemen ride,
   Or ship by landmark or by noted star.
Now had we the ten demons by our side;
   Ah, grisly company! but in the church
   With saints, with rascals in the pot-house bide.
But my whole gaze was on the pitch to search
   The valley and all its features, and those, black
   Within it, that the bubbles scald and smirch.
As dolphins, when with arching of the back,   19
   Making to mariners a sign, they bid   20
   Take thought to save the ship from coming wrack,
So, of the pain a moment to be rid,
   At whiles some sinners peered above the pitch,
   And, in less time than it lightens, hid;
And as, fringing the water of a ditch,
   The frogs stand with their muzzles only out,
   And all the rest of them is out of reach,
In such wise stood the sinners all about,
   But soon as Beardabristle hastened near
   Beneath the boiling slid in panic rout.   30
I saw, and my heart shakes yet with its fear,
   One linger, as 'twill chance that in his nook
   One frog remains while the others disappear.
And Houndscratcher up-caught him with his hook,
   Being nearest, by his hair that from the slough
   Dript tarry, and made him like an otter look.
The name of every fiend I knew by now,
   So well I marked them when they mustered first,
   And when they called each other, listened how.

19-21. *The belief that dolphins warn sailors of an approaching storm was very common.*

"O Scarletfury, let his back be pierced   40
    And opened by thy talons," all the band
    Shouted together, of those fiends acurst.
And I: "O Master, if thou may'st, demand
    Who is that lamentable wretch, whose hide
    Is fallen into his adversary's hand."
Thereon my Guide drew closer to his side,
    Asking him whence he came; he, so implored,
    "I am of the Kingdom of Navarre," replied.   *48*
"My mother placed me as servant of a lord,
    For she had borne me to a lewd wastrel   50
    Who self and substance into pleasure poured.
With good King Tybalt then I went to dwell: 52
    With jobbery there did I my purse equip,
    For which I pay now in this heat of hell."
And Swinewallow, at each side of whose lip
    Tusks like a hog's projected hideous,
    Made him to feel how one of them could rip.
Among malignant cats was come the mouse.
    But Beardabristle closed him in embrace
    And said: "Stand off, while I enfork him thus."   60
And to my Master as he turned his face
    "Ask on," he said, "if more thou wouldest know,
    Before another give him deadlier chase."
The Guide spoke then: "Now tell us, knowest thou
    Any that is a Latin 'mid your throng
    Beneath the pitch?" And he: "I left but now
One of those who to a neighbour isle belong.
    Would he still covered me! then could I scorn
    To tremble at the threat of claw and prong."
And Furnacewind cried: "Too much we have borne!" 70

---

48. Some of the early commentators ascribe to this man from
    Navarre the name of Ciampolo; but we really know of him only
    what Dante tells us.
52. "Tybalt," count of Champagne, son-in-law of Louis ix of France,
    was king of Navarre in the middle of the thirteenth century.

And with the grapnel seized upon his arm
So that a mangled sinew was off-torn.
Dragonspittle also to do his legs a harm
   Had much a mind; but their decurion wheeled   74
   With evil looks and smote them with alarm.
When into quiet they were somewhat quelled,
   My Guide to him who still was all at gaze
   Upon his wound, without delay appealed.
"Who is it whom thou didst quit, as thy word says,
   To come ashore by such a luckless road?"   80
   And he made answer: "Friar Gomita 'twas,   81
He of Gallura, vessel of every fraud,   *82*
   Who held his master's enemies in fee
   And did so to them that they all applaud.
Coin pouched he, and smoothly, he says, let them go
    free;
   Moreover in his other offices
   No jobber small, but prince of jobbers he.
Don Michel Zanche of Logodoro is
   With him; their tireless tongues each other match   90
O me! that other grins, look, on the watch.
   I would say more, but fear he longs to wreak
   His fury upon me, and my scurf to scratch."
And their great prefect turned him round to speak
   To Farfarel, who rolled his eyes alight
   With menace, saying: "Away, thou vulture-beak!"
"If you," resumed that sinner still in fright,
   "With folk of Tuscan or of Lombard race
   Would hold speech, I will bring them into sight;
But let the Evil Claws retire a space,   100
   That those who come may not their vengeance fear;

---

74. "Decurion": leader of ten.
81-90. Of "Friar Gomita" we know only that he was hanged. The
Pisans, who conquered Sardinia, divided it into four provinces,
Gallura, Logudoro, Arborea, and Cagliari. Michel Zanche is said
to have been vicar of King Enzo of Sardinia, son of Frederick II.

And I, still sitting in the self-same place,
One that I am, will gather seven here
By whistling, as, when one of us gets out,
Our wont is to make signal to appear."
Dogsnarler at that word raised up his snout
And shook his head, saying, "Hear that knave's device,
Who plots to cast him down, without a doubt."
Whereat he who was rich in artifice
Replied: "Too much a knave am I indeed   110
When I my friends to greater pains entice."
Hellequin burst forth without any heed
Of the others: "If thou jump, however fleet,
I'll follow thee, not at a gallop's speed,
But close above the pitch my wings will beat.
Leave we the height: to the bank's screen resort
And see if one can all of us defeat."
O thou that readest, thou shalt hear new sport.
All turned their eyes now toward the further side,
He first who most had wished the scheme to
thwart.   120
The Navarrese his moment well espied,
Planted his soles upon the ground, and sprung
Free in an instant, and their chief defied.
Then each of them was with compunction stung.
He most through whom their pride had been abased,
Who leapt up with "I've got thee" on his tongue.
Little it availed him; wings were quite outpaced
By terror; and the other dived under;
And he still flying lifted clear his breast.
Not otherwise the duck, aware how near   130
The falcon is upon her, diveth quick,
And he returns up angry and baulked of her.
But Frostyharrow, furious at the trick,
Kept winging after him, glad in his spite
To let the knave go, and a quarrel pick.

And when the barrator had slipt from sight,
    He turned his talons on his fellow-fiend,
    And gript they hung above the fosse in fight.
But a right sparrow-hawk, full grown, hot-spleened
    To claw him well, was the other; and falling,
        wroth   140
    In the middle of the boiling they careened.
Immediately the heat unclutcht them both;
    But to rise upward baffled all their wit,
    So clogged their wings were with the gluey broth.
Beardabristle with the rest lamenting it
    Made four fly over to the further shore
    With all their hooks; and in a trice alit
This side and that, each at his post, the four.
    They stretched their grapnels out to the limed pair
    Whose crust was burnt already to the core.   150
Thus busily embroiled we left them there.

Canto XXIII

*Dante, following in Virgil's steps, begins to fear
that they will be overtaken by the revengeful
demons. They are in fact pursued, and only escape
by hurried flight, Virgil making a glissade, with
Dante in his arms, down the slope of the next
chasm. Here are the Hypocrites pacing in copes of
lead, heavier than those devised by Frederick II
for malefactors. Two Friars of Bologna speak with
Dante; they were in 1266 installed in the office
of Podestà at Florence. Suddenly Dante catches
sight of Caiaphas crucified on the ground. One of
the Friars tells of the punishment of him and
Annas, and afterwards points out to the poets the
right path for them to take.*

Silent, lonely, and with no company,
   One before and one after, as on their way
   Journey the Minor Friars, journeyed we.   *3*
My thought, that lingered on the present fray,
   Was turned to Aesop and his fable, where   *5*
   The frog would the inveigled mouse betray.
For Yes and Yea make not a better pair
   Than that with this case, if but with good heed
   End and beginning be accoupled fair.
And, as one thought springs from another's seed,   *10*
   So out of that soon did another start
   Which made my first fear double terror breed.
Through us it is, my thought was, that these smart
   And suffer such derision as is bound
   To mortify and sting them to the heart;
And if with rage their enmity be crowned,
   They will come after us with more cruel tread
   Than, snapping at the leveret, comes the hound.
Already I felt my hair all rise in dread
   And stood with backward gaze and anxious brow, *20*
   As "Master, if thou hide not quickly," I said,
"Thyself and me, I have terror, I avow,
   Evil-Talons; they are close behind:
   I so imagine them, I hear them now."
And he: "Were I of glass and leaden-lined,
   Thine outward image were not in me shown
   Sooner than now is the image of thy mind.

---

3. "Minor Friars": Franciscans.
5. In Aesop's fable, *a frog, having offered to tow a rat across a stream, ties itself to the animal, jumps in with it, and then treacherously tries to dive to the bottom, expecting to drown its companion. While the rat is struggling to keep afloat, a kite, seeing the disturbance, swoops down and carries off both creatures. The beginning and the end of the fable, Dante says, are exactly like the recent episode.*

Already thy thoughts came among my own
  With the like motion and the self-same face,
  So that the two to one resolve have grown.   30
If the right bank so shelves down to its base
  That we may into the next pouch descend,
  We shall escape from that foreboded chase."
Of these words hardly had he made an end
  When them I saw, coming with outspread wing
  Not far off, ardent us to apprehend.
My Guide suddenly seized me, hurrying
  As a mother whom the roar and cries awake,
  Who sees the flames quite near her start and spring,
Snatches her child and flieth, for his sake
  More than her own, and has no thought to stop
  So long as even a shift on her to take;
And down the hard rock from the ridge's top
  Supine resigned him to its sloping side
  Which on one hand walls the next valley up.
Never so fast by sluice did water glide
  To make revolve the wheel of a land-mill,
  Close on the paddles gathering speed to slide,
As slid my Master down that slanting hill,
  And me upon his bosom, as his son,   50
  Not now as his companion, carried still.
Scarce had his feet down to the level won
  Of the deep hollow, when they were on the height
  Above us; but all fear of them was gone;
For the high Providence that did commit
  To them the warding of that fifth ravine
  Takes from them all the power of leaving it.
There in the moat beneath was to be seen
  A painted people who circled with slow tread
  Weeping, with drooping and defeated mien.   60
They wore cloaks with a deep hood on the head
  Over their eyes, according to the mode

Wherein the monks of Cluny are habited.
Without, these were so gilded that they glowed
   To the eye; within all lead, and so heavy
   That Frederick's were of straw to such a load.   66
O weary mantle in that eternity!   *Emperor of Sicily*
   We turned again to the left hand, and drew
   Along with them, intent on their deep sigh.
But under the aching weight so slow that crew   70
   Came on, that at each movement of the thighs
   The company abreast of us was new.
Wherefore I to my Guide: "Do thou devise
   To find one who by deed or name is known,
   And, as we go on, move around thine eyes."
And one, who recognized the Tuscan tone,
   Cried after us: "O stay, relax your speed,
   Ye who so run through this our dismal zone.
Perchance from me thou'lt have what thou dost need."
   Whereat my Guide turned round on me and said, 80
   "Delay a little, and at his pace proceed."
I stood still, and saw two whose looks betrayed
   Their mind's haste to be with me, but whom the
      throng
   And the weight that they were burdened with de-
      layed.
When they came up to us, they stood gazing long
   Askance at me, but uttered not a word;
   Then turned to each other and spoke themselves
      among:
"By the working of his throat this one appeared
   Alive; and if dead, why of the heavy shroud
   Have they permission to go undeterred?"   90
To me they spoke then: "Tuscan, to this crowd
   That comest where the hypocrites go sad,

---

66. *The leaden cloaks which Frederick* II *put upon criminals were,
in comparison with these, as light as straw.*

Be not, to tell us who thou art, too proud."
And I to them: "By Arno's water glad
    Was I born; in that city did I grow,
    And am with the body I have always had.
But ye, who are ye, from whom distils such woe
    As I behold down-dropping either cheek?
    What punishment upon you glitters so?"
And one of them replied: "Of lead so thick   100
    Our orange copes are that the balances
    By the greatness of the weights are made to creak.
Jovial Friars were we, and Bolognese;   103
    I Catalano, he Loderingo; and us,
    Though to choose one alone the custom is,
Together both at once thy city chose
    For maintenance of its peace; and how we bore
    Ourselves in office the Gardingo shows."
I began: "Friars, your misdeeds"—but more
    Said not, for one came now before mine eyes   110
    Crucified with three stakes upon that floor.
He, when he saw me, into his beard with sighs
    Blew, and contorted all his limbs as well;
    And Friar Catalano, marking this,
Said: "He, impaled, on whom thy gaze doth dwell, *115*
    Counselled the Pharisees that it was meet
    That one should suffer for the whole people.

---

*103-108. The brethren of the lay order of Beata Maria were not re-
quired to lead an ascetic life, and were nicknamed "Jovial Friars."
Catalano de' Malavolti and Loderingo degli Andalò were both
men of great authority, and successful mayors of several cities.
"Together both . . . thy city chose . . .": it was customary in Flor-
ence, as in many other cities, to choose as mayor for a term some
distinguished outsider. In 1266, however, instead of "one alone,"
two mayors, one from each party, were elected as a compromise.
"Gardingo": an old Longobard fortress in Florence. Near it were
the houses of the Uberti, which were destroyed in 1266, when the
Ghibellines left the city.*

*115-116. The evil counselor is Caiaphas, who favored the sacrifice of
Christ.*

Naked and cross-wise on the road he is set
  As thou beholdest, and must feel what load,
  Ere they have passed, is in their passing feet. 120
His father-in-law hath wretched like abode 121
  Within this fosse, with the others whose consent
  For all the Jews a seed of evil sowed."
Then I saw Virgil marvelling as he bent
  Over him outstretcht on the cross, in plight
  So abject, in the eternal banishment.
The Friar in these words did he then invite:
  "May it not displease you, if your law permit,
  To tell us if a gap be on the right
By which we both may issue and hence be quit, 130
  Nor any of the Black Angels need compel
  To come and to retrieve us from this pit."
He answered: "Nearer than thy hopes foretell
  A rock that from the encircling wall doth go
  Maketh a bridge across the valleys fell,
Save here where the arch is broken and roofless, so
  That you may mount the ruin, which is spread
  All down the slope, and heaps itself below."
The Guide stood still a little with bended head,
  Then spoke: "Maliciously did he advise 140
  Who hooks the sinners in yon seething bed."
The Friar then: "Of the devil's iniquities
  Once in Bologna I heard told, and heard
  That he is a liar and the father of lies."
Then with long strides my Guide went onward, stirred
  To trouble and with an angered look: whereat
  With the laden spirits no more I conferred,
Following the prints of his beloved feet.

---

121. "His father-in-law": *Annas*.

Canto XXIV

They set out to climb the ruin of a bridge shat-
tered by the earthquake which took place at
Christ's death on the cross. The mountain-climb
is vividly described. Dante reaches the top ex-
hausted, and they move down into the seventh
chasm, occupied by the Thieves, who are tor-
mented by serpents. One of the thieves, Vanni
Fucci, is seized by a serpent, and is instantly burnt
to ashes, but at once the ashes resume the former
shape. He tells of his crime, and makes a prophecy
about the war of the Black and White factions and
foretells an attack by Malaspina, captain of the
Black Guelfs in Florence, on Pistoia.

In that part of the young year when the Sun
  Beneath Aquarius warms his beaming locks   2
  And toward the South the nights begin to run,
And when upon the ground the hoar-frost mocks
  With likeness her white sister's effigy,   5
  But soon are blurred that limner's pencilled strokes,
The peasant, who hath nothing now laid by,
  Rises and looks and sees the fields and lanes
  All whitened; and thereat he beats his thigh,
Returns to his house and to and fro complains,   10

2-3. The sun is in Aquarius approximately from January 21 to Feb-
ruary 21. From December 21 to June 21 the nights grow shorter
in the northern hemisphere, longer in the southern.
5. "Her white sister": the snow.

Like a starved wretch who knows not what to do,
   Then again comes out and his hope regains,
Seeing what the world has changed its face into
   So briefly, and takes his crook and out of door
   Goes driving forth his lambs to pastures new;
Thus at my Guide's brow was mine clouded o'er
   When I beheld him in such anxious case;
   And ev'n so soon the salve came to the sore;
For when the ruined bridge we came to face,
   My Master turned upon me with the old   20
   Sweet look I had seen first at the mountain's base.
When with himself he had taken counsel bold,
   Opening his arms, and fixing first his eyes
   Upon the ruin, he of me took hold.
Like one at work, who measures all he tries,
   And always seems his next step to foresee,
   So, hoisting me over one boulder's rise,
He picked another rock out from the scree
   With careful eye, "Now grip on that," he said,
   "But prove first, if it well supporteth thee."   30
No passage was it for one stoled in lead;
   For hardly we, he light and I pushed on,
   Could scale the crag from spur to spur ahead.
And were it not that in that close of stone
   The ascent was shorter than on the other wall,
   I, if not he, most surely had been fordone.
But because Malebolge slanteth all
   Down toward the nethermost pit's opening, so
   Conformed is every valley, it must befall
That the one side is high and the other low.   40
   We came in the end where at the ledge we hung
   Whence the last stone was rent by the overthrow.
The breath was so milked out of my spent lung,
   When I was up, I could no further heave
   My body, and sat me down where I had clung.

"Now it behoveth lassitude to leave,"
  The Master said, "for softly on down reclined
  Or under coverlet, none can fame achieve,
Without which he who dallieth leaves behind
  Such vestige of himself on earth imprest   50
  As foam in water or smoke upon the wind.
And therefore rise! Quell now thy panting breast
  With the soul's strength that winneth every fight,
  So it be not by the body's weight deprest.
We have yet to climb a stair of longer flight.
  'Tis not enough to have escaped yon crew.
  Seek thine own good, if thou hast read me right."
I rose, and feigned me better than was true
  Furnished with breath, so that I spoke serene:
  "Go on; I am bold and strong to bear it through."   60
We climbed now on the bridge of the ravine,
  Rugged and narrow and difficult to tread
  And by far steeper than the last had been.
I talked, not to appear dispirited;
  Whereat a voice, ill-fitted to define
  Its words, came from the other fosse's bed.
I knew not what it said, though on the chine
  Of the arch I was which crosses here the moat;
  But he that spoke seemed our way to incline.
I had bent down, but my live eyes could not   70
  Pierce to the bottom through the air's dim pall.
  Wherefore I: "Master, see that we be got
To the other circle and soon dismount this wall,
  For hence I hear sounds of no meaning made
  And see down but distinguish nought at all."
"No other answer I give to thee," he said,
  "Save by deed only: for a just request
  By silence, with performance, should be paid."
The bridge we now descended from its crest,

Where to the eighth embankment it is knit;   80
  And there the chasm to me was manifest.
A fearful throng I saw within that pit
  Of serpents, and of breeds so strange beside,
  That my blood thins yet at the thought of it.
Let Libya's sand no longer be her pride,   85
  Though jacule and chelidre and cenchris there
  With amphisbaena and parea glide;
So many and so fell plagues its regions bare
  Could not, with all the land of the Ethiop
  And all the Red Sea's desert border, rear.   90
'Mid this most drear and cruel swarm, a group
  Of shades were running naked and aghast,
  Hopeless of hiding-place or heliotrope.   93
The snakes knotted their hands behind them fast,
  And with the head and tail piercing them through
  The loins, in front were clustered and enlaced.
And lo, to a sinner who near to our bank drew
  Shot up a serpent, which transfixed him, just
  Where from the shoulder-bones the neck out-grew.
Never "O" nor "I" was written in such a gust   100
  Of speed as he took fire with, all allumed,
  And then must needs drop into ash and dust.
When down to the very ground he was consumed,
  Of its own motion re-combining there
  The dust straightway its former shape resumed.
So the most famous sages do aver
  The Phoenix dies and then is born again
  When she approaches her five-hundredth year.
In her life eats she neither herb nor grain
  But only amomum and incense-tears; and nard   110

---

85. *The Libyan sands were familiar to Dante through Lucan and Ovid.*
93. *"Heliotrope": a precious stone that makes its bearer invisible.*

And myrrh for her last shrouding hath she ta'en.

And as one falls, but how he knows not, jarred   *112*
    And pulled to earth by a demon for his prize
    Or fit, by which men's faculties are marred,

Who stares about him as he makes to rise,
    All put to a deep amazement by the throes
    Of anguish he hath borne, and gazing sighs,

Such aspect had the sinner when he rose.
    O power of God, how striketh it to stun,
    And for its vindication heaps such blows!   *120*

The Guide then asked him who he was; whereon
    "From Tuscany," he answered, "did I rain
    Into this fell maw but a brief while gone.

Bestial life pleased me, not life of men,
    Mule that I was: for Vanni Fucci I am,   *125*
    Beast! and Pistoia was my fitting den."

And I to the Guide: "Bid him not shirk or sham,
    And what offence drags him down hither, ask.
    I have seen him when in blood and rage he swam."

The felon, who had heard me, assumed no mask,   *130*
    But turned intent on me his face and thought,
    Sad, as if shame had taken his soul to task.

"It hurts me," he said then, "more that I am caught
    In the miserable plight which thou dost see
    Than when from life to this world I was brought.

Refuse I cannot what thou hast asked of me.
    I am thrust down so far because I stole
    The fair adornments of the Sacristy.   *138*

112-114. "And as one falls . . .": *an epileptic. Epileptics were thought to be possessed by devils.* —"Obstruction" *of the passages between heart and brain.*

125. "Mule that I was": *Vanni Fucci was a bastard. He was a notorious ruffian, robber and a party leader.*

138-139. *In 1293 some silver statues were stolen from the cathedral of Pistoia. The crime was attributed to a certain Ranucci, who came near being hanged for it.*

Falsely the sin was laid on other's soul.

　But that this sight may not rejoice thine eyes, 140
　If ever thou be enlarged from this hell-hole,

Open thine ears and hear my prophecies.

　Pistoia first of all the Blacks is thinned.
　Then Florence changes laws and families:

Mars brings a mist from Valdimagra blind 145
　In murk of cloud and rolled in turbid rain,
　And with tempestuous burst and fury of wind

There shall be battle on the Piceno's plain; 148
　Whence the fire suddenly the mist shall cleave
　So that no White shall not be stricken or slain. 150

Know this, that thou may'st have wherewith to grieve."

145. The "mist" that Mars draws forth is Moroello Malaspina, lord of Lunigiana in the valley of the Magra.
148. The name "Piceno's plain" was applied to the territory of Pistoia.

Canto XXV

Fucci cries out in blasphemous rage, and is set upon by the serpents. Cacus, a giant robber in the Aeneid, *but here represented as a centaur, pursues him. Then three thieves appear; and on one of them, Agnello, a kind of dragon (really Cianfa who has been transformed into it) fastens itself so closely that they merge into one strange shape. Then a viper (into which Francesco de' Cavalcanti has been changed) bites Buoso degli Abati; and this time, serpent changes into man and man into serpent. Francesco had been killed at Gaville, near Florence.*

WHEN he had made an end, the thief exclaimed,
  Raising his hands with both the figs on high: 2
  "Take thou them, God; at thee, at thee they are
      aimed."
Thenceforth the serpents were no enemy
  To me; for round his neck, as if it hissed
  Thou speak'st no more! one coiled and clung thereby.
Another about his arms began to twist
  And tighten, prisoning him in front so fast,
  There was no wriggle in him that could resist.
Pistoia, ah Pistoia! thou shouldst blast   10
  Thyself to a cinder and toll thine own death-knell,
  For in evil thine old seed thou hast surpassed.   12
Through all the sombre corridors of hell
  No spirit so insolent against God I found,
  Not him ev'n, who at Thebes from the wall fell.   15
He fled, and uttered not another sound:
  And I beheld a Centaur full of storm
  Come crying: "Where, where goes he, the evil
      hound?"
I think not that Maremma holds such swarm   19
  Of snakes as clustered on his haunch and spread   20
  Even to where begins our human form.   21
Over his shoulders and behind the head
  Lay a dragon with extended wings aglow;
  On all whom it encountered fire it shed.
"He is Cacus," said my Master, "who below   25

---

2. "The figs": a coarse, insulting gesture.
12. "Thine old seed": Pistoia, according to tradition, was founded
  by the remnants of Catiline's army.
15. Capaneus.
19. "Maremma": a wild and swampy part of Tuscany.
21. The human part of the centaur.
25-30. In a lair on Mt. Aventine dwelt the bloody monster Cacus,
  son of Vulcan. When Hercules returned from the west with

The rocks and caverns of Mount Aventine
   Full often made a river of blood to flow.
He is trooped not with his brethren, by design,
   Because by trickery he enticed to pen
   The neighbouring great herd of stolen kine;   30
Wherefore his crooked works were ended then
   By the club of Hercules, who dealt him nigh
   A hundred blows, and had to endure not ten."
While thus he spoke, the Centaur hasted by;
   And under us on the path three spirits came near 35
   Whom both I and my Guide failed to espy
Till they called: "Who are ye? What do ye here?"
   Our discourse therefore halted short; and all
   Intent, to them alone did we give ear.
I knew them not; but so it did befall,   40
   As often it befalleth by some hap,
   That one had need the other's name to call,
Saying: "Where is Cianfa? What hath made him
      stop?"   43
   Whereat I, that my Guide might give full heed,
   From chin to nose my finger pointed up.
If thou art slow of faith, thou who dost read
   What I shall tell, 'tis nothing for surprise,
   Since half I doubt, I who witnessed it indeed.
While with brows raised I held them in mine eyes,
   Lo, a serpent with six feet one sinner faced   50
   And darting clamped its body entire on his.
With the middle feet his belly it embraced,

Geryon's herd, Cacus stole a part of it. Warned by their bellow-
ing, Hercules followed the cattle into Cacus' cave, and slew the
thief with a club.
35. Virgil and Dante are looking down from the bank. The three
spirits turn out to be Agnolo Brunelleschi, Buoso degli Abati, and
Puccio Sciancato. Two more come presently in the form of snakes.
43. "Cianfa" Donati was a Florentine; we have no information con-
cerning his thefts. He appears, in line 50, in the guise of a ser-
pent.

With the forefeet gript the arms and held them pent;
  Then of both cheeks its fangs had the full taste.
With the hind feet stretcht along his thighs it leant,
  And whipt its tail out in between the two
  And upwards on the loins behind him bent.
Ivy upon a tree never in-grew
  Close as that hideous creature, all up-reared,
  To the other's body did its body glue.   60
Like heated wax the shapes of them were slurred
  Together, and their mingling colours swam:
  Nor this nor that was as it first appeared.
As runneth up before the burning flame
  On paper, a brown colour, not yet black,
  And the white dieth; such their hues became.
The other two gazed on him, and "Alack!"
  Each cried, "O Agnel, how thou alterest!
  Lo, neither two nor one shape dost thou make."
The two heads were by now to one comprest,   70
  When there before our eyes two forms begin
  To mix in one where neither could be traced.
Two arms were made where the four bands had been;
  The belly and chest and legs and thighs below
  Became such members as were never seen.
Each former aspect was annulled, and lo,
  The unnatural image seemed neither and both,
  And such with languid step we watched him go.
As a lizard in the Dog-star's days of wrath
  Shunning from hedge to hedge the scorching flame 80
  Flickers like lightning if it cross the path,
So swift on the other two, with angry aim
  At the belly, a little viper all alight,
  Livid, and black as a corn of pepper, came.
On one of them it pierced with sudden bite
  That part in us whereby we first are fed,   86

86. "That part in us . . .": the navel.

[handwritten marginal note: Creatures that cannot be described]

Then, dropping down, lay stretched out opposite.
That pierced one stared on it but nothing said;
   Nay, without motion of his feet he yawned
   As if a sleep or fever on him weighed.   90
He eyed the snake, the snake him: from his wound
   The one smoked fiercely, the other from its mouth;
   Their smoke commingled in the air beyond.
Let Lucan tell no more the fate uncouth
   Of poor Sabellus and Nasidius,   95
   But stay to hear shot forth a stranger truth;
Nor Ovid boast Cadmus and Arethuse
   More; if the one he fabled into a snake,
   To a fountain the other, I grudge it not his Muse,
For never did he such transfusion make   100
   As that both persons, front to front, should find
   That each to itself could the other's substance take.
They mutually responded in such kind
   That the snake split its tail into a fork,
   And close the wounded one his feet combined.
The legs, and thighs with them, adhered so stark
   Of their own will, that soon the eye would fail
   The least division in their joins to mark.
That figure was assumed by the cleft tail
   Which opposite had melted, and its skin   110
   Grew soft, and the other hard with horny scale.
I saw the arms at the armpits enter in
   And the two feet of the serpent, which were short,
   Lengthen as much as those had shortened been.
The two hind-feet together, as they contort,
   Combine into the member man conceals:
   From his the wretch grows two feet of like sort,

---

95. In Lucan's *Pharsalia*, Sabellus, *as the result of being bitten by a
little snake in the desert, melts away like snow. Nasidius, who had
been poisoned by another serpent, swells into a shapeless globe
and bursts his armor.*

The while the smoke with altered colour steals
 Both in its veil, and on one side bestows
 The hair that from the other side it peels.   120
The one fell prostrate and the other rose,
 But not withdrew the lamps of wicked glow   122
 'Neath which these muzzles were exchanged for those.
The erect one drew his upward toward his brow,
 And from the too much matter that it gained
 Out of the flat cheeks ears started to grow.
The flesh that slipt not back but there remained
 Of its excess made rise a nose, and swell
 The lips till a right thickness they attained.
The prostrate one shot out his muzzle an ell   130
 And quite into his head drew back the ears,
 As a snail draws its horns into its shell.
The tongue, before whole, fashioned to converse
 In speech, divides; and in the other head
 The fork unites; the smoke no longer stirs.
The soul that had become a reptile fled
 With hissing noise along the valley side,
 And the other sputtered at it as it sped.   138
Toward it he turned then his new back, and cried
 Aloud to the other: "I'll have Buoso crawl   140
 Along the road where I was made to glide."
Thus I beheld the seventh pit's ballast all
 Change and re-change; and here let the surprise
 Excuse me, if ill my pen the thing recall.
And though bewilderment confused my eyes
 And bruised my perfect understanding, flee
 These did not, ere that I could recognize
Puccio Sciancato; of all the three
 Companions who came first, he only had kept

---

122. "Lamps": *glaring eyes.*
138. "The other sputtered . . .": *human saliva was thought to be poisonous to snakes.*

His form from those malign mutations free: 150
The other was he for whom Gaville wept.   151

Canto XXVI

Dante addresses his native city in shame. He had recognized five Florentines of noble family among the Thieves. Virgil leads him up the rugged path to the next chasm, the eighth, where are the Evil Counsellors, whose theft is spiritual, each imprisoned in a burning flame. One of the flames has a double tip and conceals the spirits of Ulysses and Diomed. Virgil asks one of them to speak; and Ulysses tells of his last voyage into the unknown ocean below the Equator and shipwreck near the Mount of Purgatory. This story does not agree with the Odyssey and is thought to be Dante's invention. (It suggested Tennyson's poem.)

FLORENCE, exult that thou hast grown so great
    That thy wings beat, the seas and lands around,
    And wide thy name is spread within Hell's gate!
Among the Thieves five of such note I found
    Thy citizens, whence shame comes to my cheek,
    Nor to thine honour doth it much redound.
But if the truth in dream of morning speak,   7

---

151. "The other," originally the second snake, was Francesco, nicknamed Guercio de' Cavalcanti, killed for his misdeeds by the people of Gaville, a village on the upper Arno. Gaville mourns because of the vengeance taken for his death.

7. It was a popular belief that dreams occurring just before dawn would come true.

Thou shalt in short time feel what upon thee
     Prato, and others also, thirst to wreak.   9
If it were now, not too soon would it be!   10
     Since come it must, I would that come it were,
     For, with each year, heavier it is for me.
Thence we departed; and by that same stair
     Which served for our descent, of ledges frayed,
     My Guide climbed back, and me with him up-bare.
And as our solitary way we made
     Among the juts and splinters of the scarp,
     The foot sped not without the hand to aid.
Then did I grieve, and grief returneth sharp,
     Seeing what I saw in memory, and I rein   20
     More than of wont my genius, lest it warp
And run where Virtue is not to constrain,
     So that if good star or aught better still   23
     Enrich me, I may not grudge myself the gain.
Like fire-flies that the peasant on the hill,   25
     Reposing in that season, when he who shines
     To light our world his face doth least conceal,
At that hour when the fly to gnat resigns,
     Sees glimmering down along the valley broad,
     There, where perhaps he ploughs or tends the
          vines,—   30
So numerous the flames in the Eighth Chasm glowed
     Down all its depth, laid open to mine eyes
     Soon as I came to where the bottom showed.
As he who avenged him by the bears saw rise   34
     The fiery chariot that Elijah bore
     With horses mounting straight into the skies,

---

9. "Prato" is a little town near Florence: thou shalt feel the grief
   which even thy nearest neighbors wish thee.
23. "Aught better" is divine grace.
25. In this pretty simile of the fireflies, the season which is indicated
   (lines 26-27) is the summer solstice, the hour (line 28) is dusk.
34. "He who . . .": Elisha (2 Kings 2:23-24).

For follow it with his eyes he could not more
 Than to behold only the flame serene
 Like to a little cloud above him soar;
Thus moved along the throat of that ravine   40
 Each flame, for what it stole it doth not show,
 And within each a sinner is, unseen.
I stood upon the bridge, rising tip-toe:
 Had I not caught a rock and on it leant
 I should have fallen, without thrust or blow.
The Guide, who saw me gazing thus attent,
 Said: "Within these fires are the spirits confined,
 Burned by the shroud within which they are pent."
"Master," I answered, "this had I divined
 Myself already, which thou makest plain.   50
 And ev'n now was the question in my mind:
Who is in that fire which comes so torn in twain
 As if it rose above the pyre that bare
 Eteocles beside his brother slain?"   54
He answered me: "Ulysses suffers there,   55
 And Diomed; as they braved Heaven's wrath before
 Together, now its vengeance must they share.
Within their flame tormented, they deplore
 The Horse and its deceiving ambuscade
 Which opened for Rome's gentle seed the door. 60
And they lament the guile, whereby the shade
 Of Deidamia for Achilles rues;   62

---

54. Eteocles and Polynices, the rival sons of Oedipus, contending
 for the possession of Thebes, killed each other. When their bodies
 were burned on the same pyre, the flames divided into two peaks.
55-60. Ulysses and Diomed, two of the leading heroes of the Trojan
 war, go together in their punishment, as they went together to
 expose themselves to divine wrath —"Deplore the Horse . . .": the
 wooden horse full of Greek warriors, which the Trojans were
 persuaded to take into the city. By this means Troy was destroyed,
 and Aeneas and his followers, who afterwards founded the Roman
 stock, had to flee.
62. Thetis, to save her son Achilles from the war, disguised him as

And for Palladium stolen are they paid."   *63*
"If they within those sparks a voice can use,
  Master," I said, "I pray thee of thy grace—
  A prayer that strongly as a thousand sues—
Forbid me not to tarry in this place
  Until the hornéd flame blow hitherward:
  See, toward it how the longing bends my face."
And he to me: "The thing thou hast implored   *70*
  Deserveth praise: and for that cause thy need
  Is answered: yet refrain thy tongue from word.
Leave me to speak, for well thy wish I read.
  But they, since they were Greeks, might turn aside,
  It may be, and thy voice disdain to heed."
After the fire had come, where to my Guide
  Time and the place seemed fit, I heard him frame
  His speech upon this manner, as he cried:
"O ye who are two within a single flame,
  If while I lived, merit of you I won,   *80*
  If merit, much or little, had my name,
When the great verse I made beneath the sun,
  Move not, but let the one of you be heard
  Tell where he went to perish, being undone.'
The greater horn of the ancient flame was stirred
  To shudder and make a murmur, like a fire
  When in the wind it struggles and is blurred,
Then tossed upon a flickering crest yet higher,
  As it had been a tongue that spoke, it cast
  A voice forth from the strength of its desire,   *90*

---

a girl and entrusted him to King Lycomedes of Scyros; there he
won the love of the king's daughter Deidamia, and promised that
he would be true to her. Discovered by Ulysses and Diomed, he
departed with them to the war, and forgot his promise.

63. Ulysses and Diomed stole the Palladium, an image of Pallas, on
which the fate of Troy depended.

80. Virgil assumes that he has immortalized Ulysses and Diomed in
his Aeneid.

Saying: "When I from Circe broke at last,   *91*
  Who more than a year by Gaeta (before   *92*
  Aeneas had so named it) held me fast,
Not sweet son, nor revered old father, nor
  The long-due love which was to have made glad
  Penelope for all the pain she bore,
Could conquer the inward hunger that I had
  To master earth's experience, and to attain
  Knowledge of man's mind, both the good and bad.
But I put out on the deep, open main   100
  With one ship only, and with that little band
  Which chose not to desert me; far as Spain,
Far as Morocco, either shore I scanned.
  Sardinia's isle I coasted, steering true,
  And the isles of which that water bathes the strand.
I and my crew were old and stiff of thew
  When, at the narrow strait, we could discern
  The boundaries Hercules set far in view   *108*
That none should dare beyond, or further learn.
  Already I had Sevilla on the right,   110
  And on the larboard Ceuta lay astern.
'Brothers,' I said, 'who manfully, despite
  Ten thousand perils, have attained the West,
  In the brief vigil that remains of light
To feel in, stoop not to renounce the quest
  Of what may in the sun's path be essayed,
  The world that never mankind hath possessed.
Think on the seed ye spring from! Ye were made
  Not to live life of brute beasts of the field

---

91. *Circe, daughter of the sun, was a sorceress who turned men into beasts. Ulysses visited her and compelled her to restore her victims to human form.*

92. *Aeneas named the place in memory of his nurse Caieta, who had died there.*

108. *"The boundaries": the pillars of Hercules, on either side of the Strait of Gibraltar.*

But follow virtue and knowledge unafraid. 120
With such few words their spirit so I steel'd,
   That I thereafter scarce could have contained
   My comrades from the voyage, had I willed.
And, our poop turned to where the Morning
      reigned, 124
   We made, for the mad flight, wings of our oars,
   And on the left continually we gained.
By now the Night beheld within her course
   All stars of the other pole, and ours so low, 128
   It was not lifted from the ocean-floors.
Five times the light had been re-kindled slow 130
   Beneath the moon and quenched as oft, since we
   Broached the high venture we were plighted to,
When there arose a mountain in the sea, 133
   Dimm'd by the distance: loftier than aught
   That ever I beheld, it seemed to be.
Then we rejoiced; but soon to grief were brought.
   A storm came out of the strange land, and found
   The ship, and violently the forepart caught.
Three times it made her to spin round and round
   With all the waves; and, as Another chose, 140
   The fourth time, heaved the poop up, the prow
      drowned,
Till over us we heard the waters close."

---

124. *They turn their stern to the morning and sail forth, constantly gaining on the left; that is, their course is not due west, but southwest.*

128. *"Ours": our northern pole; when they pass the equator, the North Star sinks below the sea level,*

130. *"Five times . . .": they have sailed five months.*

133. *Doubtless the mountain of Purgatory, directly opposite Jerusalem, in the middle of the Hemisphere of Water.*

Canto XXVII

Another flame appears, and a voice from it asks for news of Romagna, and Dante tells of its condition. The name of this spirit is not given, but he is Guido da Montefeltro, a distinguished Ghibelline. He tells how he was persuaded by Pope Boniface VIII to give fraudulent counsel. The poets then pass to the next chasm.

Quieted now, the flame rose all upright,
  Having no more to speak, and with the accord
  Of the sweet poet was moving from our sight
When another, that came on behind it, toward
  Its summit caused us to direct our eyes
  Because of the wild sound that from it roared.
As the Sicilian bull, that with the cries   7
  Of him (and it was justice) bellowed first
  Who with his file had shaped it in that guise,
Kept bellowing as the sufferer's voice outburst,   10
  So that although it was of brass compact
  The metal seemed with agony transpierced;
Thus from the fire at first, since a way lacked
  For issue, the despairing words up-cast
  Were changed into its language by the tract;

7. The brazen Sicilian bull, made for Phalaris, tyrant of Agrigentum, was so constructed that the shrieks of victims burned within it sounded like the bellowing of a real beast. Phalaris tried it first on its maker, Perillus.

But after they had found their road at last
  Up to the tip, imparting to the flame
  The trembling the tongue gave them as they passed,
We heard it say: "O thou at whom I aim
  My voice, who used'st speech of Lombardy   20
  Saying, 'Now go, no more of thee I claim,'
Though over-tardy I have come, maybe,
  Speak with me, so it not irk thee and if thou wilt:
  Thou seest, although I burn, it irks not me.
If into this blind world thou art but now spilt
  From that sweet Latin country whence I bore
  Hither the entire burden of my guilt,
Tell me if Romagna now have peace or war;   28
  For I was of the mountains there, between
  Urbino and where the springs of Tiber pour."   30
Still all attentive downward did I lean,
  When soft my Leader touched me on the side
  Saying, "Speak thou; a Latin this has been."
To him without ado then I replied,
  Having no need my answer to prepare:
  "O spirit that there enshrouded dost abide,
Not now is thy Romagna, and was not e'er,
  Without war in her tyrants' hearts; but blood
  Of battle in open field I left not there.
Ravenna stands as long years it hath stood,   40
  Where covering Cervia with vans outspread   41
  Polenta's Eagle over it doth brood.
The city that of the French made slaughter red   43

---

28. Romagna is the region lying between the Po, the Apennines, the
Adriatic, and the Reno.
30. The county of Montefeltro lies between Urbino and the Tuscan
Apennines.
41-42. Cervia, a town near Ravenna, was subject to the Polenta
family, whose arms contained an eagle.
43. "The city": Forlì, whose inhabitants, in 1282, had defeated
their French besiegers with great slaughter. In 1300 it was ruled
by the Ordelaffi, who had in their arms a lion with green paws.

And ere that proved its fortitude so long,
   Under the Green Paws hides once more its head.
The old mastiff of Verrucchio and the young,   *46*
   Who brought Montagna into such evil state,
   After their wont still tear where they have clung.
Guideth Lamone's and Santerno's fate   *49*
   The young Lion of the white lair, changing side   *50*
   Winter and summer, with the seasons' date.
And that city the Savio flows beside,   *52*
   Even as it lies between the hill and plain,
   Tyranny and freedom do its life divide.
Now who thou art declare to us, nor refrain
   In hardness more than others have been hard,
   So may thy name on earth its front maintain."
When for awhile the flame had shrilled and roared
   After its manner, the sharp tip it swayed
   This way and that, and then this breath out-
       poured: *60*
"If I believed that my reply were made
   To one who could revisit earth, this flame
   Would be at rest, and its commotion laid.
But seeing that alive none ever came
   Back from this pit, if it be truth I hear,
   I answer without dread of injured fame.
I was a man of arms, then Cordelier,   *67*
   Hoping, so girdled, in my ways to amend;
   And certainly that hope had come entire

46-47. The "old mastiff" is Malatesta da Verrucchio, lord of
Rimini; the "young mastiff" is his son Malatestino. In 1296 they
defeated the Ghibelline forces of Rimini, and murdered their
leader Montagna.

49. Faenza, on the Lamone, and Imola, near the Santerno, were
ruled by Maghinardo da Susinana, whose banner bore a blue lion
on a white field.

52. "That city" is Cesena.

67. "Cordelier": a Franciscan friar.

But for the Great Priest, whom may ill attend,   70
   Who brought me back into my sins of old,
   And how and why I'll have thee comprehend.
Whilst I was bones and pulp and in the mould
   My mother made for me, my deeds were those
   Of the sly fox, not of the lion bold.
All cunning stratagems and words that gloze
   I knew, and mastered the uses of deceit
   So that to earth's end rumour of it goes.
When at the age which counselleth retreat
   I saw me arrived, the which should all constrain   80
   To strike the sail and gather in the sheet,
That which before had pleased me now was pain,
   And from the world a penitent I withdrew.
   Ah, miserable! it should have been my gain.
The prince of the new Pharisees, who knew   85
   How to wage war beside the Lateran
   And not with Saracen and not with Jew,
For each one of his foes was Christian,
   And none to conquer Acre's fort had gone   89
   Nor trafficked in the land of the Soldán,   90
Regarding neither the office of his throne
   Nor the Holy Orders, nor in me that cord
   Which used to make lean those that girt it on,
As on Soracte Constantine implored   94
   Sylvester's art his leprosy to heal,
   So for my mastery me this man conjured

---

70. "The Great Priest" is Pope Boniface viii.
85. Boniface viii was waging war at home, close to his Lateran palace, with the Colonna family, who had entrenched themselves in their stronghold of Palestrina. This city was surrendered to Boniface on false promises, and then demolished.
89. No one of them had been a renegade to help the Saracens take Acre in 1291.
94. Pope Sylvester i, who had taken refuge on Mt. Soracte, near Rome, was sought out, according to the legend, to cure the Emperor Constantine of leprosy; this he did by baptism.

To cure his prideful fever, and made appeal
   To me for counsel: and I kept me mute,
   For like a drunkard seemed his words to reel.
And then he spoke: 'Let not thy heart misdoubt;   100
   Here I absolve thee. Now instruct me how I
   May Palestrina from the earth uproot.
Heaven, as thou knowest, I have authority
   To unlock and lock: for double is the key,
   Which he who came before me prized not high.'   *105*
Then that strong argument enforcing me
   To think silence the worst counsel of all,
   I said, 'Since, Father, I am cleansed by thee
Of that guilt into which I now must fall,
   Wouldst thou in the high seat hold triumphant
      head,   110
   Make large thy promise, its fulfilment small.'   *111*
Francis came afterwards, when I was dead,
   To take me; and one of the Black Cherubim
   Denied him: 'Thou wilt do me wrong,' he said.
'Among my minions must I carry him
   Because he gave the treacherous advice,
   Since when by the hair I have held him, every limb.
For the unrepentant unabsolvèd dies,
   Nor can a soul repent and will the sin
   At once; in this a contradiction lies.'   *120*
O wretched me! How startled was I then,
   When seizing me he said: 'Thou thoughtest not,
   May be, that I had a logician been!'
To Minos then he bore me; he straightway got
   His tail eight times around his horny side
   And biting on it then with anger hot,

---

105. "He who came before me . . .": *Celestine* v, *who renounced the papacy.*
111-120. St. Francis of Assisi came to claim the departing spirit; but though absolved by a Pope, Guido had not genuinely repented of his last misdeed, and therefore the absolution was invalid.

'To the thievish fire this sinner goes,' he cried.
    Therefore I, where thou seëst me, am borne
    Lost in this swathing, and in grief abide."
When he had ended thus his words forlorn,   130
    The flame departed sorrowing, all frayed
    With struggle and tossing upward its sharp horn.
I and my Guide with me passed on, and made
    Along the cliff to the other arch up-built
    Over the fosse in which their fee is paid
To those who, sowing discord, harvest guilt.

Canto XXVIII

*The ninth chasm punishes the Schismatics with
fearful mutilations, surpassing even the horrors of
the wars which from early times devastated South-
ern Italy (Apulia). First appears Mahomet, re-
garded by Dante as a perverter of Christianity.
He asks Dante to warn Fra Dolcino, an unortho-
dox fanatic, that he may be starved out (as he was)
in his stronghold by the ecclesiastical authorities
of Novara. Similarly, Pier da Medicina, who kept
the houses of Polenta and Malatesta embroiled,
asks Dante to warn two men of Fano that the
younger Malatesta (half-brother of Francesca's
husband) means to have them drowned on their
way to a conference to which he will invite them.
Next Dante is shown Curio, who, when Caesar was
at Rimini, counselled him to persist in his march
on Rome; Mosca, through whom arose the Guelf
and Ghibelline factions at Florence; and Bertran
de Born, the Troubadour, who sowed strife be-
tween Henry II of England and his eldest son
Henry, called "the young king."*

Who even in words untrammelled, though 'twere
        told
    Over and over, could tell full the tale
    Of blood and wounds before me now unrolled?
Truly there is no tongue that could avail,
    Seeing that our speech and memory are small
    And for so great a comprehension fail.
Nay, were it possible to assemble all
    Who of old upon Apulia's fated soil
    Wailed their spilt blood and friendless burial,
Wrought by the Trojans, or in that long moil   10
    Of war which heaped, as Livy writes nor errs,
    Of Roman rings so marvellous a spoil,
With those who, Robert Guiscard's serried spears
    Defying, met great hurt and sore distress,
    And those whose bones the plough still disinters
At Ceperano, where their faithlessness
    The Apulians proved, and Tagliacozzo, where
    The aged Erard conquered weaponless;
And one should make his riddled carcase bare
    And another show his limbs cut off; yet shapes   20
    Of fouler fashion in the Ninth Chasm were.
A cask that has lost side- or mid-piece gapes

10-18. "By the Trojans": the Romans, whose ancestors came from
Troy; the allusion is to their conquest of the Samnites.—The "long
moil of war" is the Second Punic War: after the battle of Cannae
Hannibal's troops took from the dead Romans more than three
thousand bushels of rings.—"Robert Guiscard": the Norman con-
queror who overran southern Italy in the eleventh century.—"At
Ceperano . . .": in the battle of Benevento, in 1266, where Man-
fred, son of Frederick II, was defeated by Charles of Anjou, and
killed; he had been deserted by the Apulian troops.—At "Taglia-
cozzo," in 1268, the Imperial forces were again defeated by
Charles of Anjou. The victory was due to the wit of a French
general, Erard (or "Alard") de Valéry.

Less wide than one I saw, chopped from the chin   23
Down to that part wherefrom the wind escapes.
The bowels trailed, drooping his legs between;
    The pluck appeared, the sorry pouch and vent
    That turns to dung all it has swallowed in.
While gazing on him I stood all intent,
    He eyed me, and with his hands opened his breast,
    Saying: "Now see how I myself have rent.   30
How is Mahomet maimed, thou canst attest.
    Before me Ali, weeping tear on tear,   32
    Goes with face cloven apart from chin to crest.
And all the others whom thou seëst here
    Were, alive, sowers of schism and of discord,
    And therefore in this wise they are cloven sheer.
There is a devil behind us who hath scored
    His mark on us, and brings each of this crew
    Again to the edge of his most cruel sword
When the forlorn road we have circled through;   40
    For all our wounds are healed of blood and bruise
    Ere any of us before him comes anew.
But who art thou who on the crag dost muse,
    Haply to postpone thine apportioned pain,
    Whatever confessed sins thy soul accuse?"
"Death comes not yet to him, nor guilty stain,"
    Replied my Master, "chastisement to wreak;
    But, that the full experience he obtain,
I, who am dead, am missioned through Hell's reek
    From zone to zone to lead him undeterred;   50
    And this is true as that to thee I speak."
More than a hundred spirits, as him they heard,
    Forgetting anguish in astonishment,
    Halted amid the fosse and on me stared.

---

23. "One I saw . . .": Mahomet.
32. "Ali": the husband of Mahomet's favorite daughter, and one of
his most zealous followers.

"Thou, then, who to the sun may'st win ascent
    Erelong, bid Fra Dolcino his granaries   56
    (Unless to hurry hither he be bent)

Replenish well, that to the Novarese
    Victory come not through the blockading snow,
    Which else it were no easy thing to seize."   60

After he had lifted up one foot to go
    Away, these words to me Mahomet said,
    Then on the ground stretched it, departing slow.

Another, who had his throat pierced through, and bled
    With nose cut off up to the eyebrows' hair,
    And had but one sole ear upon his head,

Standing in wonder with the rest to stare,
    Before the rest opened his weazand wide
    Which outwardly was crimsoned everywhere,

Saying: "Thou who art damned not and who hast not
      died,   70
    And whom I have seen on Latin earth, I trow,
    Unless in too great likeness I confide,

Remember Pier da Medicina; and oh,   73
    If ever thou revisit the sweet plain
    That from Vercelli slopes to Marcabo,

Hie thee to Fano and to her worthiest twain,
    To Guido and to Angiolello, and say
    That if the foresight given us be not vain,

Out of their ship they shall be cast away
    By a fell tyrant's cruelty and guile,   80
    Tied up in sacks nigh La Cattolica.   81

Never 'twixt Cyprus and Majorca's isle   82
    Not even by pirates or by Grecian spawn

---

56. "Fra Dolcino": see the Argument.
73-74. "Pier da Medicina": see the Argument. "The sweet plain" is the plain of the Po.
81. "Cattolica": a place on the Adriatic.
82. From one end of the Mediterranean to the other.

Saw Neptune such a crime his waves defile.   *84*

That traitor who with one eye sees alone
  And holds the city, one who is with me here
  Would wish his eyes had never looked upon,

Will summon them in parley to confer,
  And then so act that they shall need no prayer   *89*
  Or vow, Focara's stormy cape to clear."   *90*

And I to him: "Show to me and declare,
  If news of thee I carry up to the sun,
  Who is he that had the bitter sight to bear?"

Then laid he his hand upon the jaw of one
  Of his companions, and the mouth opened,
  Saying: "This is he, and all his speech is done.

He it is who, banished, made in Caesar end   *97*
  The doubt, affirming that to men prepared
  Delay is loss no patience can amend."

O how affrighted now to me appeared,   *100*
  With his tongue slit and in his gullet stopt,
  Curio, who in speech so greatly dared.

And one who at the wrist had both hands lopt
  Raising the stumps through the dim air on high
  So that their blood befouled him as it dropt,

Said: "Thou'lt remember too the Mosca's cry
  'A thing done makes an end.' Alas, how bad
  Was the seed sown for Tuscan folk thereby!"

"And for thy kin death," thereto did I add:
  So that, accumulating pain on pain,   *110*
  He went away like one with anguish mad.

But I remained to look on the sad train,
  And saw a thing which without proof more sure
  I should have fear even to tell again

---

84. "That traitor": the younger Malatesta, who had only one eye.
89-90. They need have no fear of being shipwrecked, because they
   will be already drowned.
97. "He it is who . . .": Curio (see the Argument).

Saving that conscience holdeth me secure,
  That good companion which doth fortify
  With a strong breastplate one who knows him pure.
Verily I saw and still have in mine eye
  A headless trunk that followed in the tread
  Of the others of that desolate company.   120
And by the hair it held the severed head
  That in its hand was like a lantern swayed,
  And as it looked at us, "Oh me!" it said.
Thus of itself a lamp for itself it made;
  And they were two in one and one in two;
  How this can be, He knows who is there obeyed.
When it was just at the arch and close below,
  It raised its arm high and with it the head
  That it might bring its words the nearer so,
Which were: "Behold what I have merited!   130
  Thou who, still breathing, goest the dead to view
  See if any suffer punishment as dread.
Know, that thou may'st bear tidings of me true,
  Bertran de Born am I, and the Young King   *134*
  My evil promptings to rebellion drew.
Father and son did I to quarrel bring.
  Ahitophel wrought not more on Absalom
  And David with the malice of his sting.
Such union since I made asunder come,
  I carry alas! dissevered this my brain   140
  From the live marrow it fed its vigour from.
Thus retribution's law do I maintain."

---

134. "Bertran de Born": *see the Argument.*

Canto XXIX

*The poets, as they cross to the next chasm, talk
of Geri del Bello, a kinsman of Dante. They now
come to the tenth and last bolgia, containing the
Falsifiers. Their penalty is to be afflicted with
loathsome diseases, and they lie grovelling and
helpless and inert. Dante speaks with one
(Grifolino) who promised to teach Albero of Siena
to fly, and was also an alchemist, like his com-
panion Capocchio, who derides the Sienese in an
ironic speech.*

THOSE throngs and their unheard-of wounds had made
   Mine eyes so drunk, they were with longing faint
   To tarry, and weep out what on them weighed.
But Virgil said: "Why gazest still intent?
   Why on the maimed unhappy shades below
   Still lingering is thy vision wholly bent?
Thou hast not at the other chasms done so.
   Consider, if all the tale thou wouldst complete,
   This circle two and twenty miles doth go;
The Moon already is underneath our feet;   *10*
   Near to its end the time permitted draws,
   And more is yet to see than here we meet."
"Had'st thou," I then replied, "marked but the cause
   Which made my eyes go questing with my mind,

---

*10. The moon being under their feet, the sun must be over their
heads: it is about noon in Jerusalem.*

Perhaps thou wouldst have suffered me to pause."
Meantime the Guide was going, and I behind
  Moved in his steps, now making my reply
  And adding: "There within the cavern blind
Whereon I kept so fixt a scrutiny
  I think one of my own blood makes lament   20
  For guilt which down there costs a price so high."
The Master then: "On him should not be spent
  Thy thought; let him distract thee not at all.
  Turn to others, let him stay there, where he went;
For him I saw beneath the bridge's wall
  With angry threats at thee his finger dart.
  Geri del Bello's name I heard them call.   27
So all preoccupied with him thou wert
  Who once held Hautefort, thou wouldst not thy
     head   29
  Turn to the other; and so did he depart."   30
"O my dear Guide, his violent death," I said,
  "Which hath not yet found vengeance or redress
  From any who share dishonour with the dead,
Made him indignant; therefore, as I guess,
  He went with no word spoken from my sight;
  And the more pity is in my heart's distress."
Thus talking, we won vantage of the height
  Where first the ridge the other valley shows
  Down to the bottom, were there but more light.
When we above the final cloister rose   40
  Of Malebolge's monastery, where
  All its lay-brethren it could now disclose,
A volley of strange lamentings came to tear
  My heart so barbed with pity's sudden prick

---

27. "Geri del Bello": *a first cousin of Dante's father, who was killed
by one of the Sacchetti. In 1300 his death, to Dante's shame, was
still unavenged.*
29. "Hautefort" *was the castle of Bertran de Born.*

That with my hands I covered either ear.

Pain such as if from lazarets the sick   46
  In feverish August from Chiana's fen,
  And from Maremma and Sardinia, thick

Were heaped together in a single pen
  With all their sores, was here: and all so stank   50
  As when they fester do the wounds of men.

Now we descended over the last bank
  Of the long ridge, and still were moving toward
  The left; and now my vision deeper sank

Where Justice of the infallible award,
  Ministress of the great Sire, punishes
  The falsifiers whom her scrolls record.

I think no greater pang of grief was his
  Who saw Aegina's people all infirm   59
  When the air was so charged with malign disease   60

That the animals, down to the little worm,
  Dropt dying, and afterwards the ancient folk,
  As poets for a certainty affirm,

From seed of ants reanimated woke,
  Than here to see along that valley black
  The listless spirits huddled by the rock.

This on the belly and that upon the back
  Of the other lay, and some were shifting round
  At crawling pace along the dismal track.

Step by step went we without speech or sound   70
  Looking and listening to the sick, who drooped
  Helpless to raise their bodies from the ground.

I saw two sit who one another propt,
  As pan is propt on pan for the warmth's sake,
  From head to foot bespotted and corrupt.

---

46. The swampy Valdichiana and Maremma (in Tuscany) and the
fens of Sardinia were noted haunts of malaria.

59-64. A pest sent by Juno carried off the inhabitants and even the
animals that occupied the island of Aegina; afterwards, Jupiter
restored the population by turning ants into men.

Ne'er saw I curry-comb more frenzy take
  From hand of groom for whom his master waits
  Or one who is kept unwillingly awake,
Than here did the anguished clawing upon pates
  And bodies, as each plied the nail to appease   80
  The fury of the itch that nothing yet abates.
Those fevered nails the scabby leprosies
  Scraped off, as the knife scrapes from bream the scales
  Or what fish hath them larger yet than these.
"O thou whom fury of fingers so dis-mails,"
  My Guide to one of them began, "and who
  So often makest pincers of thy nails,
Tell us if any Latian be with you
  Who are here within, so may thy nails be hard
  Eternally to avail for what they do."   90
"Latians are we whom here thou seest so marred,
  Both of us," the one answered, making moan,
  "But who art thou who hast of us regard?"
And the Guide: "I am one who, zone by zone,
  Descend, and this man living with me take
  Until all Hell be to his vision shown."
Then did the mutual prop suddenly break,
  And each of them turned toward me, with the rest
  Who chanced to have heard him; and it made them
      quake.
To me the Master all his gaze addressed,   100
  Saying: "Tell whatever thou art so inclined,"
  And I began, obeying his behest,
"So may your memory out of human mind
  There in the first world, not for ever fade
  But under many suns a life yet find,
Tell me who ye are, and in what city bred,
  Nor let your penance, loathly and foul howe'er
  It be, of that disclosure make you afraid."
"I was of Arezzo," the one answered clear,   *109*

---

109. "I was of Arezzo": Grifolino (see the Argument).

"And Albero of Siena had me burned;   110
   But what I died for hath not brought me here.
In jest, 'tis true, I said to him, 'I have learned
   To lift myself in the air and earth to skim';
   But he who craved much but small knowledge earned,

Willed I should show him the art, and for that whim,
   Because I made him not a Daedalus,
   He had me burned by one who had fathered him.
But for the alchemy I loved to use
   On earth, to this last pocket of the ten
   Minos, who may not err, condemns me thus."   120
And I to the Poet: "Now did ever men
   People as vain as the Sienese record?
   Truly the French are not by far so vain."

Whereat the other leper, who caught my word,   *124*
   Answered to me: "Except me Stricca, who   *125*
   Contrived to spend so modestly his hoard,
And Niccolò who made invention new
   Of that so costly usage of the clove
   Within the garden where such spices grew.

Except the Band of Prodigals where strove   130
   Caccia of Ascian to waste wood and vine,   *131*
   And by his wit the Abbagliato throve.
But that thou may'st know whose vote seconds thine
   Against the Sienese, sharpen thy sight
   So that thou may'st retain this face of mine.

So shalt thou know Capocchio's shade, whose might
   Of alchemy to metals gave false shape,

---

124. "The other leper" is Capocchio.

125-127. "Except me": evidently ironical. "Stricca": probably Gio-
vanni Stricca, mayor of Bologna in 1286. His brother "Niccolò"
was, apparently, the one who introduced into Siena the use of
cloves as a spice.

131-132. "Caccia of Ascian" is perhaps the poet known as Caccia da
Siena. "Abbagliato": a nickname of Bartolommeo Folcacchieri, a
brother of the poet Folcacchiero.

And thou'lt remember, if I scan thee right,
How I of Nature was so good an ape."

Canto XXX

---

*The poets are still in the tenth chasm and now
meet the Counterfeiters. Among them is one
Schicchi, who impersonated Buoso de' Donati in
order to gain, with other things, a beautiful mare
(the "lady of the herd," line 43); also Myrrha, the
story of whose incest is told by Ovid. These, who
are counterfeiters of persons, are afflicted with
madness. Next are the coiners, counterfeiters of
things, punished with dropsy. One of them, Adam
of Brescia, tells his story to Dante, and points out
Potiphar's wife, and Sinon, who betrayed Troy
to the Greeks; they are perjurers, falsifiers in
words, who are afflicted with fever. Adam and
Sinon engage in a squabble, and Virgil reproves
Dante for listening to them.*

WHAT time revengeful Juno was inflamed   1
  Through Semele against the Theban blood,
  As otherwhiles like forfeit she had claimed,
Athamas fell to so insane a mood,
  That seeing his wife go clasping in embrace   5

1-3. *Juno was enraged at Thebes on account of the love of Jupiter
and Semele, daughter of the king of that city.* "As otherwhiles
. . .": *the two instances are the destruction of Semele and the
tragic incident that follows.*
5. "His wife": *Ino, sister of Semele. Ino and Athamas had two chil-
dren, Learchus and Melicerta.*

Of either arm her two sons, "In the wood
Spread we the nets," he cried, "that lioness
    And lion cubs may in the toils be found,"
    Then stretching out his talons merciless
On the one who was named Learchus, whirled him
            round   10
    In his strong grasp and on a boulder dashed;
    And she herself with the other burden drowned.
Also when Fortune turning had abashed
    The Trojans' towering spirit and so brought low
    That king and kingdom down together crashed,
Miserable Hecuba, captive to her foe,   16
    After that she had seen her daughter die,
    And on the sea-banks by the ebb and flow
Anguished beheld her Polydorus lie,
    Howled as a dog howls, stricken in the brain,   20
    So much had sorrow wrenched her mind awry.
But never fury of Thebes or Troy had ta'en,
    To goad wild beast, much less the heart of man,
    A lodge in aught so cruel and insane
As two shades that I saw, naked and wan,
    That like a famisht swine, after escape
    Out of his sty, raging and biting ran.
The one seized on Capocchio by the nape,
    Planting his tusks there, so that, dragging him,
    It made the rugged ground his belly scrape.   30
The Aretine who remained, with every limb
    Trembling, said to me: "Gianni Schicchi it is.
    Thus harrying others goes he, goblin grim."
"Oh," said I: "so may the other spare to seize
    And tear thee, ere it dart out of our sight,
    Tell us who it is, if telling not displease."

---

16. *After the fall of Troy, Hecuba saw her daughter Polyxena slain
as a victim on the tomb of Achilles, and her son Polydorus mur-
dered and thrown into the sea.*

And he to me: "That is the ancient sprite
 Of execrable Myrrha who to her sire
 Bore love, but love which far exceeded right.
She came to sin with him in her desire,   40
 Borrowing an alien form to hide her shame
 As the other, going away there, did conspire,   *42*
That he the lady of the herd might claim,
 Buoso Donati's person to assume,
 Making a will conforming to the name."
And when the raging two were past on whom
 Mine eyes had been so fixt, they made pursuit
 Of the other spirits born to evil doom.
And I beheld one shapen like a lute
 If he had only had his groin below   50
 Lopt from the rest, where man's fork hath its root.
The dropsy's weight which disproportions so
 The limbs with humours ill-absorbed within
 That with the paunch the visage doth not go,
Held his lips open in the parching skin
 Even as 'tis with the hectic, who for thirst
 Curls the one lip up and the other toward his chin.
"O ye who are not anywise amerced,
 I know not why, in this world without hope,"
 Said he to us, "that ye may hearken first   60
To the misery of Master Adam, stop.   *61*
 Alive I had all my wishes: now, alas!
 I crave for water, for one little drop.
The mountain brooks that sparkle through the grass
 Flowing down to Arno from the Casentin   65
 And freshening all the moist earth where they pass
For ever are in my sight; nor only seen;

---

42. "The other": *Gianni Schicchi (see the Argument).*
61. "Master Adam," *a counterfeiter, was burned in 1281.*
65. *The Casentino is a district in the mountains at the head of the Arno.*

For the image of them parcheth more than this
Disease that wastes the face where flesh hath been.
The unbending Justice which doth me chastise   70
  Finds in the place where into sin I strayed
  Cause to make keener and more swift my sighs.
There is Romena, where the mint I made
  Of the false coin, stamped with the Baptist bright,   74
  For which the burning of my body paid.
But saw I here the wretched Guido's sprite   76
  Or Alessandro's or their brother's, I'd
  For Branda's fount not sacrifice the sight.
One is in already, if they have not lied
  Who go around pricked by their frenzy's goad;   80
  But what avails it me whose limbs are tied?
Were I but now so nimble that this load
  I could an inch in a hundred years drag out
  I had set myself already upon the road
To seek for him through this misshapen rout,
  Though half a mile and more it is across
  And though eleven miles it winds about.
Through them I am of the household of this fosse;
  By their persuasion I the florins struck
  That had three carats' weight in them of dross."   90
And I to him: "Who are the two sad folk
  Who, at thy right and close on thy domain,
  Like a hand plunged in icy water smoke?"
"Here were they when I dropt into this drain,"
  He answered, "and since then they have not stirred,
  And, I think, never may they stir again.
One is the false wife who chaste Joseph slurred;

---

74. *This coin had on one side the image of John the Baptist who
was the patron of Florence, on the other the lily-flower from
which it derived its name.*

76-78. *"Guido" and "Alessandro" are the counts of Romena, at
whose instigation Master Adam committed the crime. Fonte
Branda was a fountain near the walls of Romena.*

Troy's false Greek, Sinon, is the other; and hot   *98*
  In the foul fumes of fever are they blurred."
And one who of his speech took angry note,   100
  Perhaps because named with such evil scum,
  Upon the rigid belly of him smote.
It sounded like the beat of a great drum.
  And Master Adam smote him in the face,
  With arm that seemed as hard and mettlesome,
Saying to him: "Though from this cursed place
  My heaviness disableth me to go,
  I have an arm still free for such a case."
Whereat the other: "When thou wast going to
  The fire, thou hadst it not so ready there,   110
  But ready and more when coining was to do."
And he of the dropsy: "Truth of that affair
  Thou hast; but when they questioned thee in Troy
  Such witness of the truth thou didst not bear."
"If I spoke false, thou too didst falsify
  The coins," said Sinon. "For one crime I am here,
  But thou for more than all the devil's fry."
"Bethink thee of the horse, thou perjurer,"
  Replied the swollen paunch, "and be thine aches
  Sharper, that of it all the world's aware."   120
"Sharper to thee be now the thirst that cracks
  Thy tongue, and the foul rheum," the Greek replied,
  "That of thy belly a blind bastion makes."
The coiner then: "As ever, thy jaw gapes wide
  To speak ill; for if thirst is in my veins
  And water stuffs me out from side to side,
Thou hast the burning and the head that pains;
  And little prompting wouldst thou need to lap
  The mirror of Narcissus to the drains."   *129*

---

98. "Sinon" persuaded the Trojans to take the wooden horse into
the city.
129. "The mirror of Narcissus" is water.

All ear, I listened to their snarl and snap,   130
    When spoke the Master: "A little longer look,
    And soon between us shall a quarrel hap."
And when I heard the wrath in his rebuke,
    I turned, and such shame through my bosom shot
    That even now it shakes me as then it shook.
As a man dreams of hurt that he has got
    And dreaming wishes that it were a dream,
    Yearning for that which is, as if 'twere not,
Such, with no power of utterance, did I seem,
    Who wished to excuse myself and did excuse   140
    Even then, and that I had done it could not deem.
"Less shame the folly of greater fault undoes
    Than thou hast now committed," said my Guide.
    "Let thy heart therefore all its sorrow lose.
Remember I am always at thy side,
    Should fortune bring thee to some other place
    Where with like tongues men wrangle and deride.
The wish to hear them is a wish that's base."

Canto XXXI

*Dante has now visited the whole of the Eighth
Circle, with its ten concentric chasms; and ap-
proaches the central well or pit which leads to the
last and lowest circle. He seems to see a ring of
towers round the well; but Virgil explains that
these are Giants, who stand within it, and whose
upper part appears over the bank surrounding the
well. One of the Giants is Nimrod, who is by
Dante supposed to have built the Tower of Babel,
and pays for it by his unintelligible speech. After*

seeing him the poets go on round the rim of the
well to Ephialtes, and then to Antaeus, who takes
them up in his grasp and deposits them at the
bottom of the pit, in the Ninth Circle. As he leans
over he appears to Dante like the Garisenda, one
of the leaning towers of Bologna.

THE self-same tongue first dealt to me the wound
   So that it coloured both my cheeks with red,
   And then itself restoring medicine found.
Thus have I heard that by Achilles sped   *4*
   The spear, that was his father's, where it pierced
   Brought hurt and then with healing comforted.
We turned our back upon the valley accurst
   Up by the bank about its circle cast
   And without any speech the ridge traversed.
To less than night and less than day we passed,   *10*
   So that my sight not far before me went;
   But now, on high, a horn sounded a blast
So loud, it would have made the thunder faint;
   Which drew my eyes in reverse course to go
   Whence the sound came, all upon one place bent.
When Charlemagne by dolorous overthrow
   Had lost his army and sacred enterprise,
   No note so terrible did Roland blow.   *18*
Thitherward short while had I turned mine eyes,
   When many lofty towers I seemed to see;   *20*
   Whereat I: "Master, say, what city is this?"
"Because thou travellest," said he to me,
   "The murk at too great distance, thou dost err

---

4. *Virgil's tongue has the same power as the magic spear of Achilles*
and his father Peleus, which could both wound and cure.
18. *At the battle of Roncesvalles, when all was lost, Roland blew*
his horn so loud that it was heard thirty leagues away.

And thy imagination cheateth thee.

If thou arrive there, thou shalt see full clear
How much remoteness can the sense confound.
Therefore thy steps I bid thee somewhat spur."

Thereon he clasped my hand with pressure fond
And said: "I'll tell thee, ere we further go,
So that the truth of it may less astound,   30

These are not towers but Giants, and thou must know
That each and all, around the bank confined,
Down from the navel are in the well below."

As, when the mist disperses in the wind,
By little and little the eye discerns anew
Shapes of things dimly in the cloud divined,

So, as the gross, dark air I journeyed through
And toward the brink came near and nearer yet,
My error was dissolved, and my fear grew.

For as with towers on its round rampart set   40
Montereggione crowns itself, so tall   41
Around the stony circle of the pit

With half their bodies turreted the wall
The horrible Giants whose rebellious pride
Jove's thunderings out of heaven still appal.

By now the face of one I well descried,
Shoulders and breast, and of the belly a part,
And arms that hung down by his either side.

Of a truth Nature, when she left the art
Of making the like creatures, did not ill   50
From Mars such monstrous agents to divert;

And if of elephants and whales she still   52
Repents not, he that subtly reads her right
Approves the prudent working of her will.

---

41. "Montereggione," a strong castle built by the Sienese, was sur-
mounted by twelve towers.
52-54. Nature continues to produce elephants and whales, but they
have no intelligence and therefore are harmless. Her suppression
of giants, then, shows fine discrimination.

For if with the mind's instrument unite
　　Power and an evil purpose both at once,
　　Men have no means against such force to fight.
His face seemed large as the pine-cone of bronze　　*58*
　　That by St. Peter's has in Rome renown.
　　In like proportion were his other bones;　　60
So that the bank which from the middle down
　　Made him an apron, still so much displayed
　　Above, that to have reached up to his crown
Three Frieslanders in vain their boast had made.　　*64*
　　For down from where a man buckles his coat
　　Thirty large spans of him mine eye surveyed.
Raphel may amech zabi almi, throat　　*67*
　　And brutish mouth incontinently cried;
　　And they were fitted for no sweeter note.
"Stupid soul!" towards him then began my Guide,　　70
　　"Keep to thy horn, and vent thee with its sound
　　When rage or other passion shakes thy hide.
Search on thy neck until the belt be found
　　That holds it fastened, O thou soul confused.
　　See where it girdles thy huge breast around."
Then to me speaking: "He hath himself accused.
　　This is that Nimrod, through whose ill design　　77
　　One language through the world is no more used.
Leave we him standing, nor waste words of thine;
　　For every tongue to him is as to all　　80
　　Others is his, which no one can divine."
Then made we a longer journey along the wall

---

58. A pine cone of gilt bronze, which is said to have been one of
　the adornments of the Mausoleum of Hadrian, stood in Dante's
　day in the fore-court of St. Peter's.
64. "Three Frieslanders" (standing on one another's shoulders)
　would have boasted in vain that they could reach from the bank
　to the giant's hair. Frisians were noted for their tall stature.
67. These words have no meaning.
77. "Nimrod": see the Argument.

Leftward, and at a cross-bow shot beyond
    We found the next, even yet more fierce and tall.
What master it was who put him in such bond
    I cannot tell, but his right arm behind
    And the other in front of him were pinioned
With a great chain, that held him all entwined
    From the neck down, and over what was bared
    To view, far as the fifth turn seemed to wind.   90
"This proud rebellious spirit his prowess dared
    To match against the supreme might of Jove,"
    Said my Guide; "wherefore he hath such reward.
Ephialtes he, who would the adventure prove
    When that the Giants made the Gods afraid.
    The arms he shook then, now he cannot move."
"If it were possible, I should wish," I said,
    "That these mine eyes should have experience
    Of Briareus' immeasurable shade."
Whereto he said: "Antaeus not far hence   100
    Thou'lt see, who speaks and is not chained; and he
    Will lower us to the bottom of all offence.
Far beyond stands he whom thou cravest to see,
    And shackled is, and like this one he shows,
    Save that he seems of fiercer looks to be."
Never convulsion of an earthquake rose
    To shake with so much violence a tower
    As now shook Ephialtes in its throes.
Then more than ever I dreaded my death-hour,
    And nought else needed for it but the dread,   110
    Had I not seen what bonds constrained his power.
We then continued on our way that led
    Around the hollow, and to Antaeus came
    Emerging full five ells, without the head.
"O thou who in the valley of happy fame,   115

---

115. In the valley of Bagrada, near Zama, Scipio conquered Hannibal.

Bequeathing Scipio glory on the day
When routed Hannibal was put to shame,
Didst take a thousand lions once for prey,
    And through whom, hadst thou been amongst the
        host
Of thy high-warring brethren, some yet say   120
The sons of the Earth had not the victory lost,
    Set us down then, nor scorn thou to do thus,
    Where lies Cocytus locked in the deep frost.
Make us not go to Typho or Tityus!   124
    This man can give what here is languished for.
    Bend thee then down, nor curl thy lip at us.
He can thy fame yet upon earth restore:
    He lives, and him long life doth yet abide
    If to itself Grace call him not before."
Thus spake the Master, and quickly from his side   .30
    He stretched the hands which Hercules assayed
    Of old in mighty grapple, and took my Guide.
When Virgil felt their grasp upon him laid
    He said, "Come hither, and let me take thee," and
        then
    Of me and of himself one bundle made.
Such as the Garisenda seems to men   136
    Beneath its leaning, when clouds pass on high,
    And counter-wise it seemeth then to lean,
Such seemed Antaeus to me, who stood to eye
    His bending; and it frighted so my mind   140
    That any other road I longed to try.
But gently on the floor which keeps confined   142

---

124. "Typho" and "Tityus": two other giants.
136-138. "Garisenda": one of the two famous leaning towers in
Bologna. To an observer standing beneath the overhang, and look-
ing upward, a cloud passing over the tower, in the direction op-
posite to its slope, makes the structure seem to be falling.
142. "On the floor . . .": ninth circle.

Judas with Lucifer, he down at last
  Set us, nor lingered over us inclined,
But raised himself, as in a ship the mast.

Canto XXXII

---

*The Ninth Circle is formed by the frozen waters of
Cocytus, into which all the rivers of Hell descend.
It is divided into four concentric rings. The outer-
most is called Caïna, from Cain who killed his
brother, and contains those who have done vio-
lence to their own kin. The second is called
Antenora, from Antenor the Trojan, and contains
those who, like him, betrayed their country. The
other two are called Ptolomea and Giudecca. In
Caïna Dante finds the two sons of Alberto degli
Alberti frozen into the ice: they had killed each
other. Dante learns who they are from Camicion
de' Pazzi. Moving into Antenora—for there is no
material division between the rings of this circle—
he strikes his foot against the head of Bocca degli
Abbati, the traitor on the Florentine side at the
battle of Montaperti; Bocca refuses to tell his
name, though Dante discovers it, but is eager to
tell other traitors. Passing on, Dante sees two
sinners frozen in one hole, one of whom gnaws the
head of the other.*

IF I HAD rhymes to rasp and words to grate
  Congenial with the grimness of the pit
  Whereon all the other scarps collect their weight,
I should crush out the juice of my conceit

More fully; but not having them, I fall
Into fear, being constrained to tell of it.
For to portray the bottom and core of all
The world is no feat to essay in sport,
No, nor for tongues that *Mamma, Pappa,* call.   9
But may those Ladies now my verse support   10
Through whom Thebes rose up to Amphion's note
So that my words may not the truth distort.
O rabble above all others misbegot,
Who are in the place to speak of which is hard,
Better on earth ye were born sheep or goat!
When we were down within the well's dark ward
Under the Giant's feet, and yet more low,
And still on the high wall was my regard,
I heard a voice say: "Look how thou dost go!
Beware that thy feet spurn not as they pass   20
The heads of thy sad brethren worn with woe."   21
Whereat I turned, and saw a great morass
Before me and beneath, whose icy flood
Had likeness not of water but of glass.
Never in Austria did Danube broad
Darken his wintry stream with veil so thick,
Nor Don afar beneath the freezing cloud,
As there was here: for even were Tambernic   28
Or Pietrapana down upon it shot,
It would not, ev'n at the edge, have given a creak. 30
Like, when the peasant-woman dreams of what
She'll glean afield, the frogs that, every one
With muzzle out of water, croaking squat,

---

9. Not fit for a childish tongue.
10. "Ladies": the Muses, thanks to whom Amphion's lyre charmed
the rocks to move and form the walls of Thebes.
21. The "sad brethren" who thus address Dante from the ice, are
the counts of Mangona.
28-29. "Tambernic" is an unidentified mountain. "Pietrapana" is
a mountain in the Apennines.

So livid, up to where men's shame is shown,
  The desolate shades were in the ice confined,
  Setting their teeth to the stork's chattering tune.
Each of them downward held his face inclined.
  And by the mouth their bitter cold was seen
  And by the eyes the torment of their mind.
When I had looked awhile upon that scene,   40
  I turned, and at my feet saw two close-prest
  So that their hair commingled in between.
"Tell me, ye who are crushed so, breast to breast,"
  Said I, "who are ye?" And back their necks they bent,
  And when to me their gaze they had addressed,
Their eyes, before moist but with tears unspent,
  Gushed down over the lips, and what forth-welled,
  The frost bound fast, and stopt again their vent.
Log to log clamping-iron never held
  So firmly; wherefore with their heads they sparred, 50
  Butting like goats, such rage within them swelled.
And one who had both ears by cold quite marred,
  With brow still bent, said: "Why with scrutiny
  As in a glass look'st thou on us so hard?
If thou desire to learn who these two be,
  The vale wherefrom Bisenzo's waters flow   56
  They and their father Albert held in fee.   57
They issued from one body: Caina through
  Thou well may'st search and never find a shade
  More worthy to be stuck in the icy glue;   60
Not him whose breast and shadow by the blade   61
  In Arthur's hand were cloven at one blow;

---

56. The "Bisenzo" is a little stream that runs near Prato.
57. Alberto, count of Mangona. His sons quarrelled over their in-
    heritance and killed each other.
61. "Him whose breast . . .": Mordrec, the treacherous nephew of
    King Arthur, who was pierced by such a blow from him that, when
    the weapon was pulled out, a ray of sunlight traversed his body.

Not Focaccia; nor him who with his head   *63*
So blocks my sight, it can no further go,
   And Sassol Mascheroni had for name: *65*
   If thou be Tuscan, him wilt thou well know.
And lest thou tease me further speech to frame,
   Know that Camicion de' Pazzi I was,   *68*
   And wait for Carlin to excuse my shame."
Then saw I countless visages, alas!   *70*
   Purpled with cold, that made me shudder, and still
   The shudder comes when frozen pools I pass.
As we were going toward the middle still
   Where the universe concentres all its weight
   And I was trembling in the eternal chill,
Whether it was by will or chance or fate
   I know not, but as 'mid the heads I went
   Hard against one my stumbling foot I set.
"Why dost thou trample me?" it made lament;
   "If thou com'st not the vengeance to increase   *80*
   For Montaperti, why, then, me torment?"'   *81*
And I: "Wait, Master, here, that he may ease
   My mind of a certain doubt that I have had.
   Then will I haste as much as thou dost please."
The Leader stood: then spoke I to that shade
   Who still kept bitterly blaspheming there,

---

63. "Focaccia" de' Cancellieri, of Pistoia, killed one of his relatives
in a tailor's shop.

65. "Sassol Mascheroni" murdered a nephew to secure his inherit-
ance.

68-69. Of Camicion de' Pazzi nothing certain is known. He is said
to have treacherously slain a kinsman named Ubertino. "Carlino"
de' Pazzi is still alive; he was to commit his great crime in 1302,
when he was bribed to surrender to the Florentine Blacks the
castle of Pietravigne.

81. The mention of Montaperti arouses Dante's suspicions. This was
the disastrous defeat of the Florentine Guelfs in 1260 by the
Sienese Ghibellines. The rout was attributed to the traitor Bocca
degli Abati (see line 106, and the Argument).

"What art thou, who dost others so upbraid?"
"Who art thou, who dost through Antenora dare
   Come smiting others," said he, "on the cheek?
   Wert thou alive, it were too much to bear."   90
"Alive I am," replied I, "and if thou seek
   Fame, it may profit that thy name be writ
   Among the other names whereof I speak."
And he: "My craving is quite opposite.
   Take thyself off; vex me no more; be sped.
   To flatter on this slope thou hast small wit."
Then seizing him by the hair behind, I said:
   "Needs must I have thy name from thine own lip
   Or not a hair remains upon thy head."
Whence he to me: "Though all my scalp thou strip, 100
   I'll tell not who I am; I will resist,
   Though over me a thousand times thou trip."
Already I had his hair twined in my fist,
   And more than one tuft had I plucked away,
   The while he howled, nor would his face up-twist,
When another cried: "What ails thee, Bocca, say!
   Is it not enough to chatter with thy jaws?
   Must thou howl too? What fiend has thee for prey?"
"Speak not now," said I, "there's no longer cause;
   For to thy shame, accursed traitor thou!   110
   I'll tell the truth of what thy treachery was."
"Away!" he answered. "Blab, I care not how.
   But if thou get hence, let the tale be told
   Of him who had his tongue so prompt but now.
Here in his place he rues the Frenchman's gold.
   Thou canst say: 'Him of Duera I espied,   *116*
   There where the sinners ache amid the cold.'
Shouldst thou be questioned who was there beside,

---

116. *Buoso da Duera of Cremona, being bribed by the French, al-
lowed, in 1265, the army of Charles of Anjou, to pass by the
Ghibelline forces.*

Thou hast at hand the Beccheria here   *119*
   Who, with his gorget slit by Florence, died.   120
Farther on, I think, is Gianni de' Soldanier,   *121*
   Ganelon, and Tebaldello, who made the trap,   *122*
   Opening Faenza when all slept in her."
We had left him now behind, when in one gap
   Frozen together two so close I saw
   That the one head to the other was a cap.
And as upon a crust a famished jaw,
   So the uppermost, there where the brain joins with
   The nape, did eagerly the other gnaw.
Not otherwise did Tydeus' frenzied teeth   *130*
   Upon the brows of Menalippus feed
   Than he upon the skull and parts beneath.
"O thou who showest by such bestial deed
   Thy hatred upon him thou dost devour,
   Tell me why," said I; "but be this agreed,
That, if with reason thou complain so sore,
   I, knowing who ye are and what his crime,
   May yet on earth above repay thy score,
So my tongue be not withered ere the time."

---

119. *Tesauro dei Beccheria of Pavia was beheaded by the Guelfs of Florence for conducting secret negotiations with the Ghibelline exiles.*
121. *"Gianni de' Soldanier," in 1266, headed a mob against his Ghibelline associates.*
122. *"Ganelon" is the famous traitor to Charlemagne, at Roncesvalles. The Ghibelline Tebaldello surrendered to the Bolognese Guelfs his own city of Faenza.*
130. *Tydeus, one of the seven kings who attacked Thebes, was mortally wounded by Menalippus, whom he succeeded in killing. Before dying, he called for the head of his opponent, and gnawed it fiercely.*

Canto XXXIII

The two sinners are Count Ugolino and the Arch-
bishop of Pisa, both traitors. Ugolino, having the
chief power in Pisa, where he was head of the
Guelfs, allied himself with the Archbishop, the
leader of the Ghibellines, in order to get rid of his
nephew; then the Archbishop turned against him
and had him and his four sons imprisoned in a
tower and starved to death, as Ugolino now de-
scribes to Dante. After an outburst of bitter indig-
nation against Pisa, Dante passes on with Virgil to
the third ring, the Ptolomea, so called from
Ptolemy, whose treacherous act of murder is told
in the Book of Maccabees. Here they find Friar
Alberic, who invited his brother and nephew to a
feast and then had them killed; the signal to the
murderers being "Bring in the fruit." He explains
the peculiar privilege of Ptolomea, that sometimes
a man is brought there still alive, leaving a demon
in his body on earth. This is the case with him and
with Branca d'Oria, who had his father-in-law,
Michel Zanche (already met with in Malebolge),
murdered.

THAT sinner raised up from the brute repast
  His mouth, wiping it on the hairs left few
  About the head he had all behind made waste.
Then he began: "Thou willest that I renew
  Desperate grief, that wrings my very heart
  Even at the thought, before I tell it you.

But if my words prove seed for fruit to start
   Of infamy for the traitor I gnaw now
   Thou shalt hear words that with my weeping smart.
Albeit I know not who thou art, nor how   10
   Thou hast descended hither, Florentine,
   Unless thy speech deceive me, seemest thou.
Know then that I was the Count Ugolin,
   And this man Roger, the Archbishop: why
   I neighbour him so close, shall now be seen.
That by the malice of his plotting I,
   Trusting in him, was seized by treachery,
   Needs not to tell, nor that I came to die.
But what hath not yet been reported thee,
   How cruel was that dying, hear, and then   20
   Judge with what injury he hath injured me.
The narrow slit within the prison-pen
   That has from me the name of Famine's Tower
   (And it must yet imprison other men)
Had shown me through its chink the beam of more
   Than one moon, when the dream of evil taste   26
   For me the curtain of the future tore.
This man appeared as master and lord who chased   28
   The wolf, and the wolf-cubs, over the mount
   That lets not Pisan eyes on Lucca rest.   30
Hounds, trained and lean and eager, led the hunt
   Where with Gualandi and Sismondi went   32
   Lanfranchi; these he had posted in the front.
Full soon it seemed both sire and sons were spent;
   And in my vision the strained flanks grew red

---

26. *Just before dawn of the day when the door is to be nailed up,*
Ugolino has an allegorical dream; from lines 38-39 we learn that
his companions have ominous dreams, but of a more literal char-
acter.
28. *"This man": Archbishop Ruggeri.*
32-33. *Gualandi, Sismondi and Lanfranchi are the leaders of the*
Pisan Ghibellines; in the dream they figure as huntsmen.

Where by the tearing teeth the flesh was rent.
When I awoke before the dawn, in dread,
   I heard my children crying in their sleep,
   Them who were with me, and they cried for bread.
Cruel art thou if thou from tears canst keep   40
   To think of what my heart misgave in fear.
   If thou weep not, at what then canst thou weep?
By now they were awake, and the hour drew near
   When food should be set by us on the floor.
   Still in the trouble of our dreams we were:
And down in the horrible tower I heard the door
   Nailed up. Without a word I looked anew
   Into my sons' faces, all the four.
I wept not, so to stone within I grew.
   They wept; and one, my little Anselm, cried: 50
   'You look so, Father, what has come on you?'
But I shed not a tear, neither replied
   All that day nor the next night, until dawn
   Of a new day over the world rose wide.
A little of light crept in upon the stone
   Of that dungeon of woe; and I saw there
   On those four faces the aspect of my own.
I bit upon both hands in my despair;
   And they supposing it was in the access
   Of hunger, rose up with a sudden prayer,   60
And said: 'O Father, it will hurt much less
   If you of us eat: take what once you gave
   To clothe us, this flesh of our wretchedness.'
Then, not to make them sadder, I made me brave.
   That day and the one after we were dumb.
   Hard earth, couldst thou not open for our grave?
But when to the fourth morning we were come,
   Gaddo at my feet stretched himself with a cry:
   'Father, why won't you help me?' and lay numb
And there died. Ev'n as thou seest me, saw I,   70

One after the other, the three fall: they drew,
　　Between the fifth and sixth day, their last sigh.
I, blind now, groping arms about them threw,
　　And still called on them that were two days gone.
　　Then fasting did what anguish could not do."　　75
He ceased, and twisting round his eyes, thereon
　　Seized again on the lamentable skull
　　With teeth strong as a dog's upon the bone.
Ah, Pisa! thou offence to the whole people
　　Of the fair land where sound is heard of Sì,　　80
　　Since vengeance in thy neighbours' hands is dull,　　81
Caprara and Gorgona shifted be　　82
　　Into Arno's mouth, and Arno back be rolled,
　　That every living soul be drowned in thee!
For if Count Ugolin by treachery sold　　85
　　Thy forts, it was not cause thou shouldst torment
　　His little sons, whatever of him was told.
Their youth, O thou new Thebes, made innocent
　　Uguiccione and Brigata, and those　　89
　　Two others named already in that lament.　　90
We passed on, where the frost imprisons close
　　Another crew, stark in a rugged heap,

---

75. *Hunger did more than grief could do: it caused my death.*
80. *The languages of Europe were classified according to the word for "yes," Italian being the language of* sì.
81. *"Thy neighbours": Lucca and Florence, which waged bitter war against Pisa.*
82. *"Caprara and Gorgona": two small islands in the sea not far from the mouth of the Arno, beside which Pisa lies.*
85. *The archbishop represented to the Pisans that Ugolino, in 1285, had betrayed them in the matter of five strongholds which he had allowed Lucca and Florence to occupy. In reality the cession of these castles was a necessary piece of diplomacy.*
89. *Thebes being the wickedest city of the ancients, Dante calls Pisa the "new Thebes."*
90. *"Those two others": Anselmuccio and Gaddo. Gaddo and Uguccione were Ugolino's sons, Brigata and Anselmuccio his grandsons.*

Not bent down, but reversed all where they froze.
The very weeping there forbids to weep;
  And the grief, finding in the eyes a stop,
  Turns inward, to make anguish bite more deep.
For their first tears collect in one great drop,
  And like a vizor of crystal, in the space
  Beneath the brows, fill all the hollow up.
And now although, as with a callous place   100
  Upon the skin, because the cold stung so,
  All feeling had departed from my face,
It seemed as if I felt some wind to blow.
  Wherefore I: "Master, who is it moves this air?
  Is not all heat extinguished here below?"
Whereto he answered: "Soon shalt thou be where,
  Seeing the cause which poureth down the gust,
  Thine eye to this the answer shall declare."
And one sad shadow amid the icy crust
  Cried to us: "O ye souls, so cruel found,   110
  That into the last dungeon ye are thrust,
Raise the stiff veils wherein my face is bound,
  So that the grief which chokes my heart have vent
  A little, ere the weeping harden round."
Wherefore I: "Tell me, if I to this consent,
  Who thou art; if I do not succour thee,
  May I to the bottom of the ice be sent."
"I am Friar Alberic," then he answered me;   *118*
  "He of the fruits out of the bad garden,
  Who, dates for figs, receive here my full fee."   *120*
"Oh," replied I to him, "thou art dead, then,
  Already?" He answered, "I have no knowledge
  How stands my body in the world of men.
This Ptolomea hath such privilege

118-120. *"Friar Alberic": see the Argument. "Dates for figs," that
is: I am being repaid with interest, a date being worth more than
a fig.*

That often a soul falls down into this place
    Ere Atropos the fated thread abridge.   *126*
And that thou may'st more willingly the glaze
    Of tears wipe from my cheek-bones' nakedness,
    Know that, on the instant when the soul betrays,
As I did, comes a demon to possess   *130*
    Its body, and thenceforth ruleth over it
    Until the timed hour come for its decease.
The soul falls headlong to this cistern-pit:
    The body of him who winters there behind
    Perhaps among men still appears to sit.
Thou must, if newly come, call it to mind;
    It is Ser Branca d' Oria. Years enough
    Have passed since he was to his prison assigned."
"I think," I said, "that thou dost lie; whereof
    Proof is, that Branca d' Oria never died,   *140*
    And eats, drinks, sleeps, and puts clothes on and off."
"Up there with the Evil Talons," he replied,
    "Where sticky pitch is boiling in its bed,
    Not yet had Michel Zanche come to bide,
When this man left a devil in his stead   *145*
    In his own body, and in one of his house
    Who with him played the traitor and did the deed.
But stretch thy hand out hither and unclose
    My eyes for me." And I unclosed them not;
    And to be rude to him was courteous.   *150*
Ah, Genoese, who have utterly forgot
    All honesty, and in corruption abound,
    Why from the earth will none your people blot?
For with Romagna's evillest spirit I found   *154*

---

126. "Atropos": *the Fate who cuts the thread of life.*
145. *Branca's soul, leaving a devil in its stead, reached this ninth*
    circle as soon as the murdered man's soul (Michel Zanche)
    reached the eighth.
154. *Alberigo de' Manfredi.*

One of you, who, for deeds he did contrive   *155*
Even now in soul is in Cocytus drowned
And still in body appears on earth alive.

Canto XXXIV

*There remains the last ring of the circle, the
Giudecca (so named from Judas Iscariot), where
the sinners are wholly imprisoned in the ice. Here
at the centre of the earth is the monstrous form of
Lucifer, half above the ice and half below it. He
has three heads; and in his teeth are mangled the
spirits of Judas, of Brutus, and of Cassius. All has
now been seen. Dante puts his arms round Virgil's
neck; and Virgil, clinging by Lucifer's shaggy side,
lets himself down to his waist; there he turns
round (at the center of gravity in the universe),
so that his head is where his feet had been, and
climbs in the opposite direction, i.e. toward the
antipodes, which, except for the Mount of Purga-
tory, is all water. By a long passage in the rock
the poets climb up till through a round opening
they see the stars, and emerge at last in the south-
ern hemisphere on the shores of the Mount of
Purgatory surrounded by the sea.*

THE banners of the King of Hell proceed
Toward us," my Guide said. "If thine eyes avail
To espy him, forward gaze and give good heed."
As when the thick autumnal mists exhale,
Or when night draws down on our hemisphere,

155. *Branca d'Oria.*

A mill shows far away with turning sail,
Such structure to my eyes seemed now to appear;
   And, for the wind that blew, I shrank behind
   My Master, because else no rock was near.
Now was I (verse for them I fear to find)   10
   There where the frozen spirits as in glass
   Were covered wholly, and there like straw they
      shined.
Some prostrate lie, some standing in their place,
   This on its head, that on its soles upright,
   Another like a bow bends feet to face.
When we had gone so far as appeared right
   For the good Master's purpose to reveal
   To me the creature that was once so bright,
He turned about and stayed me upon my heel,
   Saying: "Behold Dis, and the place behold   20
   Where thou thy soul with fortitude must steel."
How faint I then became, how frozen cold,
   Ask me not, Reader; for I write it not,
   Because all speech would fail, whate'er it told.
I died not, yet of life remained no jot.
   Think thou then, if of wit thou hast any share,
   What I became, deprived of either lot.
The Emperor of the kingdom of despair
   From the mid-breast emerged out of the ice;
   And I may with a giant more compare   30
Than giants with those monstrous arms of his:
   Consider now how huge must be the whole
   Proportioned to the part of such a size.
If he was once fair as he now is foul,   34

30-31. *A rough computation makes Dis more than a third of a mile in stature.*

34-36. *If Lucifer's beauty, as God created him, was equal to his present ugliness, his revolt against his Creator was an act of such monstrous ingratitude as to be a fitting source of all subsequent sin and sorrow.*

And 'gainst his Maker dared his brows to raise,
    Fitly from him all streams of sorrow roll.
O what a marvel smote me with amaze
    When I beheld three faces on his head!
    The one in front showed crimson to my gaze;
Thereunto were the other faces wed   40
    Over the middle of either shoulder's height,
    And where the crest would be, their union made.
The right was coloured between yellow and white,
    The left was such to look upon as those
    Who come from where Nile flows out of the night.
Two mighty wings from under each arose
    Commeasurable with so great a bird:
    Never did sails at sea such form disclose.
Feathers they had not, but like bats appeared
    The fashion of them, and with these he flapped   50
    So that three winds were from their motion stirred.
Thence all Cocytus was in frost enwrapt.
    He wept with six eyes, and the tears beneath
    Over three chins with bloody slaver dropt.
At each mouth he was tearing with his teeth
    A sinner, as is flax by heckle frayed;   56
    Each of the three of them so suffereth.
The one in front naught of the biting made
    Beside the clawing, which at whiles so wrought
    That on the back the skin remained all flayed.   60
"That soul up there to the worst penance brought
    Is Judas the Iscariot," spoke my Lord.
    "His head within, he plies his legs without.
Of the other two, hanging with head downward,
    Brutus it is whom the black mouth doth maul.
    See how he writhes and utters not a word!
Cassius the other who seems so large to sprawl.

---

56. "Heckle": a hemp-brake.

But night again is rising; time is now   68
    That we depart from hence. We have seen all."
I clung about his neck, he showed me how,   70
    And choosing well the time and place to trust,
    When the great wings were opened wide enow,
He clutched him to the shaggy-sided bust,
    And climbed from tuft to tuft down, slipping by
    Between the matted hair and icy crust.
When we were come to that part where the thigh
    Turns on the thickness of the haunches' swell,
    My Guide with effort and with difficulty
Turned his head where his feet had been; the fell
    He grappled then as one who is mounting, so   80
    That I conceived turning back to Hell.
"Hold fast by me, for needs must that we go,"
    Said my Guide, panting like a man quite spent,
    "By such a ladder from the core of woe."
And issuing through the rock where it was rent   85
    He made me sit upon the rock's edge there;
    Then toward me moved, eye upon step intent.
I lifted up my eyes, and Lucifer
    Thought to have seen as I had left him last;
    And saw him with legs uppermost appear.   90
And if into perplexity I was cast
    Let them be judge who are so gross of wit
    They see not what the point is I had passed.
"Rise up now," said the Master, "upon thy feet.
    The way is long, and arduous the road.

---

68. By the time of Jerusalem, it is the evening of Saturday, April 9,
1300. The poets have spent twenty-four hours in their downward
journey.
85. Through the chink between Satan's thigh and the rocky bottom
of the ice, they emerge into a cavern which is situated on the
other side of the earth's center. Virgil puts Dante down on the
brink of the crevice.

The sun in mid-tierce now repairs his heat."   *96*
No palace-chamber was it that now showed
   Its flinty floor, but natural dungeon this,
   Which but a starving of the light allowed.
"Master, before I pluck me from the abyss,"   100
   Said I, when I had risen erect, "speak on
   A little, so my error to dismiss.
Where is the ice? And how is he, head prone,
   Thus fixt? And how so soon is it possible
   The sun from evening has to morning run?"   *105*
And he: "Thou dost imagine thyself still
   On the other side of the centre, where I gript
   The hair of the Worm that thrids the earth with ill.
There wast thou while with thee I downward slipt;
   But when I turned round, from that point we fled 110
   Whereonto weight from every part is heaped.
Now thou art under the hemisphere's deep bed   *112*
   Opposite that where spreads the continent
   Of land, 'neath whose meridian perishèd
The Man who sinless came and sinless went.
   Thou hast thy feet upon a little sphere,
   Whose surface is Giudecca's complement;
When it is evening there, 'tis morning here.
   And he whose hair for us a ladder made

---

96. "Tierce" embracing the three hours following sunrise, "mid-tierce" is about half-past seven o'clock in the morning.

105. As Dante presently learns, the change from evening to morning is due, not to any unusual movement of the sun, but to the altered position of the observers, who have passed from one hemisphere to the other. The difference in time between them is 12 hours.

112-117. "Hemisphere" means here hemisphere of the sky, not of the earth. It is the celestial hemisphere which covers the terrestrial Hemisphere of Water. Opposite to it is the celestial hemisphere "'neath whose meridian" lies Jerusalem, where Jesus was slain. The "sphere" of line 116 is the circular block of ice and stone immediately surrounding Satan. On the Hell side it is ice, on the other side it is stone.

Is still fixed as before and doth not stir.   120
He fell from Heaven on this side and there stayed. *121*
   And all the land which ere that stood forth dry,
   Covered itself with sea, by him dismayed,
And came to our hemisphere; and, him to fly,
   Perhaps, what on this side is seen around
   Left its place here void and shot up on high."
There is a cave that stretches underground
   Far from Beelzebub as his tomb extends,
   Known not by sight, but only by the sound
Of a stream flowing, that therein descends   130
   Along the hollow of rock that it has gnawed,
   Nor falleth steeply down, but winds and bends.
The Guide and I, entering that secret road,
   Toiled to return into the world of light,
   Nor thought on any resting-place bestowed.
We climbed, he first, I following, till to sight
   Appeared those things of beauty that heaven wears
   Glimpsed through a rounded opening, faintly bright;
Thence issuing, we beheld again the stars.

121-126. At the time of their creation, sea and land were not sep-
arated. Then Satan fell, and all the land shrank away from the
surface of the side where he descended, leaving a vast empty bed
to be filled by the sea. The ground which he traversed "perhaps"
fled away from him, and issued forth to form the Island of Purga-
tory, leaving a vacant cavern near the center.

139. The descent through Hell occupied Friday night and Saturday.
Each of the three great divisions of the poem ends with the sweet
and hopeful word "stars."

PURGATORIO

Canto I

Having emerged from Hell, Virgil and Dante find
themselves on the eastern shores of the island-
mountain of Purgatory, which is at the antipodes of
Jerusalem. It is the dawn of Easter Day, 1300.
Four stars, symbols of the cardinal virtues (perhaps
suggested by descriptions of the Southern Cross),
blaze in the sky. Cato, the Guardian of Purgatory,
appears to the poets and questions them. Being
satisfied by Virgil, he tells them to wait for the
daylight; but first Virgil is to wash Dante's face
with dew and to gird him with a reed.

Now hoisteth sail the pinnace of my wit
  For better waters, and more smoothly flies
  Since of a sea so cruel she is quit,
And of that second realm, which purifies
  Man's spirit of its soilure, will I sing,
  Where it becometh worthy of Paradise.
Here let dead Poesy from her grave up-spring,
  O sacred Muses, whom I serve and haunt,
  And sound, Calliope, a louder string   9
To accompany my song with that high chant   10
  Which smote the Magpies' miserable choir

9-11. The Magpies were the nine daughters of King Pieros; they
challenged the Muses to a contest and, being worsted by one of
them, Calliope, became so insolent that they were turned into
birds.

That they despaired of pardon for their vaunt.
Tender colour of orient sapphire
  Which on the air's translucent aspect grew,
  From mid heaven to horizon deeply clear,
Made pleasure in mine eyes be born anew
  Soon as I issued forth from the dead air
  That had oppressed both eye and heart with rue.
The planet that promoteth Love was there,
  Making all the East to laugh and be joyful,   20
  And veiled the Fishes that escorted her.   21
I turned to the right and contemplated all
  The other pole; and four stars o'er me came,   23
  Never yet seen save by the first people.
All the heavens seemed exulting in their flame.
  O widowed Northern clime, from which is ta'en
  The happy fortune of beholding them!
When from my gaze I had severed them again,
  Turned somewhat to the other pole, whose law
  By now had sunken out of sight the Wain,   30
Near me an old man solitary I saw,   31
  In his aspect so much to be revered
  That no son owes a father more of awe.
Long and with white hairs brindled was his beard,
  Like to his locks, of which a double list
  Down on his shoulders and his breast appeared.

---

21. Venus was dimming, by her brighter light, the constellation
of the Fishes; the time indicated is an hour or more before sunrise.
23-24. Dante invents here a constellation of four bright lights, cor-
responding to the Great Bear of the north. These luminaries sym-
bolize the four cardinal virtues: Prudence, Temperance, Fortitude,
and Justice. Adam and Eve before the fall ("the first people"),
dwelling at the top of the mountain of Purgatory, beheld these
stars.
31. This custodian of Purgatory (an example of that free will which
the souls in his domain are striving, by purification, to regain), is
Cato the Younger, who on earth killed himself in Utica rather
than submit to Caesar.

The beams of the four sacred splendours kist
　　His countenance, and they glorified it so
　　That in its light the sun's light was not missed.
"Who are ye, that against the blind stream go,"   40
　　Shaking those venerable plumes, he said,
　　"And flee from the eternal walls of woe?
Who hath guided you? what lamp your footsteps led,
　　Issuing from that night without fathom
　　Which makes a blackness of the vale of dread?
Is the law of the abyss thus broken from?
　　Or is there some new change in Heaven's decrees,
　　That, being damned, unto my crags ye come?"
Then did my leader on my shoulder seize
　　And with admonishing hand and word and sign   50
　　Make reverent my forehead and my knees;
Then spoke: "I come not of my own design.
　　From Heaven came down a Lady, at whose prayer,
　　To help this man, I made his pathway mine.
But since it is thy will that we declare
　　More of our state, needs must that I obey
　　And tell thee all: deny thee I would not dare.
He hath never yet seen darken his last day,
　　Yet so near thereto through his folly went
　　That short time was there to re-shape his way.   60
Even as I said, to his rescue I was sent,
　　Nor other way appeared that was not vain
　　But this on which our footsteps now are bent.
I have shown him all the sinners in their pain,
　　And now intend to show him those who dwell
　　Under thy charge and cleanse themselves of stain.
How I have brought him were too long to tell.
　　Our steps a Virtue, helping from on high,
　　That he might see thee and hear thee, did impel.
Now on his coming look with gracious eye.   70
　　He seeketh freedom, that so precious thing,

How precious, he knows who for her will die.
Thou knowest: for her sake, death had no sting
    In Utica, where thou didst leave what yet
    The great day shall for thy bright raiment bring.
The eternal laws are still inviolate;
    For he doth live, nor me doth Minos bind.   77
    But I am of the circle where the chaste eyes wait
Of Marcia, visibly praying that thy mind,
    O sainted breast, still hold her for thine own.   80
    For love of her, then, be to us inclined.
Suffer that thy seven realms to us be shown;
    And thanks of thee shall unto her be brought,
    If there below thou deign still to be known."
"Marcia was so pleasing to my thought
    Yonder," he answered, "and myself so fond,
    Whate'er she willed, I could refuse her naught.
Now no more may she move me, since beyond   88
    The evil stream she dwells, by the decree
    Made when I was delivered from that bond.   90
But if a heavenly lady hath missioned thee,
    As thou hast said, of flattery is no need.
    Enough, that in her name thou askest me.
Go then; first gird this man with a smooth reed,
    And see thou bathe his features in such wise
    That from all filthiness they may be freed.
It were not meet that mist clouded his eyes
    To dim their vision, when he goes before
    The first of those that serve in Paradise.
This little isle, there where for evermore   100
    The waters beat all round about its foot,
    Bears rushes on the soft and oozy shore.

77-79. Minos, the Judge of Hell, does not bind Virgil, who dwells
in the Limbus. "Marcia" was Cato's wife.

88-90. When Cato was released from Limbus by Christ, he became
subject to the law forbidding the blessed to be moved by the fate
of the damned.

No other plant that would put forth a shoot
   Or harden, but from life there is debarred,
   Since to the surf it yields not from its root.
And then return not this way afterward.
   The sun, at point to rise now, shall reveal
   Where the mount yieldeth an ascent less hard."
So he vanished; and I rose up on my heel
   Without word spoken, and all of me drew back   110
   Toward my guide, making with mine eyes appeal.
He began: "Son, follow thou in my track.
   Turn we on our footsteps, for this way the lea
   Slopes down, where the low banks its boundary
      make."
The dawn was moving the dark hours to flee
   Before her, and far off amid their wane
   I could perceive the trembling of the sea.
We paced along the solitary plain,
   Like one who seeks to his lost road a clue,
   And till he reach it deems he walks in vain.   120
When we had come there where the melting dew
   Contends against the sun, being in a place
   Where the cool air but little of it updrew,
My Lord laid both hands out on the lank grass
   Gently, amid the drops that it retained:
   Wherefore I, conscious what his purpose was,
Lifted to him my cheeks that tears had stained;
   And at his touch the colour they had worn,
   Ere Hell had overcast it, they regained.
Then came we down to the land's desert bourne,   130
   Which never yet saw man that had essayed
   Voyage upon that water and knew return.
There did he gird me as that other bade.
   O miracle! even as it was before,
   The little plant put forth a perfect blade
On the instant in the place his fingers tore.

Canto II

The sun rises. A boat, steered by an angel, swiftly
approaches the shore; it contains a company of
spirits brought to Purgatory. These landed, the an-
gel with the boat departs to collect other spirits at
the mouth of the Tiber. Among the newcomers
Dante recognizes a friend; it is Casella the musi-
cian. Casella is persuaded to sing, and the spirits
gather round to listen, when Cato appears and re-
bukes them for loitering, and they scatter up the
slopes of the mountain.

Now the sun touched the horizon with his flame,   *1*
　　The circle of whose meridian, at the height
　　It reaches most, covers Jerusalem;
And opposite to him in her circling, Night
　　Came up from Ganges, and the Scales with her
　　That from her hand fall as she grows in might;
So that the fair cheeks of Aurora, there   *7*
　　Where I was, gave their red and white away,
　　Sallowing, as if old age had turned them sere.

1-6. *This is one of the astronomical riddles to which our poet was*
addicted. According to medieval cosmology, Jerusalem and Purga-
tory are on opposite sides of the earth, 180° from each other:
when Jerusalem sees the sun rise, Purgatory sees it set. The river
Ganges, which flowed on the eastern confines of the inhabited
world, stands for the "east." What we are told, in a devious and
ingenious way, is that for the spectators on the island of Purgatory
the sun was rising.

7-9. *The poet transfers to the face of the goddess of dawn (Aurora)*
the changing colors of the morning sky.

We lingered yet by the ocean-marge, as they   10
    Who think upon the road that lies before
    And in their mind go, but in body stay;
And lo! as at the approach of morning frore
    Mars through the mist glimmers a fiery red
    Down in the West over the ocean-floor,
(May mine eyes yet upon that sight be fed!)   16
    Appeared, moving across the water, a light
    So swift, all earthly motion it outsped.
From which when for a space I had drawn my sight
    Away, and of my Guide the meaning sought,   20
    I saw it now grown bigger and more bright.
On either side of it I knew not what
    Of white appeared to gleam out; and below
    Another whiteness by degrees it got.
My master spoke not yet a word, till lo!
    When those first whitenesses as wings shone free
    And his eyes now could well the Pilot know,
He exclaimed: "Bend, see that thou bend the knee.
    Behold the Angel of God! Lay hand to hand!
    Such ministers henceforth thou art to see.   30
Look, how he scorneth aid that man hath planned,
    And wills not oar nor other sail to ply,
    But only his own wings from far land to land.
See how he has them stretcht up toward the sky,
    Sweeping the air with that eternal plume
    Which moulteth not as the hair of things that die."
Such an exceeding brightness did allume
    The Bird of God, who near and nearer bore,
    Mine eyes to endure him might not now presume,
But bent them down; and he came on to shore   40
    Upon a barque so swift and light and keen
    As scarcely a ripple from the water tore.

---

16. "May mine eyes . . .": after death, when my soul shall be
wafted to Purgatory.

On the heavenly Steersman at the stern was seen
   Inscribed that blissfulness whereof he knew;
   And more than a hundred spirits sat within.
Together all were singing *In exitu*
   Israel de Egypto as one host
   With what of that psalm doth those words ensue.
With the holy sign their company he crossed;
   Whereat themselves forth on the strand they threw: 50
   Swift as he came, he sped, and straight was lost.
They that remained seemed without any clue
   To the strange place, casting a wondering eye
   Round them, like one assaying hazards new.
On every side the arrowing sun shot high
   Into the day, and with his bright arrows
   Had hunted Capricorn from the mid sky,   57
When the new people lifted up their brows
   Towards us, and spoke to us: "If ye know it, show
   What path to us the mountain-side allows."   60
And Virgil answered: "Peradventure you
   Suppose we have experience of the way;
   But we are pilgrims, even as ye are too.
We came but now, a little before you, nay,
   By another road than yours, so steep and rude
   That the climb now will seem to us but play."
The spirits, who by my breathing understood
   That I was still among the living things,
   Marvelling, became death-pale where they stood.
As round a messenger, who the olive brings,   70
   Folk, to hear news, each on the other tread,
   And none is backward with his elbowings,
So on my face their gaze intently fed
   Those spirits, all so fortunate, and forgot

---

57. At dawn the constellation of Capricorn was on the meridian; it
is effaced by the rays of the rising sun.
70. Bearers of good tidings used to carry an olive branch.

Almost to go up and be perfected.

One of them now advanced, as if he sought
 To embrace me, with a love so fond and fain,
 That upon me to do the like he wrought.

O Shades, in all but aspect, void and vain!   *79*
 Behind it thrice my hands did I enlace,   *80*
 And thrice they came back to my breast again.

Wonder, I think, was painted on my face;
 At which the spirit smiled and backward drew,
 And, following it, I sprang forward a pace.

Gently it bade me pause: and then I knew
 Who it was, and prayed him pity on me to show
 And talk with me as he was used to do.

"As in the mortal body I loved thee, so
 In my release I love thee," he answered me.
 "Therefore I stay: but thou, why dost thou go?" *90*

"Casella mine, that this place I may see   *91*
 Hereafter," I said, "have I this journey made. *92*
 But how hath so much time been stolen from thee?"

And he to me: "None have I to upbraid
 If he who takes when he chooses, and whom, *95*
 This passage many times to me forbade.

For in a just will hath his will its home.
 Truly he has taken now these three months past

79-81. *Throughout Hell the souls, though without weight, are not only visible but tangible. On the lower slopes of the mountain of Purgatory, however, Dante cannot touch a shade, although two spirits can still embrace.*

91. *Of Casella we know only that he was a musician of Florence and a close friend of the poet and, perhaps, that he set to music Dante's canzone, "Love that discourseth to me in my mind" (see line 112).*

92-93. *Dante's present experience is intended to fit him to return to Purgatory after death. Casella evidently had died some time before, and Dante is astonished to see him just arrived in the other world.*

95-97. *"He who takes . . .": the angelic boatman. "In a just will . . .": the will of God.*

Whoso hath wished to enter, in all welcome.
So I, whose eyes on the sea-shore were cast   100
   Where Tiber's water by the salt is won,   *101*
   By him was gathered in benignly at last.
To that mouth now his wings he urgeth on
   Because for ever assemble in that spot
   They who are not to sink towards Acheron."
And I: "If a new law forbid thee not
   Memory and usage of the enamoured song
   Which used to soothe all wishes of my thought,
May it please thee awhile to solace with thy tongue
   My spirit that, in its mortal mask confined,   110
   The journey hither bitterly hath wrung."
"Love that discourseth to me in my mind"
   Began he then so sweetly, that the sound
   Still in my heart with sweetness is entwined.
My Master and I, and all that people around
   Who were with him, had faces so content
   As if all else out of their thoughts were drowned.
We to his notes, entranced, our senses lent:
   And lo! the old man whom all the rest revere
   Crying, "What is this, ye laggard spirits faint?   120
What truancy, what loitering is here?
   Haste to the Mount and from the slough be freed
   Which lets not God unto your eyes appear."
As doves, when picking corn or darnel seed,
   All quiet and close-crowding to that fare,
   Their strut of pride forgotten in their greed,
If anything appear their hearts to scare
   On the instant leave the food there, where it lies,
   Because they are assailed by greater care,
So saw I that new company arise,   130

---

101. The "Tiber's water" signifies allegorically the Church of Rome.
There congregate the souls of those who die in its bosom. The
souls of the unrepentant descend to Acheron.

And leave the song, and the steep slope essay,
　　Like one who goes, knowing not of where he hies:
Nor with less haste went we upon our way.

Canto III

─────────────────────────────────────

*As the two poets proceed towards the mountain,
Dante notes that he casts a shadow but that Virgil
does not. Virgil calms Dante's perplexities. They
arrive at the foot of the mountain and are baffled
by the precipitous face of it, when a troop of spirits
approaches and by these they are directed. One of
their number is Manfred, son of the Emperor Fred-
erick II and King of Sicily. He tells of his death at
the battle of Benevento and the contumely done to
his body by order of Pope Clement IV. Because he
died excommunicate, though repenting at death, he
is doomed to a long period of wandering in this
Ante-Purgatory.*

─────────────────────────────────────

Although in hurry so impetuous
　　They fled, and o'er the plain were scattered wide,
　　Turned toward the Mount where Justice probeth us,
I pressed me close unto my trusted Guide.
　　How without him could I have dared to start?
　　Who would have drawn me up the mountain-side?
Reproach of self seemed biting at his heart.
　　O honourable conscience, clear and chaste,
　　How small a fault stings thee to bitter smart!
Soon as his feet had cast aside the haste　　　10
　　Which in all action marreth dignity,

My mind, which heretofore was self-encased,
Enlarged its scope, to eager search set free,
   And I addressed me to the mount, whose head
   Loftiest rises heavenward from the sea.
The sun that was behind us flaming red
   Was broken before me in the shape that I
   Opposed obstruction to the beams he shed.
I turned me aside, put into fear thereby
   Of being abandoned, when from me alone   20
   I saw on the earth in front a shadow lie.
Already had my comforter begun,
   Turning full round: "Why art thou still afeared?
   Believ'st thou not I am with thee and guide thee on?
Now is it evening there, where is interred   25
   The body within which I shadow made.
   Naples has it, from Brindisi transferred.
If, then, before me nothing lies in shade,
   Marvel not more than at the heavens, wherein
   The light of one doth the other not invade.   30
That power disposes bodies like to mine
   In torments both of heat and frost to weep
   Which wills not that its workings we divine.
He is mad who hopes that reason in its sweep
   The infinite way can traverse back and forth
   Which the Three Persons in one substance keep.
With the *quia* stay content, children of earth!   37
   For if the whole before your eyes had lain,
   No need was there for Mary to give birth.

25-27. "Is it evening there . . .": *in Italy. Virgil died in Brindisi,
but was buried in Naples.*
30. *The nine concentric heavens are transparent.*
37-42. "Quia": *because. The meaning is: be satisfied with knowing
the effects. If man had been all-knowing, there would have been
no sin, and consequently no atonement; and, if human knowledge
had sufficed, the vain longing of the ancient sages (which torments
them through eternity) would have been satisfied.*

Ye have seen desiring without fruit, in vain,   *40*
   Men such that their desire had been at rest,
   Which now is given them for eternal pain.
Of Aristotle's and of Plato's quest
   I speak, and many more." His head he sank
   Here, and no more said, and remained distrest.
Meanwhile we had come up to the mountain's flank.
   There at its foot we found the rock so sheer,
   Vainly would legs be limber on that bank.
'Twixt Lerice and Turbia the most bare,   *49*
   Most broken landslide, for the going up,   50
   Compared to this an easy ladder were.
"Now who knows on which hand the scarp may slope
   So," said my Master, as his steps he stayed,
   "That one without wings to ascend may hope?"
And while, his forehead holding low, he made
   Scrutiny of the nature of the road,
   And I the rock above all round surveyed,
On the left hand a company now showed
   Of spirits who moved their feet toward where we were
   And yet seemed not to move, so slow they trod.   60
Said I to the Master: "Lift thine eyes, for there
   Behold one who will give us counsel soon,
   If of thyself thou hast none to declare."
He eyed them, and with gladness frankly shown
   Replied: "Let us go thither, for full slow
   They come, and thou, confirm thy hope, sweet son."
Still was that folk so far, I mean even now
   When we had made a thousand paces, as
   A good thrower with his hand would throw,
When they all pressed up to the stony mass   70
   Of the high cliff and stood, crowding and checked,
   As he who goes in doubt halteth to gaze.
"O ye, well-ended, spirits already elect,"

---

49. *Between these places the mountains descend steeply to the sea.*

Virgil began, "by that perpetual peace
    Which, as I think, ye all look to expect,
Tell us where slopes the mountain by degrees
    Such, that it may be possible to ascend;
    For him who knows most lost hours most displease."
As sheep come from the fold where they were penned
    By one, by two, by three; and, eye and nose   80
    Keeping to earth, timid the others stand;
And what the first one does the other does,
    All simple and quiet in their ignorance,
    And, if she stand still, huddle to her close;
So I beheld now moving to advance
    Toward us, the leader of that happy flock,
    With stately gait and modest countenance.
When those in front perceived how the light broke
    Its beams upon the ground on my right flank
    So that I cast a shadow upon the rock,   90
They halted and a little backward shrank;
    And those now coming after into view,
    Not knowing why, with the others all kept rank.
"Without your question, I avow to you,
    This is a man whose body ye perceive,
    Whereby on the earth the light is cloven through.
Marvel you not for this cause, but believe
    That not without power which from Heaven he took
    He seeks this wall's surmounting to achieve."
The Master thus; and that most worthy folk   100
    Said: "Turn then, and before us enter ye."
    With the back of the hand they signed, as thus they
        spoke.
And one of them began: "Whoe'er thou be,
    Turn thy face, as thou goest thus beyond:
    Consider if ever on earth thou sawest me."
I turned and fixedly looked on him: blond
    He was, and beautiful, of noble mien;

But one eye-brow was cleft by a great wound.
I disclaimed humbly ever to have seen
   His person; then "Look on my breast," he said,   110
   And showed me, above, a scar upon the skin.
Smiling he spoke: "Manfred am I, Manfred,   *112*
   The grandson of Constantia, the Empress;   *113*
   Wherefore I pray thee, when thou art homeward
      sped,
Seek my fair daughter, her who mother is
   Of the glory of Sicily and of Aragon,
   And if she have heard aught different, tell her this.
After two mortal strokes had quite fordone
   My broken frame, myself did I commit,
   Weeping, to him whose mercy spurneth none.   120
Horrible were my sins; but the infinite
   Goodness hath arms so wide in their embrace
   That it accepts that which turns back to it.
And if Cosenza's pastor, who in chase
   Of me was sent by Clement, had but once
   Read well in God the rubric of his grace,
Still at the bridge-head would my body's bones
   Be found near Benevento, as at first,
   Under the guard of the heaped, heavy stones.
Now by the rains they are washed, by winds
      dispersed   130

---

112. "Manfred am I . . .": see the Argument. Handsome, culti-
vated, winning, Manfred was the idolized chief of the Ghibellines,
and the hated and excommunicated opponent of the Papacy. In
1266, on a plain near Benevento, he was defeated and slain by
Charles of Anjou. His body was interred on the battlefield; but
Pope Clement IV sent the Archbishop of Cosenza (see line 124)
to cast out the corpse, and Manfred's remains were deposited on
the bank of the Verde river, (see line 131).
113-116. "Constantia, the Empress" was the daughter of Roger II
of Sicily, the last of the Norman kings. Manfred's "fair daughter"
is Constance (see also line 143), the mother of Frederick and
James, who became kings respectively of Sicily and Aragon.

Forth of the Kingdom, beside Verde tost,
  Whither he had borne them with quenched lights,
      accurst.
Not through their malediction is one lost
  So, that eternal love cannot relent
  So long as hope has aught of green to boast.
True it is that whoso, though he at last repent,
  In contumacy of Holy Church hath died,
  Must stay without this bank, refused the ascent,
For thirty-fold the time that in the pride
  Of his presumption he remained, unless   140
  In prayers to abridge that term he may confide.
See if thou canst not aid my happiness
  One day, revealing to my good Constance
  How thou hast seen me, and also this duress;   *144*
For here can those there much our weal advance."

---

*144. Manfred believes that his daughter will shorten by prayer his
term of exclusion.*

Canto IV

---

*The spirits point out a narrow passage in the rock
by which the poets are to ascend, and then leave
them. Climbing up with difficulty, Virgil and Dante
arrive at a terrace which runs round the mountain.
They rest awhile; and Dante is puzzled by the fact
that, though he is facing east, the sun strikes him
on the left; and Virgil explains that this is because
they are now in the southern hemisphere. Behind a
rock they find a group of spirits in listless attitudes.
One of them, Belacqua, a friend of Dante's, tells
how, because he delayed his repentance, he is de-
layed from entering into Purgatory.*

WHEN, through delight or it may be through pain   *1*
　　Conceived by some one faculty of ours,
　　That faculty doth all the soul enchain,
It seems it gives heed to no other powers;
　　And this refutes that error which believes
　　That in us one soul over another flowers;
So when the soul by the ear or the eye receives
　　What grapples it and strongly clings it round,
　　Time goes, and naught of it the man perceives.
For 'tis one power that listens to the sound   *10*
　　And another that which keeps the soul entire:
　　This one is still at large, and that one bound.
Experience of this truth did I acquire,
　　Hearing that spirit and marvelling to hear;
　　For fifty full degrees had mounted higher
The sun, and I had been all unaware,
　　When we came where those spirits to us cried
　　With one accord: "What you desire is here."
The villager will in the hedgerow-side
　　With his fork-full of brambles often block,   *20*
　　What time the grape grows dark, a gap more wide
Than was the cleft by which we scaled the rock,
　　My leader, and I after him, alone,
　　As soon as we had parted from that flock.
One goes to San Leo up, to Noli down,   *25*
　　One climbs Bismantova to Cacuma's height
　　With only feet; but this must needs be flown,

1-13. When the soul is absorbed in the operation of one of the
senses, no impressions can reach it from another sense. Those who
maintain that man has several souls are wrong: if we had two souls,
we could attend to two things at once.
25-26. "San Leo," "Bismantova" and "Cacuma" are peaks in the
Apennines.

I mean with the swift wings and feathered flight
   Of great desire, following behind that lead
   Which gave my heart hope and my feet a light. 30
Up between broken rock did we proceed.
   Its face on each hand grazed us, and below
   The ground forced us both hands and feet to need.
When we had clambered to the upmost brow
   Of the high bank, on the open mountain-side,
   "Master mine," said I, "what course make we now?"
And he to me: "See that no footstep slide.
   Only behind me gain thy ground aslant
   Till some sage escort Heaven for us provide."
The lofty summit rose, our sight to daunt,   40
   And the bold slope of it more steeply ran
   Than to the centre a line from mid-quadrant.
Weary was I, when: "Turn thee," I began,
   "O sweet father, upon me: see'st thou not
   How alone, if thou stay not, I remain?"
"Son," said he, "drag thee as far as yonder spot,"
   Pointing me out a ledge a little beyond
   Which on that side circles the mount about.
So did my courage to his spur respond
   That I behind him forced myself to crawl   50
   Till the round ledge beneath my feet I found.
There we both sat us down by the cliff-wall,
   Turned toward the East, the way that we had clomb,
   For to look back is wont to solace all.
I bent my eyes to the low shores; therefrom
   I raised them to the sun, and marvelled: lo,
   On the left hand I found his beams to come.
The poet saw well why astounded so
   Before the chariot of the light I stayed,
   Now entering between us and Aquilo.   60

60. "Aquilo": the north wind.

Wherefore: "If Castor and Pollux," now he said   *61*
 "That mirror did for its companions take,
 Whose light both upward is and downward led,
Thou wouldst have seen the blazing Zodiac   *64*
 By the two Bears revolving closer yet,
 Except it strayed forth from its ancient track.
How that is, if the power thy thought abet,
 Fix well thy mind to imagine Zion's hill
 On the earth's surface with this mountain set
So, that both have a single horizon still   *70*
 And different hemispheres; wherefore the way
 That Phaëthon to his own hurt drove so ill   *72*
Must on one side of this mount bring the day
 When it is on the other side of that,
 If thou perceivest what my words convey."
"Master mine, never did I contemplate"
 Said I, "aught clearer than I see now, just
 In that point, which it seems I stumbled at,
That of Heaven's moving circles the mid-most,
 In a certain science called the Equator's girth,   *80*
 Ever abiding 'twixt the sun and frost
For the reason that thou tellest me toward the North
 Departs hence far as the Hebrews in their turn
 Would see it toward the hottest zone of earth.
But, if it please thee, gladly would I learn
 How far we go still, since the mount rises
 Higher than my eyes are able to discern."

---

61. "Castor and Pollux" *compose the sign of* Gemini. *The clause means: if it were* June (*instead of* April).
64. *The* zodiac *comprises the belt of constellations through which the sun passes in its annual course.* "The blazing Zodiac" *is, in other words, the sun itself.*
70. "Zion's hill," *or* Jerusalem, *and the mountain of Purgatory are on opposite sides of the earth.*
72. "Phaëthon" *tried to drive the chariot of the sun.*
80-81. "A certain science": *astronomy. When it is winter in any place, the sun is on the other side of the equator from that place.*

And he: "This mountain hath such properties,
   That the first steps below are toil extreme,
   And the higher a man climbs the less it is.   90
Thus when to thee it shall so pleasant seem
   That the ascent doth smooth and easy grow,
   As in a boat that glideth with the stream,
Then is the end; thou need'st no further go.
   There of all weariness hope thou to be quit.
   No more I answer, and this for truth I know."
This word he spoke, and when he had ended it,
   A voice near sounded: "Ere that thou attain
   So far, it may be thou wilt need to sit."
At the voice, each of us turned round again,   100
   And on the left saw a great bulk of stone
   Which neither he nor I perceived till then.
Thither we approached, and there were persons strown
   In postures at the rock's back in the shade
   Listless as one who for his rest sinks down.
And one, whose looks the weariness betrayed,
   With hands clasping his knees was sitting there,
   And had his forehead low between them laid.
"O sweet my Lord," said I, "turn thine eyes here
   Upon that one who more indifferent shows   110
   Himself than if Sloth were his own sister."
Then, seeming to give heed, he turned to us,
   Moving his face only over his thigh,
   And said: "Go up now, thou who art valorous!"
I knew who it was then; and that difficulty
   Which still a little did my breath impede
   Hindered me not from going to him: when I
Had got to him, he scarce lifted his head,
   Saying: "Art satisfied then that the sun
   Driveth his chariot on thy left indeed?"   120
His indolent gestures and his curt speech won
   My lips into a little smile to part

Ere I began: "Of grief, Belacqua, none
Have I for thee now; but say why thou art
   Seated just here? Dost thou await escort,
   Or hast thou but resumed thy wonted part?"
And he: "What boots it, brother, to resort
   Up there? God's angel, sitting at the gate
   My passage to the penances would thwart.
For me, shut out, first must the heavens rotate   130
   So long as in my life their circlings were,
   Because my good sighs I delayed so late,
Unless, ere that, there succour me a prayer
   Rising out of a heart that lives in grace.
   What profits pleading that Heaven will not hear?"
The poet already had mounted from that place
   Before me, saying: "Come, thou seëst stand
   The sun at the meridian, and the pace   138
Of Night by now touches Morocco's strand."

---

138. It is noon in Purgatory, midnight in Jerusalem.

Canto V

---

*The poets, continuing the ascent, meet a band of
spirits who are astonished that Dante casts no
shadow. These all died by violence and repented
only at the last moment. Three of them speak to
Dante in turn; Jacopo del Cassero; Buonconte da
Montefeltro, who tells how his body was carried
down a stream into the Arno, through the malig-
nity of a devil who had in vain contended for his
soul; and lastly Pia de' Tolomei, done to death in
secret by her husband.*

From those shades now I had a little gone
   And was ascending where my Master led,
   When, pointing with his finger at me, one
Behind me cried: "See, it seems no light is shed
   Upon the left of the lower of those two,
   And he behaves like one who is not dead."
At that word's sound mine eyes turned back, and lo!
   They all were with amazement eyeing me,
   Me only, and where the light was broken through.
"Why dost thou let thy mind entangled be,"   10
   My Lord said, "that thou falterest on the hill?
   If here they whisper, what is that to thee?
Follow behind me and let them talk their fill:
   Stand like a tower whose summit never shakes
   For the wind's blowing, and stays immovable.
For always he in whom thought overtakes
   The former thought, his goal less clearly sees,
   Because the one the other must relax."
What could I answer save "I come"? and this
   I said, suffused with something of that hue   20
   Which sometimes wins a man forgivenesses.
Meanwhile across the mountain-side there drew
   A people chanting, a little above our course,
   The Miserere in alternation due.
When they perceived that I opposed perforce
   My body to the passage of the ray,
   They changed their chant to an "Oh" long and hoarse.
And two of them, as envoys, broke away,
   Running to meet us, and began to plead:
   "Make known to us your condition, we do pray."   30
My Master spoke then: "Backward ye may speed
   To those who sent you, and carry this report,
   That the body of this man is flesh indeed.

If because seeing his shadow they stopt short,
   As I suppose, they have their answer given.
   He is one whom it may profit them to court."   *36*
Never saw I at nightfall the clear heaven
   By kindled vapours cleft so swift in twain
   Or, in the sunset, clouds of August riven,
But in less time they had sped up again,   *40*
   And, there arrived, wheeled toward us with the rest
   Like a troop hurrying with loosened rein.
"Many is the folk that toward us cometh prest"
   The poet said: "They come to implore thy grace:
   But to go on, and going listen, is best."
"O soul that goest into blissfulness
   With those members that thou wert born with," they
   Came crying out "arrest awhile thy pace.
If ever any of us thou sawest, say,
   So that of him news thou mayst yonder bear: *50*
   Ah, why go on, ah, why wilt thou not stay?
We all were slain by violence, and were
   Sinners to the last hour's extremity.
   Then warning light from Heaven made us aware,
So that, repenting and forgiving, we
   Came out of life atoned in peace with God
   Who pierceth us with longing, him to see."
And I: "Though long I gaze on you, I could
   Recognize none: but if to pleasure you
   I can do aught, speak, spirits born for good.   *60*
This for the sake of that peace will I do
   Which following in the steps of such a guide
   From world to world I am bounden to ensue."
One spoke then: "We do all of us confide
   In thy good office, nor thine oath demand,

---

36. *They are in need of the prayers of the living, which Dante may
procure for them.*

If to the will the power be not denied.
Wherefore I, who only speak before this band,
  Pray thee, if e'er by thee be visited
  The country 'twixt Romagna and Charles's land,   *69*
Me with thy favourable prayers bestead   *70*
  In Fano, that right pleading may o'ercome
  The offences that were heavy upon my head.
There was I born: but the deep wounds, wherefrom
  Issued the blood my life had for its seat
  Were dealt me in the Antenori's home,
There where I thought me safest in retreat.
  He of Este had it done, whose anger ran
  Far beyond that which justice findeth meet.
But had I fled then toward La Mira, when
  At Oriaco I was trapped and found   *80*
  I should be yonder still with breathing men.
I ran to the marsh, and reed and mud enwound
  My feet, so that I fell, and there saw I
  A pool grow from my veins upon the ground."
Another then: "So that desire on high
  Be achieved which draws thee up the Mount, do thou
  Pity, and help me mine to satisfy.
Buonconte I am, of Montefeltro, and now   *88*
  Not Joan nor other of me has any thought.
  Wherefore 'mid these I go with humbled brow."   *90*
And I: "What chance or violence on thee wrought
  To cause thee stray so far from Campaldin,
  That no man of thy burial-place knew aught?"

69-76. *The country between* "Romagna" *and* "Charles's land," *i.e.,
the kingdom of Naples, which belonged to Charles* ii *of Anjou, is
the March of Ancona. The speaker is Jacopo del Cassero, a lead-
ing citizen of Fano. He fell out with Azzo of Este, and was mur-
dered.—*"The Antenori's home"*: Padua.*

88. *Count Buonconte of Montefeltro, a Ghibelline leader, was cap-
tain of the Aretines in the disastrous battle of Campaldino in
1289. Joan was his wife.*

"O," answered he, "below the Casentin   *94*
   A stream named Archiano runs across
   That over the Hermitage springs in Apennine.
There where its name is changed from what it was
   Did I arrive, with the throat deeply cleft,
   Fleeing on foot and bloodying the grass.
There lost I sight and there of speech was reft,   100
   Ending on Mary's name, and there did give
   My ghost up, and my flesh alone was left.
I will tell truth; tell it thou where men live.
   The angel of God took me; and he of Hell
   Cried, 'Thou from Heaven, why dost thou me deprive?
The eternal part in this man thou dost steal,
   Snatching him from me for one little tear.
   But otherwise with the other part I'll deal.'
Thou knowest how the clammy mists prepare
   And turn again to water where they find   110
   The cold condensing them in upper air.
The ill will, only on ill bent, he combined
   With cunning, and by virtue of that power
   His nature gave, he roused the mist and wind.
When day was spent, the valley he spread o'er
   From Pratomagno to the mountain-chain
   With cloud, and made the sky above to lour,
So that the charged air changed to water; rain
   Came down and to the rivulets compelled
   All of it that the earth could not contain.   120
And as it merged and into torrents swelled
   So swiftly to the royal stream it prest
   That nothing its impetuous rush withheld.
My frozen body at its mouth the crest
   Of foaming Archian found and bore me down

94-96."The Casentin" *is a mountainous district in Tuscany; the* "Hermitage" *is the monastery of Camaldoli.*

Into Arno, and loosed the cross upon my breast
I had made of me when the strong pangs came on.
  It rolled me about its bed from side to side
  Then wrapt me in all the plunder it had won."
"Ah, when, the long way ended, thou dost bide   130
  At peace, returned into the world again"
  The third after the second spirit sighed,
"Remember me, who am La Pia, then.   133
  Siena made me and Maremma unmade:
He knows who had ringed me with his jewel, when
The vows of marriage we together said."

---

*133. Pia de' Tolomei of Siena was wedded to Nello della Pietra,
who, wishing to marry another woman, murdered her in his castle
in the Tuscan Maremma.*

Canto VI

---

*Dante is beset by spirits, some of whom are named,
desiring the intercession of their friends on earth,
but gets free of them. Virgil observes a shade sit-
ting alone and apart, and asks it to show them the
quickest way of ascent. It is Sordello the thirteenth
century poet, a Mantuan like Virgil. The two em-
brace when they learn that they are of the same
city: and this provokes from Dante an impassioned
outburst of indignation at the disunited and fac-
tious state of Italy, only to be remedied by the as-
sertion of the Imperial authority; ending with a
bitterly sarcastic description of Florence and the
Florentines.*

WHEN dicers from the game of hazard rise,   *1*
   The loser keeps disconsolately at play,
   Repeats the casts and sadly groweth wise:
With the other all the people hurry away;
   One goes in front, one plucks him back, a third,
   Beside him, to be called to mind will pray.
He stops not, giving this and that a word;
   Those he extends his hand to, cease to press;
   And so he wins him riddance from that herd.
Such was I, turning here and there my face   10
   Amid the thronging of that multitude,
   And got me quit of them by promises.
There was the Aretine, who by the rude   *13*
   Sinews of Ghin di Tacco died, and there
   The other, who was drowned as he pursued.
There Frederic Novello was in prayer   *16*
   With outstretcht hands, and he of Pisa, who made
   The good Marzucco's fortitude appear.
I saw Count Orso, and that other shade,   *19*
   By envy and hatred from its body torn,   20
   As it averred, and not for faith betrayed;
Pierre de la Brosse I mean; and may this warn   22
   The Lady of Brabant, ere her life cease,
   Lest to worse company she be down-borne.

---

1. "Hazard": a game played with three dice.
13-15. "The Aretine" is Benincasa of Laterina, who was murdered by the famous robber, Ghino di Tacco, whose brother he had condemned to death. "The other" Aretine is said to be Guccio Tarlati, who was drowned in the Arno while pursuing the enemy.
16-18. "Frederic Novello," the son of Count Guido Novello, was killed in war. "He of Pisa" is the son of "Marzucco," a Pisan, whose fortitude was shown by pardoning the murderer of his son.
19. "Count Orso" of Mangona was murdered by his cousin Albert.
22. "Pierre de la Brosse" was chamberlain of Philip III of France; he was hanged through the wiles of Philip's second wife, Mary of Brabant.

When I from all these spirits had gained release
  Whose one prayer was that others pray for them
  So that their way be hastened unto peace,
I thus began: "Thou, O my Light, dost seem
  In a certain place expressly to gainsay
  That prayer may alter the decree supreme.   30
And these people who only for this pray,
  Is it idle hope, then, that they entertain,
  Or may thy words some other sense convey?"
And he to me: "That which I wrote is plain,
  And the hope these cherish fails not, if aright
  Thou wilt consider it with judgment sane.
For justice is not brought down from its height,
  Because in an instant burning love can here
  Redeem the debt these souls have to requite.
And in that case where I the law made clear,   40
  Prayer to amend fault was of none effect
  Because God was not present to the prayer.
Yet be not in so deep a question checked,
  Unless she tell thee who shall be in this
  A light between truth and the intellect.
Dost thou understand me? I speak of Beatrice.
  When to this mountain's top thou winn'st at last
  Thou shalt behold her smiling and in bliss."
And I: "My Lord, move we with greater haste,
  For now I grow not weary as I did.   50
  And see, the hill doth now a shadow cast."
"We will go onward with this day," replied
  The master, "far as we the path can track;
  But the truth is not what thy hopes confide.
Ere thou be above, thou'lt see him shining back
  Who now behind the mountain slope is gone
  So that thou causest not his rays to break.
But see yon spirit that, stationed all alone,
  All solitary, looketh toward us now:

It shall the speediest way to us make known." 60
We came to it. O Lombard spirit, how   *61*
    Disdainful and majestical thou wast!
    In moving of thine eyes how stately and slow!
No word to us approaching it addrest,
    But let us go on, watching only there
    In likeness of a lion couched at rest.
Yet Virgil toward it moved and made his prayer
    That it should point to us the best ascent;
    And that shade for his question had no care,
But of our country and where our life was spent 70
    Inquired of us; and the sweet Guide began
    "Mantua": and the shade, all self-intent,
Leapt toward him from its place, crying "Mantuan!
    I am Sordello, of thine own city."
    And each into the other's arms they ran.
Thou inn of sorrow, ah, trampled Italy!
    No Lady of domains, but brothel of shame!
    Ship without pilot on a stormy sea!
That gentle spirit was thus quick to acclaim
    His countryman and hail him there for friend 80
    Merely at the sweet sound of his city's name;
And now their days in thee the living spend
    In quarrel, and each one doth the other wound
    Of those whom one wall and one moat defend.
Search, miserable! all the shores around
    Thy coasts, and then within thy bosom look,
    If peace in any part of thee be found.
What does it profit, that Justinian took
    Thy bridle in hand, if empty be the seat?
    Were't not for this, thou hadst earned less rebuke. 90
Ah, ye that should be all-devout, and let   *91*
    Caesar sit in the saddle, if indeed

---

61. "Lombard spirit": *Sordello.*
91. "Ye that . . .": *the clergy.*

God's admonition ye do not forget,
See now this beast to what a vicious steed,
   Lacking the spur's correction, she doth grow,
   Since ye have grasped the bridle and strive to lead. *96*
O German Albert, who neglectest so   *97*
   Her who hath wild and mutinous become,
   And oughtest to bestride her saddle-bow,
May a just judgment from the stars consume   *100*
   Thy race, and be it strange and manifest,
   That thy successor tremble at thy doom.
Thou and thy father, covetous in quest
   Of lands beyond, have turned aside and choose
   That the garden of the empire be laid waste.
Come, and see Capulets and Montagues,   *106*
   Monaldi and Filippeschi, O heedless wight—
   Those losing hope and these in dread to lose.
Come, cruel! come and see the woes that blight
   Thy nobles, and their heavy wrongs amend: *110*
   Thou shalt see Santafior, how dark its plight.   *111*
Come, see thy Rome that, mourning without end,
   Widowed and desolate, crieth night and day
   "Why, Caesar mine, wilt thou not be my friend?"
Come, see how thy folk love each other: nay,
   If our affliction no compassion move,

---

96. *Ever since the clergy usurped temporal authority.*
97. *Albert of Hapsburg was elected King of the Romans in 1298 but never went to Italy to be crowned.*
100-103. *In 1307 Albert's oldest son died after a short sickness; the next year Albert himself was murdered.—"Thy successor": Henry VII, who descended into Italy.—"Thy father": Rudolf, who was as remiss as his son.*
106-107. *Dante cites a few of the great houses that were ravaged by strife: the Montecchi of Verona, Ghibellines; the Cappelletti of Cremona, of the Church party; the Monaldi and Filippeschi, rival families (Guelf and Ghibellines) of Perugia and Orvieto.*
111. *The Counts of Santafiora, a great Ghibelline family, had lost a great part of their territory to Siena.*

Come and be shamed for what men of thee say.
And be it permitted me, O highest Jove,   *118*
   Who wast on earth crucified for our sake,
   Dost thou thy just eyes otherwhere remove,   120
Or is it preparation thou dost make
   In thine unfathomed wisdom for some good
   Wholly invisible to our sight opaque?
For not a city lacks its tyrant brood,
   And every churl who would a party lead
   Grows a Marcellus for the multitude.   *126*
My Florence, thou may'st be content indeed
   At this digression, which doth touch thee not,
   So well thy folk provide against their need.
Many love justice, yet haste not to shoot   130
   The word, being well-advisèd, from the bow;
   But on thy people's lips it leapeth out.
Many to bear the common burden are slow;
   But thy folk answer to the call unbid,
   Crying "I gird me to the task and go."
Rejoice now, thou hast reason, thou amid
   Thy riches, thou at peace, thou wise of will!
   That I speak truth, the event cannot keep hid.
Athens and Lacedaemon, famous still
   For law-making and civil discipline,   140
   Showed but a small hint of the Commonweal
Compared with thee, who dost so finely spin
   That in October thou providest thread
   Which mid-November cannot hope to win.
How often thou rememberest to have shed
   Laws, coinage, customs, offices, for new,
   Cast out old members and new members bred!
And if thou wilt examine and see true,

---

118. "Highest Jove": Christ.
126. C. Claudius Marcellus was a partisan of Pompey.

Thou'lt see thyself in that sick woman's shape
　　Who, laid on down, finds no rest, and can do   150
Nothing but turn and turn, her pain to escape.

Canto VII

---

*Sordello asks Virgil who he is, and on being told,
pays homage to the great poet. Night is approach-
ing, and Sordello explains that they can only mount
by daylight; he therefore escorts them to a flowery
dell, where are princes and rulers who had neg-
lected their duties; among them he points out the
emperor Rudolf; Philip III of France and Henry of
Navarre; Peter III of Aragon; Charles I of Anjou;
and Henry III of England.*

AFTER the welcomes grave and glad had now
　　Thrice and four times been given and returned,
　　Sordello, drawing back, said: "Who art thou?"
"Before the time when toward this mountain yearned
　　The spirits worthy to go up to God,
　　My bones had by Octavian been inurned.
I am Virgil; and to no guilt else I owed
　　Loss of Heaven, save that faith I had not got."
　　Answering thus, my Guide himself avowed.
As one who hath a sudden sight of what   10
　　Makes him to marvel, who believes, nor less
　　Disbelieves, saying "It is; No, it is not";
Such seemed he, and then downward bent his face,

And in humility toward him once more came
And clasped him where the inferior should em-
    brace.   *15*
"Glory of the Latins," said he, "by whose fame
  Our tongue revealed what power was in it stored,
  Eternal praise of that place whence I am,
What merit or grace hath thee to me declared?
  If I am worthy to hear thee, tell wherefrom   *20*
  Thou comest, and, if from Hell, out of what ward?"
"Through all the circles of the sad kingdom,"
  He answered him, "I am come from that my state.
  Virtue from Heaven moved me; with it I come.
Not for things done but undone 'twas my fate
  To lose the vision of the Sun on high,
  By thee desired and known by me too late.
Down there a place is that no torments try
  But only darkness grieves, where the lament
  Hath not the sound of wail, but is a sigh.   *30*
There dwell I with the babies innocent
  Who bitten by the tooth of Death expired
  Before they were from human guilt exempt.   *33*
There dwell I among those never attired
  In the three holy virtues; without sin
  All the others they both followed and desired.   *36*
But if thou know'st and canst, give us some sign
  Whereby we may most speedily come to be
  Where Purgatory rightly doth begin."
"No set post is prescribed us," answered he.   *40*
  "It is permitted to go up and round:
  Far as I may, I will companion thee.
But see how day declines now to its bound,

---

15. *Either under the arms or at the feet.*
33. *Before baptism.*
36. *The souls in Limbus were ignorant of the three theological
virtues, but they knew the four cardinal virtues.*

And to ascend by night cannot be done;
  Best then to seek a lodge on some good ground.
Here on the right are souls gathered alone.
  If thou consent, I'll lead thee to their bower.
  Not without joy will they to thee be known."
"How?" was the answer: "he who at night-hour
  Would mount, will others stop him from his quest 50
  Or will he fail because he had not power?"
The good Sordello with his finger traced
  The ground, saying "Look, this mere line by no skill
  Wouldst thou cross over after day is past.
Not that aught else the going-up would foil,
  Except alone the darkness of the night:
  This, by disabling, trammelleth the will.
Downward by night return indeed one might,
  Descending the steep slope with footsteps blind,
  While the horizon holds day shut from sight."   60
Then my lord spoke, as wondering in his mind,
  "Lead us then where thou sayest we may be brought
  To sojourn and therein a solace find."
Short way had we proceeded from that spot,
  When I perceived the hill-side showed a scoop
  Such as here too the valleys hollow out.
"There will we go," that shade said, "where the slope
  Hath made out of itself a lap of grass,
  And there await the new day's coming-up."
Twixt steep and level a winding path there was,   70
  That led us to the shelving of that pit
  Where, more than half, the rim diminishes.
Gold and fine silver, crimson, pearly white,
  Indigo, smooth wood lustrous in the grain,
  Fresh flake of emerald but that moment split,
Could none of them in colour near attain
  The flowers and the grass in that retreat,
  As less with greater rivalleth in vain.

Not only had Nature painted all complete,
    But of a thousand fragrancies had made   80
    One new and indistinguishable sweet.

Singing *Salve Regina*, on that bed   82
    Of grass and flowers there saw I souls at rest,
    Sight of whom from without the ridge forbade.

"Before the little sun is home in nest"
    Said he who thus aside had made us go,
    "Desire not that I make you manifest.

From this ridge face and gesture will ye know
    Of each and all, better than if at once
    Received among them in the nook below.   90

He who sits highest and has an air which owns
    Neglect of those things that he should have done,
    Nor moves his mouth with the others' antiphons,

Was the emperor Rudolf, who might well have won *94*
    To heal the wounds of murdered Italy.
    Now for another saviour she hopes on.

The other, who seems to comfort him, is he
    Who ruled the country where the water springs   *98*
    Which Moldau bears to Elbe and Elbe to sea,

Ottocar named, and was in leading-strings   *100*
    Far better than full-bearded Wenceslas,
    His son, who to his sloth and lechery clings.

And that snub-nose who seems conferring close   *103*
    With him who looks so kindly, is he who fled,
    Soiling the lily, and died inglorious.

Look how he beats his breast, uncomforted!
    Behold the other, who with sighings vain

---

82. Salve Regina *is an antiphon recited after sunset.*
94. *Rudolf of Hapsburg.*
98-100. *"The country . . .": Bohemia. Ottocar* ii *was killed in* 1278.
103-104. *"That snub-nose" is Philip* iii, *the Bold, of France. He is conferring with Henry the Fat of Navarre.*

Has with his palm made for his cheek a bed.

Father and father-in-law of France's bane   *109*
   Are they; they know his foulness and his sins;   110
   Hence comes the grief that stabs them with such pain.

He who appears so burly, and singing joins   *112*
   Him of the manly nose in one accord,
   Had all worth for a girdle around his loins.

And if the youth behind him on the sward   *115*
   Had after him remained king, then indeed
   From vessel to vessel had the worth been poured;

Which may not of the other heirs be said.
   James and Frederick possess the realms, but to
   The better heritage doth none succeed.   120

Full seldom human virtue rises through
   The branches; and the Giver wills it so,
   That they to him for such a gift may sue.

Also to the high-nosed one do my words go
   Even as to Peter, who with him lifts his chant,
   Whence now Apulia's and Provence's woe.

So much less than its seed is the grown plant   *127*
   As, more than Beatrice and than Margaret,
   Constance still maketh of her husband vaunt.

The king of the simple life see yonder, set   *130*
   Aloof from the others, Harry of England; more
   Hath he to boast in the issue he begat.

He on the ground amongst them sitting lower

---

109. "France's bane": Philip IV, the Fair.

112-113. Peter III of Aragon, King of Sicily.—He "of the manly nose" is Charles of Anjou, conqueror of Naples and Sicily.

115. "The youth": Alphonse III, Peter's oldest son, who died young in 1291.

127-132. Charles II is as much inferior to Charles I as Charles I is to Peter III. Beatrice and Margaret were the successive wives of Charles I; Constance was the wife of Peter. Henry III of England was reputed to have little wit; his son, Edward I, was highly esteemed.

Is William the Marquis, with eyes upward
      thrown,   *134*
Through whom Alessandria and her war
Make Monferrato and Canavese moan."

Canto VIII

At sunset these souls join in the evening hymn; but
they appear apprehensive, and two angels in green,
with drawn swords, descend to take post on either
side of the little valley and guard them from the
visit of the serpent (of temptation). Sordello brings
Dante and Virgil among the spirits, and Dante rec-
ognizes Nino de' Visconti, and they talk together.
Dante now notes that the four stars of the morning
have disappeared and three stars (symbols of the
Theological Virtues) are shining in their place. The
snake appears, but is driven off by the angels who
swoop down like hawks. Conrad Malaspina asks
Dante for news of his country, the Val di Magra.
Dante replies that he has never been in those
lands, but praises the Malaspini for their upright-
ness. Conrad predicts that before long Dante will
know of the hospitality of his house by experience
and not only by report.

Now was the hour which longing backward bends
In those that sail, and melts their heart in sighs,
The day they have said farewell to their sweet friends,

---

134. William VII, or "Longsword," who was Marquis of Montferrat
and Canavese. In 1292 he was treacherously captured at Alessan-
dria, in Piedmont.

And pricks with love the outsetting pilgrim's eyes
    If the far bell he hears across the land
    Which seems to mourn over the day that dies,
When I let hearing from my ears be banned,
    Absorbed in gaze on one of the souls there,
    Uprisen, who craved an audience with its hand.
It joined and lifted both its palms in prayer,   10
    Fixing its eyes upon the East, as though
    'Twere saying·to God: "For naught else have I care."
Te lucis ante I heard devoutly flow
    Out of its mouth and with a note so sweet
    It caused me quite out of myself to go.
And the others then devoutly followed it,
    Sweetly, with eyes fixed on the spheres that spin
    On high, until the hymn was all complete.
Sharpen thy sight well, reader; for so thin
    Assuredly the veil of truth is now   20
    That 'tis an easy task to pass within.
I saw that noble army from below
    Upward their silent gaze thereafter send
    As if expectant, pale and humble of brow.
And I saw, issuing from on high, descend
    Two angels, each with flaming sword in hand
    Broken short off and blunted at the end.
Green as the just-born leaves ere they expand,
    Their raiment was, which they behind them trailed,
    By the green wings ever disturbed and fanned.   30
One lighting a little above us I beheld,
    And the other descended on the opposite bank,
    So that the people all in the midst were held.
Clearly their blond heads I discerned, but blank
    The eyes were in their faces, like a power
    That, dazzled by excess of splendour, shrank.
"Both are from Mary's bosom come, this bower,"
    Sordello said, "to have in ward, because

Of that snake which shall visit us at this hour."
Whereat I, knowing not by what way it was,   40
   Turned me around then and all frozen pale
   Up to the trusted shoulders pressed me close.
Sordello again: "Now down into the dell
   'Mid the great shades, to speak with them, go we:
   To see you in their midst will please them well."
I think that I descended steps but three
   And was below, when I saw one to stare,
   As if for recognition, only at me.
'Twas now the time when dusk blackens the air,
   Yet not so but that what before was lost   50
   By distance twixt his eyes and mine was clear.
Toward me he moved, and I to his accost.
   Noble Judge Nino, how my heart had ease   53
   To see that not among the damned thou wast!
We left unsaid no greeting that could please.
   Then he asked: "How long since didst thou attain
   The foot of the mountain over the far seas?"
"O," said I, "from within the dens of pain
   I came this morn: in my first life I am,
   Though by this journey the other life I gain."   60
And when this answer of mine was heard by them,
   Sordello and he backward recoiled a pace,   62
   Like folk on whom a sudden amazement came.
The one turned round to Virgil, the other to face
   One sitting there, crying: "Conrad, up now get!   65
   Come, see what God hath purposed in His grace."
Then, turned to me: "By this especial debt
   Thou owest to Him who so hides from our view

---

53. "Nino" Visconti, a grandson of the Ugolino of Inf. xxxiii, was
judge, or governor, of a Sardinian province.
62. Sordello, up to this time, has not noticed that Dante is alive.
65. Conrad Malaspina was the lord of Villafranca of the Magra.
For a century his house had been famous for its liberality to
troubadours.

His first *Wherefore,* that none may fathom it,
When thou hast passed the wide waters anew,   70
   Tell my Joan that she make for me a prayer   71
   There where the innocent are hearkened to.
Her mother, I think, for me hath no more care
   Since that day when she changed her wimples white,
   Which she, poor soul, must long again to wear.
Through her, full easy it is to judge aright
   How soon love's fire can in a woman fade
   If eye and touch keep not the flame alight.
The viper by the Milanese displayed
   Will for her tomb make not so fair a crest   80
   As would Gallura's blazoned cock have made."
Thus spoke he, in all his countenance imprest
   With the clear stamp of that most righteous zeal
   Which within due bound burneth in the breast.
My eyes went only upon the heavens to dwell,
   There where the motion of the stars is slow
   As the more near to the axle in the wheel.
My leader then: "Son, at what gazest thou
   Aloft?" And I: "At those three torches there   89
   Which make the whole pole on this side to glow."   90
And he to me: "The four stars beaming clear
   Thou sawest this morning, now upon that side
   Are sunk, and these are risen where they were."
Sordello, as he spoke, drew him aside
   To himself, saying: "Our adversary, see!"
   Pointing his finger, Virgil's eye to guide.
There, where the dell's foot is from barrier free,

71-80. Joan was Nino's only child. Nino's wife, Beatrice d'Este,
had married Galeazzo Visconti, who was driven from Milan. The
arms of the Visconti (the viper) will not adorn her tomb so well
as Nino's (the cock).

89-93. The "three torches," representing the three theological vir-
tues, appear at night. The day is ushered in by the constellation of
the four cardinal virtues.

Was a snake, such perhaps as in his guile
    Gave unto Eve food from the bitter tree.
Through grass and flowers on came the fell reptile, 100
    And now and again its head to its back it drove,
    As a beast sleeks itself, and licked the while.
I did not see, and cannot speak thereof,
    How moved the heavenly hawks; but sure am I
    That I beheld both one and the other move.
Hearing the green wings cleave the air to fly,
    The serpent fled, and the angels wheeled about
    Abreast up to their posts again on high.
The shade that to the judge when he called out
    Had drawn close, all through that assault and
        swoop   110
    From me had not once loosed its gaze devout.
"So may that lantern which doth lead thee up
    Find in thy will as much wax as needs yet
    To reach on high the enamelled mountain-top,"
It said, "if thou hast sure news to relate
    Of Val di Magra's and its neighbours' lot,
    Tell it to me, for once there I was great.
I was called Conrad Malaspina; not
    The ancient one, but truly of his descent.   *119*
    I loved my own, with love cleansed here from
        spot."   120
"O," said I, "through your land I never went;
    But where throughout all Europe do men dwell
    That its renown is not among them sent?
The fame that honoureth your house so well
    Crieth out the country, crieth out its lord,
    So that who ne'er was there can of it tell.
I swear to you, so grace my steps reward,
    Your honoured race hath ceased not forth to show

---

119. *The older and more famous Conrad Malaspina was the grand-father of the present speaker.*

The glory of the purse and of the sword.

Custom and nature privilege it so 130
   That though the guilty head the world misguides, *131*
   Sole it goes straight, nor the evil way will know."

And he: "Depart now, for the sun abides *133*
   Not seven times in the bed the Ram with all
   Four feet in season covers and bestrides

Before this courteous opinion shall
   Right in the middle of thy head be nailed—
   Nail stronger than report of men withal—

If that the course of judgment have prevailed."

---

131. "The guilty head": Rome.
233-135. *The sun will not return seven times to the sign of Aries,
the Ram: seven years will not pass.*

Canto IX

---

*Dante falls into a deep sleep and dreams that he is
carried up by an eagle into the sphere of fire. Wak-
ing suddenly, he finds himself with Virgil at a spot
higher up the mountain and just below the gate of
Purgatory proper. Virgil tells him that, while he
slept, Lucy carried him up from the valley below.
The gate of Purgatory is guarded by an angel sit-
ting on the topmost of three steps, each differently
colored. Dante goes up to the gate and humbly
craves admission. The angel inscribes the letter P
(symbol of the seven deadly sins, Peccata) seven
times on his forehead; then opens the gate with a
golden and a silver key.*

ANCIENT Tithonus' concubine by now   *1*
  At the eastern balcony was growing white
  Forth from the arms of her sweet bed-fellow.
With jewels was her forehead tiar'd bright
  Clustered in likeness of the cold creature
  That woundeth with his tail as with a bite.
And Night had made in that place where we were   7
  Two of her climbing steps, and now the third
  Hovered upon its wings inclining near,
When I, in whom something of Adam stirred,   *10*
  Sank down with body overcome by sleep,
  Where all we five were seated, on the sward.   *12*
At that time when the swallow wakes to cheep
  Her sad notes close upon the morning hour,
  Perhaps the record of old plaints to keep,
And when our mind, being a truant more
  From flesh, and with its thoughts less tangled up,
  In vision wins almost prophetic power,
I seemed in a dream to see above me stoop
  An eagle of golden plumage in the sky   *20*
  With wings stretcht wide out and intent to swoop.
He seemed above the very place to fly
  Where Ganymede was forced his mates to lose   *23*
  When he was snatcht up to the assembly on high.
Within me I thought: Perhaps only because
  Of habit he strikes here, and from elsewhere
  Scorneth to carry up aught in his claws.
Then, having seemed to wheel a little, sheer

1-6. "Ancient Tithonus' concubine" *is the lunar Aurora, i.e. the
moon's dawn.*—"The cold creature" *is the constellation of Scorpio.*
7-9. Nearly three hours have passed since nightfall.
12. Sordello, Virgil, Dante, Nino, Conrad.
*23. Ganymede was caught up by an eagle, to be cup-bearer to the
gods.*

Down he came, terrible as the lightning's lash,
And snatcht me up far as the fiery sphere.   30
Then he and I, it seemed, burnt in the flash,
And I so scorched at the imagined blaze
That needs must sleep be broken as with a crash.
Not otherwise Achilles in amaze,   34
Not knowing whither he was come, did start
And all around him turn his wakened gaze
When Scyros-wards from Chiron, next her heart,
His mother bore him sleeping, to alight
There where the Greeks compelled him to depart,
Than I now started as sleep fled me quite   40
And my face turned to death-pale suddenly,
Even as a man who freezes from affright.
Beside me was my Comfort, only he:
And lo, the sun was more than two hours high
Already, and mine eyes were turned to sea.
"Have no fear," said my Lord, "but fortify
Thyself; to a good point we have won through.
Hold thee not back, but all thy strength apply.
Thou art arrived at Purgatory now.
See there the rampart closing it around,   50
See the entrance there where it seems cleft in two.
Ere this when in thee the soul slumbered sound
Amid the dawning that precedes the day,
Laid on the flowers that prank the lower ground,
A lady came, saying 'I am Lucy; I pray   55
Let me lift up this sleeping man, to aid
And speed him the more surely upon his way.'
Sordello and the other noble natures stayed.
She took thee, and as the brightening day grew near

34-39. *To prevent Achilles from going to the Trojan war, Thetis took him in his sleep from his teacher, the centaur Chiron, to the island of Scyros.*
55. *Lucy is the symbol of Illuminating Grace.*

She mounted, and I followed in her tread.   60
Here did she set thee; her beautiful eyes made clear
  First, where the entrance in yon opening lies;
  Then she departed, and sleep went with her."
Like one who is delivered from surmise
  And changes fear to comfort in his mind
  When truth reveals itself before his eyes,
I changed me; and when from doubting disentwined
  My leader saw me, up where the rampart rose
  He moved on toward the height, and I behind.
Reader, thou see'st well how my matter grows   70
  In loftiness, and therefore marvel not
  That my art also more exalted shows.
We approached and were arriving at a spot
  Whence, there where first to me a gap appeared
  Like in a wall some crack that it hath got,
I saw a gate, and three steps mounting toward
  The gate above, coloured of divers stain,
  And a guardian who as yet spoke not a word.
And as my eyes were opened to see plain,
  I saw him seated on the topmost tread   80
  In countenance such as I could not sustain.
A naked sword within his hand he had
  Which toward us turned the rays so from the steel
  That I to face it often in vain essayed.
"There where you stand, halt, and declare your will,"
  He began saying; "who is it escorteth you?
  Beware lest coming up be to your ill."
My master spoke and answered him: "But now
  A lady of heaven who hath these things in care,
  Said to us: 'There the gate is; thither go.'"   90
"And may she for your steps all good prepare,"
  Resumed the warden in his courtesy,
  "Come ye then forward to ascend our stair."

There came we; and the first step of the three   *94*
    Was white marble, and polished with such art
    That just as I appear it mirrored me.
The second was black-purple or yet more swart,
    Of rugged stone and burnt into the grain;
    And it was cracked both lengthwise and athwart.
The third whose mass the other two sustain   100
    Seemed porphyry, from which a blazing broke
    Bright as the blood that spurts out of a vein.
The angel of God rested upon this block
    Both his feet, sitting on the threshold stone,
    Which seemed to me of adamantine rock.
Up the three steps my Leader took me on
    With my own right good will, saying: "Now entreat
    In all humility that the bolt be drawn."
Devout I flung me at the sacred feet:
    I prayed him to open to me of his grace;   110
    But first upon my bosom thrice I beat.
Seven P's upon my forehead did he trace
    With his sword's point, and: "See that thou," he said,
    "When that thou art within, these wounds efface."
Ashes or earth that comes dry on the spade
    Would be one colour with his raiment's fold;
    And from beneath it two keys he displayed.
One was of silver and the other of gold.   *118*
    First with the white, then with the yellow he wrought
    So to the gate that I was well consoled.   120
"Whenever one of these fails in the slot
    So that the lock it turneth not aright,"
    Said he to us, "this passage opens not.
More precious the one is, but great art and wit

---

94. Apparently these steps stand for the three stages of original
innocence, sin, and atonement.
118. The golden key of power and the silver key of discernment.

The other needs before the lock will stir,
  Because by this one is the knot unknit.
From Peter I hold them, and he bade me err
  Rather in opening than in keeping fast,
  If but the people cast them prostrate here."
He pushed the sacred portal's door at last,   130
  Saying: "Enter, but be warned that he who is
     found
  Looking behind him is again out-cast."   *132*
And when within their sockets turned full round
  The pivots of the sacred portal-door,
  Made of strong metal and clanging in their sound,
Tarpeia rasped not nor gave such a roar   *136*
  When good Metellus from its charge was rent,
  Whereby it was to stay despoiled and poor.
I turned me aside, on that first thunder intent;
  And *Te Deum laudamus* seemed I then   140
  To hear in voices with the sweet sound blent.
Just such an image did my senses gain
  From what I heard, as from a choir is caught
  When they to instruments accord their strain,
And now the words are clear and now are not.

---

132. "Looking behind": upon his former life.
136-138. When Caesar took possession of the Tarpeian rock from
the tribune Metellus, the gates of the temple were opened and the
rock resounded.

Canto X

---

*The poets, now admitted to Purgatory, mount by a
zigzag passage through the rock, till they reach a
terrace, which runs round the entire mountain. On*

*the outer rim is the precipitous slope; on the inner
side the cliff is adorned with reliefs in white
marble, representing types of Humility and taken
both from sacred and pagan history. Dante marvels
at their life-likeness. There now approaches a
crowd of spirits, hardly appearing human at first
because bowed down in agonized postures by the
huge rocks which they bear. These are the Proud,
expiating their sin.*

WHEN we were past the threshold of the gate
   From which the spirits' perverse desires abstain
   Because they make the crooked path seem straight,
By the loud sound I knew it shut again;
   And had mine eyes been toward it backward drawn
   What plea to excuse the fault could I maintain?
We mounted through a cloven mass of stone
   Which shifted upon one and the other side
   Like a wave fleeing and then coming on.
"Here must we use a little art," my Guide   10
   Began, "and take heed to continue close,
   This way or that, to the receding side."
This caused us so much of our steps to lose
   That the diminished moon's disk had anew
   Attained its bed, to sink into repose,
Ere from that needle's eye we had come through;   *16*
   But when we now were free of the open air
   Above, where into itself the Mount withdrew,
I weary, and both uncertain where we were,
   We stood at halt upon a level place   20
   Lonelier than roads crossing a desert bare.
From its edge, bordering on the emptiness,
   To the foot of the high bank which mounts upright

16. "That needle's eye": *the narrow passage.*

Three times a human body had spanned the space.
And so far as my eye could wing its flight
    Now on the left, now on the right, I found
    This terrace so appear unto my sight.
Our feet had not yet moved upon this ground
    When I discerned that bank (which, rising straight,
    Lacked means to ascend it as it circled round)   30
To be of shining marble and all ornate
    With chiselling, so that Polycletus, yea,   32
    Nature herself would have been shamed thereat.
The Angel that came down with the decree   34
    Of peace for ages prayed and wept for, whence
    From so long interdict Heaven was made free,
Appeared before us with such live presence,
    Graven there, gentle of gesture and of eye,
    That it seemed not an image without sense.
One would swear he said *Ave!* for there-by   40
    Was she imagined and made manifest
    Who turned the key to admit love from on high.
And in her gesture these words were expressed:
    Ecce ancilla Dei, clear as can   44
    A figure be that is on wax impressed.
"Fix not thy mind on the one place," began
    The gracious Poet, who had me, where he was,
    On that side where the heart is in a man.
Wherefore I moved mine eyes, turning my face,
    And saw, past Mary and beyond the head   50
    Of him who now bestirred me from my place,
Another story on the rock portrayed;   52

32. "Polycletus": the Greek sculptor.
34. "The Angel" is Gabriel. This example of humility represents the Virgin at the Annunciation.
44. "Behold the handmaid of the Lord," Mary's reply to Gabriel.
52-57. "Another story": King David dancing before the ark of the covenant. Uzzah, one of the drivers of the cart, seeing the ark shaken, "put forth his hand . . . and took hold of it"; where-

Wherefore I crossed by Virgil and drew near
That I might have it to my eyes displayed.
There on the very marble graven were
The cart and the oxen drawing the holy Ark,
Whereby the unchartered office prompts to fear.
In front were people, all, as I could mark,
In seven choirs banded; of my senses two
Said, one "They are mute," and one "They are sing-
ing, hark!"   60
In like manner the incense-smoke also
Which there appeared, by its imagining
Made eyes and nose at odds of Yes and No.
Before the blessed vessel went dancing
The humble Psalmist, with his dress up-girt;
In that hour was he more and less than King.
Opposite at a palace-window apart   67
Was the effigy of Michal looking on,
Like to a woman full of scorn and hurt.
I moved my feet from where I stood, to con   70
Another story with a closer eye
Which beyond Michal white upon me shone.   72
There was enacted the nobility
Of the high prince whose worth made intervene
Gregory and win him his great victory;
Trajan the Roman emperor I mean:
And a poor widow to his bridle clung
Whose tears and grief were in her gesture seen.
Round him appeared a trampling and a throng

---

upon "God smote him" for his "unchartered office": 2 Samuel
6:6.
67. His wife, Michal, "looked through a window, and saw King
David leaping and dancing before the Lord; and she despised him
in her heart": 2 Samuel 6:16.
72-74. The third example of humility is furnished by Trajan, who
acknowledged the justice of a poor widow's claim; whereupon
St. Gregory interceded with God for his salvation.

Of horsemen, and the eagles on gold brede   80
  Visibly in the wind above him swung.
'Mid them all that forlorn one seemed to plead:
  "Avenge me for my son, I supplicate,
  Who is dead, and whose death makes my heart to
    bleed."
And he appeared to answer her: "Now, wait
  Till I return." And she; "My Lord" (like one
  In whom grief presses forth importunate)
"If thou return not?" He: "It shall be done
  By one in my place." She: "And what to thee
  Is another's goodness if thou lose thine own?"   90
Wherefore he: "Comfort now, for needs must be
  That I fulfil my duty, ere I stir.
  Justice wills it, and pity holdeth me."
He, to whose sight no new thing can appear,   94
  Fashioned this visible language, to us new,
  Since such a thing never was fashioned here.
While I regarded, as I joyed to do,
  Images of humility so rare
  And for the Artist's sake precious to view,
The poet murmured, "Lo, much people there   100
  Approaching, but their steps are slow and spent.
  These will direct us to the upper stair."
Mine eyes that in their gazing were content,
  Seeing new things to their desire displayed,
  Turned, and on him immediately were bent.
Reader, I would not that thou be dismayed   106
  From good resolve, through being brought to know
  How God designeth that the debt be paid.
Consider not the nature of the woe;
  Think of the sequel, think that, at the extreme,   110

---

94. "He, to whose sight . . .": God.
106. Dante fears that the horror of the penance may divert the
reader from his "good resolution" to make amends.

Beyond the high sentence it cannot go.   *111*
I began: "Master, what I see doth seem
   Not persons, moving toward us with such gait,
   But what I know not, so my sight doth swim."
And he to me: "Their miserable state
   Of torment bows them to this crouching plight.
   So that my eyes at first were in debate.
Look hard; then disentangle with thy sight
   What comes beneath those stones: already thou
   Mayest discern how each his breast doth smite."   120
O ye proud Christians, weary and sad of brow,
   Who, tainted in the vision of the mind,
   In backward steps your confidence avow,
Perceive ye not that we are worms, designed
   To form the angelic butterfly, that goes   *125*
   To judgment, leaving all defence behind?
Why doth your mind take such exalted pose,
   Since ye disabled, are as insects, mean
   As worm which never transformation knows?
Just as a figure sometimes may be seen   130
   For corbel, roof or ceiling to sustain,
   Uniting knees to breast with nought between,
Which form unreal causeth real pain
   In him who sees it, so beheld I these
   When closely I regarded them again.
True it is they were contracted more or less
   As more or less upon their backs they bore;
   And he who seemed the most to acquiesce
Weeping appeared to say: "I can no more."

---

111. The suffering will stop at the day of judgment.
125. Cf. Matt. 22:30: "For in the resurrection they . . . are as the
angels of God in heaven."

Canto XI

The souls of the Proud repeat a paraphrase of the Lord's Prayer. Virgil asks of them the way to the nearest ascent; he is answered by Humbert Aldo-brandesco. Dante then recognizes Oderisi of Gub-bio, an illuminator of manuscripts, who discourses on the transitoriness of human fame and tells the story of Provenzan Salvani of Siena.

O OUR Father, who art in heaven above,
  Not as being circumscribed, but because toward
  Thy first creation thou hast greater love,
Hallowed thy name be and thy power adored
  By every creature, as is meet and right
  To give thanks for the sweetness from thee poured;
May upon us thy kingdom's peace alight,
  For to it of ourselves we cannot rise,
  Unless it come itself, with all our wit.
As of their will thine angels' companies   10
  Make sacrifice, as they Hosanna sing,
  So may men make of their will sacrifice.
To us this day our daily manna bring: *13*
  Else through this desert harsh must he revert
  His steps, who most to advance is labouring.
And as we pardon every one the hurt

1-3. *The Canto opens with an expanded paraphrase of the Lord's Prayer.* "Thy first creation": *the angels and the heavens.*
13. *The* "daily manna" *is spiritual food.*

That we have suffered, do thou pardon too,
    Benignant, nor remember our desert.
Try not our will, so easy to subdue,
    With the old adversary, and by thine aid   20
    Save us from him who goads it, to our rue.
This last prayer, dear Lord, is for us not made
    Any more, since remaineth now no need,
    But 'tis for those who have behind us stayed."
Thus for themselves and us, praying God-Speed
    Those shades were going beneath their burden
        bowed,
    Like the oppression that a dream may breed.
Each in his proper pain, a weary crowd,
    They circled the first terrace with their tread,
    Purging away the murk of the world's cloud.   30
And if of us good always there is said,
    What can be said and done for them by men
    Here, whose good-will is rooted and inbred?
Surely we ought to help them wash the stain
    Which they have borne hence, so that cleansed and
        light
    They may go forth the starry spheres to attain.
"Ah, so may pity and justice ease your plight
    Soon, that disburdened ye be free to stretch
    The wing that lifts you to your longing's height,
Show us on which hand we may quickest reach   40
    The stair; if there more be than the one road,
    That which is least hard show us, we beseech.
For he who comes with me, having the load
    Of Adam's flesh upon him yet to wear,
    Mounts, though against his will, in halting mode."
From whom the words came, answering the prayer
    Which to those shades he had addressed, whom still
    I followed on the path, was not made clear;
But this was said: "To the right along the hill

Come with us now and there shall ye be shown   5c
   The pass for a living person possible.
And if I were not hindered by the stone
   Which lies upon me, my proud neck to tame,
   Wherefore I needs must carry my face prone,
Him who yet lives and hath not told his name
   Would I behold, to see if 'tis a man
   I know, and make him pity this my shame.
Latin was I; son of a great Tuscan.   58
   William Aldobrandesco fathered me:
   I know not if his fame among you ran.   60
The ancient blood and feats of chivalry
   Of my forefathers puffed my pride up so
   That, careless of our common Mother's plea,
Such extreme scorn of all men did I show,
   It killed me; how, the Sienese can tell
   And every child in Campagnatico.
I am Humbert; pride not only did compel
   Me to that fate; but all my kinsfolk too,
   Dragged down by it, into disaster fell.
Here must I therefore bear this load of rue,   70
   Till God be satisfied, among the dead,
   Since 'mid the living this I did not do."
Listening I stoopt my face down to his head.
   And one of them twisted himself about,
   (Not he who spoke) beneath what on him weighed
And saw me and knew me and was calling out,
   Straining his neck to keep me in his eye
   Who, all bent down, went with them foot by foot.
"Art thou not Oderisi," then said I,   79
   "Honour of Gubbio, honour of that art,   80

58-66. *Humbert, a member of the mighty Ghibelline family of the
Aldobrandeschi, was killed by Sienese troops at his stronghold
of Campagnatico, in 1259.—"Our common Mother" is the earth.*
79. *Oderisi of Gubbio was a famous illuminator of manuscripts.*

The illuminators famed in Paris ply?"
"Brother, the pages smile more on the mart
  Which Franco of Bologna paints," said he: *83*
  "Now the honour is all his, mine only in part.
Truly I had not used such courtesy
  In life, so great desire within me burned
  To excel the rest, which overmastered me.
By such pride such a penalty is earned.
  Nor were I here, save that, having the power
  Of sinful doing, unto God I turned.   90
O idle glory of all human dower!
  How short a time, save a dull age succeed,
  Its flourishing fresh greenness doth devour!
In painting Cimabue thought indeed   *94*
  To hold the field; now Giotto has the cry,
  So that the fame of the other few now heed.
So our tongue's glory from one Guido by
  The other is taken; and from their nest of fame
  Perchance is born one who shall make both fly.
Naught but a wind's breath is the world's acclaim, 100
  Which blows now hence, now thence, as it may hap,
  And when it changes quarter changes name.
Wilt thou have more fame if old age unwrap
  Thy bones from withered flesh than if thy race
  Ended ere thou wert done with bib and pap
Before a thousand years pass,—shorter space
  To eternity than is a blinked eye-lid
  To the circle in heaven that moves at slowest pace?

---

83. *Of Franco of Bologna, an illuminator and a painter, little is known.*
94-99. *Giovanni Cimabue was regarded as the restorer of painting in Florence. Giotto, Cimabue's pupil, was the greatest painter of Dante's time. The poet Guido Cavalcanti surpassed Guido Guinicelli of Bologna. As to the general deduction of line 99, Dante must have known that the reader would immediately apply it to him.*

With him, who moves so slow before me, did   *109*
   All Tuscany once ring: and of him now   110
   Is scarcely a whisper in Siena hid,
Which he was lord of when was forced to bow
   The fury of Florence, who at that time grew
   In pride as high as now she is fallen low.
Your reputation is as grass in hue,
   Which comes and goes, and through him is it brown
   Who from the soil its springing freshness drew."
And I to him: "Thy true word softens down
   My swelling heart and healeth it of pride.
   But of whom speak'st thou, and of whose re-
      nown?"   120
" 'Tis Provenzan Salvani," he replied;
   "And he is here because so bold he had grown,
   Presuming all Siena to bestride.
Thus goes he without rest as he has gone
   Since death, and in such coin he needs must pay,
   For over-daring upon earth to atone."
And I: "If such a spirit as makes delay
   Of his repentance till life's utmost rim,
   Remains beneath and mounts not up this way,
Save hallowed prayers assist him, till such time   130
   Be measured as his years of living were,
   How was the coming hither vouchsafed him?"
"He of his own will in Siena square"   *133*
   Said he, "when most he gloried among men,
   Posted himself, all shame forsworn, and there
To liberate his friend out of the pain
   That he endured in Charles's prison tower,
   Constrained himself to tremble in every vein.

---

109. "With him . . .": Provenzano Salvani, a valiant Ghibelline
chief, who was all-powerful in Siena in 1260 and nine years later
was defeated and beheaded.
133-138. To save the life of a friend held for ransom by Charles of
Anjou, Provenzano meekly begged of the passers-by.

Darkly, I know, I speak, and say no more.

But soon thy neighbours' acts shall be for signs   140
Whereby to read the riddle thou'lt have power.

This deed delivered him from those confines."   *142*

---

142. "This deed" enabled him to enter Purgatory.

Canto XII

Virgil bids Dante leave Oderisi, with whom he has
been stepping, bowed in sympathy. They go on
their way, and Dante is now admonished by Virgil
to examine the pavement they are treading. On this
are chiselled reliefs, showing examples of pride laid
low. After they have gone some distance, they meet
the angel who guards this terrace and who with a
stroke of his wing erases one of the P's from Dante's
forehead. They ascend a stair, like the one made to
ease the ascent from Florence to San Miniato, and
Dante is surprised to find that he now mounts more
easily than he went on the level. This is because the
P (the sin of pride) has been obliterated.

LIKE oxen in the yoke, pace matching pace,

That laden spirit I accompanied

So long as the sweet Teacher gave me grace;

But when he said: "Press on now and leave his side,

For here 'tis well that each one urge with all

His might his bark, and sail and oar be plied,"

Upright, as walking maketh natural,

I made again my body, although in thought

Bowed down I still remained and shrunken small.

I had moved me, and willingly my footsteps sought 10
  My Master's, and we, stepping both as one,
  Already showed how light we were of foot,

When he admonished me: "Turn thine eyes down.
  Good will it be, the way to soothe the more,
  To see the bed thy soles are treading on."

As tombs over those buried in stone floor,
  That after may be memory of them, bear
  The portraiture of what they were before,

Wherefore men often-times weep for them there,
  Because remembrance pricks them with the smart 20
  That only the compassionate doth spur,

So saw I, but more life-like, since the art
  Did there of a diviner craftsman tell,
  The road formed by the Mount's projecting part.

I saw on one side him, who to excel
  All other creatures was created, flame
  Down, like the lightning, as from heaven he fell.   27

I saw Briareus, by celestial aim   28
  On the other side transfixed upon the ground,
  Lying with mortal frost upon his frame.   30

I saw Thrymbæus, Mars and Pallas round
  Their father, still in arms and gazing o'er
  The great limbs of the Giants strewn beyond.

I saw Nimrod under his mighty tower   34
  As if bewildered and regarding those
  Who in Shinar with him bragged of all their power.

O Niobe, into mine eyes arose   37

---

27. *Luke* 10:18: *"I beheld Satan as lightning fall from heaven."*
28-33. *Briareus was one of the giants who fought against the gods.
The carving represents the bodies of the defeated giants, upon
which Apollo ("Thymbraeus"), Pallas, Mars, and Jove are gazing.*
34. *"Nimrod": the builder of the tower of Babel in the land of
Shinar.*
37. *Niobe, proud of her seven sons and seven daughters, disparaged*

What grief, to see, carved on that floor, thy pain
Twixt seven and seven of children in death's throes!

O Saul, how there upon thine own sword slain   *40*
Didst thou appear, dead on Gilboa bare
That after felt not dew nor any rain.

O mad Arachne, so I saw thee stare,   *43*
Half-spider already, mournful on the shred
Of what thou wovest to thine own despair.

O Rehoboam, here no threatening head   *46*
Thine image showeth; but a chariot now
Hurries thee away, ere chase come, full of dread.

It showed further, the hard pavement, how   *49*
Dearly Alcmaeon made his mother pay   *50*
The unlucky necklace, to achieve his vow.

It showed how his sons rushed on him to slay   *52*
Sennacherib; and how, their father killed,
They left him in the temple where he lay.

It showed the rout and cruel carnage willed
By Queen Tomyris who to Cyrus cried: *56*
"Blood thou didst crave, with blood shalt thou be
    filled."

It showed how after Holofernes died
The Assyrians all fled headlong and dismayed;
The relic of the slaying it showed beside.   *60*

Latona, whose two children, Apollo and Diana, avenged her by
shooting all of Niobe's offspring.

43. "Arachne," who had challenged Pallas to a trial of skill in weav-
ing, was turned by her into a spider.

46. "Rehoboam": see 1 Kings 12:18.

49. Amphiaraus, to avoid going to the Theban war, hid himself, but
was betrayed by his wife Eriphyle, who had been bribed by a
golden necklace. Her son Alcmaeon killed her in vengeance for the
loss of his father.

52. Sennacherib, the haughty king of the Assyrians, was killed by
his sons "as he was worshipping."

56. "Tomyris," queen of the Scythians, to avenge the defeat of her
army, lured Cyrus and his men into an ambush and destroyed
them.

I saw Troy gaping and in ashes laid.
  O Ilion, thee how vile and desecrate
  The witness of the sculpture there betrayed!
What master of brush or point were he so great,
  Who line and shade could have so justly wed
  For every subtle mind to wonder at?
The live appeared living, and dead the dead.
  Not better he who saw the actual deed
  Saw than I, stooping, all beneath my tread.
Wax proud now and with haughty front proceed,   70
  Children of Eve, nor gaze upon the ground,
  So that your evil courses ye may heed.
More of the Mount by us was compassed round
  Already, and of the sun's path much more spent
  Than the mind reckoned, being not yet unbound,
When he who, watchful without ceasing, went
  In front of me, said: "Lift thy head upright!
  'Tis no time now to walk so all-intent.
See, an angel cometh toward us into sight
  There, and from service of the day withdrawn   80
  The sixth handmaiden homeward taketh flight.   81
Reverence over face and act put on,
  So that to send us upward may him please.
  Think, that this day never again shall dawn!"
To his monitions, ever the hour to seize,
  Was I full well used, so that to my ears
  In that matter he spoke no mysteries.
Onward to us the beauteous creature nears,
  Clad in white raiment and in countenance
  Like as at morn a trembling star appears.   90
His arms he opened, then his wings' expanse,
  Saying: "Come; nigh to this spot is the stair,
  And easy now will be the ascending hence.
To this inviting they who come are rare.

---

81. *The sixth hour of daylight.*

O human spirits, upward born to spring,
  Why fall ye down at a brief blast of air?"
He led us where the rock was cleft; his wing
  On me across the forehead did he beat,
  Then pledged me a safe path for my journeying.
As, on the right, to climb the hill that, set   100
  O'er Rubaconte, by the church is topt   *101*
  Which has the well-ruled city under it,
There is a breach amid the ascent abrupt,
  Hewn into steps made in the former time
  When stave and ledger were yet uncorrupt,
Even so the slope is made less hard to climb
  Which falls from the other cornice with steep face,
  But on both sides close presses the rock's rim.
While we were turning to the upward pass
  Voices *Beati pauperes spiritu*   110
  Sang, beyond speech to tell, so sweet it was.
Ah, different verily this avenue
  From Hell's approaches; for through singing here
  Is the entry, but down there fierce wails pursue.
Now mounting up the sacred steps we were,
  And far more lightly it seemed that now I trod
  Than earlier on the level did appear.
Wherefore I; "Master, say what is this load
  Which has been taken from me, that scarce aught
  Of toil seems now to oppress me upon the road?" 120
He answered: "When the P's thy brow has got,
  Nigh cancelled on thee yet remaining still,
  Shall, like the one, be utterly razed out,
Thou shalt be so surrendered to good-will
  That not only shall toil not tire thy feet
  But to mount up shall be delectable."
Then did I like to those who walk the street

101-102. "The church": San Miniato. "Rubaconte": *the old name of
the bridge, now called Ponte alle Grazie.* "Well-ruled" *is ironical.*

With something that they know not on their head
  Save that they doubt the signs and stares they meet,
Wherefore, to make sure, the hand comes to aid   130
  And seeks and finds, that service to afford
  For which the mere sight is not facultied;
And with the hand's spread fingers I explored
  And found but six the letters he of the keys
  Had over both the temples on me scored;
Perceiving which my Leader smiled at ease.

Canto XIII

---

*The poets arrive at the second terrace, where the
sin of Envy is punished. Voices are heard praising
the virtues of generosity and charity. Then Dante
perceives the envious sinners sitting huddled to-
gether along the side of the cliff, their eyelids
stitched up with wire; and he speaks to them.
Among the spirits is a woman, Sapia of Siena, who
tells of her envious nature and how she rejoiced at
the defeat of her countrymen, commanded by Pro-
venzan Salvani (see Canto XI) at Colle in 1269. At
the end of the canto she alludes to two abortive
schemes of the Sienese; to discover the stream of
Diana, underneath the city, and to buy the port of
Talamone.*

Now were we at the topmost of the steps
  Where for a second time is scarped all round
  The mount which, as 'tis climbed, of evil strips.
About the hill there is a cornice wound

After the fashion of the former one,
  Save that the curve of it is sooner found.
Shades there are none to see there, nor sign shown,
  So naked looks the bank and paven way,
  All the one livid colour of the stone.
"If here, for people to ask of, we should stay,"   10
  The poet was beginning, "I much doubt
  Our choice will may-be have too great delay."
The sun then with a steady gaze he sought;
  Moving, on his right side he pivoted
  And the left part of him he turned about.
"O sweet light, in whose confidence," he said,
  "I enter on the new way, do thou lead
  Our steps here as we would that they be led.
Thou warm'st the world, thou shinest on its need.
  Save other reason prompt against it, still   20
  Thy rays must be the guide that we should heed."
Over such space as here counts for a mile,
  So far there in but short time did we move,
  Being quickened by our own consenting will.
And toward us flying now were heard above,
  But not seen, spirits speaking, and they sent
  Courteous welcome to the table of love.
The first voice flying *Vinum non habent*
  Cried in its passage with a loud clear note,
  Repeating it behind us as it went.   30
And ere it had passed quite out of ear-shot
  Through distance, passed another, without cease
  Crying "I am Orestes," and it too stayed not.   33
"O," said I, "Father, what voices are these?"
  Even as I asked him, did the third begin
  Saying, "Love those who have wrought you injuries."

---

33. When the tyrant Aegisthus had condemned Orestes, whom he did not know by sight, Orestes and his friend Pylades both claimed that name, each wishing to save the other.

And the good Master: "Envy is the sin
　　Which in this circle is scourged, and to that end
　　From love are drawn the cords of discipline.
Needs must the bit the contrary intend.　　　　　　40
　　I think that thou wilt hear it, as I guess,
　　Ere by the Pass of Pardon thou ascend.　　　　　42
But fix thine eyes through the air in steadfastness,
　　And thou shalt see before us huddled folk
　　That sitting each against the cliff-side press."
Then wider than before my eyes awoke.
　　I looked in front and shades with cloaks espied
　　Not different from the colour of the rock.
And when we had come up nearer to their side
　　I heard cried "Mary, pray for us!" and "O　　　50
　　Michael" and "Peter" and "O All Saints!" cried.
I think on earth to-day no man can go
　　So hard, he were not with compassion stung
　　At what mine eyes were then constrained to know.
For when I had arrived so near that throng
　　That all their features came distinctly seen,
　　A heavy grief out of mine eyes was wrung.
With hair-cloth they seemed covered, coarse and mean,
　　And each upon the other's shoulder leant,
　　And all of them against the bank did lean.　　　60
The blind, to whom is lacking nourishment,
　　Sit so at Pardons begging for their needs,
　　And each one's head is on his neighbour bent,
So that in others quick may spring the seeds
　　Of pity, not alone by sound of words
　　But by the sight, which not less sorely pleads.
And as to them the sun no boon affords,
　　So to the spirits, there where I have said,
　　Heaven's light no bounty of itself accords.

---

42. "The Pass of Pardon" is the beginning of the ascent to the
next circle.

For the eyelids of them all with iron thread   70
 Are stitched up, as is done to a wild hawk   71
 Because its spirit stays not quieted.

I seemed to do those shades wrong, thus to walk,
 Seeing others, and myself invisible:
 Me therefore to my wisdom I betook.

What the mute craved to say, he knew full well:
 And for that cause my question did forestall,
 Saying: "Speak, but make brief what thou hast to
  tell."

Virgil came with me along the outer wall
 Of the cornice, where, because no parapet   80
 Engirdles it, on that side one may fall.

And on the other side of me were set
 The devout shades, who through the horrible seam
 Pressed drops out, so that all their cheeks were wet.

"O people assured of seeing the light supreme,"
 I, turning to them, spoke, "the only home
 Ye crave, and your solicitude's one theme,

So may grace quickly sift away the scum
 Upon your conscience, so that through it clear
 The stream of memory down-flowing may come,   90

Tell me, for gracious will it be and dear
 To me, if any among you a Latin be.
 Perchance 'twill profit him, if such be here."

"O brother mine, each of a true city
 Is citizen, but thou would'st rather say
 That made his pilgrimage in Italy."

The answer I thus heard a voice convey
 Seemed somewhat farther on from where I was,
 Wherefore I made me heard yet more that way.

'Mid the others one sat with expectant face: 100
 And if one ask How so? it was the same

---

71. *Falcons that were tamed full-grown used to have their eyes
closed in this cruel way.*

As if I saw one blind his chin upraise.
"Spirit," said I, "that dost thy nature tame
  To mount up, if from thee came the reply,
  Make thyself known to me by place or name."
"I was of Siena, and here with the others I,"
  It answered, "wash away life's guilty blot,
  Weeping to him that he to us draw nigh.
Though Sapia named, yet sapient I was not.   *109*
  Of others' suffering was I much more glad   110
  Than of all good luck that befell my lot.
And lest thou think that now deceit I add,
  Hear if, already when life downward wheeled,
  I was not, even as I tell thee, mad.
My townsmen, hard by Colle, on the field
  Were ranked in battle against their foes' attack;
  And I prayed God for that which he had willed.
There were they routed and turned fleeing back
  In defeat's bitter steps, and in that chase
  A joy surpassing all else did I take;   120
So much that, lifting my presumptuous face,
  I cried to God 'I fear thee now no more,'
  As did the merle for a brief sunshine's grace.
I craved for peace with God on the last shore
  Of life, and not yet were the debt I owed
  Abridged by my repentance in that hour,
Had Piers Pettinaio not bestowed   *127*
  On me remembrance, holy prayers to make,
  And in his charity grieved for me to God.
But who art thou who passing by wouldst seek   130
  To learn our state, and hast thine eyes unwired,
  As I believe, and usest breath to speak?"
"Sight," said I, "shall be yet from me required

---

109. "Sapia": see the Argument.
127. Only the intercession of one of her countrymen secured for her
admission to Purgatory.

Here, but for brief time, for the offence is small
   Done by these eyes through being by envy fired.
Far greater is the dread in which my soul
   Hangs of the torment lower down, the thought   *137*
   Of which doth ev'n now with its weight appal."
And she: "Who then to us up hither brought
   Thy steps, if here again thou think'st to be?"   140
   And I: "He who is with me and says naught.
And I am living, therefore ask of me,
   Spirit elect, if thou would'st that down there
   On earth my mortal feet I stir for thee."
"This is so new a thing," she said, "to hear,
   That of God's love for thee 'tis a great sign:
   Prosper me therefore sometimes with a prayer.
And I by what thou most desir'st to win
   Entreat thee, if ever Tuscan earth thou tread
   That thou restore my name among my kin.   150
Thou'lt see them among that people in folly bred
   Who trust in Talamone and there will more   *152*
   Hope lose than seeking the Diana's bed.
But most shall the Admirals lose upon that shore."

---

137. "The torment lower down" *is of the circle of pride.*
152-154. "Talamone" *and* "Diana": *see the Argument.* "The Ad-
   mirals": *those who expect to be admirals.*

Canto XIV

---

*Overhearing Dante's talk, and learning that he is
still alive, two spirits, Guy del Duca and Rinieri da
Calboli, engage him in conversation. The former,
discovering that Dante comes from the shores of*

*the Arno, describes the course of that accursed river
down a valley in which the inhabitants of each
town it passes grow ever more brutish, till it reaches
Pisa, the worst of all. He predicts what Florence is
to suffer (in 1303) at the hands of Rinieri's grand-
son, and goes on to condemn the people of his own
Romagna for their degeneracy. Virgil and Dante
leave this pair of spirits, and as they go on hear
voices in the air warning against envy.*

"Wнo is this that circles round about our hill
   Ere death have licensed him from earth to fly
   And shuts his eyes and opens them at will?"
"I know not who he is: but this know I,
   He is not alone; ask thou who art nearer him,
   And sweetly accost him, so that he reply."
Thus two shades closely huddled, limb to limb,
   There on the right of me were talking low,
   Then held upturned for speech their faces dim.
And the one said: "O Soul, that on dost go   10
   Toward Heaven, though still within the body set,
   For charity console us, and tell who
Thou art and whence thou comest; for so great
   Astonishment is in us at thy grace
   As must be at a thing known never yet."
And I: "Through Tuscan country spreads apace
   A stream from Falterona issuing   17
   And a hundred miles contenteth not its race.
This body from the banks of it I bring.
   To tell you who I am, since yet hath been   20
   But little noised my name, were a vain thing."
"If my mind rightly pierce within that screen

---

10. "The one" is Guy del Duca.
17. "Falterona": a mountain in the Apennines.

To thy intention," then to me replied
He who spoke first, " 'Tis Arno thou dost mean."
And the other said to him: "Why did he hide,   25
In speaking of that river, the name of it,
As one does, loathly matter to avoid?"
The shade thus questioned did him thus acquit:
"I know not, but indeed good cause he has.
That such a stream's name perish is most fit.   30
For from its springing, where the mountain-mass,   31
Wherefrom is torn Pelorum, swells and soars
So that few points that measure overpass,
As far as where surrendered it restores
That which the sky hath sucked up from the sea,
Whence rivers have what flows between their shores,
Virtue is cast out for an enemy
By all, yea like a viper, either from
The curst place or ingrained malignancy.
And they who have the unhappy vale for home   40
Have altered so their nature, one would swear
That into Circe's pastures they had come.
Among brute hogs, on acorns fit to fare
Rather than viand on which man subsists,
It first directs its current poor and spare.
Curs it encounters, coming downward, beasts
Whose force is feebler than their snarlings' threat,
And from them in contempt its muzzle twists.   48
It goes down, and the more it groweth great
The more it finds the dogs to wolves transformed,   50
This ill-starred gutter of accursed fate.
Its way then through deep gorges having wormed,
Foxes it finds that trap nor cunning fear,

---

25. "The other" is Rinieri da Calboli.
31. "The mountain-mass": the Apennine chain, of which Pelorum
is the continuation.
48. Toward Arezzo the Arno suddenly turns off to the west.

So have their hearts with fraud's devices swarmed.
Nor will I cease, for all another hear:
  And well for him if later he recall
  What prophecy to me discloseth clear.
I see upon those wolves thy grandson fall,   58
  To hunt them by the savage river and drive
  Along its banks and terrify them all.   60
I see him sell their flesh while yet alive,
  Then kill them like old cattle,—many a head
  Of life, himself of honour to deprive.
Bloody he comes forth from the wood of dread.
  He leaves it such that hence a thousand years
  'Tis not to its first state re-forested."
As at the announcing of great ills appears
  The face of him who listens sore disturbed,
  Whence-so-ever comes the peril to his ears,
So saw I the other soul, who held him curbed   70
  To listen, become troubled and grow sad
  When these words into itself it had absorbed.
The speech of the one, the look the other had
  Filled me with longing that their names I knew,
  And question of them, mixt with prayers, I made.
Wherefore the spirit that first spoke, now anew
  Began to speak: "Thou wouldest that I agree
  To indulge thee in what for me thou wilt not do.   78
But since God wills that his grace shine through thee
  So greatly, I will not baulk thee, and therefore
    learn   80
  That Guy del Duca it is whom thou dost see.
My blood with envy did so hotly burn,
  That did I see joy in a face upleap
  Thou wouldst have seen my face all livid turn.

---

58. "Thy grandson": the nephew of Rinieri, Fulcieri da Calboli,
who had many citizens put to death.
78. Dante has avoided giving his name.

Of my own sowing such the straw I reap.
  O human people, why the heart confide
  There where fruition ousteth partnership?   *87*
This is Rinier, the glory and the pride
  Of the house of Calboli, which house hath lacked
  All sign of heir to his virtue since he died.   90
Nor only is his blood beggared, in that tract
  'Twixt Po and Reno and sea and mountain's foot *92*
  Of the good, truth and gentle ways exact,
For all within those borders the rank shoot
  Of poison smothers, so that too late may
  The tiller come, that canker to uproot.
Good Lizio, Hal Mainardi, where are they?   *97*
  Guy di Carpigna and Traversaro, where?
  O Romagnuols all bastardized today!
When in Bologna shall a Fabbro appear?   100
  In Faenza a Bernardin di Fosco arise
  Again, fair scion for small plant to bear?
Marvel not, Tuscan, if tears fill mine eyes
  When Guy of Prata I remember, and
  Ugolin d'Azzo, and our friendship's ties,
Frederic Tignoso and his comrade band,
  The Traversari and Anastagi, names
  Extinguished, houses heirless and dismanned,
The ladies and the knights, the toils and games
  Which love and courtesy made our delight   110
  There where our hearts now wickedness inflames.
Why, O Brettinoro, didst not vanish quite,   *112*
  Since out of thee thy family is gone
  With much folk, to escape their guilt by flight?

---

87. *Upon earthly possessions.*
92. *" 'Twixt Po and Reno . . .": Romagna.*
97-107. *In these lines are enumerated sundry noble and famous citizens of Romagna in the twelfth and thirteenth centuries.*
112. *"Brettinoro" was the birthplace of Guido [Guy] del Duca.*

Bagnacaval does well, to bear no son;   *115*
  But Castracaro ill, and Conio worse,
  Since such Counts it hath troubled to breed on.
Well shall do the Pagani when their curse,   *118*
  The Demon, quits them; not that clean of shame
  May ever be their record that endures.   120
O Ugolin de' Fantolin, thy name   *121*
  Is safe, expecting no inheritor
  To blacken and by debasing it defame.
But go thy way now, Tuscan, for far more
  To weep than speak comforteth now my heart,
  So hath our converse wrung it to the core."
That those dear spirits heard our steps depart
  We knew, and therefore by their silence they
  Emboldened us, sure of the path, to start.
When we were left alone, bent on our way,   130
  Like lightning when it cuts the air in twain
  We heard a voice that smote against us say:
"By whoever findeth me shall I be slain"   *133*
  And fled, like thunder in a dying peal,
  If suddenly the cloud bursts with its rain.
And when our ears a truce from it could feel
  The second lo! with such a crash and groan
  Came, as the thunder upon thunder's heel:
"I am Aglauros who was turned to stone."   *139*
  Then I, to press close to the Poet, stept   140
  With one foot backward and not forward thrown.
Now all around the air in quiet slept;

115-117. "Bagnacavallo" *is a little place near Ravenna. The counts
  of Castrocaro (near Forlì) and Conio (near Imola) were numerous
  and ill-famed.*
118. "The Pagani," *a noble family of Faenza,* "shall do well" *to get
  no more sons,* "when their demon," *Maghinardo, shall have died.*
121. "Ugolino" *was a worthy gentleman of Faenza.*
133. *The first of the examples of envy is that of Cain.*
139. *Because she was envious of her sister Herse.*

And he was saying: "That was the hard bit
By which within his bounds man should have kept.
But ye the bait seize, so that the hook in it
Of the old Enemy draws you to his side,
And bridle or lure therefore avails no whit.
The heavens call to you and around you glide
In circle, and their eternal beauties show,
And with earth only is your eye satisfied, 150
Wherefore he who discerns all battereth you."

Canto XV

*It is now afternoon, when the poets are dazzled by
the brightness of an angel who points out to them
the next ascent. As they climb upward, Dante re-
minds Virgil of something which had perplexed
him in Guido del Duca's speech; and Virgil ex-
plains the difference between partnership in mate-
rial goods and partnership in spiritual goods. They
reach the third terrace, and Dante is caught up in
an ecstatic vision and sees examples of gentleness
(the Virgin Mary, Pisistratus, St. Stephen). He
comes to himself, and the two continue their jour-
ney, till they encounter a dark smoke which sur-
rounds them and robs them of light and air.*

As MUCH as, 'twixt the third hour and the day's 1
Beginning, is apparent of the sphere
For ever moving as a child that plays,

1-6. *It was three hours before sunset, or mid-afternoon.*

So much of the sun's course did now appear,
   Toward evening drawn, to be untravelled yet;
   And it was vespers there and midnight here.
The middle of the nose the full beam met,
   For we had made the mount's encirclement
   So far that due West now our feet were set,
When heavy on my brows seemed to be bent   10
   A brilliance such as ne'er before opprest;
   And the untold things were an astonishment.
Wherefore I raised my hands up to the crest
   Of the eyebrows, and so made the sun less great,
   Whereby was the light's overflow comprest.
As when from mirror or from water, straight
   The ray will in the opposed direction start,   *17*
   Ascending by the self-same law as that
Which it descends by, and as far depart
   From a stone's falling line in equal space,   20
   As proveth both experiment and art,
Even so reflected light upon my face
   Shining in front of me appeared to smite,
   Wherefore my eyes were swift themselves to abase.
"Sweet Father, what is that from which my sight,"
   I said, "I cannot serviceably fend,
   And which seems toward us to be moving bright?"
"Needs not," he answered, "wonder to expend
   That the heavenly retinue should dazzle still.
   He is sent, who comes to invite us to ascend.   30
Soon shall it be that when these things reveal
   Themselves, not trouble but a joy 'twill stir
   As great as nature fitteth thee to feel."
When we had reached the blessed Messenger,
   With a glad voice he called us: "Hither come
   To a stair far less steep than the others are."

---

17. A ray of light is reflected upward at the angle at which it
descends.

Already, thence departed, up we clomb.
 Beati Misericordes was sung now   *38*
 Behind, and "Joy thou, that hast overcome."
My Master and I together alone, we two,   *40*
 Were mounting, and I thought not to let slip
 Profit his words might on the way bestow,
And turned to him with question on my lip:
 "What meant the spirit of the Romagnuol
 Speaking of 'ousting' and of 'partnership'?" *45*
Then he to me: "He knows the hurt to his soul
 Of his chief vice; let it not then surprise
 If he reprove it, so to cause less dole.
For in as much as all your longing hies
 Where partnership diminisheth the share, *50*
 'Tis Envy moves the bellows for your sighs.
But did the soul's love of the highest sphere *52*
 Wrench upward your desire, then would not ye
 Within your bosom entertain that fear.
For by so many more saying 'Ours' there be,
 So much the more of good doth each possess,
 And more of love burns in that sanctuary."
"From being satisfied I fast not less
 But more," said I, "than had I question spared,
 And in my mind doubt doth the more increase. *60*
How can it be that out of a good shared
 More numerous possessors more shall win
 Of wealth than if a few had it in ward?"
And he to me: "Because thou still dost pin
 Merely upon terrestrial things thy wit,
 From very light thou drawest darkness in.
The Good ineffable and infinite
 That is on high so runneth unto love

---

38. *Matt.* 5:7: *"Blessed are the merciful."*
45. *The words of Guido del Duca in Canto* xiv, 87.
52. *"The highest sphere" is the Empyrean, the abode of God.*

As a beam comes to a body that is bright.
So much it gives as warmth it findeth of,　　　　　70
　　So that, how far so-ever love be poured,
　　The eternal goodness doth its best improve.
And the more people on high have that accord,
　　The more to love well are there, and more love is,
　　And mirror-like 'tis given and restored.
If my discourse thy hunger not appease,
　　Thou shalt see Beatrice; she thy craving thought
　　Shall free from this and all perplexities.
Strive only that the five wounds be razed out
　　Soon from thy forehead, like to the other twain,　　80
　　Which by our sorrowing are to healing brought."
I was nigh saying: "Thou content'st me," when
　　I saw me on the circle above to be,
　　So that my eyes' wish made me mute again.
There seemed I in a vision of ecstasy　　　　　85
　　On a sudden to be caught up from my feet,
　　And in a temple many a one to see,
And at the entry a lady, with the sweet
　　Gesture of a mother, saying, "O my son!
　　Why, son, didst thou thy parents thus entreat?　　90
Behold, thy father and I about have gone
　　To seek thee sorrowing"; and as there she stopt,
　　That which appeared first, disappeared: whereon
Appeared to me another woman, who dropt　　・　94
　　Those waters down her cheek which grief has stored
　　And which from indignation spring abrupt,

70-72. *The divine love runs to meet the aspiring human affection
and, uniting with it, doubles its ardor and its joy.*
85-88. *The examples of gentleness appear as ecstatic visions. The
first represents the infant Jesus, who is found in the temple dis-
puting with the doctors.*
94. *"Another woman": the wife of Pisistratus, ruler of Athens, en-
raged because a young man has dared to embrace their daughter.*

Saying: "If thou art of the city lord
  For whose name did the gods such strife declare
  And whence all knowledge sparkling is outpoured,
Avenge thee of those presumptuous arms that dare   100
  Embrace our daughter, O Pisistratus!"
  And the lord seemed with a benignant air
To answer her, serene and courteous:
  "What shall we do to him who works us ill
  If he who loves us is condemned by us?"
Then saw I people inflamed by angry will
  Slaying a youth with stones, and each one bade   *107*
  The other on, crying aloud "Kill, Kill!"
And him I saw with body already weighed
  Down unto earth by death, yet not the less   110
  Ever of his eyes gates unto heaven he made,
Praying the high Lord in such agonies
  With that look which doth pity's door undo
  That he forgive his persecutors this.
When my soul came back to the outward view
  Of what true things are outside of its thought,
  I recognized my errors not untrue.
My leader, who could see my body all wrought
  Like a man shaking sleep off from his limbs,
  Said, "What doth ail, that thou art so distraught   120
And more than half a league with eye that swims
  And legs that stagger comest on thy way
  Like him whom wine or heavy sleep bedims?"
"Sweet Father mine, listen, and if I may"
  I said, "I'll tell thee what I saw appear
  When from me thus my legs were taken away."
And he: "Had'st thou a hundred masks to wear
  Over thy face, thou couldest not but choose

---

107. For the stoning of St. Stephen, the first Christian martyr, see
Acts 7: 54-60.

To show me thy hid thoughts, how small so'er.
What thou saw'st was that thou might'st not excuse 130
Thy heart from letting in the water of peace
Which the eternal fount ever renews.
I asked 'What ails?' not with the thought that is
In him who asks and looks but with the eye,
Which, when the body is senseless, nothing sees.
I asked, that I thy feet might fortify.
So must be spurred the laggard, ever slow
The waking hour's return to profit by."
We through the evening journeying strove to throw
Our strained eyes as far forward as we could, 140
Against the beams of evening shining low.
And lo, by little and little a smoky cloud
Rolled itself onward toward us, dark as night,
And every place of refuge overflowed:
This robbed us of the pure air and of sight.

Canto XVI

The poets are now on the terrace of the Wrathful, who move in a dark cloud of stinging smoke and are heard praying for peace and mercy. One of the spirits questions them, and Dante enters into talk with him: He is Mark Lombardo, and he mourns over the corruption of the times; which prompts Dante to ask if this is due to the stars or innate human depravity. Mark replies that the stars have their influence, but man has free will; and he attributes the degeneracy of the age to the usurpation by the Papacy of the temporal power.

GLOOM of Hell, gloom of night uncomforted
　　By any star beneath a niggard sky
　　Darkened by cloud as far as cloud could spread,
Made not so thick a curtain to the eye
　　Nor to the feel such rasping frieze as made
　　The smoke that there was all our canopy.
For the eyelids to keep open in vain essayed;
　　Wherefore my Escort, trusty and sage, drew close
　　And offered me his shoulder for my aid.
Just as behind his guide a blind man goes   10
　　Lest he should stray or stumble against aught
　　Whereby he might be hurt, or life ev'n lose,
So through the bitter and foul air I fought,
　　Listening to my leader, who still would say
　　"See from my side that thou be parted not."
I heard voices; and each one seemed to pray
　　For peace and for compassion on their sin
　　To the Lamb of God who taketh sins away.
Still *Agnus Dei* did their prayers begin:
　　One word was in them all, one tone rang clear,   20
　　So that entire concord they seemed to win.
"O Master, are those spirits that I hear?"
　　Said I; and he: "Rightly dost thou conceive.
　　The knot of anger are they loosening here."
"Now who art thou who com'st our smoke to cleave
　　And speakest of us just as if still time
　　Thou didst divide and by the calend live?"   27
This by a voice was spoken. "Answer him,"
　　My Master therefore said, "and ask if he
　　Will tell us if from this point we should climb."   30
And I: "O creature that art cleansing thee

---

27. "By the calend": *after the mortal way. The calends was the first
day of each month.*

To return fair to him that made thee, thou
Shalt hear a marvel if thou follow me."
"As far I'll follow as our laws allow,"
    It answered, "and if sight the smoke confounds,
    Hearing in lieu of it unites us now."
Then began I: "With these same swathing bonds
    Which death undoes, I journey up the mount
    And did come hither through Hell's gasping wounds.
And if God hath so filled me from his fount   40
    Of grace, and wills that I behold his court
    After a fashion beyond latter wont,
Hide not from me who before death thou wert,
    But tell me, and tell me if for the pass I am
    Set rightly; and let thy words our way escort."
"I was of Lombardy; Mark was my name;
    I knew the world, and that worth did I love
    At which now no one bendeth bow to aim.
For mounting up 'tis straight on thou must move."
    Thus answered he, and added: "I pray thee   50
    That thou for me pray when thou art above."
And I: "By faith that binds my loyalty
    To thee, that which thou askest I will do:
    But a doubt bursts me unless I get me free.
'Twas simple at first, now twofold doth it grow   55
    By this thy judgment, certifying, both
    Here and elsewhere, that which I couple it to.
The world is utterly despoiled, in truth,
    Of all virtue, as thou too dost complain:
    Big with iniquity under cloud it goeth.   60
But make to me the cause, I pray thee, plain,
    That I may see it and to others show;

---

55. When the doubt was first suggested to him by the words of
Guido del Duca in Canto xiv, 37-41, it was "simple"; now it is
"twofold."

    For one sets it in Heaven, and one in man."   63
First a deep sigh that grief strained to one "Oh"
    Broke from his breast; then he began: "Brother,
    The world is blind, and of it truly art thou.
Ye, who are living, every cause refer
    Up to the stars, as if with them they swept
    All absolutely, and naught could fate deter.
Were it so, the free choice in you had slept   70
    Annulled, nor were it justice that ye still
    For good have had joy and for evil wept.
The stars do prompt the motions ye fulfil;
    I say not all, but even suppose it said,   74
    A light is given you to know good and ill,
And Free will which, though oft discomfited
    In its first battlings with the stars' decree,
    Wins in the end all, be it but rightly bred.
To a mightier power, a nobler nature, ye
    Being free are subject; which creates the mind
    In you that the stars hold not in their fee.
And therefore if the world now strayeth blind,
    In you the cause is; track and seek it there,
    And I shall be thy spy, this cause to find.
From the hands of him who wistly loves her, ere   85
    She is, forth comes, like a child frolicking
    That now weeps and now laughs without a care,
The little, the innocent soul that knows nothing
    Saving that, sprung from a Creator's joy,
    She goes to her own joy and there loves to cling.   90
Ravished at first with good that's but a toy,
    Still runs she back bewitcht to the fond bower

---

63. "Heaven" *means the stars, i.e., planetary influence.*
74. *The stars initiate only bodily impulses; they have no control over the will.*
85-86. *The subject of* "forth comes" *is* "soul" *in line* 88. *He* "who wistly loves her" *is God.*

If no guide turn her from delight's decoy.
Needs then that law bridle her wayward hour
　　And that she have a king who may far-off
　　Discern of the true city at least the tower.
The laws are: but what hand puts them to proof?　97
　　None; since the shepherd, going before, may chew
　　The cud, but hath not the divided hoof.
Wherefore the people, who see their guide pursue　100
　　What only his greedy appetite hath craved,
　　Feed upon that nor seek for pastures new.
The evil guidance whereto 'tis enslaved
　　Thou seest is that which doth the world corrode,
　　Not nature, that in you may be depraved.
Rome, that the good world made for man's abode,
　　Was used to have two suns, by which were clear
　　Both roads, that of the world and that of God.
One hath put out the other; to crozier
　　Is joined the sword; and going in union
　　Necessity compels that ill they fare,　110
Since, joined now, neither fears the other one.
　　Consider the ear of corn, if thou still doubt;
　　For every plant is by its fruiting known.
In the land where Adige and Po spread out　115
　　Their waters, before Frederick met with feud
　　Were worth and courtesy not vainly sought.
Now may pass there without solicitude
　　Whosoever hath desisted out of shame
　　To speak with good men or on them intrude.　120
True, there are still three elders in whose name

97-108. *The laws still exist, but there is no one left to execute them, since the Papacy has usurped the imperial power and joined the sword of worldly supremacy to the crozier of ecclesiastical authority. It was not so in the old days, when Rome was the seat of two brother monarchs—the Pope and the Emperor.*

115-116. *Lombardy. In 1300 Italy had known no Imperial guidance since the death of Frederick II, fifty years before.*

The old age reproves the new, and time seems hard
  Ere to a better life God carry them,
Conrad of Palazzo and the good Gerard
  And Guy of Castel, who is better styled
  'The guileless Lombard' in the Frenchmen's word.
Henceforward say that Rome's church, having willed
  Confusion of two rules, falls in a slough,
  And both she and her burden are defiled." ⸺
"O my Mark," answered I, "well reasonest thou;   130
  And why the sons of Levi were removed   131
  From the inheritance I see well now.
But what Gerard is this thou hast so approved
  For sample of the extinct race, by whose side
  The barbarous generation goes reproved?"
"Either thy speech deceives me," he replied,
  "Or thou dost tempt me, who in Tuscan tone
  Knowledge of the good Gerard hast denied.
By other surname he's to me unknown,   139
  Except his daughter Gaia give him it.   140
  Now God be with you, I come no further on.
See, raying through the smoke, now waxeth white
  The gleaming of the sun; the angel is there:
  Ere I be seen of him, I must be quit."
So he turned back, nor more from me would hear.

---

131. The "sons of Levi," or Levites, are the priests.
139. If any other epithet than "good" is needed to identify this
  Gerardo da Camino (who was captain general of Treviso), the only
  suitable one is suggested by the name of his daughter "Gaia," or
  "joyous."

Canto XVII

---

*Dante gets clear of the smoke, as the sun is setting.
And again he falls into a trance, in which appear
examples of wrath (Procne, Haman, Amata) and is
waked by an angel who shows the way of ascent to
the next terrace. The poets mount and reach the
terrace, but cannot go farther, because it is night.
Dante asks Virgil what sin is purged there. It is the
sin of spiritual Sloth. Virgil takes the opportunity
to expound the system of Purgatory. In the three
circles through which they have passed are pun-
ished Pride, Envy, and Anger—all perversions of
love or desire. Above, in three circles, are those
whose desire for temporal goods was in excess and
whose sins were Avarice, Gluttony, and Lust.*

READER, if in the mountains you have been
   Caught ever in a cloud, through which you saw
   Not otherwise than moles do through the skin,   *3*
Remember, when the vapours thick and raw
   Begin to thin themselves, how the sun's sphere
   Enters among them weakly as they withdraw,
And easily will your fancy make appear
   How I was by the sun revisited
   That now unto his setting was full near.
So, measuring with my master's faithful tread   *10*
   My steps, from such a cloud did I come out

---

3. According to Aristotle, the eye of the mole is covered by a mem-
brane which prevents it from seeing

To rays on the low shore already dead.
O Fantasy, that dost at times so rout
    Our senses that a man stays negligent
    Although a thousand trumpets sound about,
Who moves thee, if senses naught to thee present?
    There moves thee a light which of itself is shaped
    In heaven, or by a will wherefrom 'tis sent.
The sin of her who from her form escaped   *19*
    Into the bird which most delights to sing,   *20*
    Printed its traces on my fancy rapt;
And here within its own imagining
    So closeted my mind was, it could then
    Receive the imprint of no outer thing.
Within my lofty fancy I next saw rain
    One crucified, upon whose visage showed,   *26*
    In the act of dying so, a fierce disdain.
Beside him great Ahasuerus stood,
    Esther his wife, and Mordecai, he
    Who in speech and act was incorruptly good.   *30*
And as this image broke spontaneously,
    Like to a bubble when it findeth fail
    The water, under which it came to be,
Rose in my vision, making grievous wail,
    A maiden, saying: "Queen, why didst thou choose *35*
    To become naught, letting thy wrath prevail?
Thou hast slain thyself, Lavinia not to lose;
    Me now thou hast lost; I am she that sadly cries,
    Mother, for no death but thy life's dark close."
As when strikes of a sudden on closed eyes   *40*
    The day's new light, and sleep breaks at a blow

---

19. "The sin of her . . .": *Progne, who became a nightingale.*
26. *The "one crucified" is Haman, minister of King Ahasuerus.*
35. *The "Queen" is Amata, wife of King Latinus, who hanged her-*
    self on hearing a premature report of the death of her daughter
    Lavinia's intended husband.

And broken flutters ere it wholly dies,
Did my imagination even so
    Collapse, soon as a light smote on my face
    Greater by far than is our wont to know.
I turned me to discover where I was,
    When a voice saying: "Here is the ascent"
    Caused every other thought from me to pass.
And this made my desire so vehement
    To see who it was that spoke, as longing is   50
    Which only face to face can be content.
But as the sun which presses on our eyes
    And by excess veileth his form, so here
    All of their virtue failed my faculties.
"This is a heavenly spirit that, without prayer
    On our part, up the path directeth us
    And in his own light hideth himself there.
He deals with us as with himself one does;
    For he who awaits the prayer and sees the need
    Already is with the unkind ones who refuse.   60
Now let us match our feet to such God-speed
    And hasten, ere the dark come, to ascend:
    After, we could not, till day dawn, proceed."
Thus spoke my Leader, and we turned to bend
    Our footsteps to the rising of a stair.
    And soon as the first step I had attained
Near me I felt as 'twere a wing in the air
    And my face fanned, and *"Beati,"* I heard,   68
    "Pacifici," who evil wrath forswear."
Now far above us were the rays upreared,   70
    The last rays, whereupon the night ensues;
    So that the stars on many sides appeared.
Why, O my virtue, dost thou me disuse?
    I said within me, for I felt the power

68-69. Matt. 5:9. *"Blessed are the peacemakers."*

Of my legs fail me, being put in truce.
We stood where the steps mounted up no more
    And remained fixt, just as a ship embayed
    And onward driven is stranded on the shore.
And listening for a little while I stayed,
    If aught in the new circle I might hear;   80
    Then turned me to my Master round, and said:
"O sweet my Father, tell what trespass here
    Within this present circle is purified?
    If our feet halt, let thy speech persevere."
And he to me: "Love of the good, that did   85
    The scantling of its duty, is here restored:
    Here the ill-slackened oar again is plied.
But that unto thy reason all be bared,
    Turn unto me thy mind, and thou shalt get
    From our delay some good fruit for reward."   90
"Nor creature nor creator ever yet,
    My son, was without love," continued he,
    "Natural, or of the mind: thou knowest it.
The natural always is from error free;
    But the other may, through a bad object, err
    By too much force or its deficiency.
While to the prime good 'tis resolved to steer,   97
    And in the second keepeth measure due,
    Of sinful joy it cannot be the spur.
But should it swerve to evil, or pursue   100
    The good with too strong or too feeble intent,
    The creature to his Maker is untrue.
Hence may'st thou understand how love is meant
    To be in you the seed of virtue pure
    And of all works deserving chastisement.
Now, since love's gaze nothing can ever lure

85-86. *The sin punished is sloth.*
97-98. *"The prime good": heavenly blessings; "the second": worldly blessings.*

From weal of that which is its nature's seat,
All things are from self-hatred made secure.
And since none can conceive that separate
From God, and self-subsisting, any stay,   110
Him, its first cause, his creature cannot hate.
If rightly this division I assay,
Remains that the ill loved is other's woe;
And this love springs in three modes from your
          clay.   114
There is, who through his neighbour's overthrow
Hopes to excel, and only for that cause
Longs that he may from greatness be brought low.
There is, who fears power, favour, fame to lose
Because another mounts; wherefore his lot
So irks, he loves the opposite to choose.   120
And there is, who through injury grows so hot
From shame, with greed of vengeance he is burned,
And so must needs another's ill promote.
This three-formed love down under us is mourned.
Now would I have thee the other comprehend,
Which to the good speeds, but with order
          spurned.   126
Each one confusedly doth apprehend
A longed-for good, wherein the mind may rest;
And therefore each one strives to attain that end.
If laggard be the love that makes the quest   130
For sight of it or winning it, this zone
Chastises you therefor, the sin confest.
Another good there is which blesses none.
'Tis not felicity, 'tis not the Good
Essence, of all good, fruit and root alone.
The love that this good hath too hotly wooed

---

114. "In three modes": *the vices of pride, of envy, and of anger.*
126. "With order spurned": *too sluggishly toward heavenly good,*
too eagerly toward worldly good.

Is mourned above us in three circles: how
'Tis reckoned as tripartite, since I would
Thou seek it out thyself, I tell not now."

Canto XVIII

---

*Dante, still not satisfied, asks Virgil to explain more
fully the nature of love, to which his argument had
reduced every good work and also its opposite.
Virgil discourses on this theme, and solves Dante's
further doubt as to what moral merit and demerit
consist in, explaining the function of free will. It
is now near midnight, and the moon has appeared
from behind the mountain. Dante begins to drowse,
when he is startled by a throng of spirits who over-
take them, running at full speed. These are the
Slothful, expiating their sins by the hurry of their
zeal. Two of them run in front, proclaiming ex-
amples of zeal. A spirit who was Abbot of San
Zeno in Verona tells the poets to follow and they
will find the passage upward. He condemns Albert
della Scala for appointing his depraved son to the
abbacy; then rushes on. Last come two shades, pro-
claiming examples of sloth. Dante, again drowsy,
falls asleep.*

THE profound Teacher of his argument
    Had made an end, and with an earnest look
    Searched in my face if I appeared content;
And I, whom a new thirsting overtook,
    Kept silent outwardly but said within:
    "Perhaps with too much questioning I provoke."

But that most truthful Father, who had seen
   The wish too timid to disclose its thought,
   By speaking heartened my speech to begin.
Wherefore I: "Master, clearly do I note   10
   (So quickened is my vision in thy light)
   All that thy discourse hath described or taught.
Therefore, sweet Father, make more explicit
   To me, I pray thee, what this love is, whence
   Thou draw'st each good deed and its opposite."
"Direct the keen eyes of the intelligence
   Toward me," he said, "and the error thou wilt prove
   Of those, blind, who of leading make pretence.
The mind which is created apt to love,
   Soon as by pleasure it is stirred to act,   20
   To every pleasing thing is quick to move.
Your apprehension from a thing of fact
   Draweth an image, shown to the inward view,
   So that perforce it doth the mind attract.   24
And if, being turned, it is inclined thereto,
   The inclination is love: nature it is,
   Which is through pleasure knit within ye anew.
Then, just as fire to the upper region flies
   By reason of its form which, where it best
   Endureth in its matter, is born to rise,   30
Even so the mind is with desire possessed,
   Which is a motion of spirit, and cannot be,
   Till the thing loved rejoiceth it, at rest.
Now how the truth is hidden thou canst see
   Plainly, from all those people who aver   35
   That each love in itself is praiseworthy

24-29. *The senses convey to the mind the impression of some at-
tractive object in the material world; the understanding then de-
velops this impression in such a way that it is brought to the notice
of the will.*

35. *"Those people . . .": the Epicureans, who overlook the fact that
the object of desire may be evil.*

Because perhaps its matter may appear
   To be good always; but not every seal
   Is good, however good the pressed wax were."
"Thy words and my wit following at their heel"   40
   I answered him, "do love to me disclose,
   But the more big with doubt this makes me feel;
For if love from without is offered us,
   And with no other foot the soul proceed,
   No merit it is if straight or not she goes."
And he to me: "So far as reason plead
   Can I instruct thee; beyond that point, wait
   For Beatrice; for faith is here thy need.
Every substantial form which, separate   49
   From matter, is knitted up with it, doth own   50
   A faculty peculiar and innate,
Which only in its activity is known
   Nor save by its effect manifested,
   As a plant's life is by the green leaves shown.
Therefore man knows not either whence is bred
   The understanding of first hints of thought
   Nor the impulse to desire's first objects led,
Which are in you as the instinct that hath taught
   Bees to make honey; and this original bent
   Desert of praise or blame admitteth not.   60
Now, that with this will all wills else consent,
   The power that judges is inborn in you
   And ought to guard the threshold of assent.
This is the principle that holds the clue

49-62. *In scholastic language, a "substantial form" means the particu-
lar basic principle, which gives an object its separate existence; and
the substantial form of mankind is the intellective soul, whose
"faculty peculiar" is an instinct which comprises innate knowledge
and the inborn disposition to love. Hence we are not aware of the
source of our natural inclination toward all that seems good. Judg-
ment ("the power that judges") tells us which desires are right
and which are wrong.*

To merit in you, according as it can
   Good loves and guilty garner and winnow true.
Those reasoners who sought the Founder's plan
   Have recognized this inborn liberty,
   And therefore Ethic have they left to man.
Wherefore suppose that from necessity   70
   Arises every love that in you stirs,
   You have the power to curb it in your fee.
The noble virtue Beatrice avers
   To be Free Will, and therefore look that thou
   Have this in mind if she thereof converse."
The Moon, almost to midnight moving slow,
   Made the stars seem to us more rare and wan,
   Shaped like a bucket that were all aglow,
As 'gainst the heaven upon those paths she ran
   Which the sun kindles when the man of Rome   80
   Sees him at set 'twixt Sard and Corsican;
And since that noble shade, because of whom
   Pietola is more famed than Mantua town,   83
   Had freed me of that which was so burdensome,
I now, who from the questions I had sown
   Had reaped his candid and clear argument,
   Stood like a man who wanders, drowsy grown.
But suddenly this drowsiness was rent
   From off me by a throng of people, who
   Behind our shoulders were to us-ward bent.   90
As once Ismenus and Asopus knew   91
   By night a fury and trampling down their side,
   If but the Thebans did to Bacchus sue,
Such forms, by what of them I now descried,
   Were coming round that circle, forward bowed
   With speed, whom good will and a just love ride.
Soon were they on us, because that great crowd

---

83. Virgil was born at Pietola, near Mantua.
91. "Ismenus" and "Asopus" are rivers in Boeotia.

Moved at a run, as each the other chased;
   And two in front with weeping cried aloud:
"Mary to the hill country ran in haste,   100
   And Caesar, that Ilerda be subdued,
   To Spain, when he had stabbed Massilia, raced."
"On, on!" the others cried as they pursued.
   "Through faint love O let not a moment lapse,
   That grace by zeal for good may be renewed."
"O people, whose present ardour doth perhaps
   Redress the loitering ways begotten by
   Lukewarmness in you that well-doing saps,
This one who lives, and surely I do not lie,
   Would mount, if but the sun's light be restored.   110
   Tell us then where the opening may be nigh."
These were the words addressed them by my Lord.
   Then spoke one of those spirits: "Where we go,
   Follow, and of the passage be assured.
We with desire to move are smitten so
   That stay we cannot; therefore pardon us
   If as discourtesy this our duty show.
Verona's Abbot of San Zeno I was
   Under the rule of Barbarossa brave,
   Of whom Milan still talks and says Alas!   *120*
There's one with foot already in the grave
   Who soon shall rue that monastery's case
   And will lament that there to power he clave,
Because his son, in his whole body base,   *124*
   And worse in mind, and his birth also bad,
   He has set up there in the true shepherd's place."
I know not if more words or none he had,
   So far already he had pressed beyond;
   But this I heard and to retain was glad.

---

120. *The Emperor Barbarossa destroyed Milan in* 1162.
124. *"His son": Giuseppe, the son of Albert della Scala (see the Argument).*

He who in all need was my succour fond   130
   Bade me to turn and "See, these two," he said.
   "Come biting at the sin of sloth's despond."
In rear of all they cried: "The folk were dead   *133*
   For whom the sea divided and made way
   Ere Jordan saw those who inherited.
And they who chose not to endure the day
   To the last labours of Anchises' son
   To life inglorious gave their souls away."
Then when those shades so far from us had run
   That they could now be seen no more, arose   140
   A new thought in me and then another one,
And many and divers others sprang from those,
   And I so wandered in and out of them
   That all the wandering made mine eyes to close,
And thinking was transmuted into dream.

133-138. *All the Hebrews who had crossed the Red Sea perished,
except Caleb and Joshua. Some of Aeneas's companions, weary of
hardship, stayed behind in Sicily.*

Canto XIX

---

*In a dream Dante has a vision of the Siren (sym-
bolizing worldly enticements). A lady from heaven
appears in this dream; and Virgil, at her bidding,
exposes the Siren's real foulness. Dante is roused by
Virgil, the sun having now risen, and an angel
speeds them up the passage to the fifth terrace,
where are the souls of the avaricious and the prodi-
gal, lying prone on the ground. Virgil asks the way,
and is answered by one who proves to be Pope
Adrian V. He tells them that he was possessed by*

*Avarice till he reached the highest office, and then
turned to God. Dante kneels, to show his reverence,
but is told by the spirit to rise.*

In that hour when the heat of day no more
    Can warm the Moon's cold influence, and it dies
    O'ercome by the earth or whiles by Saturn's power;

When geomancers see in the East arise   *4*
    Their Greater Fortune, ere the dawn be come,
    By a path which not long dark before it lies,

In dream came to me a woman stuttering dumb,
    With squinting eyes and twisted on her feet,
    With deformed hands and cheeks of pallor numb.

I gazed on her; and as the sun's good heat   10
    Comforteth cold limbs weighed down by the night,
    So did my look make her tongue nimbly feat,

And straightened her and set her all upright
    In short time, and her ruined countenance made
    Into the colour which is love's delight.

Soon as her loosened tongue came to her aid,
    She began singing, so that for its sake
    From her voice hardly had my hearing strayed.

"I am," she said, "the sweet Siren, who make
    Mariners helpless, charmed in the mid-sea;   20
    Such pleasure in my music do men take.

I turned Ulysses from his wandering, he
    So loved my song; and who with me hath found
    Home, seldom quits, so glad is he of me."

Her lips were not yet closed upon the sound
    When came a lady in whom was holiness
    Prompt to my side, that other to confound.

---

4. "Geomancers" foretold the future by means of figures constructed
on points that were distributed by chance. One of their figures,
called "Greater Fortune," resembled a constellation.

"O Virgil, Virgil, tell me who is this?"
   Indignantly she said; and straight he went
   With eyes fixt on that honest one, to seize   30
The other, and when her garments he had rent,
   He laid her open and showed her belly creased,
   That waked me with the stench that forth it sent.
I turned my eyes, and Virgil said: "At least
   Thrice have I called thee; up, let us begone!
   Find we the opening where thou enterest."
I raised me up; high day now overshone
   The holy mount and filled each winding ledge.
   We went, and at our back was the new sun.
I followed him, like one who is the siege   40
   Of heavy thought that droops his forehead, when
   He makes himself the half-arch of a bridge.
And I heard: "Come! Here is the pass"; spoken
   With so much loving kindness in the tone
   As is not heard in this our mortal pen.
With outspread wings that shone white as a swan
   He who thus spoke guided our journeying
   Upward between the two walls of hard stone.
Stirring his plumes, he fanned us with his wing
   And named *qui lugent* blessed, for that they   50
   Shall dispense consolation, like a king.
We both had passed the angel a little way
   When, "What now ails thee that thine eyes are so
   Fixt on the ground?" my Guide began to say.
And I: "In such misgiving do I go
   From a strange dream which doth my mind possess
   So that the thought I cannot from me throw."
"Sawest thou," he said, "that ancient sorceress
   For whom alone the mount above us wails?   59
   Sawest thou how man obtains from her release?   60

---

50. "Qui lugent": *those who mourn.*
59. "Above us": *in the three upper circles.*

Let that suffice: beat the earth down with thy heels;
   Turn thine eyes toward the lure which from his
     seat   *62*
   The Eternal King spins round with the great wheels."
As a falcon, that first gazes at his feet,
   Turns at the cry and stretches him beyond
   Where desire draws him thither to his meat,
Such I became; and far as, for one bound
   Upwards, a path is cloven through the stone,
   Such went I up to where one must go round.
Soon as I was enlarged on the fifth zone   *70*
   I saw on it a weeping multitude
   With faces to the ground all lying prone.
My spirit clave unto the dust, I could
   Hear them cry out, with sighings and laments
   So that the words hardly were understood.
"O ye chosen of God, whose punishments
   Both hope and justice make less hard to bear,
   Direct our footsteps to the high ascents."
"If from the lying prone exempt ye are,
   And wish the speediest way to be revealed,   *80*
   Keep your right hands to the outside as ye fare."
This answer to the poet, who thus appealed,
   Was made a little in front of us; therefore
   I noted, as each spoke, what was concealed.
My Lord then with my eyes I turned to implore,
   Whereat his glad sign of assent I caught
   To what my eager look was craving for.
Then, free to do according to my thought,
   I passed forward above that creature there
   Whose words before had made me of him take
     note,   *90*
Saying: "Spirit, in whom weeping ripens fair

---

62. *"The lure . . .": the uplifting influence of the revolving heavens.*
70. *This is the circle of avarice and prodigality.*

That without which one cannot turn to God,   *92*
Suspend for me awhile thy greater care.
Who thou wast, tell me, and why to earth ye are bowed,
    Face down, and if thou would'st that I should win
    Aught for thee yonder, whence I tread this road."
And he: "Why turned to Heaven our backs have been
    Thou shalt learn; but first *scias quod ego*   *98*
    Fui successor Petri. Down between
Sestri and Chiaveri waters flow   *100*
    Of a fair stream, wherefrom our old estate   *101*
    Nameth the title it vaunts most to bestow.
One month, scarce more, taught me how weighs the
        great   *103*
    Mantle on him who keeps it from the dirt,
    So that all others seem a feather's weight.
Late came the day that could my soul convert,
    But when the Roman Pastor I became,
    Thus found I life to be with lies begirt.
I saw that there the heart no peace could claim,
    Nor in that life could one mount higher: of this   *110*
    Therefore the love sprang in me to a flame.
Up to that hour I, lost in avarice,
    Was miserable, being a soul in want
    Of God; thou seëst here what my forfeit is.
Here of what avarice works is made the account,
    In purge of souls converted ere the end;
    And no more bitter penalty hath the mount.
Even as our eyes on high we would not send,
    Which only upon earthly things were cast,
    So here to earth Justice hath forced them bend.   *120*

---

92. The fruit of repentance.
98. "Know that I was a successor of Peter." *The speaker is Pope Adrian* v.
101. "A fair stream": *the Lavagna river. Adrian belonged to the Fieschi family, who were counts of Lavagna.*
103. "One month": *Adrian* v *held the papal office only for 38 days.*

As avarice turned all our works to waste
   Because it quenched our love of all goodness,
   Even so Justice here doth hold us fast,
Both hands and feet, in seizure and duress;
   And so long as the just Lord hath assigned,
   So long we lie stretched-out and motionless."
I had knelt down; to speak was in my mind;
   But he, by the mere hearing, in that pause
   Being aware that I my back inclined,
Said, "Dost thou bow thy knees? and for what
     cause?"   130
   And I to him: " 'Tis for your dignity:
   My conscience pricked me, standing as I was."
"Make straight thy legs and rise up from thy knee,
   Brother," he answered: "err not; of one Lord
   I am fellow-servant with the rest and thee.
If thou hast understood that holy chord
   The Gospel sounds which *Neque nubent* saith,   *137*
   Thou mayest perceive well why I spoke that word.
Go now, and no more tarry upon thy path,
   For thou disturb'st the tears wherewith I crave   140
   To ripen what thyself didst say of faith.
A niece yonder, Alagia named, I have,   *142*
   Good in herself, so only that our house
   Her nature by example not deprave.
She only is there to assist me with her vows."

---

137. *If thou hast interpreted* Neque nubent *("They neither marry")
in the broader sense, as meaning that earthly relations are not pre-
served in the spiritual world.*
142. *"Alagia" de' Fieschi was the daughter of Adrian's brother Nic-
colò.*

Canto XX

The souls of the avaricious are so many that Dante, to pass them, must keep close to the inner side of the cliff. And as he goes, he hears a spirit celebrating examples of poverty and generosity (The Virgin Mary, Fabricius, St. Nicholas). Questioning it, the spirit discloses that it is Hugh Capet, and denounces the greed of his descendants who sat on the throne of France. Among them were Charles I of Anjou, to whom Dante attributes the death of St. Thomas Aquinas (a now discredited tradition); Charles of Valois, who, like Charles I of Anjou, invaded Italy and brought about the triumph of the Blacks in Florence and the banishment of the Whites, including Dante: also Philip the Fair, who gave Pope Boniface VIII up to his enemies and who attacked the Order of the Templars. The spirit then tells how at night they proclaim warning examples of avarice. The poets depart, and suddenly the whole mountain quakes and a cry of "Glory to God on high" ascends on every side. Dante is awed and wonders what this may mean.

Ill fights a will against a better will;
 Wherefore against my wish, his to content,
 The sponge dipt in the water I did not fill.
Onward I moved me, and on my Leader went,
 Keeping the rock close, where a space was clear,
 As on a wall one hugs the battlement;
For those who are distilling, tear by tear
 Through the eyes the evil of the world's disease

On the other side approach the edge too near.

She-wolf of old, a curse upon thee seize,   10
    That more than any other beast hast prey,
    For none thy hollow hunger can appease.

O Heaven, whose revolutions, as men say,
    Change the condition of this world below,
    When comes he who shall drive her quite away?

Now were we going with short steps and slow
    And I with the prone shades preoccupied,
    Whom I heard piteously beweep their woe.

And so it chanced, I heard "Sweet Mary" sighed
    In front of us with so profound a moan   20
    As if a woman in her travail cried;

Continuing: "So little didst thou own,
    As one may well perceive by that poor inn
    Where thou didst lay thy sacred burden down."

"O good Fabricius," next I heard begin,   25
    "Virtue with poverty didst thou prefer
    To the possession of much wealth with sin."

These words sounded so pleasant in my ear
    That I drew further on, to be acquaint
    With that spirit whose voice I seemed to hear.   30

It spoke now of that bounty of the saint
    And of the damsels Nicholas endowed   32
    To save the honour of their youth from taint.

"O spirit that discoursest so much good,
    Tell me who thou art, and why alone," said I,
    "These worthy praises thou renew'st aloud.

Thy words shall lack not recompense on high
    If I return the now short space to tread,
    Of life which yonder to its end doth fly."

---

25. "Fabricius": the Roman consul famous for his incorruptibility.
32. St. Nicholas, on three successive nights, secretly threw into the
window of his neighbor's house enough money to provide dowries
for his three daughters.

And he: "I'll tell thee, not for any aid   **40**
  That I expect from there, but I salute
  Grace shining in thee so, ere thou art dead.
Of that malignant tree was I the root
  Wherewith all Christian lands are shadowed o'er,
  So that but rarely is plucked from it good fruit.
But if Douay, Lille, Ghent and Bruges had power,
  Not long would vengeance for the treachery wait: **47**
  From him who judgeth all, this I implore.
Hugh Capet was I in my former state.   *49*
  Of me the Philips and the Louises   **50**
  Are born, by whom France has been ruled of laté.
Son was I of a butcher of Paris:
  When the ancient kings to an end had dwindled, all
  Save one, who gave himself to the gray dress,   *54*
I found firm in my hands the reins to pull
  Of the realm's government, and such resource
  From new possessions, and of friends so full,
That to the widowed crown in time's due course
  The head of my son was promoted; whence
  The anointed brows of those inheritors.   **60**
So long as the great dowry of Provence   *61*
  Had not yet robbed of shame my dynasty,
  Small power it had, but yet did no offence.
Its rapine from that day began to ply
  Violence and fraud; and then seized for amends
  Ponthieu and Normandy and Gascony.
Charles enters Italy; in his turn he sends

---

47. *They would soon wreak vengeance on Philip the Fair, who had
conquered Flanders.*
49. *"Hugh Capet," king of France from 987 to 996, was the
founder of the Capetian line.*
54. *The last of the Carolingians became a monk.*
61-66. *"The great dowry of Provence": Charles of Anjou contrived to
marry Beatrice, heiress of Provence. The history of his reign be-
came a chronicle of crimes.*

His victim Conradin to death; thereon   68
   Thrusts Thomas back to heaven, for amends.

I see a day, soon after this is done,   70
   That brings another Charles forth out of France   71
   To make both him and his the better known.

Forth comes he, alone, without arms save the lance
   That Judas jousted with; so true his aim,
   The paunch of Florence bursts at its advance.

Thence shall he gain, not lands, but sin and shame,
   Upon himself so much the heavier
   As he the lighter reckoneth such blame.

The other, who from his ship a prisoner   79
   Came, I see sell his daughter, as pirates do   80
   With other girl-slaves, haggling over her.

O Avarice, what more have we to rue
   From thee, since thou our race didst so persuade
   That even to its own flesh it is untrue?

That future ill and past may seem outweighed,   85
   I see Alagna by the Lilies ta'en,
   And in his Vicar Christ a captive made.

I see him scorned and mocked at once again;
   I see the vinegar, the gall, renewed,
   And him 'twixt living malefactors slain.   90

I see the second Pilate's cruel mood
   Grow so insatiate that without decree
   His greedy sails upon the Temple intrude.

O my Lord, when shall I rejoice to see

68-69. *Charles of Anjou put to death Conradin, a lad of sixteen, grandson of Frederick II.*

71. *"Another Charles": Charles of Valois (see the Argument).*

79. *A third Charles—Charles II, king of Apulia—sold his young daughter Beatrice in marriage to the old Marquis of Ferrara.*

85-93. *The crowning infamy of the race shall be the seizure of Pope Boniface VIII at Anagni (Alagna) by two creatures of Philip the Fair. The fate of Christ was renewed in that of his Vicar. Then Philip, that "second Pilate," directed his "greedy sails" toward the Order of the Templars.*

The chastisement which, being hidden from us,
Makes sweet thine anger in thy secrecy?

What I was saying of that only spouse   97
Of the Holy Ghost, and which a question bred
In thee, and turned thee toward me for a gloss,

This as response to all our prayers is said   100
As long as day lasts; but when night doth fall
An opposite strain we take up in its stead.

Pygmalion's story then do we recall,   *103*
Whom gluttonous of gold, his appetite
Made traitor and thief, and parricide withal;

And avaricious Midas' wretched plight,
Which came for answer to his greedy prayer;
At which we laugh forever, as 'tis right.

Fool Achan each remembers then, who bare   *109*
The stolen spoils away, so that the pain   110
Of Joshua's wrath seems still to bite him here.

Sapphira and her husband we arraign;   *112*
We praise the hoof-kicks Heliodorus had:
And all the mount execrates in refrain

Polymnestor, who smote Polydorus dead.
Last of all cry we: 'Crassus, thou dost know;
Say, did the taste of gold make thy mouth glad?' *117*

Sometimes we talk, one loud and the other low,
According as the impulse spurreth speech
At greater or at lesser pace to go.   120

---

97. *Having replied to Dante's first question (line 35), Hugh proceeds to answer his second (line 36). Cf. Matt. 1:20: "that which is conceived in her [Mary] is of the Holy Ghost."*

103. *Pygmalion, brother of Dido, killed her husband for the sake of his wealth.*

109. *Achan, having stolen some of the spoils of Jericho, was stoned to death at Joshua's command.*

112–113. *"Her husband": Ananias (see Acts 5:1-10). "Heliodorus": see Macc. 3: 7, 25-27.*

117. *Crassus, triumvir with Caesar and Pompey, was famous for his wealth and his greed.*

The good, then, that by day we tell of each
   Not I alone rehearsed, but at that hour
   None else near did his voice so loudly pitch."
From him we had already gone before,
   And now were striving to surmount the path
   So far as was permitted to our power,
When, like a thing that falling tottereth,
   I felt the mountain tremble, and ice-cold fear
   Seized on me, as on one going to his death.
Delos quaked not so violently, I swear,   *130*
   In that time ere her nest Latona made
   Therein, the two eyes of the heavens to bear.
Then from all parts a shout my ears dismayed
   Such that the Master drew him to my side
   Saying: "While I guide thee, be not thou afraid."
Gloria in excelsis Deo they all cried,
   By what from those near by I understood,
   Whose words could through the shouting be descried.
Motionless stood we in suspended mood,
   Like to the shepherds who first heard that chant, 140
   Until the trembling ceased and naught ensued.
Then took we again the pathway pure of taint,
   Eyeing the shades which on the terrace lay,
   Returned already to their wonted plaint.
No ignorance ever fretted me to pray
   For knowledge with so troublesome a sting,
   If my remembrance go not here astray,
As then I seemed to feel while pondering;
   And, for our haste, question I ventured not,
   Nor of myself could I see anything.   150
Thus I went on, fearful and full of thought.

---

130. *Delos, before Latona took refuge there to bring forth Apollo
and Diana (sun and moon, "the two eyes of heaven"), was a wan-
dering island.*

Canto XXI

*The poets, hastening along, are overtaken by a
spirit, who greets and questions them. Virgil ex-
plains their errand, and asks the cause of the trem-
bling of the mountain. The shade explains that this
happens when a soul, feeling itself purged of its
sin, is free to rise from Purgatory. This has just
happened to himself. Virgil asks the shade who he
is, and he tells them that he is Statius the poet, and
speaks warmly of his debt to Virgil's poetry. Dante
smiles, and on further question it is revealed that
he is in Virgil's presence, and Statius does obei-
sance to the Master.*

THE natural thirst which is unquenchable
　　Save by the water the Samaritan　　　　　　　2
　　Poor woman asked the boon of at the well
Wrought on me; and now, my Leader in the van,
　　Haste urged me up the encumbered path to press,
　　And grief for the just vengeance through me ran;
And lo! as Luke for our sake witnesses
　　How Christ appeared to those two on the way,
　　Already risen out of the tomb's recess,
To us, intent on those who prostrate lay,　　　　10
　　Appeared a shade and close behind us drew;
　　Nor were we aware till first we heard it say
To us: "My brothers, God give peace to you!"

2. "The water": *the water of truth.* "The Samaritan": *see Luke
24:13-15.*

Immediately we turned; and Virgil gave
  Back unto him the sign that fits thereto,
And then began: "Into the blest conclave
  May the just court bring thee in peace up there
  Which me into eternal exile drave."
Said the other, while we strode on, "If ye are
  Shades not on high acceptable to God,   20
  Who hath led you up so far along his stair?"
My Teacher then: "If the signs traced in blood
  On this man by the angel thou hast read,
  Thou'lt see 'tis fit that he reign with the good.
But since she, who spins night and day the thread, 25
  Had not yet wholly drawn for him the skein
  For each on Clotho's distaff firmly laid,
His spirit, which is thy sister as it is mine,
  Because it sees not in our mode, could not
  Alone ascend and up the mountain win.   30
Wherefore was I fetched out of Hell's wide throat
  To attend and guide him, and I guide him still
  Beyond, as far as my lore serve his lot.
But tell us, if thou knowest, why the hill
  Shuddered but now, and why all seemed to cry
  Down to its oozy base as with one will."
Thus asking, did he thread the needle's eye
  Of my desire, and merely with the hope
  The fasting of my thirst became less dry.
That spirit began: "Naught on this sacred slope   40
  Can happen which its order overrides,
  Nor is aught suffered outside custom's scope.
Free from all variation it abides.   43
  What of itself to itself Heaven taketh here

---

25. Lachesis, the second of the three Fates, spins the thread of life,
    which Clotho prepares and Atropos cuts off.
43. Purgatory is exempt from physical change, and only spiritual
    causes operate there.

May operate as cause, and naught besides,
Since neither rain nor hail falls anywhere
  Nor snow nor any dew nor rime herein
  Higher than the three steps of the short stair.
No cloud appeareth, whether dense or thin,
  Nor lightning flash, nor Thaumas' daughter, she 50
  Who yonder oft is wont to change her scene.
Nor higher than the topmost of the three   52
  Steps that I spoke of, where are set the feet
  Of Peter's vicar, can dry vapour be.
Down lower the quaking may be little or great
  By reason of the winds in the earth that hide,
  I know not how; here quaked it never yet.
It quakes here when some soul feels purified
  So that it may stand up or upward move,
  And by such cry is it accompanied.   60
Its will alone gives of the cleansing proof,   61
  Which, all free now to change its company,
  Seizes the soul and makes it glad thereof.
It wills indeed before, but is not free
  From that desire God's justice against will
  Sets, as toward sin once, now to its penalty.
And I who have lain under these pains until
  Five hundred years and more passed, have but
     known
  Now, for the better threshold a free will.
Hence didst thou feel the earthquake, and thereon 70
  The pious spirits hear around us praise
  The Lord, and may be speed them upward soon."

---

50. "Thaumas' daughter": *Iris, the rainbow.*
52-54. "Three steps": *before the gate of Purgatory.* "Peter's vicar": *the angel at the gate.*
61-66. *A soul in Purgatory is held there only by its own conditioned will. As soon as this conditioned will, or desire, coincides with the absolute will, i.e., the eternal inclination to seek blessedness, the penitent knows that his expiation is over.*

Thus to us spoke he; and since the draught repays
    With more pleasure, the more the thirst was great,
    I could not tell how much he helped my case.
And the sage Leader: "Now I see the net
    That holds you here, and how 'tis broken, too;
    Why it quakes here, and why ye all shout elate.
May it please thee now that I be acquainted who
    Thou wast, and let thy words to me unfold   80
    Why here thou hast lain so many ages through."
"What time brave Titus, in the cause enrolled   82
    Of the highest King, avenged the wounds whence
        came
    Flowing the blood which was by Judas sold,
With the most lasting, most exalting name
    Yonder I had," replied that other one,
    "If not with faith yet, amplitude of fame.
So sweet a soul my song had, that anon
    Rome drew me from my own Toulouse away;
    And there the myrtle for my brows I won.   90
Statius the folk there name me still today.   91
    Of Thebes, then of Achilles' might, I sung,
    But fell with the second burden on the way
Seed to my ardour were the sparks that sprung
    To fire me from the flame divine that more
    Than a thousand hath with inspiration stung.
Of the Aeneid I speak, mother which bore,
    Nurse which in art trained me up; lacking it,
    To balance a drachm's weight I had not power.
To have lived when Virgil lived, I would submit   100
    Willingly in this bondage still to be

82-84. *The capture of Jerusalem by the Emperor Titus was regarded as a vengeance for the crucifixion of Christ.*

91-93. *Statius was a Latin poet of the first century of our era. Of his two great epics, the Thebaid and the Achilleid, the second is unfinished.*

A sun's course more than will my debt acquit."
These words turned Virgil with a look toward me,
   A look that silently "Be silent" said:
   But all is not done by the will's decree;
For on the passion wherefrom each is bred
   Laughter and tears follow so close that least
   In the most truthful is the will obeyed.
I barely smiled, like one whose lips attest;
   Whereat the shade was mute and in the eyes   110
   Looked at me, where the mind is most exprest,
And: "So be accomplished thy great enterprise,"
   Said he, "Why did thy face a moment gone
   From me a gleam of laughter not disguise?"
Now am I caught on both sides; by the one
   Made to be mute, by the other thus conjured
   To speak: wherefore I sigh, and am all known
Unto my master, and: "Be reassured,
   Fear not to speak," he said, "but speak and ease
   The great desire he hath to hear thy word."   120
Wherefore I: "May be that thy wonder is,
   O ancient spirit, at my smiling then.
   But thee I'll have a greater marvel seize.
This one who guides mine eyes the heights to ken
   Is that same Virgil from whose fountain stream
   Thou drankest force to sing of gods and men.
If for my smile thou suppose other theme,
   Leave it for untruth and thyself persuade,
   It was those words which thou didst speak of him."
About my Teacher's feet he would have laid   130
   His arms, and bent; but he said: "Do it not,
   Brother; thou art a shade, and see'st a shade."
And he, uprising: "Now thou knowest what
   Profound love toward thee warmeth my heart-strings
   When I our nothingness have so forgot,
Handling the shadows as substantial things."

Canto XXII

Mounting the rocky stair, at which an angel has erased another P from Dante's forehead, the three reach the sixth terrace, where Gluttony is punished. Virgil asks Statius how it was he could be guilty of avarice; and Statius explains that his was the opposite sin of prodigality, for both are expiated in the same circle; and he further explains how he became a Christian. He then asks Virgil about the fate of the ancient poets, and Virgil tells him that they are in Limbo, and some of the people of Statius' Thebaid are with them. Their talk is interrupted at sight of a tree, full of fruit, on which a fountain sprays. A voice coming out of it recites examples of temperance.

B<small>Y</small> now we had left the angel in his place,
  Him who had turned us to the sixth circle,
  Having first razed a scar from off my face,
And had proclaimed those spirits blessed who dwell
  In longing after righteousness (and this
  With *sitiunt* only his words effected well);   6
And lighter than through the other passages
  I found my body move, so that untired
  I followed the swift spirits up with ease,
When Virgil: "Love, that is by virtue fired,   10
  To fire another love did never fail,

---

6. "Sitiunt": Matt. 5:6, "Blessed are they which . . . thirst after righteousness."

If but it have shown forth the flame desired;
Wherefore from that first hour when Juvenal   *13*
   Who of thy affection brought to me report
   Came down into Hell's border among us all,
My good will toward thee hath been of such sort
   As never yet to one unseen did bind,
   So that to me now these stairs will seem short.
But tell me, and let me a friend's forgiveness find
   If my rein slacken in too great confidence,   *20*
   And talk with me henceforth in friendly kind,
How could thy breast find room for the offence
   Of avarice, when so much wisdom throve
   In thee by virtue of thy diligence?"
These words made Statius a little move
   Toward laughter at the first; then he replied:
   "Each word of thine is a dear token of love,
But often are things apparent that provide
   For doubting false material, because
   Of the true reasons that beneath them hide.   *30*
Thy asking shows me that thou didst suppose
   Me avaricious yonder; it may be
   By reason of that circle where I was.
Know then that avarice was removed from me
   Too far; and for a thousand moons the wage
   Of this excess I have paid in penalty.
And had I not set straight my pilgrimage
   When I had pondered what thou criest out,
   As if at human nature thou didst rage,
'O hallowed hunger of gold, why dost thou not   *40*
   The appetite of mortal men control?'
   To turn in the sad jousts had been my lot.
Then knew I how too far flights can cajole

---

13. The Latin poet *Juvenal* was a contemporary of Statius.
40-41. Cf. Aeneid III, 56-57: "*Quid non mortalia pectora cogis, Auri
  sacra fames?*"

The hands to squander, and I repented then
   Of this and other evils in my soul.

How many with shorn hair will rise again   *46*
   Through the ignorance forbidding them to win
   Repentance in their life or life's last pain!

Know that the fault that meeteth any sin   *49*
   By direct opposition, is with it   50
   Condemned, and drieth here its fulsome green.

Wherefore if I among the folk was set
   Who wail their avarice, so to cleanse my stain,
   It hath befallen me for its opposite."

"Then too when thou didst sing the strife insane
   Of the twin Sorrows that Jocasta bore,"   *56*
   Spoke on the singer of the rustic strain,

"That chant of thine sustained by Clio's lore,   *58*
   Argues that faith, without which good works fail
   Of their effect, had not yet taught thee more.   60

If so, what sun, what candle did avail
   To annul thy darkness, so that thou didst steer
   Behind the Fisher afterwards thy sail?"   *63*

And he to him: "Thou first didst to the clear
   Springs of Parnassus in its caves invite;   *65*
   Then thy light brought me to God's presence near.

Thou didst as he who travels in the night,
   Who bears a lamp behind him, nor befriends
   Himself, but those who follow leads aright,

When thou didst say, 'The world itself amends;   *70*
   Justice returns and the first age of man,

---

46. "With shorn hair": a symbol of prodigality.
49. Prodigality is a sin, as well as avarice.
56. By the "twin Sorrows" of Jocasta are meant her two sons, Eteocles and Polynices.
58. "Clio": the Muse of history.
63. The "Fisher" is St. Peter.
65. Parnassus is the mountain sacred to the Muses.
70. "When thou didst say": in Virgil's Bucolics, IV, 4.

And a new progeny from Heaven descends.'
Through thee became I poet and Christian:
  But that my drawing may be better shown,
  My hand shall colour what the sketch began.
Already the whole world was ripe to own
  The true belief, that fruit whereof the seed
  By the heralds of the eternal realm was sown.
And thy words, that I touched on, so agreed
  With the new preachers, that upon me grew   80
  The custom to frequent them at my need.
They then became so holy in my view
  That when Domitian persecuted them
  Their lamentation my tears also drew.
And while I trod on yonder earth, I came
  Oft to their succour, and their upright way
  Caused me all other doctrines to contemn.
And ere my poem had brought the Greeks to stay   88
  Upon the rivers of Thebes, baptized I was,
  But dared not to the world my faith betray,   90
Long time professing paganism: because
  Of this lukewarmness must I the fourth ring
  Circle until four hundred years should pass.
Thou therefore, who didst lift the covering
  Which hid such great good from me, (and time to
    spare
  The ascent allows us for our communing,)
Tell me now where is our old Terence, where   97
  Caecilius, Plautus, Varius, if thou know'st,
  And if they are damned, tell me what ward they
    share."
"They, Persius, I and many another ghost,"   *100*
  Answered my Guide, "are with the Greek, that one

---

88. *This episode marks the middle of the* Thebaid.
97-101. *Various Latin dramatists.*—"Persius": *the Latin satirist.*—
"The Greek" *is Homer.*

Whom with their milk the Muses suckled most,
In the first circle of the blind dungeon.
  Oft of the mount we talk, whose haunted ground
  Our nursing mothers keep their vigil on.   *105*
Euripides with Antiphon is found   *106*
  There, Agathon also, and Simonides
  And other Greeks whose brows the laurel crowned.
There, of thy people, Antigone one sees,   *109*
  Deiphile, and Argia, and the sad   110
  Ismene, living in past miseries.
She is there who showed Langia where it sprayed; *112*
  There is Tiresias' daughter, and there Thetis,
  And with her sisters Deidamia's shade."
Now both the poets began to hold their peace
  And round them eager looks afresh to turn,
  Having from walls and climbing won release.
Already four handmaidens of the morn   *118*
  Were left behind, and the fifth upward still
  Steered at the chariot-pole its blazing horn,   120
When said my Leader: "I think to the outer sill
  'Tis well that our right shoulders should be bent
  And that we circle, as is our wont, the hill."
Thus habit was our guidance there; we went
  Forward, the less to misgiving inclined
  Because that worthy spirit gave assent.   *126*
They journeyed on in front, and I behind
  Alone, and to their discourse listened well,
  Which gained me knowledge of poetic mind.

---

105. "Our nursing mothers": the Muses.
106-107. The Greek lyric poet, Simonides, is mentioned with the Greek tragic poets, Euripides, Antiphon, and Agathon.
109. By "thy people" Virgil means the characters in Statius' poems.
112-113. Hypsipyle who pointed out the fountain of Langia to Adrastus. "Tiresias' daughter" was Manto (Inf. xx, 55).
118. Four hours of daylight.
126. "That worthy spirit": Statius.

But soon the pleasant converse broken fell   130
  Before a tree, which in the mid-road now
  We found, with bounteous fruit, sweet to the smell.
As a pine narrows up from bough to bough
  So did this taper downward stage by stage;
  As I suppose, that none may up it go.
Upon the side where there was no passage
  A crystal liquor from the cliff sprang free
  And sprinkled all the upper foliage.
As the two poets drew near to the tree
  A voice within it from the green leaves there,   140
  Cried: "Of this food ye shall have scarcity."
Then: "Mary at the wedding had more care
  That seemly and complete should be the feast   *143*
  Than of her own mouth, which now speaks your
      prayer.
Rome's antique women were content with taste
  Of water for their drink; Daniel of old   *146*
  Despised food and in wisdom was increased.
The first age was as beautiful as gold.
  It made acorns with hunger savour sweet
  And every brook with thirst a nectar hold.   150
Honey and locusts were the only meat
  That in the wilderness the Baptist knew,
  And therefore is he glorious, and so great
As in the gospel is revealed to you."

---

143. The story of Mary at the wedding feast in Cana is an example
of temperance.
146. Dan. 1:8-17.

Canto XXIII

The cry is heard of spirits who now overtake the pilgrims. Gluttons in life, they are now emaciated to an extreme degree, reminding Dante of Ery-sichthon, punished with hunger by Demeter, and of Mary, a Jewess, who devoured her own child during the siege of Jerusalem. So it is only by the voice that Dante recognizes the friend of his youth, Forese Donati. Each is eager to learn about the other. Forese explains the nature of the punish-ment in this circle; and tells how it is through the intercession of his widow Nella that he has been spared the long delay in Ante-Purgatory; and de-nounces the dissoluteness of the women of Flor-ence, shameless as those of Barbagia, a wild district in Sardinia.

WHILE I was thus fixing mine eyes at gaze
  Through the green foliage, even as is done
  By him who on the small birds wastes his days,
My more than father said to me: "My son,
  Come now, the time allotted to our need
  Must to more profitable use be won."
I turned my face, and foot with no less speed,
  Toward the two sages, who as they conferred
  Made me the cost of going not to heed.
And lo, a weeping and a singing heard,   10
  Labia mea, Domine, that filled my ear   11

---

11. Ps. 51:15: "O Lord, open Thou my lips."

In such mode that delight and grief it stirred.
"O sweet father, what is it that I hear?"
  Said I; and he: "Shades loosening the knot
  Of their old debt perchance thus persevere."
Even as pilgrims full of their own thought
  O'ertaking unknown people upon the road
  Turn themselves round to eye them, and tarry not,
So behind us, moving more quickly, a crowd
  Of spirits coming up and passing by,   20
  Mute and devout, at us their wonder showed.
Each one was dark and hollow in the eye,
  Pallid of face, and with the flesh so lost
  As made the skin with the bones' form comply.
I think not Erysichthon at such cost   25
  Was shrivelled to the outer rind by drouth
  Of hunger, when he dreaded it the most.
I said within me, thinking in my ruth,
  "Behold the folk that lost Jerusalem
  When Mary upon her own child fleshed her tooth." 30
Their eye-sockets seemed rings without a gem.
  He who reads "omo" in the face of man   32
  Would clearly there have recognized the "m."
Who would believe, did none to him explain,
  That scent of fruit and of a liquid spring
  By gendering desire could thus ordain?
I stood astonished at their famishing,
  The cause not yet being manifest that made
  Their leanness and their scabby shrivelling,
When lo! from the deep hollow of a head   40
  A shade turned on me eyes of fixèd quest.
  Then, crying aloud, "What grace is this?" it said.

---

25. "Erysichthon": see the Argument.

30. "Mary": see the Argument.

32-33. Capital M, resembled two O's side by side. Inasmuch as this figure is not unlike a nose between two eye-sockets, it was said that man ("omo") had his name written in his face.

Him from his aspect had I never guessed,
  But in his voice was given to me the clue
  Of what was in his countenance suppressed.
This spark within me kindled all anew
  Familiarity with lip and cheek
  So altered; and Forese's face I knew. 48
"Ah, stare not," pleading he began to speak,
  "At the dry skin which the scab blotches so 50
  Nor at the flesh that on me is so to seek.
Truth of thyself tell me, and who those two
  Shades are, thou hast there for companions.
  Speak with me, I entreat thee, and be not slow."
Then I: "Thy face which dead I wept for once
  Grieves me not less, nay, tears it moves me to,
  Seeing it now so drawn upon the bones.
Say then, in God's name, what so strippeth you.
  Make me not talk while I am marvelling still.
  Ill can he speak who other things would do." 60
And he: "A virtue from the eternal will
  Descends into the water and the tree
  We have left behind, whereby I waste thus ill.
And those who, singing, weep, as thou dost see,
  That appetite they followed with such heat,
  Holy again through hunger and thirst shall be.
The scent that from the apple comes so sweet
  And from the sprinkling of the leaves with spray
  Fires us with craving both to drink and eat.
And not once only, while the appointed way 70
  We circle, is renewed for us the pain—
  I say pain, but I ought 'solace' to say—
For that Will leads us to the tree again
  Which led Christ to say 'Eli' and be glad, 74

---

48. "Forese" Donati: see the Argument.
74. "Eli": Matt. 27:46: "My God, my God, why hast Thou forsaken me?"

Freeing us with the blood out of his vein."
And I: "Forese, from that day which made
   Exchange of worlds for thee to a better mode
   Of life, five years till now thou hast not had.
If power to sin more had its period
   Ended in thee before the hour came on   80
   Of the good grief which re-weds us to God,
How art thou come so high, and how so soon?
   I had thought to find thee on yonder terraces
   Where time repairs itself by time alone."
Wherefore he answered me: "My Nella 'tis   85
   Brought me to drink thus, by her gushing tears,
   Of the sweet wormwood of the penances.
With her devout prayers and those sighs of hers
   She has drawn me from the shore where one must
      wait,
   And from the other circles freed my fears.   90
My widow, whom I loved with love so great,
   Is to God dearer, and more his love doth win,
   As in good works the lonelier is her state.
Barbagia in Sardinia ne'er hath been   94
   Immodest in its women as today
   Is the Barbagia that I left her in.
O sweet brother, what would'st thou have me say?
   A time to come already I see indeed,
   Wherefrom this hour shall not be far away,
In which from pulpit shall it be forbid   100
   To the unashamed women of Florence then
   To go showing the breast with paps not hid.
What woman of Barbary, what Saracen,
   Did ever need, to make her go covered,
   Spiritual or other regimen?
But if the unabashed ones were assured

---

85. "Nella": see the Argument.
94. "Barbagia": a wild region in Sardinia.

Of what swift heaven prepares for them on high
  Their mouths would open and their howls be heard.
If my fore-sight deceives not, they shall cry
  In sorrow, ere he clothes his cheek with down   110
  Who now is quieted with lullaby.
Ah, brother, hide thee not, let all be known!
  Thou seëst, not only I but this folk all
  Are gazing where thou intercept'st the sun."
Then I to him: "If thou to mind recall
  What thou wast with me and I was with thee,   *116*
  Still heavy will the present memory fall.
From that life he who goes in front of me
  Turned me the other day, when full and round
  The sister of him there showed herself to be."   *120*
I pointed to the sun. "Through the profound
  Night, from the real dead convoyed was I
  In real flesh that still is upward bound.
Thence hath his aid supported me thus high,
  Circle by circle, to ascend the Hill
  Which straightens you whom the world bent awry.
So long he means to comrade me, until
  I shall be there where shall be Beatrice:
  Without him thence must I the rest fulfil.
Virgil is who hath assured me this"   130
  I pointed to him; "and this other shade   *131*
  Is he for whom shook in each precipice
Your realm, from which his quittance now is paid."

---

116. "And I was with thee": *Forese and Dante had led together a
    sinful life.*
120. "The sister of him": *the moon.*
131. "This other shade": *Statius.*

Canto XXIV

*Dante asks about Forese's sister Piccarda and learns
that she is in Paradise. Forese then points out to
him certain shades of note. Among them is Buona-
giunta, a poet of Lucca, who predicts that a lady,
Gentucca, will make Lucca pleasing to Dante. He
goes on to speak of the "sweet new style" of the
Florentine school of poets to which Dante be-
longed, superior in naturalness and sincerity to the
school of Jacopo of Lentini in Sicily (called The
Notary), Guittone of Arezzo, and Buonagiunta him-
self. Dante speaks of the miseries of Florence, and
Forese foretells the death of his brother Corso Do-
nati, leader of the Blacks, and chief cause of those
miseries. Dante next observes another tree, from
which comes a voice reciting examples of gluttony;
the Centaurs, and the Hebrews rejected by Gideon
(Judges, 7). As the three poets go on silently, they
hear a voice, and Dante is dazzled by the resplend-
ent apparition of the Angel of Temperance.*

Speech made not going, nor going speech more slow,
  But in our talk we went with manful stride
  Like to a ship when winds behind it blow;
And me through the eyes' pits in amazement eyed
  The thronging shades, who appeared things twice
    dead
  When they were of my living certified.
And my discourse continuing, I said:

"Perchance he mounts more slowly upon his way   *8*
    Than he would else do, for another's aid.
But, if thou know'st, where is Piccarda, say;   *10*
    And say if I see any whom I should
    Note well, of these whose eyes so on me stay."
"My sister who was beautiful and good,
    I know not which most, triumphs now to wear
    Her glad crown in Olympus' high abode."
So said he: and then: " 'Tis not forbidden here
    To name each one, since so drained out and dim
    Our likeness is, by reason of our fare.
This one is Buonagiunta" pointing at him,   *19*
    "Buonagiunta of Lucca, and, next, the face   *20*
    That more than the others showeth scale and seam,
Had Holy Church within his arms' embrace:
    He was of Tours, and purges off by fast
    Bolsena's eels and the sweet wine's disgrace."
Many another he showed me, first and last,
    And to be named thus all contented were,
    It seemed, for none a dark look on us cast.
I saw, biting for hunger the empty air,
    Ubaldin dalla Pila, and Boniface,   *29*
    Who pastured with his staff folk near and far   *30*
I saw Master Marchese, who once had space   *31*
    To drink at Forlì with less dry a throat,
    Nor, even so, could with his thirst keep pace.
As a man does who, looking, takes chief note
    Of one, to him of Lucca did I do,

---

8. *Statius* "mounts more slowly" *in order to be longer with Virgil.*
10. "Piccarda": *see the Argument.*
19-20. "Buonagiunta": *a poet of Lucca.* "The face . . .": *Pope Martin IV.*
29. "Ubaldin dalla Pila": *a Ghibelline leader.* "Boniface" de' Fieschi: *an archbishop of Ravenna.*
31. "Master Marchese": *mayor of Faenza in* 1296.

Who most, it seemed, for my acquaintance sought.

I thought I heard, as he was muttering low,
   "Gentucca," there where he could feel the smart   *38*
   Of the high justice which displumes them so.

"O soul," said I, "who something wouldst impart   *40*
   To me, do so, that I may understand,
   And with thy speech content me and thine own
      heart."

"A woman, who wears not yet the wimple's band,
   Is born," said he, "who shall my city endear
   To thee, however by men's tongues arraigned.

This prophecy with thee thou art to bear.
   If in my muttering thou wast doubtful of
   The truth, the thing's self shall yet make it clear.

But tell me, I pray, if I see him who wove
   Out of his heart the new rimes that begin   *50*
   Ladies that have intelligence of love."   *51*

And I to him: "I am one who hearkens when
   Love prompteth, and I put thought into word
   After the mode which he dictates within."

"O brother," he said, "I see what knot deterred
   The Notary and Guittone and me too,   *56*
   Baulked of the new sweet style I have lately heard.

For now I see well how the pen with you
   Follows him who dictateth close behind,
   Which our pens truly were not wont to do;   *60*

And he who seeks to look beyond can find
   No difference else 'twixt one and the other style."
   Thereat he held his peace, and seemed resigned.

Even as cranes that winter along the Nile
   Now make themselves a squadron in the air,

---

38. "Gentucca": see the Argument (she is also the "woman" of line
43). "There where . . ." in the mouth.
51. The first canzone of the Vita Nuova.
56. "The Notary and Guittone": see the Argument.

Then fly at greater speed and go in file,
So all the people that had gathered there,
    Turning away their faces, forward prest:
    Fleet both through leanness and their wish **they were.**
And as the runner who becomes distrest   70
    Lets his companions pass him and walks on
    Till he have eased the panting of his chest,
Forese let the holy flock be gone,
    And asking: "How long shall it be before
    Again I see thee?" in step with me went on.
"I know not what of life I may have more"
    Replied I, "but return not so soon but
    My wish will waft me sooner to the shore,
Because the place where I to live was put
    Is, day by day, of all good more despoiled   80
    And seems ordained in misery to rot."
"Now go," said he, "for him who is most embroiled 82
    I see dragged at the tail of a strong beast
    Down towards the vale where sin is unassoiled.
The beast goes faster at every step, increased
    In speed, until it breaks him on the ground
    And leaves his body hideously defaced.
Yon wheels shall have not long to circle round"
    He raised his eyes to heaven "ere that be clear
    To thee, which my words may not more expound. 90
Remain thou now behind, for time is dear
    In this kingdom, so that too much I lose,
    At equal pace with thee thus loitering here."
As sometimes at a gallop toward his foes
    Forth from a troop a rider, bent to snatch
    The honour of the first encounter goes,
So with great strides from us did he detach;

82-87. *Corso Donati, the great leader of the Blacks, who in 1308 was accused of treason and condemned. In Dante's version, Corso is kicked to death by the animal that is hauling him.*

And I in the way remained with but the two,
Those marshals of the world that had no match.
When he was gone so far out of our view   100
That my eyes after him pursuing yearned
Even as did my mind his words pursue,
Laden and living branches I discerned
Of another apple-tree, not far away,
Seeing that but then had I thither turned.
I saw folk under it raise their hands; and they
Were crying toward the leaves I know not what,
Like children that futile and eager pray,
And he who is prayed answers them not a jot,
But so to make their craving very keen   110
Holds their desire on high and hides it not.
They, as if undeceived, departed then.
And now we came to the great tree, which, dumb,
Rejects so many prayers and tears of men.
"Pass ye on, and no further this way come!
Higher up there is a tree whose taste was tried   *116*
By Eve, and this same plant was raised therefrom."
Thus from among the branches some one cried.
Virgil and Statius and I, close-prest
Together, passed on the ascending side.   120
"Remember," it said, "those monsters, all unblest, *121*
Formed in the clouds, who when they had gorged
    their fill
Fought against Theseus with their double breast,
And the Hebrews, at the drinking weak of will,
Whom Gideon for his comrades would not choose *125*
When he came down on Midian from the hill."
So, skirting one of the two edges close,

---

116. The tree of knowledge.
121-123. "Those monsters, . . . who . . . fought against Theseus"
are the Centaurs.
125. Of the Hebrews ready to fight against Midian, Gideon chose
only those who drank without kneeling: Judg. 12:4-7.

We passed, hearing what gluttons' faults once sowed
And after reaped a recompense of woes.

Once more at large upon the empty road   130
Full thousand and more paces on, each one
Lost in his thoughts, without a word we strode.

"What ponder ye three, as ye go alone?"
Said a sudden voice; whereat I shook in dread
As a young beast does, into panic thrown.

To see who it was, I lifted up my head;
And never yet was seen in furnaces
Molten metal or glass to glow so red

As I saw one who was saying, "If ye please
To mount, here turn ye to ascend the height.   140
This way they go who would go into peace."

His aspect had all taken away my sight.
Wherefore I turned, back to my teachers drawn,
As one who by his ear is guided right.

And as, annunciation of the dawn,
The breeze of May awakeneth, sweet to smell,
Impregnated from flower and grassy lawn,

A wind full on the forehead did I feel
Touching me, and distinct I heard the plumes   *149*
That made ambrosial fragrance on me steal.   150

And I heard cry: "Blessed those, whom illumes
So much of grace that never palate's lust
Makes them exceed by kindling of its fumes,
Hungering always so far as is just."

---

149. "The plumes": of the Angel of Temperance.

Canto XXV

It is afternoon of the third day. One by one the poets mount the stair; and Dante, perplexed to know how it is that immaterial shades, not needing food, can suffer hunger and become emaciated, lays the problem before Virgil, who refers it to Statius. Statius then expounds a theory, derived from Aristotle and Aquinas, of the formation of the body, into which the rational soul is infused by the Creator, drawing into its substance the vital functions it finds already there (the vegetative and sensitive souls). At death the soul, freed from the flesh but retaining memory, intelligence and will and the other faculties in a dormant state, goes at once to its appointed place, whether Tiber-mouth or Acheron, and impresses its form upon the air; and this aerial body, the "shade," forms organs for every sense. The philosopher to whom Statius refers as erroneously supposing the intellectual faculty to be separate from the soul is Averroes. They have now arrived at the seventh and uppermost circle, that of the Lustful. Here they have to go warily because of a great fire burning on their path, into which spirits are passing, while voices from within the flames celebrate examples of chastity (the Virgin, Diana).

An hour 'twas that indulged no loitering,
    For now the sun had to the Bull resigned,
    Night to the Scorpion, the meridian ring;
Wherefore as he does, who looks not behind

But goes straight on, whatever his eye sees,
   If sharp necessity spur on his mind,
So through the gap we entered by degrees,
   And one before the other took the stair
   That unlinks climbers by its narrowness.
And as the young stork lifts its wing to dare   10
   The flight it wishes, and attempteth not
   To leave the nest, and drooping flutters there,
Such was I, with desire to ask both hot
   And chilled; and last came to the gesture shown
   By him whose lips prepare to speak his thought.
My sweet Father, for all we hasted on,
   O'erlooked it not, but said: "Discharge the bow
   Of speech which thou hast to the iron drawn."
Then, set at ease, I opened lips, and: "How,"
   Began I, "can one famish and be pined   20
   There, where of food there is no need to know?"
"If thou hadst Meleager called to mind,   22
   Consumed with the consuming of a brand,
   Thou would'st not here so much discordance find.
And if thou thinkest how your image, scanned
   Within the mirror, stirs quick as you stir,
   What seems hard would seem easy to understand.
But that thou may'st reach haven in thy desire,
   Lo, Statius here; and him do I adduce
   And pray him to thy wounds to minister."   30
"If I unfold to him," answered Statius,
   "Where thou art, the eternal sight, that I
   Cannot deny thee shall be my excuse."
Then he said: "Son, if thou thy mind apply
   And well absorb my words, they shall afford
   Light to thee on the *How* thou art troubled by.

---

22. *The life of Meleager was made by the fates to depend on that of
a firebrand.*

Blood perfected, which never is drunk or stored   37
   By thirsting veins and is left over, as if
   'Twere food which thou removest from the board,
Takes in the heart a virtue informative   40
   To all the human members, like that blood
   Which courses through the veins to make those live.
Refined yet more, it flows down where 'tis good
   Not to speak but be silent, and thence pours
   Into another's blood in natural mode.
There the one is mingled with the other's course,
   Ordained, one to be passive, the other to act
   Because it comes from a so perfect source.
Thereto joined, it begins its part to enact,
   Coagulating first, then quickening whole   50
   What for material it had made compact.
The active virtue growing into a soul   52
   Like a plant's, only with the difference
   That this is on the way, that at the goal,
So works that it has motion now and sense
   Like a sea-fungus; then sets out to find
   For the powers it is the seed of, instruments.
Now, son, the virtue expandeth unconfined
   Which from the heart of the begetter flows
   Where nature all man's members hath designed. 60
But how from animal it human grows
   Thou see'st not yet: and this point caused a wit
   Wiser than thou art wrongly to suppose;
So that he falsely by his teaching split
   The possible intellect from the soul, since no

37-51. *Man's blood contains potentially all the parts of his frame. Some of it remains intact and unsullied in the heart, retaining its complete formative power. This "perfected blood" becomes the parent seed.*

52-60. *The embryo's life is at first merely that of a plant—the "vegetative soul." Then the senses are developed, and its life is that of the "sensitive soul." Both "souls" are perishable.*

Organ he found that was possessed by it.
Open thy breast to coming truth, and know
   That when the articulation of the brain
   Is consummated in the embryo,
The First Mover turns to it, glad and fain   70
   Over such art of nature, and, to abound
   In virtue, inbreathes a spirit of new strain,   72
Which, drawing what it there has active found
   Into its substance, makes one soul complete
   That lives and feels and on itself turns round.
And that thou may'st less marvel at this, the heat
   Of the sun consider, that becometh wine
   When with it the vine's flowing juices meet.
When Lachesis hath no more thread to spin   79
   It sheds the flesh, and bears away therefrom   80
   Virtually both the human and divine:
The other faculties inert and dumb;
   And will and memory and intelligence,
   Which now in act far keener have become.
It stays not, but is borne in its suspense
   To one or the other shore, in wondrous mode.   86
   Here first it learns what path it must take thence.
Soon as 'tis circumscribed by its abode,
   The formative virtue radiates without let
   As much as in the living members showed.   90
And as the air when it is charged with wet,
   Through another's ray that it reflects, reveals
   The divers colours in their glory set,
Thus here the neighbouring air itself anneals
   Into that form which, by the virtue it owes,
   The still surviving soul upon it seals.

---

72. The "spirit of new strain" is the "rational soul" (see the Argument).
79. "Lachesis": the Fate.
86. "To one or the other shore": to the bank of Acheron or of Tiber (see the Argument).

And then like to the flame that, following close
    The fire, wherever it shifteth, to it cleaves,
    So the new form after the spirit goes.
Since visible aspect it therefrom receives,   100
    Well is it called a shade, and thence its own   *101*
    Organ to each sense, even to sight, it gives.
We speak, we laugh, by this, and this alone;
    By this we liberate the tears and sighs
    Thou mayst have heard about the mount make moan.
The shade takes form as the desires devise
    And the other stings of feeling that we share.
    And this it was occasioned thy surprise."
And now we had come to the last twisting stair
    And to the right hand had wheeled round our
        steps,   110
    And all our thoughts were turned to other care.
Here from the bank an arrowy fire outleaps   *112*
    And from the ground beats up a blast whose brawl
    Bends the flames backward and at distance keeps.
Thus on the free side must we needs go all,
    One after the other; and the fire I feared
    On this side, and on that side feared to fall.
My Leader said: "Along this place keep guard
    With the curb tight over the eyes, for sore
    Mishap might come, if one but a little erred."   120
Summae Deus clementiae at the core   *121*
    Of the great burning I heard chanted, so
    That to turn thither it made me hunger more.
And through the flames I beheld spirits go.
    Wherefore I eyed them and my steps, at feud
    Each moment, as my glance went to and fro.
After the end which doth that hymn conclude

---

101. "A shade": see the Argument.
112. "An arrowy fire": *the symbol of purification from lust.*
121. "God of clemency supreme."

They *Virum non cognosco* cried aloud;   *128*
  Then with soft voices all the hymn renewed.
That finished, they cried on: "To Dian vowed   *130*
  The wood was, whence was Helice in shame   *131*
  Driven, who had Venus' poison in her blood."
Then, to their chanting turned, they cried the name
  Of women and of husbands who were chaste,
  As virtue and marriage do their fealty claim.
This ritual, I think, for them doth last
  For all the time the fire upon them glows.
  And with such cure and diet of such taste
Behoveth that the wound at last should close.

---

128. "I know not a man," is the reply of Mary to the angel at the Annunciation. After each singing of the hymn the souls call aloud an example of chastity.
131. The nymph Helice had been seduced by Jupiter.

Canto XXVI

Proceeding along the circle, the three poets go in single file, keeping to the outer edge, because of the fire. Dante's shadow makes the flames seem redder, which astonishes the spirits. One of them, who is Guido Guinicelli, questions Dante, whose attention is however distracted by a throng coming towards them who greet the others briefly; they are those who were guilty of unnatural lust, while the sin of the first group was "hermaphrodite," or bi-sexual, but infringed human law. This is explained by Guinicelli, who now makes himself known and is greeted with reverence by Dante as his "father" in poetry (as the sons of Hypsipyle recognized and embraced their mother in Statius' poem). But Guinicelli deprecates his praise and points to the shade

of Arnaut Daniel, the Provençal poet, as a better
craftsman in verse, surpassing his rival Giraut de
Borneuil of Limoges. Guinicelli disappears into the
flame, and Dante greets Arnaut, who replies in the
Provençal tongue.

WHILE thus along the road's edge we progressed
   One after one, "By my instruction's light"
   Said the good Master, "see thou profitest."
The sun smote on my shoulder from the right
   And with his beams by now was changing fast
   The whole face of the West from blue to white.
And redder with the shadow that I cast
   The flames appeared; and this small sign alone
   Many, I saw, took heed of as they passed.
This was the cue for them to speak upon: 10
   And of me, among themselves, they made comment:
   "No shadowy body this one seems to own."
Far as they could, then, certain of them went
   Toward me, still watchful not to issue out
   There where the burning would no more torment.
"O thou that goest behind the others, not
   From indolence but for reverence may-hap,
   Answer me, who have fire within my throat.
Not I alone will drink thine answer up,
   For all these have a greater thirst for it   20
   Than for cold brooks Indian or Ethiop.
Say how it is that thou thyself dost set
   As a wall against the sun, as if ensnared
   Thou wert not in the meshes of Death's net."
Thus one spoke; and already I had declared
   Myself, had not the intentness of my gaze
   Been drawn to a new thing which then appeared.
For where the middle road was all ablaze

People were coming with face fronting these
    Who made me stand and linger in my amaze.   30
Each shade I see on either side to press,
    And without staying, and content with scant
    Greeting, I see them one another kiss.
Even so within their dusky troops an ant
    Noses another, if haply it may spy
    Their journey out or what their luck may grant.
Soon as they put the friendly greeting by,
    Before the first step of the speeding foot
    Each of them strives which shall the loudest cry.
"Sodom and Gomorrah" the new-comers shout.   40
    The rest, "Pasiphae entereth the cow   41
    That the young bull may hasten to her rut."
Like cranes that, some to the Rhipean snow
    Would fly, some to the sandy regions,—they
    Shunning the frost, and those the hot sun's glow—
One part go on, the other come away,
    And weeping to their first chants they recur
    And to the words it fits them most to say.
And those same ones who did me first implore
    With listening intentness in their mien   50
    Were drawing close up to me as before.
I, who now twice their eagerness had seen,
    Began: "O spirits that have security
    Of reaching in the end the state serene,
My members, whether green or ripe they be,
    Remain not yonder upon earth confined
    But with their blood and joints are here with me.
Upward I go, to be no longer blind.
    There is a lady above who hath won me grace;   59
    Hence in your world my mortal self ye find.   60

---

41. "Pasiphae," cursed by Venus with a passion for a bull, satisfied
her lust by concealing herself in a wooden cow.
59. "A lady": the Virgin Mary.

But so may your supreme wish come to pass
  Sooner, so that the heaven may harbour you
  Which brims with love and spreads in amplest space,
That yet my pen may write it, tell me who
  Ye are, and what that multitude is there
  Which goes behind your backs away from you?"
Not otherwise the embarrassed highlander
  Grows dazed and round about him stareth dumb,
  Wild and uncouth amid the city's stir,
Than each shade did now in his looks become.   70
  But when they were disburdened of that strain,
  And lofty hearts are soon relieved therefrom,
"Blessed thou," that first shade began again,
  "Who for a better death art taking in
  Store of experience out of our domain.
The people who come not with us had that sin
  For which Caesar of old as he passed by
  Heard in his triumph called behind him 'Queen!'   78
Therefore do they reproach themselves and cry
  'Sodom,' as thou hast heard, at parting hence,   80
  And with their shame the burning magnify.
For us, hermaphrodite was our offence.
  But since we observed not human law (our blood
  Pursuing like a beast the lusts of sense)
We read, to our reproach and for our good,
  Parting, the name of her who did imbrute
  Herself in the imbruted frame of wood.
Thou knowest our guilty acts now and their fruit.
  If chance thou would'st by name know who we are,
  There is no time to tell, nor could I do it.   90
Of me indeed I will content thy prayer.
  I am Guido Guinicelli and purge me in flame   92

---

78. A charge of sodomy.
92. "Guido Guinicelli": the most important Italian poet before
Dante.

Because, ere the end, my sins repented were."

Then such as in Lycurgus' grief became   *94*
  Two sons, rejoiced their mother again to see
  So became I (yet not so high I aim),

When I heard name himself the father of me
  And of others, my betters, who have wrought
  Ever of love sweet rhyme so graciously.

Without hearing or speech, in musing thought   *100*
  I went, a long time gazing on him still,
  Yet, for the fire, no nearer to him sought.

When with beholding I had fed my fill,
  I offered all his wishes to obey
  With that oath which persuades another's will.

And he to me: "Such trace, by what men say,
  Thou leavest printed in me, and one so clear,
  That Lethe cannot drown or make it grey.   *108*

But if 'twas truth thy words just now did swear,
  Tell me what is the cause why in thy speech   *110*
  And look thou showest that thou hold'st me dear."

And I to him: "Your own sweet ditties, which,
  So long as modern use is not let die,
  The ink that they were written in shall enrich."

"O brother," said he, "He who is singled by   *115*
  My finger (he pointed to a spirit in front)
  Wrought better in the mother-tongue than I.

Whether in verses of love or prose romaunt
  He surpassed all; and let the fools contend
  Who make him of Limoges of more account.   *120*

To rumour rather than to truth they bend
  Their faces, fixt in their opinion's seat

---

94. *Hypsipyle's two sons saved her from the rage of Lycurgus (see the Argument).*

108. *"Lethe": the river of oblivion.*

115. *"He who . . .": Arnaut Daniel, a twelfth-century troubadour.*

120. *Giraut de Borneuil of Limoges: a younger contemporary of Arnaut.*

Ere art or reason they can apprehend.

Thus many an elder did Guittone treat,   *124*
   Shouting as one, their votes for him to pledge,
   Till truth, with most, conquered the counterfeit.

Now if thou hast such ample privilege
   That to the cloister it admitteth thee
   Where Christ is Abbot of the blest college,

A Paternoster do thou say for me   130
   So far as need for us be of such aid
   In this world, where to sin we are no more free."

Then, perhaps giving place to another shade
   Close by him, through the flames he disappeared
   Like fish that into the deep water fade.

Him who was pointed at I a little neared
   And told him what desire upon my side
   Held for his name a grateful place prepared.

And with a willing frankness he replied:
   "Your courteous request pleases me so,   140
   I have no power nor will from you to hide.

I am Arnald, and I weep and singing go.
   I think on my past folly and see the stain,
   And view with joy the day I hope to know.

I pray you by that Goodness which doth deign
   To guide you to the summit of this stair
   Bethink you in due season of my pain."

Then he shrank back in the refining fire.

---

124. *Guittone d'Arezzo: a prolific imitator of the Provençal school.*

Canto XXVII

Night is coming on, when the Angel of Chastity appears and tells Dante that he cannot go further without passing through the fire. He is terrified, remembering deaths by burning that he had witnessed on earth; and even Virgil's encouragement cannot overcome his fears till he is reminded that Beatrice awaits him beyond. The three pass through the fire and emerge at the place of ascent. Another angel warns them to hasten, as the sun is setting. Each now makes a bed for himself on a step of the stair. Dante sleeps, and dreams of Leah and Rachel, types of the active and contemplative life; foreshadowing the meeting with Matilda and Beatrice which is to come. He wakes with morning, and at the summit Virgil tells him that his mission is ended and that Dante now needs no guide or instructor.

As when his first beams tremble in the sky   *1*
   There, where his own Creator shed his blood,
   While Ebro is beneath the Scales on high,
And noon scorches the wave on Ganges' flood,
   Such was the sun's height; day was soon to pass;
   When the angel of God joyful before us stood.
Outside the flames, above the bank, he was.
   Beati mundo corde we heard him sing   *8*
   In a voice more living far than comes from us.

1-5. *The time described is the approach of sunset.*
8. *Matt. 5:8: "Blessed are the pure in heart."*

Then "None goes further, if first the fire not sting.   10
    O hallowed spirits, enter unafraid
    And to the chant beyond let your ears cling."
When we were near him, this to us he said.
    Wherefore I, when I knew what his words meant,
    Became as one who in the grave is laid.
Over my clasping hands forward I leant,
    Eyeing the fire, and vivid to my mind
    Men's bodies burning, once beheld, it sent.
Then toward me turned them both my escorts kind;
    And Virgil said to me: "O my son, here   20
    Torment, may-be, but death thou shalt not find.
Remember, O remember . . . and if thy fear
    On Geryon into safety I recalled,
    What shall I do now, being to God more near?
If thou within this womb of flames wert walled
    Full thousand years, for certainty believe
    That not of one hair could they make thee bald.
And if perchance thou think'st that I deceive,
    Go forward into them, and thy faith prove,
    With hands put in the edges of thy sleeve.   30
Out of thy heart all fear remove, remove!
    Turn hither and come confidently on!"
    And I stood fixed and with my conscience strove.
When he beheld me still and hard as stone,
    Troubled a little, he said: "Look now, this same
    Wall is 'twixt Beatrice and thee, my son."
As Pyramus at the sound of Thisbe's name
    Opened his dying eyes and gazed at her
    Then, when the crimson on the mulberry came,   39
So did I turn unto my wise Leader,   40
    My hardness melted, hearing the name told

---

39. *The mulberry turned red on being spattered with the blood of
Pyramus, who stabbed himself when he thought Thisbe slain by a
lion (Ovid, Met., IV, 55-166).*

Which like a well-spring in my mind I bear.
Whereon he shook his head, saying: "Do we hold
    Our wish to stay on this side?" He smiled then
    As on a child by an apple's bribe cajoled.
Before me then the fire he entered in,
    Praying Statius that he follow at his heel
    Who for a long stretch now had walked between.
When I was in, I had been glad to reel
    Therefrom to cool me, into boiling glass,   50
    Such burning beyond measure did I feel.
My sweet Father, to give me heart of grace,
    Continued only on Beatrice to descant,
    Saying: "Already I seem to see her face."
On the other side, to guide us, rose a chant,
    And we, intent on that alone to dwell,
    Came forth there, where the ascent began to slant.
And there we heard a voice *Venite* hail   58
    Benedicti patris mei out of light   59
    So strong, it mastered me and made me quail.   60
"The sun departs," it added; "comes the night.
    Tarry not; study at good pace to go
    Before the west has darkened on your sight."
Straight rose the path within the rock, and so
    Directed onward, that I robbed the ray
    Before me from the sun, already low.
I and my sages few steps did assay
    When by the extinguished shadow we perceived
    That now behind us had sunk down the day.
And ere the horizon had one hue received   70
    In all the unmeasured regions of the air,
    And night her whole expansion had achieved,
Each of us made his bed upon a stair,
    Seeing that the nature of the mount o'ercame

58-59. Matt. 25:34: "*Come, ye blessed of my Father . . .*"

Alike the power to ascend and the desire.
As goats, now ruminating, though the same
    That, before feeding, brisk and wanton played
    On the high places of the hills, grow tame,
Silent, while the sun scorches, in the shade,
    Watched by the herd that props him hour by hour 80
    Upon his staff and, propt so, tends his trade;
And as the shepherd, lodging out-of-door,
    Watches night-long in quiet by his flock,
    Wary lest wild beast scatter it or devour;
Such were we then, all three, within that nook,
    I as a goat, they as a shepherd, there,
    On this and that side hemmed by the high rock.
Little could there of the outside things appear;
    But through that little I saw the stars to glow
    Bigger than ordinary and shine more clear.   90
Ruminating and gazing on them so
    Sleep took me; sleep which often will apprize
    Of things to come, and ere the event foreknow.
In the hour, I think, when first from Eastern skies
    Upon the mountain Cytherea beamed   95
    Whom fire of love forever glorifies,
A lady young and beautiful I seemed
    To see move through a plain and flower on flower
    To gather; singing, she was saying (I dreamed),
"Let them know, whoso of my name inquire,   100
    That I am Leah, and move my fingers fair
    Around, to make me a garland for a tire.
To glad me at the glass I deck me here;
    But never to her mirror is untrue
    My sister Rachel, and sits all day there.

---

95. "Cytherea" is Venus, whose star shines before sunrise.
100. Dante is about to visit the Garden of Eden, the abode of in-
nocence and harmless activity. Consequently the active and the
contemplative life are revealed to him in the form of Laban's
daughters, Leah and Rachel.

She is fain to hold her beauteous eyes in view
    As me with these hands I am fain to adorn:
    To see contenteth her, and me to do."
Already, through the splendour ere the morn,
    Which to wayfarers the more grateful shows,   110
    Lodging less far from home, where they return,
The shadows on all sides were fleeing, and close
    On them my sleep fled; wherefore, having seen
    The great masters risen already, I rose.
"That apple whose sweetness in their craving keen *115*
    Mortals go seeking on so many boughs
    This day shall peace to all thy hungers mean."
Words such as these to me did Virgil use;
    And no propitious gifts did man acquire
    For pleasure matching these, to have or choose.   120
So came on me desire upon desire
    To be above, that now with every tread
    I felt wings on me growing to waft me higher.
When under us the whole high stair was sped
    And we unto the topmost step had won,
    Virgil, fixing his eyes upon me, said:
"The temporal and the eternal fire, my son,
    Thou hast beheld: thou art come now to a part
    Where of myself I see no farther on.
I have brought thee hither both by wit and art.   130
    Take for thy guide thine own heart's pleasure now.
    Forth from the narrows, from the steeps, thou art.
See there the sun that shines upon thy brow;
    See the young grass, the flowers and coppices
    Which this soil, of itself alone, makes grow.
While the fair eyes are coming, full of bliss,
    Which weeping made me come to thee before,
    Amongst them thou canst go or sit at ease.
Expect from me no word or signal more.

---

115. "That apple . . .": *earthly happiness.*

Thy will is upright, sound of tissue, free: 140
To disobey it were a fault; wherefore
Over thyself I crown thee and mitre thee."   142

Canto XXVIII

Dante sees before him the Earthly Paradise, which crowns the Mount, and sets out to explore "the divine forest." The grass is full of flowers, and birds sing on the boughs. He is stopped by the stream of Lethe, and on the farther side of it perceives a lady gathering flowers and singing. She is Matilda (as we learn from Canto XXXIII), a lady generally identified with a Countess of Tuscany (1046-1115), supporter of Pope Gregory VII, but here representing the active life and the guide of Dante towards Beatrice (the contemplative life). Dante asks her to explain how it is that wind blows and water runs at a height where, according to Statius, there is no disturbance and no rain. She satisfies his curiosity and tells him how the water is supernaturally constant and replenished, pouring from a fountain which on one side is called Lethe and has the property of obliterating memory of sin, and on the other Eunoë, which restores the memory of good deeds. Here, she adds, was the abode of man in his state of innocency.

Now eager to search out through all its maze
The living green of the divine forest
Which to my eyes tempered the new sun's rays,
I left the mountain's rim, nor stayed to rest

142. *I make thee thine own Emperor and Pope.*

But took the plain by slow and slow degrees
  Where with sweet smells all the earth around is blest.
Gentle air, having no inconstancies
  Within its motion, smote upon my brow
  With no more violence than a gracious breeze;
And trembling to the touch of it, each bough   10
  Was bending all its foliage toward that side
  Where the holy Mount casteth its first shadow;   12
Yet not so far from upright was blown wide
  But that the small birds on the topmost spray
  All their sweet art continually still plied,
And from a full throat singing loud and gay
  Welcomed the first thrills in the leaves, that bore
  A burden to the descant of their lay
Such as swells up along Chiassi's shore,   19
  From branch to branch of the pine-forest blown,   20
  When Æolus has loosed Sirocco's roar.
Already my slow steps had borne me on
  So far within that immemorial wood
  That I could no more see whence I had gone;
And lo! a stream that stopped me where I stood;
  And at the left the ripple in its train
  Moved on the bank the grasses where it flowed.
All waters here that are most pure from stain
  Would qualified with some immixture seem
  Compared with this, which veils not the least
    grain,   30
Altho' so dark, dark goes the gliding stream
  Under the eternal shadow, that hides fast
  Forever there the sun's and the moon's beam.
With my feet halting, with my eyes I passed
  That brook, for the regaling of my sight

12. *The direction is the west.*
19-22. *The pine grove of "Chiassi": the old port of Ravenna;
"Sirocco": the southeast wind; "Acolus": the king of the winds.*

With the fresh blossoms in their full contrast.
And then appeared (as in a sudden light
   Something appears which from astonishment
   Puts suddenly all other thoughts to flight)
A lady who all alone and singing went,   40
   And as she sang plucked flowers that numberless
   All round about her path their colours blent.
"I pray thee, O lovely Lady, if, as I guess,
   Thou warm'st thee at the radiance of Love's fire,—
   For looks are wont to be the heart's witness,—
I pray thee toward this water to draw near
   So far," said I to her, "while thou dost sing,
   That with my understanding I may hear.
Thou puttest me in remembrance of what thing
   Proserpine was, and where, when by mischance   50
   Her mother lost her, and she lost the spring."   51
Even as a lady turns round in the dance
   With feet close to each other and to the ground
   And hardly foot beyond foot doth advance,
Toward me with maiden mien she turned her round
   Upon the floor of flowers yellow and red,
   Holding the while her modest eyes earth-bound.
My supplication then she comforted,
   So near approaching, that her song divine
   Reached me with meaning to the music wed.   60
Soon as she came to where the grasses line
   The fair stream's bank and stand wet in its wave,
   She accorded me to lift her eyes to mine.
I think not that the light such glory gave
   Beneath the eye-lids of Venus, being hit
   So strangely by the dart her own boy drave.   66

---

40. "A lady": Matilda.
51. When Proserpine, the daughter of Ceres, was suddenly carried off to the lower world by Pluto, she had been picking flowers.
66. "Her own boy": Cupid.

Erect, she smiled from the bank opposite,
   Disposing in her hands those colours fair
   Which that land bears without seed sown in it.
Three paces the stream parted me from her;   70
   But Hellespont, where Xerxes bridged the strait 71
   That still makes human vaunt a bridle wear,
Endured not from Leander keener hate,
   'Twixt Sestos and Abydos full in foam,
   Than this from me, because it closed the gate.
"It may be," she began, "since new ye come
   And see me smiling in this place elect,
   Made for mankind to be their nest and home,
That wonder and some misgiving hold you checkt;
   But the psalm *Delectasti* beams a ray   80
   Which haply shall discloud your intellect.
And thou who art first and didst beseech me, say
   If there is aught that doth thy question rouse,
   Behold! I am here thy mind's thirst to allay."
"The running water," I said, "and rustling boughs
   Perplex me, appearing to serve other laws
   Than what a new belief made me espouse."
Then she: "I'll tell thee how from its own cause
   Cometh to pass what doth thy wonder tease,
   And purge away the mist that gives thee pause. 90
The Supreme Good, who himself alone doth please,
   Made man good, and for goodness, and this clime
   Gave him for pledge of the eternal peace.
By his default he sojourned here small time:
   By his default, for tears, labour and sweat
   He exchanged honest laughter and sweet pastime.
And lest the tumults that beneath it beat,

71-74. *Xerxes, king of Persia, crossed the Hellespont; this river swelled between Leander in Abydos and his beloved Hero in Sestos.*
80. *The psalm proclaims the final triumph of the righteous.*

From water and earth by exhalation bred,
  Which follow, far as they can rise, the heat,
Should vex the peace man here inherited,   100
  This mount thus far up toward the heavens rose,
  And, barred secure from storm, lifts up its head.
Now since all the air in one smooth circuit flows,   *103*
  And, save its circle is broken by some fret,
  Revolving with the primal motion goes,
Such motion, striking here, where without let
  In living air this peak upholds its height,
  Makes the wood sound, since it is thickly set,
And all the plants, so smitten, contain such might
  In them, that with their virtue the air they strew   110
  Which scatters it abroad in circling flight.
The rest of the earth, according to its due
  Of soil and climate doth conceive and bear
  Trees of each kind and each diverse virtue.
No marvel will it then on earth appear,
  (This known,) when some plant without seed hath
      struck
  Invisibly its root, to burgeon there.
Know that the blest plain whereon thou dost look
  Is pregnant of all seed beneath the skies
  And bears fruit in it no hand there doth pluck.   120
The water which thou seëst doth not rise
  From veins, that mist, by cold condensed, restores,
  Like rivers that now gain, now lose in size,
But issues from a spring's unfailing stores
  Which God's will, plenishing it, still re-makes
  So that on either side it freely pours.
On this side it streams virtue such as takes

103-108. *The two mobile elements—air and fire—are swept around
the earth by the heavens in their "primal motion," or daily circuit.
On the surface of the earth the air encounters many obstacles; but
this mountain-top receives the atmospheric current unobstructed.*

Soilure of sin out of the memory;
On the other, memory of good deeds awakes.
On this side, Lethe, the other, Eunoë   *130*
Its name is; nor comes healing from this well
Unless upon both sides it tasted be.
This savour doth all savours far excel.—
Now, though it may be all thy thirstiness
Is quenched, even were this all that I should tell,
I give thee this corollary as a grace;
Nor do I think my words shall less be prized
By thee, that they exceed my promises.
They who in old time dreaming poetized
Of the felicity of the Age of Gold   *140*
On Helicon perchance this place agnized.
Innocent here was man's first root of old;
Here blooms perpetual Spring, all fruits abound:
This is the nectar whereof each hath told."
Then full upon my poets I moved me round;
And I perceived that they with smiles had learned
The interpretation that her discourse crowned.
To the fair lady then my face I turned.

---

130. "Lethe" and "Eunoë": see the Argument.
140-142. The golden age was "poetized" by the ancient poets. When
they sang of Parnassus ("Helicon"), they may have been dimly
conscious of the real origin of man.

Canto XXIX

---

*Matilda is proceeding along the stream, while
Dante keeps pace with her on the other side, when
she calls his attention to a brilliant light and a*

*music which are approaching. At first dazzlingly
indistinct, the light resolves itself into a mystical
procession, heralded by Seven Candlesticks, "the
seven spirits of God," followed by four and twenty
elders, symbolizing the books of the Old Testa-
ment, and four Beasts, symbolizing the Gospels.
The last escort the triumphal car of the Church,
drawn by a Gryphon (representing the twofold na-
ture of Christ). By the wheels are dancing, on one
side the three theological virtues and on the other
the four active virtues. Then come elders, rose-
crowned, who typify the remaining books of the
New Testament; St. John closing the whole pro-
cession. When Dante is abreast of the car, the pro-
cession is stopped by a peal of thunder.*

Singing, like to a lady in love's dream,
  She with the closing words continued on
  Blessed are they whose sins are pardoned them.
Like nymphs that used to wander, each alone,
  Amid the shadowing green from tree to tree,
  One seeking, and one hiding from, the sun,
Against the motion of the stream moved she
  Upon the bank; and I with her abreast
  Made little step with little step agree.
Not to a hundred had our steps increased   10
  When both the banks so curved as to compel
  My feet to turn aside unto the East.
Thus went we, and were not far when it befell
  The Lady toward me turning full about
  Said: "Now, my brother, look and listen well!"
And lo! a sudden splendour dazzled out
  From all sides of the forest through the trees,
  So that, if it were lightning, I made doubt.
But since the lightning, as it comes, ceases,

And this, remaining, ever intenser grew,   20
   Within my thought I said: "What thing is this?"
And a sweet melody ran thrilling through
   The luminous air; which in my righteous zeal
   Made me the hardihood of Eve to rue,
Who, but a woman newly formed to feel,
   Alone, where all earth and all heaven obeyed,
   Presumed to abide not under any veil,   27
Beneath which had she in devotion stayed,
   I should of those ineffable delights
   Supp'd sooner, and with me longer had they
     delayed.   30
While thus I went mid the first sounds and sights
   Of the eternal pleasance, hesitant
   In joy that longed to reach yet heavenlier heights,
Before us, under the green boughs aslant,
   The air glowed as a fire glows in a blast,
   And the sweet sound was heard now as a chant.
O Virgins holy and high, if ever fast,   37
   And cold, and vigil, I for you endured,
   Now am I spurred to claim reward at last.
Helicon's founts for me be full out-poured,   40
   With all her choir Urania me uphold   41
   To attempt in verse things scarce to thought assured.
A little farther on seven trees of gold
   Feigned to be such by reason that the tract
   Dividing us from them the sight cajoled.
But when a nearer vision had unpacked
   The general image, which our fancies gloze,
   So that of no particular it lacked,
The power that argument for reason shows
   Perceived them candlesticks, even as they were,   50

---

27. "Any veil": of ignorance.
37. "O Virgins . . .": the Muses.
41. "Ur..a": the Muse of astronomy.

And clear the words into "Hosanna" rose.

In beauty on high the pomp was flaming there,
  Brighter by far than is the moon's mild blaze
  In her mid month through the clear midnight air.

I turned me backward filled full of amaze
  To the good Virgil, and for answer read
  No less a weight of wonder in his gaze.

Then to the things of glory again my head
  I turned, and they came moving on so slow,
  They had been passed by a bride newly wed.   60

The Lady cried to me: "Why dost thou glow
  To look but on the living lights in awe,
  Nor seekest what comes after them to know?"

Then saw I people in white apparel draw
  Nearer, as if one led them, rank by rank:
  Such whiteness upon earth none ever saw.

The water glittered bright on my left flank,
  And gave to me my left side, if my face
  Looked into it, like a mirror, from the bank.

When on my shore I had found such vantage-place   70
  That only the stream's width kept me confined,
  The better to behold, I stayed my pace.

I saw the flames come onward, and behind
  Leave the air as if by painted colour sleeked
  That a brush trails, to each its tint assigned,

So that the air remained in order streaked
  With seven bands, the hues the Sun hath dyed
  His bow, and Delia her girdle freaked.   78

To rearward, farther than the eye descried,
  These banners streamed; as I computed it,   80
  Ten paces might the outermost divide.   81

---

60. *They would have been outstripped by a wedding procession.*
78. *"Delia": Diana, the moon.*
81. *"The outermost": the two outer ones, representing "wisdom"
and "fear of the Lord."*

Under so fair a sky as I have writ,
  Came four and twenty elders, two by two,
  And they wore crowns of the white lilies knit.
"Among the daughters of Adam blessed thou,   *85*
  And blessed," they continued in their song,
  "Thy beauties, the eternal ages through."
Soon as the flowers and the fresh grass along
  The other bank, opposite to my eye,
  Were cleared of those elect ones and their throng, *90*
As star comes after star into the sky,
  Four living creatures followed in their train,   *92*
  Crowned with green leaves, slowly advancing nigh.
Each with six wings was plumed, the plumy grain
  Filled full of eyes; and even such would gleam   *95*
  The eyes of Argus, could they live again.
But further to define the forms of them,
  I spare to spend rhymes, reader, nor can aim
  At lavishness, constrained to other theme.
But read Ezekiel, who their form and frame   *100*
  Paints as he saw them, from the region cold
  Coming upon the wind in cloud and flame.
As thou upon his page dost find them scrolled,
  So were they here; but for the wings they wore,
  John is with me, and hath the difference told.   *105*
The midmost of the space between the four
  Contained a car on two wheels, triumphing,
  Which at his neck a Gryphon onward bore.   *108*
And he stretcht upward one and the other wing

85-87. *The books of the Old Testament anticipate the greeting to Mary uttered at the time of the Annunciation.*
92. *The four animals represent the Gospels.*
95. *The hundred-eyed Argus was the guardian of Io.*
100. *Ezekiel 1:4-6; 2:12.*
105. *In the Revelation of St. John 4:6-8, the animals have six wings.*
108. *"A Gryphon": see the Argument.*

'Twixt three and three and mid band, lest he
    might,   110
  By cleaving it, to any an injury bring.
They rose so high that they were lost to sight.
  As far as he was bird, his limbs were scaled
  With gold, the rest was vermeil mixt with white.
With car so fair never was Rome regaled
  By Africanus, nor Augustus, nay,   116
  The Sun's own car beside it would be paled,
The Sun's own car that perished, driven astray,
  At Earth's devout prayer fallen in flames extinct,
  When Jove let justice have her secret way.   120
Beside the car's right wheel came dancing linked
  Three ladies in a ring; so red was one,   122
  That scarce in fire her form had been distinct:
The next was like as if her flesh and bone
  Were made all of an emerald; the third
  Seemed snow on which the air had newly blown.
And now the red to lead the rest appeared,
  And now the white; and from the chant which led
  They took the time, as slow or quick they heard.
By the left wheel came four with festal tread,   130
  In purple, following in their order due
  One of them, who had three eyes in her head.
After the passing of this retinue
  I saw two aged men, unlike arrayed,
  But like in mien, reverend and grave to view.
One showed him a familiar of that trade   136

116-120. "Africanus": *Publius Cornelius Scipio. Phaëthon, the un-successful driver of the chariot of the sun, was stricken down by Jove.*

122-125. *Red is the color of Charity.* "The next" *is Hope, the third is Faith.*

130. *The four cardinal virtues: Prudence (who leads), Temperance, Justice, and Fortitude.*

136-139. *The "familiar" of Hippocrates, the Greek doctor, repre-*

Ennobled by supreme Hippocrates
Whom Nature for her dearest creatures made.
Contrary care the other seemed to please:
    He bore a sword so keen and bright, its glance   140
    Made, even across the stream, fear on me seize.
Then saw I four, of aspect humble, advance;   *142*
    And behind all was an old man alone
    Coming, with piercing visage, in a trance.
And all these seven had a like raiment on
    With the first troop, but round about the head
    A garlanding of lilies had they none,
Of roses rather, and other blossoms red.
    One from short distance viewing them would swear
    That over the eyes a fire upon them fed.   150
Now when the car came opposite me, the air
    Thundered; and this folk in their solemn lines,
    Seeming forbidden, did no farther dare,
Halting in that place with the van's ensigns.   *154*

---

sents the book of the Acts of the Apostles. "The other" *represents*
the Epistles of Paul.
142-144. "Four": the minor Epistles. The "old man" stands for the
Revelations of St. John.
154. "The van's ensigns": the candlesticks.

Canto XXX

Like the stars of Ursa Minor which guide sailors to
port, the Seven Candlesticks, stars of the empy-
rean, control the movements of those in the proces-
sion; and the elders who preceded the car now turn
toward it, and one (who represents the Song of
Solomon) calls on Beatrice to appear. Angels are

*seen scattering flowers, and in the midst of them a
veiled lady clad in the colors of Faith, Hope, and
Charity. It is Beatrice; and Dante experiences the
same agitation in her presence, though her face is
not revealed, as when he first saw her. Overcome,
he turns for comfort to Virgil; but Virgil has
now disappeared; and Beatrice addresses Dante by
name, severe in look and in speech. Frozen by her
reproaches, he is melted by the compassion of the
angels, to whom Beatrice tells of Dante's life and
disloyalty to her.*

Now when those Seven of the First Heaven stood
    still   1
  Which rising and declension never knew
  Nor veil of other mist than the evil will,
And which apprized each there what he should do,
  Even as the starry Seven in lower air   5
  Guide him to port who steereth by them true,
The people in whom truth doth itself declare,
  Who first between it and the Gryphon came,
  Turned to the car, as if their peace were there.
And one, as if Heaven prompted that acclaim,   10
  Veni, sponsa, de Libano chanted thrice,   11
  And after him all the others cried the same.
As at the last trump shall the saints arise,
  Crying alleluias to be re-attired
  In flesh, up from the cavern where each lies,
Upon the heavenly chariot so inspired
  A hundred sprang *ad vocem tanti senis,*   17

1-4. "The First Heaven": the Empyrean.—"The evil will": man's
    sinfulness.—"There": in the procession of the Church.
5-6. As the Ursa Minor guides the helmsman.
11. "Come with me from Lebanon, my spouse."
17. "At the voice of so great an elder."

Messengers of eternal life, who quired

Singing together *Benedictus qui venis,*   *19*

    While from their hands flowers up and down were
        thrown,   *20*

    And *Manibus O date lilia plenis.*   *21*

I have seen ere now at the beginning dawn

    The region of the East all coloured rose,

    (The pure sky else in beauty of peace withdrawn)

When shadowed the sun's face uprising shows,

    So that the mists, attempering his powers,

    Let the eye linger upon him in repose;

So now for me amid a cloud of flowers

    That from the angels' hands up-floated light

    And fell, withinside and without, in showers,   *30*

A lady, olive-crowned o'er veil of white,

    Clothed in the colour of a living flame,

    Under a mantle green, stole on my sight.

My spirit that a time too long to name

    Had passed, since, at her presence coming nigh,

    A trembling thing and broken it became,

Now by no recognition of the eye

    But virtue invisible that went out from her

    Felt old love seize me in all its mastery.

When smote my sight the high virtue that, ere   *40*

    The years of boyhood were behind me laid,

    Already had pierced me through, as with a spear,

With such trust as a child that is afraid

    Or hurt, runs to his mother with his pains,

    I turned me to the left, to seek me aid

And say to Virgil: "Scarce one drop remains

    Of blood in me that trembles not: by this

    I recognize the old flame within my veins."

But Virgil had from us his company's

---

19. "Blessed is he that cometh" (in the name of the Lord).
21. "Oh, give lilies with full hands!"

Sweet solace taken, Virgil, father kind,   50
  Virgil, who for my soul's weal made me his.
Nor all that our first mother had resigned   52
  Availed to keep my cheeks, washed with the dew,
  From tears that once more stained them, welling
    blind.
"Dante, that Virgil leaves thee, and from thy view
  Is vanished, O not yet weep; weep not yet,
  For thou must weep, another stab to rue."
Like the admiral who on poop or prow is set,
  To eye his men, in the other ships dispersed,
  And comes, each heart to embolden and abet,   60
So on the left side of the car, when first
  I turned, hearing my own name in my ear
  (Which of necessity is here rehearsed)
I found the gaze of her I had seen appear
  Erewhile, veiled, in the angelic festival,
  Toward me, this side the stream, directed clear;
Howbeit the veil she had from her head let fall,
  With grey leaf of Minerva chapleted,
  Disclosing her, did not disclose her all.
Still severe, standing in her queenlihead,   70
  She spoke on, as one speaks whose purpose is
  To keep the hottest word awhile unsaid.
"Look on me well: I am, I am Beatrice.
  How, then, didst thou deign to ascend the Mount?
  Knewest thou not that, here, man is in bliss?"
I dropt mine eyes down to the lucent fount,
  But seeing myself there, drew them back in haste
  To the grass, heavy upon my shame's account.
As to a child a mother looks stern-faced,
  So to me seemed she: pity austere in thought   80
  Hath in its savour a so bitter taste.
She ceased then, and from every angel throat

52. Not all Eden.

Straightway *In te, Domine, speravi* rose 83
But beyond *pedes meos* they passed not.
As on the chine of Italy the snows 85
Lodged in the living rafters harden oft
To freezing, when the North-East on them blows,
Then, inly melted, trickle from aloft,
If from the shadeless countries a breath stirs, 89
Like in the flame a candle melting soft, 90
So was I, without sighs and without tears,
In presence of their singing who accord
Their notes to music of the eternal spheres;
But when I was aware of the sweet chord
Of their compassion, more than if they spoke
Saying, "Lady, why this shame upon him poured?"
The ice that round my heart had hardened woke
Warm into breath and water, and from my breast
In anguish, through mouth and through eyes, out-
broke.
She, standing ever in her still'd arrest 100
Upon the car's same side, to the array
Of those compassionate beings these words addrest:
"Ye so keep watch in the everlasting day
That neither night stealeth from you, nor sleep,
One step that the world takes upon its way;
Therefore my answer shall the more care keep
That he, there, understand me amid those tears,
So that transgression equal sorrow reap.
Not only by operation of great spheres 109
Which to some certain end each seed uptrain 110

83-84. Ps. 31: "In thee, O Lord, do I put my trust." Verse 8 ends
with: "Thou hast set my feet in a large room."
85. "The chine of Italy" is the Apennine range.
89. "The shadeless countries": the African desert.
109-112. The "great spheres" are the revolving heavens, which de-
termine the disposition of every human being. God also bestows
upon every individual a special degree of grace.

According as the starry voice it hears,
But bounty of heavenly graces, which for rain
  Have exhalations born in place so high
  That our eyes may not near to them attain,
This man was such in natural potency,
  In his new life, that all the ingrained good   *116*
  Looked in him to have fruited wondrously.
But so much groweth the more rank and rude
  The soil with bad seed and unhusbanded,
  The more it hath from earth of hardihood.   *120*
His spirit some time my countenance comforted
  With look of my young eyes for its support,
  Drawing him, the right path with me to tread.
Soon as the threshold I had passed, athwart
  The second period, and life changed its home,   *125*
  Me he forsook, with others to consort.
When from the flesh to spirit I had clomb
  And beauty and virtue greater in me grew,
  Less dear to him, more strange did I become;
And with perverted steps on ways untrue   *130*
  He sought false images of good, that ne'er
  Perform entire the promise that was due.
Nor helped me the inspiration won by prayer
  Whereby through dream or other hidden accost
  I called him back; so little had he care.
So low he sank, all means must I exhaust,
  Till naught for his salvation profited
  Save to be shown the people that are lost.
For this I broached the gateway of the dead,
  For this with tears was my entreaty brought   *140*
  To him, by whom his feet were hither led.
The ordinance of high God were set at naught

---

116. "New life": young life.
125. "The second period": begins at 25. Her "life changed" the
temporal home for the eternal.

If Lethe were passed over into peace,
    And such viand enjoyed, without some scot
Of penitence that may the tears release."

Canto XXXI

---

*Dante, accused by Beatrice, confesses his sin and is
filled with penitence. Overwhelmed by the severity
of Beatrice's words, and by his own remorse, he
falls senseless. When he recovers from his faint, he
finds that Matilda is drawing him across Lethe
stream, in which she immerses him. The four
dancers (the four cardinal virtues) lead him up to
the Gryphon, where Beatrice is standing; in her
eyes the Gryphon is mirrored, now in one form
now in the other. The other three (the Theological
Virtues) then come forward, dancing, and implore
Beatrice to smile upon her faithful servant.*

"O THOU who art yon-side the sacred stream,"
    Turning her speech to point at me the blade
    Which even the edge had made so sharp to seem,
She spoke again, continuing undelayed.
    "Say, say if this be true; for, thus accused,
    Confession must thereto by thee be made"
Whereat my faculties were so confused
    That the voice stirred and faltered and was dead
    Ere it came free of the organs that it used.
Short time she endured; "What think'st thou?" then she
        said.   10
    "Answer, for in thee the sad memories

By the water are not yet discomfited."   *12*
Fear and confusion's mingled miseries
   Constrained out of my mouth a "Yes" so low
   That to understand it there was need of eyes.
As the arbalast that snaps both string and bow,
   When to a too great tautness it is forced,
   And shooting hits the mark with feebler blow,
So under this so heavy charge I burst,
   Out of me letting gush the sighs and tears;   *20*
   And in its vent my voice failed as from thirst.
Wherefore she questioned: "Within those desires
   I stirred in thee, to make thee love the Good
   Beyond which nought is, whereto man aspires,
What moats or what strong chains athwart thy road
   Didst thou encounter, that of hope to pass
   Onward, thou needs must strip thee as of a load?
And what solace or profit in the face
   Of the others was displayed unto thine eye
   That thou before them up and down must pace?"   *30*
After the drawing of a bitter sigh
   Scarce had I voice an answer to essay,
   And lips with difficulty shaped reply.
Weeping I said: "Things of the passing day,
   Soon as your face no longer on me shone,
   With their false pleasure turned my steps away."
And she: "If thou wert silent, nor didst own
   What thou avowest, not less were record
   Of thy fault made: by such a judge 'tis known.
But when the sinner's own mouth has outpoured   *40*
   The accusation, in our court the wheel   *41*
   Against the edge is turned back on the sword.
Howbeit, that now the shame thou carry still
   For thine error, and at the Siren's plea

---

12. "The water": of Lethe.
41-42. *The sword of justice is blunted, i.e., tempered with mercy.*

Another time thou be of stronger will,
Lay aside the seed of weeping; hark to me.
  Hear how my buried body should have spurred
  And on the opposite path have furthered thee.
Nature or art never to thee assured
  Such pleasure as the fair limbs that did house   50
  My spirit, and now are scattered and interred.
And if the highest pleasure failed thee thus
  By my death, at such time what mortal thing
  Ought to have drawn thee toward it amorous?
Truly oughtest thou at the first arrow's sting
  Of those lures, to rise after me on high,
  Who was no more made in such fashioning.
Nay, nor should girl or other vanity   58
  Of such brief usage have thy wings down-weighed
  To wait for other coming shafts to fly.   60
The young bird waiteth two or three indeed;
  But in the eyes of the full-fledged in vain
  The net is spread and the arrows vainly speed."
As boys that dumb with shamefastness remain,
  Eyes to ground, listening to their faults rehearsed,
  Knowing themselves in penitence and pain,
So stood I; and she said: "From what thou hear'st
  If thou art grieving, lift thy beard and look,   68
  And thou shalt by a greater grief be pierced."
With less resistance is a stubborn oak   70
  Torn up by wind (whether 'twas ours that blew
  Or wind that from Iarbas' land awoke)   72
Than at her bidding I my chin up-drew;
  And when by "beard" she asked me for my face,

---

58. Is the "girl" to be taken literally, or does she symbolize some
  intellectual pursuit inconsistent with the spiritual ideal? The ques-
  tion remains open.
68. "Beard": chin.
72. "Iarba" was king of Libya.

The venom in the meaning well I knew.   75
And when to expose my features I could brace
   My spirit, I saw those primal Essences   77
   Reposing from their strewings in their place.
And mine eyes, hardly as yet assured of these,
   Were 'ware of Beatrice, turned toward that beast   80
   Which in two natures one sole person is.
Under her veil beyond the stream I wist
   That she surpassed her ancient self yet more
   Than when amongst us she surpassed the rest.
The nettle of penitence pricked me now so sore
   That, of all things, that which did most pervert
   To love of it, I had most hatred for.
The recognition gnawed so at my heart
   That I fell conquered, and what then of me
   Became, she knows who had devised the smart.   90
Then when my heart restored the faculty
   Of sense, the lady I had found alone   92
   I saw above me, and "Hold," she said, "hold me."
To the neck into the stream she had led me on
   And, drawing me behind her, went as light
   Over the water as a shuttle thrown.
When I was near the bank of blessed sight
   Asperges me my ears so sweetly graced   98
   I cannot recollect it, far less write.
The fair lady opened her arms, embraced   100
   My head, and plunged me underneath the flow,
   Where swallowing I must needs the water taste,
Then raised me and presented me, bathed so,

---

75. *The implication that the beard is inconsistent with Dante's
   youthful vagaries.*
77. "Primal Essences": the angels.
80. "That beast": the Gryphon.
92. "The lady": Matilda.
98. "Purge me": Ps. 51:7.

Within the dancing of the beauteous Four;   *104*
   And each an arm about me came to throw.
"Here we are nymphs, in the sky stars: before
   Beatrice descended to the world, we were
   Ordained to be her handmaids evermore.
We'll lead thee to her eyes; but the Three there,   *109*
   Whose gaze is deeper, in the blissful light   110
   That is within, shall make thine own more clear."
Thus singing they began, and me then right
   Up to the Gryphon's breast with them they led
   Where Beatrice was standing opposite.
"See that thou spare not of thy gaze," they said.
   "We have set thee afore the emeralds to stand   *116*
   Wherefrom for thee Love once his armoury fed."
Thousand desires, hotter than flame, constrained
   The gaze of mine eyes to the shining eyes
   Which on the Gryphon only fixed remained.   120
As in the glass the sun, not otherwise
   The two-fold creature had its mirroring
   Within them, now in one, now the other guise.   *123*
Think, Reader, if I marvelled at this thing,
   When I beheld it unchanged as at first
   Itself, and in its image altering.
While in a deep astonishment immersed
   My happy soul was tasting of that food
   Which, itself sating, of itself makes thirst,
Showing themselves as if of loftiest blood   130
   In their demeanour, the other three came then
   Dancing to the angelic air they trod.
"Turn, Beatrice, turn thy sainted eyes again,"

---

104. "The beauteous Four": *the cardinal virtues.*
109. "The Three": *the theological virtues.*
116. "The emeralds": *the eyes of Beatrice.*
123. *Now with its human, now with its divine, bearing—the two component parts of the nature of Christ.*

So were they singing, "to thy servant leal
Who to see thee so many steps hath ta'en.
Of thy grace do us this grace, to unveil
To him thy mouth, so that he may discern
The second beauty which thou dost conceal."   *138*
O splendour of the living light eterne,
Who is there that beneath Parnassus' shade   *140*
Has grown pale or has drunk of that cistern
That would not seem to have his mind o'er-weighed
Striving to paint thee as thou appeared'st where
To figure thee, heaven's harmonies are made,
When thou didst unveil to the open air?

---

138. "The second beauty" *is the mouth, the first beauty being the* *eyes.*

Canto XXXII

Dazzled to blindness for a while by the eyes of Beatrice, Dante becomes aware that the procession has wheeled round and is returning to face the sun. The Gryphon moves the car, and Dante follows it, with Matilda and Statius, through the wood. They come to a tree, despoiled of flowers and leaves; and the Gryphon fastens the car to the trunk of it; whereon it puts forth all its foliage again. Dante falls into a sleep and waking sees Beatrice guarding the car, the Gryphon having ascended to heaven, while the seven Virtues make a ring round her. An eagle swoops down on the tree, stripping it of its flowers and leaves once more. Then a vixen leaps into the car, but is put to flight by Beatrice. The eagle descends again, enters the car and leaves it clothed with his plumage. Between the wheels

*the earth gapes and a dragon comes forth and
wrenches off part of the car. The remnant of the
car is again covered in an instant by the plumes;
from it seven heads emerge; and seated on the car
appear a harlot and a giant, by whom it is dragged
away.*

*These actions and transformations typify crises
and vicissitudes in the history of the Church. The
harlot represents the Papacy under Boniface VIII
and Clement V, the giant the French monarchy.*

So FASTENED were mine eyes, and so intent
   The ten years' thirst of longing to abate,
   That the other senses were annulled and spent,
And they on this side and on that side set
   Walls of unheeding (so to itself allured
   The holy smile, drawing the ancient net)—
When needs must they be against my will conjured
   Unto my left hand by those Goddesses,   8
   Because from them a "Too fixt!" I had heard;
And the condition which impoverishes   10
   The eyes but lately smitten by the sun
   Caused for a space the sight of mine to cease.
But when to less things by comparison
   My sight was re-established, less I mean
   Than the great splendour I was forced to shun,
I saw the glorious army, that had been
   Wheeled to the right, returning to confront
   The seven flames in their place and the sun's sheen.
As, for retreat, with shields to bear the brunt,
   A squadron wheels and turns with the ensign, ere 20
   It can accomplish the full change of front,
That soldiery of the heavenly kingdom there,

---

8. "Those Goddesses": the three Christian Virtues.

Which made the van, all passed us by before
The turning of the pole had turned the car.

While to the wheels the ladies came once more
The Gryphon moved the blessed charge onward,
Yet not so that one feather shook therefor.

The fair lady who drew me to the ford,   28
Statius, and I, were following the wheel
That with a smaller arc its orbit scored.   30

As thus we thrid the high wood, where none dwell
Through her who trusted to the snake's deceit,
Music of angels timed our paces well.

Perhaps in three flights takes a space as great
A shaft loosed from the string as we had gone,
When Beatrice alighted on her feet.

I heard all murmur "Adam"; and anon
They made a circle about a tree, made bare   38
Of flower and leaf on branches every one.

Its summit, which expands the more in air   40
The loftier it grows, would for its height
Make the Indians in their woods admiring stare.

"Blest art thou, Gryphon, that with beak and bite   43
Thou tearest naught from this sweet-tasting wood
Seeing how ill the belly griped from it."

Thus as about the stalwart tree they stood
Cried the others, and the twy-formed beast cried too;
"So is preserved the seed of all things good."

And turning round upon the pole he drew,
He halted it beneath the widowed stem,   50
And that which came from it left bound thereto.

As plants on earth when downward falls on them   52

---

28. "The fair lady": *Matilda.*
30. *The right wheel, inasmuch as the chariot is turning to the right.*
38. "A tree": *the Tree of Law.*
43-45. *Christ himself is careful not to trespass on the field of temporal power.*
52. "When downward falls . . .": *in the spring.*

The great light, mingled with the radiance
   Which comes behind the heavenly Carp to beam,
Swell inly, and each renews its own substance
   And its own colour ere the Sun anew
   His steeds beneath another star advance,
So the reviving tree into a hue
   Less than of rose, more than of violet,
   Through its so desolated branches grew.   60
I understood it not, nor may repeat
   The hymn, which then that people chanted, here,
   Nor did my sense outlast the whole of it.
If I could picture how the eyes severe
   Were lulled to sleep, hearing of Syrinx tell,   65
   The eyes whose too long vigil cost so dear,
I would portray how into sleep I fell,
   As one whose painting with his model vies:
   But who paints drowsing let him paint it well.
Wherefore I pass to where I opened eyes.   70
   I say, a splendour rent sleep's veil away,
   And summons of a voice: "What dost thou? Rise!"
As, to behold some flower of the apple-spray   73
   Which makes the angels for its fruit athirst
   And makes in heaven perpetual marriage-day,
Peter and John and James were led, and first
   Quite overpowered, came to themselves again
   At that word which a greater sleep dispersed,
And saw their company diminished then
   By Moses and Elias also, and eyed   80
   Their master's raiment altered in its grain,
So came I to myself; and I espied

---

65. *The hundred eyes of Argus were put to sleep by Mercury's song
   of the nymph Syrinx.*
73-78. *"Some flower of the apple-spray": a foretaste of Christ's glory.
   The scene has been transformed. A change as wonderful as when
   Peter, John, and James, who had witnessed the Transfiguration of
   Christ, recovered from their fright (Matt. 17:1-8).*

That pitying one bent o'er me, who my foot
Had led along the stream and been my guide.
And I said: "Where is Beatrice?" all in doubt.
    Whereon she answered me: "Behold her there
    Sitting under the new leaf on its root.
Behold the company encircling her!
    The rest after the Gryphon mount on high
    With a profounder song and sweeter air."   90
And if her words were further poured forth, I
    Know not, since she, who from all other sound
    Had shut me out, was now before mine eye.
Alone she sat upon the very ground,
    Left there, the chariot to watch and ward
    Which by the twy-formed beast I had seen bound.
The seven nymphs round her made for her a guard
    With those lights in their hands which, burning free,
    Neither by North or South wind may be marred.
"Here for short time a forester, with me   100
    Shalt thou an everlasting citizen
    Of that Rome, whereof Christ is Roman, be.   102
Upon the car keep thine eyes fastened then,
    And what thou seest, when thou returnest, write
    That it may profit the evil life of men."
Thus Beatrice: and I with my whole might
    Whither she willed, devoted at the feet
    Of her commands, gave both my mind and sight.
Never did fire from clouds that gathering meet,
    When from the region that is most remote   110
    It rains, come down with suddenness as fleet
As I saw swoop the bird of Jove; he shot   112
    Down through the tree; the bark of it he rent,

---

102. "Of that Rome . . .": the city of God.
112. "The bird of Jove": the eagle (the emblem of the Roman Empire), whose descent represents here the persecution of the Christians.

And the flowers too and the fresh foliage smote.
And all his force upon the car he spent,
   Which staggered like a ship by tempest chased
   And now to starboard now to larboard sent.
Then I beheld into the hollow haste
   Of the triumphal wain a vixen, lean   *119*
   As if of no good food she knew the taste.   120
But with upbraiding for her sins unclean
   My lady turned her to such flight thereon
   As bones may compass with no flesh between.
And then from there, whence down he first had flown,
   The eagle I saw descend into that ark   *125*
   And leave it plumed with feathers of his own.
And such as comes from a heart grieving dark
   A voice issued from heaven, and thus it spoke:
   "How ill thou art laden, O my little barque!"
Then it appeared to me that, as the earth broke   130
   'Twixt the two wheels, a dragon made his way   *131*
   Therefrom and through the car his tail up-stuck.
And like a wasp which draws the sting away,
   Drawing to himself the venomed tail, he drew
   Part of the floor forth, and so trailed astray.
That which remained, like soil enlivened new
   With grass, the feathers (haply offered by
   Benign intention) once more overgrew,
And all was clothed therewith before mine eye,
   Both one and the other wheel and pole, so soon   140
   That the mouth opens longer for a sigh.
The holy shrine, this transformation done,
   Put forth heads pushing through its parts; and o'er
   The pole were three, and in each corner one.

---

119. *The vixen stands for Heresy.*
125. *The return of the eagle symbolizes the donation of Constantine.*
131-147. *Here is recorded a great schism, either the secession of the*
   Greek Church or the Mohammedan movement. The seven heads
   represent the seven capital vices.

The first had horns as of an ox, the four
   A single horn that from the forehead rose·
   Never was seen such prodigy before.
Secure as fortress on a mountain shows,
   Upon it a loose harlot sat enthroned   *149*
   With quick glances around under her brows.   150
As if that by none else should she be owned,
   I saw a towering giant standing by: *152*
   Somewhile they kissed together and were fond.
But when she turned on me her wanton eye,
   A scourge on her that savage paramour
   From head to the foot-soles began to ply.
Then full of jealousy and in anger sore
   He loosed the monster and dragged it through the
      wood
   So far that the trees only from the whore
And the new beast a shield before me stood.   160

---

149. "A loose harlot": see the Argument.
152. "A giant": see the Argument.

Canto XXXIII

---

*The Seven Virtues lament the triumph of evil
forces, but Beatrice tells them that though she de-
parts, it is only for a time. Leaving the tree with
the Seven, and followed by Dante, Statius, and Ma-
tilda, she speaks graciously to Dante and proph-
esies the future when one, represented by the Ro-
man numerals DUX, shall rescue Italy from her
present corruptions: this is conjectured to be the
emperor Henry VII. But she sees that Dante does
not understand her enigmatic discourse, since his*

mind has been dulled as if hardened by the petrify-
ing waters of the Elsa. He asks why she speaks so
darkly, and she replies that it was to show him how
inadequate is the philosophy he has followed:
henceforth she will speak more clearly. It is now
noon. Beatrice bids Matilda lead Dante to the foun-
tain from which both Lethe and Eunoë flow. He
drinks of Eunoë and is forthwith ready to mount on
his further journey to Paradise.

D<small>EUS</small>, *venerunt gentes;* thus, now three,   *1*
  Now four, with voice and weeping, alternate
  Began those ladies a sweet psalmody;
And Beatrice, sighing and compassionate
  Listened with look so altered, at the cross
  Scarce was the change on Mary's face more great.
But when those nymphs, for her to interpose,
  Yielded her place, up to her full height she,
  In colour like a flame, on her feet rose.
"*Modicum, et non videbitis me*   *10*
  Et iterum, dear sisters mine," she said,
  "*Modicum, et vos videbitis me.*"
Then all the seven before her she arrayed,
  And merely by her nod before her brought
  Me and the lady and the sage who stayed.   *15*
Thus she went on, and I believe that not
  Ten steps upon the ground by her were paced
  When with her eyes upon mine eyes she smote.
And with a tranquil countenance: "Make more haste"
  She adjured me, "so that if I speak with thee   *20*
  Thou wilt for hearkening be the better placed."

---

1. *Ps.* 79:1: "O God, the heathen are come into Thine inheritance."
10-12. *John* 16:16: "A little while, and ye shall not see me: and
again, a little while, and ye shall see me."
15. "The lady": Matilda. "The sage": Statius.

Soon as I was, where duty bade me be,
 With her, she said: "Brother, why ventureth
 Thy tongue not, now thou art near, to question me?"
As with those who from reverence bate their breath
 Before their betters, so that, being unstrung,
 They bring not the voice living to the teeth,
So it happed to me; and with a halting tongue
 I said to her: "My need, Madonna, you
 Well know, and what things to its good belong." 30
And she to me: "I would that thou eschew
 Both fear and shame and rid thee of their cloak,
 So that thou speak no more as dreamers do.
Know that the vessel which the serpent broke   34
 Was and is not; but let the guilty weigh   35
 This well: God fears no sops to avert his stroke.
Not for all time without an heir shall stay
 The eagle who left the plumage on the car,   38
 Whence it became a monster, and then a prey.
For surely I see, what now I tell thee, a star   40
 That, safe from barrier and impediment,
 Shall bring us times, already now not far,
When a Five Hundred Ten and Five forth sent   43
 By God shall slay the thief and also him,
 That giant, who with her in whoredom went.
Perhaps my prophecy, obscure in theme
 As Sphinx or Themis, may persuade thee less
 Since in like mode it maketh thy mind·dim;
But soon the events shall be the Naiades   49

---

34. The "vessel" is the chariot.
35. "The guilty": Clement and Philip shall both be stricken down.
38. "The eagle": the Empire; Dante considered Frederick II the last
Roman Emperor.
43. The number DXV gives DUX, the Latin word for "leader." An
emperor, ordained by God, is soon to correct the Papacy and over-
throw the power of France.
49. Dante erroneously believed that the "Naiades," or water-nymphs,
were the successful guessers of the Sphinx's riddle.

That, without ruin of the flocks or scaith   50
　　To corn, shall solve this riddle's knottedness.
Note thou: as these words go forth on my breath,
　　Their purport do thou unto them declare
　　Who live that life which is a race to death.
And when thou writest these things, have a care
　　Not to conceal how thou hast seen the boughs
　　Which here have twice been ravaged and made bare.
Whoso despoils that tree or rends it, does
　　Offence to God, since he in act hath curst
　　What God created holy for His use.   60
For biting of it did in pain and thirst
　　Five thousand years and more the first soul yearn 62
　　For Him who in himself the bite amerced.
Thy wit sleeps if it faileth to discern
　　That tree for a special cause to be so high
　　And at the top to growth inverted turn.
If the vain thoughts thy mind is crusted by
　　Had not been water of Elsa and not made   68
　　Their pleasure a Pyramus to the mulberry,   69
By heed to so great circumstances paid   70
　　Thou wouldst have found thy moral sense admit
　　God's justice in the tree that he forbade.
But since I see dulled into stone thy wit
　　And, stony, into stain of colour wrought
　　Such that the light of my word dazzles it,
I also will that, if not written, thy thought
　　Bear it within thee, for the cause wherefore
　　The staff with palm encircled home is brought."   78
And I: "As wax is under the seal's power,
　　Keeping unchanged the figure it imprest,   80

62-63. "The first soul": Adam. "For Him": Christ.
68. "Water of Elsa": see the Argument.
69. As the blood of Pyramus stained the mulberry.
78. "The staff" which the pilgrims bring back from the Holy Land.

My brain is stamped by you for evermore.
But why doth your word, longed-for without rest,
    Soar now so far beyond my vision's reach,
    That the more keen, the vainer is its quest?"
"That thou may'st see," she said, "what the schools
        teach
    Which thou hast followed, and may'st come to know
    How vain its power to keep pace with my speech,
And see your way from the divine way so
    Far separate as is that heaven remote
    Which speeds the highest, from the earth below." 90
Wherefore I answered: "I remember not
    That I estranged myself ever from you,
    Nor prick of conscience therefrom have I got."
"And if in this thy memory tells not true,"
    Smiling she answered, "art thou not acquaint
    How thou this day of Lethe hast drunken new?
And if for fire the smoke is argument,
    Clearly doth this forgetfulness a flaw
    Prove in thy will, on other things intent.
But naked verily shall be my saw   100
    Henceforth, so far as shall befit thy case,
    Uncovering it unto thy vision raw."
Both more resplendent and with slower pace
    The sun held the meridian circle above
    Which varieth still with the observer's place,
When halted (as he halts and doth not move
    Who goes with folk to escort them and defend,
    If he finds aught new or the trace thereof)
The seven ladies, at a shadow's end
    Pale as beneath black branches and green growth 110
    The mountains over their cold brooks extend.
Before them Tigris and Euphrates both
    I seemed to see from one spring welling twinned
    And parting as friends part, lingering and loth.

"O light! O glory of all human kind,
    What are these waters that from one source fleet
    And self from self into the distance wind?"
At such a prayer was said to me: "Entreat
    Matilda that she tell thee"; and here replied,
    As one who doth himself from blame acquit,   120
The fair lady: "This and things beside
    Have been told him by me; and I can swear
    That these from him no Lethe waters hide."
And Beatrice: "Perhaps a greater care
    That often putteth memory to rout
    Hath made his mind dim-eyed and unaware.
But behold Eunoë, which there floweth out: 127
    Lead him to it, and, as thou art wont to use,
    Revive his virtue faint to death with doubt."
As noble soul that maketh no excuse   130
    But makes another's will her will, when she
    The outward sign of it straightway construes,
So the fair lady, having taken me,
    Set forth and spoke to Statius in his place:
    "Come with him," gracious as a queen may be.
If, Reader, for the writing were more space,
    That sweet fount, whence I ne'er could drink my fill,
    Would I yet sing, though in imperfect praise.
But seeing that for this second canticle
    The paper planned is full to the last page,   140
    The bridle of art must needs constrain my will.
Back from that wave's most holy privilege
    I turned me, re-made, as the plant repairs
    Itself, renewed with its new foliage,
Pure and disposed to mount up to the stars.

[handwritten marginalia: Confession of Dante / purified]

---

127. *Dante's memory of the good must be revived by Eunoë.*

PARADISO

Canto I

The poet invokes the aid of Apollo in attempting the hardest part of his theme, the description of Paradise.

On earth, in Italy, it is evening; but at the summit of the Mount of Purgatory it is near noon about the time of the vernal equinox; the sun being in Aries, a propitious conjunction. Dante and Beatrice are suddenly transported to the sphere of fire, between the earth and the moon. Dante is so "transhumanized" that he is now able to hear the music of the spheres; but at first he is bewildered, not understanding, till Beatrice explains that he has left the earth behind. He is still puzzled to know how it is that he has risen, more swiftly than air or fire, against the laws of gravitation. Beatrice tells him that the instinct implanted in the soul is to rise, as fire rises, towards heaven; this belongs to the order of the universe, in which each part has its own function. Dante has been liberated from the distractions which, through man's possession of free will, sometimes cause the soul to be diverted from its aim.

THE glory of Him who moveth all that is
　Pervades the universe, and glows more bright
　In the one region, and in another less.
In that heaven which partakes most of His light
　I have been, and have beheld such things as who

Comes down thence has no wit nor power to write;
Such depth our understanding deepens to
   When it draws near unto its longing's home
   That memory cannot backward with it go.
Nevertheless what of the blest kingdom   10
   Could in my memory, for its treasure, stay
   Shall now the matter of my song become.
For the last labour, good Apollo, I pray,
   Make me so apt a vessel of thy power
   As is required for gift of thy loved bay.   15
One of Parnassus' peaks hath heretofore
   Sufficed me; both now shall I need forthwith
   For entering on the last arena-floor.
Enter into my bosom, and in-breathe
   Such force as filled thee to out-sing the strain   20
   Of Marsyas when thou didst his limbs unsheathe.   21
O divine power, if thou so far sustain,
   That I may show the image visibly
   Of the holy realm imprinted on my brain,
Thou'lt see me come to thy beloved tree   25
   And there the leaves upon my temples fit
   Which I shall earn both through the theme and thee.
So few times, Father, is there plucked of it
   For Caesar or for poet triumphing
   (Fault and reproach of human will and wit),   30
That in the joyous Delphic god must spring   31
   A joy new-born, when the Peneian frond
   With longing for itself doth any sting.
A small spark kindles a great flame beyond:
   Haply after me with better voice than mine

handwritten marginalia: to give an image of heaven

---

15. "Loved bay": Daphne, loved and pursued by Apollo, was changed to a laurel.
21. "Marsyas": a satyr, who was defeated and then flayed by Apollo.
25. "Thy beloved tree": the laurel.
31-32. "The joyous Delphic god": Apollo. "The Peneian frond": the laurel.

Such prayer shall plead, that Cirrha may respond. 36
The world's lamp rises upon men to shine   37
    By divers gates, but from that gate which makes
    Four circles with three crosses to conjoin,
With happier star joined, happier course it takes,   40
    And more to its own example can persuade,
    Moulding and stamping it, the mundane wax.
Almost this gate had morning yonder made
    And evening here; and there that hemisphere   44
    Was all white, and the other part in shade,
When, turned on her left side, I was aware
    Of Beatrice, fixing on the sun her eyes:
    Never on it so fixed was eagle's stare.
And as a second ray will always rise
    Where the first struck, and backward seek ascent, 50
    Like pilgrim hastening when he homeward hies,
So into my imagination went
    Through the eyes her gesture; and my own complied,
    And on the sun, past wont, my eyes were bent.
Much is permitted there which is denied
    Here to our faculties, thanks to the place   56
    Made for mankind to own, and there abide.
Not long I endured him, yet not so brief space
    But that I saw what sparkles round him shone
    Like molten ore fresh from the fierce furnace;   60
And, on a sudden, day seemed added on
    To day, as if He, who such things can do,
    Had glorified heaven with a second sun.
Beatrice was standing and held full in view

---

36. "Cirrha" stands for Delphi, Apollo's abode.
37-44. In these lines Dante describes the season. The sun, being almost in the sign of Aries, has the most benign influence on the earth.
44-45. Here Dante tells the hour: it was noon in Eden, midnight in Jerusalem.
56. "Thanks to the place": Eden.

The eternal wheels, and I fixed on her keen   65
  My eyes, that from above their gaze withdrew.
And at her aspect I became within
  As Glaucus after the herb's tasting, whence   68
  To the other sea-gods he was made akin.
The passing beyond bounds of human sense   70
  Words cannot tell; let then the example sate
  Him for whom grace reserves the experience.
If I was only what thou didst create   73
  Last in me, O Love whose rule the heavens attest,
  Thou know'st, who with thy light didst lift my state.
When that the wheel which thou eternizest
  In longing, held me with the harmony   77
  Which thou attunest and distinguishest,
So much of heaven was fired, it seemed to me,
  With the sun's blaze that never river or rain   80
  Widened the waters to so great a sea.
The new sound and the great light made me fain
  With craving keener than had ever been
  Before in me, their cause to ascertain.
She then, who saw me as I myself within,
  My mind's disturbance eager to remit,
  Opened her lips before I could begin,
And spoke: "Thou makest thyself dense of wit
  With false fancy, so that thou dost not see
  What thou would'st see, wert thou but rid of it.   90
Thou'rt not on earth, as thou supposest thee:
  But lightning from its own place rushing out

---

65. "The eternal wheels": *the revolving heavens.*
68. *The fisherman Glaucus, tasting of a certain herb, became a sea-god.*
73. *Dante is not sure whether he took his body with him to Heaven, or left it behind.*
77. *The swift motion of the Primum Mobile, the outermost sphere of the material universe, is due to the eagerness of every one of its parts to come into contact with every part of God's own Heaven, the Empyrean.*

Ne'er sped as thou, who to thy home dost flee."   93
If I was stript of my first teasing doubt
  By the brief smiling little words, yet freed
  I was not, but enmeshed in a new thought.
And I replied: "I am released indeed
  From much amazement; yet am still amazed
  That those light bodies I transcend in speed."
She, sighing in pity, gave me as she gazed   100
  The look that by a mother is bestowed
  Upon her child in its delirium crazed,
And said: "All things, whatever their abode,
  Have order among themselves; this Form it is
  That makes the universe like unto God.
Here the high beings see the imprint of His
  Eternal power, which is the goal divine
  Whereto the rule aforesaid testifies.
In the order I speak of, all natures incline
  Either more near or less near to their source   110
  According as their diverse lots assign.
To diverse harbours thus they move perforce
  O'er the great ocean of being, and each one
  With instinct given it to maintain its course.
This bears the fiery element to the moon;
  This makes the heart of mortal things to move;
  This knits the earth together into one.
Not only creatures that are empty of
  Intelligence this bow shoots towards the goal,
  But those that have both intellect and love.   120
The Providence, that rules this wondrous whole,
  With its own light makes the heaven still to stay 122
  Wherein whirls that which doth the swiftest roll.

---

93. "Thy home": the Empyrean.
110. "Their source": God.
122-125. "The heaven": the Empyrean, within which the swift
  Primum Mobile revolves. "That cord": the bowstring of instinct.

And thither now upon the appointed way
  We are borne on by virtue of that cord still
  Which means a joyful mark, shoot what it may.
True it is that as the form oftentimes ill
  Accordeth with the intention of the art,
  The matter being slow to serve the will,
So aside sometimes may the creature start;   130
  For it has power, though on this course impelled, *131*
  To swerve in purpose toward some other part
(And so the fire from cloud may be beheld
  To fall), if the first impulse of its flight
  To earth be wrested, by false pleasure held.
Thou should'st not marvel, if I esteem aright,
  More at thy rising than at streams we see
  Fall to the base down from a mountain's height;
Marvel it were if thou, from hindrance free,
  Had'st sat below, resolved there to remain,   140
  As stillness in live flame on earth would be."
Thereon toward heaven she turned her gaze again.

---

131. "For it has power": *the free will.*

Canto II

---

*From the sphere of fire Dante and Beatrice rise to
the Heaven of the Moon with unimaginable speed,
like the flight of a bolt from a crossbow. (The move-
ments are described in inverted order to suggest its
instantaneous swiftness.) They enter the pearllike
substance of the moon; and Dante wonders how,
still in the body, he can penetrate into it—a mys-
tery like the union of divine and human nature in
Christ. He now asks Beatrice the cause of the*

*spots in the moon, first giving the explanation he
had hitherto maintained, that they are due to den-
sity and rarity. Beatrice refutes his error and then
gives the true account. Each sphere is quickened
and governed by the Intelligence presiding over it;
and the Intelligence of the eighth heaven distrib-
utes its influence among the fixed stars. But this in-
fluence is modified by the character of the bodies it
enters; hence the variation in degree of brilliance
among the stars; hence also the brightness and dim-
ness in the moon.*

*In refuting Dante's explanation Beatrice en-
forces theory by experiment, the modern method,
here praised as the fountainhead of the arts. This is
remarkable in a medieval poem.*

O YE, EMBARKED in a small skiff, who long
　To listen, having followed on its way
　My boat, that goes continuing in song,
Turn again home to sight of shore and bay!
　Trust not the deep; for peradventure there
　By losing me ye might be left astray.
The sea I sail none yet did ever dare.
　Minerva wafts, Apollo leads me on,
　And the nine Muses show me either Bear.　9
Ye other few, who have raised your necks for boon　10
　Of the angels' bread betimes, given to sustain　11
　The life lived here (and surfeit none hath known),
Ye well may trust your bark to the salt main,
　Keeping the furrow of my keel, before
　The wake behind it is smoothed out again.

---

9. "Either Bear": the constellations of the Great and Little Bear, by
which sailors are guided.
11. "The angels' bread": sacred knowledge.

The glorious ones that fared to Colchis shore,   *16*
  When they saw Jason ply the ploughman's trade,
  Stood marvelling much; but ye shall marvel more.
The inborn thirst, which never is allayed,
  For the God-moulded realm, bore us on high   **20**
  Swift almost as ye see heaven's motion made.
Beatrice was gazing up; on her gazed I.
  Perhaps in such space as a bolt is spent
  And flies and from the peg is loosed to fly,
I saw me arriving where a marvel bent
  My sight all to itself: and she, because
  Nothing from her was hidden of my intent,
Turned—and her joy like to her beauty was—
  To me, and "Turn to God in thanks," she said,
  "Who with the first star hath united us."   *30*
It seemed a cloud all round about us spread,
  Luminous, dense, compact, and burnished bright,
  Like diamond with a sunbeam on it shed.
The everlasting pearl enclosed us quite
  Within itself, as water of a well
  Receives, remaining whole, a ray of light.
If I was body,—and on earth none could tell
  How one substance another can admit,
  Which must be, if body into body steal—
The more in us should longing's flame be lit   **40**
  To see that Essence wherein we perceive   *41*
  How our nature and God in one were knit.
There shall be seen that unto which we cleave
  By faith, not proven in argument; self-shown
  As is the simple truth that all believe.

16-18. *The Argonauts were amazed to see Jason compel two monstrous bulls to draw a plow.*
30. "The first star": *the moon.*
41. *In the "Essence" of Christ the human and the divine nature are miraculously united (see the Argument).*

"My Lady," I answered, "more devoutly none
   Could thank Him, and I thank Him yet again,
   Who hath removed me from yon mortal zone.
But tell me, what are those dark spots that stain
   This body, which down there on the earth's floor   50
   Make folk to fable of the burden of Cain?"
She smiled a little, and then said: "If the lore
   Of mortals err in its imagining,
   Where sense hath no key to unlock the door,
Truly the barb of wonder should not sting
   Thy mind henceforth, since, following after sense, 56
   Reason, thou see'st, hath all too short a wing.
But tell me what thine own intelligence
   Conceives." And "What appears diverse," said I,
   "Is caused, I think, by bodies rare or dense."   60
And she: "Indeed thou'lt see thy guess to lie
   Submerged in error, if thou give good ear
   To the argument I shall oppose it by.
Many are the lights displayed in the eighth sphere, 64
   Which both in quality and in magnitude
   May be observed a diverse look to wear.
If this from dense and rare alone ensued,
   All with one virtue, equal less or more
   In distribution, would be found imbued.
But needs must be that diverse virtues flower   70
   From formal principles; and these, save one,   71
   Would on thy reasoning wholly lose their power.
Further, did rareness cause the spots alone
   Of which thou askest, either in some part were
   This planet starving of its matter shown,.
Or, as in a body is disposed each layer

---

56. "Following after sense": since even under the guidance of the
senses.
64. "The eighth sphere" is that of the fixed stars.
71. "Formal principles": inherent characters.

Of fat and lean, so in its volume it
Would have leaves interchanging here and there.
Were the first true, it would be seen transmit   79
   In his eclipse the light from the sun's face,   80
   As when his beams any rare body hit.
This is not so. Take then the other case;
   And if it chance that I refute this too,
   Thy supposition tumbles from its base.
If this rare quality extend not through,   85
   There must be a limit where its opposite
   Forbiddeth it to pierce the residue;
And thence that other's ray pours back its light
   Like colour from the glass returning, where
   It keeps the lead behind it out of sight.   90
Now thou wilt say that the ray showeth here
   More dim than what from the other parts is sent
   Because from further back reflected there.
From this objection may experiment
   Deliver thee, if thou its virtue try,
   (Source wherefrom stream the arts that you invent).
Take three mirrors; and set two equally
   At distance from thyself; and let the last,
   Further removed, between these front thine eye.
Turned towards them, have a light behind thee
     placed,   100
   Illumining the mirrors, all the three;
   And back to the eye from each it will be cast.
Though the more distant image come to thee
   Less great in magnitude, thou wilt behold
   How of an equal brightness it must be.

---

79. "Were the first true . . .": *if the layers did extend through the moon, we should see the sun shining through them at the time of a solar eclipse.*
85. *If the layers did not extend, the dense matter would reflect the light.*

Now, as the element that goes to mould
   The snow, beneath warm beams is left in loss
   Both of the former whiteness and the cold,
Thee in thine intellect left naked thus
   I mean to inform with living light that glows   110
   Before thee sparkling as a bright star does.
Within the heaven of the divine repose
   Circles a body, in whose virtue lies   *113*
   The being of all that its confines enclose.
The following heaven, which has so many eyes,   *115*
   Portions that being through divers essences
   Distinct from it, though it must all comprise.
The other wheels by various differences
   Dispose the inborn characters they show
   Unto their ends and fruitful purposes.   120
These organs of the universe, then, go
   From grade to grade, as now thou see'st is done,
   For from above they take, but work below.
Note well how through this passage I have gone
   Advancing to the truth, thy heart's desire,
   That thou may'st henceforth keep the ford alone.
Perforce the blessed Movers must inspire,
   As do the craftsman's purposes his tool,
   The virtue and motion of each holy gyre.
The heaven so many lights make beautiful   130
   Receives the image, and makes thereof its seal,
   From the deep mind that is its motion's rule.
And as the soul which in your dust ye feel
   Through members differing and conformed thereby
   To divers powers, is thus diffused piecemeal,
So does the Intelligence display on high

---

113. *The "body" which revolves inside the Empyrean is the Primum Mobile, from which all the rest of the world derives its special mode of being.*
115. *"The following heaven": the starry sphere.*

   Its goodness, multiplied through stars, while round
      It rolls itself on its own unity.
And diverse virtue makes diverse compound
      With the precious body into which it flows,   140
      Wherewith, as life in you, it is close-bound.
Because of the glad nature whence it grows
      The mingled virtue through the body beams
      As gladness through the living pupil shows.
From this comes, not from dense and rare, what seems
      The difference you see 'twixt light and light.
      This is the formal principle that schemes,
Conformed to its own goodness, dim and bright."

Canto III

*Dante becomes aware of faces appearing eager to
speak to him. At first he supposes them to be reflec-
tions (unlike Narcissus, who supposed his reflection
to be real). One of these spirits is Piccarda, about
whom Dante had asked her brother Forese in Pur-
gatory (Canto XXIV). She is with those placed in
the sphere of the Moon because of vows broken or
imperfectly performed. Dante asks if those who are
in this lowest sphere ever crave for a more exalted
place in Paradise. She tells him that this is impos-
sible; it is of the essence of their bliss merely to ful-
fill the divine will: "In His will is our peace." And
she goes on to tell how she took the veil in the Or-
der of Saint Clare, but was forcibly taken from her
convent (to be married to a noble). Among these
spirits is the Empress Constance, who also was torn
from her convent and married to Henry VI, the sec-
ond of the three "whirlwinds" from Suabia (line*

119); the first being Frederick Barbarossa, and the
third Frederick II; all these emperors were men of
tempestuous energy.

THAT Sun which fired my bosom of old with love   *1*
   Had thus bared for me in beauty the aspect sweet
   Of truth, expert to prove as to disprove;
And I, to avow me of all error quit,
   Confident and assured, lifted my head
   More upright, in such measure as was fit.
But now appeared a sight that riveted
   Me to itself with such compulsion keen
   That my confession from my memory fled.
As from transparent glasses polished clean,   *10*
   Or water shining smooth up to its rim,
   Yet not so that the bottom is unseen,
Our faces' lineaments return so dim
   That pearl upon white forehead not more slow
   Would on our pupils its pale image limn;
So I beheld faces that seemed aglow
   To speak, and fell into the counter-snare
   From what made love 'twixt man and pool to grow. *18*
No sooner had I marked those faces there,
   Than, thinking them reflections, with swift eyes   *20*
   I turned about to see of whom they were,
And saw nothing: again, in my surprise,
   I turned straight to the light of my sweet Guide,
   Who smiling, burned within her sainted eyes.
"Marvel not at my smiling," she replied,
   "To contemplate thy childlike thought revealed
   Which cannot yet its foot to truth confide,

1. "That Sun": Beatrice.
18. "Man": Narcissus (see the Argument).

But moves thee, as ever, on emptiness to build.
   True substances are these thine eyes perceive,
   Remitted here for vows not all fulfilled.   30
Speak with them therefore, hearken and believe,
   For the true light which is their happiness
   Lets them not swerve, but to it they must cleave."
And I to the shade that seemed most near to press
   For converse, turned me and began, as one
   Who is overwrought through longing in excess:
"O spirit made for bliss, who from the sun
   Of life eternal feelest the sweet ray
   Which, save 'tis tasted, is conceived by none,
It will be gracious to me, if I may   40
   Be gladdened with thy name and all your fate."
   And she, with laughing eyes and no delay:
"Our charity no more locks up the gate
   Against a just wish than that Charity   44
   Which would have all its court in like estate.
On earth I was a Virgin Sister: see
   What memory yields thee, and my being now
   More beautiful will hide me not from thee,
But that I am Piccarda thou wilt know,
   Who with these other blessed ones placed here   50
   Am blessed in the sphere that moves most slow;
For our desires, which kindle and flame clear
   Only in the pleasure of the Holy Ghost,
   To what he appointeth joyfully adhere;
And this which seems to thee so lowly a post
   Is given to us because the vows we made
   Were broken, or complete observance lost."
Then I to her: "Something divinely glad
   Shines in your marvellous aspect, to replace
   In you the old conceptions that I had;   60
I was slow therefore to recall thy face:

---

44. "That Charity": of God.

But what thou tell'st me helpeth now to clear
  My sight, and thee more easily to retrace.
But tell me: you that are made happy here,
  Do ye to a more exalted place aspire,
  To see more, or to make yourselves more dear?"
She smiled a little, and with her smiled that choir
  Of spirits; then so joyous she replied
  That she appeared to burn in love's first fire:
"Brother, the virtue of love hath pacified   70
  Our will; we long for what we have alone,
  Nor any craving stirs in us beside.
If we desired to reach a loftier zone,
  Our longings would be all out of accord
  With His will who disposeth here His own.
For that, these circles, thou wilt see, afford
  No room, if love be our whole being's root
  And thou ponder the meaning of that word.
Nay, 'tis of the essence of our blessed lot
  In the divine will to be cloistered still   80
  Through which our own wills into one are wrought,
As we from step to step our stations fill
  Throughout this realm, to all the realm 'tis bliss
  As to its King, who wills us into His will;
And in His will is perfected our peace.
  It is the sea whereunto moveth all
  That it creates and nature makes increase."
Then saw I how each heaven for every soul
  Is paradise, though from the Supreme Good
  The dews of grace not in one measure fall.   90
But as may hap, when sated with one food
  Still for another we have appetite,
  We ask for this, and that with thanks elude,
Such words and gesture used I that I might
  Learn from her what that web was where she plied
  The shuttle and yet drew not the head outright.

"Perfect life and high merit have enskied
   A Lady above," she said, "whose rule they take   *98*
   In your world who in robe and veil abide,
That they till death may, sleeping and awake,   100
   Be with that Spouse who giveth welcome free
   To all vows love may for His pleasure make.
To follow her, a young girl, did I flee
   The world and, closed within her habit, vowed
   Myself to the pathway of her company.
Afterwards men, used to evil more than good,   *106*
   Tore me away, out of the sweet cloister;
   And God knows then what way of life I trod.
This other splendour whom thou see'st appear
   To thee on my right side, who, glowing pale,   110
   Kindles with all the radiance of our sphere,
Can of herself tell also the same tale.
   She was a Sister; from her head they tore
   Likewise the shadow of the sacred veil.
She was turned back into the world once more
   Against her will, against good usage too;
   Yet still upon her heart the veil she wore.
This is the light of the great Constance, who   *118*
   From Suabia's second whirlwind was to bring
   To birth the third Power, and the last ye knew." 120
Thus spoke she to me, and then began to sing
   Ave Maria, and singing disappeared,
   As through deep water sinks a heavy thing.
My sight, which followed far as it was powered,
   When it had lost her, turned and straightway shot
   To the other mark, more ardently desired,
And Beatrice, only Beatrice, it sought.

---

98. "A Lady above": *St. Clare, the friend of St. Francis; she founded
   the order that bears her name.*
106. "Men": *her brother Corso Donati and his followers.*
118. "The great Constance": *see the Argument.*

But she upon my look was flaming so
   That at the first my sight endured it not;
And this made me for questioning more slow.   130

Canto IV

*Two questions perplex Dante's mind; but, equally
desirous to learn the answer to each of them, he
is paralyzed into silence. Beatrice, reading his
thoughts, gives them utterance. One of Dante's
doubts refers to Plato's theory, in the* Timaeus, *that
each soul returns after death to the star from which
it came. This involves a poisonous heresy, since the
orthodox view is that the blessed all have their
home in the Empyrean, though they show them-
selves to Dante in the different spheres. The other
question is prompted by the lower place assigned
to those who were forced to break their vows;
which seems inconsistent with divine justice. Bea-
trice explains the difference between the absolute
and the relative will.*

*At the end of the canto Dante asks whether a
person, by other good deeds, may compensate for
broken vows.*

BETWEEN two foods, each near in like degree
   And tempting, would a man starve ere he chose
To put one to his teeth, though choice were free.
And so between two wolves, his ravening foes,
   In equal dread of both, would stand a lamb:
So would a hound stand still between two does.

Hence, if I held my peace, I take no blame
   Upon me, in like perplexity bemused,
   Since help was none, nor therefor merit claim.
I held my peace; but my desire suffused   10
   My face, together with my question's need,
   Warmer than if articulate speech I used;
And Beatrice did as Daniel, when he freed   13
   Nebuchadnezzar from the wrath that made
   His heart unjustly will a cruel deed.
"I see how one and the other desire," she said,
   "So draw thee that thy trouble is knotted fast
   Within itself, and thou art speechless stayed.
Thou arguest: 'If the good will in me last,
   By what reason can violence from without   20
   Lessen for me the merit long amassed?'
Also it is perplexing to thy thought
   That to the stars the souls seem to fly home,
   According to the doctrine Plato taught.
These are the questions that thy will benumb
   With equal burden; therefore first I treat
   Of that which holds in it the worst venom.
Not Seraphs who in God most inly meet,
   Not Moses, Samuel, nor whichever John   29
   Thou choose, not Mary even, have a seat   30
In other heaven than those the spirits have won
   Who here but now made themselves visible;
   Nor more or less years to their being run.
But all make beautiful the first circle
   And have sweet life, albeit of divers taste,
   Since more and less the eternal breath they feel.
They showed themselves here, not because they are
   placed

---

13. "Daniel" *revealed the forgotten dream of Nebuchadnezzar, sav-*
   ing the astrologers from the anger of the king.
29. "Whichever John . . .": *the Baptist and the Evangelist.*

In this allotted sphere; rather to show
The heavenly sphere that is exalted least.
Speech to your wit must needs be tempered so,   40
Since but from things of sense it apprehends
What it makes apt for the intellect to know.
Scripture to your capacity condescends
For this cause, and a foot and hand will feign
For God, yet something other it intends.
Thus Holy Church portrays to you as men
With human look Michael and Gabriel
And the other who made Tobit whole again.   48
What of the souls Timaeus has to tell
Is not like that which is apparent here;   50
For what he says it seems he thinks as well.   51
He says the soul returns to its own star,
Himself believing it was severed thence
When Nature made it form for flesh to wear.
Haply his opinion is of other sense
Than his words sound, and maybe has in it
Import of no derisory pretence.
If to these spheres he means the souls remit
The honour of their influence and the blame,
Perhaps his bow upon some truth may hit.   60
Ill understood, this principle overcame
Nigh all the world; and on that erring plea
It gave to Jove, Mars, Mercury a name.
The other matter of thy perplexity
Hath the less poison, since from me to veer
Its mischief could not have perverted thee.
That heavenly justice should unjust appear
In the eyes of mortal beings is argument
Of faith; no heresy corrupteth here.
But seeing that your understanding, bent   70

---

48. *Raphael, who cured the blindness of Tobit.*
51. *Because Plato seems to understand it literally.*

Upon this truth, can pierce to it unconfused,
I'll make thee, according to thy wish, content.
If violence is, when he who is abused   73
Nowise connives with what he is mastered by,
Then these souls were not on that count excused.
For the will cannot, if it wills not, die,
But does as in the fire's flame nature does
Though violence wrest it thousand times awry.
Should it, then, bend, little or much, it thus
Abets the violence; and so did these,   80
Who still might have regained the holy house.
If their will had stayed perfect in duress,
Like that which upheld Laurence on the grid,   83
Or Mucius, to his own hand pitiless,
It would have driven them, soon as they were freed,
Upon the road whence they were dragged before;
But so entire a will is rare indeed.
Now by these words, if thou hast reaped their lore
As thou should'st do, the argument falls down
Which would have teased thee many a time more; 90
But now another pass is to be won,
Fronting thine eyes, such that thou would'st not, ere
Thou wert full weary, win through it alone.
I have set within thy mind this surety clear,
That souls in bliss never may lie, since they
Are to the primal truth forever near.   96
And then thou mightest hear Piccarda say
That Constance kept devotion to the veil,
So that in this she seems to say me nay.
Many times ere now, brother, it befell   100
That to escape some danger a man was brought

---

73. *Beatrice begins by establishing a definition of violence.*
83-84. *St. Laurence was a Christian martyr. Mucius Scaevola burned off his own right hand.*
96. *"The primal truth": God.*

To do against his wish things blameable,
Even as Alcmaeon, on whom his father wrought   *103*
  By his entreaties, his own mother slew:
  Not to lose piety, he set pity at naught.
At this point I would have thee hold it true
  That violence commingles with the will
  And no excuse holds for the work these do.
Will absolute consents not to the ill,
  But it consents so far as it's in dread,   110
  If it recoil, of a wrong greater still.
When, then, Piccarda utters on this head
  Her thought, she means the absolute will, and I
  The other, so that both the truth have said."   *114*
Such was the sacred stream that rippled by,
  Issuing from the spring whence all truth flows,
  Both one and the other desire to satisfy.
"O loved of the First Lover, O goddess, whose
  Discourse," said I then, "floods me and bathes me
    round
  And warms my spirit till more and more it glows, 120
My love is not to such degree profound
  As to suffice to render grace for grace:
  May he who sees, and can, thereto respond!
Nothing can satiate, I now see, unless
  The True illumine it, the mind of men:
  Beyond that, no truth can enlarge its place.
Therein it rests like wild beast in his den,
  Soon as it reaches it; and reach it may:
  Else every human longing were in vain;
Hence the doubt groweth, like a sucker, say,   130
  At Truth's foot; it is nature's urging, which
  Spurs us from height to height on the upward way.

---

103. Alcmaeon, to avenge his father, killed his mother.
114. "The other": the relative will.

This prompts me, this emboldens, to beseech
   With reverence, Lady, that of one truth yet
   That is obscure to me thou deign to teach.
I would fain know if one may pay the debt
   For broken vows with other deeds upright
   Which may not come short, in your balance set."
Beatrice looked on me with eyes of light
   Filled so divinely with love's spark ablaze   140
   That, vanquished, all my powers were put to flight;
And I became as lost with downcast gaze.

Canto V

*In answer to Dante's last question, Beatrice tells
him that it is impossible to make sufficient compen-
sation for broken vows, because the vow means the
surrender of the most precious gift of all, that of
free will. It is however allowed to substitute other
meritorious service for the "matter" of the vow;
that is the service undertaken in the vow's fulfill-
ment; but only on condition that it is authorized
by the Church (see Purgatorio, Canto IX, for the
"white and yellow keys") and that what is com-
muted is in the proportion of six to four, compared
with the service it is substituted for. Vows are not
to be undertaken lightly; the tragic dilemma of
Jephthah, and of Agamemnon when he sacrificed
his daughter, is adduced in illustration.*

   *Suddenly Beatrice and Dante are caught up into
the Heaven of Mercury, where are the souls of the
ambitious. One of these spirits, who is Justinian,
addresses Dante.*

"IF I FLAME on thee in love's fervency
   Beyond all that is seen in earthly mood,
   So that I quell the courage of thine eye,
Marvel not: this from perfect sight ensued,
   That, even as it apprehends, can win
   To set foot on the apprehended good.
I see clear how already glows within
   Thine understanding the eternal light,
   Which only and always kindles love, once seen.
And even if other lure your love invite   10
   'Tis nothing but some vestige left from that,
   Ill-recognized, which through it showeth bright.
Thou would'st know if amends may be so great
   For broken vows, with other service paid,
   As to safeguard the soul from claim of debt."
So Beatrice began this canto, and stayed
   No more than one who breaks not off his theme;
   And onward thus the sacred message led.
"Of all the gifts God in His bounty extreme
   Made when creating, most conformable   20
   To His own goodness, and in His esteem
Most precious, was the liberty of the will,
   With which creatures that are intelligent
   Were all endowed, they only, and are so still.
Now thou can'st see, following this argument,
   The high worth of the vow, so it not lacked,
   When thou consented'st to it, God's consent.
For when is sealed 'twixt God and man the pact,
   This treasure, being such as I explain,
   Is sacrificed, and that by its own act.   30
How then can compensation here obtain?
   If thou think'st to use well thine offering, thou

Would'st do a good work from ill-gotten gain.   *33*

Of this chief point thou art certified; but now,
  Since Holy Church hath dispensation made,
  Which seems this truth I have told to disavow,

Still must thou be at table a while delayed,
  Because what thou hast taken of tough food
  Requires for thy digestion further aid.

Open thy mind to what I tell thee, and brood   *40*
  Thereon within; for knowledge none can vaunt
  Who retains not, although he have understood.

Two things essential the conditions want;
  The one is that whereof the sacrifice   *44*
  Consists; the other is the covenant.

To cancel this last, nothing can suffice
  Save keeping it; that this point thou may'st heed,
  I made my words about it so precise.

Therefore the Jews could not escape the need
  To sacrifice, though the thing offered might   *50*
  In part at least be exchanged, as thou can'st read.

The other thing, which I as 'matter' cite,
  May well be such that no offence may be
  If another matter be exchanged for it.

But let none shift the burden wilfully
  From off his back, if at the turning sticks   *56*
  Either the white key or the yellow key.

Let him hold all exchange as folly's tricks,
  Unless the thing that's taken up include
  The thing laid down, as four's contained in six.   *60*

---

33. *Thou art like a thief who is trying to do good deeds with ill-gotten gain.*

44-45. *"The one . . .": the thing promised. The "other" element, in a vow, is the act of agreement.*

56-57. *The "turning" of the "white key" of discrimination and the "yellow key" of authority signifies ecclesiastical permission.*

Whatever therefore by its own worth would   *61*
   Weigh so that every counter-poise weighed short
   By other spending cannot be made good.
Let mortals never take the vow in sport:
   Keep faith, nor let your eyes, in doing this,
   As Jephthah's with his first-vowed gift, distort;   *66*
Who should have rather said: 'I did amiss'
   Than, keeping faith, do worse. And thou canst trace
   Such folly in the great chieftain of Greece,   *69*
Whence Iphigenia wept for her fair face   *70*
   And made simple and wise to weep her too,
   Hearing of that vow kept in such a case.
Christians, walk more wary in what you do,
   Not like a feather blown at the wind's bent,
   Nor think that every water cleanses you.
Ye have the Old and the New Testament;
   Ye have the Shepherd of the Church for guide;
   With these for your salvation be content.
If evil greed aught else to you have cried,
   Be men, not witless sheep, so that the Jews   *80*
   Among you may not mock you and deride.
Do not as the lamb does who will refuse
   His mother's milk, and silly in wantonness,
   Do battle with himself, himself to amuse."
Thus, as I write, to me spoke Beatrice;
   Then turned in all her longing's radiance
   To the region where the world most living is.   *87*
Her silence and transfigured countenance
   Imposed a hush upon my craving wit
   That had new questionings ready in advance: *90*

61-63. *If the obligation is the most precious of our possessions (our free will), nothing can be substituted for it.*

66. "As Jephthah . . .": see Judg. 9:31.

69. *Agamemnon erred when he sacrificed his daughter to obtain from the Gods a favorable wind.*

87. *The Empyrean.*

And sudden as an arrow that hath hit
  The target ere the bowstring cease to thrill,
  We flew, and on the second realm alit.   *93*
There I beheld such joy my lady fill,
  When in this heaven she stept into its blaze,
  It made the planet glow more lucent still.
And if the star laughed out with altered rays,
  What then did I, whose mortal character
  Was liable to mutation's every phase?
As in a fish-pond which is still and clear   100
  The fishes draw to what comes from outside
  In such sort that they think their food is there,
So thousand splendours, ay, and more beside,
  I saw drawn toward us; and from each was heard
  "Lo one, by whom our loves are magnified."
And as each one of them to us-ward neared
  The shade was seen with joy to overflow
  By the effulgence that from it appeared.
Reader, if what I start to tell thee now
  Were broken off, consider how intense   110
  A craving would torment thee more to know;
And thou can'st ask of thine intelligence
  How much I longed to hear from these their state,
  Soon as they were discovered to my sense.
"O happy born, whom grace lets contemplate
  The thrones of the eternal triumph, ere
  For thee thy militancy reach its date,
The light pervading heaven through every sphere
  Kindles us all; of us then, if it please
  To be enlightened, take thy fill and hear."   120
Such words were said to me by one of these
  Devout souls; and by Beatrice; "Speak, speak!
  Have no fear; trust as in divinities."
"I see how in thine own light thou dost seek

---

93. "Second realm": *the Heaven of Mercury.*

To nest thee, and that it streameth through thine
    eye;
Such sparkles, as thou smilest, from it break:
But who thou art I know not, neither why,
    Great soul, thou art stationed in this sphere veiled
      o'er
    From mortals by another's rays on high."   *129*
This I said, turning to the first splendour   *130*
    That had addressed me; and its luminousness
    Became thereat far livelier than before.
Like as the sun, which hides him in excess
    Of light, when once the heat has nibbled thin
    The dense, dull mists that overspread his face,
So did the sacred presence hide within
    Its beams, by joy increased in radiance,
    And, close enclosed thus, gave me answer in
The manner that the following canto chants.

---

129. "By another's rays . . .": the Heaven of Mercury is veiled by
the sun.

Canto VI

---

*Justinian tells Dante who he is, and what he had
done as a Law-giver. He then speaks of the achieve-
ments of Rome, symbolized by the Roman Eagle;
and recounts her history, from the westward jour-
ney of the Trojans and their settlement in Italy to
the time of the earlier Caesars, and the destruction
of Jerusalem by Titus. This last is conceived of as
punishment of the Jews for having put Christ to
death; but the crucifixion was itself the punish-
ment of mankind, in Christ's person, for "the an-*

*cient sin" of Adam and was inflicted by Pilate as
representative of the Roman Empire, regarded by
Dante as a divine institution. Justinian recounts this
history in order to denounce the factions of Dante's
day who would break up the unity of the Empire;
the Guelfs, under their leader "the new Charles"
(Charles II of Apulia) who would replace the
"world's great ensign," the Eagle, by the lilies of
France; and the Ghibellines, who want to appro-
priate it for their party. Justinian then explains that
the spirits who are assigned to "this little planet,"
Mercury, are there because they were ambitious of
fame and honor and not only aiming at the glory of
God; hence placed in a lower sphere. He concludes
with the story of Romeo, minister of Raymond
Berenger of Provence, whose four daughters were,
through his efforts, married to four kings; but being
falsely accused, he was driven into exile. The last
lines perhaps allude obliquely to Dante's own exile.*

When Constantine had turned the Eagle's head   1
   Against heaven's course which it of old pursued
   With him who took Lavinia to his bed,
Twice a hundred years and longer posted stood
   The bird of God at Europe's last confine,
   Neighbouring the mountains whence it first issued,
And under shadow of the wings divine
   Kept there from hand to hand continued reign,
   Till by succession's change it came to mine.
Caesar I was, and am Justinian,   10
   Who by the will of Primal Love possessed
   Pruned from the laws the unneeded and the vain.

1-3. *The Roman Eagle, having followed Aeneas from Troy to Italy,
was carried by Constantine from Rome to Byzantium.*
10. *"Justinian": Emperor of the East in the sixth century under
whose direction was achieved a great compilation of Roman law.*

And, ere my mind was to the task addressed,
   One nature only in Christ did I suppose,
   Not more, and in such doctrine acquiesced.
But blessed Agapetus, he who was
   Chief Pastor then, by his discourses drew   *17*
   My mind, and taught me the pure faith to espouse.
Him I believed; and what by faith he knew
   Is clear to me, as clear 'tis to your wit   *20*
   That contradictories are, one false, one true.
So soon as with the Church I moved my feet,
   It pleased God of his grace to inspire me for
   The high task, and I gave me whole to it.
Arms to my Belisarius I made o'er,   *25*
   Who in Heaven's right hand such auxiliar had,
   It was a sign I should not use them more.
To thy first question now is the answer made,
   And here it stops; but that which from it flows
   Constrains me something furthermore to add,   *30*
That thou may'st see with how much reason goes
   Against the ever-sacred standard he   *32*
   Who claims it his, or he whose schemes oppose.
See what great virtue hath won it fealty
   Of reverence, beginning from the day
   When Pallas died to give it sovereignty.   *36*
Thou knowest how in Alba it kept sway
   Three hundred years and more, until was fought
   Between the three and three the final fray.   *39*
Thou know'st what from the Sabine rape it wrought *40*

17-18. "Chief Pastor": *Pope*. "The pure faith": *the dual nature of
Christ.*
25. "Belisarius": *Justinian's great general.*
32. "The ever-sacred standard": *the Imperial Eagle.*
36. *To avenge the death of his friend Pallas, Aeneas slew Turnus and
gained possession of Latium.*
39. "Between the three and three . . .": *the three Curiatii, who
fought for Alba Longa against the three Horatii, the champions of
Rome.*

Through seven reigns, down to Lucretia's woe,
  Conquering the neighbour peoples round about;
And what, borne by Rome's champions, it could do
  Against Brennus and against Pyrrhus,   *44*
  And the other princes, its confederate foe,
When, sur-named from his rough curls, Quinctius, *46*
  Torquatus, Decii and Fabii, vied
  In fame that I embalm most gladly thus.
It smote to earth next the Arabians' pride,   *49*
  Who followed Hannibal across the torn   50
  Rocks of the Alps, wherefrom thou, Po, dost glide.
Youthful in triumph under it were borne
  Scipio and Pompey; and bitter doom it meant
  To that hill, underneath which thou wast born. *54*
Then near the time when all heaven was intent
  That in its own peace earth should also share,
  Caesar seized hold of it by Rome's consent:
And what it did from Var to Rhine, Isère
  Knows well the memory of, and Saône, and Seine,
  And every valley feeding Rhône from far.   60
What it did after it left Ravenna, when
  It leapt the Rubicon, was flight so fast
  That neither tongue could follow it, nor pen.
Toward Spain it swung the files of war, and passed
  Next toward Durazzo, and Pharsalia struck,
  So that hot Nile felt it, and was aghast.   *66*
Antandros, Simois, which it first forsook,
  It saw again, where Hector's ashes lie;   *68*

---

44. "Brennus": *leader of the Gauls.* "Pyrrhus": *king of Epirus.*
46. "Quinctius" *was called Cincinnatus from his unkempt shock of hair.*
49. "The Arabians": *the Carthaginians.*
54. "To that hill": *Fiesole.*
66. Caesar's victory at Pharsalia was felt in Egypt, where Pompey was murdered.
68. "It* [the Eagle] *saw again": when Caesar was pursuing Pompey, he stopped to visit the Troad.*

Then, woe to Ptolemy! its plumes it shook,
On Juba pounced, like flame out of the sky,   70
   Then toward your West wheeled and went storming
     on
   Where sounded the Pompeian trumpet's cry.
For what, with its next bearer, it had done,   73
   Brutus and Cassius howl in hell beneath:
   Modena and Perugia it made groan.
Cleopatra for that cause still anguisheth,
   Who, lost in fear of what she fled before,
   Took from the aspic sudden and black death.
With him it sped on to the Red Sea shore,
   With him stablisht the world in peace so great   80
   That his own temple on Janus closed the door.   81
But what the Eagle, whose prowess I relate,
   Had done before, and what it yet should do
   Through all the mortal realm of its estate,
Seems small and dim, if with profounder view
   In the third Caesar's hand 'tis looked upon   86
   With undisturbed eye and intention true:
For Justice, whose live breath on me has blown,
   Vouchsafed it, in the hand of him I mean,
   The glory of vengeance, God's wrath to atone.   90
What I repeat here may thy wonder win:
   Thereafter under Titus it made speed
   To avenge the vengeance on the ancient sin:
And when the biting Lombard fangs made bleed   94
   The Holy Church, under its wings in haste
   Came Charlemagne victorious to her need.
Those, then, whom I arraigned erewhile, thou may'st

---

70. "Juba": king of the Numidians.
73. The "next bearer" of the Eagle was Augustus.
81. The temple of Janus was closed only in time of peace.
86. "The third Caesar": Tiberius, under whom Christ was crucified.
94. Charlemagne came to the aid of the Church against the Longo-
   bards.

Judge now, and their delinquencies assay,
Which are the cause of all the ills ye taste.
Against the world's great ensign these array   100
The yellow lilies; those to a faction's force
Annex it; which is worse, were hard to say.
Under another standard plot your course,
Ghibellines! for he follows this one ill
Who between it and justice makes divorce.
And let not this new Charles set out to quell   *106*
The Eagle with his Guelfs, but those claws dread
That from a lordlier lion stript the fell.
Ofttimes ere now have sons inherited
Woe from their fathers' fault; nor let him dream   110
God will his own arms for those lilies shed.
This little planet has for diadem   *112*
Good spirits who were active, to the end
That fame and honour should accrue to them.
When the desires, on these things nourished, bend
Aside so, needs must that the rays that soar
From the true love less ardently ascend.
But the commeasuring of our wages' score
With our desert doth to our bliss belong,
Because we see them neither less nor more,   120
Whereby the living justice is so strong
To sweeten our affection's pure intent
That it may not be warped to any wrong.
Divers voices on earth are sweetly blent;
So in our life the divers seats accord
To make among these wheels one sweet concent.
Within the pearl that thou art turned toward
Shineth the shining light of Romeo, whose   *128*
So goodly achievement had such ill reward:

---

106. "This new Charles": *see the Argument.*
112. "This little planet": *Mercury.*
128. "Romeo" of Villeneuve: *see the Argument.*

But the Provençals, his malicious foes,   130
   Have not the laugh: and ill indeed they fare
   Who make of others' good deeds their own loss.

Four daughters had Count Raymond Berenger,
   All queens; this Romeo won for him, a man
   Humble of station and a pilgrim there.

By crooked words was he persuaded then
   To call to account this good servant and just
   Who paid him five and seven for every ten.

Old and poor, thence, an outcast, was he thrust;
   And if the world knew what a heart he bore   140
   Within him, begging life from crust to crust,

Much as it praises, it would praise him more."

Canto VII

*After Justinian and his companion spirits have re-
sumed their place in the celestial dance, Beatrice
dispels certain difficulties which had arisen in
Dante's mind concerning the doctrine of Redemp-
tion. The first is the question: Why, if Christ was
justly put to death, could it be just to punish those
who did this? Beatrice explains that he was justly
punished as regards his human nature, unjustly as
being God. The next question is: Why did God
choose this particular mode of redeeming mankind
and not some other mode? The answer is that man
could only recover what he lost by the Fall either
through atoning himself for Adam's sin (and no of-
fering of his was adequate) or through the divine
mercy. But God combined "the two ways," both
mercy and justice, for by Christ's incarnation and
death man recovered the means of being pardoned,*

while at the same time justice was satisfied. Bea-
trice goes on to enlighten Dante on another point,
and explains the difference between those created
things which are corruptible and those which are
incorruptible—the latter being acted upon immedi-
ately by the Divine Power, the former by the sec-
ondary influences of the stars.

"Hosanna, Holy God of Hosts, to thee,
    Who from the loftiest heaven illuminest
    These kingdoms' flames in their felicity!"
So, turning, by its own song re-possest,
    That spirit appeared to sound its chant of praise,
    On whom two splendours, twinned in lustre, rest.   **6**
And it and the others stept into their maze,
    Dancing, like sparks, of speed ineffable;
    And sudden distance veiled them from my gaze.
A doubt held me; and I said inly "Tell,   **10**
    O tell it to her! Tell my lady," I said,
    "Who slakes my thirst with sweet drops from her
        well."
But the overmastering reverence in me bred,
    Though but by *Be* and *ice,* again deprest,   *14*
    Like to a drowsing man's, my drooping head.
Beatrice bore that I was thus distrest
    A short time; such a smile then rayed from her
    As would make one, in fire that burnt him, blest.
"According to my thought, which cannot err,
    How vengeance that is just can justly be   **20**
    Chastised, provoketh in thy mind demur.
Soon from this doubt will I deliver thee.

---

6. "Two splendours": of natural intelligence and of illuminating grace.
14. "*Be* and *ice*": Beatrice.

Hearken thou to my words, for I have brought
A gift, to make thee of most high doctrine free.
Because that man who ne'er was born brooked not   25
To curb his will to his profit, he condemned
Himself; condemned, too, all his seed begot.
Wherefore mankind lay in great error penned
Down there for many an age and sick thereof,
Until it pleased the Word of God descend;   3)
And there that nature, which had dared remove
From its creator, he to himself annealed
By the sole act of his eternal love.
Now turn thy sight to what is now revealed.
This nature, with its maker joined, as first
Created, not a grain of ill concealed;
But by itself it had been banished erst
From Paradise, because it swerved aside
From truth, and its own way of life reversed.
And thus the penalty the Cross applied,   40
If measured by the nature taken on,
Was never in its sting more justified.
In like manner was never such wrong done,
Having regard to Him who suffered there,
In whom this nature was condensed to one.
Thus from one act diverse effects appear:
At the one death God and the Jews were glad:
Therewith earth shook and the heavens were laid
bare.
It should not then perplex thee, when 'tis said
At any time that vengeance justly wrought   50
In a just court with vengeance was repaid.
But now I see thy mind from thought to thought
Ravelled within thee and in great desire
Waiting for the untying of the knot.
Thou sayest: 'I understand well what I hear;

---

25. "That man": Adam.

But for what cause God willed this mode alone
    For our redemption, is to me not clear.'
This decree, Brother, is not to be shown
    To the eyes of him whose unperfected wit
    Hath not in love's flame into ripeness grown.   60
But since this target many engage to hit
    But few clearly discern, I will expound
    How such mode was the worthier and more fit.
The Divine Bounty, in which no shadow is found
    Of envy, as it burns from inward, spills
    Eternal beauties sparkling all around.   66
That which immediately from it distils
    Thereafter knows no end, since its imprint
    Remaineth ever on whatso thing it seals.
That which immediate raineth without stint   70
    From it, is all free, since it is removed
    From power of new things in the firmament.   72
Being more conformed to it, 'tis the more loved;
    For the holy ardour that irradiates all
    Lives most in what most like to itself is proved.
Vantaged with all these bounties is man's soul:
    And should one thing fail that is requisite,
    From its nobility it needs must fall.
Sin only is that which disfranchises it,
    And makes it unlike to the Sovereign Good,   80
    So that with that light 'tis but faintly lit
Nor can regain the station where it stood
    Unless with suffering of just penalties
    For ill joys it fill up what sin made void.
Your nature forfeited these dignities
    When its first seed sinned wholly and was cast

---

60. Only an infinitely loving mind can comprehend what impelled
    God to sacrifice himself for man.
66. "Eternal beauties": men and angels.
72. The "power of new things . . .": of the stars.

From them, as it was cast from Paradise;
And they could be recovered (if thou hast
   Subtly considered it) by no way save
   One or the other of these fords be past: 90
Either that God in graciousness forgave,
   Or else that man by his own will and deed
   For his own folly satisfaction gave.
Deep in the deep, eternal counsel feed
   Thy fixt eyes now, and close as thy mind may
   Let it to every word of mine give heed.
Man in his circumscription could not pay
   The debt, since not so deep might he descend,
   Were he, thereafter, humbly to obey,
As, disobeying, he aspired to ascend: 100
   For the which cause, from rendering the due
   Atonement by his own act he was banned.
Needs then must God by His own ways renew   *103*
   Man's life and its integrity restore;
   I mean, by one way or by both the two.
But as the deed commends itself the more
   The more it makes the goodness to appear
   Of the heart, whence it issued, of the doer,
The Divine Goodness, whereof all things bear
   The seal, designed then all its paths to assay   110
   That it might lift you up where once ye were;
Nor 'twixt the final night and the first day   *112*
   Did aught of such a grandeur come to pass
   Nor ever shall, on one or the other way.
God gave Himself with larger bounteousness
   To enable man to lift himself again
   Than if he had only pardoned of his grace;
And Justice must all other modes disdain
   Except the Son of God humbled Him so

---

103. "His own ways": Mercy and Justice.
112. Between Judgment and Creation.

That He became incarnated in man. 120
Now backward to a certain point I go
    To enlighten thee and fill full thy desire,
    So that thou mayest perceive this as I do.
Thou say'st: 'I see the water, I see the fire,
    The air, and the earth, and their comminglings, come
    All to corruption and short time endure;
And yet these were created things: wherefrom
    Follows, if it be truth thou dost declare,
    They should be safe from that corruption's doom.'
The angels, Brother, and this untainted star 130
    In which thou art, one may 'created' call
    Even as entirely in their being they are;
But the elements which thou hast named, and all
    The things that they have mingled to compound,—
    Created virtue hath informed them all. 135
Created was the matter in them found,
    Created was the informing power, whose worth
    Is in the stars about them rolling round.
The life of every brute and plant on earth
    Is by the quick beams of the sacred fires 140
    From its combining potencies drawn forth.
But the Supreme Benignity inspires
    Directly your life, making it to love
    Itself, and kindling it to fresh desires.
For thee this argument may further prove
    Your resurrection, if the thought be weighed
    How human flesh was formed to breathe and move,
When the first parents both of them were made."

---

135. "Created virtue": *the secondary power of the stars.*

Canto VIII

*Dante and Beatrice have now arrived in the third
heaven, that of Venus. A band of spirits, abandon-
ing their circling movement, come to meet them;
and one spirit addresses Dante as one he had known
on earth, quoting the first line of a canzone by the
poet. This is Charles Martel (d. 1295), King of
Hungary; he tells of the several kingdoms to which
he was heir; of the "Sicilian Vespers," the mas-
sacre provoked by the misrule of his grandfather;
and of the folly of his brother Robert in encourag-
ing the rapacity of his Catalonian mercenaries.
His allusion to the degeneracy of the avaricious
Robert from his generous father leads Dante to ask
about the cause of degeneracy in families. Charles
explains that diversity is necessary for social life,
variety of function requiring variety of character.*

THE world was, to its peril, wont to hold
  That the fair Cyprian rayed love's fever round,   2
  Where with her the third epicycle rolled;
Wherefore not only were her rites renowned
  With sacrifice and votive ceremony
  By the ancient people in ancient error bound:
Dione too was hymned, and Cupid; she
  As being her mother, he her son; and how
  He sat, they told, fondled on Dido's knee.

2-3. "The fair Cyprian": Venus.—"Epicycle": the circuit of a re-
volving sphere carrying the planet.

And after her of whom I prelude now   10
  They chose to name the star which woos the sun
  Now with the nape turned toward him, now the
    brow.
All unaware that we had thither flown
  I soon had proof that we were there, because
  A rarer beauty in my Lady shone.   15
And as within a flame a sparkle shows,
  And in a voice is caught a voice's note,
  If one holds on and the other comes and goes,
I saw in that light other torches float,
  Circling (I deemed) more or less swiftly past,   2
  In measure as interior vision taught.
From freezing cloud never descended blast,
  Visible or not, so swiftly, it would not seem
  As loitering or obstructed in its haste
To whoso witnessed those divine lights gleam
  Toward us, abandoning the circle stirred
  To motion first in the high Seraphim.
And among those who most in front appeared
  Sounded "Hosanna"; so that envious
  I am still, to hear once more what then I heard.   30
Then one brought himself nearer, and spoke thus   31
  Alone: "All we are ready to fulfil
  Thy pleasure, that thou may'st have joy of us.
We in one gyre with the Heavenly Princes wheel,
  In the one circling, the one thirst of love,
  To whom thou from the world didst make the appeal:
Ye who by intellect the third heaven move.
  And our love brims so, that for thy content
  A little of quiet no less sweet shall prove."
When my gaze had been offered reverent   40

---

15. Beatrice, who symbolizes Revelation, grows in loveliness as she
    and Dante rise from sphere to sphere.
31. "One": Charles Martel (see the Argument).

Up to my Lady, and she had reassured
  And satisfied them with her own consent,
They turned back to that light which had outpoured
  Itself so freely; and "Say, who are ye," impressed
  With a profound affection, was my word.
How greatly in splendour and in size increased
  I saw it at the new bliss which, when so
  I spoke, was added to its blissful feast!
Transfigured thus, it spoke: "The world below
  Held me not long; and much would not have
            happed,   50
  Had it been longer, that now comes in woe.
My bliss concealeth me from thee, enwrapt
  Within its beams, that make for me a hood,
  Like worm that in its swaddling silk is lapt.
Much didst thou love me, and for reason good;
  For had I stayed below, I would have shown
  More of my love to thee than leaf and bud.
Of that left bank, washed by the streaming Rhône   58
  When Sorgue has joined it, I should have been lord
  In the due time, and therewithal should own   60
That horn too of Ausonia which is towered   61
  With Bari, Gaeta and Catona, down
  From where to sea Tronto and Verde are poured.
Upon my brows already flamed the crown
  Of all the land by Danube's water crost   65
  After its German banks it has outgrown.
And beautiful Trinacria, whose coast   67
  'Twixt Pachynus and Pelorus is o'erhung
  (Beside the gulf that Eurus vexes most)

---

58. "Of that left bank . . .": Provence.
61. "That horn . . . of Ausonia": (Italy) is the Kingdom of Naples.
65. "Of all the land . . .": Hungary.
67-69. "Trinacria" is Sicily.—"Pachynus and Pelorus": two capes.—
  "Eurus": the east wind.

Not from Typhoeus' breath but fume up-flung   70
   Of sulphur, would still look to have its kings   71
   Through me from seed of Charles and Rudolf sprung,
Had not ill rule, which chafes so the heart-strings
   Of subject-peoples, moved Palermo in chime
   To cry *Death! Death!* with eager clamourings.
And if my brother had foresight in time,   76
   Ere now he had rebuffed the starveling greed
   Of Catalonia, lest it injure him.
And verily should provision now be made
   By him or another, lest upon his ship,   80
   Already o'erladen, heavier load be laid.
His nature, liberal stem's too niggard slip,
   Has need of soldiery of such a brood
   As lusteth not its coffers to equip."
"Since I believe that the beatitude
   Which thy words flood me with, my liege, complete,
   There where indeed begins and ends all good,
Is seen by thee as I see it, more sweet
   It is to me; and this too I hold dear
   That contemplating God thou seëst it.   90
Thou hast made me glad; make then this one thing
    clear,
   For with thy speech a question is entwined,
   How a sweet seed a bitter fruit may bear."
Thus I: and he to me: "If to thy mind
   I show a truth, thou'lt have before thine eyes,
   All manifest, what now thou hast behind.

---

70. *The darkness from Aetna is not due to the struggles of the giant
Typhoeus, but to the effect of the sun's heat.*

71. *Sicily would now be awaiting a line of kings descended from
the grandfather and the father-in-law of Charles Martel, if the
revolution of 1282, called the Sicilian Vespers, had not driven
Charles's people from the island.*

76. *"My brother": Robert, who is represented as having adopted the
traditional miserliness of Catalonia.*

The Good which moves and, moving, satisfies
   The realm thou climbest, by its foresight still
   On these vast bodies works in wondrous wise.   *99*
Nor for the natures only is there skill   100
   To make provision, but along with them
   The all-perfect mind provideth too their weal.
Wherefore whatever this bow shoots, the same
   Alights ordained to a provided end,
   Even as a thing directed to its aim.
Were this not so, the heaven thou dost ascend
   Would so produce its own effects, that these
   Were ruins and not works that art has planned.
This cannot be, unless the Intelligences,
   That move these stars, from imperfection ail   110
   And ail, too, the first cause of their disease.   *111*
Would'st thou that I more of this truth unveil?"
   And I: "Not so; it is impossible,
   I see, that Nature, where the need is, fail."
Whence he again: "Would it be worse now, tell,
   For man on earth were he no citizen?"
   "Yes," I replied; "here in no doubt I dwell."
"And can that be, unless it be that men
   Diversely live with diverse offices?
   No, if aright your master guides his pen."   120
Thus far he went deducing by degrees,
   And then concluded: "Therefore must we own
   Your effects rooted in diversities.
One is born Solon, and a Xerxes one,   *124*
   Melchisedec another, or he who flew
   Soaring into the sky, and lost his son.

---

99. *God has embodied his providence in the stars.*
111. *A defect in the work of the stars would imply a fault in their*
Maker.
124-126. *One is born a legislator, another a general, another a priest,*
another a mechanic (Daedalus, who lost his son Icarus while they
were flying through the air).

The circling nature, which imprinteth true   *127*
  The mortal wax, plieth its art with heed,
  But careth not what inn it cometh to:
Whence Esau is found separate in seed   130
  From Jacob, and Quirinus comes from so   *131*
  Base father that from Mars is claimed his breed.
And the begotten nature would but go
  The way of its begetter, if the power
  Of providence o'erruled it not below.
Now that which was behind thee is before,
  But that thou may'st know that thou pleasurest me,
  With a corollary will I wrap thee o'er.
Nature, if she find fortune not agree
  With her intents, like any other seed   140
  Moved from its own soil, fails her destiny;
And if the world beneath us took but heed
  And followed the foundation Nature lays,
  Its people would from misery be freed.
But ye perversely in religion place
  Him born to gird the sword upon his side,
  And make him king who should a pulpit grace;
Wherefore from the right road ye wander wide."

---

127. "The circling nature": *the spheres.*
131. "Quirinus," *or Romulus, was the son of such a poor father that his paternity was ascribed to the god Mars.*

Canto IX

Dante apostrophizes Clemence, Charles's daughter, still living and Queen of France, assuring her of retribution to be exacted for the wrongs suffered by Charles's family.
  Another spirit now makes itself known: Cunizza

da Romano, sister of the notorious tyrant, "the fiery
brand," Ezzelin. She tells of the crimes of the
people of her country, especially of the bishop of
Feltro who gave up to execution a number of Fer-
rarese who had taken refuge with him. (Malta, line
54, was the name of several prisons; here perhaps
one at Bolsena.) Fulk is the name of the next spirit
to appear. He was born at Marseilles, but without
naming the place lets it be inferred from elaborate
geographical indications. First a troubadour, then a
monk, Fulk ended as a bishop. Like Cunizza, he
feels no remorse for the amours of his youth. He
points out the spirit of Rahab the harlot, and de-
nounces the corruption of the Papacy and priest-
hood. (The "accursed flower," line 130, is the lily
stamped on the golden florin.)

A<small>FTER</small> thy Charles, beautiful Clemence, thus
   Had solved my doubt, he spoke of treachery soon
   To afflict his seed and bring them cruel loss.
But "Hold thy peace," he said; "let time roll on."
   So I can tell naught, save that, to requite
   Your wrongs, shall chastisement be duly done.
Already the spirit of that sacred light
   Had turned unto the Sun which thrills it through,
   As to that Good whence all things drink delight.
Ah, souls deceived and impious creatures! You   10
   Whose hearts from so great good pervert your aim
   And twist your foreheads unto things untrue!
And lo, another of those splendours came
   Toward me, and signified its good intent
   To please me, by its brighter outward flame:
The eyes of Beatrice, which were wholly bent
   Upon me, as before, made me assured
   That my desire should have her dear assent.

"Ah, swiftly," said I, "proof to me accord   *19*
  That I can on thy mind reflect my mind,   *20*
  Blest spirit! and give my longing its reward."
Whereon the light, by me still undivined,
  Out of its depths, whence rose its singing first,
  Went on, as one whose joy is to be kind:
"In that part of the Italian land, immersed   *25*
  In sin, that is between Rialto set
  And Piave and Brenta, where their springs outburst
Rises a hill, and soars to no great height;
  Whence once a fiery brand rushed down, to war   *29*
  Upon that region and to ravage it.   *30*
Out of one root with it was I born there.
  Cunizza was I called; and here I glow,
  Since I was conquered by this burning star.
But for the cause of this my lot I owe   *34*
  No grief, but shrive myself in happiness:
  Hard saying, maybe, to your crowd below.
Of this dear jewel, luminous in bliss,   *37*
  Which in our heaven neighboureth me most near,
  Great fame remains; and ere it perishes
Five times shall come again the hundredth year.   *40*
  Think, should a man not make himself excel
  So that the first life may a second rear?
Not such high aim the present rabble who dwell   *43*
  'Twixt Adige and Tagliamento choose,
  Nor yet repent beneath the tyrant's flail.

19-21. *Answer me without waiting to be questioned.*
25. *"In that part . . .": the March of Treviso, in the northeast corner of Italy.*
29. *"A fiery brand": Ezzelin (see the Argument).*
34. *"The cause": the influence of Venus.*
37. *"This dear jewel": Fulk of Marseilles, who reappears in line 67.*
40. *Five centuries shall pass. Dante probably thought the world would come to an end at about that time.*
43. *"The . . . rabble who dwell . . .": the citizens of Treviso.*

But soon shall Padua by the reedy ooze   *46*
  Stain the stream watering Vicenza red,
  Since duty still the froward folk refuse;

And where Cagnano and Sile join their bed   *49*
  One lordeth it and goes with head held high,   *50*
  To catch whom even now the net is spread.

Feltro shall wail its pastor's perfidy—   *52*
  A crime so foul, that Malta's deep dungeons
  Held never a doer of like infamy.

Exceeding wide and big would be the tuns
  Sufficient to contain Ferrara's blood,
  And weary who should weigh it, ounce by ounce,

Which that suave priest shall lavish in a flood
  To prove his party zeal; and such expense
  Shall be congenial to that country's brood.   60

Above are Mirrors—Thrones ye call them—whence *61*
  God in his judgments shineth on us here,
  So that these words commend them to our sense."

She ceased then; and like one whose thoughts appear
  Gone elsewhither, she turned, as the wheel turned
  And in its circle again included her.

The other Joy, of whom I had newly learned   67
  As something precious, made my eyes as glad
  As a fine ruby on which a sunbeam burned.

Joy doth in heaven splendour to shining add,   70
  As smiles on earth; but down below the shade   71
  Outwardly darkens as the mind is sad.

"God sees all; and thy sight, blest spirit," I said,

46-47. *In 1314 the Paduans attacking Vicenza were defeated by Can Grande of Verona.*
49. "*And where* . . .": *at Treviso.*
50. "*One lordeth* . . .": *Rizzardo, a powerful lord, who was to be murdered by an assassin.*
52. "*Its pastor*": *the bishop of Feltro (see the Argument).*
61. *The "Thrones" are the angels that direct the Heaven of Saturn.*
67. "*The other Joy*": *Fulk (see line 37).*
71. "*Down below*": *in Hell.*

"Is deep in Him, so that no harbourings
  Of secret wish thy vision may evade:
Why doth thy voice then, which forever sings
  To charm Heaven, with those Flames' devout
      concert   77
  Which make themselves a cowl of the six wings,
Not satisfy the longing of my heart?
  I would not now be waiting thy request   80
  Were I so in thee as in me thou art."
Then he began to speak: "That mightiest   82
  Of valleys that the expanding water brims
  Out of the ocean wreathed about Earth's breast
So far between its shores' estrangement streams
  Against the sun, it is meridian there
  Which at its starting-point horizon seems.
Of that valley was I a coast-dweller
  'Twixt Ebro and Magra, which, with course soon
      done,   89
  Parts Genoese from Tuscan villager.   90
Almost alike for rise and set of sun
  Lies Bugia and the place from which I came,   92
  That once with warm blood made its harbour run.
Fulk was I called by those that knew my name;
  And this heaven taketh my imprint to wear
  As I from its imprinting do the same.
For Belus' daughter burned not fierier,   97
  Wronging Sichaeus and Creusa both,
  Than I, so long as curled my youthful hair,
Nor Rhodopeian maid, ensnared by the oath   100

---

77. "Those Flames": the six-winged Seraphim.
82-83. "That mightiest of valleys": the Mediterranean.
89. Between the Spanish river Ebro and the Italian Magra.
92. "Bugia": a town on the north coast of Africa. "The place": Marseilles.
97-102. "Belus's daughter": Dido. All the following are examples of passionate love.

Demophoön swore, nor Hercules when he
  Held Iole enclosed in his heart's troth.
Yet here is no repentance, only glee;
  Not for the sin, washed from our memories,
  But for the Power which planned and could foresee.
We contemplate the art which beautifies
  Result so great, and we discern the Good
  Which turns the world below back toward the skies.
But that thou may'st reap all the plenitude
  Of thy desires, engendered in this sphere,   110
  Behoves yet more to say, ere I conclude.
Thou long'st to know who lives in that light here
  Which near to me so sparkles in its bliss
  As the sun's ray glitters on water clear.
Know that within there Rahab is at peace;   115
  And having joined our order she bestows
  Her seal upon it in the loftiest place.
To this heaven, where the shadow your earth throws
  Comes to a point, first soul to be retrieved
  Of any, she with Christ triumphant rose;   120
And meet it was that she should be received
  In some heaven, palm of victory supreme
  That was with those two nailèd palms achieved, 123
Because in Joshua's war she prospered him
  Toward his first glory in the Holy Land,
  Which to the papal memory is grown dim.
Thy city, which was planted by his hand   127
  Who first presumed his maker to abhor,
  And from whose envy woe and wail expand,
Puts forth and propagates the accursed flower   130
  Which leads both sheep and lambs astray; and 'tis

---

115. *The story of Rahab, a harlot who hid Joshua's spies, is related in Josh. 2.*
123. *By lifting up both hands.*
127. *"Thy city": Florence, a plant of the devil.*
130. *"The accursed flower": see the Argument.*

Not the wolves now, but shepherds, that devour.
The Gospel and great Doctors are for this
  Forsaken, and only the Decretals read   *134*
  With zeal, as many a margin testifies.
To this the Pope and Cardinals are wed:
  They in their thoughts never to Nazareth come,
  There, whither Gabriel his wings outspread.
But Vatican and the other parts of Rome
  That are its holy places, where lie hid   140
  Soldiers of Peter, each beneath his tomb,
Shall of this whoredom speedily be rid."   *142*

134. "The Decretals" (Canon Law) are studied for financial profit.
142. "Whoredom": the unholy union of a corrupt Papacy and the
  Church.

Canto X

*Dante and Beatrice are borne aloft to the fourth
heaven, that of the sun. Here are the theologians.
The Canto begins with an exhortation to the reader
to admire the beauty and precision of the order of
the universe; the first lines referring to the three
Persons of the Trinity. A band of twelve spirits
make themselves into a circle or garland round
Dante and Beatrice in the center. One of these,
Thomas Aquinas, names the others, one by one.
They are Albertus Magnus of Cologne, Gratian,
Peter Lombard, Solomon, Dionysius the Areopa-
gite, Orosius, Boethius, Isidore of Seville, the Ven-
erable Bede, Richard of St. Victor, and Sigier of
Brabant.*

On His Son gazing, with the Love that still
  From one and from the other's breath proceeds,
  The Power primordial and ineffable
Made with such order all that circling speeds
  Through mind or space, that he who looks on it
  Cannot but taste Him, as thereon he feeds.
With me, then, Reader, lift thou up thy sight
  To the high spheres, directed to that part
  Where the two motions on each other smite.   9
Rejoice there to adore that Master's art   10
  Who inly holds it in so dear esteem
  That never will his eye from it depart.
See how diverges there, as branch from stem,   13
  The oblique circle which the planets tread
  To minister to the world invoking them.
And were their path not bent, the heaven would shed
  Much of its influence idly, and well-nigh
  Would every potency on earth be dead.   18
If from the straight farther or less awry
  Were the diverging, many a flaw would strain   20
  The world's whole order, down here and on high.
Now on thy bench, Reader, do thou remain,
  Thinking on what thou hast foretasted there
  If thou would'st banquet ere thou tire thy brain.
I have set before thee: feed now on this fare;
  For that matter to which my pen I vow
  Now wresteth to itself all of my care.
The greatest minister of Nature, who   28
  Imprinteth on the world the heavens' power

---

9. "The two motions": the diurnal and the annual revolutions of the
  sun.
13. "Diverges": at Aries the ecliptic slants across the equator.
18. There would be no seasons, and hence no generation.
28. "The greatest minister": The sun.

And whose light measures time for us below. *30*
Conjoined with that sign spoken of before, *31*
 Was circling through the spirals whereupon
 He, day by day, shows at an earlier hour. *33*
I was with him; yet had awareness none
 Of the ascent more than a man is made
 Aware of his first thought ere 'tis begun.
'Tis Beatrice by whom I thus am sped
 From good to better, in such instant flight
 That over time her action is not spread. *39*
How must those spirits be in their nature bright, *40*
 Which in the sun, where I had entered thus,
 Were visible not by colour but by light!
Vainly invoked were art, lore, genius,
 Things unimaginable here to show:
 But faith believes, and longing kindles us.
And if imagination be too low
 For such heights, 'tis no wonder: never yet
 Did eye conceive what could the sun out-glow.
So lucent the Fourth Household there was set *49*
 Where their High Father feasts them all their
  days, *50*
 Showing how he breathes and how he doth beget.
And Beatrice began: "Give thanks, give praise
 To the angels' Sun, who to this sun of sense
 Hath by His favour deigned thy feet to raise."
Never was heart of mortal so propense
 To all devotion and to render glad
 Itself to God with impulse so intense
As at those words the heart of me was made;
 And so entire was my love given Him, that

31. "That sign": *Aries.*
33. "Shows at an earlier hour": *in the spring.*
39. *Revelation (Beatrice) enlightens us instantaneously.*
49. "The Fourth Household": *is the fourth order of the blest, the theologians.*

Beatrice, eclipsed, passed to oblivion's shade.   60
Her it displeased not; but she smiled thereat,
  So that the splendour of her smiling eyes
  Split my absorbed mind on things separate.
Then saw I living, dazzling flames devise
  In us a centre and in themselves a crown,
  Sweeter in voice than radiant in their guise.
So girdled is Latona's daughter shown   67
  Sometimes, when vapour has so charged the air
  That it retains the thread that makes her zone.
Many a jewel beautiful and rare   70
  Is in the court of Heaven from which I come,
  Such that they may not be transferred elsewhere.
Such was the song those lights sang in their home.
  Who is not fledged that he may fly at last
  Up thither, may expect news from the dumb.
When, singing so, three times those suns had passed
  In circle around us, burning as before,
  Like stars next to the poles that stay stedfast,
They seemed like ladies whom the dancing-floor
  Still detains, silent, listening in the pause   80
  Until they catch the sound of strings once more.
And within one I heard a voice: "Because
  The ray of grace, whereby true love in men
  Is kindled and thereon with loving grows,
Multiplied in thee shineth out so plain
  That it conducts thee up the stair divine
  Which none goes down save to mount up again,
Whoso refused thee of his vial's wine
  For quenching of thy thirst were no more free
  Than water that descends not to the brine.   90
Thou would'st learn what flowers on this garland be   91
  The blossom, ringing with enraptured gaze

---

67. "Latona's daughter" *is Diana, the moon.*
91. "This garland": *the ring of shining spirits.*

The lady who for Heaven emboldens thee.

A lamb once of the sacred flock I was,   *94*
    Which Dominic leadeth on the path whereby
    He thriveth well who from the path not strays.

See on the right the one to me most nigh,
    My brother and master; Albert of Cologne
    Was he, and Thomas of Aquino I.   *99*

If thou would'st have the rest likewise be known,   *100*
    Do thou behind my words come with thine eyes
    Circling around the blessed garland's zone.

The next flame issues smiling from the wise
    Gratian, who so aided with his lore   *104*
    Both courts, that it well pleases Paradise.

The other who at his side adorns our choir
    Was that Peter, who with the poor widow   *107*
    Offered his mite for Holy Church to store.

The fifth light which in beauty excelleth so   *109*
    Breathes from such love, that all on earth beseech, *110*
    With hungry longing, news of it to know.

Within there is the lofty mind to which
    Was given such wisdom that, if truth be true,
    A second never could that vision reach.

Next shines the candle coming into view   *115*
    Which in the body saw most deep within
    The angels' nature and the work they do.

In the next little radiance smiles serene

---

94. The speaker, St. Thomas Aquinas, belonged to the Dominican order.

99. Albert Magnus of Cologne was the greatest scholar of the Middle Ages.

104. Gratian, in the first half of the twelfth century, did much to establish an agreement between religious and civil law.

107. "Peter" Lombard, who wrote famous doctrinal excerpts, compared his work to the widow's mite.

109. "The fifth light": of Solomon.

115. "The candle" is Dionysius the Areopagite, the great authority on the orders of the angels.

That pleader for the Christian times, from whose *119*
Fine-wrought discourse Augustine chose to glean. *120*
Now if from light to light thy mind's eye goes,
    Attending on the praises I record,
    Already for the eighth thy thirsting grows.
There in the vision of all good outpoured
    The sainted soul rejoices, that strips bare   *125*
    The world's deceit to whoso hears his word.
The body it was hunted from down there
    Lies in Cieldauro, and, released, it came   *128*
    From torture and exile to this peace by prayer.
Further thou can'st behold the breathing flame   *130*
    Of Isidore, of Bede, of Richard burn,   *131*
    Who in contemplation more than man became.
The one from whom thine eyes to me return
    Is the illumined spirit in whose grave thought
    Slow seemed to come the death he hoped to earn.
'Tis Sigier's eternal light, who taught   *136*
    In the Straw Street, and there for all to hear
    Syllogized truths that hatred on him brought."
Then as a clock, which calleth to us clear
    At the hour when God's bride, having risen to tell *140*
    Her love, sings matins in her bridegroom's ear,
Where one part pulls the other and strikes the bell,
    Sounding its *ding-ding* in so sweet a tone
    As makes love in the attunèd spirit swell,

---

119. "That pleader": Paulus Orosius, whose work supplements St.
Augustine's City of God.
125. "The sainted soul" is Boethius.
128. St. Peter in "Cieldauro": a church in Pavia.
131. St. Isidore wrote a very useful encyclopedia. The Venerable
Bede was the author of an important historical work. Richard of
St. Victor composed a treatise On Contemplation.
136. "Sigier" of Brabant, a daring philosopher of the thirteenth cen-
tury, was condemned for heresy.
140. "God's bride": the Church.

So did I see the glorious wheel roll on
    And render voice to voice, in harmony
    And in a sweetness never to be known
Save where joy tastes its own eternity.

Canto XI

*While on earth men pursue their petty ambitions
in law, medicine (the "Aphorisms" of Hippocrates),
the priesthood, etc., Dante felicitates himself on
being with Beatrice in Heaven. St. Thomas Aquinas
now recounts to him the story of the life of St.
Francis of Assisi; of his devotion to Lady Poverty;
his foundation of the Franciscan Order, his minis-
try and death. St. Thomas then speaks of the other
great Captain of the Church, St. Dominic, and of
the corruption which has spread among his fol-
lowers.*

Distracted mortals! of what paltry worth
    Are the arguments whereby ye are so prone
    Senselessly to beat down your wings to earth!
One wooed the Law, one the Aphorisms, one
    Coveted the priesthood, and another pressed
    Through force or fraud to acquire dominion;
One plunder, and one business, quite possessed;
    One in the pleasures of the carnal sty
    Grew weary; another his own ease caressed;

145. "The glorious wheel": of twelve counseling prophets.

The while, from all these things delivered, I   10
  In heaven with Beatrice in this manner met
  Was entertained in glory upon high.
Each spirit, when he had made the ring complete,
  Coming again where he before had been,
  Stopt, like a candle in the socket set.
And straightway, from within that blessed sheen
  Which first had spoken to me, smiling there
  And glowing more intense, I heard begin:
"Even as in me its lustre shineth clear,
  So gazing into the eternal light   20
  I see thy thoughts and what their promptings are,
Thou questionest: and, that thou construe right
  My words, would'st have me more at large re-tell
  In sifted phrase, clearer to earthly sight,
What I but now was saying, 'He thriveth well,'
  And where I said: 'No second ever rose.'
  And here on some distinctions must we dwell.
The providence, which doth the world dispose
  By counsel, wherein mortal scrutiny
  Is baffled ere it can the depths unclose,   30
So that the spouse of him, who with loud cry   31
  And with the blessed blood made her his bride,
  Might go toward her Belov'd unfalteringly,
Sure in herself and closer to his side,
  Appointed in her favour captains two
  Who each on either hand should be for guide.
The one was all seraphic heart a-glow,   37
  The other, by the wisdom he attained,
  A splendour of cherubic light below.
Of the one I tell, because they who commend   40
  Either, praise both, choose which-so'er they will,
  For all their works were to a single end.

---

31. "The spouse": the Church, which Christ wedded on the Cross.
37-38. "The one": St. Francis of Assisi. "The other": St. Dominic.

Between Tupino and the dropping rill,   *43*
   Blessed Ubaldo's chosen mountain-nook,
   A fertile slope hangs from a lofty hill,
Whence cold and heat come to Perugia's folk
   Through Porta Sole, and behind it weep
   Nocera and Gualdo for the oppressor's yoke.   *48*
From this slope, where it breaketh most the steep,
   A sun was born into the world, as this   *50*
   Is seen somewhiles from Ganges to upleap;
Wherefore, who speaks of that place speaks amiss   *52*
   Saying *Ascesi*—a falling short that were—
   But *Orient* would name truly what it is.
Not yet from his uprising was he far
   When he began to make earth feel a breath
   Of comfort stirring from his virtue rare.
For, young, he ran to face his father's wrath
   For a certain lady's sake, to whom no hand   *59*
   Unlocketh pleasure's gate, more than to death,   *60*
And in his spiritual court to stand   *61*
   Where *coram patre* faith to her he swore;
   And love from day to day his ardour fanned.
A thousand and a hundred years and more
   She, robbed of her first husband, unrenowned,   *65*
   Unwooed, till he came, scorn of all men bore.
And nought availed to hear that she was found   *67*

---

43. *Assisi is situated between the river Tupino and the Chiascio;
St. Ubald had his hermitage near by.*
48. *The little towns of "Nocera and Gualdo" "weep . . . for the
. . . yoke" of the Apennines.*
50. *This real "sun," where Dante now is.*
52-54. *The Tuscan form for Assisi, "Ascesi" (which also means "I
have risen"), is less fit a word than "Orient," or Dayspring.*
59. *He espoused Lady Poverty.*
61-62. *Summoned before the episcopal court of Assisi, St. Francis
stripped off his clothes.—"Coram patre": before his father.*
65. *"She": Poverty.—"Her first husband": Christ.*
67-69. *"Amyclas," a poor fisherman, was not afraid when Caesar
knocked at his door.*

Calm with Amyclas, though by that voice hailed
Which made the whole world tremble at its sound;
Nor constancy nor fearlessness availed   70
    So daring that, where Mary stayed below,
    She wept, high on the cross where Christ was nailed.
Lest too obscurely I continue, know
    Francis and Poverty for these lovers true;
    In my explicit speech accept them so.
Their concord and the joy their faces knew
    Made love and wonder and gentle, sweet regard
    To sacred thoughts the inviting avenue:
So first the venerable Bernard bared   79
    His feet, and to such great peace swiftly hied,   80
    And thought he went slow, though he ran so hard.
O fecund good! O riches undescried!
    Barefoot goes Giles, barefoot Sylvester, toward   83
    The bridegroom, following him: so charms the bride.
Thence took his way this father and this lord,
    He and his lady and all now of his house
    Already girded with the humble cord.
No abjectness of heart abashed his brows
    That he was Peter Bernardone's son,   89
    Nor that he seemed such wondrous scorn to arouse; 90
But like a king his staunch resolve anon
    He told to Innocent, and from him the impress   92
    Of the first signet on his Order won.
When the humble folk began so to increase,
    Following him, whose marvellous life and death
    Were better sung in glory of Heaven's high peace,
Then by Honorius with a second wreath   97

---

79. "Bernard": the first disciple of St. Francis.
83. "Giles" and "Sylvester": two early disciples.
89. "Peter B.," St. Francis's father, was a rich tradesman.
92. "Innocent" III: the Pope who reluctantly sanctioned St. Francis's Rule.
97. Pope "Honorius" III. "A second wreath": the final sanction.

Was this chief shepherd's holy purpose deckt
At prompting of the Eternal Spirit's breath.
When he, in thirst of martyrdom, erect   *100*
   Stood in the presence of the proud Soldan
   And preached Christ and the band of his elect,
Seeing the people were too crude a clan
   To be converted, he, not tarrying more,
   Returned to garner ripe Italian grain.
On the rough rock 'twixt Tiber and Arno shore
   He took that final imprint of the rood   *107*
   From Christ, which for two years his body bore.
When it pleased Him who chose him for such good
   To draw him up to his reward above,   110
   Earned when he took on him that lowlihood,
To his brethren, as to rightful heirs thereof,
   His most dear lady he trusted, and to her
   Bade them to cleave with ever-faithful love;
And from her bosom the high soul and clear,
   To its own realm returning willed to flit,
   And for its body wished no other bier.
Consider now who he was, who was fit   *118*
   Colleague to captain on deep seas the bark
   Of Peter, steering to the goal aright.   120
Such and no other was our Patriarch;
   Wherefore who follow him as he commands
   Taketh aboard good wares, as all can mark.
But greedy has grown his flock for new viands,   *124*
   So that it cannot but go uncontrolled
   And become scattered on high pasture-lands;
And the more wide astray over the wold

100-102. *In 1219 St. Francis accompanied the crusaders to Egypt,
where he preached before the Sultan.*
107. *"That final imprint": the Stigmata, or marks of Christ's five
wounds.*
118. *"Who he was": St. Dominic.*
124. *"His flock": the Dominicans.*

The sheep, departing from him, go to feed,
   The emptier of milk they come to fold.
Some are there, dreading harm, who do indeed   130
   Cleave to the shepherd; but so few they are,
   That for their cowls but little cloth they need.
Now if my voice have not seemed faint and far,
   If all thy mind on what I said is bent,
   If thou hast listened with attentive ear,
In part thy wish must surely be content;
   For thou shalt see the plant they chip away,
   And see too the correction that was meant
In 'where he thriveth, if his feet not stray.'"

Canto XII

*A second band of spirits appear, and form a circle
outside the first. One of these is St. Bonaventura.
He, a Franciscan, sings the praises of St. Dominic,
just as Aquinas, a Dominican, had celebrated St.
Francis. After telling of Dominic's birth in Spain,
his unworldliness and his fervent preaching against
the Albigenses, he goes on to condemn the degen-
eracy of his own, the Franciscan, order. He then
names those famous theologians who are with him.*

Soon as the blessed flame had with the last
   Word spoken stayed the utterance of its tongue,
   The sacred mill began to circle past;   3
Nor one full revolution had it swung

3. "The sacred mill": the ring of spirits.

Before another enclosed it in a ring,
  And motion chimed with motion, song with song;
Song that surpasseth all our Muses sing,
  Our Sirens, in those dulcet pipes sustained,
  As the sun's beams the beams they backward fling.
Even as the frail film of the cloud is spanned   10
  By two bows parallel and like in hue,
  When Juno to her handmaid gives command,   *12*
Outer from inner being born anew,
  Like that lost nymph repeating sound for sound   *14*
  Whom love consumed, as sun consumes the dew;
And presage then is with assurance crowned
  By the pact God with Noah certified
  That the world never shall again be drowned;
So did these ever-living roses glide
  In circle, a double garland, joy-possessed;   20
  So the outermost to the innermost replied.
Soon as the dance and heavenly revel ceased
  Both of the singing and the flaming, loopt
  About us,—light caressing and caressed,—
All by one impulse at one moment stopt,
  Like the eyelids that must needs in unison,
  As pleasure prompts, be lifted or be dropt,
A voice that came out of the heart of one
  Of the new lights turned me, as tractable   *29*
  As needle to the star, to where it shone,   *30*
And spoke: "The love I glow with bids me tell
  Of the other Leader on account of whom
  That voice hath celebrated mine so well.   *33*
'Tis fit that, where the one is, the other come,
  That, as together to the uttermost

---

12. "Her handmaid": Iris, the rainbow.
14. "That lost nymph": Echo, who wasted away to a voice.
29. "Needle": of a compass.
33. St. Thomas, for love of his own leader, St. Dominic, has been praising St. Francis.

They strove, together may their glory bloom.
The army of Christ, which at so dear a cost   *37*
    Was armed afresh, behind the standard strayed,
    A lagging, scattered, and mistrustful host,
When the Emperor who reigns forever made   *40*
    Provision for His soldiers in their hour
    (By grace alone, not that 'twas merited);
And, as hath been said, came to His bride's succour
    With two champions, by whose deed, whose word,
    The folk regained the path and footing sure.
In that land where the sweet west wind is stirred   *46*
    To open the fresh foliage to the light,
    And therewith Europe shows her re-attired,
Not far from where the waves of ocean smite
    Behind which, when his weary course he quits,   *50*
    The sun at times hideth from all men's sight,
The fortune-favoured Calaroga sits   *52*
    With the great shield protecting her repose
    Whereon the lion, who subdues, submits.
Therein was born the enthusiast amorous
    Of Christian faith, the saintly wrestler, kind
    Unto his own, severe unto his foes.
So charged, soon as created, was his mind
    With quickening power, that in the womb it led
    His mother a prophetic tongue to find.   *60*
When at the sacred font were perfected
    The espousals pledged between the faith and him,
    Where, dowried each with mutual weal, they wed,
The lady assenting for him, in her dream
    Beheld the marvel of the fruit's reward

---

37. "At so dear a cost": *by Christ's atonement.*
46. "In that land . . .": *Spain.*
52-54. "Calaroga": *a town in Old Castile, whose shield has two lions.*
60-66. *Before his birth, his mother had prophetic dreams; so had his godmother at his baptism which is conceived here as a wedding.*

Wherewith he and his heirs should come to teem;
And, that his name should with himself accord,
 They called him, prompted by a spirit from here,
 By the possessive of his only Lord.   *69*
Dominic was he named; and I aver   *70*
 He was a husbandman chosen by Christ
 To tend His garden and be His helper there.
Messenger and familiar of Christ
 He showed him; for his love's first loyalties
 Clung to the first great counsel given by Christ. *75*
Often, awake and silent on his knees,
 His nurse would find him on the floor, as who
 Should there be saying: 'I am come for this.'
O father of him called truly Felix! O
 Mother of him called also truly Joan   *80*
 (If the word rightly they interpret so)!
Not for the world for which men now toil on
 After him of Ostia and Thaddeus; nay,   *83*
 But for the love of the true bread alone,
A mighty teacher soon, he went his way
 About the vineyard to restore the vine
 Which, tended ill, fast withers and goes gray.
And from the Seat which once was more benign *88*
 To the honest poor (not that itself forswore,
 But through him who degenerate sits therein); *90*
Not to dispense, for seven, three or four;   *91*
 Not for the gift of the first vacancy;
 Not for the tithes belonging to God's poor
He asked, but licence and authority

---

69. Dominicus *means "of the Lord."*
75. *The "counsels" of Christ are poverty, continence, and obedience.*
80. *Joan signifies in Hebrew "the grace of Lord."*
83. *"Him of Ostia" (Enrico da Susa) and "Thaddeus": two famous
 professors.*
88. *"The Seat": the Papal chair.*
91. *To dole out in charity only part of the money on hand.*

Against error to combat for what nursed 95
Those twice twelve flowers that here engarland thee.
With doctrine and with will then, both endorsed
With the apostolic office, forth he went
Swift as a torrent from some high vein forced.
On stocks and stumps of heresy he spent 100
His vehemence, most impetuously where
Most stubborn was the opposed impediment.
Springing from him then divers runnels fair
Water the Catholic orchard near and far,
So that its saplings breathe more living air.
If such as this was one wheel of the car
In which the Holy Church made her defence
And won on the open field her civil war,
Plain enough must appear the excellence
Of the other one about whom Thomas told, 110
Before my coming, in so courteous sense.
But, where the topmost of the wheel once rolled, 112
The track deserted shows now not a hint;
So that, where once was crust, is now but mould.
His household, who marched on, treading the print
His feet made, has so turned itself about
That the toe strikes on the heel's former dint;
And soon shall it appear what crop is got
From careless tillage, when the tares begin
Their plaint that from the barn they are shut out. 120
I well know that who searches close and keen
Our volume, might yet find a page to cull
Where he might read 'I am as I have been';
But not Casál's or Acquasparta's school 124
Breeds such, for these our scripture's meaning turn;

---

95. "What nursed . . .": the Faith.
112. "The wheel" is St. Francis. His track is deserted by the Franciscans.
124-125. "Casale" and "Acquasparta": the homes of the leaders of two Franciscan factions. "Scripture": the Rule of St. Francis.

So that one shirks, and the other cramps, its rule.
I am the spirit of Bonaventura, born
   In Bagnoregio; in great offices
   The temporal care ever I had in scorn.
Illuminato, Austin, look! are these,   *130*
   Of the first brethren vowed barefoot to go,
   Friended with God and with the cord made His.
Hugh of St. Victor is here with them also,   *133*
   And Peter Mangiadore and Peter of Spain,
   Who in his twelve books spreadeth light below;
Nathan the prophet; the metropolitan   *136*
   Chrysostom; Anselm; Donat, who was guide
   To the first art, nor held it in disdain.
Rabano is here; and, shining at my side,
   Joachim the Calabrian abbot, great   *140*
   In gift, through whom the spirit prophesied.
So mighty a Paladin I celebrate,
   Moved by the ardour and the courtesy
   Of brother Thomas and his speech discreet;
And moved is all this company with me."

---

130. *Two early followers of St. Francis.*
133-134. *"Hugh of St. Victor": a famous theologian.—"Peter Man-*
   giadore": the author of a commentary on the Bible.—"Peter of
   Spain," a great logician, became Pope John XXI.
136-140. *St. John "Chrysostom" was Metropolitan of Constanti-*
   nople. St. Anselm, Archbishop of Canterbury, was a keen theolo-
   gian.—"Donat" was a grammarian.—"Rabano": a Biblical com-
   mentator.—"Joachim," Abbot of Flora in Calabria, founded a new
   branch of the Cistercians.

Canto XIII

In two concentric circles the twenty-four theologians dance, singing, round Dante and Beatrice. When their chant and movement are completed, the spirit of St. Thomas again addresses Dante. He has solved one of Dante's difficulties and now undertakes to solve the other, which arose from his having said that Solomon had no peer in wisdom. He is aware of Dante's objection that Adam and Christ in His human nature were supreme in wisdom, being directly created by God; but he explains that the wisdom Solomon asked for and obtained was not the speculative wisdom of a philosopher but the practical wisdom necessary to the office of a king. He closes with a warning against hasty judgments and rashly adopted opinions.

Let him imagine, who desires to grasp
    What now I saw (and let him, while I speak,
    Hold the image like a rock firm in his clasp),
Fifteen stars, which in divers regions prick
    The dark with lustre of such vividness
    That it wins through the air, however thick;
Imagine, too, that Wain, for which the embrace   7
    Of our heaven so sufficeth, night and morn,
    That, turning on its pole, it shows not less;
Imagine, too, the mouth of that bright horn   10

---

7. "That Wain": the Great Bear or Dipper.
10. "That bright horn": the Little Bear.

Which starteth from the central axle-spike
Round which the prime revolving wheel is borne,
To have made themselves two constellations, like
    What Minos' daughter hung in heaven to blaze   *14*
    When she felt death's cold frost upon her strike;
And one within the other to have its rays,
    And both in such a manner to spin past
    That they should circle upon opposing ways;
And he will have as in a shadow traced
    The real constellations, the two rings,   20
    Dancing around the point where I was placed,
Since it as much transcends our happenings
    As the most swift of all the heavens whirled round *23*
    Is swifter than Chiana's oozy springs.
Bacchus nor Paean did their chanting sound,   *25*
    But three persons in the divine nature
    And it and the human in one person found.
Circling and song by now completed were;
    And the hallowed flames their heed on us bestowed,
    Rejoicing to alternate care with care.   *30*
Broke then the hush of divine spirits who glowed
    In concert, that flame which had told about *32*
    The wondrous life of the poor man of God.
It said: "Now that the one sheaf of thy doubt
    Is threshed and garnered up, sweet love anew
    Inviteth me to beat the other out.
Thou hold'st that in the breast wherefrom God drew *37*
    The rib to mould that lovely cheek and chin

---

14. "Minos' daughter": *Ariadne, whose crown was turned into a
constellation.*
23-24. "The most swift . . .": *the Primum Mobile. The "Chiana"
is a sluggish stream in Tuscany.*
25. "Paean": *Apollo.*
32-33. "That flame": *St. Thomas.* "The poor man": *St. Francis.*
37-38. "The breast" *of Adam, whence was taken the "rib" to form
Eve.*

Whose palate cost the world unending rue,
And in that breast which, when the spear drove in,   *40*
   Made satisfaction, after and before,
   Such as to dip the scale against all sin,
Such light as human nature skills to store
   Was by that Virtue all infused, which made
   One and the other human by its power.
Therefore thou wonderest at the thing I said
   When I declared the wisdom which hath seat   *47*
   In the fifth light no second to have had.
Open thine eyes to the answer I now complete.
   Thou shalt see thy belief and my reply   *50*
   In truth, as in the circle's centre, meet.
That which not dieth and that which can die
   Reflect but that idea in their gleam   *53*
   Which in His love our Sire begets on high.
That living radiance which so sends its beam
   From its bright source, that it parts not from it
   Nor from the Love that is en-threed with them,
Doth of its bounty its own rays unite,
   As though in a mirror, in nine subsistences,   *59*
   Itself remaining one eternal light.   *60*
Thence it descends to the least potencies   *61*
   Downward from act to act, becoming soon
   Such as makes only brief contingencies.
And these contingencies may well be shown
   To be the things engendered by the stress
   Of moving heaven, from seed or else unsown.   *66*

---

40. "That breast": of Christ.
47. "The wisdom": of Solomon.
53. "That idea": *"In the beginning was the Word."*
59. The *"nine subsistences" are the nine orders of angels.*
61-63. "To the least potencies": *to the elements.* "Brief contingencies": *perishable things.*
66. "Moving heaven": *Nature. Animals and vegetables* "from seed," *minerals without seed.*

Their wax and that which doth the wax impress
   Vary; beneath the ideal stamp we find,
   Therefore, a brilliance now more and now less;
Whence comes it that, though of the self-same kind, 70
   Trees in their fruiting better are or worse;
   And ye are born with diverse gifts of mind.
Were the heavens operant in propitious course,
   And perfect and precise the moulded wax,
   The seal's full brilliance would shine out perforce;
But Nature's rendering ever something lacks,
   Working as the artist who hath skill by dint
   Of his art's practice but a hand that shakes.
Yet if the fervent Love dispose and print
   The lucent vision of the primal Power, 80
   There is perfection without flaw or stint.
So the dust of the earth was made worthy of yore 82
   Of all perfection breathing flesh can win;
   And thus the Virgin's womb its burden bore.
Thy opinion therefore I commend; I mean,
   That the human nature never was nor can
   Be such as was in those two persons seen.
Now here if my discourse no further ran,
   'How comes it then, that this one had no peer?'
   Would be the words with which thy speech
      began. 90
But, that what still is not clear may be clear,
   Think who he was and what cause moved him (when
   He was commanded Ask!) to make his prayer.
I have not argued so that 'tis not plain
   He was a king, who therefore wisdom chose, 95
   That equal to his office he might reign.

82-84. *This happened when God formed Adam, and when Christ
was conceived.*
95. *The gift which Solomon obtained was not general intelligence
but kingly prudence.*

'Twas not to know what numbers may compose
    Heaven's movers here; nor if *necesse* could   *98*
    With a contingent in *necesse* close;

Nor whether a *primus motus* be allowed;   *100*
    Nor if in a half-circle could be made
    A triangle that no right angle showed.

Hence, if thou note all that I say and said,
    Royal prudence is that vision without peer
    To which the arrow of my intention sped.

And if on 'rose' thy gaze be fastened clear,   *106*
    Thou'lt see that it hath solely in regard
    Kings, which are many and the good kings rare.

With this distinction then, accept my word,
    Which thus consists with what faith bids thee say 110
    Of the first father and our Delight adored.

Ever let this, like lead, thy feet down-weigh
    To make thee, where thou see'st not clear, move slow,
    Like one who is weary, both to Yea and Nay.

For he among the foolish stands right low
    Who affirms without distinction or denies,
    With whichsoever case he has to do;

Since often it haps that rashness of surmise
    Leadeth the judgment on false roads to start;
    Then fond desire the understanding ties.   120

On voyage worse than vain doth he depart
    (Since he returns not such as he sets out),
    Who fishes for the truth and lacks the art.

Of this are proofs the world hath not forgot,
    Parmenides, Melissus, Bryson—great   *125*
    Multitudes going, who where they went knew not.

---

98. "Nor if *necesse* . . .": *a scholastic problem in logic.*
100. "A *primus motus*": *a motion independent of any cause.*
106. "On 'rose' ": "A second never could that vision reach" (Par. x, line 114).
125. *Greek philosophers criticized by Aristotle.*

Such was Sabellius' and such Arius' fate,   *127*
    And fools who were to Scripture as a sword
    Reflecting crooked, faces that are straight.
Let not the people be too self-assured   *130*
    In judging early, as who should count the rows
    Of green blades in the field ere they matured.
For I have seen how first the wild-brier shows
    Her sprays, all winter through, thorny and stark,
    And then upon the topmost bears the rose;
And I have seen ere now a speeding barque
    Run all her sea-course with unswerving stem
    And close on harbour go down to the dark.
Let no Dame Bertha or Sir Martin deem,   *139*
    Because they see one steal and one give all,   *140*
    They see as divine forethought seëth them;
For the one yet may rise and the other fall."

---

127. "Sabellius" and "Arius" are heretical theologians.
139. "Dame Bertha or Sir Martin": "Tom, Dick, and Harry."

Canto XIV

Beatrice begins to speak to Dante; and since she speaks from the center of the circle of spirits and St. Thomas from the circle, the image is suggested to Dante of the movement of water in a bowl, moving outward or inward according as the bowl is struck from outside or inside. What is in Dante's thought is apparent to Beatrice before he has formulated it: he wants to know if the glorified body, after the resurrection, will retain its luster eternally; and, if it does, will the eyes endure to look on its brilliance. She asks the spirits to satisfy him

on these points; and Solomon answers both ques-
tions in the affirmative. Other spirits now appear, at
first faintly descried like stars at evening, and they
form themselves into a third circle round the other
two.

 Dante and Beatrice now mount to the fifth
heaven. It is the heaven of Mars; and here the
spirits of warriors and martyrs appear in the form
of a dazzling cross.

From centre up to rim, and so' from rim
 To centre, water moves within a bowl
 As struck from outside or inside the brim.
Into my mind what thus I speak of stole
 Upon a sudden, as to an end was brought
 The speech of Thomas's illustrious soul,
Because of the similitude I caught
 From his discourse and that of Beatrice,
 Whom it pleased, after him, to speak her thought:
"This man needs (though to tell what need is his 10
 Neither with voice, nor in thought yet, hath power)
 To pierce to another truth's deep mysteries.
Tell him, then, if the light, whence comes to flower
 Your being, is destined to remain with you
 Eternally, as in the present hour;
And if it still remaineth, tell him how
 When you in body are visible again
 It may no injury to your vision do."
As, all at once, the dancers in a chain,
 By a gust of gladness urged and drawn along, 20
 More blithely step and lift a louder strain,
So at entreaty so devout and strong
 The sacred circles yet more joyous grew
 In their revolving and their wondrous song.

Whoso laments that, to live there anew,
  We here must die, has known not what regale
  Is in the freshness of the eternal dew.

That One and Two and Three who ever shall   *28*
  Live and reign ever as Three and Two and One,
  Not circumscribed but circumscribing all,   *30*

Thrice by those spirits, by each and every one,
  Was hymned with such melodious acclaim,
  'Twere full reward for all good ever done.

And I heard breathe from the divinest flame   *34*
  Of the inmost, smaller circle a voice, modest
  As haply on Mary from the angel came,   *36*

Answering thus: "As long as lasts the feast
  Of Paradise, so long, by our love lit,
  Shall we in such a radiancy be drest.

Its brightness answereth our ardour's heat,   *40*
  Ardour the vision; and that shall be as great
  As, beyond worth, it has grace given to it.

When flesh in glorified and sainted state
  Shall be re-clothed, our persons in esteem
  Shall be more pleasing, being then complete;

Whence shall increase whate'er the Good Supreme
  On us of undeserved light shall bestow,
  Light which conditions us to look on Him.

The vision then must needs intenser grow,
  Intenser the ardour which from vision came,   *50*
  And thence the light's intenser overflow.

But like the coal that giveth out the flame   *52*
  Which by its living glow is overcome,
  So that it keeps its aspect still the same,

28-30. *The mystery of the Trinity.*
34. "From the . . . flame": *of Solomon.*
36. "The angel": *Gabriel.*
40-43. "Answereth": *is proportionate.* "The vision": *of God.*
"When . . .": *on the Judgment Day.*
52. *The coal glows through the flame that envelops it.*

So this effulgence wherein now we bloom
   Shall by outshining flesh be conquered quite,
   Which all this while lies in an earthly tomb.
Nor shall such light have power to daze our sight;
   For the organs of the body shall acquire
   Strength to support all that may most delight."   60
So quick and eager seemed then either choir
   To cry Amen, that thus they seemed to announce
   Plainly for their dead bodies their desire;
Not only for their own sake, but perchance
   For mother and father and others who were dear
   Ere they became flames in the eternal dance.
And lo! around, surpassing what was there,
   A lustre, all of equal brilliance, grew
   Like brightness on the horizon growing clear.
As in the sky, when evening still is new,   70
   Comes the apparition of faint-shining things   71
   So that the sight seems and yet not seems true,
Methought that I perceived there new beings
   Making themselves a circle like a wreath
   Outside the other two resplendent rings.
O very sparkle of the Holy Breath!
   How swiftly furnace-bright it grew to be,
   Such as my daunted eyelids fell beneath!
But Beatrice disclosed herself to me
   Smiling in beauty such that I leave this   80
   Among those sights barred to my memory.
Therefrom mine eyes regained their faculties;
   And, raising them, I saw me now transferred
   Sole with my lady to a loftier bliss.
That I was lifted higher was averred
   By the star's fiery smile, whose kindled face
   Redder to me than is his wont appeared.
With my whole heart and that unvoiced address

---

71. "Things": stars, faint in the twilight.

Which all men own, burnt sacrifice I made
    To God, such as befitted this new grace.   90
Nor did the sacrificial ardour fade
    Out of my bosom, ere I knew my vows
    Accepted, and my offering perfected;
For with such redness, and so luminous,
    Splendour appeared within two beams; whereat
    I cried: "O Sun that dost adorn them thus!"
As 'twixt the poles, with lesser lights and great
    Patterned, the Galaxy so whitely glows   98
    That thereof sages question and debate,
So in the depth of Mars were clustered those   100
    Full beams to make the venerated sign   101
    Which quadrants, joined within a round, compose.
Here memory overcomes all wit of mine;
    For that cross in such glory beaconed Christ
    That I must all comparison resign:
But whoso takes his cross and follows Christ
    Shall one day pardon this my helpless case
    When he shall see that flashing forth of Christ.
From horn to horn, and between top and base,
    Moved lights that sparkled in a livelier sort   110
    When each the other came to meet and pass.
So here on earth we see, level and thwart,
    Rapid and slow, with varying aspect freaked,
    The particles of bodies long and short   114
Dance through the ray wherewith is often streaked
    The shadow, which against the glare of noon
    Men's art contrives, their comfort to protect.
As viol and harp in harmony commune
    With many strings that chime sweet on the ear

---

98. "The Galaxy": *the Milky Way.*
101-102. "The . . . sign": *the Cross.* "Quadrants": *two diameters of a circle.*
114. "The particles": *the bits of dust dancing in a ray of sunshine in a dark room.*

Of one who apprehendeth not the tune,   120
So from the lights I there beheld appear
   Was harmonized a music on the Rood
   That ravished me, though the import was not clear.
I knew the hymn to be of lofty mood
   For 'Rise' and 'Conquer' came into my ken
   As to whoso hears but hath not understood.
There was I so enamoured, that till then
   I had not been by anything possessed
   That with such sweetness did my soul enchain.
It may be I seem too boldly to protest,   130
   Slighting those eyes of beauty and delight   131
   Gazing on which my longing is at rest;
But he who minds him that the more the height
   The more power the quick seals of beauty use,
   And that I had not turned yet to their light,
May excuse that which for my own excuse
   I accuse me of, and know I tell truth here;
   For naught I say the holy joy eschews,
Since, as it mounteth, so it glows more clear.

131-134. "Those eyes" and "the quick seals of beauty" are Beatrice's
eyes, which become more potent from sphere to sphere.

Canto XV

A star detaches itself from the right arm of the cross
and descends to the foot of it. It is the soul of
Dante's ancestor Cacciaguida. After he has wel-
comed Dante with affection, Dante excuses him-
self from thanking Cacciaguida in words, because,
unlike the spirits in Paradise, he is conscious of a

*disparity between his feeling and the power to ex-
press it. His ancestor then describes the Florence of
his own time, its simple manners and familiar life,
and contrasts with it the extravagance and dissipa-
tion of the present.*

A GRACIOUS will whereinto is distilled
   Forever love that righteous thoughts inspire,
   As base greed in the bad will is fulfilled,
Imposed a silence upon that sweet lyre,   *4*
   And made the sound of sacred strings to cease
   Whereof Heaven's right hand pulls and slacks the
      wire.
How shall those beings honest prayers dismiss
   Who, to encourage me to make my prayer
   To them, of one accord now held their peace?
'Tis well that he without end should despair   10
   Who for the love of what cannot endure
   Eternally, of this love strips him bare.
As through the evening sky, serene and pure,
   Will trail from time to time a sudden blaze   *14*
   And the idle eyes from their repose allure,
Seeming a star that from its region strays,
   Save that from that place, where it seemed to ignite,
   No star is lost, and it but short time stays,
So from the arm that stretches on the right
   Down that cross to its foot a star began   20
   To glide from the full cluster, blazing bright,
Nor swerved the jewel from its ribbon's span,   22
   But shooting down the radiant strip it shone
   Like fire behind an alabaster pane.

---

4. "Lyre": the spirits of the Cross.
14. "A sudden blaze": a meteor.
22. The bright spirit did not go outside the Cross.

So fondly, if trust our greatest Muse hath won,   25
　Anchises' shade proffered his arms' embrace,
　When in Elysium he perceived his son.
"O my own blood! O brimming with God's grace!
　To whom was ever twice, as unto thee,
　The gate thrown open of Heaven's holy place?"   30
So that light spoke: I hearkened heedfully:
　Then to my lady turned again mine eyes;
　And on both sides amazement mastered me.
For such a smile was glowing in her eyes,
　Methought with mine the deepest depth to sound
　Both of my grace and of my paradise:
Then, joy to hear and see, the spirit crowned
　His proem with things added, which my mind
　Understood not, his speech was so profound.
Neither was this obscurity designed,   40
　But of necessity; for his thought I know
　Ranged high above the mark of mortal kind.
And when the bow of ardent love was so
　Unbent, that his discourse descended toward
　The target of our intellect below,
What first I comprehended was this word:
　"Blessed be thou, O Three and One, that hast
　Such courtesy upon my seed outpoured!"
Then followed: "A dear hunger from long past
　Drawn from the great Book's reading, wherein
　　white   50
Nor black is ever changed from first to last,
Thou hast assuaged, my son, within this light
　Wherein I speak to thee: thanks be to her
　Who with wings plumed thee for the lofty flight.
Thou deem'st that thy thought passeth to me clear

25-27. "Our greatest Muse": Virgil, who, in the Aeneid, describes
　the meeting of Aeneas and the shade of his father, Anchises.
50. "The great Book": of Fate.

From him who is First, as five and six expand
From one, provided this is known for sure.
Who I am, therefore, thou dost not demand,
Nor why I seem more full of happiness
Than any other in this rejoicing band: 60
Rightly thou thinkest; for both great and less
In this life on the mirror gaze, wherein,
Before thou think'st, thou dost thy thought express.
But that the sacred love I watch within
With constant gaze, and which doth in me breed
Sweet longing, may the more fruition win,
Let thy voice firm, joyous and bold proceed;
Utter the will, utter the wish whereto
My answer hath already been decreed."
I turned me round to Beatrice; and she knew   70
Before I spoke, and smiled me a signal, whence
The wings of my desire more urgent grew.
I began: "Feeling and Intelligence,
When the Prime Equality was to you made known,
For you were poised, equal in influence,   75
Because the sun that warmed you and on you shone
With heat and light hath such an equal might
That it makes beggary of comparison.
But reason and feeling in our mortal plight
(And well ye know the impediments that thwart) 80
Unequally are feathered for their flight.
Hence I, who am mortal, feel that I have part
In this disparity, and must thank thee for
Thy fatherly welcome only in my heart.
Yet, living topaz, thee I may implore,
Who dost this jewel beyond price begem,
That with thy name thou gladden me yet more."
"O leaf of mine!" thus he commenced his theme,

---

75. *The blest have no wish which they have not intelligence to ful-
fill.*

"In whose arrival happiness I knew,
  Merely awaiting thee, I was thy stem."   90
Continuing: "He from whom thy kindred drew   91
  Their name, and who hath passed the hundredth year
  Circling the Mount's first cornice for his rue,
Was my son, father to thy grandfather;
  And fit it is that thy good works abate
  The weariness that he hath yet to bear.
Florence within the ancient cincture sate   97
  Wherefrom she still hears daily tierce and nones,
  Dwelling in peace, modest and temperate.
She wore no chain or crownet set with stones,   100
  No gaudy skirt nor broidered belt, to gather
  All eyes with more charm than the wearer owns.
Nor yet did daughter's birth dismay the father;
  For dowry and nuptial-age did not exceed
  The measure, upon one side or the other.
There was no house too vast for household need;
  Sardanapalus was not come to show   107
  What wanton feats could in the chamber speed.
Nor yet could over Montemalo crow   109
  Your Uccellatoio, which, as it hath been   110
  Passed in its rise, shall in its fall be so.
Bellincion Berti girdled have I seen   112
  With leather and bone: and from her looking-glass
  His lady come with cheeks of raddle clean.
I have seen a Nerli and a Vecchio pass
  In jerkin of bare hide, and hour by hour

91-93. "He from whom . . .": *Alighiero, son of Cacciaguida.* "The Mount's first cornice": *the circle of Pride, in Purgatory.*

97-98. "The ancient cincture": *the old city walls, beside which stood the ancient Abbey, whose bell marked the hours ("tierce and nones") for the Florentines.*

107. "Sardanapalus," *king of Assyria, was notorious for his luxury.*

109-111. *Rome was not yet surpassed in splendor by Florence.*

112. "Berti": *a worthy citizen.*

Their wives the flax upon the spindle mass.
O fortunate! for each one was secure
    Of her own burial-place; none in her bed
    Deserted yet because of France's lure.   120
One would keep watch over the cradle's head,
    And, soothing, babble in that fond idiom
    Which maketh each new father and mother glad.
One, as the tresses off the distaff come,
    Would tell the story in her children's ear
    Of Trojans, of Fiesole, and Rome.
Cianghella or Lapo Salterello there   127
    As singular a portent would have been
    As now Cornelia, Cincinnatus, were.
To so comely a life and so serene   130
    Of citizens that to their city's claim
    Replied with loyalty, a so pleasant inn,
Mary, invoked with cryings on her name,
    Gave me; and in your ancient Baptistery
    Christian and Cacciaguida I became.
Moronto and Eliseo brothered me;
    My wife came to me from the vale of Po:
    It was from her thy surname was to be.
Then in the train of Conrad did I go,   *139*
    The emperor, who belted me his knight;   140
    Such honour my good service raised me to.
With him I went, the iniquity to fight
    Of those usurping infidels who rule
    (Fault of the Pastors) what is yours by right.
There was I stript free by that people foul
    Of the world's swathing of deceitfulness,
    The love of which corrupteth many a soul,
And came from martyrdom into this peace."

---

127. "Cianghella" and "Lapo" were notorious for their immodesty
139. "Conrad" III, of Swabia, leader of the crusade of 1147.

Canto XVI

Cacciaguida informs Dante, in response to his question, of the date at which he lived, and tells him about the population of Florence, then so much smaller than in Dante's time; the city being contained in the space between the battered statue of Mars on the Ponte Vecchio and the church of St. John the Baptist. Cacciaguida goes on to enumerate the great Florentine families of his day and to tell of their decline, attributed by him to admixture of blood from outside the city.

The "great baron" (line 128), who made so many knights, is Ugo il Grande, Marquis of Tuscany. Buondelmonte was killed at the instance of Mosca (see Inferno, Canto XXVIII) at the foot of the statue of Mars. The arms of Florence, originally white lilies on a red field, were changed by the Guelfs to red lilies on white.

O THOU small dignity of noble blood!
  If thou make men to glory in thee below
  Here, where we faint, pursuing the true good,
Never will I account it wonder now;
  For where desire warps not, being immune
  (I mean in Heaven), that pride did I avow.
Truly thou art a garment shrinking soon;
  So that, if naught daily to thee accrue,
  Time goes about thee with the shears that prune.
With that which Rome permitted first, the *You*   *10*

10. "The You": the respectful "voi" instead of the familiar "tu."

(In which her citizens least persevere),
  I now began to address that soul anew;
Whence Beatrice, withdrawn a pace less near,
  Smiled, and seemed like to her who, standing by,
  Coughed at the first fault told of Guinevere.   *15*
"You are my father," I said, "you fortify
  My heart to speak out boldly all I will;
  You lift me, so that I am more than I.
My mind with gladness from so many a rill
  Brims, it exults that, being so full-stored,   *20*
  It can contain all, nor be burst and spill.
O tell me then, firstling of mine adored!
  What ancestry was yours, and what the date
  Whereof your years of boyhood could record.
Tell me of the sheepfold of St. John, how great   *25*
  It was then, and who in it were the folk
  Accounted the most worthy of highest seat."
As a coal quickens, at the wind's soft stroke
  Breathed into flame, so now began to glow
  That light at the caressing words I spoke.   *30*
And as to the eye its beauty appeared to grow
  So with a voice more sweet and gentle made
  But using not the modern mode we know,
He spoke: "From that day when was *Ave* said   *34*
  To the birth in which my sainted mother earned
  Deliverance, and the burden of me shed,
Five hundred fifty and thirty times returned
  This star to its own Lion, and with its face
  Of fire beneath his paws rekindling burned.

---

15. In the Old French romance of Launcelot du Lac, the Dame de
  Malehaut coughed on hearing the impassioned speech of Guine-
  vere.
25. "St. John" the Baptist: the patron saint of Florence.
34. "From that day . . .": from the Annunciation to the birth of
  Cacciaguida (in 1091), Mars returned 580 times to the constella-
  tion of Leo.

My ancestor and I had for birth-place   40
    That last ward, first upon his onward way   *41*
    Reached by the runner in your annual race.
Of my forbears let this be enough to say:
    Of who they were, and whence, 'twere seemlier
    To hold one's peace, rather than make display.
'Twixt Mars and Baptist all who at that time were   46
    Capable of arms would in their number sum
    But a fifth part of those now living there.
But the citizens, mixt now from Campi and from   49
    Certaldo and Filigne, had their blood   50
    Then, to the least of craftsmen, pure of scum.
How much better it were to have that brood
    For neighbours rather, and that your boundary
    At Trespiano and Galluzzo stood,
Than, having them inside, the stench to aby
    Of Aguglion's churl and him of Signa, one
    Who for a jobbery sharpens still his eye!
Had but that clergy, most degenerate known,
    Not been to Caesar as a stepmother
    But tender as a mother to her son,   60
One, Florentine now, buyer and barterer,
    To Simifonte had been made to pack,   62
    Where his grandfather plied for a mean hire;
The Conti in Montemurlo would be back,
    The Cerchi in Acone parish still,
    Nor Valdigreve a Buondelmonte lack.
Confusion of persons ever was and will
    Be that from which the city's woes derive,
    As from superfluous food the body's ill;

---

41. "That last ward": *the Mercato Vecchio.*
46. " 'Twixt Mars and Baptist": *see the Argument.*
49-50. "Campi . . . , Certaldo and Filigne": *towns belonging to Florence.*
62. "Simifonte": *a stronghold in Val d'Elsa, annexed by Florence in 1202.*

And a blind bull falls with more headlong dive   70
   Than a blind lamb, and often a single sword
   Cuts sharper and with a wider sweep than five.
If Luni and Urbisaglia thou regard,   73
   How they are fallen, and how Chiusi too,
   And with them Sinigaglia, not so hard
A thing will it appear, nor strange and new
   (Since cities have a term to which they tend)
   To hear how families themselves undo.
All your affairs, like you, on death depend,
   Though this some long-enduring things conceal;   80
   And briefly come your own lives to their end.
And as the moon's heaven rolling in its wheel
   Covereth and uncovereth without cease
   The shores, so Fortune does with Florence deal.
Therefore no marvel shall appear in this
   Which I shall tell of each high Florentine
   Whose fame is hidden among Time's secrecies.
I have seen Ughi and Catellini shine,   88
   Filippi, Greci, Ormanni, and by their side
   The Alberichi, all noble in their decline;   90
Seen Soldanieri's and the Arca's pride
   And the Sannella; houses old as great;
   Ardinghi and Bostichi with them vied.
Over the gate, now burdened with the weight   94
   Of a new felony, so fraught with shame,
   That soon the ship will jettison its freight,
The Ravignani dwelt, from whom there came
   Count Guy, and whosoever since hath ta'en
   On him the lofty Bellincione's name.
He of La Pressa knew how to rule men;   100

73-75. "Luni and Urbisaglia" were fallen cities; "Chiusi" and "Sini-
   gaglia" were in decay.
88-93. Old families that have declined or disappeared.
94. "Over the gate . . .": in 1280 the Cerchi, leaders in party strife,
   bought the palace of the Counts Guidi.

And in the house of Galigaio were
   The gilded hilt and pommel, even then.
High stood Sacchetti, Giuochi, pillared Vair,
   Fifanti and Barucci and Galli, and those
   Who of the cheating bushel blushed to hear.   *105*
Still great the stock was whence Calfucci rose;
   And to the curule office still were drawn
   Sizii and men of Arrigucci's house.
O how great have I seen these, now undone
   By pride! and, with the balls of gold made fair,   *110*
   Flowered Florence in the triumphs they had won.
Such were the sires of them who now, whene'er
   Your church's bishopric is vacant, keep
   Prolonged consistory, and fatten there.
The insolent tribe that like a dragon leap
   On him who flies them, but to him whose mien
   Shows tooth or purse are milder than a sheep,
Was rising, though from small folk; Ubertin
   Donato was but little pleased to know
   His father-in-law had made him of their kin.   120
Already to the market-place below
   Had Caponsacco come down from the hill;
   Giuda, Infangato, yet had worth enow.
I'll tell a thing true, though incredible:
   One entered the small circuit by a gate   *125*
   That took its name from the Pear's blazon still.
Each one who shares the fair arms of the great   *127*
   Baron, whose virtue and whose renown, revived,
   The feast-days of St. Thomas celebrate,

---

105. "Who of the cheating bushel . . .": the Chiaramontesi, who
disgraced themselves as salt commissioners.
110. "The balls of gold": on the shield of the Lamberti family.
125-126. "The small circuit": the old city walls. "A gate": The Porta
Peruzza.
127-128. "The great Baron" is Hugh the Great (see the Argument),
who died in 1001, on St. Thomas's day.

Knighthood and privilege from him derived,   130
    Though that one now joins with the populace   131
    Who for the escutcheon a gold fringe contrived.
Gualterotti and Importuni throve apace;   133
    And, had they still abstained from neighbours new,
    The Borgo now were a more peaceful place.
The house from which arose your weeping, through 136
    The just wrath that hath murdered you and set
    A term to all the joyous life ye knew,
Was honoured, and the houses with it knit.
    O Buondelmonte, ill didst thou to flee   140
    Those nuptials, when another prompted it!
Glad had been many, who now must mournful be,
    If God thy body had into Ema thrown   143
    The first time that the city welcomed thee.
Yet fit it was that to that battered stone,   145
    Which guards the bridge, our Florence should present
    A victim in the last peace she hath known.
With these folk and with those who with them went
    I beheld Florence in such peace immersed
    That she knew no occasion to lament.   150
With these I saw her people in justice nursed
    And glory, so that never was espied
    The lily upon a victor's lance reversed,   153
No, nor by feud and faction crimson-dyed."

---

131. *The knight who "now joins with the populace" is Giano della Bella.*

133. *These families also fell from their high estate.*

136-141. "*The house": the Amidei. The bloody feud between the Amidei and the Buondelmonti divided all Florence for a long time. One Buondelmonte had forsaken his betrothed, one of the Amidei.*

143. *The "Ema" is a little stream.*

145. "*That battered stone": the statue of Mars at the foot of which Buondelmonte was killed.*

153. "*The lily": see the Argument.*

Canto XVII

*Dante now tells of the warnings he had received
(from Farinata and Brunetto Latini in Hell, and
from other souls in Purgatory), about his future;
and he now asks his ancestor to tell him plainly
what are the calamities he is to undergo. He thus
learns of his banishment from Florence; of his ref-
uge with the Della Scala family at Verona, where
Can Grande della Scala (here warmly eulogized)
was to be his chief patron and protector; and of the
annoyance to be caused him by his fellow-exiles.
Cacciaguida encourages the poet to complete his
poem and publish it, in spite of the offense it will
give to many persons opprobriously named in it and
branded with Dante's scorn.*

As came to Clymene, intent upon   1
  The truth of what against him had been said,
  Who still makes father chary toward his son,
Such was my need, and so my thought was read
  By Beatrice and by the sacred lamp
  Which for my sake had from its station sped.
Wherefore my Lady: "Let no scruple damp
  Thy desire's flame, but let it issue free,
  Bearing clear impress of the inward stamp;
Not that our knowledge by thy words may be   10

1-3. Phaëthon, having been told that Apollo was not really his father,
went to his mother Clymene to find out the truth. Apollo's indul-
gence had tragic results, when he allowed Phaëthon to drive the
chariot of the sun.

Increased, but that thy tongue inure to tell
   Thy thirst, that we may mix the cup for thee."
"Dear root of mine, who art lifted up to dwell
   So high, that, as to earthly mind 'tis clear
   Two obtuse fit not in one triangle,
So dost thou see contingent things, or e'er   *16*
   Themselves are, gazing on the point beyond
   To which all times are present, now and here.
While I by Virgil was companioned
   Over the mountain where the souls are healed,   *20*
   And journeyed down the dead world underground,
Words, grave in import, of what lies concealed
   In time to come were said to me, although
   Four-square I feel me against all hazard steeled.
My wish, then, were content if thou would'st show
   What fortune nears me and makes of me its quest:
   Foreseen, the arrow strikes a duller blow."
To that same light by which I had been addressed
   I spoke thus; and in promptness to obey
   The will of Beatrice was my will confessed.   *30*
By no such oracle, saying Yea and Nay,   *31*
   As the fond folk were limed with, ere was slain
   The Lamb of God who taketh sins away,
But in transparent speech, precise and plain,
   Answered me that paternal love, in light
   Hidden, and revealed by its own smile again.
"Contingency, concerned only to write   *37*
   In the volume of your matter, and nothing higher,
   Is all portrayed in the eternal sight,
Yet cannot thence Necessity acquire   *40*
   More than the eye that is reflecting her

---

16. "Contingent": *casual things, whether they be past, present, or future.*
31. *In no ambiguous terms, such as heathen prophets used.*
37. "Contingency": *the whole sequence of casual events.*

Can the ship's motion down the tide inspire.
From thence into my sight, as into the ear
   Harmonies of an organ softly start,
   Comes what for thee the approaching times prepare.
As by his stepmother's perfidious art   *46*
   Cruelly was Hippolytus driven out
   From Athens, so must thou from Florence part.
This they have willed; this they already plot;
   And soon shall it be done by him who brews   *50*
   That plot, where daily Christ is sold and bought.
The common cry shall, after its wont, accuse
   The wronged party; but justice shall be near
   To testify how Truth exacts her dues.
Thou shalt leave all that thou hast loved most dear;
   This is the arrow, shooting from the bow
   Of banishment, which thou hast first to fear.
How bitter another's bread is, thou shalt know
   By tasting it; and how hard to the feet
   Another's stairs are, up and down to go.   *60*
And what shall on thy shoulders heaviest sit
   Shall be the crew, stupid and venomous,   *62*
   With whom thou shalt have fallen into that pit;
For, ingrates all, frenzied and impious,
   They'll turn against thee; but thereafter soon
   They and not thou shall have blood-reddened brows.
Their brutishness shall by their works be known,
   So that thou shalt be honoured and preferred
   To have made a party of thyself alone.
Thy first hostel and refuge from that herd   *70*
   In the great Lombard's favour shalt thou find   *71*
   Who on the Ladder bears the sacred Bird.

---

46. "His stepmother": *Phaedra.*
50. "By him who . . .": *Pope Boniface* VIII.
62. "The crew": *the Whites, Dante's fellow exiles.*
71. "The great Lombard": *Bartolommeo della Scala, whose shield bore a ladder and an eagle.*

For he shall hold thee in regard so kind,
    That of the giving and asking 'twixt you two,
    That shall come first which oftenest lags behind.
And one there is thou shalt see with him, who   76
    Was at his birth so stamped with this strong star   77
    That he is destined deeds of note to do.
Hardly of him yet is the world aware
    Because of his young age, for years have rolled   80
    But nine around him in their course; but ere
The Gascon's guile great Harry have cajoled,   82
    Some sparkles of his virtue shall be shown
    In grudging not laborious days nor gold
Later, shall his magnificence be known,
    So that his enemies will not repress
    Their tongues from telling what things he hath done.
Look to him; wait his gracious offices!
    Through him shall many taste an altered lot,
    The beggar and the rich exchanging place.   90
And of him thou shalt bear, but tell it not,
    A record in thy mind." And he told things
    Which those who see with their own eyes shall doubt.
Then he added: "Son, these are the commentings
    On what thou hast been told; the snares now see
    Ambushed behind few years' revolving rings.
But I would have thee of envy of neighbours free,
    Since thy life shall be futured to outrun
    By far, the avenging of their perfidy!"
When, by his saying no more, that sainted one   100
    Showed he had finished setting of the woof
    Across the warp I proffered, I began,
Like one who, in uncertainty of proof,

---

76. "One there is": Can Grande (see the Argument).
77. "This strong star": Mars.
82. "The Gascon": Pope Clement v. "Harry": the Emperor Henry
VII.

Longs with great longing for a counsellor
Who sees, and wills uprightly, and who has love.
"I see, my father, Time against me spur
    To deal me a blow, such as falls heaviest
    On him who goes unwary and self-secure.
'Twas well with foresight, then, to arm me, lest,   *110*
    If the most dear place I am forced to lose,
    I may not, through my song, lose all the rest.
Down in the world of never-ending throes
    And up the mountain from whose radiant height,
    My Lady's eyes uplifting me, I rose,
And, after, through the heaven from light to light,
    I have learnt that, which, if it all be penned,
    In many will a bitter taste excite;
And if to truth I am a flinching friend,
    I fear to lose life among those to whom
    This world will be an old world, come to its end." 120
The enclosing radiance it was smiling from—
    My treasure I had there discovered—flashed
    Like beams that from a golden mirror come,
Then answered me: "Conscience, that is abashed
    By shame, its own or others', will in each,
    'Tis true, who reads thee, feel some frailty lashed;
Yet none the less, cast falsehood from thy speech
    Quite out; make thy whole vision manifest;
    And let them scratch wherever is the itch.
For if thy voice be pungent at first taste   130
    Yet shall it leave a vital sustenance
    After the mind has leisure to digest.
Thy cry shall come with the wind's vehemence
    That strikes full on the loftiest peaks alone;
    Honour not small shall be thy recompense.
Therefore to thee have on these spheres been shown,
    And on the Mount, and in the Vale of Dread,

---

110. "The most dear place": *Florence.*

Only such souls as have acquired renown,
Since the hearer's spirit is not comforted
    Nor knits its faith by an example mean   140
    Which hath its roots obscure and darkly hid,
Nor by what proof else is not plainly seen."

Canto XVIII

*Cacciaguida points out to Dante a number of illus-
trious souls, who appear as stars on the cross, and
move as they are named. Dante and Beatrice now
ascend from the heaven of Mars to the "temperate
star" of Jupiter, the sixth heaven, where are spirits
conspicuous for justice. The lights in which the
spirits are hidden form themselves into the pattern
of an eagle.*

*At the end of the Canto Pope John XXII is de-
nounced for his love of money. The Florentine
florin was stamped with the image of St. John the
Baptist; and in the concluding lines the Pope is
ironically represented as being so devoted to this
coin that he has forgotten Peter and Paul.*

THAT blessed mirror was now lost in joy
    Of its own thought; and savouring mine, I stood
    Tempering the bitter with the sweet alloy;
And she whom I was following unto God
    Said: "Change thy thought! Remember I am near
    To Him who of all wrong lifts off the load!"
I turned me to the sound, loving and dear,
    Of my own Comfort; and what love then shone

In the holy eyes I leave unwritten here,
Not because I mistrust my speech alone   10
  But memory, which returns not to excel
  Itself so far, save it be guided on.
Only this of that moment I can tell,
  That my affection, as she filled my gaze,
  Was freed from all else only on her to dwell,
While the eternal joy which beamed its rays
  Immediate on the beauty of Beatrice
  Rapt me with its reflection on her face.
And vanquishing me with a smile of bliss
  She spoke to me: "Turn now and listen anew!   20
  Not only in my eyes is Paradise."
As sometimes in the very features' hue
  Appears the affection, if it be so strong
  As to possess the whole soul through and through,
So in the glow the sacred flame outflung   25
  To which I turned, a craving I could see
  In it, a little our converse to prolong.
He began: "In this fifth tier of the tree   28
  Which from its top lives, and can never lose
  One leaf, and puts forth fruit continually,   30
Are blessed spirits whose names were glorious
  On earth, before into this heaven they came,
  Such as would richly furnish every Muse.
Gaze therefore on the cross: he whom I name
  Shall on its arms that suddenness enact
  Which happeneth when the cloud lets forth the
    flame."   36
Gliding along the cross a light I tracked
  At Joshua's naming; spoken, it was done;
  Nor did I learn the word before the act.

---

25. "The sacred flame": *Cacciaguida.*
28. *The fifth "tier" of the tree of the heavens is Mars.*
36. *As lightning flashes across a cloud.*

At mighty Maccabeus' name there shone   40
   Another, whirling bright before my eyes;
   And gladness whipt the top, as round it spun.
For Charlemagne and Roland in like wise
   Two more were followed by my earnest look,
   As the eye follows a falcon as it flies.
Next William, Rainouart, and then the Duke   46
   Godfrey, and Robert Guiscard, did their part,
   When swift along the cross my sight they took.
The soul I had spoken with I now saw dart
   Among the other lights, with whom it vied,   50
   Showing how great in Heaven's choir was its art.
I turned me thereupon to my right side
   To see in Beatrice what I was to do,
   Whether by speech or gesture signified.
And I beheld her eyes so clear and true,
   So joyous, that the semblance which she wore
   Surpassed all former wont, and the last too.
And as a man, by feeling hour by hour
   In the doing of good works increased delight,
   Perceives his virtue growing more and more,   60
So I perceived that this my circling flight   61
   With the heaven had widened its circumference,
   Seeing this wonder yet more wondrous-bright.
Such a change as pale cheeks experience
   When a lady, suddenly from shame relieved,
   Sheddeth the brief blush from her countenance
Was in my eyes, when turning I perceived

---

40. Judas "Maccabaeus" *delivered his people from the tyranny of the Syrians.*
46-47. *"William," Count of Orange, is the hero of a group of Old French epics. "Rainouart": a knight of Saracen birth, but baptized. "Godfrey" of Bouillon: the leader of the first crusade. "Robert Guiscard": a Norman conqueror.*
61-63. *Thus from an increase of Beatrice's loveliness I inferred that I had risen to a greater and swifter sphere.*

The whiteness round me of the temperate star,   68
The sixth, whereinto I had been received.
And in that torch of Jove, I was aware   70
Of sparkles from the love within it warm,
Spelling our speech to me in letters there.
As birds that risen above a stream in swarm,
As though rejoicing to have fed them well,
Take now a round and now a different form,
Those holy beings the lights made visible
Sang flying, and in the shaping of their throng
Became now *D*, and now *I*, and now *L*.
They moved first to the notes of their own song;
Then, as each letter, one by one, was made   80
Complete, they paused and held awhile their tongue.
O Goddess Pegasea who hast arrayed   82
Genius in glory, and given it long renown,
As it for city and realm does with thine aid,
Lend me thy light, that so I may set down
In right relief their shapes as limned in Heaven:
Through these few verses let thy power be known!
Then they disposed themselves in five times seven
Vowels and consonants; and my mind held fast
Each member as in the alphabet 'twas given.   90
DILIGITE JUSTICIAM was traced   91
The first of all, in verb and noun displayed;
QUI JUDICATIS TERRAM was the last.
Then in the *M* of the fifth word arrayed
They halted, so that Jove was made to seem
Silver with patterning of gold inlaid.
And I saw other lights descending gleam

---

68. The change is from the red light of Mars to the whiteness of
Jupiter.
82. "O Goddess Pegasea": O Muse.
91-94. They spell the first verse of the Book of Wisdom: Love
righteousness, ye that be judges of the earth. The "M" is the sym-
bol of Monarchy.

On the *M*'s top and come there to a stand,
Hymning, I think, the Good that draweth them.
As at the beating of a smouldering brand   100
Innumerable sparks rise, from whose flight
Fools in their folly an augury demand,
Seemed thence to rise a thousand sparks of light
And mount, some much, some little, according as
The Sun which kindled them ordained their height.
And when each quieted in its place, my gaze
Beheld that figured fire present the crest,
And neck beneath it that an eagle has.   *108*
He who paints there hath none to guide the wrist *109*
But guides himself; from him, we call to mind,   110
The instinct is informed that builds the nest.
The other blessèd, seeming first designed
To shape a lily in flower upon the *M*,
Moved slightly and with the pattern were combined.
O sweet star, with how many and rare a gem
Didst thou prove that the justice we obey
Proceedeth from the heaven thou dost begem!
Therefore the Mind that set thee upon thy way,
And prompts thy power, I pray to watch wherefrom
Issues the smoke that tarnishes thy ray,   120
That once again the enkindled wrath may come
On the hucksters in the temple that was reared
And walled with miracle and martyrdom.
O hosts of Heaven I contemplate, be heard
Your prayers to aid all those on earth, led on
By bad example, who have strayed and erred!
Once war was made with swords; now it is done
By the withholding in this place and that   *128*

---

108. "An eagle": *the Imperial Eagle.*
109. "He who paints there" *is God.*
128. "By the withholding . . .": *of the sacraments, by means of excommunications.*

Of bread the all-pitying Father bars from none.
Thou who recordest but to obliterate,   *130*
   Consider that Peter and Paul, who died to save
   The vineyard thou hast spoiled, are living yet.
Thou can'st well say: "So ardently I crave
   For him who willed to live apart from all   *134*
   And whom a dance brought to a martyr's grave,
That I know not the Fisherman, nor Paul."

---

130. "*Thou who . . .*": Pope John xxii, who issued and revoked
  many excommunications.
134. "*For him . . .*": St. John the Baptist (see the Argument).

Canto XIX

---

*The symbolic Eagle speaks with one voice, though
representing the many spirits composing it. It ad-
dresses Dante, and explains that no mind of mortal
is capable of understanding the Divine Justice, and
what on earth may seem justice is not so in Heaven.
Only true believers in Christ can attain to Paradise;
but many who profess Christ are less near to him
than some who never heard his name. Follows a
denunciation of certain unjust rulers.*

BEFORE me in beauty appeared with wings displayed
   The image which those souls, all woven in one,
   Exulting in their sweet fruition, made.
Each one was as a little ruby stone
   Whose core by the sun's brilliance should be lit
   So that reflected in my eyes it shone.

And that which now I must to speech commit
  No voice ever communicated, nor
  Ink wrote, nor fancy comprehended it.
For I beheld and heard the beak outpour   10
  Words, and his voice was uttering "I" and "My"
  When in conception it was "We" and "Our."
And it began: "Justice and piety
  Have raised me into the glory of that state
  Which no ambition dareth to outvie.
On earth I have left my memory so great
  That 'mid the evil people it is renowned,
  Though the example none perpetuate!"
As one may feel in many coals abound
  One heat, so from those many loves there went   20
  Out of that image only a single sound.
Then I: "O ye perpetual flowers content
  In the eternal gladness! ye who make
  Your odours all seem to me one sweet scent,
Breathe on me and break the fast wherewith I ache
  And which hath kept me long in hunger lean
  Because on earth it found no food to take.
I know that if, as in a mirror seen,
  In other realm the divine justice glow,   29
  Yours apprehends it with no veil between.   30
How eager I am to hearken, ye well know,
  And what the doubt is and solicitude
  Which caused this fast of mine from long ago."
Like falcon that emerges from the hood
  To turn his head, and clap his wings, and preen
  His plumes, and show the mettle in his blood,
So looked to me that Emblem which had been
  Woven of the praises of divine grace, filled
  With songs that Heaven knows and rejoices in.

---

29. "In other realm": the angelic order of the Thrones, in the sphere
of Saturn.

Then it began: "He who the compass wheeled   *40*
  Round the world's edges, and within that space
  Mapped out so much, both hidden and revealed,
Could not so deeply His potency impress
  On the whole universe, but that His word
  Must still remain in infinite excess.
Which proveth that the first proud being erred,   *46*
  In that, creation's highest, he would not bend
  To await the light, and so fell unmatured.   *48*
Each lesser nature, then, if thou perpend,
  Is a too scant receptacle for that Good   *50*
  Which is its own measure, and hath no end.
Wherefore our vision, which can be the abode
  Of but one ray proceeding from the Mind
  With which all things are filled as with a flood,
Cannot have such power in its natural kind
  But that it knows its origin to lie   *56*
  Far beyond what appears to it defined.
Wherefore the sight that your world liveth by
  Penetrates not the eternal justice more
  Than into the ocean penetrates the eye;   *60*
For though it sees the bottom from the shore,
  On the open sea it cannot: none the less
  It is there; but the depth conceals the floor.
There is no light save from that perfect peace
  Which never is clouded: it is else darkness,
  Shadow of the flesh, or poison of its disease.
This glimpse sufficeth of the secret place
  Which hath from thee the living Justice hid
  Whereof thy questioning ceased not to harass;
For thou didst say: 'On Indus bank is bred   *70*

---

40. "He who . . .": God.
46. "The first proud being": *Lucifer.*
48. "The light": of grace.
56. "Its origin": *the divine Mind.*

A man, and there is no one there to tell
   Of Christ; no one to write, no one to read:
Good purposes his every act impel,
   So far as human faculty perceives,
   Without sin in his life, and words as well.
Without faith, unbaptized, the world he leaves.
   Where is this justice that condemns the man?
   Where is his trespass, if he not believes?'
Now who art thou with a judge's eyes to scan,
   On thy bench sitting a thousand miles away,   80
   This case with the short sight of a mere span?
For him who would engage me in subtle play,
   Were not the Scripture beyond all appeal,   *83*
   This were fine cause for doubt to say its say.
O minds gross as of brutes! The Primal Will,
   In itself good, to its own self, which is
   The Sovereign Good, forever cleaveth still,
All then is just which is attuned to this;
   To no created good does it adhere,
   But from its radiance is that good's increase."   90
As just above her nest circles in air
   The stork, after her youngling brood is fed,
   And as the one she has fed looks up to her,
So did (while I too lifted up my head)
   The blessed image move its wings amain,
   Urged by so many wills together wed.
Wheeling, it sang, and said: "Like this my strain
   To thee who understandest not a word,
   The eternal judgment is to mortal men."
When those bright fires of the Holy Spirit stirred   100
   No more, that ensign of the empery
   Which made the Romans by the world revered
Spoke once again: "None ever rose to see

---

83. *If you mortals had not the Bible to guide you, there would be no
end to your sophistries.*

This realm who had not the belief in Christ
After or before the nailing on the tree.
But look! how many are crying: 'Christ! Christ!'
Who at the day of judgment shall be far
Less near to him than such as knew not Christ.
The Ethiop such Christians will not spare
When the assembled companies divide,   110
The one forever rich, the one stript bare.
How shall the Persians challenge your kings' pride
When they shall see that volume, wherein stand
Recorded their dispraises, opened wide!
There shall be seen 'mid the acts of Albert's hand 115
That one which soon shall move the accusing pen,
Whereby Prague's kingdom shall be desert land.
There shall be seen the woe which he on Seine, 118
By making the false coinage, is to bring,
Who by the tusk of wild boar shall be slain. 120
There shall be seen the ambition maddening
With thirst so quenchless Englishman and Scot, 122
Whose frontiers content not either king;
Seen too the soft lascivious lives that rot
Both him of Spain and of Bohemia him   125
Who never has known virtue and wills it not;
Seen too the cripple of Jerusalem,   127
His goodness noted with a One, whereas
The adverse page is noted with an M;
Seen too the avarice and the craven ways 130
Of him who rules the Isle of Fire, the isle 131

115-116. "Albert": of Austria. "That one": the devastation of Bohemia in 1304. "The accusing pen": of the recording angel.

118-120. Philip the Fair, who had debased the coinage of the realm, died from a fall occasioned by a wild boar.

122. The wars of Edward I and Edward II against the Scots.

125. Ferdinand IV of Castile and Wenceslaus IV.

127-129. Charles II of Naples, titular king of Jerusalem. "With an M": one thousand.

131. Frederick of Aragon, king of Sicily.

Whereon the old Anchises closed his days;
And to underscore how paltry he is and vile,
  His record in contracted letters writ
  Shall on a small space all the matter pile.
And all shall know what foul deeds they commit,
  His uncle and brother, such deeds as deflower   *137*
  A race so famous and two crowns with it.
And he of Portugal, he of Norway's power   *139*
  Shall be known there, and he of Rascia, who   *140*
  Saw coin of Venice in an evil hour.
O happy Hungary, if her strength but grew
  Her maimers to defy! Happy Navarre,
  If round her she her mountain rampart drew!   *144*
And none should doubt what presages prepare
  For Nicosia and Famagusta woes,   *146*
  Who groan even now at him they have to bear,
This beast, who step by step with the others goes."

---

137. James, king of Majorca and Minorca, and James II of Aragon.
139-140. Dionysius of Portugal and Haakon of Norway. The king of
   "Rascia"—a state made up of parts of Serbia, Bosnia, and Croatia
   —was a certain Stephen Ouros, who counterfeited the Venetian
   ducat.
144. If she could make the Pyrenees a bulwark against France.
146. "Nicosia and Famagusta": two towns in Cyprus, which are al-
   ready bewailing their dissolute king, Henry II of Lusignan.

Canto XX

---

*The Eagle names six spirits pre-eminent for their
justice. They form the Eagle's eye and eyebrow.
David is in the pupil of the eye, and in the eye-
brow are Trajan, Hezekiah, Constantine, William II*

of Sicily, and Ripheus the Trojan. Dante is puzzled,
because Trajan and Ripheus, whom he conceived
of as pagans, are found in Paradise: and the Eagle
explains to him how it is that they are there; end-
ing with an admonition against hasty judgment.

WHEN he who illumines all the world descends   1
  So far, departing from our hemisphere,
  That day on all sides vanishes and ends,
The heaven, which he alone before lit clear,
  With myriad lights all kindled at one flame
  Immediately begins to reappear.
Into my mind this act of heaven came
  When the Ensign that the world's great chiefs
      obeyed   8
  Silent within the blessed beak became;
Because from all those living lights, arrayed   10
  In growing brilliance, songs began to float
  Which from my memory lapse and falling fade.
O Love, whose sweet smile hath thy raiment wrought,
  How ardent wast thou in those fluted tones
  Breathed only by the breath of holy thought!
Soon as the precious and resplendent stones
  Which I beheld the sixth lamp to begem
  Had hushed the angelic chiming antiphons,
I seemed to hear the murmur of a stream
  When clear from ledge to ledge the waters drop   20
  Showing how its springs within the mountain teem.
And as from sound the music taketh shape
  At the lute's neck, or in the pipes the air
  That, penetrating, enters at the stop,

---

1. "He who . . .": the sun.
8. "The Ensign": the Eagle.

So with no pause to baulk the waiting ear
   Rose the Eagle's murmur with resounding tone
   Up through its neck, as if it hollow were.
There it became voice as a way it won
   Out from the beak in words articulate
   Such as the heart craved that I wrote them on.   30
"That part in me which looks unflinching at
   The sun in mortal eagles," thus it spoke:
   "This must thou now fixedly contemplate.
For of the fires from which my form I make
   Those wherewith the eye sparkles in my head
   In all their ranks the loftiest station take.
He from whose light the pupil's fire is fed
   Was the singer of the Holy Spirit, who bare   38
   The Ark, from city unto city led.   39
He knoweth now his song's desert, so far   40
   As in his own conception 'twas begun,
   By its being matched with recompense so rare.
Of five, who make the eyebrow's arch, the one
   Who of all closest to the beak is set   44
   Brought comfort to the widow for her son.
He knoweth now how dearly costeth it
   Not to be Christ's liege, by experience
   Of this sweet life and of its opposite.
He who comes next in the circumference   49
   Of which I speak, on the ascending curve,   50
   Postponed death by his earnest penitence.
He knoweth now that nothing maketh swerve
   The eternal judgment when a prayer's just plea
   Below, makes for to-day to-morrow serve.

---

38. "The singer": *David*.
39. "The Ark": *of the Covenant*.
44-48. *Trajan (see Purg. x, 56) was allowed to resume his body long
    enough to embrace the true faith.*
49-51. *The effect of a petition in one's own behalf is illustrated by a
    Biblical character, King Hezekiah.*

The next became Greek, with the laws and me,　　55
　　In good intention which had evil fruit,
　　Ceding the Pastor such a realm in fee.
He knoweth now that Heaven doth not impute
　　To him what ills from his good deeds derive,
　　Even though the world be stricken to the root.　　60
On the arc's down-slope, that one of the five
　　Thou seëst was William, whom that land bewails　62
　　Which weeps that Charles and Frederick are alive.
He knoweth now with what love Heaven hails
　　The just king, and in measure as he glows
　　Still proveth how that love on him prevails.
Down in the erring world who would suppose
　　Ripheus the Trojan should the fifth be found　　68
　　Within the orb the sacred lights compose?
He knoweth now enough, and far beyond　　70
　　What the world sees, of the divine grace there,
　　Although its depth his vision cannot sound."
Like the small lark who wantons free in air,
　　First singing and then silent, as possessed
　　By the last sweetness that contenteth her,
So seemed to me the image, deep-impressed
　　With the Eternal Pleasure, by whose will
　　Each thing in its own nature is expressed.
Though the doubt in me was discernible,
　　As coloured things through glass are, yet its thirst　80
　　Endured not to wait silent and be still,
But from my mouth "What things are these?" it forced
　　By the mere pressure of its vehemence:
　　A festive sparkling then I saw outburst.
And with its eye yet more enkindled thence

55-57. Constantine, ceding Rome to the Pope and transferring the
　　capital to Byzantium, made himself, the Eagle, and the laws Greek.
62-63. William II of Sicily, Charles II of Naples and Frederick of
　　Aragon (see Purg. XIX, 127-131).
68. "Ripheus": an inconspicuous character in the Aeneid.

The blessed Ensign answered without pause
  Lest he might keep me wondering in suspense:
"I see that thou believ'st these things because
  I tell them; but the 'how' thou seëst not,
  And, though believed, they keep their secret close. 90
Thou art as he who apprehends by rote
  The thing he names, but cannot thereby come
  To the essence, save another solve the knot.
Regnum coelorum suffereth violence from   *94*
  Warm love and hope, living in stedfastness,
  Which even the divine will overcome,
Not in the way that man doth man oppress,
  But conquers it because it wills that same,
  And, conquered, conquers with its own kindness.
On the eyebrow's arch the first and the fifth flame *100*
  Cause thee to marvel, seeing above thy head
  The region of the angels bright with them.
Not Gentiles, as thou thinkest, did they shed
  The flesh, but Christians, having faith for prop
  In feet which were to bleed or which had bled. *105*
For the one from Hell, whence none returneth up *106*
  Ever to right will, back to his bones repaired;
  And this was the reward of living hope;
Of living hope, whose potency inspired
  Prayers made to God to raise him from the dead, *110*
  That his will thus might waken and be stirred.
The glorious soul I speak of, having stayed
  Once more a brief while in the body on earth,
  Believed in Him who had the power to aid,
And, in believing, such a flame sent forth

---

94. "Regnum coelorum": *the kingdom of heaven.*
100. "The first and the fifth": *Trajan and Ripheus.*
105. *They had faith in the feet of Christ, one before and one after the crucifixion.*
106. "The one from Hell": *the soul of Trajan.*
110. "Prayers made to God": *by St. Gregory.*

Of very love, that at death's second sting
It became worthy to enter into this mirth.
The other, by the grace which, issuing
From so profound wells that no creature yet
Pierced with his eye down to the primal spring,   120
On righteousness below his whole heart set,
So that God's grace, unveiling more and more,
Showed him the sure redemption of man's debt.
Believing in it, he no longer bore
The pagan superstition's filthy blight
And chided the corrupted folk therefore.
And those three ladies, who rejoiced thy sight   *127*
At the right wheel, made baptism for him
A thousand years ere the baptismal rite.
Predestination! how remote and dim   130
Thy root lies hidden from the intellect
Which only glimpses the First Cause Supreme!
And you, ye mortals, keep your judgment checked,
Since we, who see God, have not therefore skill
To know yet all the number of the elect.
To us such wanting is delectable
Because our good in this good is refined,
That, what God willeth, that we also will."
With such sweet medicine was I medicined
By the celestial image, to make clear   140
The short sight of my unillumined mind.
As the strings touched by the good lute-player
Attend upon the singer's voice, whereby
The song with added pleasure takes the ear,
So, while it spoke, comes back to memory
That the two blessed spirits to the words
Made their flames tremble in one harmony
Even as the winking of the eyes concords.

---

127. "Those three ladies": *the three Christian Virtues.*

Canto XXI

*Dante and Beatrice ascend into the seventh heaven.
This is the heaven of Saturn, where are those who
passed their lives in holy contemplation. Dante dis-
cerns a ladder, the top of which is out of sight, on
which are spirits descending and ascending. One of
these is the soul of Peter Damian, who tells Dante
about his life of retirement and austerity before, in
his last years, against his wish, he was made a
Cardinal. He contrasts the luxurious habits of the
clergy with the simple lives of the Apostles.*

My lady's face once more had occupied
  My eyes, and with them all my mind was turned
  Rapt from the thought of anything beside.
She did not smile. "Were I to smile," she warned,
  "Thou would'st be as Semele, when her eyes' desire 5
  She had, and straightway was to ashes burned;
Because my beauty, which from stair to stair
  Of the eternal palace flames afresh,
  As thou hast seen, the more it mounteth higher,
Were it not tempered, would upon thee flash 10
  So that thy mortal senses in that light
  Would be as boughs beneath the thunder's crash.
We have risen to the seventh splendour's height
  Which underneath the burning Lion's breast 14

5-6. "Semele," having insisted on beholding her lover, Jupiter, in all
  his heavenly majesty, was burned to ashes by his splendor.
14. "The burning Lion": the constellation of Leo.

Rays its beams downward, mingled with his might.
Behind thine eyes let thy mind also rest,
   And make them to be mirrors of the thing
   Which in this mirror thou encounterest."   *18*
He who should know what was the pasturing
   My sight had in her look beatified,   *20*
   When I turned now to a new soliciting,
Would, weighing one against the other side,
   Recognize what delight 'twas to adhere
   To the command of my celestial Guide.
Within the crystal's ever-circling sphere—
   Named after its bright regent, him whose reign   *26*
   Made wickedness to die and disappear,—
Coloured like gold which flashes back again
   The sun, I saw a ladder stand, that seemed
   So high that the eye followed it in vain.   *30*
Moreover on the rungs descending gleamed
   So many splendours that each several star
   From heaven, methought, collected thither,
      streamed.
As rooks, after their natural habit, fare
   Forth all together at beginning day
   To warm their feathers chilled by the night air;
Then some, without returning, wing away,
   Some to the boughs they have their nests among
   Return, and others circling make a stay;
Such a behaviour had that sparkling throng,   *40*
   It seemed to me, coming in bands abreast,
   Soon as they lighted on a certain rung.
And that one which most near to us came to rest
   Became so bright that I said in my thought:
   "I see the love to me thou signallest;
But she who 'how' and 'when' to me hath taught

---

18. "This mirror": *Saturn.*
26. "Its bright regent" *is Saturn, who ruled in the Golden Age.*

For speaking and for silence, stayeth still;
Therefore, though fain, I do well to ask naught."
Then she, my silence being visible
To her, through sight of Him who seëth all, 50
Said to me: "Now thy warm desire fulfil."
And I began: "My merit is too small
To be accounted worthy of thy reply;
But for her sake who suffereth this, O soul,
O blessed life, who hidden in thy joy
Abidest, make thou known to me the cause
That brings thee to a place to me so nigh;
And say why in this circling wheel is pause
From the sweet symphony of Paradise 59
Which through the others so devoutly rose." 60
"Thou hast," he answered, "mortal ears and eyes.
For the same reason no voice singeth here
That thou hast seen no smile in Beatrice.
Down the rungs thus far of the sacred stair
I have descended but to make thee glad
With speech and with the glowing light I wear.
Nor did more love a greater fervour add;
For equal love, or greater, burns above,
As in these flaming lustres is displayed;
But the high charity which prompts our love 70
To serve the sovereign purpose, doth assign
To each its office, as thine eyes can prove."
"O sacred lamp," I said, "I well divine
How in this court free love sufficeth you
For following Heaven's fore-ordained design.
But this is where I cannot find the clue;
Why to this office the eternal power
Predestined thee of all this retinue."
I had not come to the last word before
The light made of its centre an axle-tree 80

---

59. "Symphony": *the hymns sung in the preceding spheres.*

And whirled like a swift mill-stone round that core.
The love which was within it answered: "See,
   A divine light with pressure like a sting
   Penetrates through this which embowels me,
The virtue of which, my vision strengthening,
   Lifts me above myself to contemplate
   The Supreme Essence, its far source and spring.
Thence comes the rapture that I radiate;
   For to my vision, in measure as 'tis clear,
   The clearness of my flame I match and mate.   90
But that soul which is most illumined here
   In heaven, that seraph of most fixed regard
   On God, could not content thee in thy desire,
Since what thou askest lies so deep in ward
   Of the eternal ordinance's abyss
   That from created vision it is barred.
When thou returnest to the world, take this
   Monition, that it never more presume
   To set foot to invade such mysteries:
The mind, which here shines, there is thick with
      fume;   100
   Consider therefore how below it could
   What it could not, though Heaven should it illume."
The stricture of his words had so subdued
   My questioning, that from all else I refrained
   Save the asking who he was, in humble mood.
"Between the two shores of Italian land
   Rise crags, not far from thy birth-place, so high   *107*
   That far above the thunder's noise they stand,
Shaped to a hump called Catria; and thereby
   Is found a hallowed hermitage below   110
   Where there was worship only of Deity."
His third discourse to me he opened so,

107-109. "Crags": the northern part of the Apennines. "Catria": a
spur between Urbino and Gubbio.

And then, continuing: "Here, on God intent,
  So stedfast in his service did I grow
That with but the olive's juice for nutriment
  I passed serene through heat and frost, being filled
  With contemplative thought, therein content.
That cloister used abundantly to yield
  Souls to these heavens: now 'tis so bare and mean,
  That soon its emptiness must be revealed.   120
In that place was I Peter Damian,
  And in Our Lady's house on the Adrian shores   *122*
  Peter the Sinner had I also been.
Little was left me of my mortal course
  When I was called and dragged unto the hat   *125*
  Which ever is passed down from bad to worse.
Barefoot and lean came Cephas, came the great   *127*
  Vessel of the Holy Spirit, glad to sup
  At whatsoever inn they halted at.
Pastors to-day need one to hold them up   130
  On this side and on that, and one to lead
  (So heavy are they), and one behind to prop.
They have their palfreys with long mantles hid,
  So that two beasts go under the one hide:
  O Patience, what endurance dost thou need!"
As he was speaking, more flames I espied
  From rung to rung, each whirling round, descend,
  Their beauty in their revolving magnified.
About this one they came, and made an end
  Of motion, uttering a cry profound   140
  Like nothing here; nor could I comprehend,
Since all my sense was in the thunder drowned.

---

122. *The monastery of Santa Maria, near Ravenna.*
125. *"The hat": the cardinal's hat.*
127-128. *"Cephas": St. Peter. "The great Vessel": St. Paul.*

Canto XXII

---

*The thunderous cry which had so dismayed the
poet is, Beatrice tells him, the expression of Heav-
en's wrath at the corruption just described, and a
prayer for its punishment.*

*Dante is addressed by St. Benedict, who tells
of his founding of the monastery on Monte Cas-
sino, after he had driven out the pagan worship;
and then bewails and condemns the corruption of
the monks of the Order he had founded. When the
Saint has disappeared among his companions, the
poet and his conductress are snatched up into
the eighth heaven, that of the Fixed Stars: thence
Dante, at Beatrice's command, looks back over all
the way he had come from the earth, and the sys-
tem of the seven spheres. He smiles to see how in-
significant appears the earth from such a height.*

I TURNED, numbed with amazement, to my Guide
　For comfort, as a little child who runs,
　　As always, there where it can most confide;
And as a mother succoureth her son's
　Pale cheeks and panting breath and forehead hot
　　With her own voice, that reassures at once,
She said: "Thou art in Heaven, know'st thou it not?
　And know'st thou not, Heaven is all holiness,
　　And what is done here from good zeal is wrought?
How the song would have changed thee, thou can'st
　　　guess,   10
　And (had I not refrained) by smiling I,

Seeing that this shout puts thee in such distress.
If thou had'st caught the prayers within the cry,
    Already would the chastisement appear
    Disclosed, which thou shalt witness ere thou die.
The sword cuts not in haste which smites from here
    On high, nor tarrieth, save as those conceive
    Who wait for it in longing or in fear.
But turn to the others; now may'st thou perceive
    Many illustrious spirits, if thou raise   20
    Thine eyes and lead them where I give thee leave."
As was her pleasure, I lifted up my gaze,
    And saw a hundred little spheres collect
    And grow more beautiful with mutual rays.
I stood as one who in himself hath checked
    The pricking of desire, nor makes him bold
    To speak, from fearing too much to expect,
And the most large and luminous to behold
    Of all those pearls advanced to solace me
    With what I craved might of itself be told.   30
I heard then from within it: "Didst thou see,
    As I, what loving-kindness burns in us,
    Thy thoughts had been expressed in utterance free.
But lest by waiting thou a moment lose
    On the high journey, my word but replies
    To the thought that found thy tongue so scrupulous.
That mountain on whose slope Cassino lies   37
    Was once frequented on its top by folk
    Obdurate in their dark idolatries.
And I am he who first bore up that rock   40
    The name of Him who brought down among men
    The truth which lifteth us, on high to look.
Grace so abundant overshone me then
    That I reclaimed the villages about

37-39. *St. Benedict in 528 erected two chapels in a temple of Apollo,
and converted the heathen.*

From the impious worship's world-seducing reign.
These others, all contemplatives at root,
 Were quickened by that warm enkindling fire
 Which giveth birth to holy flower and fruit.
Here is Macarius, here Romualdus, here   *49*
 My brothers, who refrained their feet and stayed 50
 Within the cloister and kept their hearts entire."
And I: "The affection which thou hast displayed,
 Speaking with me, and the benign intent
 Which by your glowing you have each conveyed
Dilate me and make me newly confident
 As when the sun the rose encourages
 To open to the utmost of its bent.
Wherefore I pray thee, Father, assure me this,
 That of thy grace I may be favoured so
 That thou unveil thy likeness as it is."   60
Then he: "Brother, thy high desire to know
 Shall in the last sphere its fulfilment win
 Where the others are fulfilled, and mine also.
There perfected and ripe and whole within
 Is each desire; and there, and there alone,
 Is every part as it hath ever been.
For it is not in space; poles it hath none;
 And mounting to it reaches up our stair;
 For this cause is it from thy sight withdrawn.
Jacob the patriarch far up even to there   70
 Was given to see its upper part extend,
 And in his vision troops of angels bear;
But on it none now lifteth foot to ascend
 From low earth: and on earth remaineth still
 My Rule, a waste of parchments without end.
Walls that were once an abbey now conceal
 A den of thieves, and every monkish hood
 Is a sack, full to bursting with bad meal.

---

49. St. Macarius of Alexandria and St. Romualdus of Ravenna.

But taking of hard usury is at feud
    Less with God's pleasure than what maketh fall 80
    Into such greed the monks' demented brood;
For whatsoever the Church holds is all
    For the poor people who God's name invoke,
    Nor for one's kin, nor some yet viler soul.
So frail the flesh is among mortal folk
    That good beginning lasts not on to mould
    The acorn from the seedling of the oak.
Peter began with neither silver nor gold,
    And I with prayer and fast gathered my band,
    And Francis his with humbleness enrolled. 90
And if in its beginning each be scanned,
    And if thou scrutinize what things deprave,
    Thou wilt behold black where the white was planned.
Yet Jordan turned-back and the fleeing wave
    God willed, were marvel of a mightier kind
    Than here were the recovery that should save."
So saying, into his company behind
    He merged; the company close round him came;
    Then all were swept up like a whirl of wind.
And the sweet Lady urged me after them, 100
    With a sign only, up that stair to spring;
    Her power my earthiness so overcame.
Now here, where up and down our motioning
    Is nature's work, was ever motion guessed
    To match the sudden swiftness of my wing.
So may I, Reader, to that triumph blest
    Return, for sake of which my weight of sin
    I wail, and often beat upon my breast,
Thou had'st not quicker plucked out and thrust in
    The fire thy finger, than I saw the sign 110
    Which follows next the Bull, and stood therein.

110-111. "The sign": Gemini (the Twins). Dante has risen to the
heaven of the fixed stars.

O glorious stars! Light pregnant with divine
   Virtue, which I in recognition thank   *113*
   For whatsoever genius is mine,

With you he mounted and with you he sank,   *115*
   The father to whom mortal life is owed,
   When first the air of Tuscany I drank.

And then, when favour was on me bestowed
   To enter the great wheel which turns your skies,
   Your region was appointed my abode.   120

To you devoutly now my spirit sighs   *121*
   To acquire virtue for the trial hard
   Which draws me on to essay that enterprise.

"Thou draw'st so near to the ultimate reward,"
   Said Beatrice, "that nothing should remit
   Thine eyes' intense and undisturbed regard;

And therefore, ere thou further enter it,
   Look down and see how great the world's extent
   Which I already have set beneath thy feet,

So that thy heart may all it can present   130
   Of joy unto the joyous throng that nears
   In triumph through the rounded firmament."

My sight through each and all of the seven spheres
   Turned back; and seeing this globe there manifest,
   I smiled to see how sorry it appears;

And I approve that judgment as the best
   Which least accounts it, and that man esteem
   Most worthy, who elsewhere brings his thoughts to
      rest.

I saw the daughter of Latona gleam   *139*
   Without that shade which I had pondered on   140
   And which had made her rare and dense to seem.

---

113. "Which I in recognition thank": *Gemini, the house of Mercury, bestows a taste for learning.*
115. *The sun was rising with Gemini when Dante was born.*
121. *Dante invokes the aid of his native constellation.*
139. *Diana, the moon.*

The strong love of thy son, Hyperion,   *142*
   I there sustained, and saw how in a ring
   Maia and Dione close beside him shone.
Next there appeared to me Jove's tempering
   Between his father and son; and I could note
   Their places and their station's varying.
And all the seven were shown me, and I thought:
   How swift they are in moving and how great,
   And each one from the other how remote!   *150*
The small round floor which makes us passionate   *151*
   I, carried with the eternal Twins, discerned,
   From hill to harbour, plain to contemplate:
Then to the beauteous eyes my eyes returned.

---

*142-146. "Hyperion" is often called the father of the sun.—"Maia":
the mother of Mercury.—"Dione": the mother of Venus.—"His
father and son": Saturn and Mars.*
151. "The small round floor": the inhabited part of the earth.

Canto XXIII

The Triumph of Christ is made visible. Christ ascends out of sight, followed by the Virgin, round whom circles the archangel Gabriel.

Still as the bird, 'mid the belovèd leaves,
   Reposing on the nest of her sweet brood
   Through night, which all things from our vision
      thieves,
Who, to have longed-for sight of them renewed

And once again to find them, where she may
  (Hard toil she taketh pleasure in), their food,
Fore-runs the time, high on the open spray,
  And warm with love awaits the earliest light,
  Only intent that dawn may bring the day;
So was my Lady, standing all upright   10
  And stretched in yearning toward the region where
  The sun shows least of hasting in his flight.
And eyeing the suspense in her rapt air,
  I was like one who wants, and who is fain
  Of what he has not, and with hope must bear.
But short the space was between *when* and *then,*
  I mean between the expectancy I had
  And seeing in heaven splendour on splendour gain.
"Behold the assembled hosts," Beatrice said;
  "Behold Christ triumphing, and all the fruit   20
  These spheres have in their circling harvested."
Joy in her aspect was so absolute,
  And such a flame shone in her countenance,
  That words are idle, and I must needs be mute.
As in a full moon's tranquil brilliance
  Trivia smiles among the nymphs who paint   26
  Eternally Heaven's uttermost expanse,
Over a myriad lamps preëminent
  I saw one Sun which kindled each and all,   29
  As light from our sun to the stars is lent;   30
And through the living light shone forth the whole
  Irradiated Substance, so intense   32
  Upon my eyes, I needs must let them fall.
O Beatrice, dear Guide! sweet Influence!
  She said to me: "What masters now thy sight
  Is power against which nothing hath defence.

---

26. "Trivia" *is one of the names of Diana: the moon.*
29. "One Sun": *Christ.*
32. "Substance": *the humanity of Christ.*

Within there is the wisdom and the might
   Which between earth and heaven the pathways
      found
   Longed-for of old with longing infinite."
As fire is from the fettering cloud unbound,   40
   Expanding till it needs must overflow,
   And, against nature, rushes to the ground,
So did my mind amid these feasts outgrow
   Itself, and was dilated, and became
   What recollection hath no skill to show.
"Open thine eyes and look on what I am!
   Thou hast seen things which of thy weakness make
   Strength to sustain my smile, nor fear the flame."
I was like one who comes to himself awake
   From a forgotten vision, and is stirred   50
   Vainly to bring it to his memory back,
When—worthy of such great thanksgiving—I heard
   This proffered boon, which nothing can erase
   From that book where the past is registered.
Were all those tongues now sounding in her praise
   Which Polyhymnia and her sisters made   56
   Rich with the sweetest milk that ever was,
Not by a thousandth of the truth their aid
   Could hymn the holy smiling of the eyes
   And what pure light from the holy face it rayed; 60
Therefore in picturing forth Paradise
   Needs must the sacred poem take a leap,
   As when some barrier on the pathway lies.
But he who thinks how heavy a theme to grip
   Is here for mortal, shouldering such a weight,
   Will think no blame if sometimes the foot slip.
No passage for a little barque is that
   Which my adventurous keel is set to plough,

---

56. "Polyhymnia and her sisters": *the Muses.*

Nor for a pilot losing heart thereat.

"Why does my face enamour so, that thou   70
  On the fair garden hast no glance bestowed
  Which flowers beneath Christ's rays? Behold it now!

Here is the Rose, wherein the Word of God   73
  Made itself flesh; and there the lilies are
  Whose fragrance lured to follow the good road."

So Beatrice; and I, all prompt to hear
  Her counsels and obey them, once again
  Betook me to the fluttering eyelids' war.

As, with my eyes in shadow, I have seen
  A meadow of flowers flashed over by the sun,   80
  When cloud breaks and a pure ray glides between,

Many a clustered splendour, blazed upon
  By ardent beams, was to my eyes revealed,
  Although I saw not whence the blazing shone.

O benign Power, who hast these spirits sealed,
  Thou didst withdraw thee on high, that to my sight,
  So feebly empowered, this room thou mightest yield.

The name of the fair flower, which day and night   88
  My lips continually invoke, compelled
  My mind to gaze upon the greatest light;   90

And when distinct in both mine eyes were held
  The glory and grandeur of the living star
  Which excels there as down here it excelled,

A fire descended out of heaven from far   94
  Shaped in a circle like a coronal,
  Which turned and turned as it engirdled her.

Whatever music sounds most sweet of all
  On earth, and draws the soul most in desire,
  Would seem cloud crackling in the thunder's brawl

Compared with the resounding of that lyre   100

73-74. "The Rose": Mary. "The lilies": the Apostles.
88. "The name": the mention of Mary.
94. The "fire" is perhaps the Archangel Gabriel.

Whereby the beautiful Sapphire was crowned   *101*
   Which makes the clearest heaven all one sapphire.
"I am angelic love and circle round
   The sublime joy, which breathes out from the womb
   Wherein the world's desire its hostel found.
And I shall circle, Lady of Heaven, till home
   Thou thy son follow into the sphere supreme
   And make it more divine since thou art come."
Thus the encircling melody of flame
   Sealed itself up, and the other lights in praise   *110*
   Made all the air re-echo Mary's name.
The royal mantle of all the wheeling maze   *112*
   Of the universe, whose ardour burns most hot,
   Most quickened in God's breath and in His ways,
Had the inner border of it so far remote
   Above, that in my vision's narrower scope,
   Where I was stationed, I discerned it not.
Therefore my eyes' endeavour might not hope
   To accompany the crownèd flame beyond,
   As after her own seed she mounted up.   *120*
And as the child who toward his mother fond
   Stretches his arms when he has milked her breast—
   The spirit flaming outward to respond—
Each of those white fires strained into a crest
   Its flame, so that the affection infinite
   They had for Mary was made manifest.
There for a while they lingered in my sight
   Singing *Regina Coeli*, in tone so steeped   *128*
   In sweetness, I still taste of the delight.
O how immense is the abundance heaped   *130*
   Into those bursting coffers, which on earth

---

101. "The Sapphire" is Mary.
112. "The royal mantle": the Empyrean.
120. "Her own seed": Christ.
128. "Regina Coeli": "Queen of Heaven," an antiphon.

Were sowers of the good grain to be reaped!
Here joy they in their treasure, earned in dearth
    Of exile, when they wept in Babylon,   *134*
    Where gold was left aside as nothing worth.
Here triumphs, under the exalted Son
    Of God and Mary, in his victory,
    With the ancient council and the later one,   *138*
He who of so great glory holds the key.

Canto XXIV

Among the innumerable company of the Blessed
(who sing and dance in circles and are here called
"Carols") one spirit detaches itself: it is St. Peter;
and at the request of Beatrice he examines Dante
on the subject of Faith. Peter is well content with
the poet's answers.

O CHOSEN band, to the great supper called
    Of the blessed Lamb who giveth you to feast
    So that desire in you is still forestalled,
If by the grace of God this man foretaste
    Of that which falleth from your table, ere
    The days appointed him of life have ceased,
Think on his boundless longing, and then spare
    Some drops for his bedewing from those pools   8

---

134. The "exile" of "Babylon" is the earthly life.
138-139. With the souls of the Old and the New Covenant, the
    Prophets and the Apostles. "He who . . .": St. Peter.
8-9. Give him a few drops from the fount of Truth, upon which his
    thought is bent.

Ye drink of, whence comes that which is his care."
Thus Beatrice: forthwith those blissful souls,   10
   Flaming like to a comet in the sky,
   Shaped themselves into spheres upon fixt poles;
And as within a clock's machinery
   The wheels so turn that to the observer's sense
   The first seems to be still, the last to fly,
Those Carols, dancing in the difference
   Of their revolving motion, swift or slow,
   Told me the measure of their affluence.   18
And from the one which seemed the most to grow
   In beauty I saw so happy a fire shine out,   20
   It left not one there of more dazzling glow.
Three times round Beatrice it twined about,
   Accompanied with singing so divine
   That fantasy to me re-tells it not.
Therefore my pen must skip, and I resign:
   Imagination, and our speech much more,
   Is of too vivid hue for shades so fine.
"O sister mine, who dost this boon implore,
   Thou hast unbound me from this beauteous sphere
   By thy devotion and love's ardent power."   30
Soon as the blessèd flame stayed itself near,
   Directed toward my Lady, its breath began
   Discoursing, even as I repeat it here.
And she: "Eternal light of that great man
   To whom our Lord the keys at parting gave,
   Which He brought down, of joy's supreme domain,
Test thou this man on points both light and grave,
   As pleases thee, how he the Faith conceives,
   By which thou once didst walk upon the wave.   39
If rightly he loves, hopes rightly, and believes,   40

---

18. "Affluence": gladness.
39. Through faith Peter "walked on the water, to go to Jesus" (Matt. 14:46).

This is not hidden from thee, since thine eye,
　Where thou art, each thing true-portrayed perceives;
But since this realm reckons its lieges by
　The true faith, now to speak of it he ought,
　This chance being given its truth to glorify."
Just as the bachelor arms him in his thought,　　　*46*
　Mute, till the master shall the question pose,
　To adduce the proof, but to determine not,
I, while she spoke, armed me with reasonings close
　To be prepared for such a questioner　　　*50*
　And such profession as I now disclose.
"Speak, O good Christian, and thyself declare!
　Faith, what is it?" Whereat my brows inclined
　Up to the light which breathed thus on the air.
I turned to Beatrice, and she promptly signed
　To me that nothing should I now repress
　But pour forth all the fountain in my mind.
"Now may the Grace that grants me to confess,"
　I began, "to the Church's high captain,
　Enable me my thoughts well to express."　　　*60*
And I continued: "As the truthful pen
　Of thy dear brother wrote for our behoof,　　　*62*
　Who, with thee, led Rome the good path to gain,
Faith is the substance of things hoped, and proof
　Of things invisible to mortal sight;
　This seems to me the essential truth thereof."
Then I heard: "Thou conceiv'st of it aright,
　If thou grasp why among the substances　　　*68*
　And then among the proofs he counted it."
And I thereon: "The profound mysteries,　　　*70*

---

46. "The bachelor": *the candidate for a degree of doctor in theol-ogy.*
62. St. Peter's "dear brother" *is St. Paul.*
68-69. *Why did St. Paul call Faith first a "substance" and then a "proof"?*
70-78. *Faith, from the human point of view, is a belief; and, in*

Which here to me are by their bounty shown,
    Are upon earth so hidden from our eyes
That there their being is in belief alone,
    On which is founded the high hope we share;
    Therefore as substance is it named and known.
And needs from this belief must we infer,
    Deducing without further vision's aid;
    Therefore of proof it has the character."
Then I heard: "If whatever is purveyed
    By teaching were so understood below,   80
    There were no room left for the sophist's trade."
This was breathed forth from that love-kindled glow,
    Which added: "Needs no further to traverse
    This coin's alloy and weight, examined now;
But tell me if thou hast it in thy purse."
    Then I: "Yes, truly; so bright and so round,
    No hint of doubt is in the stamp it bears."
Thereupon issued from the light profound
    That beamed on me: "This gem of heavenly hue,
    On which all virtue is builded and enthroned,   90
Whence came it to thee?" And I: "The abundant dew *91*
    Of the Holy Spirit which is so outpoured
    Upon the ancient parchments and the new
Is argument compelling my accord
    With such precise proof that, compared with it,
    All demonstration else appeareth blurred."
Then heard I: "The ancient and the newer Writ,
    Whose testaments have such conviction brought,
    Why dost thou them as word of God admit?"
And I: "The proofs that truth to me have taught   100
    Are the works following, for which Nature ne'er   *101*

---

theological questions, takes the place of evidence in worldly syl-
logisms.
91-93. "The abundant dew": inspiration. "Parchments": Testaments.
101. "The works following": the miracles.

Heated the iron nor on anvil smote."
The answer came: "Say who, that these works were,
    Assureth thee? The same things, and naught else,
    That need proof do the proof to thee declare."
"If the world," said I, "without miracles
    Turned Christian, then a miracle is born
    That all the rest a hundred times excels;
For thou didst enter hungry, poor, forlorn,
    Into the field, to sow there the good plant   *110*
    Which, once a vine, is now a bush of thorn."
This ended, rose through all the spheres the chant
    Of the high holy Court: "Praised, God, be thou!"
    In music making there its own descant.
And that great Baron, who had drawn me now,   *115*
    Examining, from branch to branch, till we
    Were coming to the last leaves on the bough,
Resumed: "The Grace which in love's courtesy
    Wooeth thy mind, hath loosed indeed thy tongue
    To expound thy thought as it behoveth thee;   *120*
Nor find I fault those arguments among
    Thus far; but now thou needs must persevere
    To tell what thou believ'st and whence 'tis sprung."
"O holy father, spirit who seëst here
    What thou didst so believe as to outrun   *125*
    More youthful feet, seeking the Sepulchre,"
I began, "thou would'st have me to make known
    The essence of my faith, alert and whole,
    And askest also what 'tis built upon.
I answer: I believe in one God, sole,   *130*
    Eternal, that, unmoved, all heaven doth move
    With love and with desire to the one goal.
For such belief I hold physical proof
    And metaphysical; 'tis given me too

---

115. "That great Baron": St. Peter.
125. *Faith impelled St. Peter to enter the Sepulchre before John.*

By verity which raineth from above
Through Moses, through the Psalms and Prophets,
    through
  The Gospel, and through you who wrote, I wis,   *137*
  When the ardent Spirit fondly adopted you.
In three eternal persons, and in these
  One essence, I believe; so one, so trine,   140
  That with it may be joined both *are* and *is*.
With the unfathomable state divine
  I speak of, often has stamped on me its mark
  The evangelic doctrine's great design.
And this is the beginning; this, the spark
  Which, after, into livelier flame shall swell
  To shine in me as stars shine in the dark."
Then as a lord, at news which pleases well,
  Taketh his servant to his bosom prest
  Rejoicing, soon as he has told his tale,   150
So blessing me, and singing as it blest,
  Thrice circled round me, soon as I had ceased,
  The apostolic light at whose behest
I had spoken; so my words its joy increased.

---

137. "You": the Apostles.

Canto XXV

St. James examines Dante on the subject of Hope.
Beatrice answers for him, to spare his modesty, and
says he has this virtue in full measure and has on
that account been privileged to behold Paradise. As
to the nature of Hope, Dante himself answers. This

examination ended, Beatrice points out to Dante
the spirit of St. John, which dazzles him so that for
the moment he is as one blind.

IF EVER it happen that the sacred song   *1*
　Whereto both heaven and earth have set a hand,
　Whereby I am lean, these many years and long,
O'ercome the cruelty which keeps me banned
　From the fair sheepfold where I slept, a lamb,   *5*
　Foe to the wolves that raven through the land,
With different voice now, nor with fleece the same,
　Shall I return, poet, and at the fount   *8*
　Of my baptizing shall the chaplet claim,
Because into the faith that makes the account   *10*
　Of souls to God I won then; for which worth
　Peter wreathed such a light about my front.
Thereafter toward us moved a splendour forth   *13*
　Out of that sphere whence we had seen issue
　The first fruits of Christ's vicars left on earth.   *15*
Whereon my Lady, full of gladness new,
　Said to me: "Look; look! see the Baron move
　For whose sake is Galicia journeyed to."   *18*
As when by its companion comes a dove
　To settle close, and each one to its mate,   *20*
　Turning and cooing, poureth forth its love,
So the one prince, so glorious and great,
　I saw received by the other, while that food
　They lauded, spread above, their souls to sate.

---

1. "The sacred song": the Divine Comedy.
5. "The fair sheepfold": Florence.
8-9. "The fount": the Church of San Giovanni, in Florence. "The chaplet": the laurel crown.
13-15. "A splendour": St. James. "The first fruits": St. Peter.
18. The grave of St. James at Compostella in Galicia was a favorite place of pilgrimage.

But when the welcome was complete, they stood
  Each of them silent *coram me,* so bright   26
  And burning that my sight was all subdued.
 Smiling then, Beatrice spoke: "Illustrious light,
  To whom 'twas given the bounteous largess
  Of our celestial palace once to write,   30
Do thou make Hope to sound in this high place:
  Thou knowest that thou as often hast pictured it
  As Jesus showed the three that special grace."   33
"Lift up thy head, and confidently quit
  Thyself! For whatso mortal dares to soar
  Hither, our rays must ripen and complete."
The second flame this comfort breathed: wherefore   37
  I lifted up mine eyes unto the hills
  Which beat them down by too much weight before.
"Since, ere death, of His grace our Emperor wills   40
  That face to face thou should'st His Nobles see
  In the most secret hall His presence fills,
That having seen this Court in verity
  Thou in thyself and others mayest breed
  Stronger the hope on earth enamouring thee,
Say what this is, and how therewith the seed   46
  Flowers in thy mind; and say whence comes this
      thing."
  Thus further did the second light proceed;
And that compassionate one who set my wing,
  Guiding its feathers, on a flight so vast,   50
  Fore-ran my answer, herself thus answering:
"Church Militant hath not a child to boast
  Of greater hope; 'tis writ in the Sun's beam

---

26. "Coram me": *before me.*
30. "To write": *in the Epistle of James there are some references to divine liberality.*
33. "The three": *Peter, James and John.*
37-38. "The second flame": *St. James.* "The hills": *the two Apostles.*
46. "Say what this is": *Hope.*

Which radiateth over all our host.
Therefore from Egypt to Jerusalem   55
　'Twas granted him to come, to look on her,
　Before his soldier's service end for him.
The other two points asked by thee, which were
　Not for the sake of knowing, but to record
　How much this virtue to thy heart is dear,   60
I leave to him; for they will not be hard,
　Nor theme for vain-glory: let him reply
　Therefore, and God this grace to him accord."
Like pupil answering teacher eagerly,
　Prompt in those points wherein he is most expert,
　To give proof of his quality, "Hope," said I,
"Is certain expectation that the heart
　Has of the future glory; the effect
　Of divine grace and precedent desert.
Me did the light from many stars direct;   70
　He first distilled it into me with his breath,   71
　Singer supreme of the supreme Prefect.
For 'let them put their trust in thee' he saith
　In his psalm, 'all who know thy name'; and who
　Knoweth it not, if he possess my faith?
Then didst thou into me instil his dew   76
　In thine epistle, so that I overflow
　And upon others spill your rain anew."
While I was speaking, a quick-throbbing glow
　In that fire's living bosom was revealed,   80
　Like lightning in its sudden come-and-go.
Then spoke its breath: "The warm love still not quelled
　For that dear virtue, which companioned me
　Even to the palm and the issue of the field,   84

---

55. By "Egypt" is meant life on earth.
71. "He": David.
76. "Thou": St. James.
84. "The palm": of martyrdom. "The field": the battlefield of life.

Bids me breathe to thee, who find'st felicity
  In her; and me it pleases that thou tell
  What thing it is that Hope has promised thee."
And I: "The old Scripture and the new as well
  Set up the goal, pointing to Hope at hand,
  Of all the souls God wills with Him to dwell.   90
Isaiah says that each in his own land
  Shall in a double garment be arrayed;   92
  And this delectable life is his own land.
Also in far distincter mode conveyed
  (Where of the white apparelling he wrote),
  Thy brother hath this revelation made."   96
Just on the close of these words, I heard float
  A singing from above *Sperent in te;*   98
  Whereunto answered every Carol's note.
Then 'mid them brightened so intense a ray   100
  That, if the Crab such crystal could enclose,
  Winter would have a month of one sole day.
Blithe as a maiden rises up and goes
  To join the dance, not flaunting, but to do
  That honour to the new bride which she owes,
So did that brightened splendour join the two,
  Who dancing wheeled in measure, at such pace   107
  As to the ardour of their love was due.
It sang and danced itself into its place:
  My Lady held them in her gaze confined   110
  As a bride stays, silent and motionless.
"This is he, this, who on the breast reclined

92. "In a double garment": *the effulgence of the soul and the clarified body.*
96. "Thy brother": *St. John, in Rev. 3:5 and 7:9-17.*
98. "Will put their trust in Thee."
100. "A ray": *the light of St. John. If the constellation of Cancer (the Crab) contained a star as bright as this, night would be as light as day.*
107. *The three representatives of the Christian virtues dance before Beatrice.*

Even of our Pelican; 'tis he who bore   *113*
    The great charge from the cross to him con-
        signed."   *114*
My Lady thus; but moved her eyes no more,
    Intent in contemplation and delight,
    After her words than she had done before.
As he who, gazing, strives with all his might
    To see the sun eclipsed for a brief while,
    And who by seeing is bereft of sight,   120
So did I strive with the last flame, until
    I heard a voice: "Why dazzlest thou thine eyes
    To see that, which hath no place here to fill?   *123*
Earth in earth is my body, and there lies
    With the others, till our number shall comport
    With what the eternal purposes devise.
With both robes in the blessed cloister's court
    Are the two lights which alone rose from ground; *128*
    And this I bid thee to your world report."
Hearing this voice, the circle flaming round   130
    Was stilled, and with it that sweet mingling-up
    Of threefold breath in one harmonious sound,   *132*
As, to forestall fatigue or some ill hap,
    The oars, that till then smote the water sheer,
    All at the one blast of a whistle stop.
Ah, how my mind was shaken and in fear
    When now I turned to look on Beatrice!
    For now I could not see her, though so near
I was to her, and in the world of bliss.

---

113. The "Pelican" was a symbol of Christ.
114. John was entrusted with the care of Mary.
123. Dante believes, mistakenly, that John was taken up to Heaven
in the flesh.
128. "The two lights": *Christ and Mary. Theirs are the only human
bodies now in Heaven.*
132. "Threefold breath": *of Peter, James, and John.*

Canto XXVI

*Dante is examined by St. John on the subject of
Love. When he has given his answers, there is a
sound of sweet singing; and Dante's sight is re-
stored to him. A fourth spirit has now appeared and
joined the three Apostles. Beatrice tells Dante that
this is the spirit of Adam. Though Dante has not
expressed his desire for enlightenment, Adam per-
ceives it and answers his unspoken questions. He
tells how long it is since he was placed in the Gar-
den of Eden, how long he remained there, what
was the true cause of the Fall, and what language
he spoke.*

Wʜɪʟᴇ my extinguished sight perplext me yet,
  A breath came forth that held me, hearkening tense,
  Out of the effulgence that extinguished it,
Saying: "Until thou hast again the sense
  Of sight which on me was discomfited,
  'Tis well that converse be thy recompense.
Begin then; say whereto thy soul is wed.
  Consider, and be assured that sight suppressed
  In thee is but confounded and not dead;
Because the lady, who through this region blest   10
  Leads thee, hath in her look compassionate
  The virtue Ananias' hand possessed."   12
I said: "At her good pleasure, soon or late,
  Let cure come to the eyes which, when she brought

---

12. *Ananias cured St. Paul of his blindness.*

The fire I burn with always, were the gate.
The Good which utterly contents this Court
  Is Alpha and Omega of all lessons Love   *17*
  Reads me, of lighter or more deep import."
And that same voice which I had felt remove
  Fear at the dazzling I was daunted by   20
  Put me in mind further to speak thereof,
And said: "A finer sieve thou needs must try
  To explain this matter; thou must say who bent
  Thy bow, aimed at a target set so high!"
And I "By philosophic argument
  And with authority from thence imbrued   26
  Such love must needs stamp on me its imprint;
For the good, soon as 'tis perceived as good,
  Enkindles love and makes it more to live,
  The more of good it can itself include.   30
Therefore to the Essence, whose prerogative   31
  Is, that what good outside of it is known
  Is naught else but a light its own beams give,
More than elsewhither must in love be drawn
  The mind of him whose vision can attain
  The verity the proof is founded on.
This verity to my intellect is made plain
  By Him who to that prime love testifies   38
  Which all the eternal substances maintain.
Made plain it is by word of the Author wise,   40
  Who, speaking of Himself, to Moses said:
  'I will make all good pass before thine eyes';
Made plain by thee too, when thy prelude led   43

---

17. *Rev. 1:8:* "*I am Alpha and Omega, the beginning and the end-ing, saith the Lord.*"
26. *By revealed Truth.*
31. *Since love is attracted by goodness, and all goodness is in God, he must be the primal object of love.*
38-40. "*Him who . . .*": *Aristotle.* "*The Author*": *God.*
43. "*Thy prelude*": *probably the Gospel of John.*

All other voices like a herald's cry,
   And over earth Heaven's secret trumpeted."
I heard: "Through human intellect and by
   Authorities in sure accord with it
   Thy sovereign love of loves seeks God on high.
But tell me further if other cords have knit
   Thee unto Him, so that thou may'st declare   50
   With what close teeth this love on you has bit."
Not hidden was the sacred purpose here
   Of the Eagle of Christ; nay, well could I divine   53
   Whither he intended me to persevere.
Hence I resumed: "Those bitings, that incline
   The heart to God by the power that they bring,
   All with the yearning of my love, combine.
For the being of the world, and my being,
   The death which He, that I might live, endured,
   And hope, whereto the faithful, as I, cling,   60
Joined with that living knowledge, have secured
   That from the sea of the erring love retrieved
   On the shore of the right love I stand assured.
I love the leaves wherewith is all enleaved
   The Eternal Gardener's garden, great and least,
   In the measure of the good from Him received."
A marvellous sweet singing, when I ceased,
   Through heaven resounded; and my Lady too
   Cried "Holy, Holy, Holy," with the rest;
And as a sharp light breaketh sleep in two,   70
   The visual spirit running forth to meet
   Splendour that thrills the membranes through and
      through,
And he who has been awaked recoils from it,
   Dazed by that suddenness, which makes him quail
   Till reasoning come to succour his defeat,

---

53. "The Eagle of Christ" is John.

So from mine eyes did Beatrice every scale
  Remove with her own ray, so luminous
  That over a thousand miles it might prevail;
Whence clearer than before my vision was;
  And now I asked, like one well-nigh dismayed,   80
  Concerning a fourth light I saw with us.
My Lady then: "In those bright beams arrayed
  Gazes on his creator, rapt in joy,
  The first soul that the prime power ever made."   84
And as the bough, when the wind rushes by,
  Bendeth its topmost leaves and then is raised
  By its own virtue, and once more springeth high,
So all the while that she was speaking, mazed
  I was, and then again was fortified
  By wish to speak, which burned me as I gazed.   90
Forthwith: "O fruit alone born ripe," I cried,
  "O thou who hast, our far progenitor,
  Both daughter and daughter-in-law in every bride,
Devoutly as I may, do I implore
  That thou speak to me; my desire thou see'st;
  And, to hear thee the sooner, I say no more."
Sometimes an animal, covered up at rest,
  Quivers till, through whatever wraps him, all
  The motions of his impulse are exprest;
And in like manner that first human soul   100
  Disclosed to me through its own covering
  How for my pleasure it gladdened at my call;
And from it breathed: "Without thy uttering
  I can discern thy wish better than thou
  See'st what to thee is the most certain thing,
Because I see it in the mirror true   106
  Which can the likeness of all things present
  Though none of these its likeness ever drew.

---

84. "The first soul": Adam.
106. "In the mirror true": in God.

Thou would'st be told how long a time was spent
   Since in the garden high I was enclosed   110
   Where she there led thee to the long ascent;   *111*
And how long on its joys my eyes reposed;
   And why by the great wrath I was out-cast;
   And what language I used and had composed.
Know now, my son, that not the tree's mere taste
   Was in itself cause of so hard exile,
   But only the ordered limit overpast.   *117*
From that place whence thy lady impelled Virgil,
   While for this choir I pined, four thousand, three
   Hundred and two gyres did the sun fulfil.   120
Nine hundred times and thirty, wheeling, he   *121*
   Through all the lights in turn his pathway took
   While upon earth it was my lot to be.
Wholly extinguished was the tongue I spoke
   Long ere the unachievable monument   *125*
   Was looked to be achieved by Nimrod's folk.
For never a thing that reason can invent
   Forever endures, because man's will is weak
   And, following the heaven, on change is bent.
It is a natural act that man should speak;   130
   But this or that way Nature leaves to you,
   As pleases most, whatever end you seek.
Ere I descended to the eternal rue
   YAH was the name on earth of Him Supreme
   Wherefrom the gladness clothing me I drew.
EL was He named thereafter, as doth beseem;   *136*
   For mortal use is as the leaves upon
   The bough, which drop, and others follow them.

---

111. "She there . . .": *Beatrice.*
117-118. *Adam's sin was not gluttony, but disobedience caused by
pride.* "From that place . . .": *the Limbus.*
121-122. "He": *the sun.* "The lights": *the signs of the Zodiac.*
125. "The unachievable monument": *the Tower of Babel.*
136. "EL" *is the Hebrew name.*

On the highest mount that the wave beateth on   *139*
  Was I, with life first pure and then impure,   *140*
    From the first hour to that which, when the sun
Changes his quadrant, follows the sixth hour."

Canto XXVII

*The luster clothing the spirit of St. Peter begins to
dilate and to redden. This is from indignation at
the avarice, ambition, and venality of modern
Popes. ("Cahorsins and Gascons," line 58, refers
to Clement V, a Gascon, and John XXII, of Ca-
hors.) The host of spirits vanishes; and Beatrice
bids Dante look down for a moment to see how far
they had come on their upward journey. Both are
then wafted into the ninth heaven, that of the Pri-
mum Mobile: Beatrice explains the nature of this
sphere, and laments the perversity of mankind, with
their desires set upon ignoble things, not from de-
pravity of nature but for lack of right government.*

"To THE Father and to the Son and Holy Ghost
Glory!" burst forth from all the heavenly spheres,
So sweet, my spirit in ecstasy was lost.
What I saw seemed a smile of the universe;
  So that the intoxicating ecstasy
  Entered me both by the eyes and by the ears.
O joy! unutterable felicity!

139-142. Adam lived in the Garden of Eden only about six hours.

O life entire in love and peace! and O
Riches assured, from every craving free!
Before mine eyes the four torches a-glow   *10*
Stood; and the one which first to me came near
Began more vivid and intense to grow,

And made itself in aspect to appear
As Jupiter would seem if he and Mars   *14*
Were birds and could exchange the plumes they
    wear.

The Providence, which here for each prepares
The time and the office, had imposed a hush
On every side through all the quiring stars,

When this I heard: "If that I change and flush
Marvel thou not; for thou shalt soon divine   *2(*
On all these, as I speak, as deep a blush.

He who the place usurpeth that was mine   *22*
On earth, mine, mine, now vacant in the sight
Of the Son of God, has made my grave decline

Into a sewer, well-nigh choked outright
With blood and filth; wherein the Arch-Renegade, *26*
Who fell from here, down there taketh delight."

With such a colour as on a cloud is laid
At morning or at evening, opposite
The sun, I saw the whole heaven overspread.   *30*

And as a virtuous lady, herself quit
Of self-reproach, at other's fault will seem
Abashed, though merely at report of it,

So Beatrice changed her countenance; I deem
Such an eclipse it was that darkened o'er
Heaven, when on earth suffered the Power Supreme.

10-11. The lights of Peter, James, John, and Adam.—"The one which . . .": *the flame of St. Peter.*
14-15. If Jupiter would turn red and Mars white.
22. "He who . . .": Pope Boniface VIII.
26-27. "The Arch-Renegade": Satan.—"Down there": *in Hell.*

Then he proceeded; not now as before,
    But with a voice so altered in its mood
    That even his aspect was not altered more.
"The spouse of Christ was not upon my blood   *40*
    And that of Linus and of Cletus fed,
    That for the gain of gold she might be wooed;
But Sixtus, Pius, Calixtus, Urban bled
    After much weeping 'mid the faithful band,
    That they might gain this blissful life instead.
It was not our will that on the right hand
    Of our successors one part of Christ's flock   *47*
    Should be, and one part on the other stand;
Nor that the keys which in my charge I took
    Should on a standard be the ensign flown   *50*
    In battle urged against baptizèd folk;
Nor that my image should for seal be shown
    On lying privileges, bought and sold:
    I flash and redden, seeing these things done.
From here above preying on every fold
    In shepherds' clothing wolves are seen to slink:
    O succour of God, thy hand why dost thou hold?
Cahorsins and Gascons make ready to drink   *58*
    Our blood: O in beginning once so bright,
    To what ignoble ending dost thou sink!   *60*
But the high Providence, which with Scipio's might   *61*
    Rescued the glory of the world for Rome,
    Soon will bring help, if I conceive aright.
Open thy mouth, my son, when, overcome
    By mortal weight, thou shalt return below,
    And what I hide not, do not thou shrink from."

40-46. "The spouse of Christ": the Church.—Linus and Cletus were
    Bishops of Rome.—Sixtus and the others were also martyrs.
47. The two parts "of Christ's flock" are the Guelfs and the Ghibel
    lines.
58. See the Argument.
61. Scipio the younger, who conquered Hannibal.

As in our air the vapours downward snow,   67
 Frozen in flakes, at that time when the horn
 Of the heavenly Goat is touched by the sun's glow,
So, jewelling the ether, upward borne   70
 In flakes of fire, those vapours triumphing
 Shone, which had come to make with us sojourn.
Their semblances my sight was following,
 And followed till the space between increased
 So vast, it failed on further flight to wing.
Whereat the Lady, who saw me now released
 From gazing up, said to me: "Downward send
 Thy sight, and see how far thou hast been displaced."
From the hour at which I had first looked down, I
   kenned
 That I had moved by now through the whole arc 80
 Which the first climate makes from middle to end; 81
Ulysses' mad adventure I could mark
 Past Cadiz, and this side almost, the shore
 Europa left, her sweet load to embark;
And more I had seen of this small threshing-floor,
 But now the sun beneath me in his career
 Was parted from me by one sign or more.
The enamoured mind, fain ever to confer
 With my loved Lady, more than ever sure
 Of its want, burned to gaze once more on her.   90
And all that art or nature makes to allure
 The eyes and, feasting them, the mind entrance,
 In human lineaments or portraiture,
Combined would seem but insignificance
 Beside the divine pleasure I beheld

67-72. *These lines present the strange picture of an inverted snow-storm.*—"*The heavenly Goat*" *is Capricorn.*
81-84. *The earth was divided into seven strips, or "climates."*—"*Ulysses' mad adventure*": *cf. Inf. xxvi, 90-142.*—"*This side*" *is the Phoenician shore, where Europa mounted on the back of Jupiter.*

When I turned toward her smiling countenance.
And power, that in that look abounding welled,
    From the fair nest of Leda shot me far   *98*
    And into the most swift of heavens propelled.
Its parts, the nearest and remotest, are   100
    So uniform, I have no skill to tell
    Which of them Beatrice chose for my place there;
But she to whom my wish was visible,
    Began, smiling in such a happiness
    That God's own joy seemed on her lips to dwell:
"The nature of the world which, motionless
    At core, the wheeling of the rest maintains,   *107*
    Starteth from here the running of the race;
Else this heaven no locality contains
    Save the divine mind, whence enkindled glows   110
    The love that turns it and the power it rains.
Light and love clasp it in one circle close,   *112*
    As it the other spheres; and this circuit
    He only who girds it understands and knows.
None other its speed determines; but by it
    Are measured all the others, just as ten
    Is measured, when to half and fifth part split.
And how Time in such vessel can contain
    Its roots, while in the rest its leaves emerge,
    May now to thine intelligence be plain.   120
O Covetousness, so hasty to submerge
    Mortals, that each and all are powerless
    To draw their eyes forth from thy blinding surge!
The will indeed in men still flourishes;
    But drenchings of continual rain convert
    Sound plums into a wrinklèd rottenness.

98-99. "The fair nest": *the constellation of Gemini.*—"The most swift of heavens": *the ninth, or Primum Mobile.*
107. "At core": *on the earth.*
112-114. *The ninth heaven is surrounded only by the Empyrean, which is the Mind of God.*

For faith and innocence are in the heart
   Of children only; both aside are cast
   Before a beard upon the cheeks may start.
Many a stammering child observeth fast   130
   Who, after, when his tongue is freed, will chew
   Any food, any month, in glutton haste.
And many a stammerer loves and hearkens to
   His mother, who, when full speech in him flows,
   Longeth to see her buried out of view.
So, soon as it is seen, the white skin grows
   Black on the beauteous daughter of him whose
      sway   137
   With morning comes and with the evening goes.
Then, lest thou make a marvel of such decay,
   Think that on earth is now no governance;   140
   Wherefore the human family runs astray.
But ere from winter January advance   142
   To spring, through the hundredth part which ye
      neglect,
   From these high spheres so great a light shall lance
That destiny, which we so long expect,   145
   Shall turn the poops to where the prows have stood;
   And then the fleet shall steer a course direct,
And a sound fruit shall follow upon the bud."

---

137. "Of him . . .": the sun, whose "beauteous daughter" is the
   human race.
142. If an error in the Julian calendar had not been corrected in
   1582, the month of January, in the course of less than 90 cen-
   turies, would have been pushed into the spring.
145. Once more we have a vague prophecy of violent reformation.

Canto XXVIII

Dante is privileged to see the Divine Essence, re-
vealed as a single point of intensely shining light.
In this ninth heaven, moving round that Point are
nine orders of angels, in nine concentric circles of
light. These orders are the Intelligences, who are
the Movers of the various spheres: they are di-
vided into three hierarchies: Seraphs, Cherubs,
Thrones; Dominations, Virtues, Powers; Princi-
palities, Archangels, and Angels; as set forth by St.
Dionysius. The swiftness and brightness of the
circles are the measure of their excellence; and the
joy of the angels is proportioned to their sight.

    The doubling of the chess-board squares (line
93) alludes to the inventor of chess, who asked
from a king as a reward a grain of wheat doubled
as many times as there were squares on the board.
The king was amazed at the millions to which the
numbers added up.

WHEN she who hath imparadised my mind
  Had stript the truth bare, and its contraries
  In the present life of wretched mortal-kind,
As one who, looking in the mirror, sees
  A torch's flame that is behind him lit
  Ere in his sight, or in his thought, it is,
And turns to see if the glass opposite
  Have told him truth, and findeth it agree
  Therewith, as truly as note and measure fit;
So is recorded in my memory   10

That I turned, looking on those eyes of light
  Whence Love had made the noose to capture me.
And when I turned, and when there smote my sight
  What is revealed within that sphere supreme
  If the eye upon its circling fix aright,
I saw a Point, of so intense a beam
  That needs must every eye it blazes on
  Be closed before its poignancy extreme.
Whatever star to the eye is smallest known
  Would seem a moon, were it beside this placed   20
  As star beside star, in comparison.
Close, perhaps, as the halo seems to invest
  The lustre with whose tinge it is impearled
  Where the surrounding air is mistiest,
At such a distance round the Point there whirled
  A ring of fire so swift, it had surpassed
  The motion which most swiftly girds the world.   27
And round this was a second circle traced;
  Round that a third, and then a fourth began;
  A fifth the fourth, a sixth the fifth enlaced.   30
Followed the seventh, of so ample a span
  That Juno's messenger, completely shown,   32
  Had been too narrow its compass to contain:
So the eighth and ninth; and each revolving zone
  Moved the more slowly according as it was,
  In numbering, at more distance from the one;
And that ring glowed most lively and luminous
  Which from the pure spark was removed the least,
  Being most within its truth, as I suppose.
My Lady, who saw perplexity persist   40
  In my suspense, said: "From that point of light
  Dependeth Heaven, and all things that exist.
Look on that circle most conjoined with it;

---

27. "The motion": of the Primum Mobile itself.
32. "Juno's messenger" is Iris, the rainbow.

And know, its motion is so swift by aid
  Of love, whose kindling spurs its onward flight."
And I to her: "Were the universe arrayed   46
  In the order that I see these rings denote,
  This proffered food had my desire allayed;
But in the world of sense we have learned to note
  That the encircling spheres are more divine   50
  As from the centre they are more remote.
If my desire, then, in this wondrous shrine
  Of beings angelic must be quieted,
  Which hath but love and light for its confine,
Needs must I hear still why the example bred   *material*   55
  By the exemplar differeth therefrom   *angelic
  For, by myself, I gaze on it unfed."   hierarchy*
"If thy weak fingers find it troublesome
  To untie this knot, 'tis nothing to surprise;
  So hard, from being untried, it has become."   60
My Lady thus; then: "Take and recognise
  The truth I tell thee, if thou would'st be content,
  And subtle wit about it exercise.
The corporal circles vary in their extent
  According to the virtue, more or less,
  Whence all these parts receive their nourishment.
The greater goodness will more greatly bless;
  The greater body greater blessing steeps,
  If like perfection all its parts possess.
Therefore this one which onward with it sweeps   70
  The rest of the universe, must answer to
  The circle that most love and knowledge keeps.
If thou thy measure round the virtue drew,
  Not round the seeming substance that thy sense

46-51. The light and speed of the girdles are proportionate to their
    proximity to the Point, whereas in the material universe the nearest
    sphere is the slowest.
55. The angelic circles are the pattern of the material spheres.
70. "This one": the Primum Mobile.

Doth as a circle to thy mind construe,
Thou would'st perceive a marvellous congruence
  Of great with more, and small with less, appear   77
  In each heaven, with its own Intelligence."
As, purifying the hemisphere of air,
  A brilliancy remains when Boreas blows   80
  From his more lenient cheek, and washes fair
The tarnish of the dull mist, to disclose
  Heaven laughing out, triumphant and serene,
  And each horizon all its beauty shows,
So was it with me, when so clear had been
  Vouchsafed me answer by my Lady's grace;
  And like a star in heaven the truth was seen.
And now, when she fell silent for a space,
  Thick as the sparks from molten iron sped
  So did the sparks about the circles chase.   90
Their fiery course each spark accompanied,
  So many in number that the doubling told   92
  Of chess-board squares had been out-myriaded.
From choir to choir I heard Hosanna rolled
  To that fixt Point which holds them in their home,
  Hath held them ever, and shall forever hold.
Seeing into my mind a question come,
  She said: "The circles of the first degree
  The Seraphim and Cherubim illume:
So swift they follow their own bonds, to be   100
  Like to the Point as most they can; and can
  The more, the higher they have risen to see.
Those other loves, which move around their span,
  Are named Thrones of the godhead they attest,
  Completing the first triad with their train.

77. "Of great [size] with more [intelligence]."
80. *The northeast wind, the clearest of Boreas' threefold blast.*
90. "The sparks": *the individual angels.*
92. "The doubling": *see the Argument.*
100. "Their own bonds": *the respective rings.*

And thou should'st be assured that these are blest
  In measure as their sight plumbs the abyss
  Of truth, where the intellect is stayed at rest.
Hence may be seen how the celestial bliss   *109*
  Is founded on the act that seëth God,   *110*
  Not that which loves, which cometh after this.
Of this sight merit is the measuring-rod,
  Which grace begetteth, married to good will;
  So, rank on rank, each fills its own abode.
The second triad, blossoming in soil
  Of that eternal spring, which no unkind   *116*
  Night-frost of Aries cometh to despoil,
Warbles Hosanna without end, combined
  In triple melody, that sounds on three
  Orders of bliss whereof it is entwined.   120
Three godheads are within that hierarchy;
  First Dominations; Virtues next to them,
  And Powers, the third of the orders fronting thee.
In the two last-but-one that dance and flame
  Are Principalities and Archangels:
  The last is all Angelic feast and game.
Upward these orders gaze; and so prevails
  Downward their power, that up toward God on high
  All are impelled, and each in turn impels.
Dionysius set himself so ardently   *130*
  To fix upon these orders his regard,
  He named them and distinguished them as I.
But Gregory parted from him afterward,

109-114. Grace begets good will, together they constitute merit,
merit determines the degree of sight, and sight is the source of
love.
116-117. "No . . . night-frost of Aries": no autumn.
130-138. "Dionysius" the Areopagite, the great authority for the or-
ders of the angels, was thought to have derived his information
from St. Paul (cf. line 138). St. Gregory (line 133) arranged the
angelic orders differently.

Though at himself he smiled when all things were
   In heaven to his enlightened eyes unbarred.
And if on earth a mortal could declare
   A truth so secret, be not stupefied;
   For he imparted it who saw it here
With much of truth about these gyres beside."

Canto XXIX

*Beatrice enlightens Dante on various points that
troubled him. He learns from her that the creation
was not a temporal process: God revealed Himself
in eternity. Pure "act" (the angels), pure poten-
tiality (matter), and the two united in the mate-
rial heavens, all came into being simultaneously.
Jerome erred in supposing that the angels were
created long before the rest of the universe. In con-
trast with the pure vision of the angels, preachers
on earth cloud the minds of their hearers with
pedantic questions and trivial inventions.*

WHEN both Latona's children, covered by   *1*
   The Ram and by the Scales, together make
   One complete girdle of the horizon sky,
Not longer than the one and the other take,
   Poised from the zenith, ere they disunite
   That girdle, and both their hemisphere forsake,

1-6. At the vernal equinox, at dawn and at sunset. the sun and the
moon ("Latona's children") are exactly balanced for an instant on
opposite sides of the horizon.

Beatrice held her peace with smile alight
   Upon her features and eyes fixèd clear
   Upon the Point which had o'erwhelmed my sight.

Then she: "I ask not what thou long'st to hear,   10
   But tell thee; I can all thy longing name
   Here, where is centred every *when* and *where*.   12

Not increase of His own good to proclaim
   (Which is not possible) but that His own
   Splendour might in resplendence say *I Am;*

In His eternity, where time is none,
   Nor aught of limitation else, He chose
   That in new loves the eternal Love be shown.   18

Nor, ere that, lay He dulled as in repose;
   For not before nor after, thou must know,   20
   Did God move on the waters as they rose.

Into existence, which no flaw could show,
   Form and its matter, simple or mixt withal,   23
   Sprang, as three arrows from a three-stringed bow.

And as in glass, in amber, or crystal,
   A ray of light will instantly pervade
   The whole without one moment's interval,

So its Sire's threefold operation rayed
   Into its being, entire, immediate,
   With no distinction of beginning made.   30

And with the substances was concreate
   Order, and welded with them; and these crowned 32
   The world in which pure act was animate.

In the lowest place mere potency was found;
   Between them, potency was twined with act
   In withies that may never be unwound.

---

12. God *is the center of all our conceptions of space and time.*
18. *"In new loves": in the creation of the angels.*
23. *The angels, the earth, and the heavens (see the Argument).*
32-34. *"And these crowned . . .": at the top were the angels, which are pure intelligence. "Mere potency" is characteristic of brute matter.*

From Jerome you have heard of a long tract   *37*
  Of time, wherein the angels' ranks appeared,
  While all else of the universe yet lacked;
But what I tell hath many a page averred   *40*
  (Keep watch, and thou thyself the truth shall feel)
  Of those whose pens the Holy Spirit stirred.
Reason also may perceive it in some deal,
  Which would not grant that for so long an age
  The Movers should of their completion fail.   *45*
Now, where these Loves were chosen, at what stage,
  And how, thou know'st; so that a triple flame
  Of thy desire already I assuage.
Nor could one count till he to twenty came   *49*
  So soon as of the angels did one part   *50*
  Disturb your matter's elemental frame.
The rest remained; and then began this art
  Which thou perceivest, in such joy immerst
  That never from their circlings they dispart.
The Fall had its beginning in the accurst
  Arrogance of him whom thou didst see compressed *56*
  With all the world's weights down upon him forced.
Those thou see'st here were humble, and thus confessed
  The Goodness that empowered them to aspire
  To be with so great understanding blest;   *60*
Therefore their vision was exalted higher
  With grace illumining and their own desert,
  So that they have their will firm and entire.
Nor must thou doubt what I for sure assert
  That to receive grace is desert indeed
  In measure as 'tis taken to the heart.
On this consistory now thy thought may feed

---

37. "From Jerome . . .": see the Argument.
45. "The Movers": the angels.
49. The rebellious angels fell before one could count twenty; the others accepted grace.
56. "Of him": Satan.

In contemplation, if my science fills
  Thy garner full, without ulterior aid.
But since the fashion of your schools instils   70
  The doctrine that the angelic nature's kind
  Is such as understands, remembers, wills,
I will speak on, that pure into thy mind
  The truth may come, which there below hath been
  Dimmed, and with ambiguities entwined.
These beings, since they first had joy therein,
  On God's face have their constant vision kept,
  Wherefrom nothing is hidden or unseen.
Hence no new object comes to intercept   79
  Their sight; nor need they single memories,   80
  Dividing thought, ever to recollect;
So that on earth men dream with open eyes,
  Some in good faith, some unbelieving; and they
  Are those on whom reproach the heavier lies.
Your speculation keeps not the one way
  Down there; so far desire for prominence
  Transports you and the craving for display.
Yet even this to Heaven is less offence
  And more endurable than when Holy Writ
  Is cast aside or wrested from its sense.   90
They think not how much blood the sowing of it
  In the world cost, nor what blessèd reward
  Is theirs, who humbly to its rule submit.
Each vies with the other to bring out a hoard
  Of fond inventions, which the preachers take
  And furbish: of the Gospel not a word.
One says the moon returned upon her track   97
  At the passion of Christ, and hid from view

79-81. *Nothing ever intervenes between their minds and the image of all things in God.*
97-102. *To explain the darkness at the Crucifixion, some say that the moon left its course to make an eclipse; the truth is that the sun hid its own rays.*

The sun, whose light was thus from earth held back;
And lieth, for the light itself withdrew,   *100*
   So that the darkness of eclipse made fear
   Spaniard and Indian even as the Jew.
Lapo and Bindo are names not commoner
   In Florence than the fables preached in turn
   From pulpit after pulpit, year by year,
So that the sheep, who know nothing, return
   From pasture fed with wind; yet are not they
   Excused because their loss they never learn.
Christ to His first assembly did not say:
   'To proclaim trifles go ye forth a-field,'   110
   But gave them truth to build on, day by day.
That and that only filled their mouths, and pealed
   To battle for the faith, their glorious work,
   In which the Gospel was both spear and shield.
Now they go forth to preach with quip and quirk,
   And if a good laugh they contrive to win,
   The puffed hood covers a contented smirk.
But the cowl hideth such a bird within   *118*
   That, if the crowd could see it as it is,
   They'd see what pardon they confided in;   120
Through which this folly on earth hath such increase
   That without warrant of authority
   They rush to catch at any promises.
Therewith grows fat the pig of Antony,   *124*
   And others too of yet more swinish kind,
   Paying with money unstampt by the die.
Enough of this digression! Turn thy mind
   Back to the main path, that the way we go
   Be shortened with the time to us assigned.
The angelic nature mounts in number so   130

---

118 "Such a bird": *the devil, waiting for the preacher's soul.*
124. "The pig of Antony": *the degenerate monks of the order of*
   St. Antony, *who is generally represented with a hog under his feet.*

Past measure, that no speech was ever skilled,
　　Nor mortal thought, to cast so far a throw;
And if thou note what Daniel has revealed,　　　　*133*
　　Thou wilt perceive that the determinate
　　Number is in his myriads concealed.
The primal light whose beams irradiate
　　This nature, is absorbed through avenues　　　*137*
　　Many as the splendours whereto it is mate;
And since on the mind's vision love ensues,
　　That sweetness glows within them fiery-bright　　*140*
　　Or warm, according to the mode they use.
See now the Eternal Virtue's breadth and height,
　　Since it hath made itself so vast a store
　　Of mirrors upon which to break its light,
Remaining in itself one, as before."

---

133. Dan. 7:10: "Thousand thousands ministered unto him, and ten
thousand times ten thousand stood before him."
137. Every angel constituting a species by itself, no two perceive God
alike.

Canto XXX

---

*At daybreak Dante and Beatrice find themselves
taken up from "the greatest body" (the Primum
Mobile) into the Empyrean, beyond the spheres.
This heaven is revealed symbolically as a river of
light, streaming between banks of flowers. Dante's
eyes are strengthened by "drinking" of this light;
whereupon the image is transformed, and appears
as a round sea of light, above which Paradise is dis-
covered as a vast white rose, within which are as-
sembled the "two courts" of Heaven, the Angels
and the Redeemed. Beatrice points out to Dante*

*the seat awaiting Henry VII of Luxemburg, who
was to become Emperor in 1308 and to die in 1313.
The Canto ends with a reference to Pope Clement's
deceitful conduct towards Henry, already men-
tioned in Canto XVII (line 82).*

Pᴇʀʜᴀᴘs six thousand miles away is spread   *1*
  The blaze of noon, and this world more and more
  Inclines its shadow almost to a level bed,
When over us the heavens' unfathomed core
  Begins to alter, so that one by one
  Stars lose their faint path down to this low floor,
And as the brightest handmaid of the Sun
  Comes onward, so the closing heavens efface
  Light after light, till the most fair is gone;
Even so the Triumph that forever plays   10
  About the Point which overwhelmed me quite,
  Seeming embraced by what it doth embrace,
By little and little stole out of my sight;
  So that, by vacancy of vision led,
  And love, I turned to Beatrice for light.
If all of her that heretofore is said
  Could in a single perfect praise be quit,
  'Twere still too narrow to suffice my need.
The beauty I saw not only exceeds our wit
  To measure, past all reach, but I aver   20
  He only who made it fully enjoyeth it.
And I avow me more defeated here
  Than by his theme's height and the exacted cost
  Comic or tragic poet ever were.
As the sun doth to the eyes that tremble most,

1-7. *Dante is about to describe the aspect of the sky, with the stars
gradually fading, a little before dawn. "This low floor": the earth's
surface. "Handmaid": Aurora, the dawn.*

So doth to me the thought of the sweet smile,
  Whereby, shorn of itself, my mind is lost.
From the first day when I beheld her, while
  She was in this life, till this vision blèst,
  Never from her did aught my song beguile;   *30*
Yet needs must be relinquished further quest
  To follow in verse her beauty; it now forgoes,
  As must each artist to his last power prest.
For mightier notes than this my trumpet blows
  So lofty I leave her, to assay the height
  Of the arduous theme, which draws now toward its
    close.
With the gesture of a guide, whose goal's in sight,
  She spoke: "We from the greatest body move,   *38*
  Emerging in the heaven that is pure light;
Light of the understanding, full of love,   *40*
  Love of the true good, full of joy within,
  Joy that transcends all the heart conceiveth of.
Thou shalt see either soldiery therein   *43*
  Of Paradise; the one in the aspect they
  Shall at the Judgment by thine eyes be seen."
As sudden lightning throws in disarray
  The visual spirits, so that the eye is reft
  Of power to grasp even things that strongest stay,
The living light in such a radiant weft
  Enwound me and with such glory overcame,   *50*
  That in it all was burnt and nothing left.
"Ever doth the Love which stills this heaven acclaim
  Its own with salutation like to this,
  Preparing so the candle for its flame."
No sooner did these brief words on me seize,
  Than I became aware that I had aid

---

38. "The greatest body": the Primum Mobile.
43. "Either soldiery": the army of the souls that resisted temptation,
and the host of good angels that triumphed over the bad.

To overpass my proper faculties.
And such new vision of the sense it made
   That there is no intensity, my sight
   Could not have borne to endure it unafraid.   60
And I beheld, shaped like a river, light
   Streaming a splendour between banks whereon
   The miracle of the spring was pictured bright.   63
Out of this river living sparkles thrown
   Shot everywhere a fire amid the bloom
   And there like rubies gold-encrusted shone;
Then as if dizzy with the spiced perfume
   They plunged into the enchanted eddy again:
   As one sank, rose another fiery plume.
"The high desire that burns thee now to attain   70
   To the true knowledge of the things thou see'st
   Pleaseth me more, the stronger it doth strain.
But thou must needs even of this water taste
   Ere thou the parch of so great thirst appease."
   So spoke mine eyes' Sun to me, and scarce had
      ceased
When she added: "The river and the topazes
   That enter and issue, and the smiling flowers,
   Are of their truth foreshadowing prefaces.
Not that in these things are unripened powers,
   But in thyself is that which doth impede,   80
   Since not yet to such height thy vision towers."
No child is there that flings him at such speed
   With face turned to the milk, if he awake
   Far later than his wont, as at my need
I did, more perfect mirrors still to make
   Of mine eyes, bending to the wave profound
   That floweth for our full salvation's sake.
Soon as mine eyes within the eyelids' bound

63-64. The spring flowers are the souls of the just. The "living
sparkles" are the angels.

Had drunk of it, immediately shone
   The length of it translated into round.   90
And then, as maskers in their masks are shown
   Different of feature, if they cast aside
   The assumed appearance that was not their own,
So into festal aspect glorified
   Sparkles and flowers changed: both Heaven's courts
      I saw
   Revealed before me opening far and wide.
O Splendour of God, by whose largess I saw
   With these mine eyes truth realmed in triumph, fill
   My lips with power to re-tell how I saw.
There is light yonder which makes visible   100
   Creator to creation, that alone
   In seeing Him can in its own peace dwell.
In the figure of a circle it stretcheth on
   And out, so far that its circumference
   Would be too wide a girdle for the sun.
All of it is one radiant effluence,
   Reflected downward from the First Moved Sphere,
   Whose virtue and energy proceedeth thence;
And as a hill looks down upon a mere
   As if its own adornments to enjoy,   110
   When grass and flowers are richest, mirrored there,
So over the light and round and round did I
   See mirrored on a thousand tiers all those
   Of us permitted to return on high.
And if the least degree so greatly glows,
   What measure shall suffice for the amplitude
   Of the extremest petals of this Rose?   *117*
The breadth, the height, my vision could include
   Undazzled, and that joy which blooms for aye,
   Its quality and its sum, I understood.   120

---

117. The vast, cuplike theater is called a "Rose," and its sections
"petals."

Near and far adds not there nor takes away,
   For where God governeth immediate
   The natural law runs not, and hath no sway.
To the yellow of the Rose whose leaves dilate,   *124*
   Tier over tier, perfumed with praises quired
   To the Sun that doth eternal spring create,
Me, like to one made mute, who yet desired
   To speak, Beatrice onward drew and cried:
   "Look on the assemblage of the white-attired!
Behold our City, and how it circleth wide!   130
   Behold our seats, so filled full that but few,
   Yet to be numbered there, their place abide.
On that great seat thine eyes are drawn unto
   By the crown hung already over it
   Ere at this wedding-feast thyself art due,
The soul, on earth imperial, shall sit
   Of the high Henry, coming to enforce   *137*
   Right ways on Italy, though she is yet unfit.
A blind greed hath bewitched you with its curse
   And made you like the child who perishes   140
   Of hunger, and peevish drives away his nurse.
The prefect of the court of Heaven's decrees   *142*
   Shall then be one who in open and secret ways
   Shall not be such as with his course agrees;
But in the holy office but short space
   Shall God endure him: soon shall he be thrown   146
   Where Simon Magus hath his own just place,
And thrust him of Anagna deeper down."

---

124. *The sea of light that forms the bottom of the arena.*
137. *Henry VII attempted to restore the balance of power and the Imperial authority in Italy (see the Argument).*
142-144. *"The prefect": Pope Clement V (see the Argument).—* "His": Henry's.
146-148. *Clement V shall fall into the eighth circle of Hell, where simonists are punished.—He "of Anagna" is Boniface VIII.*

Canto XXXI

Further description of the Rose of Paradise, into and out of which the angels flit like bees about a flower. Dante, having taken in its general form, turns to Beatrice to inquire more particularly about it. But Beatrice has disappeared, and in her place is an old man, who proves to be St. Bernard, and who points out Beatrice, now in her appointed seat above. Next, he bids Dante contemplate the beauty of the Virgin.

IN FORM, then, of a radiant white rose
    That sacred soldiery before mine eyes   2
    Appeared, which in His blood Christ made His
        spouse.
But the other host which seëth and, as it flies,
    Singeth His glory who enamours it
    And the goodness which its greatness magnifies,
Like bees, which deep into the flowers retreat
    One while, and at another winging come
    Back thither where their toil is turned to sweet,
Descended into the great flower, a-bloom   10
    With petal on petal, and re-ascended thence
    To where its love forever hath its home.
Their faces all were as a flame intense,
    Their wings of gold, the rest so pure a white

2-4. "That sacred soldiery": the Redeemed.—"The other host": the angels.

That never snow could dazzle so the sense.
Into the flower descending from the height
Through rank on rank they breathed the peace, the
glow,
They gathered as they fanned their sides in flight.
And, spite of the interposing to and fro
Of such a throng 'twixt high heaven and the
flower,   20
Vision and splendour none had to forgo;
For the divine light pierceth with such power
The world, in measure of its complement
Of worth, that naught against it may endure.
This realm of unimperilled ravishment
With spirits thronged from near times and from far
Had look and love all on the one mark bent.
O triple Light, which in a single star
Shining on them their joy can so expand,
Look down upon this storm wherein we are!   30
If the barbarian, coming from such land   31
As every day by wheeling Helice
And her belovèd son with her, is spanned,
Seeing Rome and her stupendous works,—if he
Was dazed, in that age when the Lateran   35
Rose, builded to outsoar mortality,
I, who was come to the divine from man,
To the eternal out of time, and from
Florence unto a people just and sane,
How dazed past measure must I needs become!   40
Between this and my joy I found it good,
Truly, to hear naught and myself be dumb.
And as the pilgrim quickens in his blood
Within the temple of his vow at gaze,

31-33. "Such land": the North. "Helice" and "her . . . son" Arcas
are the Great and the Little Bear.
35. "The Lateran": the old Papal palace in Rome.

Already in hope to re-tell how it stood,
So traversing the light of living rays
  My eyes along the ranks, now up I led,
  Now down, and now wandered in circling ways.
I saw faces, such as to love persuade,
  Adorned by their own smile and Other's light   50
  And gestures that all dignity displayed.
The general form of Paradise my sight
  Had apprehended in its ambience,
  But upon no part had it rested quite;
I turned then with a wish re-kindled thence
  To ask my Lady and to be satisfied
  Concerning things which held me in suspense.
One thing I thought, another one replied:
  I thought to have seen Beatrice, and behold!
  An elder, robed like to those glorified.   60
His eyes and cheeks of benign gladness told,
  And in his bearing was a kindliness
  Such as befits a father tender-souled:
"Where is she?" I cried on a sudden in my distress.
  "To end thy longing, Beatrice was stirred,"
  He answered then, "to bring me from my place.
Her shalt thou see, if to the circle third   67
  From the highest rank thine eyes thou wilt up-raise,
  There on the throne whereto she hath been pre-
      ferred."
Without reply I lifted up my gaze   70
  And saw her making for herself a crown
  Of the reflection from the eternal rays.
From the highest sky which rolls the thunder down
  No mortal eye is stationed so remote,

---

60. "An elder": St. Bernard, a great mystic of the twelfth century,
famous for his devotion to the Blessed Virgin.
67. The first circle is that of Mary, the second that of Eve, the third
that of Rachel, beside whom Beatrice sits.

Though in the deepest of the seas it drown,
As then from Beatrice was my sight; but naught
   It was to me; for without any veil
   Her image down to me undimmed was brought.
"O Lady, in whom my hopes all prosper well,
   And who for my salvation didst endure   80
   To leave the printing of thy feet in Hell,
Of all that I have seen, now and before,
   By virtue of what thy might and goodness gave,
   I recognise the grace and sovereign power.
Thou hast drawn me up to freedom from a slave   *Prayer*
   By all those paths, all those ways known to thee *to*
   Through which thou had'st such potency to save. *Beatrice*
Continue thy magnificence in me,
   So that my soul, which thou hast healed of scar,
   May please thy sight when from the body free."   90
So did I pray; and she, removed so far
   As she appeared, looked on me smiling-faced;
   Then to the eternal fountain turned her there.
Whereon the holy Elder: "That thou may'st
   Consummate this thy journey, whereunto
   Prayer and a holy love made me to haste,   96
Fly with thine eyes this heavenly garden through!
   Gazing on it shall better qualify
   Thy vision, the light upward to pursue.
The Queen of Heaven, for whom continually   100
   I burn with love, will grant us every grace
   Since Bernard, her own faithful one, am I."
Like one, some Croat perhaps, who comes to gaze
   On our Veronica with eyes devout,   104
   Nor sates the inveterate hunger that he has,
So long as it is shown, but says in thought,

---

96. The "prayer and a holy love" are Beatrice's.
104. The "Veronica" is the true image of the Savior, left on a ker-
chief. It was shown at St. Peter's in Rome.

"My Lord Christ Jesus, very God, is this
   Indeed Thy likeness in such fashion wrought?"
Such was I, gazing on the impassioned bliss
   Of love in him who even in this world's woe   110
   By contemplation tasted of that peace.   *111*
"Child of Grace," he began, "thou wilt not know
   This joyous being in its felicity
   If thine eyes rest but on the base below.
Look on the farthest circles thou can'st see,
   Till thou perceive enthroned the Queen, to whom
   This realm devoteth its whole fealty."
I raised my eyes; and as in morning bloom
   The horizon's eastern part becometh bright
   And that where the sun sinks is overcome,   120
So with my eyes climbing a mountain's height,
   As from a valley, I saw on the utmost verge
   What outshone all else fronting me in light.
As that point where the car is to emerge,   *124*
   Which Phaëthon drove ill, glows fieriest
   And softens down its flame on either marge,
So did that oriflamme of peace attest   *127*
   The midmost glory, and on either side
   In equal measure did its rays arrest.
And at that mid-point, with wings opened wide,   130
   A myriad angels moved in festive play,
   In brilliance and in art diversified.
There, smiling upon dance and roundelay,
   I saw a Beauty, that was happiness
   In the eyes of all the other saints' array.
And if in speaking I had wealth not less
   Than in imagining, I would not dare

---

111. St. Bernard in his meditations had a foretaste of the peace of Heaven.
124. "The car": of the sun.
127. "That oriflamme," i.e., golden pennant, is the streak of light on Mary's side.

To attempt the least part of her loveliness.
When of my fixt look Bernard was aware,
 So fastened on his own devotion's flame, 140
 He turned his eyes with so much love to her *141*
That mine more ardent and absorbed became.

Canto XXXII

---

*Bernard explains the conformation of the Celestial
Rose. It is divided down the middle, and across; on
one side are male, on the other female, saints. Be-
low the horizontal division are the souls of beatified
children. That Dante may be vouchsafed a vision
of Deity itself, Bernard makes supplication to the
Virgin, and bids Dante accompany him in his
prayer.*

Rapt in love's bliss, that contemplative saint
 Nevertheless took up the instructor's part,
 Uttering these sacred words with no constraint:
"The wound that Mary closed, and soothed its smart, *4*
 She, who so beautiful sits at her feet,
 Opened, and yet more deeply pressed the dart.
In the order making the third rank complete
 Rachel thou can'st distinguish next below
 With Beatrice in her appointed seat.
Sara, Rebecca, Judith, and her too, 10

---

141. "To her": on Mary.
4-5. "The wound": of original sin. "She": Eve.

Ancestress of the singer, whose cry rose   *11*
  Miserere mei for his fault and rue,—   *12*
These thou beholdest tier by tier disclose,
  Descending, as I name them each by name,
  From petal after petal down the Rose.
And from the seventh grade downward, following them,
  Even as above them, Hebrew women bide,
  Parting the tresses on the Rose's stem;
Because, according as faith made confide   *19*
  In Christ, these serve as for a party-wall   *20*
  At which the stairs of sanctity divide.
On this side, where the flower is filled in all
  Its numbered petals, sit in order they
  Who waiting on Christ Coming heard His call;
On the other side, where certain gaps betray
  Seats empty, in semicircle, thou look'st on
  Such as in Christ Come had their only stay.
And as on the one side the glorious throne
  Of the Lady of Heaven and the other thrones as well
  Below it make partition, so great John   *30*
Sits over against her, ever there to dwell,
  Who, ever holy, endured the desert's fare,
  And martyrdom, and then two years in Hell.   *33*
Beneath him, chosen to mark the boundary there
  Francis and Benedict and Augustine shine
  And others, round by round, down even to here.
Now marvel at the deep foresight divine!
  For the faith's either aspect, equal made,   *38*
  Shall consummate this garden's full design.

---

11. "Ancestress": *Ruth;* "the singer": *David.*
12. "Miserere mei": "Have mercy upon me."
19. *On one side of the partition are the Hebrews (line 24), on the other the Christians (line 27).*
33. "In Hell": *the Limbus.*
38. "Either aspect": *the Old Church and the New.*

And know that downward from the midmost grade   40
   Which runneth the two companies betwixt
   They sit there by no merit that they had
But by another's, on conditions fixt;   43
   For these are spirits that were all released
   Ere they had made a true choice, unperplext.
And by their faces this is manifest
   And also by their voices' childish note,
   If looking heedfully thou listenest.
Now thou art doubting, and doubt makes thee mute; 49
   But for thy sake will I the coil undo   50
   Wherein thou art bound by subtlety of thought.
Within this kingdom's compass thou must know
   Chance hath no single point's determining,
   No more than thirst, or hunger, or sorrow,
Because eternal law, in everything
   Thou see st, it stablisht with such close.consent
   As close upon the finger fits the ring;
Wherefore these children, hastened as they went
   Into the true life, are not without cause
   Within themselves more and less excellent.   60
The King, through whom this realm hath its repose
   In so great love and such felicities,
   That no rash will on further venture goes,
Creating all minds in His own eyes' bliss,
   At His own pleasure dowers them with grace
   Diversely; on this point let the fact suffice.
This is made known to you, clear and express,
   In Holy Writ, by those twins who, ere birth,   68

43-45. "But by another's": one's parents. "Released": from the flesh.
These are the spirits of children who died before the age of moral
responsibility.
49. Dante is wondering why some have higher seats than others. He
learns that the degree of beatitude is determined by predestination.
68. "Those twins": Jacob and Esau.

In the womb wrestled in their wrathfulness.

According to the colour figuring forth   70
  In the hair such grace, the sublime Light must needs
  Chaplet their heads according to their worth.

Wherefore without reward for any deeds
  Their places are to different ranks assigned,
  Differing only in what from gift proceeds.

In the early ages parents' faith, combined
  With innocence, sufficed and nothing more
  To wing them upward and salvation find.

The first age being completed, other power
  Was needed for the innocent males to attain   80
  By virtue of circumcision, Heaven's door.

But when the time of grace began its reign,
  Having not perfect baptism of Christ,
  Such innocence below there must remain.   84

Look now upon the face most like to Christ!
  For only its radiance can so fortify
  Thy gaze as fitteth for beholding Christ."

I saw rain over her such ecstasy
  Brought in the sacred minds that with it glowed— 89
  Created through the heavenly height to fly—   90

That all I had seen on all the way I had trod
  Held me not in such breathless marvelling
  Nor so great likeness vouched to me of God.

And that Love which at its first down-coming   94
  Sang to her: "Hail, O Mary, full of grace!"
  Now over her extended either wing.

The divine song echoed through all the space,
  Answered from all sides of the Blessed Court

70-72. *Our halo in Heaven is proportionate to the grace bestowed on us at birth.*
84. "Below there": *in the Limbus.*
89. "The sacred minds": *the angels.*
94. "That Love which . . .": *the angel Gabriel.*

So that serener joy filled every face.

"O holy father, who for my comfort   100
   Hast deigned thy sweet allotted place to quit,
   With me in this low station to consort,

What is that angel who with such delight
   Looketh our Queen in the eyes, lost in love there
   So that he seems one flame of living light?"

To his instruction thus did I repair
   Once more, who drew from Mary increasingly
   Beauty, as from the sun the morning star.

"Blitheness and buoyant confidence," said he,
   "As much as angel or a soul may own,   110
   Are all in him; so would we have it be.

For he it is who brought the palm-leaf down
   To Mary, when the burden of our woe
   In flesh was undertaken by God's Son.

Now with thine eyes come with me, as I go
   Discoursing, and the great patricians note
   Of the empire that the just and pious know.

Those two above, most blessed in their lot
   By being nearest to the august Empress,   119
   Are of our rose as 'twere the double root.   120

He on the left who has the nearest place
   Is that father, through whose presumptuous taste 122
   The human tribe tasteth such bitterness.

That ancient Father of Holy Church thou may'st
   See on the right, to whom Christ gave in trust
   The keys of this, of all flowers loveliest.

And he who, ere he died, saw all the host   127
   Of grievous days prepared for that fair spouse
   Won by the nails and by the lance's thrust,

---

119. "Empress": Mary.
122-124. "That father": Adam. "That ancient Father": St. Peter.
127-129. St. John, the author of the Apocalypse. "Spouse": the
Church. "The nails and . . . the lance": of Christ's Passion.

Sits by him; by the other, see repose   *130*
   That leader under whom was fed by manna
   The ungrateful people, fickle and mutinous.

And, sitting over against Peter, Anna   *133*
   Looks on her daughter, so content of soul,
   She moveth not her eyes, singing Hosanna;

And opposite the greatest father of all
   Sits Lucy, who stirred the lady of thy troth,   *137*
   When, eyes down, thou wert running to thy fall.

But stop we here as the good tailor doth
   (Since of thy sleeping vision the time flies),   *140*
   Cutting the gown according to the cloth;

And turn we to the Primal Love our eyes,
   So that, still gazing toward Him, thou may'st pierce
   Into His splendour, far as in thee lies.

Yet, lest it happen that thou should'st reverse,
   Thinking to advance, the motion of thy wing,
   A prayer for grace needs must we now rehearse,

Grace from her bounty who can the succour bring.   *148*
   And do thou with thy feeling follow on
   My words, that close to them thy heart may
      cling."   *150*

And he began this holy orison.

130-131. "By him": Peter. "By the other": Adam. "That leader":
  Moses.
133. "Anna": St. Anna, mother of Mary.
137. "The lady of thy troth": Beatrice.
148. "From her bounty": the Blessed Virgin's.

Canto XXXIII

---

*The prayer of St. Bernard to the Virgin Mary. The
prayer is granted; and then Dante prays to God
that some trace of the dazzling glimpse of the
divine mystery of Trinity in Unity may be com-
municated to men through his verse.*

"Maiden and Mother, daughter of thine own Son,   1
  Beyond all creatures lowly and lifted high,
  Of the Eternal Design the corner-stone!
Thou art she who did man's substance glorify
  So that its own Maker did not eschew
  Even to be made of its mortality.
Within thy womb the Love was kindled new
  By generation of whose warmth supreme
  This flower to bloom in peace eternal grew.   9
Here thou to us art the full noonday beam   10
  Of love revealed: below, to mortal sight,
  Hope, that forever springs in living stream.
Lady, thou art so great and hast such might
  That whoso crave grace, nor to thee repair,
  Their longing even without wing seeketh flight.
Thy charity doth not only him up-bear
  Who prays, but in thy bounty's large excess

---

1. A great part of this beautiful prayer was copied by Chaucer in
the Second Nun's Tale, 29-84.
9. "This flower": the Rose of the Blessed.

Thou oftentimes dost even forerun the prayer.
In thee is pity, in thee is tenderness,
  In thee magnificence, in thee the sum   20
  Of all that in creation most can bless.

Now he that from the deepest pit hath come   22
  Of the universe, and seen, each after each,
  The spirits as they live and have their home,

He of thy grace so much power doth beseech
  That he be enabled to uplift even higher
  His eyes, and to the Final Goodness reach.

And I who never burned with more desire
  For my own vision than for his, persist
  In prayer to thee—my prayers go forth in choir,   30

May they not fail!—that thou disperse all mist
  Of his mortality with prayers of thine,
  Till joy be his of that supreme acquist.

Also I implore thee, Queen who can'st incline
  All to thy will, let his affections stand
  Whole and pure after vision so divine.

The throbbings of the heart do thou command!
  See, Beatrice with how many of the blest,
  To second this my prayer, lays hand to hand."

Those eyes, of God loved and revered, confest,   40
  Still fixt upon him speaking, the delight
  She hath in prayer from a devoted breast.

Then were they lifted to the eternal light,
  Whereinto it may not be believed that eye
  So clear in any creature sendeth sight.

And I, who to the goal was drawing nigh
  Of all my longings, now, as it behoved,
  Felt the ardour of them in contentment die.

Bernard signed, smiling, as a hand he moved,
  That I should lift my gaze up; but I knew   50

---

22. "He that . . .": Dante.

Myself already such as he approved,
Because my sight, becoming purged anew,
     Deeper and deeper entered through the beam
     Of sublime light, which in itself is true.
Thenceforth my vision was too great for theme
     Of our speech, that such glory overbears,
     And memory faints at such assault extreme.
As he who dreams sees, and when disappears
     The dream, the passion of its print remains,
     And naught else to the memory adheres,   60
Even such am I; for almost wholly wanes
     My vision now, yet still the drops I feel
     Of sweetness it distilled into my veins.
Even so the sunbeam doth the snow unseal;
     So was the Sibyl's saying lost inert   65
     Upon the thin leaves for the wind to steal.
O supreme Light, who dost thy glory assert
     High over our imagining, lend again
     Memory a little of what to me thou wert.
Vouchsafe unto my tongue such power to attain   70
     That but one sparkle it may leave behind
     Of thy magnificence to future men.
For by returning somewhat to my mind
     And by a little sounding in this verse
     More of thy triumph shall be thence divined.
So keenly did the living radiance pierce
     Into me, that I think I had been undone
     Had mine eyes faltered, from the light averse.
And I recall that with the more passion
     I clove to it, till my gaze, thereat illumed,   80
     With the Infinite Good tasted communion.
O Grace abounding, whereby I presumed

---

65. The Cumaean "Sibyl" was accustomed to write her prophecies
on loose tree-leaves.

To fix upon the eternal light my gaze
So deep, that in it I my sight consumed! 84
I beheld leaves within the unfathomed blaze
Into one volume bound by love, the same 86
That the universe holds scattered through its maze.
Substance and accidents, and their modes, became
As if together fused, all in such wise 89
That what I speak of is one simple flame. 90
Verily I think I saw with mine own eyes
The form that knits the whole world, since I taste,
In telling of it, more abounding bliss.
One moment more oblivion has amassed 94
Than five-and-twenty centuries have wrought
Since Argo's shadow o'er wondering Neptune passed.
Thus did my mind in the suspense of thought
Gaze fixedly, all immovable and intent,
And ever fresh fire from its gazing caught.
Man at that light becometh so content 100
That to choose other sight and this reject,
It is impossible that he consent,
Because the good which is the will's object
Dwells wholly in it, and that within its pale
Is perfect, which, without, hath some defect.
Even for my remembrance now must fail
My words, and less than could an infant's store
Of speech, who at the pap yet sucks, avail;
Not that within the living light was more
Than one sole aspect of divine essence, 110
Being still forever as it was before.

84. I became blind to all else.
86. God is the Book of the Universe.
89. God, containing all things, is a perfect unit.
94-96. In the first moment after my awakening I forgot more of my
vision than mankind has forgotten, in 2500 years, of the story of
the Argonauts.

But the one semblance, seen with more intense
  A faculty, even as over me there stole
  Change, was itself transfigured to my sense.
Within the clear profound Light's aureole   *115*
  Three circles from its substance now appeared,
  Of three colours, and each an equal whole.
One its reflection on the next conferred
  As rainbow upon rainbow, and the two
  Breathed equally the fire that was the third.   *120*
To my conception O how frail and few
  My words! and that, to what I looked upon,
  Is such that "little" is more than is its due.
O Light Eternal, who in thyself alone
  Dwell'st and thyself know'st, and self-understood,
  Self-understanding, smilest on thine own!
That circle which, as I conceived it, glowed
  Within thee like reflection of a flame,
  Being by mine eyes a little longer wooed,
Deep in itself, with colour still the same,   *130*
  Seemed with our human effigy to fill,
  Wherefore absorbed in it my sight became.
As the geometer who bends all his will
  To measure the circle, and howsoe'er he try   *134*
  Fails, for the principle escapes him still,
Such at this mystery new-disclosed was I,
  Fain to understand how the image doth alight
  Upon the circle, and with its form comply.
But these my wings were fledged not for that flight,
  Save that my mind a sudden glory assailed   *140*

---

115. *The threefold oneness is disclosed by the symbol of three mysterious rings occupying exactly the same place.*
120. *"The third": the Holy Ghost, who emanates equally from Father and Son.*
134. *The problem is the squaring of the circle.*

And its wish came revealed to it in that light.
To the high imagination force now failed;
  But like to a wheel whose circling nothing jars   *143*
  Already on my desire and will prevailed
The Love that moves the sun and the other stars.

143-145. *Circular motion symbolizes faultless activity. Dante's individual will is merged in the World-Will of the Creator.*

LA VITA NUOVA

Translated by D. G. Rossetti

La Vita Nuova

(*The New Life*)

IN THAT part of the book of my memory before the
which is little that can be read, there is a rubric, saying,
"Here beginneth the New Life." Under such rubric I
find written many things; and among them the words
which I purpose to copy into this little book; if not all
of them, at the least their substance.

II

Nine times already since my birth had the heaven of
light returned to the selfsame point almost,[1] as concerns
its own revolution, when first the glorious Lady of my
mind was made manifest to mine eyes; even she who
was called Beatrice by many who knew not wherefore.[2]
She had already been in this life for so long as that,
within her time, the starry heaven had moved towards
the Eastern quarter one of the twelve parts of a degree:
so that she appeared to me at the beginning of her ninth
year almost, and I saw her almost at the end of my ninth
year. Her dress, on that day, was of a most noble colour,
a subdued and goodly crimson, girdled and adorned in
such sort as best suited with her very tender age. At that
moment, I say most truly that the spirit of life,[3] which
hath its dwelling in the secretest chamber of the heart,

---

1. *Dante first met Beatrice in 1274, when he was nine years old.—*
   "The heaven of light" is the sun.
2. *A literal rendering of these words is ". . . by many who knew*
   not how she was called." The key to the whole passage is the
   meaning of the name Beatrice, "She who confers blessing."

began to tremble so violently that the least pulses of my
body shook therewith; and in trembling it said these
words: "Here is a deity stronger than I; who, coming,
shall rule over me." At that moment the animate spirit,[3]
which dwelleth in the lofty chamber whither all the
senses carry their perceptions, was filled with wonder,
and speaking more especially unto the spirits of the
eyes, said these words: "Your beatitude hath now been
made manifest unto you." At that moment the natural
spirit,[3] which dwelleth there where our nourishment is
administered, began to weep, and in weeping said these
words: "Alas! how often shall I be disturbed from this
time forth." I say that, from that time forward, Love
quite governed my soul; which was immediately es-
poused to him, and with so safe and undisputed a lord-
ship, (by virtue of strong imagination) that I had noth-
ing left for it but to do all his bidding continually. He
oftentimes commanded me to seek if I might see this
youngest of the Angels: wherefore I in my boyhood
often went in search of her, and found her so noble and
praiseworthy that certainly of her might have been said
those words of the poet Homer, "She seemed not to be
the daughter of a mortal man, but of God." [4] And albeit
her image, that was with me always, was an exultation
of Love to subdue me, it was yet of so perfect a quality
that it never allowed me to be overruled by Love with-
out the faithful counsel of reason, whensoever such
counsel was useful to be heard. But seeing that were I
to dwell overmuch on the passions and doings of such
early youth, my words might be counted something
fabulous, I will therefore put them aside; and passing

---

3. "The spirit of life," "the animate spirit," and "the natural spirit"
were, in medieval physiology, fluid substances governing the or-
gans of the body. They had their seat, respectively, in the heart,
in the brain and in the liver.
4. Iliad, xxiv, 258.

many things that may be conceived by the pattern of these, I will come to such as are writ in my memory with a better distinctness.

III

After the lapse of so many days that nine years exactly were completed since the above-written appearance of this most gracious being, on the last of those days[5] it happened that the same wonderful lady appeared to me dressed all in pure white, between two gentle ladies elder than she. And passing through a street, she turned her eyes thither where I stood sorely abashed: and by her unspeakable courtesy, which is now guerdoned in the Great Cycle,[6] she saluted me with so virtuous a bearing that I seemed then and there to behold the very limits of blessedness. The hour of her most sweet salutation was certainly the ninth of that day; and because it was the first time that any words from her reached mine ears, I came into such sweetness that I parted thence as one intoxicated. And betaking me to the loneliness of mine own room, I fell to thinking of this most courteous lady, thinking of whom I was overtaken by a pleasant slumber, wherein a marvellous vision was presented to me: for there appeared to be in my room a mist of the colour of fire, within the which I discerned the figure of a lord of terrible aspect[7] to such as should gaze upon him, but who seemed therewithal to rejoice inwardly that it was a marvel to see. Speaking he said many things, among the which I could understand but few; and of these, this: "I am thy master." In his arms it seemed to me that a person was sleeping,

---

5. *This second meeting took place on May Day, 1283.*
6. "Great Cycle": *the eternal world.*
7. "A lord of terrible aspect": *Love.*

covered only with a blood-coloured cloth; upon whom looking very attentively, I knew that it was the lady of the salutation who had deigned the day before to salute me. And he who held her held also in his hand a thing that was burning in flames; and he said to me, "Behold thy heart." But when he had remained with me a little while, I thought that he set himself to awaken her that slept; after the which he made her to eat that thing which flamed in his hand;[8] and she ate as one fearing. Then, having waited again a space, all his joy was turned into most bitter weeping; and as he wept he gathered the lady into his arms, and it seemed to me that he went with her up towards heaven: whereby such a great anguish came upon me that my light slumber could not endure through it, but was suddenly broken. And immediately having considered, I knew that the hour wherein this vision had been made manifest to me was the fourth hour[9] (which is to say, the first of the nine last hours) of the night. Then, musing on what I had seen, I proposed to relate the same to many poets who were famous in that day: and for that I had myself in some sort the art of discoursing with rhyme, I resolved on making a sonnet, in the which, having saluted all such as are subject unto Love, and entreated them to expound my vision, I should write unto them those things which I had seen in my sleep. And the sonnet I made was this:

To every heart which the sweet pain doth move,
    And unto which these words may now be brought
    For true interpretation and kind thought,
    Be greeting in our Lord's name, which is Love.

---

8. Legends of eaten hearts were common in medieval literature.
9. "The fourth" of the twelve hours of night is the hour between 9 and 10 P.M.

Of those long hours wherein the stars, above,
    Wake and keep watch, the third [10] was almost nought
    When Love was shown me with such terrors fraught
    As may not carelessly be spoken of.
He seem'd like one who is full of joy, and had
    My heart within his hand, and on his arm
    My lady, with a mantle round her, slept;
Whom (having waken'd her) anon he made
    To eat that heart; she ate, as fearing harm.
    Then he went out; and as he went, he wept

*This sonnet is divided into two parts. In the first part
I give greeting, and ask an answer; in the second, I
signify what thing has to be answered to. The second
part commences here, "Of those long hours."*

To this sonnet I received many answers, conveying
many different opinions; of the which, one was sent by
him whom I now call the first among my friends;[11] and
it began thus, "Unto my thinking thou beheld'st all
worth." And indeed, it was when he learned that I was
he who had sent those rhymes to him, that our friend-
ship commenced. But the true meaning of that vision
was not then perceived by any one, though it be now
evident to the least skilful.

IV

From that night forth, the natural functions of my
body began to be vexed and impeded, for I was given
up wholly to thinking of this most gracious creature:
whereby in short space I became so weak and so re-

10. Here Rossetti has mistranslated. It should read "the fourth";
(see footnote 9).
11. "The first among my friends": Guido Cavalcanti. In addition
to his, two other answers to Dante's sonnet are preserved, those
of Cino da Pistoia and Dante da Majano.

duced that it was irksome to many of my friends to look upon me; while others, being moved by spite, went about to discover what it was my wish should be concealed. Wherefore I, (perceiving the drift of their unkindly questions,) by Love's will, who directed me according to the counsels of reason, told them how it was Love himself who had thus dealt with me: and I said so, because the thing was so plainly to be discerned in my countenance that there was no longer any means of concealing it. But when they went on to ask, "And by whose help hath Love done this?" I looked in their faces smiling, and spake no word in return.

V

Now it fell on a day, that this most gracious creature was sitting where words were to be heard of the Queen of Glory;[12] and I was in a place whence mine eyes could behold their beatitude: and betwixt her and me, in a direct line, there sat another lady of a pleasant favour; who looked round at me many times, marvelling at my continued gaze which seemed to have *her* for its object. And many perceived that she thus looked: so that departing thence, I heard it whispered after me, "Look you to what a pass *such a lady* hath brought him"; and in saying this they named her who had been midway between the most gentle Beatrice, and mine eyes. Therefore I was reassured, and knew that for that day my secret had not become manifest. Then immediately it came into my mind that I might make use of this lady as a screen to the truth: and so well did I play my part that the most of those who had hitherto watched and wondered at me, now imagined they had found me out.

12. *In a church.*

By her means I kept my secret concealed till some years were gone over; and for my better security, I even made divers rhymes in her honour; whereof I shall here write only as much as concerneth the most gentle Beatrice, which is but a very little.

VI

Moreover, about the same time while this lady was a screen for so much love on my part, I took the resolution to set down the name of this most gracious creature accompanied with many other women's names, and especially with hers whom I spake of. And to this end I put together the names of sixty the most beautiful ladies in that city where God had placed mine own lady; and these names I introduced in an epistle in the form of a *sirvent*,[13] which it is not my intention to transcribe here. Neither should I have said anything of this matter, did I not wish to take note of a certain strange thing, to wit: that having written the list, I found my lady's name would not stand otherwise than ninth in order among the names of these ladies.

VII

Now it so chanced with her by whose means I had thus long time concealed my desire, that it behoved her to leave the city I speak of, and to journey afar: wherefore I, being sorely perplexed at the loss of so excellent a defence, had more trouble than even I could before have supposed. And thinking that if I spoke not somewhat mournfully of her departure, my former counter-

---

13. A "sirvent": the serventese was a poem of service or honor in the Provençal style. Dante's sirvent has not come down to us.

feiting would be the more quickly perceived, I deter-
mined that I would make a grievous sonnet thereof;[14]
the which I will write here, because it hath certain
words in it whereof my lady was the immediate cause,
as will be plain to him that understands. And the sonnet
was this:

All ye that pass along Love's trodden way,
    Pause ye awhile and say
    If there be any grief like unto mine:
    I pray you that you hearken a short space
    Patiently, if my case
    Be not a piteous marvel and a sign.

Love (never, certes, for my worthless part,
    But of his own great heart,)
    Vouchsafed to me a life so calm and sweet
    That oft I heard folk question as I went
    What such great gladness meant:—
    They spoke of it behind me in the street.

But now that fearless bearing is all gone
    Which with Love's hoarded wealth was given me;
    Till I am grown to be
    So poor that I have dread to think thereon.

And thus it is that I, being like as one
    Who is ashamed and hides his poverty,
    Without seem full of glee,
    And let my heart within travail and moan.

*This poem has two principal parts; for, in the first, I
mean to call the Faithful of Love in those words of*

---

14. This is not a regular sonnet, it is a doubled sonnet, composed
of two sextets followed by two quatrains. The poem on p. 556 is
a sonnet of the same sort.

Jeremias the Prophet, "Is it nothing to you, all ye that pass by? behold, and see if there be any sorrow like unto my sorrow," and to pray them to stay and hear me. In the second, I tell where Love had placed me, with a meaning other than that which the last part of the poem shows, and I say what I have lost. The second part begins here: "Love (never, certes)."

VIII

A certain while after the departure of that lady, it pleased the Master of the Angels to call into His glory a damsel, young and of a gentle presence, who had been very lovely in the city I speak of: and I saw her body lying without its soul among many ladies, who held a pitiful weeping. Whereupon, remembering that I had seen her in the company of excellent Beatrice, I could not hinder myself from a few tears; and weeping, I conceived to say somewhat of her death, in guerdon of having seen her somewhile with my lady; which thing I spake of in the latter end of the verses that I writ in this matter, as he will discern who understands. And I wrote two sonnets, which are these:

Weep, Lovers, sith Love's very self doth weep,
    And sith the cause for weeping is so great;
    When now so many dames, of such estate
    In worth, show with their eyes a grief so deep:
For Death the churl has laid his leaden sleep
    Upon a damsel who was fair of late,
    Defacing all our earth should celebrate,—
    Yea all save virtue, which the soul doth keep.
Now hearken how much Love did honour her.
    I myself saw him in his proper form
    Bending above the motionless sweet dead,

And often gazing into Heaven; for there
  The soul now sits which when her life was warm
  Dwelt with the joyful beauty that is fled.

*This first sonnet is divided into three parts. In the
first, I call and beseech the Faithful of Love to weep;
and I say that their Lord weeps, and that they, hearing
the reason why he weeps, shall be more minded to listen
to me. In the second, I relate this reason. In the third,
I speak of honour done by Love to this Lady. The
second part begins here, "When now so many dames";
the third here, "Now hearken."*

Death, alway cruel, Pity's foe in chief,
  Mother who brought forth grief,
  Merciless judgement and without appeal!
  Since thou alone hast made my heart to feel
  This sadness and unweal,
  My tongue upbraideth thee without relief.

And now (for I must rid thy name of ruth)
  Behoves me speak the truth
  Touching thy cruelty and wickedness:
  Not that they be not known; but ne'ertheless
  I would give hate more stress
  With them that feed on love in very sooth.

Out of this world thou hast driven courtesy,
  And virtue, dearly prized in womanhood;
  And out of youth's gay mood
  The lovely lightness is quite gone through thee.

Whom now I mourn, no man shall learn from me
  Save by the measure of these praises given.
  Whoso deserves not Heaven
  May never hope to have her company.

This poem is divided into four parts. In the first I address Death by certain proper names of hers. In the second, speaking to her, I tell the reason why I am moved to denounce her. In the third, I rail against her. In the fourth, I turn to speak to a person undefined, although defined in my own conception. The second part commences here, "Since thou alone"; the third here, "And now (for I must)"; the fourth here, "Whoso deserves not."

IX

Some days after the death of this lady, I had occasion to leave the city I speak of, and to go thitherwards where she abode who had formerly been my protection; albeit the end of my journey reached not altogether so far. And notwithstanding that I was visibly in the company of many, the journey was so irksome that I had scarcely sighing enough to ease my heart's heaviness; seeing that as I went, I left my beatitude behind me. Wherefore it came to pass that he who ruled me by virtue of my most gentle lady was made visible to my mind, in the light habit of a traveller, coarsely fashioned. He appeared to me troubled, and looked always on the ground; saving only that sometimes his eyes were turned towards a river which was clear and rapid, and which flowed along the path I was taking. And then I thought that Love called me and said to me these words: "I come from that lady who was so long thy surety; for the matter of whose return, I know that it may not be. Wherefore I have taken that heart which I made thee leave with her, and do bear it unto another lady, who, as she was, shall be thy surety"; (and when he named her, I knew her well). "And of these words I have spoken, if thou shouldst speak any again, let it be in such sort as that none shall perceive thereby that thy love was feigned for her, which thou must now feign for another." And when he had spoken thus, all my imagining was gone suddenly, for it seemed to me that Love became a part of myself: so that, changed as it were in mine aspect, I rode on full of thought the whole of that day, and with heavy sighing. And the day being over, I wrote this sonnet:

A day agone, as I rode sullenly
    Upon a certain path that liked me not,
    I met Love midway while the air was hot,
    Clothed lightly as a wayfarer might be.
And for the cheer he show'd, he seem'd to me
    As one who hath lost lordship he had got;
    Advancing tow'rds me full of sorrowful thought,
    Bowing his forehead so that none should see.
Then as I went, he call'd me by my name,
    Saying: "I journey since the morn was dim
    Thence where I made thy heart to be: which now
I needs must bear unto another dame."
    Wherewith so much pass'd into me of him .
    That he was gone, and I discern'd not how.

This sonnet has three parts. In the first part, I tell how I met Love and of his aspect. In the second, I tell what he said to me, although not in full, through the fear I had of discovering my secret. In the third, I say how he disappeared. The second part commences here, "Then as I went"; the third here, "Wherewith so much."

X

On my return, I set myself to seek out that lady whom my master had named to me while I journeyed sighing. And because I would be brief, I will now narrate that

in a short while I made her my surety, in such sort that
the matter was spoken of by many in terms scarcely
courteous; through the which I had oftenwhiles many
troublesome hours. And by this it happened (to wit: by
this false and evil rumour which seemed to misfame
me of vice), that she who[15] was the destroyer of all evil
and the queen of all good, coming where I was, denied
me her most sweet salutation, in the which alone was
my blessedness. And here it is fitting for me to depart
a little from this present matter, that it may be rightly
understood of what surpassing virtue her salutation was
to me.

XI

To the which end I say that when she appeared in
any place, it seemed to me, by the hope of her excellent
salutation, that there was no man mine enemy any
longer; and such warmth of charity came upon me that
most certainly in that moment I would have pardoned
whosoever had done me an injury; and if one should
then have questioned me concerning any matter, I could
only have said unto him "Love," with a countenance
clothed in humbleness. And what time she made ready
to salute me, the spirit of Love, destroying all other
perceptions, thrust forth the feeble spirits of mine eyes,
saying, "Do homage unto your mistress," and putting
itself in their place to obey: so that he who would,
might then have beheld Love, beholding the lids of
mine eyes shake. And when this most gentle lady gave
her salutation, Love, so far from being a medium be-
clouding mine intolerable beatitude, then bred in me
such an overpowering sweetness that my body, being
all subjected thereto, remained many times helpless and

---

15. "She who . . .": Beatrice.

passive. Whereby it is made manifest that in her salutation alone was there any beatitude for me, which then very often went beyond my endurance.

XII

And now, resuming my discourse, I will go on to relate that when, for the first time, this beatitude was denied me, I became possessed with such grief that parting myself from others, I went into a lonely place to bathe the ground with most bitter tears: and when, by this heat of weeping, I was somewhat relieved, I betook myself to my chamber, where I could lament unheard. And there, having prayed to the Lady of all Mercies, and having said also, "O Love, aid thou thy servant," I went suddenly asleep like a beaten sobbing child. And in my sleep, towards the middle of it, I seemed to see in the room, seated at my side, a youth in very white raiment, who kept his eyes fixed on me in deep thought. And when he had gazed some time, I thought that he sighed and called to me in these words: "My son, it is time for us to lay aside our counterfeiting." And thereupon I seemed to know him; for the voice was the same wherewith he had spoken at other times in my sleep. Then looking at him, I perceived that he was weeping piteously, and that he seemed to be waiting for me to speak. Wherefore, taking heart, I began thus: "Why weepest thou, Master of all honour?" And he made answer to me: "I am as the centre of a circle, to the which all parts of the circumference bear an equal relation; but with thee it is not thus." [16] And thinking upon his words, they seemed to me obscure; so that again com-

16. With this dark saying Love, most probably, bids Dante to keep to one center, by devoting himself exclusively to Beatrice.

pelling myself unto speech, I asked of him: "What thing
is this, Master, that thou hast spoken thus darkly?" To
the which he made answer in the vulgar tongue: "De-
mand no more than may be useful to thee." Whereupon
I began to discourse with him concerning her salutation
which she had denied me; and when I had questioned
him of the cause, he said these words: "Our Beatrice
hath heard from certain persons, that the lady whom I
named to thee while thou journeyedst full of sighs, is
sorely disquieted by thy solicitations: and therefore this
most gracious creature, who is the enemy of all disquiet,
being fearful of such disquiet, refused to salute thee.
For the which reason (albeit, in very sooth, thy secret
must needs have become known to her by familiar ob-
servation) it is my will that thou compose certain things
in rhyme, in the which thou shalt set forth how strong
a mastership I have obtained over thee, through her;
and how thou wast hers even from thy childhood. Also
do thou call upon him that knoweth these things to bear
witness to them, bidding him to speak with her thereof;
the which I, who am he, will do willingly. And thus she
shall be made to know thy desire; knowing which, she
shall know likewise that they were deceived who spake
of thee to her. And so write these things, that they shall
seem rather to be spoken by a third person; and not
directly by thee to her, which is scarce fitting. After the
which, send them, not without me, where she may have
a chance to hear them; but have them fitted with a
pleasant music, into the which I will pass whensoever it
needeth." With this speech he was away, and my sleep
was broken up. Whereupon, remembering me, I knew
that I had beheld this vision during the ninth hour of
the day; and I resolved that I would make a ditty, be-
fore I left my chamber, according to the words my
master had spoken. And this is the ditty that I made:

Song, 'tis my will that thou do seek out Love,
    And go with him where my dear lady is;
    That so my cause, the which thy harmonies
Do plead, his better speech may clearly prove.

Thou goest, my Song, in such a courteous kind,
    That even companionless
    Thou may'st rely on thyself anywhere.
And yet, an thou wouldst get thee a safe mind,
    First unto Love address
    Thy steps; whose aid, mayhap, 'twere ill to spare:
Seeing that she to whom thou mak'st thy prayer
Is, as I think, ill-minded unto me,
And that if Love do not companion thee,
Thou'lt have perchance small cheer to tell me of.

With a sweet accent, when thou com'st to her
    Begin thou in these words,
    First having craved a gracious audience:
"He who hath sent me as his messenger,
    Lady, thus much records,
    An thou but suffer him, in his defence.
Love, who comes with me, by thine influence
Can make this man do as it liketh him:
Wherefore, if this fault *is* or doth but *seem*
Do thou conceive: for his heart cannot move."

Say to her also: "Lady, his poor heart
    Is so confirm'd in faith
    That all its thoughts are but of serving thee:
'Twas early thine, and could not swerve apart."
    Then, if she wavereth,
    Bid her ask Love, who knows if these things be.
And in the end, beg of her modestly
To pardon so much boldness: saying too:—

"If thou declare his death to be thy due,
  The thing shall come to pass, as doth behove."

Then pray thou of the Master of all ruth,
  Before thou leave her there,
  That he befriend my cause and plead it well.
  "In guerdon of my sweet rhymes and my truth"
  (Entreat him) "stay with her;
  Let not the hope of thy poor servant fail;
  And if with her thy pleading should prevail,
  Let her look on him and give peace to him."
  Gentle my Song, if good to thee it seem,
  Do this: so worship shall be thine and love.

This ditty is divided into three parts. In the first, I tell it whither to go, and I encourage it, that it may go the more confidently, and I tell it whose company to join if it would go with confidence and without any danger. In the second, I say that which it behoves the ditty to set forth. In the third, I give it leave to start when it pleases, recommending its course to the arms of Fortune. The second part begins here, "With a sweet accent"; the third here, "Gentle my Song." Some might contradict me, and say that they understand not whom I address in the second person, seeing that the ditty is merely the very words I am speaking. And therefore I say that this doubt I intend to solve and clear up in this little book itself, at a more difficult passage, and then let him understand who now doubts, or would now contradict as aforesaid.*

XIII

After this vision I have recorded, and having written those words which Love had dictated to me, I began to

---

17. "At a more difficult passage": see footnote 27.

be harassed with many and divers thoughts, by each of which I was sorely tempted; and in especial, there were four among them that left me no rest. The first was this: "Certainly the lordship of Love is good; seeing that it diverts the mind from all mean things." The second was this: "Certainly the lordship of Love is evil; seeing that the more homage his servants pay to him, the more grievous and painful are the torments wherewith he torments them." The third was this: "The name of Love is so sweet in the hearing that it would not seem possible for its effects to be other than sweet; seeing that the name must needs be like unto the thing named: as it is written: 'Names are the consequents of things.'" [18] And the fourth was this: "The lady whom Love hath chosen out to govern thee is not as other ladies, whose hearts are easily moved." And by each one of these thoughts I was so sorely assailed that I was like unto him who doubteth which path to take, and wishing to go, goeth not. And if I bethought myself to seek out some point at the which all these paths might be found to meet, I discerned but one way, and that irked me; to wit, to call upon Pity, and to commend myself unto her. And it was then that, feeling a desire to write somewhat thereof in rhyme, I wrote this sonnet:

All my thoughts always speak to me of Love,
    Yet have between themselves such difference
    That while one bids me bow with mind and sense,
    A second saith, "Go to: look thou above";
The third one, hoping, yields me joy enough;
    And with the last come tears, I scarce know whence:
    All of them craving pity in sore suspense,

---

18. "Names are the consequents of things" (i.e., they share the same nature): a frequent statement in the disputes of the schoolmen and in glosses on the civil law.

Trembling with fears that the heart knoweth of.
And thus, being all unsure which path to take,
  Wishing to speak I know not what to say,
  And lose myself in amorous wanderings:
Until, (my peace with all of them to make,)
  Unto mine enemy I needs must pray,
  My lady Pity, for the help she brings.

*This sonnet may be divided into four parts. In the
first, I say and propound that all my thoughts are con-
cerning Love. In the second, I say that they are diverse,
and I relate their diversity. In the third, I say wherein
they all seem to agree. In the fourth, I say that, wishing
to speak of Love, I know not from which of these
thoughts to take my argument; and that if I would take
it from all, I shall have to call upon mine enemy, my lady
Pity. "Lady" I say as in a scornful mode of speech. The
second begins here, "Yet have between themselves"; the
third, "All of them craving"; the fourth, "And thus."*

XIV

After this battling with many thoughts, it chanced
on a day that my most gracious lady was with a gather-
ing of ladies in a certain place; to the which I was con-
ducted by a friend of mine; he thinking to do me a great
pleasure by showing me the beauty of so many women.
Then I, hardly knowing whereunto he conducted me,
but trusting in him (who yet was leading his friend to
the last verge of life), made question: "To what end are
we come among these ladies?" and he answered: "To
the end that they may be worthily served." And they
were assembled around a gentlewoman who was given
in marriage on that day; the custom of the city being
that these should bear her company when she sat down

for the first time at table in the house of her husband.
Therefore I, as was my friend's pleasure, resolved to
stay with him and do honour to those ladies. But as soon
as I had thus resolved, I began to feel a faintness and a
throbbing at my left side, which soon took possession of
my whole body. Whereupon I remember that I covertly
leaned my back unto a painting that ran round the walls
of that house; and being fearful lest my trembling should
be discerned of them, I lifted mine eyes to look on those
ladies, and then first perceived among them the excel-
lent Beatrice. And when I perceived her, all my senses
were overpowered by the great lordship that Love ob-
tained, finding himself so near unto that most gracious
being, until nothing but the spirits of sight remained to
me; and even these remained driven out of their own
instruments because Love entered into that honoured
place of theirs, that so he might the better behold her.
And although I was other than at first, I grieved for the
spirits so expelled which kept up a sore lament, saying:
"If he had not in this wise thrust us forth, we also shoulc
behold the marvel of this lady." By this, many of her
friends, having discerned my confusion, began to won-
der; and together with herself, kept whispering of me
and mocking me. Whereupon my friend, who knew not
what to conceive, took me by the hands, and drawing
me forth from among them, required to know what ailed
me. Then, having first held me at quiet for a space until
my perceptions were come back to me, I made answer
to my friend: "Of a surety I have now set my feet on
that point of life, beyond the which he must not pass
who would return." Afterwards, leaving him, I went
back to the room where I had wept before; and again
weeping and ashamed, said: "If this lady but knew of
my condition, I do not think that she would thus mock
at me; nay, I am sure that she must needs feel some

pity." And in my weeping I bethought me to write certain words in the which, speaking to her, I should signify the occasion of my disfigurement, telling her also how I knew that she had no knowledge thereof: which, if it were known, I was certain must move others to pity. And then, because I hoped that peradventure it might come into her hearing, I wrote this sonnet:

Even as the others mock, thou mockest me;
    Not dreaming, noble lady, whence it is
    That I am taken with strange semblances,
    Seeing thy face which is so fair to see:
For else, compassion would not suffer thee
    To grieve my heart with such harsh scoffs as these.
    Lo! Love, when thou art present, sits at ease,
    And bears his mastership so mightily,
That all my troubled senses he thrusts out,
    Sorely tormenting some, and slaying some,
    Till none but he is left and has free range
To gaze on thee. This makes my face to change
    Into another's; while I stand all dumb,
    And hear my senses clamour in their rout.

This sonnet I divide not into parts, because a division is only made to open the meaning of the thing divided: and this, as it is sufficiently manifest through the reasons given, has no need of division. True it is that, amid the words whereby is shown the occasion of this sonnet, dubious words are to be found; namely, when I say that Love kills all my spirits, but that the visual remain in life, only outside of their own instruments.[19] And this difficulty it is impossible for any to solve who is not in equal guise liege unto Love; and, to those who are so, that is manifest which would clear up the dubious

---

19. "Their own instruments": the eyes.

words. And therefore it were not well for me to expound
this difficulty, inasmuch as my speaking would be either
fruitless or else superfluous.

XV

A while after this strange disfigurement, I became
possessed with a strong conception which left me but
very seldom, and then to return quickly. And it was this:
"Seeing that thou comest into such scorn by the com-
panionship of this lady, wherefore seekest thou to be-
hold her? If she should ask thee this thing, what answer
couldst thou make unto her? yea, even though thou
wert master of all thy faculties, and in no way hindered
from answering." Unto the which, another very humble
thought said in reply: "If I were master of all my
faculties, and in no way hindered from answering, I
would tell her that no sooner do I image to myself her
marvellous beauty than I am possessed with the desire
to behold her, the which is of so great strength that it
kills and destroys in my memory all those things which
might oppose it; and it is therefore that the great an-
guish I have endured thereby is yet not enough to
restrain me from seeking to behold her." And then,
because of these thoughts, I resolved to write somewhat,
wherein, having pleaded mine excuse, I should tell her
of what I felt in her presence. Whereupon I wrote this
sonnet:

The thoughts are broken in my memory,
 Thou lovely Joy, whene'er I see thy face;
 When thou art near me, Love fills up the space,
 Often repeating, "If death irk thee, fly."
My face shows my heart's colour, verily,
 Which, fainting, seeks for any leaning-place

Till, in the drunken terror of disgrace,
The very stones seem to be shrieking, "Die!"
It were a grievous sin, if one should not
Strive then to comfort my bewilder'd mind
(Though merely with a simple pitying)
For the great anguish which thy scorn has wrought
In the dead sight o' the eyes grown nearly blind,
Which look for death as for a blessed thing.

This sonnet is divided into two parts. In the first, I tell the cause why I abstain not from coming to this lady. In the second, I tell what befalls me through coming to her; and this part begins here, "When thou art near." And also this second part divides into five distinct statements. For, in the first, I say what Love, counselled by Reason, tells me when I am near the lady. In the second, I set forth the state of my heart by the example of the face. In the third, I say how all ground of trust fails me. In the fourth, I say that he sins who shows not pity of me, which would give me some comfort. In the last, I say why people should take pity; namely, for the piteous look which comes into mine eyes; which piteous look is destroyed, that is, appeareth not unto others, through the jeering of this lady, who draws to the like action those who peradventure would see this piteousness. The second part begins here, "My face shows"; the third, "Till, in the drunken terror"; the fourth, "It were a grievous sin"; the fifth, "For the great anguish."

XVI

Thereafter, this sonnet bred in me desire to write down in verse four other things touching my condition, the which things it seemed to me that I had not yet made manifest. The first among these was the grief that possessed me very often, remembering the strangeness which Love wrought in me; the second was, how Love many times assailed me so suddenly and with such strength that I had no other life remaining except a thought which spake of my lady; the third was, how when Love did battle with me in this wise, I would rise up all colourless, if so I might see my lady, conceiving that the sight of her would defend me against the assault of Love, and altogether forgetting that which her presence brought unto me; and the fourth was, how when I saw her, the sight not only defended me not, but took away the little life that remained to me. And I said these four things in a sonnet, which is this:

At whiles (yea oftentimes) I muse over
  The quality of anguish that is mine
  Through Love: then pity makes my voice to pine
  Saying, "Is any else thus, anywhere?"
Love smiteth me, whose strength is ill to bear;
  So that of all my life is left no sign
  Except one thought; and that, because 'tis thine
  Leaves not the body but abideth there.
And then if I, whom other aid forsook,
  Would aid myself, and innocent of art
  Would fain have sight of thee as a last hope,
No sooner do I lift mine eyes to look
  Than the blood seems as shaken from my heart,
  And all my pulses beat at once and stop.

This sonnet is divided into four parts, four things being therein narrated; and as these are set forth above, I only proceed to distinguish the parts by their beginnings. Wherefore I say that the second part begins, "Love smiteth me"; the third, "And then if I"; the fourth, "No sooner do I lift."

XVII

After I had written these last three sonnets, wherein I spake unto my lady, telling her almost the whole of my condition, it seemed to me that I should be silent, having said enough concerning myself. But albeit I spake not to her again, yet it behoved me afterward to write of another matter, more noble than the foregoing.[20] And for that the occasion of what I then wrote may be found pleasant in the hearing, I will relate it as briefly as I may.

XVIII

Through the sore change in mine aspect, the secret of my heart was now understood of many. Which thing being thus, there came a day when certain ladies to whom it was well known (they having been with me at divers times in my trouble) were met together for the pleasure of gentle company. And as I was going that way by chance, (but I think rather by the will of fortune,) I heard one of them call unto me, and she that called was a lady of very sweet speech. And when I had come close up with them, and perceived that they had not among them mine excellent lady, I was reassured; and saluted them, asking of their pleasure. The ladies were many; divers of whom were laughing one to another, while divers gazed at me as though I should speak anon. But when I still spake not, one of them, who before had been talking with another, addressed me by my name, saying, "To what end lovest thou this lady,

20. Here ends the first section of the Vita Nuova, in which Dante's condition is described, and Beatrice is addressed directly. The second section is devoted to praising Beatrice's soul, and the third to her memory.

seeing that thou canst not support her presence? Now tell us this thing, that we may know it: for certainly the end of such a love must be worthy of knowledge." And when she had spoken these words, not she only, but all they that were with her, began to observe me, waiting for my reply. Whereupon, I said thus unto them: "Ladies, the end and aim of my love was but the salutation of that lady of whom I conceive that ye are speaking; wherein alone I found that beatitude which is the goal of desire. And now that it hath pleased her to deny me this, Love, my Master, of his great goodness, hath placed all my beatitude there where my hope will not fail me." Then those ladies began to talk closely together; and as I have seen snow fall among the rain, so was their talk mingled with sighs. But after a little, that lady who had been the first to address me, addressed me again in these words: "We pray thee that thou wilt tell us wherein abideth this thy beatitude." And answering, I said but thus much: "In those words that do praise my lady." To the which she rejoined, "If thy speech were true, those words that thou didst write concerning thy condition would have been written with another intent." Then I, being almost put to shame because of her answer, went out from among them; and as I walked, I said within myself: "Seeing that there is so much beatitude in those words which do praise my lady, wherefore hath my speech of her been different?" And then I resolved that thenceforward I would choose for the theme of my writings only the praise of this most gracious being. But when I had thought exceedingly, it seemed to me that I had taken to myself a theme which was much too lofty, so that I dared not begin; and I remained during several days in the desire of speaking, and the fear of beginning.

XIX

After which it happened, as I passed one day along a path which lay beside a stream of very clear water, that there came upon me a great desire to say somewhat in rhyme; but when I began thinking how I should say it, methought that to speak of her were unseemly, unless I spoke to other ladies in the second person; which is to say, not to *any* other ladies, but only to such as are so called because they are gentle, let alone for mere womanhood. Whereupon I declare that my tongue spake as though by its own impulse, and said, "Ladies that have intelligence in love." [21] These words I laid up in my mind with great gladness, conceiving to take them as my commencement. Wherefore, having returned to the city I spake of, and considered thereof during certain days, I began a poem with this beginning, constructed in the mode which will be seen below in its division. The poem begins here:

Ladies that have intelligence in love,
   Of mine own lady I would speak with you;
   Not that I hope to count her praises through,
   But telling what I may, to ease my mind.
   And I declare that when I speak thereof
   Love sheds such perfect sweetness over me
   That if my courage fail'd not, certainly
   To him my listeners must be all resign'd.
   Wherefore I will not speak in such large kind
   That mine own speech should foil me, which were
      base;

---

21. This famous canzone is quoted and discussed, as the first example of Dante's "sweet new style," in Purg. XXIV, 49-63.

But only will discourse of her high grace
In these poor words, the best that I can find,
With you alone, dear dames and damozels:
'Twere ill to speak thereof with any else.

An Angel, of his blessed knowledge, saith
  To God: "Lord, in the world that Thou hast made,
A miracle in action is display'd
By reason of a soul whose splendors fare
Even hither: and since Heaven requireth
Nought saving her, for her it prayeth Thee,
Thy Saints crying aloud continually."
Yet Pity still defends our earthly share
In that sweet soul; God answering thus the prayer:
"My well-belovèd, suffer that in peace
Your hope remain, while so My pleasure is,
There where one dwells who dreads the loss of her:[22]
And who in Hell unto the doom'd shall say,
'I have look'd on that for which God's chosen pray.'"

My lady is desired in the high Heaven:
  Wherefore, it now behoveth me to tell,
Saying: Let any maid that would be well
Esteem'd keep with her: for as she goes by,
Into foul hearts a deathly chill is driven
By Love, that makes ill thought to perish there;
While any who endures to gaze on her
Must either be made noble, or else die.
When one deserving to be raised so high
Is found, 'tis then her power attains its proof,
Making his heart strong for his soul's behoof
With the full strength of meek humility.

---

22. "One dwells who dreads the loss of her": *Dante himself. It has
been much discussed whether or not the two following lines con-
tain a forecast of the* Commedia.

Also this virtue owns she, by God's will:
Who speaks with her can never come to ill.

Love saith concerning her: "How chanceth it
  That flesh, which is of dust, should be thus pure?"
  Then, gazing always, he makes oath: "Forsure,
  This is a creature of God till now unknown."
  She hath that paleness of the pearl that's fit
  In a fair woman, so much and not more;
  She is as high as Nature's skill can soar;
  Beauty is tried by her comparison.
  Whatever her sweet eyes are turn'd upon,
  Spirits of love do issue thence in flame,
  Which through their eyes who then may look on them
  Pierce to the heart's deep chamber every one.
  And in her smile Love's image you may see;
  Whence none can gaze upon her steadfastly.

Dear Song, I know thou wilt hold gentle speech
  With many ladies, when I send thee forth:
  Wherefore, (being mindful that thou hadst thy birth
  From Love, and art a modest, simple child,)
  Whomso thou meetest, say thou this to each:
  "Give me good speed! To her I wend along
  In whose much strength my weakness is made strong."
  And if, i' the end, thou wouldst not be beguiled
  Of all thy labour, seek not the defiled
  And common sort; but rather choose to be
  Where man and woman dwell in courtesy.
  So to the road thou shalt be reconciled,
  And find the lady, and with the lady, Love.
  Commend thou me to each, as doth behove.

*This poem, that it may be better understood, I will
divide more subtly than the others preceding; and*

*therefore I will make three parts of it. The first part is a
proem to the words following. The second is the matter
treated of. The third is, as it were, a handmaid to the
preceding words. The second begins here, "An Angel";
the third here, "Dear Song, I know." The first part is
divided into four. In the first, I say to whom I mean to
speak of my lady, and wherefore I will so speak. In the
second, I say what she appears to myself to be when I
reflect upon her excellence, and what I would utter if
I lost not courage. In the third, I say what it is I purpose
to speak, so as not to be impeded by faint-heartedness.
In the fourth, repeating to whom I purpose speaking, I
tell the reason why I speak to them. The second begins
here, "And I declare"; the third here, "Wherefore I will
not speak"; the fourth here, "With you alone." Then,
when I say "An Angel," I begin treating of this lady:
and this part is divided into two. In the first, I tell what
is understood of her in heaven. In the second, I tell
what is understood of her on earth: here, "My lady is
desired." This second part is divided into two; for, in
the first, I speak of her as regards the nobleness of her
soul, relating some of her virtues proceeding from her
soul; in the second, I speak of her as regards the noble-
ness of her body, narrating some of her beauties: here,
"Love saith concerning her." This second part is divided
into two; for, in the first, I speak of certain beauties
which belong to the whole person; in the second, I speak
of certain beauties which belong to a distinct part of the
person: here, "Whatever her sweet eyes." This second
part is divided into two; for, in the one, I speak of the
eyes, which are the beginning of love; in the second, I
speak of the mouth, which is the end of love. And, that
every vicious thought may be discarded herefrom, let
the reader remember that it is above written that the
greeting of this lady, which was an act of her mouth,*

was the goal of my desires, while I could receive it. Then, when I say, "Dear Song, I know," I add a stanza as it were handmaid to the others, wherein I say what I desire from this my poem. And because this last part is easy to understand, I trouble not myself with more divisions. I say, indeed, that the further to open the meaning of this poem, more minute divisions ought to be used; but nevertheless he who is not of wit enough to understand it by these which have been already made is welcome to leave it alone; for certes I fear I have communicated its sense to too many by these present divisions, if it so happened that many should hear it.

XX

When this song was a little gone abroad, a certain one of my friends, hearing the same, was pleased to question me, that I should tell him what thing love is; it may be, conceiving from the words thus heard a hope of me beyond my desert. Wherefore I, thinking that after such discourse it were well to say somewhat of the nature of Love, and also in accordance with my friend's desire, proposed to myself to write certain words in the which I should treat of this argument. And the sonnet that I then made is this:

> Love and the gentle heart are one same thing,
>   Even as the wise man in his ditty saith.[23]
>   Each, of itself, would be such life in death
>   As rational soul bereft of reasoning.
> 'Tis Nature makes them when she loves: a king
>   Love is, whose palace where he sojourneth

---

23. "The wise man" is Guido Guinizelli (1230-1276), one of the forerunners of the "sweet new style." "His ditty" is his famous poem Al cor gentil ripara sempre amore ("Unto the gentle heart Love aye repairs").

Is call'd the Heart; there draws he quiet breath
At first, with brief or longer slumbering.
Then beauty seen in virtuous womankind
    Will make the eyes desire, and through the heart
    Send the desiring of the eyes again;
Where often it abides so long enshrined
    That Love at length out of his sleep will start.
    And women feel the same for worthy men.

*This sonnet is divided into two parts. In the first, I
speak of him according to his power. In the second, I
speak of him according as his power translates itself into
act. The second part begins here, "Then beauty seen."
The first is divided into two. In the first, I say in what
subject this power exists. In the second, I say how this
subject and this power are produced together, and how
the one regards the other, as form does matter.*[24] *The
second begins here, "'Tis Nature." Afterwards when I
say, "Then beauty seen in virtuous womankind," I say
how this power translates itself into act; and, first, how
it so translates itself in a man, then how it so translates
itself in a woman: here, "And women feel."*

XXI

Having treated of love in the foregoing, it appeared
to me that I should also say something in praise of my
lady, wherein it might be set forth how love manifested
itself when produced by her; and how not only she
could awaken it where it slept, but where it was not she
could marvellously create it. To the which end I wrote
another sonnet; and it is this:

---

24. Dante here borrows the philosophical language of the schoolmen
to explain how the activity of love (the "power") in its "subject"
(the gentle heart) is awakened by the sight of a beautiful and vir-
tuous human being.

My lady carries love within her eyes;
  All that she looks on is made pleasanter;
  Upon her path men turn to gaze at her;
  He whom she greeteth feels his heart to rise,
And droops his troubled visage, full of sighs,
  And of his evil heart is then aware:
  Hate loves, and pride becomes a worshipper.
O women, help to praise her in somewise.
Humbleness, and the hope that hopeth well,
  By speech of hers into the mind are brought,
  And who beholds is blessed oftenwhiles.
The look she hath when she a little smiles
  Cannot be said, nor holden in the thought;
  'Tis such a new and gracious miracle.

This sonnet has three sections. In the first, I say how this lady brings this power into action by those most noble features, her eyes; and, in the third, I say this same as to that most noble feature, her mouth. And between these two sections is a little section, which asks, as it were, help for the previous section and the subsequent; and it begins here, "O women, help." The third begins here, "Humbleness." The first is divided into three; for, in the first, I say how she with power makes noble that which she looks upon; and this is as much as to say that she brings Love, in power, thither where he is not. In the second, I say how she brings Love, in act, into the hearts of all those whom she sees. In the third, I tell what she afterwards, with virtue, operates upon their hearts. The second begins, "Upon her path"; the third, "He whom she greeteth." Then, when I say, "O women, help," I intimate to whom it is my intention to speak, calling on women to help me to honour her. Then, when I say, "Humbleness," I say that same which is said in the first part, regarding two acts of her mouth,

one whereof is her most sweet speech, and the other her
marvellous smile. Only, I say not of this last how it
operates upon the hearts of others, because memory
cannot retain this smile, nor its operation.

XXII

Not many days after this, (it being the will of the
most High God, who also from Himself put not away
death,) the father of wonderful Beatrice,[25] going out of
this life, passed certainly into glory. Thereby it hap-
pened, as of very sooth it might not be otherwise, that
this lady was made full of the bitterness of grief: seeing
that such a parting is very grievous unto those friends
who are left, and that no other friendship is like to that
between a good parent and a good child; and further-
more considering that this lady was good in the supreme
degree, and her father (as by many it hath been truly
averred) of exceeding goodness. And because it is the
usage of that city that men meet with men in such
a grief, and women with women, certain ladies of
her companionship gathered themselves unto Beatrice,
where she kept alone in her weeping: and as they passed
in and out, I could hear them speak concerning her,
how she wept. At length two of them went by me, who
said: "Certainly she grieveth in such sort that one might
die for pity, beholding her." Then, feeling the tears upon
my face, I put up my hands to hide them: and had it
not been that I hoped to hear more concerning her,
(seeing that where I sat, her friends passed continually
in and out,) I should assuredly have gone thence to be
alone, when I felt the tears come. But as I still sat in
that place, certain ladies again passed near me, who

25. Beatrice's father, *Folco Portinari, a wealthy Florentine, died on
December 31, 1289.*

were saying among themselves: "Which of us shall be joyful any more, who have listened to this lady in her piteous sorrow?" And there were others who said as they went by me: "He that sitteth here could not weep more if he had beheld her as we have beheld her"; and again: "He is so altered that he seemeth not as himself." And still as the ladies passed to and fro, I could hear them speak after this fashion of her and of me. Wherefore afterwards, having considered and perceiving that there was herein matter for poesy, I resolved that I would write certain rhymes in the which should be contained all that those ladies had said. And because I would willingly have spoken to them if it had not been for discreetness, I made in my rhymes as though I had spoken and they had answered me. And therefore I wrote two sonnets; in the first of which I addressed them as I would fain have done; and in the second related their answer, using the speech that I had heard from them, as though it had been spoken unto myself. And the sonnets are these:

You that thus wear a modest countenance
    With lids weigh'd down by the heart's heaviness,
    Whence come you, that among you every face
    Appears the same, for its pale troubled glance?
Have you beheld my lady's face, perchance,
    Bow'd with the grief that Love makes full of grace?
    Say now, "This thing is thus"; as my heart says,
    Marking your grave and sorrowful advance.
And if indeed you come from where she sighs
    And mourns, may it please you (for his heart's relief)
    To tell how it fares with her unto him
Who knows that you have wept, seeing your eyes,
    And is so grieved with looking on your grief
    That his heart trembles and his sight grows dim.

This sonnet is divided into two parts. In the first, I call and ask these ladies whether they come from her, telling them that I think they do, because they return the nobler. In the second, I pray them to tell me of her: and the second begins here, "And if indeed."

Canst thou indeed be he that still would sing
   Of our dear lady unto none but us?
   For though thy voice confirms that it is thus,
   Thy visage might another witness bring.
And wherefore is thy grief so sore a thing
   That grieving thou mak'st others dolorous?
   Hast thou too seen her weep, that thou from us
   Canst not conceal thine inward sorrowing?
Nay, leave our woe to us: let us alone:
   'Twere sin if one should strive to soothe our woe,
   For in her weeping we have heard her speak:
Also her look 's so full of her heart's moan
   That they who should behold her, looking so,
   Must fall aswoon, feeling all life grow weak.

This sonnet has four parts, as the ladies in whose person I reply had four forms of answer. And, because these are sufficiently shown above, I stay not to explain the purport of the parts, and therefore I only discriminate them. The second begins here, "And wherefore is thy grief"; the third here, "Nay, leave our woe"; the fourth, "Also her look."

XXIII

A few days after this, my body became afflicted with a painful infirmity, whereby I suffered bitter anguish for many days, which at last brought me unto such weakness that I could no longer move. And I remember that

on the ninth day, being overcome with intolerable pain,
a thought came into my mind concerning my lady: but
when it had a little nourished this thought, my mind
returned to its brooding over mine enfeebled body. And
then perceiving how frail a thing life is, even though
health keep with it, the matter seemed to me so pitiful
that I could not choose but weep; and weeping I said
within myself: "Certainly it must some time come to
pass that the very gentle Beatrice will die." Then, feel-
ing bewildered, I closed mine eyes; and my brain began
to be in travail as the brain of one frantic, and to have
such imaginations as here follow. And at the first, it
seemed to me that I saw certain faces of women with
their hair loosened, which called out to me, "Thou shalt
surely die"; after the which, other terrible and unknown
appearances said unto me, "Thou art dead." At length,
as my phantasy held on in its wanderings, I came to be
I knew not where, and to behold a throng of dishevelled
ladies wonderfully sad, who kept going hither and thither
weeping. Then the sun went out, so that the stars
showed themselves, and they were of such a colour that
I knew they must be weeping: and it seemed to me that
the birds fell dead out of the sky, and that there were
great earthquakes. With that, while I wondered in my
trance, and was filled with a grievous fear, I conceived
that a certain friend came unto me and said: "Hast thou
not heard? She that was thine excellent lady hath been
taken out of life." Then I began to weep very piteously;
and not only in mine imagination, but with mine eyes,
which were wet with tears. And I seemed to look to-
wards Heaven, and to behold a multitude of angels
who were returning upwards, having before them an ex-
ceedingly white cloud: and these angels were singing
together gloriously, and the words of their song were
these: "Hosanna in the highest": and there was no more

that I heard. Then my heart that was so full of love said unto me: "It is true that our lady lieth dead": and it seemed to me that I went to look upon the body wherein that blessed and most noble spirit had had its abiding-place. And so strong was this idle imagining, that it made me to behold my lady in death; whose head certain ladies seemed to be covering with a white veil; and who was so humble of her aspect that it was as though she had said, "I have attained to look on the beginning of peace." And therewithal I came unto such humility by the light of her, that I cried out upon Death, saying: "Now come unto me, and be not bitter against me any longer: surely, there where thou hast been, thou hast learned gentleness. Wherefore come now unto me who do greatly desire thee: seest thou not that I wear thy colour already?" And when I had seen all those offices performed that are fitting to be done unto the dead, it seemed to me that I went back unto mine own chamber, and looked up towards heaven. And so strong was my phantasy, that I wept again in very truth, and said with my true voice: "O excellent soul! how blessed is that that now looketh upon thee!" And as I said these words, with a painful anguish of sobbing and another prayer unto Death, a young and gentle lady, who had been standing beside me where I lay, conceiving that I wept and cried out because of the pain of mine infirmity, was taken with trembling and began to shed tears. Whereby other ladies, who were about the room, becoming aware of my discomfort by reason of the moan that she made, (who indeed was of my very near kindred,) led her away from where I was, and then set themselves to awaken me, thinking that I dreamed, and saying: "Sleep no longer, and be not disquieted." Then, by their words, this strong imagination was brought suddenly to an end, at the moment that I was about to say, "O Bea-

trice! peace be with thee!" And already I had said, "O
Beatrice!" when being aroused, I opened mine eyes, and
knew that it had been a deception. But albeit I had in-
deed uttered her name, yet my voice was so broken with
sobs, that it was not understood by these ladies; so that
in spite of the sore shame that I felt, I turned towards
them by Love's counselling. And when they beheld me,
they began to say, "He seemeth as one dead," and to
whisper among themselves, "Let us strive if we may not
comfort him." Whereupon they spake to me many sooth-
ing words, and questioned me moreover touching the
cause of my fear. Then I, being somewhat reassured,
and having perceived that it was a mere phantasy, said
unto them, "This thing it was that made me afeard";
and told them of all that I had seen, from the beginning
even unto the end, but without once speaking the name
of my lady. Also, after I had recovered from my sick-
ness, I bethought me to write these things in rhyme;
deeming it a lovely thing to be known. Whereof I wrote
this poem:

A very pitiful lady, very young,
   Exceeding rich in human sympathies,
   Stood by, what time I clamour'd upon Death;
   And at the wild words wandering on my tongue
   And at the piteous look within mine eyes
   She was affrighted, that sobs choked her breath.
   So by her weeping where I lay beneath,
   Some other gentle ladies came to know
   My state, and made her go:
   Afterward, bending themselves over me,
   One said, "Awaken thee!"
   And one, "What thing thy sleep disquieteth?"
   With that, my soul woke up from its eclipse,
   The while my lady's name rose to my lips:

But utter'd in a voice so sob-broken,
  So feeble with the agony of tears,
  That I alone might hear it in my heart;
  And though that look was on my visage then
  Which he who is ashamed so plainly wears,
  Love made that I through shame held not apart,
  But gazed upon them. And my hue was such
  That they look'd at each other and thought of death;
  Saying under their breath
  Most tenderly, "Oh, let us comfort him":
  Then unto me: "What dream
  Was thine, that it hath shaken thee so much?"
  And when I was a little comforted,
  "This, ladies, was the dream I dreamt," I said.

"I was a-thinking how life fails with us
  Suddenly after such a little while;
  When Love sobb'd in my heart, which is his home.
  Whereby my spirit wax'd so dolorous
  That in myself I said, with sick recoil:
  'Yea, to my lady too this Death must come.'
  And therewithal such a bewilderment
  Possess'd me, that I shut mine eyes for peace;
  And in my brain did cease
  Order of thought, and every healthful thing.
  Afterwards, wandering
  Amid a swarm of doubts that came and went,
  Some certain women's faces hurried by,
  And shriek'd to me, 'Thou too shalt die, shalt die!'

"Then saw I many broken hinted sights
  In the uncertain state I stepp'd into.
  Meseem'd to be I know not in what place,
  Where ladies through the street, like mournful lights,
  Ran with loose hair, and eyes that frighten'd you

By their own terror, and a pale amaze:
The while, little by little, as I thought,
The sun ceased, and the stars began to gather,
And each wept at the other;
And birds dropp'd in mid-flight out of the sky
And earth shook suddenly;
And I was 'ware of one, hoarse and tired out,
Who ask'd of me: 'Hast thou not heard it said? . . .
Thy lady, she that was so fair, is dead.'

"Then lifting up mine eyes, as the tears came,
  I saw the Angels, like a rain of manna,
  In a long flight flying back heavenward;
Having a little cloud in front of them,
After the which they went and said, 'Hosanna!'
And if they had said more, you should have heard.
Then Love spoke thus: 'Now all shall be made clear:
Come and behold our lady where she lies.'
These idle phantasies
Then carried me to see my lady dead:
  And standing at her head
  Her ladies put a white veil over her;
And with her was such very humbleness
That she appeared to say, 'I am at peace.'

"And I became so humble in my grief,
  Seeing in her such deep humility,
  That I said: 'Death, I hold thee passing good
Henceforth, and a most gentle sweet relief,
Since my dear love has chosen to dwell with thee:
Pity, not hate, is thine, well understood.
Lo! I do so desire to see thy face
That I am like as one who nears the tomb;
  My soul entreats thee, Come.'
Then I departed, having made my moan;

And when I was alone
I said, and cast my eyes to the High Place:
'Blessed is he, fair soul, who meets thy glance!'
. . . . Just then you woke me, of your complaisaùnce."

This poem has two parts. In the first, speaking to a person undefined, I tell how I was aroused from a vain phantasy by certain ladies, and how I promised them to tell what it was. In the second, I say how I told them. The second part begins here, "I was a-thinking." The first part divides into two. In the first, I tell that which certain ladies, and which one singly, did and said because of my phantasy, before I had returned into my right senses. In the second, I tell what these ladies said to me after I had left off this wandering: and it begins here, "But uttered in a voice." Then, when I say, "I was a-thinking," I say how I told them this my imagination; and concerning this I have two parts. In the first, I tell, in order, this imagination. In the second, saying at what time they called me, I covertly thank them: and this part begins here, "Just then you woke me."

XXIV

After this empty imagining, it happened on a day, as I sat thoughtful, that I was taken with such a strong trembling at the heart, that it could not have been otherwise in the presence of my lady. Whereupon I perceived that there was an appearance of Love beside me, and I seemed to see him coming from my lady; and he said, not aloud, but within my heart: "Now take heed that thou bless the day when I entered into thee; for it is fitting that thou shouldst do so." And with that my heart was so full of gladness, that I could hardly believe it to be of very truth mine own heart and not another. A short while after these words which my heart spoke to me with the tongue of Love, I saw coming towards me a certain lady who was very famous for her beauty, and of whom that friend whom I have already called the first among my friends had long been enamoured.[26] This lady's right name was Joan; but because of her comeliness (or at least it was so imagined) she was called of many *Primavera* (Spring), and went by that name among them. Then looking again, I perceived that the most noble Beatrice followed after her. And when both these ladies had passed by me, it seemed to me that Love spake again in my heart, saying: "She that came first was called Spring, only because of that which was to happen on this day. And it was I myself who caused that name to be given her; seeing that as the Spring cometh first in the year, so should she come first on this day, when Beatrice was to show herself after the vision of her servant. And even if thou go about to consider her right name, it is also as one should say, 'She shall come first'; inasmuch as her name, Joan, is taken from that John who went before the True Light, saying: 'I am the voice of one crying in the wilderness: Prepare ye the way of the Lord.' " And also it seemed to me that he added other words, to wit: "He who should inquire delicately touching this matter, could not but call Beatrice by mine own name, which is to say, Love; beholding her so like unto me." Then I, having thought of this, imagined to write it with rhymes and send it unto my chief friend; but setting aside certain words which seemed proper to be set aside, because I believed that his heart still regarded the beauty of her that was called Spring. And I wrote this sonnet:

---

26. The friend is Guido Cavalcanti.

I felt a spirit of love begin to stir
  Within my heart, long time unfelt till then;
  And saw Love coming towards me, fair and fain,
  (That I scarce knew him for his joyful cheer,)
Saying, "Be now indeed my worshipper!"
  And in his speech he laugh'd and laugh'd again.
  Then, while it was his pleasure to remain,
  I chanced to look the way he had drawn near,
And saw the Ladies Joan and Beatrice
  Approach me, this the other following,
  One and a second marvel instantly.
And even as now my memory speaketh this,
  Love spake it then: "The first it christen'd Spring;
  The second Love, she is so like to me."

This sonnet has many parts: whereof the first tells how I felt awakened within my heart the accustomed tremor, and how it seemed that Love appeared to me joyful from afar. The second says how it appeared to me that Love spake within my heart, and what was his aspect. The third tells how, after he had in such wise been with me a space, I saw and heard certain things. The second part begins here, "Saying, 'Be now'"; the third here, "Then, while it was his pleasure." The third part divides into two. In the first, I say what I saw. In the second, I say what I heard: and it begins here, "Love spake it then."

XXV[27]

It might be here objected unto me, (and even by one worthy of controversy,) that I have spoken of Love as

---

27. This chapter, of great interest as an early specimen of literary criticism, is poetically a digression. Dante maintains that the poetic personification of Love is permissible, so long as the underlying meaning is not obscured.

though it were a thing outward and visible: not only a
spiritual essence, but as a bodily substance also. The
which thing, in absolute truth, is a fallacy; Love not be-
ing of itself a substance, but an accident of substance.
Yet that I speak of Love as though it were a thing tan-
gible and even human, appears by three things which
I say thereof. And firstly, I say that I perceived Love
coming towards me; whereby, seeing that *to come* be-
speaks locomotion, and seeing also how philosophy
teacheth us that none but a corporeal substance hath
locomotion, it seemeth that I speak of Love as of a
corporeal substance. And secondly, I say that Love
smiled; and thirdly, that Love spake; faculties (and
especially the risible faculty) which appear proper unto
man: whereby it further seemeth that I speak of Love
as of a man. Now that this matter may be explained, (as
is fitting,) it must first be remembered that anciently
they who wrote poems of Love wrote not in the vulgar
tongue, but rather certain poets in the Latin tongue. I
mean, among us, although perchance the same may
have been among others, and although likewise, as
among the Greeks, they were not writers of spoken lan-
guage, but men of letters, treated of these things. And
indeed it is not a great number of years since poetry
began to be made in the vulgar tongue; the writing of
rhymes in spoken language corresponding to the writing
in metre of Latin verse, by a certain analogy. And I say
that it is but a little while, because if we examine the
language of *oco* and the language of *sì*[28] we shall not
find in those tongues any written thing of an earlier date
than the last hundred and fifty years. Also the reason
why certain of a very mean sort obtained at the first
some fame as poets is, that before them no man had
written verses in the language of *sì*: and of these, the

---

28. The Provençal and the Italian languages.

first was moved to the writing of such verses by the wish
to make himself understood of a certain lady, unto
whom Latin poetry was difficult. This thing is against
such as rhyme concerning other matters than love; that
mode of speech having been first used for the expression
of love alone. Wherefore seeing that poets have a li-
cence allowed them that is not allowed unto the writers
of prose, and seeing also that they who write in rhyme
are simply poets in the vulgar tongue, it becomes fitting
and reasonable that a larger licence should be given to
these than to other modern writers; and that any meta-
phor or rhetorical similitude which is permitted unto
poets, should also be counted not unseemly in the
rhymers of the vulgar tongue. Thus, if we perceive that
the former have caused inanimate things to speak as
though they had sense and reason, and to discourse one
with another; yea, and not only actual things, but such
also as have no real existence, (seeing that they have
made things which are not, to speak; and oftentimes
written of those which are merely accidents as though
they were substances and things human;) it should
therefore be permitted to the latter to do the like; which
is to say, not inconsiderately, but with such sufficient
motive as may afterwards be set forth in prose. That
the Latin poets have done thus, appears through Virgil,
where he saith that Juno (to wit, a goddess hostile to
the Trojans) spake unto Æolus, master of the Winds;
as it is written in the first book of the Æneid, "*Æole,
namque tibi*" etc.; and that this master of the Winds
made reply: "*Tuus, o regina, quid optes Explorare la-
bor; mihi iussa capessere fas est.*" And through the
same poet, the inanimate thing speaketh unto the ani-
mate, in the third book of the Æneid, where it is writ-
ten: "*Dardanidæ duri*" etc. With Lucan, the animate

thing speaketh to the inanimate; as thus: *"Multum, Roma, tamen debes civilibus armis."* In Horace man is made to speak to his own intelligence as unto another person; (and not only hath Horace done this, but herein he followeth the excellent Homer,) as thus in his Poetics: *"Dic mihi, Musa, virum"* etc. Through Ovid, Love speaketh as a human creature in the beginning of his discourse *De Remediis Amoris,* as thus: *"Bella mihi, video, bella parantur, ait."* By which ensamples this thing shall be made manifest unto such as may be offended at any part of this my book. And lest some of the common sort should be moved to jeering hereat, I will here add, that neither did these ancient poets speak thus without consideration, nor should they who are makers of rhyme in our day write after the same fashion, having no reason in what they write; for it were a shameful thing if one should rhyme under the semblance of metaphor or rhetorical similitude, and afterwards, being questioned thereof, should be unable to rid his words of such semblance, unto their right understanding. Of whom, (to wit, of such as rhyme thus foolishly,) myself and the first among my friends do know many.

XXVI

But returning to the matter of my discourse. This excellent lady, of whom I spake in what hath gone before, came at last into such favour with all men, that when she passed anywhere folk ran to behold her; which thing was a deep joy to me: and when she drew near unto any, so much truth and simpleness entered into his heart, that he dared neither to lift his eyes nor to return her salutation: and unto this, many who have felt it can bear witness. She went along crowned and clothed with humility, showing no whit of pride in all that she heard and saw: and when she had gone by, it was said of many, "This is not a woman, but one of the beautiful angels of Heaven!" and there were some that said: "This is surely a miracle; blessed be the Lord, who hath power to work thus marvellously." I say, of very sooth, that she showed herself so gentle and so full of all perfection, that she bred in those who looked upon her a soothing quiet beyond any speech; neither could any look upon her without sighing immediately. These things, and things yet more wonderful, were brought to pass through her miraculous virtue. Wherefore I, considering thereof and wishing to resume the endless tale of her praises, resolved to write somewhat wherein I might dwell on her surpassing influence; to the end that not only they who had beheld her, but others also, might know as much concerning her as words could give to the understanding. And it was then that I wrote this sonnet:

My lady looks so gentle and so pure
  When yielding salutation by the way,
   That the tongue trembles and has nought to say,
   And the eyes, which fain would see, may not endure.
And still, amid the praise she hears secure,
  She walks with humbleness for her array;
  Seeming a creature sent from Heaven to stay
  On earth, and show a miracle made sure.
She is so pleasant in the eyes of men
  That through the sight the inmost heart doth gain
  A sweetness which needs proof to know it by:
And from between her lips there seems to move
  A soothing spirit that is full of love,
  Saying for ever to the soul, "O sigh!"

This sonnet is so easy to understand, from what is afore narrated, that it needs no division: and therefore, leaving it,

XXVII

I say also that this excellent lady came into such favour with all men, that not only she herself was honoured and commended; but through her companionship, honour and commendation came unto others. Wherefore I, perceiving this and wishing that it should also be made manifest to those that beheld it not, wrote the sonnet here following; wherein is signified the power which her virtue had upon other ladies:

For certain he hath seen all perfectness
  Who among other ladies hath seen mine:
  They that go with her humbly should combine
  To thank their God for such peculiar grace.
So perfect is the beauty of her face
  That it begets in no wise any sign
  Of envy, but draws round her a clear line
  Of love, and blessed faith, and gentleness.
Merely the sight of her makes all things bow:
  Not she herself alone is holier
  Than all; but hers, through her, are raised above.
From all her acts such lovely graces flow
  That truly one may never think of her
  Without a passion of exceeding love.

This sonnet has three parts. In the first, I say in what company this lady appeared most wondrous. In the second, I say how gracious was her society. In the third, I tell of the things which she, with power, worked upon others. The second begins here, "They that go with

her"; the third here, "So perfect." This last part divides
into three. In the first, I tell what she operated upon
women, that is, by their own faculties. In the second,
I tell what she operated in them through others. In the
third, I say how she not only operated in women, but in
all people; and not only while herself present, but, by
memory of her, operated wondrously. The second be-
gins here, "Merely the sight"; the third here, "From all
her acts."

XXVIII

Thereafter on a day, I began to consider that which
I had said of my lady: to wit, in these two sonnets afore-
gone: and becoming aware that I had not spoken of
her immediate effect on me at that especial time, it
seemed to me that I had spoken defectively. Where-
upon I resolved to write somewhat of the manner
wherein I was then subject to her influence, and of what
her influence then was. And conceiving that I should
not be able to say these things in the small compass
of a sonnet, I began therefore a poem with this begin-
ning:

Love hath so long possess'd me for his own
    And made his lordship so familiar
    That he, who at first irk'd me, is now grown
    Unto my heart as its best secrets are.
    And thus, when he in such sore wise doth mar
    My life that all its strength seems gone from it,
    Mine inmost being then feels thoroughly quit
    Of anguish, and all evil keeps afar.
    Love also gathers to such power in me
    That my sighs speak, each one a grievous thing.
    Always soliciting
    My lady's salutation piteously.

Whenever she beholds me, it is so,
Who is more sweet than any words can show.

XXIX

"How doth the city sit solitary, that was full of people! how is she become a widow!" [29]

I was still occupied with this poem, (having composed thereof only the above-written stanza,) when the Lord God of justice called my most gracious lady unto Himself, that she might be glorious under the banner of that blessed Queen Mary, whose name had always a deep reverence in the words of holy Beatrice. And because haply it might be found good that I should say somewhat concerning her departure, I will herein declare what are the reasons which make that I shall not do so. And the reasons are three. The first is, that such matter belongeth not of right to the present argument, if one consider the opening of this little book. The second is, that even though the present argument required it, my pen doth not suffice to write in a fit manner of this thing. And the third is, that were it both possible and of absolute necessity, it would still be unseemly for me to speak thereof, seeing that thereby it must behove me to speak also mine own praises: a thing that in whosoever doeth it is worthy of blame. For the which reasons, I will leave this matter to be treated of by some other than myself.[30] Nevertheless, as the number nine, which number hath often had mention in what hath gone before, (and not, as it might appear, without reason,) seems also to have borne a part in the manner of her death: it is therefore right that I should say somewhat

---

29. *Lamentations of Jeremiah*, 1:1.
30. *Dante may be referring here to a canzone on the death of Beatrice by Cino da Pistoia.*

thereof. And for this cause, having first said what was
the part it bore herein, I will afterwards point out a
reason which made that this number was so closely
allied unto my lady.

XXX

I say, then, that according to the division of time in
Italy,[31] her most noble spirit departed from among us in
the first hour of the ninth day of the month; and accord-
ing to the division of time in Syria, in the ninth month
of the year: seeing that Tismim, which with us is Octo-
ber, is there the first month. Also she was taken from
among us in that year of our reckoning (to wit, of the
years of our Lord) in which the perfect number was
nine times multiplied within that century wherein she
was born into the world: which is to say, the thirteenth
century of Christians. And touching the reason why this
number was so closely allied unto her, it may peradven-
ture be this. According to Ptolemy, (and also to the
Christian verity,) the revolving heavens are nine; and
according to the common opinion among astrologers,
these nine heavens together have influence over the
earth. Wherefore it would appear that this number was
thus allied unto her for the purpose of signifying that,
at her birth, all these nine heavens were at perfect
unity with each other as to their influence. This is one
reason that may be brought: but more narrowly con-
sidering, and according to the infallible truth, this num-
ber was her own self: that is to say by similitude. As

---

31. *"In Italy." Here Rossetti adopted an incorrect reading. Read:
"In Arabia."—In this chapter Dante has recourse to three differ-
ent calendars in order to trace the mystical number nine in the
date of Beatrice's death. (She actually died not on June 9 but on
June 8, 1290.)*

thus. The number three is the root of the number nine;
seeing that without the interposition of any other num-
ber, being multiplied merely by itself, it produceth nine,
as we manifestly perceive that three times three are
nine. Thus, three being of itself the efficient of nine, and
the Great Efficient of Miracles being of Himself Three
Persons (to wit: the Father, the Son, and the Holy
Spirit), which, being Three, are also One:—this lady
was accompanied by the number nine to the end that
men might clearly perceive her to be a nine, that is, a
miracle, whose only root is the Holy Trinity. It may be
that a more subtile person would find for this thing a
reason of greater subtilty: but such is the reason that I
find, and that liketh me best.

XXXI

After this most gracious creature had gone out from
among us, the whole city came to be as it were widowed
and despoiled of all dignity. Then I, left mourning in
this desolate city, wrote unto the principal persons
thereof, in an epistle, concerning its condition; taking
for my commencement those words of Jeremias: "How
doth the city sit solitary!" And I make mention of this,
that none may marvel wherefore I set down these words
before, in beginning to treat of her death. Also if any
should blame me, in that I do not transcribe that epistle
whereof I have spoken, I will make it mine excuse that
I began this little book with the intent that it should
be written altogether in the vulgar tongue; wherefore,
seeing that the epistle I speak of is in Latin, it belongeth
not to mine undertaking: more especially as I know that
my chief friend, for whom I write this book, wished
also that the whole of it should be in the vulgar tongue.

XXXII

When mine eyes had wept for some while, until they were so weary with weeping that I could no longer through them give ease to my sorrow, I bethought me that a few mournful words might stand me instead of tears. And therefore I proposed to make a poem, that weeping I might speak therein of her for whom so much sorrow had destroyed my spirit; and then I began "The eyes that weep."

That this poem may seem to remain the more widowed at its close, I will divide it before writing it; and this method I will observe henceforward. I say that this poor little poem has three parts. The first is a prelude. In the second, I speak of her. In the third, I speak pitifully to the poem. The second begins here, "Beatrice is gone up"; the third here, "Weep, pitiful Song of mine." The first divides into three. In the first, I say what moves me to speak. In the second, I say to whom I mean to speak. In the third, I say of whom I mean to speak. The second begins here, "And because often, thinking"; the third here, "And I will say." Then, when I say, "Beatrice is gone up," I speak of her; and concerning this I have two parts. First, I tell the cause why she was taken away from us: afterwards, I say how one weeps her parting; and this part commences here, "Wonderfully." This part divides into three. In the first, I say who it is that weeps her not. In the second, I say who it is that doth weep her. In the third, I speak of my condition. The second begins here, "But sighing comes, and grief"; the third, "With sighs." Then, when I say, "Weep, pitiful Song of mine," I speak to this my song, telling it what ladies to go to, and stay with.

The eyes that weep for pity of the heart
    Have wept so long that their grief languisheth
    And they have no more tears to weep withal:
    And now, if I would ease me of a part
    Of what, little by little, leads to death,
    It must be done by speech, or not at all.
    And because often, thinking, I recall
    How it was pleasant, ere she went afar,
    To talk of her with you, kind damozels,
    I talk with no one else,
    But only with such hearts as women's are.
    And I will say—still sobbing as speech fails—
    That she hath gone to Heaven suddenly,
    And hath left Love below, to mourn with me.

Beatrice is gone up into high Heaven,
    The kingdom where the angels are at peace;
    And lives with them; and to her friends is dead.
    Not by the frost of winter was she driven
    Away, like others; nor by summer-heats;
    But through a perfect gentleness, instead.
    For from the lamp of her meek lowlihead
    Such an exceeding glory went up hence
    That it woke wonder in the Eternal Sire,
    Until a sweet desire
    Enter'd Him for that lovely excellence,
    So that He bade her to Himself aspire:
    Counting this weary and most evil place
    Unworthy of a thing so full of grace.

Wonderfully out of the beautiful form
    Soar'd her clear spirit, waxing glad the while;
    And is in its first home, there where it is.
    Who speaks thereof, and feels not the tears warm

Upon his face, must have become so vile
As to be dead to all sweet sympathies.
Out upon him! an abject wretch like this
May not imagine anything of her—
He needs no bitter tears for his relief.
But sighing comes, and grief,
And the desire to find no comforter,
(Save only Death, who makes all sorrow brief,)
To him who for a while turns in his thought
How she hath been among us, and is not.

With sighs my bosom always laboureth
On thinking, as I do continually,
Of her for whom my heart now breaks apace;
And very often when I think of death,
Such a great inward longing comes to me
That it will change the colour of my face;
And, if the idea settles in its place,
All my limbs shake as with an ague-fit;
Till, starting up in wild bewilderment,
I do become so shent
That I go forth, lest folk misdoubt of it.
Afterward, calling with a sore lament
On Beatrice, I ask, "Canst thou be dead?"
And calling on her, I am comforted.

Grief with its tears, and anguish with its sighs
Come to me now whene'er I am alone;
So that I think the sight of me gives pain.
And what my life hath been, that living dies,
Since for my lady the New Birth's begun,
I have not any language to explain.
And so, dear ladies, though my heart were fain,
I scarce could tell indeed how I am thus.
All joy is with my bitter life at war;

Yea, I am fallen so far
That all men seem to say, "Go out from us,"
Eyeing my cold white lips, how dead they are.
But she, though I be bow'd unto the dust,
Watches me; and will guerdon me, I trust.

Weep, pitiful Song of mine, upon thy way,
  To the dames going, and the damozels,
  For whom, and for none else,
Thy sisters[32] have made music many a day.
Thou, that art very sad and not as they,
  Go dwell thou with them as a mourner dwells.

XXXIII

After I had written this poem, I received the visit
of a friend [33] whom I counted as second unto me in the
degrees of friendship, and who, moreover, had been
united by the nearest kindred to that most gracious
creature. And when we had a little spoken together, he
began to solicit me that I would write somewhat in
memory of a lady who had died; and he disguised his
speech, so as to seem to be speaking of another who was
but lately dead: wherefore I, perceiving that his speech
was of none other than that blessed one herself, told
him that it should be done as he required. Then after-
wards, having thought thereof, I imagined to give vent
in a sonnet to some part of my hidden lamentations: but
in such sort that it might seem to be spoken by this
friend of mine, to whom I was to give it. And the sonnet
saith thus: "Stay now with me," etc.

This sonnet has two parts. In the first, I call the Faith-

---

32. "Thy sisters": other poems of analogous subject.
33. Probably Manetto Portinari, one of the five brothers of Bea-
    trice.

*ful of Love to hear me. In the second, I relate my miser-
able condition. The second begins here, "Mark how they
force."*

Stay now with me, and listen to my sighs,
　　Ye piteous hearts, as pity bids ye do.
　　Mark how they force their way out and press through;
　　If they be once pent up, the whole life dies.
Seeing that now indeed my weary eyes
　　Oftener refuse than I can tell to you,
　　(Even though my endless grief is ever new,)
　　To weep, and let the smother'd anguish rise.
Also in sighing ye shall hear me call
　　On her whose blessed presence doth enrich
　　The only home that well befitteth her:
And ye shall hear a bitter scorn of all
　　Sent from the inmost of my spirit in speech
　　That mourns its joy and its joy's minister.

XXXIV

But when I had written this sonnet, bethinking me
who he was to whom I was to give it, that it might ap-
pear to be his speech, it seemed to me that this was but
a poor and barren gift for one of her so near kindred.
Wherefore, before giving him this sonnet, I wrote two
stanzas of a poem: the first being written in very sooth
as though it were spoken by him, but the other being
mine own speech, albeit, unto one who should not look
closely, they would both seem to be said by the same
person. Nevertheless, looking closely, one must perceive
that it is not so, inasmuch as one does not call this most
gracious creature *his lady*, and the other does, as is
manifestly apparent. And I gave the poem and the son-

net unto my friend, saying that I had made them only for him.

The poem begins, "Whatever while," and has two parts. In the first, that is, in the first stanza, this my dear friend, her kinsman, laments. In the second, I lament; that is, in the other stanza, which begins, "For ever." And thus it appears that in this poem two persons lament, of whom one laments as a brother, the other as a servant.

Whatever while the thought comes over me
  That I may not again
  Behold that lady whom I mourn for now,
  About my heart my mind brings constantly
  So much of extreme pain
  That I say: "Soul of mine, why stayest thou?
  Truly the anguish, Soul, that we must bow
  Beneath, until we win out of this life,
  Gives me full oft a fear that trembleth:
  So that I call on Death
  Even as on Sleep one calleth after strife,
  Saying: 'Come unto me. Life showeth grim
  And bare; and if one dies, I envy him.' "

For ever, among all my sighs which burn,
  There is a piteous speech
  That clamours upon Death continually:
  Yea, unto him doth my whole spirit turn
  Since first his hand did reach
  My lady's life with most foul cruelty.
  But from the height of woman's fairness, she,
  Going up from us with the joy we had,
  Grew perfectly and spiritually fair;
  That so she spreads even there

A light of Love which makes the Angels glad,
And even unto their subtle minds can bring
A certain awe of profound marvelling.

XXXV

On that day which fulfilled the year since my lady
had been made of the citizens of eternal life, remember-
ing me of her as I sat alone, I betook myself to draw the
resemblance of an angel upon certain tablets.[34] And
while I did thus, chancing to turn my head, I perceived
that some were standing beside me to whom I should
have given courteous welcome, and that they were ob-
serving what I did: also I learned afterwards that they
had been there a while before I perceived them. Per-
ceiving whom, I arose for salutation, and said: "Another
was with me." Afterwards, when they had left me, I set
myself again to mine occupation, to wit, to the drawing
figures of angels: in doing which, I conceived to write
of this matter in rhyme, as for her anniversary, and to
address my rhymes unto those who had just left me. It
was then that I wrote the sonnet which saith, "That
lady": and as this sonnet hath two commencements, it
behoveth me to divide it with both of them here.

*I say that, according to the first, this sonnet has three
parts. In the first, I say that this lady was then in my
memory. In the second, I tell what Love therefore did
with me. In the third, I speak of the effects of Love.
The second begins here, "Love, knowing"; the third
here, "Forth went they." This part divides into two. In
the one, I say that all my sighs issued speaking. In the
other, I say how some spoke certain words different
from the others. The second begins here, "And still." In*

---

34. Robert Browning's poem "One Word More" is based on this
incident.

this same manner is it divided with the other begin-
ning, save that, in the first part, I tell when this lady
had thus come into my mind, and this I say not in the
other.

First Commencement

That lady of all gentle memories
    Had lighted on my soul;—whose new abode
    Lies now, as it was well ordain'd of God,
    Among the poor in heart, where Mary is.

Second Commencement

That lady of all gentle memories
    Had lighted on my soul;—for whose sake flow'd
    The tears of Love; in whom the power abode
    Which led you to observe while I did this.
Love, knowing that dear image to be his,
    Woke up within the sick heart sorrow-bow'd,
    Unto the sighs which are its weary load,
    Saying, "Go forth." And they went forth, I wis;
Forth went they from my breast that throbb'd and
      ached;
    With such a pang as oftentimes will bathe
    Mine eyes with tears when I am left alone.
And still those sighs which drew the heaviest breath
    Came whispering thus: "O noble intellect!
    It is a year to-day that thou art gone."

XXXVI

Then, having sat for some space sorely in thought
because of the time that was now past, I was so filled
with dolorous imaginings that it became outwardly
manifest in mine altered countenance. Whereupon, feel-

ing this and being in dread lest any should have seen
me, I lifted mine eyes to look; and then perceived a
young and very beautiful lady, who was gazing upon
me from a window with a gaze full of pity, so that the
very sum of pity appeared gathered together in her.[35]
And seeing that unhappy persons, when they beget
compassion in others, are then most moved unto weep-
ing, as though they also felt pity for themselves, it came
to pass that mine eyes began to be inclined unto tears.
Wherefore, becoming fearful lest I should make mani-
fest mine abject condition, I rose up, and went where
I could not be seen of that lady; saying afterwards
within myself: "Certainly with her also must abide most
noble Love." And with that, I resolved upon writing a
sonnet, wherein, speaking unto her, I should say all that
I have just said. And as this sonnet is very evident, I
will not divide it.

Mine eyes beheld the blessed pity spring
　　Into thy countenance immediately
　　A while agone, when thou beheld'st in me
　　The sickness only hidden grief can bring;
And then I knew thou wast considering
　　How abject and forlorn my life must be;
　　And I became afraid that thou shouldst see
　　My weeping, and account it a base thing.
Therefore I went out from thee; feeling how
　　The tears were straightway loosen'd at my heart
　　Beneath thine eyes' compassionate control.
And afterwards I said within my soul:
　　"Lo! with this lady dwells the counterpart
　　Of the same Love who holds me weeping now."

35. Here begins the episode of "the gentle lady," whose sympathy
caused Dante to forget Beatrice for a while. Its allegorical in-
terpretation, on which Dante insisted at a later period of his life,
has been the subject of endless discussions.

XXXVII

It happened after this, that whensoever I was seen
of this lady, she became pale and of a piteous counte-
nance, as though it had been with love; whereby she
remembered me many times of my own most noble
lady, who was wont to be of a like paleness. And I
know that often, when I could not weep nor in any way
give ease unto mine anguish, I went to look upon this
lady, who seemed to bring the tears into my eyes by the
mere sight of her. Of the which thing I bethought me
to speak unto her in rhyme, and then made this sonnet:
which begins, "Love's pallor," and which is plain with-
out being divided, by its exposition aforesaid.

Love's pallor and the semblance of deep ruth
    Were never yet shown forth so perfectly
    In any lady's face, chancing to see
    Grief's miserable countenance uncouth,
As in thine, lady, they have sprung to soothe,
    When in mine anguish thou hast look'd on me;
    Until sometimes it seems as if, through thee,
    My heart might almost wander from its truth.
Yet so it is, I cannot hold mine eyes
    From gazing very often upon thine
    In the sore hope to shed those tears they keep;
And at such time, thou mak'st the pent tears rise
    Even to the brim, till the eyes waste and pine;
    Yet cannot they, while thou art present, weep.

XXXVIII

At length, by the constant sight of this lady mine
eyes began to be gladdened overmuch with her com-

pany; through which thing many times I had much un-
rest, and rebuked myself as a base person: also, many
times I cursed the unsteadfastness of mine eyes, and
said to them inwardly: "Was not your grievous condi-
tion of weeping wont one while to make others weep?
And will ye now forget this thing because a lady looketh
upon you? who so looketh merely in compassion of the
grief ye then showed for your own blessed lady. But
whatso ye can, that do ye, accursed eyes! many a time
will I make you remember it! for never, till death dry
you up, should ye make an end of your weeping." And
when I had spoken thus unto mine eyes, I was taken
again with extreme and grievous sighing. And to the
end that this inward strife which I had undergone might
not be hidden from all saving the miserable wretch who
endured it, I proposed to write a sonnet, and to com-
prehend in it this horrible condition. And I wrote this
which begins "The very bitter weeping."

*The sonnet has two parts. In the first, I speak to my
eyes, as my heart spoke within myself. In the second, I
remove a difficulty, showing who it is that speaks thus:
and this part begins here, "So far." It well might receive
other divisions also; but this would be useless, since it
is manifest by the preceding exposition.*

"The very bitter weeping that ye made
    So long a time together, eyes of mine,
    Was wont to make the tears of pity shine
    In other eyes full oft, as I have said.
But now this thing were scarce rememberèd
    If I, on my part, foully would combine
    With you, and not recall each ancient sign
    Of grief, and her for whom your tears were shed.
It is your fickleness that doth betray
    My mind to fears, and makes me tremble thus

What while a lady greets me with her eyes.
Except by death, we must not any way
    Forget our lady who is gone from us."
So far doth my heart utter, and then sighs.

XXXIX

The sight of this lady brought me into so unwonted
a condition that I often thought of her as of one too
dear unto me; and I began to consider her thus: "This
lady is young, beautiful, gentle, and wise: perchance it
was Love himself who set her in my path, that so my
life might find peace." And there were times when I
thought yet more fondly, until my heart consented unto
its reasoning. But when it had so consented, my thought
would often turn round upon me, as moved by reason,
and cause me to say within myself: "What hope is this
which would console me after so base a fashion, and
which hath taken the place of all other imagining?"
Also there was another voice within me, that said: "And
wilt thou, having suffered so much tribulation through
Love, not escape while yet thou mayest from so much
bitterness? Thou must surely know that this thought
carries with it the desire of Love, and drew its life from
the gentle eyes of that lady who vouchsafed thee so
much pity." Wherefore I, having striven sorely and very
often with myself, bethought me to say somewhat
thereof in rhyme. And seeing that in the battle of
doubts, the victory most often remained with such as in-
clined towards the lady of whom I speak, it seemed to
me that I should address this sonnet unto her: in the
first line whereof, I call that thought which spake of her
a gentle thought, only because it spoke of one who was
gentle; being of itself most vile.

In this sonnet I make myself into two, according as

*my thoughts were divided one from the other. The one
part I call Heart, that is, appetite; the other, Soul, that
is, reason; and I tell what one saith to the other. And
that it is fitting to call the appetite Heart, and the reason
Soul, is manifest enough to them to whom I wish this
to be open. True it is that, in the preceding sonnet, I
take the part of the Heart against the Eyes; and that
appears contrary to what I say in the present; and there-
fore I say that, there also, by the Heart I mean appetite,
because yet greater was my desire to remember my most
gentle lady than to see this other, although indeed I
had some appetite towards her, but it appeared slight:
wherefore it appears that the one statement is not con-
trary to the other. This sonnet has three parts. In the
first, I begin to say to this lady how my desires turn all
towards her. In the second, I say how the Soul, that is,
the reason, speaks to the Heart, that is, to the appetite.
In the third, I say how the latter answers. The second
begins here, "And what is this?" the third here, "And
the heart answers."*

A gentle thought there is will often start,
    Within my secret self, to speech of thee;
    Also of Love it speaks so tenderly
That much in me consents and takes its part.
"And what is this," the soul saith to the heart,
    "That cometh thus to comfort thee and me,
    And thence where it would dwell, thus potently
Can drive all other thoughts by its strange art?"
And the heart answers: "Be no more at strife
    'Twixt doubt and doubt: this is Love's messenger
    And speaketh but his words, from him received;
And all the strength it owns and all the life
    It draweth from the gentle eyes of her
    Who, looking on our grief, hath often grieved."

XL

But against this adversary of reason, there rose up in me on a certain day, about the ninth hour,[36] a strong visible phantasy, wherein I seemed to behold the most gracious Beatrice, habited in that crimson raiment which she had worn when I had first beheld her; also she appeared to me of the same tender age as then. Whereupon I fell into a deep thought of her: and my memory ran back according to the order of time, unto all those matters in the which she had borne a part; and my heart began painfully to repent of the desire by which it had so basely let itself be possessed during so many days, contrary to the constancy of reason. And then, this evil desire being quite gone from me, all my thoughts turned again unto their excellent Beatrice. And I say most truly that from that hour I thought constantly of her with the whole humbled and ashamed heart; the which became often manifest in sighs, that had among them the name of that most gracious creature, and how she departed from us. Also it would come to pass very often, through the bitter anguish of some one thought, that I forgot both it, and myself, and where I was. By this increase of sighs, my weeping, which before had been somewhat lessened, increased in like manner; so that mine eyes seemed to long only for tears and to cherish them, and came at last to be circled about with red as though they had suffered martyrdom; neither were they able to look again upon the beauty of any face that might again bring them to shame and evil; from which things it will appear that they were fitly guerdoned for their unsteadfastness.

---

36. "About the ninth hour" is a mistranslation. What Dante's text indicates is "the time of nones," approximately noon.

Wherefore I, (wishing that mine abandonment of all such evil desires and vain temptations should be certified and made manifest, beyond all doubts which might have been suggested by the rhymes aforewritten,) proposed to write a sonnet, wherein I should express this purport. And I then wrote, "Woe's me!"

I said, "Woe's me!" because I was ashamed of the trifling of mine eyes. This sonnet I do not divide, since its purport is manifest enough.

Woe's me! by dint of all these sighs that come
    Forth of my heart, its endless grief to prove,
    Mine eyes are conquer'd, so that even to move
    Their lids for greeting is grown troublesome.
They wept so long that now they are grief's home
    And count their tears all laughter far above:
    They wept till they are circled now by Love
    With a red circle in sign of martyrdom.
These musings, and the sighs they bring from me,
    Are grown at last so constant and so sore
    That Love swoons in my spirit with faint breath;
Hearing in those sad sounds continually
    The most sweet name that my dear lady bore,
    With many grievous words touching her death.

XLI

About this time, it happened that a great number of persons undertook a pilgrimage, to the end that they might behold that blessed portraiture bequeathed unto us by our Lord Jesus Christ as the image of His beautiful countenance,[37] (upon which countenance my dear lady now looketh continually). And certain among these pilgrims, who seemed very thoughtful, passed by a path

---

37. *This image is the Veronica (Cf. Par., xxxi, 103 ff.).*

which is wellnigh in the midst of the city where my
most gracious lady was born, and abode, and at last
died. Then I, beholding them, said within myself:
"These pilgrims seem to be come from very far; and I
think they cannot have heard speak of this lady, or
know anything concerning her. Their thoughts are not
of her, but of other things; it may be, of their friends
who are far distant, and whom we, in our turn, know
not." And I went on to say: "I know that if they were
of a country near unto us, they would in some wise seem
disturbed, passing through this city which is so full of
grief." And I said also: "If I could speak with them a
space, I am certain that I should make them weep be-
fore they went forth of this city; for those things that
they would hear from me must needs beget weeping in
any." And when the last of them had gone by me, I
bethought me to write a sonnet, showing forth mine
inward speech; and that it might seem the more pitiful,
I made as though I had spoken it indeed unto them.
And I wrote this sonnet, which beginneth: "Ye pilgrim-
folk." I made use of the word *pilgrim* for its general
signification; for "pilgrim" may be understood in two
senses, one general, and one special. General, so far as
any man may be called a pilgrim who leaveth the place
of his birth; whereas, more narrowly speaking, he is
only a pilgrim who goeth towards or frowards the House
of St. James.[38] For there are three separate denomina-
tions proper unto those who undertake journeys to the
glory of God. They are called Palmers who go beyond
the seas eastward, whence often they bring palm-
branches. And Pilgrims, as I have said, are they who
journey unto the holy House of Gallicia; seeing that no
other apostle was buried so far from his birth-place as
was the blessed Saint James. And there is a third sort

38. At the shrine of Santiago de Compostela, in Spain.

who are called Romers; in that they go whither these whom I have called pilgrims went: which is to say, unto Rome.

This sonnet is not divided, because its own words sufficiently declare it.

Ye pilgrim-folk, advancing pensively
 As if in thought of distant things, I pray,
 Is your own land indeed so far away
 As by your aspect it would seem to be—
That nothing of our grief comes over ye
 Though passing through the mournful town midway;
 Like unto men that understand to-day
 Nothing at all of her great misery?
Yet if ye will but stay, whom I accost,
 And listen to my words a little space,
 At going ye shall mourn with a loud voice.
It is her Beatrice that she hath lost;
 Of whom the least word spoken holds such grace
 That men weep hearing it, and have no choice.

XLII

A while after these things, two gentle ladies sent unto me, praying that I would bestow upon them certain of these my rhymes. And I, (taking into account their worthiness and consideration,) resolved that I would write also a new thing, and send it them together with those others, to the end that their wishes might be more honourably fulfilled. Therefore I made a sonnet, which narrates my condition, and which I caused to be conveyed to them, accompanied with the one preceding, and with that other which begins, "Stay now with me and listen to my sighs." And the new sonnet is, "Beyond the sphere."

*This sonnet comprises five parts. In the first, I tell
whither my thought goeth, naming the place by the
name of one of its effects. In the second, I say wherefore
it goeth up, and who makes it go thus. In the third, I
tell what it saw, namely, a lady honoured. And I then
call it a "Pilgrim Spirit," because it goes up spiritually,
and like a pilgrim who is out of his known country. In
the fourth, I say how the spirit sees her such (that is,
in such quality) that I cannot understand her; that is
to say, my thought rises into the quality of her in a
degree that my intellect cannot comprehend, seeing
that our intellect is, towards those blessed souls, like
our eye weak against the sun; and this the Philosopher
says in the Second of the Metaphysics.*[39] *In the fifth,
I say that, although I cannot see there whither my
thought carries me—that is, to her admirable essence—
I at least understand this, namely, that it is a thought
of my lady, because I often hear her name therein. And
at the end of this fifth part, I say, "Ladies mine," to
show that they are ladies to whom I speak. The second
part begins, "A new perception"; the third, "When it
hath reached"; the fourth, "It sees her such"; the fifth,
"And yet I know." It might be divided yet more nicely,
and made yet clearer; but this division may pass, and
therefore I stay not to divide it further.*

Beyond the sphere which spreads to widest space
   Now soars the sigh that my heart sends above:
   A new perception born of grieving Love
   Guideth it upward the untrodden ways.
When it hath reach'd unto the end, and stays,
   It sees a lady round whom splendours move
   In homage; till, by the great light thereof
   Abash'd, the pilgrim spirit stands at gaze.

---

39. "The Philosopher": Aristotle.

It sees her such, that when it tells me this
  Which it hath seen, I understand it not,
  It hath a speech so subtile and so fine.
And yet I know its voice within my thought
  Often remembereth me of Beatrice:
  So that I understand it, ladies mine.

XLIII

After writing this sonnet, it was given unto me to behold a very wonderful vision; wherein I saw things which determined me that I would say nothing further of this most blessed one, until such time as I could discourse more worthily concerning her. And to this end I labour all I can; as she well knoweth. Wherefore if it be His pleasure through whom is the life of all things, that my life continue with me a few years, it is my hope that I shall yet write concerning her what hath not before been written of any woman.[40] After the which, may it seem good unto Him who is the Master of Grace, that my spirit should go hence to behold the glory of its lady; to wit, of that blessed Beatrice who now gazeth continually on His countenance, who is blessed throughout all ages.

---

40. *This is the first announcement, and the germ, of The Divine Comedy. The closing lines of the Vita Nuova were paraphrased by Dante in the letter he addressed to Can Grande della Scala, in sending him the Paradiso.*

THE RHYMES

*Translated by D. G. Rossetti
and others*

Editor's Note

Dante's poems—his "Rhymes"—were never collected by their author. They belong to every period of the poet's life. The main group, however, of which the first four poems in the present edition are a sample, were certainly written at the time of La Vita Nuova. They are similar in inspiration, theme, and style. If Dante chose to exclude them from his youthful work, it was only for artistic considerations.

Another group of love-poems, of which the sonnet "Two ladies to the summit of my mind" is an example, belong to a much later and more meditative period. Two poems included here give particular evidence of the range of Dante's poetry. The first, "To Forese Donati," is a jocose sonnet which Boccaccio must have prized. The second, "To the dim light and the large circle of shade," shows how Dante could sing not only the purgatory of love and its paradise, but its inferno as well—the burning cruelty of a passion unheeded.

(When not otherwise indicated, the poems are given in the translation by D. G. Rosetti.)

To Guido Cavalcanti

Guido, I wish that Lapo, thou, and I,
　　Could be by spells convey'd, as it were now,
　　Upon a barque, with all the winds that blow
Across all seas at our good will to hie.
So no mischance nor temper of the sky
　　Should mar our course with spite or cruel slip;
　　But we, observing old companionship,
To be companions still should long thereby.
And Lady Joan, and Lady Beatrice,[1]
　　And her the thirtieth on my roll, with us
　　　　Should our good wizard set, o'er seas to move
　　　　And not to talk of anything but love:
And they three ever to be well at ease
　　As we should be, I think, if this were thus.

A Garland Have I Seen[2]

A garland have I seen
　　So fair, that every flower
　　Will cause my sighs to flow.

Lady, I saw a garland borne by you,
　　Lovely as fairest flower;
　　And blithely fluttering over it, beheld
　　A little angel of Love's gentle quire,
　　Who sung an artful lay,

---

1. "And Lady Joan, and Lady Beatrice": *D. G. Rossetti misread this line. The right reading is: "And Lady Joan, and Lady Lagia." Dante avoids mentioning Beatrice's name; he only designates her as "the thirtieth on [his] roll."*
2. *Translated by C. Lyell.*

621

Which said, who me beholds
Shall praise my sovereign lord.

Let me be found where tender floweret blooms,
  Then will my sighs break forth.
  Then shall I say, my lady fair and kind
Bears on her head the flowerets of my Sire;
  But to increase desire,
  Soon shall my lady come
  Crowned by the hand of Love.

Of flowers these new and trifling rhymes of mine
  A ballad have composed;
  From them, to win a grace, they have ta'en a robe
That never to another hath been given:
  Therefore let me entreat,
  When ye shall sing the lay,
  That ye will do it honor.

Upon a Day, Came Sorrow

Upon a day, came Sorrow in to me,
  Saying, "I've come to stay with thee awhile";
  And I perceived that she had usher'd Bile
And Pain into my house for company.
Wherefore I said, "Go forth— away with thee!"
  But like a Greek she answer'd, full of guile,
  And went on arguing in an easy style.
Then, looking, I saw Love come silently,
Habited in black raiment, smooth and new,
  Having a black hat set upon his hair;
And certainly the tears he shed were true.
  So that I ask'd, "What ails thee, trifler?"

Answering he said: "A grief to be gone through;
   For our own lady's dying, brother dear."

Whence Come You?

Whence come you, all of you so sorrowful?
   An' it may please you, speak for courtesy.
   I fear for my dear lady's sake, lest she
Have made you to return thus fill'd with dule.
O gentle ladies, be not hard to school
   In gentleness, but to some pause agree,
   And something of my lady say to me, `
For with a little my desire is full.
Howbeit it be a heavy thing to hear:
   For love now utterly has thrust me forth,
With hand for ever lifted, striking fear.
   See if I be not worn unto the earth:
Yea, and my spirit must fail from me here,
   If, when you speak, your words are of no worth.

To Forese Donati[1]

If you should hear her cough, the luckless mate
   Of Bicci, whom his friends Forese call,
   You'd say that she was used to hibernate
   In northern climes, where ice envelops all.

---

1. In this youthful poem Dante pokes fun at his friend and relative
Forese Donati, with whom he exchanged salacious sonnets, and
at his wife, Nella, whose perpetual cold he attributes to her hus-
band's neglect. (To marry "into Count Guido's house" was an
idiom for marrying into a wealthy family.) It will be remembered
that, in Purg. XXIII, Dante makes amends for this sonnet, and
beautifully praises Nella, who had become a widow, as the only
virtuous woman in Florence.—Translated by C. H. Grandgent.

Mid-August finds her in catarrhal state:
   Imagine what she is in spring and fall!
   At night, beneath the suffocating weight
Of quilts and comforters in vain she'll crawl.
Her cough, her cold, her every other ill
   Spring not from wasted humors in her veins,
   But from desertion in her lonely nest.
Her mournful mother cries, repining still:
   "I could have married her, with little pains,
   Into Count Guido's house—had I but guest!"

Master Brunetto[1]

Master Brunetto, this my little maid
   Is come to spend her Easter-tide with you;
   Not that she reckons feasting as her due—
Whose need is hardly to be fed, but read.
Not in a hurry can her sense be weigh'd,
   Nor 'mid the jests of any noisy crew:
   Ah! and she wants a little coaxing too
Before she'll get into another's head.
But if you do not find her meaning clear,
   You've many Brother Alberts hard at hand,
     Whose wisdom will respond to any call.
Consult with them and do not laugh at her;
   And if she still is hard to understand,
     Apply to Master Giano last of all.

---

1. *This sonnet, which D. G. Rossetti erroneously believed to have been sent by Dante to Brunetto Latini with a copy of the Vita Nuova, was actually written for another Brunetto (or Betto) Brunelleschi.*

Two Ladies

Two ladies to the summit of my mind
  Have clomb, to hold an argument of love.
  The one has wisdom with her from above,
For every noblest virtue well design'd:
The other, beauty's tempting power refined
  And the high charm of perfect grace approve:
  And I, as my sweet Master's will doth move,
At feet of both their favors am reclined.
Beauty and Duty in my soul keep strife,
  At question if the heart such course can take
    And 'twixt two ladies hold its love complete.
    The fount of gentle speech yields answer meet,
  That Beauty may be loved for gladness' sake,
And Duty in the lofty ends of life.

To the Dim Light[1]

To the dim light and the large circle of shade
I have clomb, and to the whitening of the hills
There where we see no color in the grass.
Natheless my longing loses not its green,
It has so taken root in the hard stone
Which talks and hears as though it were a lady.

---

1. This sestina, whose metrical structure fits admirably the poet's feelings, belongs to a section of Dante's poems traditionally called "Rime pietrose" ("Stony rhymes"). They are all addressed to a woman called Pietra (a word which, in Italian, means "stone"), who refuses cruelly to heed the poet's love. We have reasons to believe that, behind their allegorical virtuosities, the "Rime pietrose" reflect a very earthly passion.

Utterly frozen is this youthful lady
Even as the snow that lies within the shade;
For she is no more moved than is a stone
By the sweet season which makes warm the hills
And alters them afresh from white to green,
Covering their sides again with flowers and grass.

When on her hair she sets a crown of grass
The thought has no more room for other lady;
Because she weaves the yellow with the green
So well that Love sits down there in the shade—
Love who has shut me in among low hills
Faster than between walls of granite-stone.

She is more bright than is a precious stone;
The wound she gives may not be heal'd with grass:
I therefore have fled far o'er plains and hills
For refuge from so dangerous a lady;
But from her sunshine nothing can give shade—
Not any hill, nor wall, nor summer-green.

A while ago, I saw her dress'd in green—
So fair, she might have waken'd in a stone
This love which I do feel even for her shade;
And therefore, as one woos a graceful lady,
I wooed her in a field that was all grass
Girdled about with very lofty hills.

Yet shall the streams turn back and climb the hills
Before Love's flame in this damp wood and green
Burn, as it burns within a youthful lady,
For my sake, who would sleep away in stone
My life, or feed like beasts upon the grass,
Only to see her garments cast a shade.

How dark soe'er the hills throw out their shade,
Under her summer-green the beautiful lady
Covers it, like a stone cover'd in grass.

To Cino da Pistoia[1]

I thought to be for ever separate,
　　Fair Master Cino, from these rhymes of yours;
　　Since further from the coast, another course,
My vessel now must journey with her freight,
Yet still, because I hear men name your state
　　As his whom every lure doth straight beguile,
　　I pray you lend a very little while
Unto my voice your ear grown obdurate.
The man after this measure amorous,
　　Who still at his own will is bound and loosed,
　　How slightly Love him wounds is lightly known.
If on this wise your heart in homage bows,
　　I pray you for God's sake it be disused,
　　So that the deed and the sweet words be one.

---

1. Cino da Pistoia (1270-1336), one of the minor poets of the
school of "the sweet, new style," was a personal friend of Dante.

LATIN PROSE WORKS

Editor's Note

De Vulgari Eloquentia *is a treatise in Latin on the "vernacular tongue," that is, the Italian language.* Dante *most probably worked at* De Vulgari Eloquentia *between 1304 and 1306, but left it unfinished, in the middle of the second of the four parts, or "books," he had planned to write. The aim of* De Vulgari Eloquentia *is to establish Italian as a literary language, on equal footing with Latin. The first "book" deals with language in general, its origin and its history. It also attempts an interesting classification of the Italian dialects. Dante maintains that the "courtly speech"—namely the literary Italian used by the best poets from Frederick II to Guido Cavalcanti and to himself—is the only one suitable to become the national tongue. The unfinished second "book" deals with problems of style, and poetic forms, particularly the canzone.* De Vulgari Eloquentia *is still grounded in medieval thought; yet many of its chapters anticipate with peculiar insight the scientific approach to matters of language and style.*

De Monarchia, *a Latin treatise in three parts written around 1313, is the definitive statement of Dante's political ideas. It shows how the rivalry between the Papacy and the Empire had been the cause of all calamities, since the Church, at the time of Constantine, usurped the temporal power. The only way to achieve universal peace is to recognize the supremacy of a universal monarchy (the Holy Roman Empire) dependent only on God, although respectful of the spiritual power of the Church. A division of authority between its temporal guide (the Emperor) and its spiritual guide (the Pope) will lead mankind to happiness first on earth then in heaven.*

Dante's extant letters are all in Latin, which is why they are traditionally called his Epistles. *The political epistles (V and VI), of which this edition includes essential passages, are notable for their prophetic tone. Among the letters of a more personal character, Epistle IX was defined by Giuseppe Mazzini as a model of integrity for all political exiles.*

From De Vulgari Eloquentia

SPEECH IS PECULIAR TO MAN

(BOOK I, CHAPTER II)

THIS [the vernacular] is our true first speech. I do not, however, say "our" as implying that any other kind of speech exists beside man's; for to man alone of all existing beings was speech given, because for him alone was it necessary. Speech was not necessary for the angels or for the lower animals, but would have been given to them in vain, which nature, as we know, shrinks from doing. For if we clearly consider what our intention is when we speak, we shall find that it is nothing else but to unfold to others the thoughts of our own mind. Since, then, the angels have, for the purpose of manifesting their glorious thoughts, a most ready and indeed ineffable sufficiency of intellect, by which one of them is known in all respects to another, either of himself, or at least by means of that most brilliant mirror in which all of them are represented in the fulness of their beauty,[1] and into which they all most eagerly gaze, they do not seem to have required the outward indications of speech. And if an objection be raised concerning the spirits who fell,[2] it may be answered in two ways. First we may say that inasmuch as we are treating of those things which are necessary for well-being, we ought to pass over the fallen angels, because they perversely refused to wait for the divine care. Or secondly (and better), that the devils themselves only need, in order to

---

1. This "mirror" is God.
2. The fallen angels: Satan and his companions.

disclose their perfidy to one another, to know, each of another, that he exists, and what is his power: which they certainly do know, for they had knowledge of one another before their fall.

The lower animals also, being guided by natural instinct alone, did not need to be provided with the power of speech, for all those of the same species have the same actions and passions; and so they are enabled by their own actions and passions to know those of others. But among those of different species not only was speech unnecessary, but it would have been altogether harmful, since there would have been no friendly intercourse between them.

And if it be objected concerning the serpent speaking to the first woman, or concerning Balaam's ass, that they spoke, we reply that the angel in the latter, and the devil in the former, wrought in such a manner that the animals themselves set their organs in motion in such wise that the voice thence sounded clear like genuine speech; not that the sound uttered was to the ass anything but braying, or to the serpent anything but hissing.

But if any one should argue in opposition, from what Ovid says in the fifth book of the *Metamorphoses* about magpies speaking, we reply that he says this figuratively, meaning something else. And if any one should rejoin that even up to the present time magpies and other birds speak, we say that it is false, because such action is not speaking, but a kind of imitation of the sound of our voice, or in other words, we say that they try to imitate us in so far as we utter sounds, but not in so far as we speak. If accordingly any one were to say expressly "Pica" [magpie], and "Pica" were answered back, this would be but a copy or imitation of the sound made by him who had first said the word.

And so it is evident that speech has been given to man alone. . . .

IS OUR NATIVE TONGUE
THE BEST IN THE WORLD?

(BOOK I, CHAPTER VI)

SINCE human affairs are carried on in very many different languages, so that many men are not understood by many with words any better than without words, it is meet for us to make investigation concerning that language which that man who had no mother,[3] who was never suckled, who never saw either childhood or youth, is believed to have spoken. In this as in much else Pietramala[4] is a most populous city, and the native place of the majority of the children of Adam. For whoever is so offensively unreasonable as to suppose that the place of his birth is the most delightful under the sun, also rates his own vernacular (that is, his mother-tongue) above all others, and consequently believes that it actually was that of Adam. But we, to whom the world is our native country, just as the sea is to the fish, though we drank of Arno before our teeth appeared, and though we love Florence so dearly that for the love we bore her we are wrongfully suffering exile—we rest the shoulders of our judgment on reason rather than on feeling. And although as regards our own pleasure or sensuous comfort there exists no more agreeable place in the world than Florence, still, when we turn over the volumes both of poets and other writers in which the world is gener-

---

3. The first man, Adam.
4. "Pietramala" was a village in the Apennines. The ironical expression means "in any insignificant place."

ally and particularly described, and take account within ourselves of the various situations of the places of the world and their arrangement with respect to the two poles and to the equator, our deliberate and firm opinion is that there are many countries and cities both nobler and more delightful than Tuscany and Florence of which we are a native and a citizen, and also that a great many nations and races use a speech both more agreeable and more serviceable than the Italians do. Returning therefore to our subject, we say that a certain form of speech was created by God together with the first soul. And I say "a form," both in respect of words and their construction and of the utterance of this construction; and this form every tongue of speaking men would use, if it had not been dissipated by the fault of man's presumption, as shall be shown further on.

In this form of speech Adam spoke; in this form of speech all his descendants spoke until the building of the Tower of Babel, which is by interpretation the tower of confusion; and this form of speech was inherited by the sons of Heber, who after him were called Hebrews. With them alone did it remain after the confusion, in order that our Redeemer (who was, as to his humanity, to spring from them) might use, not the language of confusion, but of grace. Therefore Hebrew was the language which the lips of the first speaker formed.

THE STANDARD ITALIAN LANGUAGE

(BOOK I, CHAPTER XVI)

AFTER having scoured the heights and pastures of Italy, without having found that panther which we are in pursuit of,[5] in order that we may be able to find her, let

5. The "panther" symbolizes a language fitted for the whole of

us now track her out in a more rational manner, so that
we may with skilful efforts completely enclose within
our toils her who is fragrant everywhere but nowhere
apparent.

Resuming, then, our hunting-spears, we say that in
every kind of things there must be one thing by which
all the things of that kind may be compared and
weighed, and which we may take as the measure of all
the others; just as in numbers all are measured by unity
and are said to be more or fewer according as they are
distant from or near to unity; so also in colors all are
measured by white, for they are said to be more or less
visible according as they approach or recede from it.
And what we say of the predicaments which indicate
quantity and quality, we think may also be said of any
of the predicaments and even of substance; namely, that
everything considered as belonging to a kind becomes
measurable by that which is simplest in that kind.
Wherefore in our actions, however many the species into
which they are divided may be, we have to discover
this standard by which they may be measured. Thus, in
what concerns our actions as human beings simply, we
have virtue, understanding it generally; for according to
it we judge a man to be good or bad; in what concerns
our actions as citizens, we have the law, according to
which a citizen is said to be good or bad; in what con-
cerns our actions as Italians, we have certain very simple
standards of manners, customs, and language, by which
our actions as Italians are weighed and measured. Now
the supreme standards of those activities which are
generically Italian are not peculiar to any one town in
Italy, but are common to all; and among these can now
be discerned that vernacular language which we were

Italy, which, in previous chapters, Dante has failed to discover
in any of the local dialects.

hunting for above, whose fragrance is in every town, but whose lair is in none. It may, however, be more perceptible in one than in another, just as the simplest of substances, which is God, is more perceptible in a man than in a brute, in an animal than in a plant, in a plant than in a mineral, in a mineral than in an element, in fire than in earth. And the simplest quantity, which is unity, is more perceptible in an odd than in an even number; and the simplest color, which is white, is more perceptible in orange than in green.

Having therefore found what we were searching for, we declare the illustrious, cardinal, courtly, and curial[6] vernacular language in Italy to be that which belongs to all the towns in Italy but does not appear to belong to any one of them, and by which all the municipal dialects of the Italian are measured, weighed, and compared.

THE WORTHY SUBJECTS:
ARMS, LOVE, AND VIRTUE

(BOOK II, CHAPTER II)

AFTER having proved that not all those who write verse, but only those of the highest excellence, ought to use the illustrious vernacular, we must in the next place establish whether every subject ought to be handled in it, or not; and if not, we must set out by themselves those subjects that are worthy of it. . . .

We must discuss what things are greatest; and first in respect of what is useful. Now in this matter, if we carefully consider the object of all those who are in search of

---

6. "Illustrious, cardinal, courtly, and curial": Dante wants his standard Italian to be a language exalted, cleansed from the peculiarities of the single dialects, and worthy to be spoken at a royal court as well as in the courts of justice.

what is useful, we shall find that it is nothing else but safety. Secondly, in respect of what is pleasurable; and here we say that that is most pleasurable which gives pleasure by the most exquisite object of appetite, and this is love. Thirdly, in respect of what is right; and here no one doubts that virtue has the first place. Wherefore these three things, namely, safety, love, and virtue, appear to be those capital matters which ought to be treated of supremely, I mean the things which are most important in respect of them, as prowess in arms, the fire of love, and the direction of the will. And if we duly consider, we shall find that the illustrious writers have written poetry in the vulgar tongue on these subjects exclusively. . . .

THE TRAGIC STYLE

(BOOK II, CHAPTER IV)

. . . LET us treat of the tragic style. We appear then to make use of the tragic style when the stateliness of the lines as well as the loftiness of the construction and the excellence of the words agree with the weight of the subject. And because, if we remember rightly, it has already been proved that the highest things are worthy of the highest, and because the style which we call tragic appears to be the highest style, those things which we have distinguished as being worthy of the highest song are to be sung in that style alone, namely, Safety, Love, and Virtue, and those other things, our conceptions of which arise from these; provided that they be not degraded by any accident.

Let every one therefore beware and discern what we say; and when he purposes to sing of these three subjects simply, or of those things which directly and simply follow after them, let him first drink of Helicon, and then, after adjusting the strings, boldly take up his *plectrum* and begin to ply it.[7] But it is in the exercise of the needful caution and discernment that the real difficulty lies; for this can never be attained to without strenuous efforts of genius, constant practice in the art, and the habit of the sciences. And it is those [so equipped] whom the poet in the sixth book of the Aeneid describes as beloved of God, raised by glowing virtue to the sky, and sons of the Gods, though he is speaking figuratively. And therefore let those who, innocent of art and science, and trusting to genius alone, rush forward to sing of the highest subjects in the highest style, confess their folly and cease from such presumption; and if in their natural sluggishness they are but geese, let them abstain from imitating the eagle soaring to the stars.

From De Monarchia

THE AUTHOR'S PURPOSE

(BOOK I, CHAPTER I)

IT WOULD seem that all men on whom the Higher Nature has stamped the love of truth must make it their chief concern, like as they have been enriched by the toil of those who have gone before, so themselves in like manner to toil in advance for those that shall be hereafter, that posterity may have of them whereby to be enriched.

For he who, himself imbued with public teachings,

---

7. "Helicon" *is one of the resorts of the Muses. The* "plectrum" *is a small quill for striking the strings of the lyre.*

yet cares not to contribute aught to the public good, may be well assured that he has fallen far from duty; for he is not "a tree by the streams of waters, bearing his fruit in due season," but rather a devouring whirlpool, ever sucking in, and never pouring back what it has swallowed. Wherefore, often pondering these things with myself, lest I should one day be convicted of the charge of the buried talent, I long not only to burgeon, but also to bear fruit for the public advantage, and to set forth truths unattempted by others. For what fruit would he bear who should demonstrate once more some theorem of Euclid; who should strive to expound anew felicity, which Aristotle has already expounded; who should undertake again the apology of old age, which Cicero has pleaded? Naught at all, but rather would such wearisome superfluity provoke disgust.

And inasmuch as amongst other unexplored and important truths the knowledge of the temporal monarchy is most important and least explored, and (for that it stands in no direct relation to gain) has been attempted by none; therefore am I minded to extract it from its recesses; on the one hand that I may keep vigil for the good of the world, and on the other that I may be the first to win for my glory the palm of so great a prize. A hard task in truth do I attempt, and beyond my strength, trusting not so much in my proper power as in the light of that giver who giveth to all liberally and upbraideth not.

THE UNIVERSAL EMPIRE

(BOOK I, CHAPTER II)

FIRST, therefore, we have to consider what the temporal monarchy means; in type to wit, and after intention. The temporal monarchy, then, which is called empire is "a unique princedom extending over all persons in time," or, "in and over those things which are measured by time"; and there rise three main inquiries concerning the same: for in the first place we may inquire and examine whether it is needful for the well-being of the world; in the second, whether the Roman people rightfully assumed to itself the function of monarchy; and in the third, whether the authority of the monarchy depends immediately upon God, or upon some other minister or vicar of God.

But inasmuch as every truth which is not a first principle is demonstrated by reference to one that is, it behoves us in every inquiry to be clear as to the first principle to which we are to return by analysis, in order to establish the certainty of all such propositions as may afterwards be laid down. And inasmuch as the present treatise is an inquiry, it would seem that before all else we must investigate the first principle in the strength of which what follows is to be established.

Be it known, then, that there are some things, in no degree subject to our power, about which we can think, but which we cannot do; such are mathematics, physics, and divinity; but there are some which are subject to our power, and which we can not only think about, but can also do; and in the case of these the doing is not undertaken for the sake of thinking, but the latter for the former, since in such cases the doing is the goal.

Since, then, the present matter is concerned with polity, nay, is the very fount and first principle of right polities, and since all that concerns polity is subject to our power, it is manifest that our present matter is not primarily concerned with thinking, but with doing. Again, in the case of anything that is done it is the ultimate end which constitutes the first principle and cause of the whole thing, for it is that end which, in the first instance, sets the agent in motion; so it follows that the whole theory of the means which make for the end must be derived from the end itself. Thus there is one theory of cutting wood to build a house, and another to build a ship. That thing, then, if there is any, which is the goal of the entire civilization of the human race, will give us this first principle, a reduction to which will be held a sufficient explanation of everything to be proved hereafter. But it would be folly to suppose that there is a goal of this civilization and a goal of that, but no one goal of all civilizations.

THE GOAL OF MANKIND IS UNIVERSAL PEACE

(BOOK I, CHAPTER IV)

IT HAS been sufficiently shown that the work proper to the human race, taken as a whole, is to keep the whole capacity of the potential intellect constantly actualized, primarily for speculation, and secondarily (by extension, and for the sake of the other) for action.

And since it is with the whole as it is with the part, and it is the fact that in sedentary quietness the individual man is perfected in knowledge and in wisdom, it is evident that in the quiet or tranquillity of peace the human race is most freely and favorably disposed towards the work proper to it (which is almost divine, even as it is said "Thou hast made him a little lower than the angels"). Whence it is manifest that universal peace is the best of all those things which are ordained for our blessedness. And that is why there rang out to the shepherds from on high, not riches, not pleasures, not honors, not length of life, not health, not strength, not beauty, but peace. For the celestial soldiery proclaims, "Glory to God in the highest; and, on earth, peace to men of good will." Hence, also, "Peace be with you" was the salutation of him who was the salvation of man. For it was meet that the supreme saviour should utter the supreme salutation. And likewise his disciples saw good to preserve this custom, and amongst them Paul, as all may see in his salutations.

Our exposition, then, has made clear what is the better means (or rather the best) whereby the human race attains to its proper work. And thus we perceive the directest means of approach to that whereto as to their ultimate goal all our doings are directed, which directest means is universal peace. Therefore let this underlie the following arguments, as that first principle which we needed (as aforesaid) for a mark, set up in advance; into which, as into the most manifest truth, whatsoever is to be proved must be resolved.

NECESSITY OF A WORLD POWER

(BOOK I, CHAPTER V)

AND now, to resume what we said at the outset, three main questions are raised and discussed about the temporal monarchy, more commonly called the empire; concerning which, as already declared, we purpose to make inquiry, in the order indicated above, under the first principle now laid down. Let us therefore first discuss whether a temporal monarchy is needful for the well-being of the world.

Now against its being needful there is no force either of argument or of authority, whereas most powerful and most patent arguments establish that it is. Of which let the first be drawn from the authority of the Philosopher in his *Politics*.[1] For there his venerable authority asserts that when more things than one are ordained for a single purpose, needs must one of them guide or rule, and the others be guided or ruled. And to this not only the glorious name of the author, but inductive argument also forces assent.

For if we consider an individual man, we shall see that this is true of him; since whereas all his faculties are ordained for felicity, the intellectual faculty is the guide and ruler of all the others, else he cannot attain to felicity. If we consider the family, the goal of which is to prepare its members to live well, there must needs be one to guide and rule whom they call the pater-familias, or his representative; according to the philosopher when he says, "Every house is ruled by the oldest." And it is his task, as Homer says, to rule over all the rest, and to impose laws on his housemates; whence the proverbial curse, "May you have a peer in your house." If we consider a district, the end of which is helpful co-operation both in persons and in appliances, one must needs be the guide of the rest, whether he be imposed upon them by another or rise to eminence out of themselves, with the consent of the rest. Else not only do they fail to attain the mutual support they aim at, but sometimes when several strive for pre-eminence, the whole district is brought to ruin. And if we consider a city, the end of which is to live well and suitably, there must be a single rule, and this not only in a rightly ordained polity, but even in a wrong one. For if it be otherwise not only is the end of civil life missed, but the very city itself ceases to be what it was. If finally we consider a special kingdom, the end of which is the same as that of the city, only with better assurance of tranquillity, there must be

1. "The Philosopher" *is Aristotle.*

one king to rule and govern, else not only do they in the kingdom fail to reach the goal, but the kingdom itself lapses into ruin, according to that saying of the infallible truth, "every kingdom divided against itself shall be laid waste." If, then, this is so in these cases and in every other case in which a single end is aimed at, the proposition laid down above is true.

Now it is admitted that the whole human race is ordained for a single end, as was set forth before. Therefore there must be one guiding or ruling power. And this is what we mean by monarch or emperor. Thus it appears that for the well-being of the world there must be a monarchy or empire.

THE WORLD COURT

(BOOK I, CHAPTER X)

WHERESOEVER contention may arise there must needs be judgment, else there were an imperfection without its proper perfector; which is impossible, since God and nature fail not in things necessary. Now between any two princes, one of whom is in no way subject to the other, contention may arise, either through their own fault or that of their subjects, as is self-evident. Wherefore there must needs be judgment between such. And since the one may not take cognizance of what concerns the other, the one not being subject to the other (for a peer has no rule over his peer), there must needs be a third of wider jurisdiction who, within the compass of his right, has princedom over both. And such a one will either be the monarch or not. If he is, the proposition is established. If not, he again will have a co-equal outside the compass of his jurisdiction; and these two will again need a third; and so we shall either go on to infinity (which may not be), or must come to the first and highest judge by whose judgment all contentions may be solved, either mediately or immediately. And he will be monarch or emperor. Therefore monarchy is necessary for the world. And this reasoning was perceived by the Philosopher[2] when he said, "Things love not to be ill-disposed; but a multiplicity of princedoms is ill; therefore, one prince."

FREEDOM UNDER THE LAW

(BOOK I, CHAPTER XII)

AND the human race when most free is best disposed. This will be clear if the principle of freedom be understood. Wherefore be it known that the first principle of our freedom is freedom of choice, which many have on their lips but few in their understanding. For they get as far as saying that free choice is free judgment in matters of will; and herein they say the truth; but the import of the words is far from them, just as is the case with our teachers of logic in their constant use of certain propositions, given by way of example in Logic; for instance, "A triangle has three angles equal to two right angles."

Therefore I say that judgment is the link between apprehension and appetite. For first a thing is apprehended, then when apprehended it is judged to be good or bad, and finally he who has so judged it pursues or shuns it. If, then, the judgment altogether sets the appetite in motion, and is in no measure anticipated by it, it is free. But if the judgment is moved by the appetite, which to some extent anticipates it, it cannot be free, for it does not move of itself, but is drawn captive by

---

2. "The Philosopher" *is again Aristotle.*

another. And hence it is that brutes cannot have free judgment because their judgments are always anticipated by appetite. And hence too it may be seen that the intellectual substances whose wills are immutable, and separated souls departing from this life in grace, do not lose their freedom of choice because of the immutability of their wills, but retain it in its most perfect and potent form.

When we see this we may further understand that this freedom (or this principle of all our freedom) is the greatest gift conferred by God on human nature; for through it we have our felicity here as men, through it we have our felicity elsewhere as deities. And if this be so, who would not agree that the human race is best disposed when it has fullest use of this principle? But it is under a monarch that it is most free. As to which we must know that that is free which exists "for the sake of itself and not of some other," as the Philosopher has it in his work, *De Simpliciter Ente*.[3] For that which exists for the sake of something else is conditioned by that for the sake of which it exists, as a road is conditioned by the goal. It is only when a monarch is reigning that the human race exists for its own sake, and not for the sake of something else. For it is only then that perverted forms of government are made straight, to wit democracies, oligarchies, and tyrannies, which force the human race into slavery (as is obvious to whosoever runs through them all), and that government is conducted by kings, aristocrats (whom they call *optimates*), and zealots for the people's liberty. For since the monarch has love of men in the highest degree, as already indicated, he will desire all men to be made good, which cannot be under perverted rulers. Whence the Philosopher in his *Politics*

---

3. "De Simpliciter Ente" *is another title for Aristotle's Metaphysics.*

says, "Under a perverted government a good man is a bad citizen, but under a right one, a good man and a good citizen are convertible terms." And such right governments purpose freedom, to wit that men should exist for their own sakes. For the citizens are not there for the sake of the consuls, nor the nation for the sake of the king, but conversely, the consuls for the sake of the citizens, the king for the sake of the nation. For just as the body politic is not established for the benefit of the laws, but the laws for the benefit of the body politic, so too they who live under the law are not ordained for the benefit of the legislator, but rather he for theirs, as saith the Philosopher again in what has been left by him on the present matter. Hence it is clear that, albeit the consul or king be masters of the rest as regards the way, yet as regards the end they are their servants; and the monarch most of all, for he must assuredly be regarded as the servant of all. Hence it may begin to appear at this point how the monarch is conditioned in laying down the laws by the end set before him.

Therefore the human race is best disposed when under a monarchy. Whence it follows that for the well-being of the world the existence of a monarchy is necessary.

THE POWER OF THE CHURCH IS SPIRITUAL

(BOOK III, CHAPTER XV)

THAT which is against the nature of anything is not in the number of its virtues, since the virtues of each thing follow its nature, for the attainment of its end. But virtue to authorize rule over our mortality is contrary to the nature of the church. Therefore it is not of the number of her virtues. . . .

The form of the church is no other than the life of Christ, embraced both in his words and in his deeds. For his life was the idea and exemplar of the church militant, especially of pastors, and most of all of the supreme pastor, whose it is to feed the lambs and sheep. Whence he himself in John, when bequeathing the form of his life, says, "I have given you an example that as I have done to you so should ye also do." And specifically to Peter when he had committed to him the office of pastor, as we learn from the same source, he said, "Peter, follow thou me." But Christ in the presence of Pilate renounced any such regimen as that in question. "My kingdom," said he, "is not of this world. If my kingdom were of this world, my servants would fight that I should not be given over to the Jews. But now my kingdom is not hence."

Which is not so to be understood as though Christ, who is God, were not lord of this kingdom; since the Psalmist says, "For the sea is his and he made it. And his hands established the dry land"; but that as the exemplar of the church he had no charge of this kingdom. As though a golden seal were to say of itself, "I am not the standard in any class," which saying would not hold concerning it in so far as it is gold, since as gold it is the standard in the class of metals; but it holds concerning it in so far as it is a definite stamp capable of being received by impression.

It is therefore the formal principle of the church to say and to feel that same. And to say or feel the opposite is obviously counter to its form, or to its nature, which is the same thing. Whence we gather that the power of authorizing this kingdom is counter to the nature of the church. . . . The authority of the empire by no means depends on the church.

From The Epistles

THE BONDAGE OF LOVE

(EPISTLE III)

Dante writes to Lord Moruello, Marquis Malaspina.[1]

For fear that the master should have no knowledge of the captivity of the servant, and of the graciousness of the affection that commands him, and for fear that confused narrations, which are often wont to become seedbeds of false opinion, should declare the captive to be neglectful of his duty, it has pleased me to address to the sight of your magnificence the concatenation of this present rescript.

It chanced, then, that when I had parted from the threshold of that court (for which I was afterwards to sigh) wherein, as you have often marked with wonder, I had leave to follow the offices of liberty, no sooner had I set my feet by the streams of the Arno, in security and carelessness, than straightway behold a woman appeared to me, descending like a lightning flash, strangely harmonious with my condition both in character and in person. Oh, how was I struck dumb at her apparition! But my stupor yielded to the terror of the thunder that followed. For like as thunders straightway follow flashes from heaven, so when the flame of this beauty had ap-

---

1. *Dante was a frequent guest at the court of the Malaspina between 1306 and 1308, and he worked there at his literary treatise the Convivio (The Banquet). This letter tells how a casual encounter with a lady in the Apennines broke off Dante's undertaking. The Convivio is an unfinished work.—Dante sent with this letter a beautiful canzone, "Amor da che convien pur ch'io mi doglia."*

peared, Love laid hold of me, terrible and imperious; raging, moreover, like a lord banished from his fatherland returning after long exile to what is all his own! For he slew or banished or enchained all opposition in me. He slew that praiseworthy determination in the strength of which I held aloof from women, those instruments of his enchantment; and the unbroken meditations wherein I was pondering on things both of heaven and of earth, he relentlessly banished as things suspected; and finally, that my soul might never again rebel against him, he chained my free will; so that I needs must turn not whither I would, but whither he wills. Love, therefore, reigns within me, and there is no power to oppose him. And how he rules me you must inquire below, outside the boundary of these presents.

THE DIVINE MISSION OF HENRY VII

(EPISTLE V)

On the kings of Italy all and several, on the senators of her fostering city, on her dukes, marquises, counts, and peoples, the humble Italian Dante Alighieri, the Florentine, exiled counter to his deserts, imploreth peace.

Lo NOW is the acceptable time wherein arise the signs of consolation and peace. For a new day beginneth to glow, showing forth the dawn which is even now dissipating the darkness of our long calamity; and already the breezes of the east begin to blow, the lips of heaven glow red, and confirm the auspices of the nations with a caressing calm. And we, too, shall see the looked-for joy, we who have kept vigil through the long night in the desert. For peace-bringing Titan shall arise, and Justice,

which, without the sun hath languished like the helio-
trope, will revive again so soon as he shall brandish his
first ray. All they who hunger and thirst shall be satisfied
in the light of his rays, and they who love iniquity shall
be confounded before his shining face. For the strong
lion of the tribe of Judah hath lifted up his merciful ears,
and, taking pity on the wail of universal captivity, hath
raised up a second Moses to snatch his people from the
burdens of the Egyptians, leading them to the land that
floweth with milk and honey.

O Italy! henceforth rejoice; though now to be pitied
by the very Saracens, yet soon to be envied throughout
the world! because thy bridegroom, the solace of the
world and the glory of thy people, the most clement
Henry, Divus and Augustus and Caesar, is hastening to
the bridal. Dry thy tears and remove the marks of grief,
O thou fairest one; for nigh at hand is he who shall re-
lease thee from the prison of the impious, and, smiting
the malicious, shall destroy them with the edge of the
sword, and shall give out his vineyard to other hus-
bandmen such as shall render the fruit of justice at time
of harvest. . . .

O blood of the Lombards, put off thy contracted
barbarism, and if aught of the seed of the Trojans and
the Latins remain, give place thereto, lest when the
eagle from above shall come swooping down like a thun-
derbolt he find his own nestlings cast out and the place
of his proper offspring seized by crows. Ah, see to it,
ye tribe of Scandinavia, that so far as lieth in you, ye
learn to long for his presence at whose coming ye now
rightly tremble! Nor let illusive greed seduce you, siren-
like, doing to death, by some charm, the vigil of reason.
"Come before his face with confession of submission,
and rejoice in penitential psalmody," remembering that
"whoso resisteth the power resisteth the ordinance of

God," and whoso fighteth against the divine ordinance kicketh against a will co-equal with omnipotence; and "it is hard to kick against the prick."

But ye who grieve under oppression, uplift your heart; for your salvation is nigh at hand. Take the harrow of fair humility, and breaking up the clods caked by the heat of your wrath, make level the acre of your minds, lest haply the celestial shower, anticipating the seed ere ye have sown it, fall from on high in vain; that the grace of God leap not back from you like the daily dew from a rock; but rather, that ye conceive like a fertile valley, and thrust forth the green, the green, that is, that bears the fruit of true peace; that when your land is keeping spring in this verdure, the new ploughman of the Romans may, with the more love and confidence, yoke the oxen of his counsel to the plough. . . .

But if a stubborn mind demandeth further proof, not yet assenting to the truth, let it examine the words of Christ, even when already bound; for when Pilate urged on him his power, our Light declared that office to come from above of which he who then bore it in the vicarious authority of Caesar made his boast. Walk not, therefore, as the Gentiles walk in the vanity of their thought, clouded in darkness, but open the eyes of your mind and see that the Lord of heaven and earth hath ordained to us a king. He it is whom Peter, the vicar of God, exhorteth us to honor, whom Clement, the present successor of Peter, doth illuminate with the light of the apostolic benediction; that where the spiritual ray sufficeth not there the splendor of the lesser luminary may give light.

TO THE INFAMOUS FLORENTINE

(EPISTLE VI)

Dante Alighieri, the Florentine, exiled counter to his deserts, to the most infamous Florentines within.[2]

. . . You, who transgress divine and human law, whom a dire rapaciousness hath found ready to be drawn into every crime—doth not the dread of the second death pursue you? For ye first and alone, shunning the yoke of liberty, have murmured against the glory of the Roman prince, the king of the world and the minister of God, and on the plea of prescriptive right have refused the duty of the submission which ye owed, and have rather risen up in the insanity of rebellion! Or are ye ignorant in your madness and your spleen that public rights have limitation only with the limitation of time, and can be called to no reckoning by prescription? For the sanctions of the laws proclaim aloud, and human reason perceiveth by searching out, that the supremacy over public things, howsoever long neglected, can never lose its force, nor, however emaciated, be overcome. For that which maketh for the advantage of all cannot perish, nor even be weakened, without detriment to all. The which God and nature wills not, and the consensus of mortals would utterly abhor. Wherefore, then, stirring up so vain a thought as this, do ye, a second race of Babylonians, desert the compassionate empire and seek to establish new kingdoms, making the civic life of

---

2. *This is an excerpt from the famous letter, seething with boundless indignation, which Dante sent to his fellow-citizens, when he realized that Florence was heading the resistance against Emperor Henry VII (cf. the Introduction to this volume).*

Florence one, and that of Rome another? . . . But if the requital of your evil enterprises is not a terror to you, let this then terrify your stubborn minds, that not only wisdom but the beginning thereof hath been taken from you as a penalty for your sin. For no condition of the delinquent is more terrible than when he doeth after his will shamelessly and without fear of God. Full often, in truth, is the impious man smitten with this punishment, that he should be forgetful of himself in death, since he hath been forgetful of God in life. . . .

The fortifications which ye have not reared in prudence against necessity, but changed at random and for wantonness, . . . these ye shall mournfully gaze upon as they fall in ruins before the battering-ram, and are burnt with fire. Ye shall see that populace which now doth rage hither and thither, for and against, then of one mind clamoring dire threats against you, for they may not be hungry and timid at one same time. Ye shall look upon the grievous sight of your temples, thronged with the daily concourse of matrons, given up to the spoiler; and of your wondering and unknowing little ones, destined to expiate the sins of their sires. And—if my presaging mind be not deceived, as it announceth that which it hath learned from truth-telling signs, and arguments that may not be gainsaid—your city, worn out with long-drawn sufferings, shall be given at last into the hands of the aliens, the greatest part of you scattered in death and captivity, while the few that are left to endure their exile shall look on and weep. . . .

Oh, most wretched offspring of Fiesole! Oh, Punic barbarism once again! Do the things that I have touched on strike too little terror into you? Nay, I believe that, for all the hope ye simulate in countenance and lying word, ye tremble in your waking hours and ever start from your slumbers shuddering at the omens that have crept into your dreams or rehearsing the counsels of the daytime. But if in your well-merited trepidation ye regret your madness, but yet grieve not for it, be it further imprinted on your minds (that the streamlets of fear and woe may flow into the bitterness of repentance) that this baton-bearer of the Roman estate, this divine and triumphant Henry, thirsting not for his own but for the public ease, hath shrunk on our behalf from no arduous task, freely sharing in our sufferings, as though the prophet Isaiah had pointed the finger of prophecy upon him, after Christ, when by the revelation of the Spirit of God he foretold "truly he hath borne our weaknesses and hath carried our woes." Therefore, if ye cease to dissemble, ye yourselves perceive that the time is at hand for most bitter remorse for your rash undertakings. Yet may not late penitence, of such a sort, give birth to pardon. Rather is it itself the beginning of seasonable chastisement. For the saying is: The sinner is smitten that he may come back to the way without backsliding.

Written the day before the Kalends of April, on the confines of Tuscany, under the source of the Arno, in the first year of the most auspicious progress to Italy of Henry the Caesar.

But we marvel what may be the cause of this so sluggish delay. Victor long ago in the valley of the Po, thou dost desert, pass over, and neglect Tuscany. . . .

Be ashamed to be entangled so long in a little narrow plot of the world, and thou for whom all the world looketh! And let it not escape the vision of Augustus that the tyranness of Tuscany is strengthened in the confidence of delay and daily exhorting the pride of the malignant ones, gathereth new strength and addeth audacity to audacity.

TO THE EMPEROR HENRY VII

(EPISTLE VII)

*Of the most sacred triumphant one, and sole lord,
Lord Henry, by divine providence king of the Ro-
mans, ever Augustus, his most devoted servants
Dante Alighieri the Florentine, exiled counter to
his deserts, and all the Tuscans generally who de-
sire the peace of the land, and do kiss the feet.*[3]

1. As testifieth the unmeasurable love of God, the in-
heritance of peace hath been left us, that in its marvel-
lous sweetness the hardships of our warfare might be
softened, and by its practice we might earn the joys of
the triumphant fatherland. But the envy of the ancient
and implacable foe, who plotteth ever and in secret
against the prosperity of man, by persuading some to
forfeit their heritage of their own will, hath, in the
guardian's absence, impiously stripped us others thereof
against our will. Hence we have long wept by the
streams of Confusion, and without ceasing have im-
plored the protection of the righteous king, that he
should scatter the following of the cruel tyrant and re-
establish us in our just rights. And when thou, successor
of Caesar and of Augustus, leaping over the ridges of
the Apennines, didst bring back the venerated Tarpeian
standards,[4] forthwith our long sighing desisted and the
floods of our tears were dried. And, even as the rising of
the longed-for Titan, the new hope of a better age
flashed upon Latium. . . .

---

3. Dante, *in this letter, directly addresses the Emperor, who was
then besieging Cremona, and reproves him for his delay to crush
his real foe, "the poisonous hydra," Florence.*
4. *"Tarpeian standards": the Roman eagle.*

Dost thou not know, most excellent of princes, and from the watch tower of highest exaltation dost thou not perceive where the fox of this stench skulks in safety from the hunters? For the culprit drinketh not of the headlong Po, nor of thy Tiber, but her jaws do ever pollute the streams of the torrent of Arno; and (knowest thou not perchance?) this dire plague is named Florence. She is the viper that turns upon the entrails of her mother. She is the sick sheep that infects the flock of her lord with her contagion. She is the foul and impious Myrrha that burns for the embraces of her father Cinyras. She is that passionate Amata who rejected the wedlock decreed by fate, and feared not to summon to herself the son-in-law that fate denied her; who called him forth to war, in her madness, and at last, expiating her evil deeds, hanged herself in the noose.[5] In truth, with the fierceness of a viper she is striving to rend her mother, for she hath sharpened the horns of rebellion against Rome, who created her in her image and after her likeness. In truth doth she breathe out poisonous fumes, exhaling infection whence the neighboring sheep pine even without knowing it, whilst she with her false blandishments and fictions draweth her neighbors to her and bewitcheth them when drawn. . . .

Come, then, banish delay! thou lofty scion of Jesse. Take to thee confidence from the eyes of the Lord God of Sabaoth, before whom thou standest, and lay this Golias low with the sling of thy wisdom and the stone of thy strength; for when he falleth, night and the darkness of fear shall overwhelm the camp of the Philistines; the Philistines shall flee, and Israel shall be delivered. Then

---

5. As Myrrha sought the incestuous embraces of her father, so is Florence the Pope's mate.—Amata (Florence) rejected the heaven-decreed marriage with Aeneas (Henry VII), and gave herself to her son-in-law, Turnus (King Robert of Naples).

shall our heritage, the taking away of which we weep without ceasing, be restored to us again. And even as we now groan, remembering the holy Jerusalem, exiles in Babylon, so, then, citizens, breathing again in peace, we shall look back in our joy upon the miseries of Confusion.

Written in Tuscany, under the source of the Arno, fourteen days before the Kalends of May, 1311, in the first year of the most auspicious progress to Italy of the divine Henry.

BETTER EXILE THAN DISHONOR

(EPISTLE IX)

To a Florentine friend.[6]

WITH grateful mind and close attention did I perceive from your letter, received with due reverence and affection, how deeply you have my recall at heart. And thereby you have bound me under the closer obligation because it so rarely chanceth that exiles find friends. But I go on to answer the contents of it. And if my answer be not such as perchance the pusillanimity of certain might seek, I would beg you, in all affection, to winnow it in your judgment before you pronounce upon it.

This, then, is what has been indicated to me by the letters of your nephew and mine, and many other friends, as to the decree recently passed in Florence concerning the pardon of the exiles: That if I will consent to

---

6. *In this famous letter to an unidentified friend, Dante indignantly rejects the infamous conditions the Florentine rulers had attached to his recall from exile. The most probable date of this letter is 1315.*

pay a certain sum of money, and be willing to bear the brand of oblation,[7] I may be absolved and may return at once. Wherein are two things ridiculous and ill-advised, O father! I say ill-advised by those who have expressed them; for your letter, more discreetly and advisedly drawn up, contained no hint of them.

Is this the glorious recall whereby Dante Alighieri is summoned back to his fatherland after suffering well-nigh fifteen years of exile? Is this the reward of innocence manifest to all the world, of unbroken sweat and toil in study? Far be it from the familiar of philosophy, this abject self-abasement of a soul of clay! To allow himself to be presented at the altar, as a prisoner, after the fashion of some Ciolo[8] or other infamous wretch. Far be it from the preacher of justice, when he hath suffered a wrong, to pay his coin to them that inflicted it as though they had deserved well of him.

Not this the way of return to my country, O my father! but if another may hereafter be found by you or any other, which hurts not Dante's fair fame and honor, that will I accept with no lagging feet. If no such path leads back to Florence, then will I never enter Florence more. What then? May I not gaze upon the mirror of the sun and stars wherever I may be? Can I not ponder on the sweetest truths wherever I may be beneath the heaven, but I must first make me inglorious, nay infamous, before the people and the state of Florence? Nor shall I lack for bread.

---

7. "The brand of oblation": this ceremony consisted in presenting the repentant as an offering to St. John.
8. "Ciolo": of this man we can only infer that he had submitted abjectly.

A Bibliographical Note

THE following works by Dante do not appear in the present volume: *The Eclogues*—two verse compositions in Latin, in the Virgilian manner, which are part of a poetic correspondence between the aged poet and a young scholar of Bologna, Giovanni Del Virgilio, and which throw light on Dante's last years and have a place in the history of pastoral literature; *Quaestio de aqua et terra*—a "paper" in Latin on a question of scholastic physics which Dante read in Verona in 1320; and *Il Convivio* ("The Banquet")—an unfinished treatise in Italian, containing Dante's exegesis of three of his own *canzoni*. Of Dante's minor works, "The Banquet" is undoubtedly the most central for the insights it offers into the poet's literary and aesthetic positions, and for its treatment of allegory.

Until recently, the standard edition of Dante's work in the original was *Le Opere di Dante, Testo critico della Società Dantesca Italiana* (IInd ed., Florence, 1960), published on the seven hundredth anniversary of the poet's death, under the editorship of G. Vandelli. A new, authoritative edition of the *Commedia* was commissioned by the same sponsor, and readied by Giorgio Petrocchi. It appeared in 1966–68 in three volumes, as part of the festivities honoring the poet's birth. The text is accompanied by numerous notes and by an admirable philological apparatus. As for Dante's "minor" works, the following ought to be consulted: *Le Rime*, ed. by G. Contini (IInd ed., Turin, 1960); *Il Convivio*, ed. by G. Busnelli and G. Vandelli, in two volumes (Florence, 1934); *De Vulgari Eloquentia*, ed. by P. G. Ricci (IInd ed., Florence, 1957); and *De Monarchia*, ed. by G. Vinay (Florence, 1950). The only complete English translation in prose is included in several volumes of the "Temple Classics" (London, 1964), with text translation and commentaries by H. Oelsner, T. Okey, P. H. Wicksteed, and A. G. F. Howell.

Translations of the *Commedia* in English are too numerous to be listed here. Among them, however, three clearly deserve to be singled out: the well-known, easily accessible Modern Library edition by Carlyle-Wicksteed, with its useful notes and commentary; John D. Sinclair's rendition (New York, 1961) for its faithfulness to the original; and C. S.

Singleton's accurate prose translation, part of a six-volume tome, a scholarly endeavor destined to remain, for a long time to come, a basic reference tool, particularly because of its massive, three-volume, line-by-line commentary. For an analysis of the quality of the English versions of the *Commedia* one must turn to Gilbert F. Cunningham's two-part study, *The Divine Comedy in English: A Critical Biography* (London and New York, 1965 and 1967).

There are numerous introductory studies on Dante. The best of these are the eminently usable *Dante* (Westport, Conn., 1976), by Thomas G. Bergin; *Dante* (London and New York, 1966), by Francis Fergusson; Michele Barbi's shorter *Life of Dante* (Berkeley, Calif., 1954; London, 1955); and Paget Toynbee's *Dante Alighieri: The Poet and Works* (ed. by C. S. Singleton, London and New York, 1965).

Turning to basic reference works, the standard studies are: Umberto Cosmo, *Handbook of Dante Studies* (Oxford, 1950), of great value to the novice reader; Paget Toynbee's *A Dictionary of Proper Names and Notable Matters in the Works of Dante* (IInd ed. revised by C. S. Singleton, Oxford, 1968) and E. H. Wilkins, T. G. Bergin, *et al.*, *A Concordance to the Divine Comedy of Dante Alighieri* (London and Cambridge, Mass., 1965), are essential to the specialist.

T. S. Eliot's main essay on Dante is included in his *Selected Essays* (London and New York, 1932). Those interested in the historical, philosophical, and theological background of Dante's work may profit from George Santayana's *Three Philosophical Poets* (London, 1910; Cambridge, Mass., 1947), Etienne Gilson's *Dante the Philosopher* (London and New York, 1949), Karl Vossler's *Mediaeval Culture: An Introduction to Dante and His Times* (London and New York, 1958), H. Flanders Dunbar's *Symbolism in Medieval Thought and Its Culmination in the Divine Comedy* (New York, 1961), Bruno Nardi's *Nel mondo di Dante* (Rome, 1944), Paul R. Ruggiers' *Florence in the Age of Dante* (Norman, Okla., 1964), Edmund G. Gardner's *Dante and the Mystics* (London, 1913), Joseph A. Mazzeo's *Medieval Cultural Tradition in Dante's "Divine Comedy"* (Ithaca, N.Y., 1960), Bruno Nardi's *Dante e la Cultura Medievale* (Bari, 1949).

The reader seeking illumination on Dante's works will do well to consult some of the specialized studies that have appeared over the last decades (valuable for their scholarship and critical originality): J. E. Shaw, *Essay on the Vita Nuova* (Princeton, N.J., 1929; London, 1930); Charles S. Singleton, *An Essay on the "Vita Nuova"* (Baltimore, Md., 1978); Francis Fergusson, *Dante's Drama of the Mind: A Modern Reading of the Purgatorio* (Princeton, N.J., 1952; London, 1953); Bernard Stambler's *Dante's Other World* (New York, 1957; London, 1958); Joseph A. Mazzeo's *Structure and Thought in the "Paradiso"* (Ithaca, N.Y., and London, 1958). The seminal essay by Erich Auerbach, "Figura," may be read in *Scenes from the Drama of European Literature* (New York and London, 1959); by the same author see also *Dante, Poet from the Secular World* (Chicago and London, 1961). Charles S. Singleton's *Dante's "Commedia." Elements of Structure* (Baltimore, Md., 1978) is a thoroughly convincing study of Dante's allegory, while his *Journey to Beatrice* (Baltimore, Md., 1977) is an absorbing analysis of crucial figures and events of the "Purgatory."

The "problem" of allegory remains one of the central issues frequently holding the key to interpretation of Dante's masterpiece, and four more serious studies on the subject have clearly underscored this point: Robert Hollander's *Allegory in Dante's "Commedia"* (Princeton, N.J., 1969); Jean Pépin's *Dante et la Tradition de l'Allégorie* (Montreal, 1970); Francis Fergusson's *Trope and Allegory: Themes Common to Dante and Shakespeare* (Athens, Ga., 1977); and Giuseppe Mazzotta's *Dante: Poet of the Desert. History and Allegory in the "Divine Comedy"* (Princeton, N.J., 1977).

A thorough descriptive bibliography of Dante scholarship in the United States may be found in the *Annual Report of the Dante Society* (Cambridge, Mass.), now *Dante Studies*, ed. by A. L. Pellegrini, published by the State University of New York at Binghamton. *Studi Danteschi* is the main journal of Dante studies in Italy (Florence).

—Sergio Pacifici

Queens College and City University of New York, Graduate Center, 1981